Elisabeth Carpenter lives in Preston with her family. She completed a BA in English Literature and Language with the Open University in 2011. She was awarded a Northern Writers' New Fiction award (2016), and was longlisted for the Yeovil Literary Prize (2015 and 2016) and the Mslexia Women's Novel Award (2015). Libby loves living in the north of England, and sets most of her stories in the area. She currently works as a bookkeeper. Her debut novel, *99 Red Balloons*, became a bestseller in 2017 and received widespread acclaim from both reviewers and readers.

You can follow Elisabeth on Twitter @LibbyCPT

11 MISSED CALLS

Debbie disappeared over thirty years ago, while on holiday in Tenerife. Her daughter Anna, only a baby at the time, has struggled all her life to make sense of it, filling a scrapbook with pages and pages of facts about her mother that she has gleaned from others' recollections. But then Anna's stepmother Monica receives a strange email saying it's time to tell the truth. And it's signed 'Debbie'. Anna realises she's never been told the full story of what happened that night on the cliff. Confused and upset, she turns to her husband Jack — but when she finds a love letter from another woman in his wallet, it's clear there's no one left to help her — least of all her own family . . .

Books by Elisabeth Carpenter
Published by Ulverscroft:

99 RED BALLOONS

ELISABETH CARPENTER

11 MISSED CALLS

Complete and Unabridged

CHARNWOOD
Leicester

First published in Great Britain in 2018 by
Avon
London

First Charnwood Edition
published 2019
by arrangement with
Avon
A division of HarperCollins*Publishers*
London

A catalogue record for this book is available from the British Library.

ISBN 978–1–4448–4215–9

Published by
F. A. Thorpe (Publishing)
Anstey, Leicestershire

Set by Words & Graphics Ltd.
Anstey, Leicestershire
Printed and bound in Great Britain by
T. J. International Ltd., Padstow, Cornwall

This book is printed on acid-free paper

In memory of:

Daniel and Dorothy Sweeney
Patricia and Stanley Carpenter
Michael Carpenter
Julia Thorn

Prologue

Monday, 28 July 1986
Tenerife, Canary Islands
Debbie

The rock I'm standing on is only twelve inches long — just a foot stopping me falling into the water nearly five hundred feet below. The stone is cool under my bare feet.

It's quiet; there aren't many cars going past behind me. It must be late, or early. There's a lovely warm breeze, one you don't get in England when it's dark. If it gets stronger, it might push me over the edge. Hitting water from this height is meant to be like landing on tarmac.

I've always been afraid of heights. What a strange time to conquer my fear. Nathan said this part of the cliffs is called La Gran Caída. Perhaps the name will be imprinted on my soul, alongside Bobby's and Annie's. I thought that when I had children, I'd become a better person. I think I've always had a badness, a sadness, inside me.

Why are my thoughts everywhere? They need to be here. I'm ridiculous, silly; my mother's right. She's always right. I'm useless to everyone. Everyone will be happier without me. Especially the children.

1

Oh God, no.

I can't think about the children.

They have Peter. I'd only let them down again. What if I were left on my own with Annie again? I might kill her.

They'll forget me soon enough. They're young enough to erase me from their memory.

Breathe, breathe.

I'm surprised by how calm I am.

It's like my mind was coated in tar, but now it's been wiped clean.

I close my eyes.

So, this is how it ends.

I thought I'd be scared if ever I fell from such a height, but if I jump there'll be nothing I can do about it.

The warm breeze skims my face again. I should be with my children right now, lying next to them, watching them sleep.

But I can't. I'm not good enough for them. They'll end up hating me.

Bobby, Annie, you were the loves of my life.

'Debbie! For God's sake, what are you doing?'

Is that the voice inside my head again?

I close my eyes. I don't want anyone to stop me. I just want darkness.

Don't look back. I can't look back.

'Debbie, come away from there!'

Before I have time to think, I'm turning around.

'Oh,' I say. 'It's you.'

1

Present Day

Anna

My mother, Debbie, has been missing for thirty years, ten months and twenty-seven days. It's her birthday the day after tomorrow — two days after mine. I'm three years older than she was when she was last seen. She disappeared so long ago, that my father doesn't talk about her any more. I have always taken scraps of information from my stepmother, Monica, and my grandfather, who will *never give up hope*.

But they have run out of new things to say about her. I was just over one month old when she left. I have no memories of my own, but I have a box. Inside it are random objects, music records, and photographs that belonged to her. There's also a scrapbook with pages and pages of facts I wrote about her: *She had dark hair, like mine. She was five foot five (two inches taller than me). She had her ears pierced twice in each ear. (Gran didn't like it and had no idea where she got the money, at fifteen, to do that.) She liked The Beatles and Blondie. She wasn't very happy at the end.*

I started the list when I was eleven, so my first entries are naive and in the past tense. What I would like to know now is: *What made you* leave? and *Do you ever think of us?* But of course, no one can answer those questions but her.

The letterbox rattles, shaking me out of my thoughts. Sophie runs to the front door. The envelopes look huge in her little hands.

'There are loads more cards for you, Mummy,' she says.

She hands me the three pastel-coloured envelopes. I examine the handwriting on each one to see if I recognise it. I don't know why I do it to myself every year. If the writing is unfamiliar, I get butterflies and a feeling of anticipation. What if this is the day she contacts me? What if it is today that I find out that she's not dead — that she did something so terrible she had to protect us from the truth?

It is wishful thinking. I have made up so many stories in my head over the years. They get more absurd every time: she died the night she disappeared; she's in prison for drug smuggling; she's living in a South American village after suffering from amnesia.

I place the birthday cards on the table.

'Are you not going to open them?' asks Sophie.

'We'll wait till Grandad arrives. He'll be here in a minute.'

Birthdays make me think of her even more. I often wonder what my mother would look like now if she were alive. I try not to look out for her any more. Not after it got me into so much trouble last time.

A few months ago, I told Sophie she was dead. It was the worst thing I could have said, but I didn't want her thinking she had a grandmother

4

out there in the world that wasn't interested in her. I hadn't meant to say it.

'When are you going to leave *me*, Mummy?' Sophie had said.

'Never,' I said.

'But Granny Debbie left you and Uncle Robert.'

'Not on purpose.'

'Did you lose her?'

'I suppose we did,' I said, stroking her hair to take the sting out of it.

'Is she in heaven, then? That's what my friend Lila said about her nana. She had to go to church and then after the singing and the crying, they went outside and the wooden box she was in went into the ground. At least three metres under the grass, she said. But she wasn't allowed to watch that bit — it was what her cousin told her. He's twelve so he saw everything. Is that what happened to Granny?'

'Yes,' I said. 'I'm sorry about your friend Lila.'

Sophie shrugged. 'She's okay. She's on the gold step now. But we all don't mind. It was her first time. She might be naughty again next week.'

'Everyone's naughty sometimes, Sophie. But be kind to her, will you?'

'Yeah.'

She's sitting at the kitchen table now, making her own birthday card for me.

Sometimes I worry I might have the same thoughts as Debbie — that I will abandon everyone, leave in the middle of the night without being able to stop myself.

I hear Dad's car pull up outside.

5

'Grandad!' shouts Sophie, as the car door slams shut.

Just the one door: Monica's not with him.

They usually do everything together now they're both retired.

I open the front door, and Sophie squeezes between me and the door frame as we watch Dad walk down the front path. He's tall, but he always keeps his head down, like he wants to blend in with the background.

He looks up before the step.

'I didn't realise there'd be a welcoming committee!' he says, bowing slightly.

He's trying to look happy for Sophie and me, but the smile is only present on his lips. It's a manner so familiar to me that it's almost normal.

'Happy birthday, love,' he says, before kissing my cheek, and stepping inside.

He ties a silver balloon to the end of the bannister and places a gift bag on the floor.

'Am I allowed to play with it?' Sophie says, standing on the bottom stair, and blowing the balloon sideways.

'Maybe later,' I say. 'I'll put the kettle on.'

Dad and Sophie follow me into the kitchen.

'But it's your birthday,' says Dad, 'and it's a Saturday. Let's have a drop of fizz.'

Sophie sits back at the table.

'Why's Grandad talking posh?'

'I don't know.'

Dad pulls out a bottle of champagne from my gift bag and hands it to me. It's already chilled. He nudges me aside and reaches into the cupboard for three wine glasses. It's like he can't stop moving.

'You know how I feel about birthdays, Dad. I don't want a fuss.'

'Course you do — it's your thirtieth! We had champagne on your twenty-first, remember? I take it Jack's at work . . . on a Saturday? I've never known a conveyancing solicitor work a weekend in my entire life.' Dad glances at me and raises his eyebrows. 'Anyway, your brother should be here any minute.'

I don't say that Robert probably won't drink either. Robert would think that ordering a taxi so he can enjoy a few glasses of champagne during the day is one step towards anarchy, lack of self-control, and being on the verge of a nervous breakdown.

He has always been the same. Robert was six when Debbie disappeared. Everyone says it's harder for him, because he remembers. When I was little, Robert told me that Dad was arrested after we came back to England — that, for a few days, it was like he had lost two parents. He probably doesn't remember telling me; he's barely mentioned it since. He hates talking about her now. He couldn't understand why, until only a few years ago, I had pictures of her everywhere. Most of those photographs are in the loft now.

'Where's Monica?' I say. 'Is she ill again?'

He fills the glasses halfway, waiting for the bubbles to melt before he tops them up. We're not usually the champagne kind of family.

'No — well, not physically — it's just . . . we've had an email. I can't tell you what was in it until Robert gets here. He won't be long.'

'An email? Why didn't you just forward it to me, or tell me over the phone? Does Leo know?'

Leo is our stepbrother — Monica's son — but he lives in America with his father.

'No, no. We wouldn't tell him without you two knowing first.' He paces along the small space between the sink and the kitchen table. 'I did wonder whether it was the right day to do this, but I couldn't face you today without telling you.'

'What does it say?'

He narrows his eyes and purses his lips.

'Is it about Debbie?' I say.

He nods slowly.

My legs start to shake. It feels like the blood has run cold in my face. I lean against the back of a chair.

What could an email say about her? If her remains had been found, or if she were still alive — it wouldn't be in a casual email. Maybe this is how it's done these days — especially if she were found in Tenerife. Has a dog found her while searching for a bone? Or has she been discovered in a hospital somewhere — her memory wiped by an accident?

I must stop thinking.

Dad wouldn't open champagne if it were bad news, would he?

I open my mouth; I almost don't want to say it out loud.

'Is she dead?' I whisper, so Sophie doesn't hear.

'Anna, love, just be patient. Please. He'll be here soon.'

8

Why did he not just say no — put me out of my misery?

My stomach is churning. Deep breath. Breathe, breathe.

He looks at his watch and we stand wordlessly, with only the sound of the wine bubbling, losing its fizz. Briefly, the mask slips from his face when he thinks I'm not looking — I have seen it often over the years: the sadness of remembering something lost.

'Sophie,' I say. 'I'll put a film on for you while we wait for Uncle Robert. Then we can have some cake.'

'Cake?'

'Yes, love.'

She takes my hand, and we go into the living room. I flick on the television, but it takes too long to find a film — my hands are shaking.

'Just put the kids' channel on,' she says, her head tilted to the side as she looks at me.

'Good plan. Thanks, sweetheart.'

She's only six, but she can be so perceptive at times. I pull the living-room door closed as much as I can without her panicking that I am going to abandon her.

Dad's looking at the clock when I walk back into the kitchen.

'It's not like Robert to be ten minutes late,' he says. 'Why don't you open your present? Monica's so excited about it.'

'Why isn't she here then?'

'She thought she'd give us some space while I tell you the news.'

'That's very understanding of her.'

Dad narrows his eyes for a second. Perhaps I was too sarcastic. Monica has been married to my father since I was eleven, but she has always been in my life. My mother is *presumed dead* in the eyes of the law.

'She hasn't taken it well,' he says. 'She didn't even want me to read it.'

'What? Wasn't it addressed to you?'

I follow him as he walks out of the kitchen and into the hall. He peers through the window next to the front door.

'Dad?'

He is saved by the bell. I open the door to Robert.

'Happy Birthday, Anna,' he says, unwrapping his scarf — he's never without one. 'Hotter than I thought it'd be today. Should've gone with the cotton.'

Robert hands me a birthday card, which will contain fifteen pounds.

'Come on through to the kitchen, you two,' says Dad, walking straight there.

'What's going on?' says Robert, draping his jacket along the stairs. He glances at the balloon on the end of the bannister. 'You really should get a coat stand or something.'

'He's got an email,' I say, 'about Debbie.'

Robert's shoulders slump; he lowers his head, his eyes scanning the wooden floor of the hall.

'Is it good news or bad?' he says, finally looking up at me.

'I don't know. But he opened champagne.'

'That could mean anything.'

He links his arm through mine and guides me

through to the kitchen.

'What do you mean by that?' I hiss.

Dad's leaning against the kitchen cupboards — he's already pulled out two chairs.

'Ssh,' Robert says to me, sitting on the chair nearest Dad.

'Okay.' Dad clasps his hands together. 'Sorry about this, Anna — it being on your birthday and all.'

'She hates birthdays anyway,' says Robert.

'This came through yesterday.' He picks up a brown envelope from the kitchen counter behind him, and takes out two sheets of A4. 'Well, Monica received it a few days ago — I only saw it yesterday. I've done a copy for both of you.'

'Why didn't she show it to you straight away?' I say to Dad.

He just shrugs.

My brother snatches one of the sheets from Dad's hand.

'Robert!' I say, taking the other.

I glance down quickly. There are only a few lines.

I read it properly.

Dear Monica,
It's time to tell the truth.
Debbie x
The memories of shells and sweet things are sometimes all we have left.

'Is this it?' says Robert, standing up. 'It's a crank letter. You've had them before, haven't you, Dad?'

'What?' I say. 'No one said anything to me.'

'I suppose they didn't want to upset you,' Robert says.

I frown at him, making a note in my mind to ask Monica about it next time I see her.

'But what if it's not?' I say quietly. 'My memory box is covered in shells.'

Robert tuts. 'That could mean anything. You're just making it significant because it means something to you. It's like these charlatan psychics. If Debbie were alive, why would she make contact now after so long?'

'Something might've happened,' I say to Dad. 'It says *it's time*. Why did she address it to Monica and not you?'

Dad shakes his head.

'I've no idea what it means,' he says. 'Neither does Monica. We'll just have to wait and see if she sends something else.'

'If it's even a *she* who wrote it,' says Robert. 'It could be anyone.'

'Did you reply?' I say.

We both look up at Dad.

'I . . . I think Monica might have. I've been a bit shaken by it all, to be honest.'

'It sounds a bit sinister,' I say. 'What does Monica think it means?'

Dad takes one of the glasses of champagne and takes a large sip.

'Like I said, she doesn't know.'

Robert looks at me and shrugs.

'That's because it's a load of crap.'

'Uncle Robert!' Sophie runs into the kitchen and jumps onto Robert's lap. 'Did you just say *crap*?'

'Of course not!' says Robert. 'I said *slap*.'

'Which isn't much better,' says Dad, rubbing the top of Sophie's head.

I walk into the living room and switch off the television. I look down at the email again. Monica received it days ago, yet didn't show Dad. I look out of the window, leaning against the glass. I don't know what I expect to see outside. But a thought strikes me.

Monica knows more than she is letting on.

2

3 a.m. Thursday, 26 June 1986
Debbie

I've been looking at the same page of this stupid magazine for over an hour, trying to read the words under the crappy night-light above my head, but I keep daydreaming. The article's about making the perfect chocolate roulade, and getting the timings right for all the 'trimmings' on Christmas day. It's from one of the women's magazines Mum has been saving for months — or maybe years, judging by the state of them. She's still trying to convince me that *Good House-keeping* will make me a more fulfilled person and a better mum. But there's nothing more depressing than reading about Christmas in June. I don't know why she thinks I'd be interested in things like this — she's not the best cook herself. I'm nearly twenty-seven, not forty-seven. I should be reading about George Michael or the G spot.

I throw it onto the bed tray, but it slips off. The sound is amplified by a rare moment of silence on the maternity ward. I hold my breath in the hope that it cancels out the splat of the magazine onto the floor. Please, no one wake up. This peace is mine right now, and I don't want anyone else to ruin it. My normal life is far from peaceful.

14

Annie looks like a little doll; she's been so quiet. It must be the pethidine. She's got the same podgy fingers that Bobby had — they're like tiny tree trunks. I didn't think she'd suit the name. I'd suggested Gemma or Rebecca, but Peter wanted to call her Anna after his late mother. It's just right for her.

I've lost track of time and I've only been here for one night. The sky is purple; is it nearly morning or is it still dusk?

It's hardly ever quiet in here, but they're all asleep now. The new mothers try to feed as quietly as possible, but they're amateurs, all three of them. And it's never completely dark. They like to keep the light on above their heads. Perhaps they're afraid that if it goes out, their babies will disappear.

I pick up the magazine, as quickly as I can with damn painful stitches, and place it on my cabinet. There are seven birthday cards, still in their envelopes, ready for me to open tomorrow, or is it today? Is it terrible that I'm glad I'm not sharing my birthday — to be relieved that Annie arrived two days earlier than her due date? It probably is, but I'll keep that selfish thought in my head. It's one of many, anyway.

⋆   ⋆   ⋆

'Debbie.'

My mind wakes up, but I leave my eyes closed. It's so hot. I'm on a beach, lying on sand in a cove that only I know about.

'Debbie.'

15

Was that a voice in my head? I open one eye to find a nurse bending over me.

'Oh God,' I say. 'The baby.'

I sit up as quickly as I can. How could I be so careless falling asleep so heavily? The nurse rests a cold hand on my wrist.

'Baby's fine,' she says. 'There's a phone call for you.'

I swing my legs so they're dangling over the side of the bed. The nurse pushes the payphone towards me and gives me the handset.

'Debs, it's me.' It's Peter. 'How's Annie? Did she wake much in the night? I wish I could be there. Shall I ask if you can come home early?'

It takes a few moments to digest Peter's words. He must've thought of them during the night, to be saying them all at once. Being with children does that; makes you go over things in your mind, with no adult to talk to. He's not used to it being just Bobby and him.

'No, no,' I say. 'It's fine. She's being as good as gold.'

Good as gold? I sound like my mother.

'I can't make the afternoon visiting times today,' he says, 'but I'll be there at seven tonight. I'll drop Bobby off at school, then I'll work straight through. Is that all right? I have to make sure I can spend at least a week at home when you both come out.'

'That's fine. Monica's visiting this afternoon.'

'Good, good.'

'I have to go now, though. They're bringing lunch round.'

'Really?'

16

'Bye, Peter.'

I place the handset back into the cradle. I hate making small talk, especially while a whole maternity ward can hear me shouting down the payphone. The nurse doesn't say anything, even though when I look at the clock on the wall it's only eight in the morning, and four hours from lunchtime. I suppose she's seen everything, so I don't feel as embarrassed as I should. I've spent so long lying to Peter — *Yes, I'm fine* and *Yes, I've always wanted two children* — that it comes naturally to me.

Why is he taking a whole week off? He's branch manager now at Woolies — surely they can't be without him for that long. I'm sure he didn't with Bobby, though that time is a blur. I don't think I can remember anything — I might've forgotten how to look after a tiny baby.

The woman in the bed next to me is snoring so loudly, it's like being at home. A silver chain her boyfriend bought her is dangling off the hospital bed. 'I can't wear necklaces at night,' she said yesterday, 'in case they strangle me in my sleep.' I was about to tell her that I was afraid of spiders to make her feel better, but I remembered Mum saying I shouldn't make everything about me. 'It's called empathy,' I said. 'Ego,' she said. She's too humble for her own good. I blame Jesus — she loves him more than life itself.

Yesterday, she whispered, 'Mothers are so much older these days.' (Some of her opinions aren't as Christian as they should be.) 'Women want everything now,' she said. 'They all want to be men.'

It was, of course, a stupid thing to say in a maternity ward. And she was an older mother herself.

An assistant is coming round to change the water jugs.

'It's good that you're dressed,' she says to me. 'Makes you feel a bit more together, doesn't it?'

I look down at my *Frankie Says Relax* T-shirt and red tartan pyjama bottoms. My mouth is already open when I say, 'Yes.'

She looks at my birthday cards, displayed on the cabinet. I can't even remember opening them.

'Happy Birthday, lovey,' she says.

It's only then I realise that Peter forgot my birthday.

★   ★   ★

At last, Annie makes a feeble sound as though she can't be bothered.

'I know, little girl,' I say. 'Sometimes it's more effort than it's worth, waking up.'

I pick her up and out of the plastic fish tank (that's what Bobby called it when he visited yesterday) and put the ready-prepared bottle to her lips, settling back into the pillows. She suckles on it — probably going too fast, too much air — but I let her. She's going to be a feisty little thing, I can tell.

Everyone else wanted me to have a girl. No one believed me when I said I didn't mind, that healthy was all that mattered. But I would've been happy with two boys, I'm sure. It seems

18

longer than nearly six years since I had Bobby — I was only twenty-one, but I felt so grown-up. He's so loving, so sensitive. 'Perfect little family now,' said Mum. 'One of each.' And I should feel that, shouldn't I?

But I don't.

3

Anna

I used to have dreams that Debbie was dead and had come back to life. Sometimes she would be rotting, sometimes she would be an unwelcome guest as the family was sitting around the table for Sunday lunch. I don't remember seeing her happy in my dreams. When I was eight, I used to have the same nightmare, over and over. I still remember it now. Our house was burning down, and a woman stood at my bedroom doorway screaming. Robert came to my side that night and sang 'Hush, Little Baby'. I thought it childish the morning after, but at the time it soothed me. He said that Debbie sang it to me in the middle of the night a few times when I wouldn't sleep.

I can't sleep now. My mind won't be still.

If Debbie were alive, then it would mean it was my fault that she left. She was fine until I came into the world. Not that anyone has said as much, but Dad, Robert — they all probably think it is down to me that she isn't here any more. Perhaps I was a mistake.

I can't stop thinking about her. I wish I hadn't put all of Debbie's photographs in the loft. Jack would call me crazy if I got the ladder down at three o'clock in the morning.

What would she look like now? Would she still hate me?

Random thoughts like these always come into my head when I try not to think of her.

A few years after we married, Jack told me I was obsessed with her.

'I know,' I said.

'It's not enough that you're aware of it,' he said. 'You have to change it.'

Yesterday, he came home after Dad and Robert had left, and Sophie had gone to bed. Dad asked why a conveyancer would be called out to work on a Saturday, but I've stopped probing Jack about it. He must be so busy at work that he forgot my birthday. He knows I hate birthdays, which is his usual excuse. I should tell him that *it's not enough that you're aware of it*.

We met when I was twenty-two and Jack was twenty-four, at a Spanish evening class. I only went on Monica's suggestion. 'You're too young to be stuck in all day on your own, love,' she said. 'I don't like seeing you so lonely.'

I had been desperate to meet someone, perhaps have children — a family of my own. I'm not sure I would be in so much of a rush, had I the chance to start again; I was far too young, but I had no friends and hardly ever went out. I had just finished university and was applying for at least twenty jobs a week.

Before the first class, Monica took me into Boots to have a makeover.

'Could you do something with her eyebrows?' she said to the lady dressed in white — plastered in thick foundation and bright-red lipstick. 'They've gone a bit wild.'

'Monica!' I said through gritted teeth, as I sat on a pedestal for everyone in the shop to see.

'We might as well, while we're here.'

After my face had been transformed, Monica took me to the hairdressers: my first visit for several years.

'She has beautiful hair,' Monica said to the stylist, 'but perhaps we could put some highlights at the front . . . to frame her lovely face.'

On the way home, I caught sight of myself in her car's vanity mirror and got a fright. I didn't look like me any more.

When I walked into the classroom that evening, I thought Jack was the teacher. He was standing at the front, talking to the students with such confidence. But when he opened his mouth, he spoke with a broad Yorkshire accent and was worse at Spanish than I was. I learned that he'd stayed in Lancashire after university, after his parents *abandoned* him to go and live in Brighton.

Jack said I wasn't like other women he met. 'You're an innocent, Anna. It's like you've been sheltered from the world.'

But that was my act — the character I chose to present to others at that time. Self-preservation. I didn't even look like the real me. I could act like I had no silly fears — of heights, swimming pools, and other irrational things. But I couldn't pretend forever.When I confessed my greatest fears three months later, Jack hadn't laughed at me. 'They're perfectly reasonable phobias,' he'd said. 'But life's about risk sometimes.'

Jack's parents moved away so long ago — Sophie has only met them six times. They think it's enough to send my daughter ten pounds in a card for her birthday and Christmas.

I think because Jack isn't close to *his* parents, there's no love lost between him and *my* dad. When he's drunk, Jack often ponders out loud whether my dad had anything to do with my mother's disappearance, and rolls off the possible ways in which it could have happened.

'Why else,' he said one night, 'would he end up married to Debbie's best friend?'

I switch off when he starts talking like that. He has stopped saying sorry about it in the morning — if he remembers saying it at all. I console myself that he's only so boorish when he's had a drink.

'Dad . . . well, Monica . . . got an email from someone saying they're my mother,' I said to him when he got in last night. I was sitting at the kitchen table — the champagne, which had long gone flat, still in three glasses.

'Is that why you've taken to drink?' he said, shrugging off his suit jacket and hanging it on the back of a chair.

'It's not funny,' I said.

I thought he would be more surprised. It was like his mind was elsewhere.

He grabbed the glass with the most wine in, and downed half of it. He winced.

'It's flat.' He pulled out a chair and sat down. 'Do you think it's really her? It can't be, surely. It must be some lunatic wanting a bit of attention.'

'I've no idea if it is or isn't. How would I know that?'

Jack raised his eyebrows. He hates anything that borders on histrionic.

'If it is,' I said, 'then it means she left us . . . That she left me.'

I saw the briefest flicker of irritation on his face. He gets like that when I talk about Debbie in that way. He hates people with a *poor me* attitude. It's bad enough that I have a fear of swimming pools and spiders. I don't want to be a victim. I have tried to overcome that feeling all my life.

He pulled off his tie, in the way he always does: wrenching it off with one hand, while grimacing as though he were being strangled. Who's the victim now, eh? I thought to myself.

'What a day,' he said, as usual. 'Have you got a copy of the email?'

'Yes. Dad gave me and Robert a print-out. I wonder if we could trace the email address. Do you think I should ring Leo?'

'Will he care?'

'Course he'll care . . . he grew up with us. At least, until I was ten.'

'Sharing a bedroom with *your* brother would make anyone want to flee the country.'

I don't laugh.

'I'll look at the email later,' he said. 'I've had a really long day. Is there anything in for tea?'

I looked at him for a few seconds, waiting for him to realise. But he didn't. Sophie had claimed the balloon my dad gave me; it was floating from her bedpost. My cards were on top of the fridge, but Jack hadn't noticed them.

I stood.

'I'm going to bed,' I said. 'There's a new volunteer starting tomorrow.'

He snorted. 'Ah, the ex-con. And on a Sunday as well.' He made the sign of the cross with his left hand. 'Lock up your handbag.'

'Yes, very funny,' I said as I walked towards the door. 'It's part of the offender-rehabilitation programme Isobel's been going on about.'

His chair scraped on the stone floor as he stood.

'Guess I'll just stick a pizza in the oven then.'

I tried to stomp up the stairs, but failed in bare feet. *Happy sodding birthday, Anna.*

I look at him next to me in bed now, jealous of his ability to sleep soundly at this hour. He's never had anything big to worry about. It's 3.45 a.m. If I get up now, I'll be a wreck later, but I can't lie here with only my thoughts.

I manage to avoid all the creaking floorboards and make it quietly downstairs to the kitchen. The ticking of the clock is too loud. On the table, Jack's plate is covered with pizza crusts, and crumbs litter the floor under the chair.

The three wine glasses are now empty. Why the hell did he want to drink flat champagne? I go to the fridge to count the bottles of beer left: there were six, and now there are none. No wonder he's sleeping so soundly. I don't know why he's drinking so much when he's looking after Sophie tomorrow. He's usually the sensible one.

25

I sit opposite his empty chair. It's wearing the jacket that Jack was earlier. His right pocket is slightly open, and the top of his wallet is peeking out.

Before I know it, I'm out of my seat.

The wallet slips out of Jack's pocket so easily, it's like it was waiting for me. Inside is a picture of Sophie and me. It's old — from Sophie's first birthday. I look quite together in the photo, which is surprising considering what I was going through. There are some receipts — the usual expenses he claims: newspapers, dinner. I scan the food he ate at lunchtime yesterday: steak, crème brûlée, and one small glass of pinot noir. Only one meal, but quite an extravagant one — on my birthday. I almost give up searching, but I feel like I am missing something.

There is a compartment I've not noticed before: to the side and underneath his cards. I wedge my fingers inside it. There's something there. I grasp it, using my fingers as tweezers, and pull it out.

It's a note. The paper is blue, with black lines — like the old-fashioned Basildon Bond writing pad my grandmother used. The creases are crisp; it's not been read many times. I unfold it and look straight to the name at the bottom: Francesca.

I read the rest of the letter.

This woman definitely knows my husband.

4

Friday, 27 June 1986
Debbie

Peter's holding Annie while I pack. I almost don't want to leave the hospital. With Bobby, I wanted to go home straight away, but regretted it as soon as I got back.

Ever since I gave birth to him, I've been scared that I'll die any minute. I go to bed and, most nights, I think I won't wake up. Sometimes I'm exhausted, but when my mind feels sleep begin — it's like I'm slipping from life, and I'm jolted awake. I can't sleep for hours after.

At least in hospital I'm safe. Plus, people give you food to eat, and you don't have to worry about housework. As much as Peter said he'd become one of these New Men who help tidy up and change nappies, it didn't happen. Now I know what's waiting for me when I get home.

I had a little routine here. I got to know Stacy in the next bed. Actually ... *know* is exaggerating it a bit. We watched *Coronation Street* together, and both our babies decided to sleep through it, which was a miracle in itself. Stacy couldn't get over Bet Lynch being in the Rovers when it was on fire. I told her that it's not real life, but she was having none of it. I put a cushion between us when she said she fancied

27

Brian Tilsley — it still gives me shivers thinking about it.

'Was it horrible spending the whole of your birthday in hospital?' says Peter.

'It wasn't too bad,' I say.

I smile at him, so he'll probably think it's because of Annie that I didn't mind, because she's enough of a present. He gives me a smile back. He thinks he can read my mind. I look at him and he's the same lovely-looking man I've been with for years. I love him. Why are my thoughts telling me different? It's like they're betraying me.

I zip up my suitcase; the clothes inside'll smell of hospital when I open it up. I'll probably feel sentimental about it.

'It's too warm in here,' I say.

He smiles again. Perhaps he likes the fact I'm suffering for our child — even after being pregnant and giving birth. Perhaps he's right. It was a relatively quick labour — I've not endured enough to deserve the life I'll go back to: swanning about the house all day watching *Sons and Daughters*, *The Sullivans*, and all the other soaps he reckons I watched during those long weeks when my maternity leave started.

'Good luck,' says Stacy, lying in the next bed, baby fast asleep in her arms — her only child.

'Good luck,' I say, to be friendly. 'Not that you'll need it.'

'We should meet up for coffee sometime,' she says.

'Yes, we should.'

I pick the baby up from the bed and Peter and

I leave the ward. I didn't give Stacy my telephone number because we'll never get together. People suggest it all the time and they never mean it. I'm not sure if I'll regret it or not.

Annie's wrapped up in the shawl we used for Bobby on his first day out into the world. We're in the lift and Annie's not opened her eyes since leaving the ward. She's going to miss her first proper glimpse of sky if she's not careful.

'There, there,' I say, stroking her soft, plump cheek.

'Don't wake her, Debs,' says Peter. 'The bright light might startle her.'

'Don't be silly. She's got to see it some time.'

The lift doors open and there are people everywhere.

'Can we pop into the shop to get a souvenir?' I say.

I don't wait for Peter.

'Is Annie not souvenir enough?'

I pretend I didn't hear. I want something to put in her little keepsake box, like I did for Bobby. Someday she'll look at it and know that I cared enough.

On the counter, there's a selection of pens. I pick one up that has a boat sailing up and down. She'll like that, I know she will. I'd have loved my mum to have bought me anything that wasn't on a birthday or Christmas, even if it were practical.

'A pen's got nothing to do with hospitals,' says Peter.

'They're hardly going to sell stethoscopes and hypodermic needles.'

I smile at the lady behind the counter, but she

doesn't smile back. She's not amused. I'm used to it. Peter's always telling me not to be so honest in public.

★　★　★

I wind the window down because it's as hot in the car as it was in the hospital. I'm holding on to Annie tightly on the back seat. Peter's driving at about ten miles an hour. It's a good job our house is only five minutes away.

I'm staring at Annie, willing her eyes to open, and it seems she's telepathic: her eyes don't even squint in the daylight.

'Welcome to the world, little girl.'

I say it quietly, so Peter doesn't hear. I'm keeping this moment for me.

★　★　★

They're due here at three. The house looks okay; I have the baby as an excuse not to bother about it so much. If it were my mum visiting, I'd make it a bit messier — if only to give her something to do. She likes to feel useful.

Bobby's waiting by the window. His little hands are around the cat's neck as it lies on the back of the settee. Annie's in the pram next to him by the window — the midwife said it's the best way to get the jaundice out of her.

'Are you sure you don't mind Monica and Nathan coming round?' says Peter. 'I tried to put them off, but she wouldn't listen.'

'It's fine, it's fine.'

Sometimes I think Peter knows about my secret, but he doesn't seem to let on.

He says I look good, *considering*, but I don't feel it. I can't move quickly with these damn painful stitches; I walk like I've drenched my trousers in starch. I'd planned what to wear when they came round, but my blouse gaped too much at the front. I'm like a cow that needed milking two days ago, and my breasts are leaking so much. So now, I'm wearing a jumper, in June, with two green paper towels from the hospital stuffed in each cup of my bra.

'They're here,' shouts Bobby, jumping down from the settee, scaring the cat.

'I'll go,' says Peter, as though he's doing me a huge favour by answering the door.

I hear them in the hallway — Monica's whispering in case Annie's asleep, but Peter's talking normally because *we've* decided to talk at a regular volume during the day so as not to make the baby used to silence. It took Bobby three years to learn that there didn't have to be quiet in order to sleep.

I'm not the first person Nathan looks at when he walks in the room. His eyes are on the floor until his gaze reaches the pram wheels, and only then does he look up. He almost tiptoes, which isn't really necessary on the carpet.

'Well aren't you a pretty little thing?' he says.

Monica's in my face and I almost jump, until I realise she's kissing my cheek.

'I know I saw you in the hospital,' she says, 'but bloody well done, you.'

She hands me a Marks & Sparks carrier bag

that she's filled with magazines, Ferrero Rocher, and a mini bottle of Snowball. Is it too early to open it?

'You don't need to whisper, everyone,' shouts Peter, as though there were a crowd in the room. 'We're doing this thing . . . '

I let him explain. It's embarrassing. It's like we're pretending to be New Age parents when we're probably the opposite. Does Nathan think I'm boring now — worrying about babies and what sort of noise is acceptable?

'Did you see the match on Sunday?' Peter says to Nathan.

'Oh God, don't mention it,' says Monica. 'He's not stopped moaning about it all week.'

'Bloody hand of God,' says Nathan. 'I'm not watching any more World Cup. I just can't believe . . . ' He shakes his head.

Monica sits and pulls Nathan down towards the settee by his hand; he lands next to her. Peter goes to the kitchen, and Monica leans towards me, her hands on her knees.

'Peter's so good, isn't he?'

I glance at Nathan; he's still not looking at me.

'He is,' I say. 'He's the best.'

Monica tilts her head. They've left Leo at his friend's so they can have a *proper visit*. She's so nice to me, she's been such a good friend. I suddenly have this sense of remorse and a crushing feeling of shame about the thoughts I've been having. She gets down onto her knees and reaches into her pocket for a rectangular tissue.

'It's only normal,' she says. 'I cried for days after I had Leo.'

I hadn't realised I was crying.

I pat my face dry and look at Nathan above the tissue.

He narrows his eyes when he looks at me.

Was that hatred? Does he think I'm weird? I've always been inappropriate. I feel like I'm in the wrong life. I should be with Nathan, not Peter. He was with me first, after all.

There was a girl in my class at school who died in a car crash when she was fourteen. I'll always remember her name: Leslie Pickering. It's terrible that I think about her at times like this, and I don't know why I do. I think to myself: *she never has to go through this*, and I wish I were her. These thoughts scare me.

'It's just . . . just . . . '

I think of poor Leslie Pickering's parents. I bet they wish *I* were dead instead of her, too.

My face is in my hands. Why am I doing this in front of them?

Monica pats my knees and rubs them like I need warming.

'We need to arrange a night out,' she says.

I look up. Nathan wrinkles his nose.

'Don't be stupid, Monica,' he says. 'She's just had a baby — why the hell would she want a night out?'

I sit up a bit straighter and stuff the tissue up my sleeve.

'Mind your language in front of Bobby,' says Monica. 'What about Lytham Club Day tomorrow instead? We could let the boys go on a few rides.'

'Actually, that doesn't seem such a bad idea,' I

say, pretending I want to go outside — that I wouldn't care if everyone saw me walking like I've a horse missing between my legs. I could take some painkillers. 'I've been in the house for too long. I could do with getting out.'

I try to make eye contact with Nathan, but after a few minutes, it gets silly. I'm ridiculous. Because it's all in my head. Why would he want me? A mother who's just given birth to her second child, and a wife who's supposed to be in love with her husband. I'm a joke.

5

Anna

Sheila, the volunteer who comes in nearly every day, is in the back room of the bookshop, filling the kettle and sighing to herself. I don't want to be here either. I need to be investigating the address that Debbie sent the email from.

It was at the end of primary school that I started the scrapbook filled with facts about her. I thought if I kept a list, then it would keep her alive — it was something tangible. As soon as I learned something new, I would write it down. There must be over a hundred snippets of information in there. Sometimes things would slip out of Dad or Robert's mouth and I would repeat it again and again in my head till I could find a pen and paper. Grandad never said much about Debbie, though. I never had to carry a notebook when I went to his house. Perhaps he thought he was being kind.

Grandad usually comes into the bookshop on a Sunday after the ten o'clock Mass. He sits at the counter if he can wrestle Sheila out of the way. He said he wasn't really into religion until Gran died nearly twenty years ago. He's been to church every Sunday since.

My grandmother was sixty-nine when she had her first, fatal heart attack. I was ten, nearly

35

eleven. She used to talk about my mother all the time. 'I want you to remember all the little bits,' she said, 'in case I'm not around for long enough.' It was as though she'd predicted her own death. She was the one who helped me create the scrapbook. 'Your brother's still too hurt to hear all of this. I don't see that changing any time soon, Lord help him,' she said. 'But I'm glad you want to know. Frank can't talk about her for long . . . He hides in his office.'

Grandad's office is a little wooden shed he built in their back yard.

I wonder how he is taking the news about the note from Debbie. Dad must have told him by now, yet Grandad's not answering his telephone or replying to his emails or texts. My messages are coming up as *read*, so I know he's okay. But it's not like him to ignore anything. He loves technology — he was the person who explained the workings of the Internet to me. 'We are all closer together because of this,' he said. 'Though sometimes it makes us realise we're worlds apart.'

The new volunteer is five minutes late. How can she expect to be taken seriously if she's not punctual? She's meant to be embarking on a new start. That's what my boss, Isobel, said. I might be the manager of this bookshop, but sometimes Isobel sends volunteers here because she wants to appear more Christian than she really is.

At least it takes my mind off the letter for five minutes. Or rather, letters: plural. Why are different aspects of my life falling apart at exactly the same time? Can't things go well for more than one day?

I put Jack's letter back in his wallet last night, but only after I had taken a photo of it on my mobile phone. *To the love of my life.* That's what she called him. It wasn't dated, so I can't tell if it is old or new. There were no references to any events past or present. I try to think back to when Jack and I got together, to remember names of past girlfriends, but I can't. I don't think we even mentioned our exes; it didn't seem important once we found each other.

If the volunteer isn't here in three minutes, I'll look at the letter on my phone ag —

'Annie Donnelly?'

I didn't even hear the door open. A woman is standing in front of me. She is taller than me and in her late fifties, at a guess. She's without make-up and her face looks weather-beaten and tanned, as though she spends her weekends outdoors. Her hair is dark, and her skin has a healthy glow that I will never have, being in this bookshop all the time.

'It's Anna,' I say, a little more harshly than I intended.

I slide off the stool behind the counter.

'Sorry.' Her voice is quiet, but she returns my gaze. 'I'm Ellen.'

'It's eight minutes past.'

I'm not usually so spiky, but already I get the impression she doesn't want to be here. She glances at the clock behind me, then looks at her wrist.

'My watch is behind . . . since the clocks went forward. I must've set it wrong.'

'Right.' I try not to waver from her gaze.

The clocks went forward nearly three months ago, but I don't mention it.

'Follow me into the back,' I say, leading her into the small stockroom. Every spare space on the twenty-three long shelves is crammed with books.

'I'll get to my spot behind the counter,' says Sheila, carrying her cup of tea.

'Do you want to see my CV?' asks Ellen, blinking so much now, it's like there is something in her eyes. She reaches into her handbag before I reply, and hands me a brown envelope. 'It sounds worse than it was.'

'Excuse me?'

'What they say I did. Did Isobel tell you?'

She means her criminal record. I've seen enough crime dramas to know that everyone says, *I didn't do it.*

'No. Isobel has this thing about confidentiality — she takes it seriously. If you want to tell me when you're ready, then that's up to you. As Isobel took it upon herself to get your references, you don't have to tell me anything.'

I really want to ask what she was in prison for, but the words won't come out. I'm the manager — I can't engage in gossip.

'Oh,' says Ellen.

I've said too much, mentioning Isobel and her *confidentiality*, which I over exaggerated. She goes on about data protection, but she's the biggest gossip I know.

We look at each other as I wait for Ellen to tell me all about it. She breaks my stare, looking instead at all the books on the shelves.

'What do you want me to do?' she says.

I try not to look disappointed — it might be on her CV. Though I doubt most people would count being in prison as an occupation.

I point to the table, which has three huge boxes of books on it.

'These need sorting into categories and putting on the shelves, which are labelled with different genres, and fiction and non-fiction. Would you like a cup of tea first? My grandmother always used to say . . . '

I walk towards the kitchenette, not bothering to finish my sentence. Ellen's already unpacking the books. I was boring myself anyway.

The sound of the kettle masks my opening her envelope. There is only one thing I want to check. If my mother were alive, she would be fifty-eight tomorrow. I look at the back of Ellen's head. There is a photo of Robert in one of our old albums, where he's gluing plane parts together; Debbie is sitting with her back to the camera — her long dark hair is pulled into a bun, so it looks like it's shorter. Ellen looks just like her from behind.

I peek at the top of her CV. I see it.

I read it again to make sure.

Ellen has the same date of birth as my mother.

★　★　★

Sheila sniffs and remains on her perch behind the till.

'I don't *have* to go in the back if I don't want to,' she says. 'If she wants to say hello, she'll have to come in here.' She leans forward. 'She could be a murderess for all we know.' She whispers as quietly as a church bell.

I could argue that Ellen probably isn't a convicted killer, and that being the veteran volunteer of the bookshop with twelve years' service, Sheila should make an effort to welcome her, but I don't. It will fall on deaf ears, as things like this usually do with her — she pretends, at times convenient to her, that she's hard of hearing.

Instead, I say, 'How many people do you know that have the same birth date as you?'

It's like I can hear the index cards sifting in her mind as her eyes drift away into the past.

'Mavis Brierly,' she says. 'Fattest girl at school, though I don't know how; no one had much money to buy so much food. After that, I met a woman in the maternity ward when I was expecting Timothy — can't remember her name . . . began with a 'C', if I remember rightly. So, two people. Though they're probably dead now. Most people I know are.'

I shouldn't have asked her; I shouldn't be thinking like this.

The last time it happened was six years ago. It was the woman who used to work in the bakery a few doors down from the shop I used to work in. If it hadn't been for Jack, I'd have a restraining order against me.

'Okay,' I say. 'So, it's not as unusual as I thought.'

'Obviously not. There are only three hundred and sixty-five days in a year, and millions of people in this world.' She leans towards me again. 'Why do you ask? Has Tenko in there got the same birthday as you?'

'Sheila! You must stop talking like that. Everyone deserves a second chance.'

Ellen clears her throat. She's standing at the doorway.

'This book,' she says. 'I think it might be valuable. It's a *Harry Potter* first edition.'

Sheila picks up a pen and writes on the notepad next to the till on the counter. She pushes it towards me when she's finished. *She's probably a thief.*

My face grows hot as I rip the sheet from the pad. I screw it up and drop it into the bin, before ushering Ellen back into the storeroom. She can't have seen what Sheila wrote, but she will have noticed the whispering, and the silence that followed her presence.

'I'm so sorry about that,' I say, in case she read it. 'I'll give Sheila a warning. I don't want you to feel uncomfortable.'

Ellen sits at the table and places the book in front of her.

'It's okay. I'm used to it,' she says. 'There was one person in particular who targeted me when I was inside: Jackie Annand. She never liked me. But that's another life. I'm here now.'

She looks up at me and smiles. She has the same eyes as Sophie.

6

Wednesday, 2 July 1986
Debbie

We need to bin this digital alarm clock. Even when I close my eyes, I can still see the angry red numbers reminding me I'm not asleep. It's one fifteen in the morning. If I go by her previous feeds, Annie'll be waking again at three thirty. I could go and heat a bottle ready, in case she wakes early.

I keep checking she's still breathing. She's only a foot away, in her basket. What if I fall asleep too deeply, roll off the bed and crush her? No, no that couldn't happen — I've not fallen out of bed since I was a child. But you never know. I shuffle away from the edge a bit.

I close my eyes, but my mind is busy with too much crap. My body's exhausted — why won't my brain listen to it? It's no good. The memory of last Saturday keeps coming back to me. I wish I'd never gone with them to Lytham Club Day. There were too many people around — everyone stared at me. *You shouldn't be outside.* I bet that's what they were thinking.

I watched Bobby and Leo on the little rides, while Nathan, Monica and Peter went on the waltzers. It was too warm. The children's rollercoaster went round and round and round, hundreds of times. I had to sit on the grass.

Peter and the others came over, swaying.

'That was amazing,' said Monica. 'I haven't been on one of those since I was a teenager.'

'You have to go on something, Debs,' said Peter.

I ended up climbing onto the lorry that had been converted into a two-storey 'fun' house with the boys. Bobby took me by the hand and pulled me up the stairs.

'You'll love it, Mummy,' he said.

Halfway up the stairs, my legs started to shake. Why hadn't I realised how high it would be up there? The eyes on the faces painted on the walls watched me. I tried to cover them with my hands as I walked past, but there were too many. Their gaze followed me until we reached the outside part of the upper level.

I held the rail opposite.

Peter and Monica stood waving at us; I couldn't let go to wave back.

It was too high. I couldn't breathe. A cold sweat covered my body.

Oh God, I thought. I'm going to die.

I kneeled on the metal floor. The ringing in my ears got louder.

'Mummy? Mummy? Are you okay?'

Breathe, breathe.

I put my head close to my chest, closing my eyes.

I don't know how many minutes passed before Bobby's hand touched my shoulder.

'Is it too high for you, Mummy?' he said. 'Don't worry. I'll help you down. I used to be like this when I was four.'

He reached down for my hand; I looked up at him.

My breathing gradually slowed.

'I'm sorry, Bobby.' I looked around, relieved I could get the words out of my mouth. The sound in my ears faded. 'Come on, love. Let's find something fun for you to go on next.'

I don't know what happened to me that day.

Am I dying? I feel numb and my body doesn't feel like mine any more. That day, I could barely breathe — there must be something wrong with me. My mind might be shutting down first.

1.23 a.m.

Oh God. I might go insane with tiredness. In an article in one of Mum's magazines, it said if you can't get to sleep, get up and make a milky drink, but I can't find the energy.

After counting three hundred and fifty-six sheep, I turn onto my back and look up to the ceiling. This is torture. I bet Monica never had this.

I can't believe I was trying to catch Nathan's eye on Friday. What was I hoping to achieve? My face feels hot with the memory of it. He doesn't even know how I feel — *I* don't even know how I feel. Monica wouldn't have noticed anyway. She was too busy being amazed by how great Peter is.

'We should get a microwave too, Nath,' she'd said. 'We could have jacket potatoes every day, then.'

He'd rolled his eyes at her back, but frowned when he realised that I saw him.

Go away, Nathan, I'd thought to myself, fully aware that — as always — my feelings were as fickle as Preston sunshine. There'd been a smash of china in the kitchen, and Monica had jumped up immediately.

'Are you all right, Peter?'

It was my turn to roll my eyes. I glanced at Nathan, but he was looking at the impression Monica had left on the settee. I wondered, then — as I do now, in the darkness — if he'd had the same thought that I did. That perhaps Monica was in love with my husband.

★   ★   ★

'*Get up! Get up!*'

I sit up quickly.

'I'm coming, Uncle Charlie,' I say without thinking.

But there's no one here. The bedroom is semi-lit by daylight filtering through the curtains. Annie's basket is empty — so is Peter's side of the bed.

Why did I call out for Uncle Charlie? My mum's brother has been dead for years.

I battle with the cover, tangled in my legs, almost tripping out of bed.

Bobby's duvet is made up as though he's not slept in it.

'Peter!' I shout as I run down the stairs. I push open the living-room door, and there, sitting in the armchair holding Annie, is my mother.

Bobby's sitting on the floor, eating dry Rice Krispies, and watching *Picture Box* on the telly.

That's not right — it can't be after nine thirty.

'Is this on tape?' I ask Mum.

She looks to the heavens.

'Course not, love. Since when have you seen me operating machinery? And shouldn't your first question be why Bobby's not at school?' She doesn't wait for me to reply. 'He said he wasn't feeling very well. The baby must've kept him up all night.'

'What? No, that can't be right. Where's Peter?' I'm still standing at the door in my nightie; she'll tell me to get dressed any minute now. 'Has he popped to the corner shop?'

'He's at work.'

'Really? Has a week passed already? That went quickly.'

Mum's eyes widen, and she shakes her head a little.

'I do wonder about you sometimes,' she says. 'You have not been asleep for a whole week. He popped into work for an emergency — said he wanted you to catch up on your rest.'

She sits Annie up, rubbing her little back.

She knows I didn't mean that, but she's doing me a favour by being here, so I don't argue with her. Part of me wishes I *had* slept for a week. 3.15–9.30 a.m. — that means I've had six hours and fifteen minutes' sleep. A record. I haven't slept that long since I was four months pregnant.

'I was just joking about sleeping that long,' I say.

I know she doesn't believe me. She probably thinks I'm not coping. It's family legend that the day after I was born, she was up and about doing

46

housework, or sheafing wheat in the fields or whatever.

'Do you know what'll do you some good?'

I glance at the ceiling. 'What?'

'Getting a bit of exercise. I've been doing it every morning with what's-her-name on TV-am.'

'You mean Mad Lizzie? Have you heck been doing aerobics, Mum.'

'Well, I watch her do it while I have a cup of tea. Her energy's infectious.'

'She'd make me feel worse,' I whisper, turning to look at myself in the hall mirror. Before Mum has a chance to mention it, I say, 'I'll just have a quick wash and get dressed.'

As I put my foot on the first stair, she hollers, 'Best run a bath, Deborah. You look like you could do with one.'

*   *   *

I stare at my face in the bathroom mirror until it becomes a boring collection of features that could belong to a stranger. My body has been hijacked for so long, it's going to be months before I feel like it's mine again.

Mum thought I believed I'd slept for a whole week. I have my moments, but I'm not that ditzy. She probably remembers the time I swallowed an apple seed when I was pregnant with Bobby. I telephoned her in a panic that it might harm him — everything scared me then.

'What do you think will happen, Deborah? That an apple tree will grow inside you?'

I've since learned that apple seeds contain

47

cyanide, so I'll be sure to tell her that if she brings it up again.

The steam from the bath starts to blur the glass.

'*You know it's not meant to be like this.*'

A man's voice. It sounded like Uncle Charlie again. But what if it's not him — what if it's God trying to speak to me?

I open the bathroom door.

'Mum? Is that you?'

Silence.

There's nobody upstairs. What's happening to me?

I dress quickly, putting on whatever's on the back of the chair in the bedroom.

Downstairs, Mum has dressed Bobby, and a sleeping Annie is in her pram under the window. Mum looks up at me as I loiter at the living-room door again, as though it's not my house.

'Are you all right?' says Mum. 'You look as though you've forgotten something.'

'I'm fine.'

I walk straight to the kitchen without saying another word. After the *sleeping for a week* conversation, I can't tell her what's actually worrying me; she wouldn't understand. The voice I heard sounded as though it was outside of my head, but there was no one there. I feel like someone's watching me all the time.

I don't know what's real and what's not any more.

7

Anna

It has been five days since I read the email and I still can't find the right words to write back. I searched the loft for the box of Debbie's things, but I couldn't find it anywhere. This morning, Jack suggested it might be in the storage unit with the rest of the belongings we haven't seen for years. I must not have looked at her things for over three years. Jack promised he would go over later to collect what he can find.

I pull up outside Dad and Monica's to collect Sophie. I haven't seen nor heard from Monica since last week. I should have brought her a box of chocolates or something to let her know I'm thinking of her — that I appreciate all that she's done for me.

Growing up, neither I nor Robert called her *Mum*. Robert had always known her as Monica, so I must have copied him. 'Why do you call your mum by her first name?' friends used to ask. 'She just likes it that way,' I'd say, too embarrassed to tell the truth.

Monica never treated us any differently to Leo. It must have annoyed him. I haven't heard from him in months — he's been living in America near his dad for almost ten years. It must be so hard for Monica, Leo being so far away.

Dad opens the door before I have the chance to ring the doorbell.

'Good day, love?' he asks, as though it is a normal, unremarkable day.

How can he act so nonchalant? My mother is alive! Perhaps he's worried about Monica. Leo's been gone for so long, and now my mother might be coming back to replace her. Like *she* did to Debbie.

I put my head around the living-room door. Sophie raises her hand in greeting, chewing something without taking her eyes off the television. There's a plate next to her with an unopened tangerine.

'Not bad, thanks,' I say. 'Is that chocolate she's eating?'

Dad's hovering in the hallway and doesn't answer my question.

'Do you want a cup of tea, or do you want to head straight off?'

'Are you trying to get rid of me?'

I follow him into the kitchen. He puts the kettle on and beckons me to stand closer to him. He waits until the water starts to hiss until he speaks.

'Monica's not feeling too well,' he says.

He points to the kettle, then up to the ceiling. What he means is that the walls are very thin in their three-bedroomed terraced house — you can hear next door sneezing, and I dread to think what else.

'Shall I take her up a drink?' I ask.

Making yourself heard whilst trying to be quiet is harder than it seems.

Dad shakes his head. 'Best leave her to it, love.'

'It's okay,' I say, pouring hot water into the teapot. 'I want to see Monica for myself. I'll take her up a digestive.'

Dad doesn't look happy, but what is he going to do? Wrestle me to the ground to stop me? I pour tea into a china cup, and milk into a little jug, and place them on a tray with a biscuit she probably won't eat. I carry them upstairs, everything rattling.

I balance the tray on the palm of one hand and knock on their bedroom door with the other. There's no reply. She used to do this a lot when she and Dad had arguments about the boys when they were teenagers. Robert and Leo didn't get on most of the time. They had to share a bedroom. Robert's side was reasonably tidy; Leo's not so much.

I knock again.

'Monica, it's me, Anna.'

Still no reply.

I open the door. My eyes go directly to their bed, but she's sitting in the chair that faces the window. I place the tray on the little table, and sit on the footstool next to her.

'Have you been crying?' I ask.

She blinks several times.

'Oh, hello, Anna. I'm sorry. I'm not with it today.'

'That's okay. Is it the news about Debbie?'

I can't call Debbie *my mother* in front of her. It feels disloyal to Monica; she has always been here for me.

51

'Yes, I suppose it is,' she says. 'It's all come as a bit of a shock.'

I pick up the cup of tea and offer it to her.

'I've put two sugars in it.'

She purses her lips in a smile. 'You're too good to me. I don't deserve it.'

'Of course you do. Who else would put up with Robert and me?'

There is an answer that hangs in the air that neither of us even jokes about: *Not my mother.*

'You know,' she says, 'I felt tremendous guilt getting together with your dad after your mother left. She was my best friend, you know. I met her in the third year of secondary school. I'd just moved up north, and spent the first couple of days sitting on my own at dinner time. Then Debbie came over to me — of course, she was Deborah, then. Her mum, you see, she always wanted her to be Deborah, never Debbie.'

I love hearing Monica talk about my mother like this. Grandad still calls her Deborah — when he talks about her, that is.

'Has Dad told Grandad about the email?'

Monica drops a splash of tea onto her skirt as she sips from her cup. She frowns, disorientated at being interrupted.

'I imagine so. You'll have to ask him.'

I take the tea cup away from her as she dabs at the blotch.

'Where was I? Oh yes, at school. She walked up to me, her dark, wavy hair flowing behind her — you've got her hair, you know, the exact same. She looked stunning. Who looks so beautiful while they're a schoolgirl? Back then it was different — kids weren't allowed to wear make-up to school, and I had terrible spots. Debbie thought she was hideous, but she was never hideous. She was a joy to be around . . . well, until the end . . . Anyway, when she met my eye that day, I was sitting on a bench near the Maths block. I had to turn around to check it was me she was talking to. 'I hear you're from London,' were her first words to me. 'I'd love to go there,' she said.'

'What did you two used to get up to?'

I have asked the question so many times, but Monica never complains. Sometimes, there will be something I've never heard before.

'We didn't get up to much really. In the first summer we spent together, we were fourteen. All we did was talk about boys, though the ones at our school could never compare to David Cassidy.' She smiles at me. 'He was famous in the seventies — Google him. We were so naive. We read about boys and sex from a book, for God's sake. *Forever* by Judy Blume — though we'd heard about most things by sixteen.' She returns her gaze to the window. 'We didn't spend much time at her house. Ithink she was ashamed, but she needn't have been — her parents were lovely.'

'Why would she feel ashamed?'

'Her parents sent her to a school in the next town — she mixed with other people than those on her estate.' She looks at me and places a hand on mine. 'I'm not saying that it's right or anything, for her to have felt like that. It's just how it was. Her parents were older than most when she was born. When she was growing up, they focused on what was best for her. I wish my parents had been like that, but Debbie felt embarrassed that they showed so much interest in her life. It made her lonely, I think. She didn't have many friends. She was like you, really.'

'A loner, you mean?'

'No, no. As if I'd say something like that to you.' She squeezes my hand, rubbing the top of it with her thumb. 'She chose her friends carefully . . . was wary of other people. Her parents sheltered her from the big bad world, protected her from the hardship they suffered.' Monica sighs. 'Time goes by too quickly. She was always there for me. Until the end. It was all my fault.'

My ears tingle with a new bit of the story — she has never mentioned any cross words between them.

'What do you mean it was your fault?'

'Has your dad never talked about the troubles we had?'

'He doesn't talk about her much at all, let alone any problems.'

'Thinking about it . . . I don't know if Peter would want me to say anything to you about it.' Monica's not looking at me any more. 'We haven't talked about it for such a long time, I don't know what he remembers. Memories can get distorted . . . hold you back, you know? Such a horrible time.'

Monica is staring out of the window again. It's like a mist has covered her eyes, between the past and the present. I follow her gaze. Mr Flowers, from the house opposite, has dropped his keys; he's trying to pick them up using the end of his walking stick. I should go out and help him, but I want to hear what Monica has to say.

'I've said too much. Your father never wanted you to find out anything bad about Debbie. He blames himself, too, I imagine. There's a lot that's been airbrushed from Debbie's history.'

'What do you mean?'

She sits up and reaches for a tissue to wipe away the fresh tears.

Dad's heavy footsteps are on the stairs.

Monica leans over and puts a hand on my shoulder.

'Please don't tell your dad I told you anything, will you? He'd kill me if he found out I mentioned anything.'

'I'm sure he wouldn't mind. You've hardly said anything.'

She leans against the back of the chair.

'I loved her, you know. She was like a sister to me.'

Dad turns the handle of the bedroom door. I put a smile on my face, so that when he opens the door, he'll think everything is fine.

* * *

I put the key into our front door, and remember the letter hidden in Jack's wallet. I have spent the past week worrying about it, but barely thought of it today. Does that mean I don't care about him any more? I need to confront him, but that would mean admitting I was snooping again. I can't have him think I'm not coping. It can't be like last time. I nearly lost everything.

I let Sophie in through the door before me. She looks so small in her little grey school pinafore — her cute little legs. I can't lose my little girl; I must keep it together — pretend everything is okay. But I make a mental note to go through all of Jack's contacts on Facebook to see if there's anyone by that name — there can't be many. I have never met anyone called Francesca.

I reach into Sophie's school bag and take out her reading book. She skips through to the kitchen and sits at the table next to Jack. I place the book in front of Sophie and she begins reading quietly to herself.

'You're back early,' I say.

I glance around the kitchen. Jack's put all the dirty dishes into the dishwasher and the empty beer bottles into the recycling. The worktops have been wiped clean and the bin has been emptied.

There's a carrier bag of food on the counter. I peek inside: ingredients for a spaghetti bolognese and a bottle of red wine. I kiss the top of Jack's head and we almost clash as he jolts in surprise.

'Did you remember at last?' I say to him.

'Remember what?' He winks and walks out of the kitchen, coming back seconds later with a bouquet of flowers and a small gift bag.

'I'm so sorry, Anna,' he says. 'I've had the present in the boot of my car for days. I was mortified when I got to work this morning, saw it, and realised the date.' He hands me the bunch of roses. 'I got these as an extra — to say sorry.' He strokes my cheek. 'Are you going to open your present?'

'I might save it for later — when I can really appreciate it.'

He's smiling for the first time in weeks — I don't want to spoil it by mentioning anything about love letters from strange women. He's still looking at me, but his eyes glaze over.

'Are you all right?' I say.

He tilts his head to one side, blinking his thoughts away. 'I was about to ask you the same thing. After that email — '

'I'm fine.' I don't want to talk about it in front of Sophie. I nod in the direction of our daughter, her little head down in concentration.

'If you put Sophie to bed,' says Jack, 'I can nip out to the storage unit and get that box of things you were looking for the other day.'

'That would be great. Thank you.'

It seems I'm not the only one pretending we're all right. I know he's tried to make it better with the flowers, but I know there is something he's hiding from me.

It was four years ago when I first searched Jack's belongings. Sophie was asleep, and Jack had nipped to the bathroom. He'd just used his phone and the pin number wasn't needed so I picked it up. There were several texts from a woman.

Jack caught me looking, though I was hardly subtle. I was standing in the middle of the living room with his phone in my shaking hands.

'What are you doing, Anna?' he'd said.

'I was just borrowing your phone — mine's out of battery.'

I didn't look up. He walked towards me quickly, holding out his hand for me to give him the phone, but I held on to it.

'But we're at home,' he said. 'Use the landline.'

'Who's Samantha?'

'What? Give me the phone, Anna. You can't just go through people's things.'

He lifted his hand to grab it, but I put my hand behind my back.

'You're my husband, Jack. We shouldn't have secrets.'

He folded his arms slowly.

'There are boundaries, Anna. People have boundaries. Haven't you learned that from what happened with Gillian Crossley?'

'That's nothing like this. And you said we'd never mention it. It was two years ago.'

He tilted his head to the side.

'I know. But sometimes I get scared you'll do something like that again. She said you were stalking her. It's happened one too many times.'

'That's below the belt, Jack. You know I wasn't well. I had counselling. I know the signs, when to get help.'

He stared at me.

'You'd tell me if things were getting on top of you, wouldn't you? I love you. I'm not your enemy.'

I glanced at the photographs on the wall: of Jack and me, of Sophie.

'I know. I'm just tired.' I brought my hand round and handed him the phone. 'But who is

Samantha? I'm sure any wife would want to know who the woman texting her husband is.'

He shook his head, grabbing the phone from my hands.

'A new solicitor at work. And if you'd read the texts properly you'd have seen that.'

My face burned.

Later, when he was asleep, I checked his firm's website and there she was: Samantha Webster, Solicitor — her arms folded in a serious pose for the camera.

I look at him now, listening to Sophie read, and you wouldn't think he was hiding something. If I were to admit I had searched his wallet, he would accuse me of *relapsing*. But what happened all those years ago has taught me one thing: two can play at that game.

★   ★   ★

Monica used to say that if a boy caused you so much heartache, then they weren't the right one for you. My first heartbreak was aged twelve. I lay on my bed, listening to LeAnn Rimes belting out 'How Do I Live' to drown out the sound of the boys arguing in the room next to my head. Monica knocked at the door.

'Are you okay, Anna? You've not come down for your tea.'

'Fine,' I shouted over the noise.

She walked in, closed the door, and opened the curtains and the window.

'A bit of fresh air is what's needed in here,' she said. She sat on the edge of my bed and swiped the hair from my face. 'What's wrong, love?'

'Nothing.'

'I've plated your dinner up. I'll leave it on the side. Just heat it up in the mike when you're ready to come down.'

She didn't move from the bed, was still stroking my hair.

'Thanks.'

'If you want to talk about it, I'm here.'

'Hmm.'

The song ended, but it started again because I'd put it on repeat.

'Is it your friends, Annie? Have they all ganged up on you again?'

I shook my head. That hadn't happened in months, but it wasn't them this time.

'A boy?'

I shrugged, my shoulders cushioned against the pillow.

'It's hard, isn't it?' she said.

'I suppose.'

I had to blink quickly so my tears didn't fall out of my eyes.

'Hannah said yes to a date with him. She knew I liked him.'

In the end, I couldn't stop the tears falling.

'Oh, love.'

I sobbed into the pillow. Monica lay down next to me, put her arms around me, and I cried into her jumper.

'Let it all out, sweetheart.'

We lay like that for ten minutes. The song played another two times, and I finally stopped crying.

60

'He wasn't the right one for you, that's all. The One will come along and he'll like you right back.' She stood up. 'Talk to me about it whenever you want. I've been there. School is tough, I know. It'll pass quickly enough.'

Now I blink away the tears that have formed in my eyes as I hear Jack's car pull up outside. I open the front door quietly and watch him open the boot and take out the box.

Is he being nice because he feels guilty, or because he genuinely wants to help me? Heartache sounds too indulgent when you've been with a person for years. I might not like Jack sometimes, but he's my family. I love him. Perhaps that's why I haven't confronted him: I don't want to hear the truth.

He's trying hard to be quiet, so he doesn't wake Sophie. I stand aside as he carries the box into the house as though it were a boulder. I shove my hands underneath and take it from him. It's not that heavy at all, but I pretend it is as I lower it to the ground.

'Careful — it's weighty,' he says.

'It's okay. I'm used to carrying boxes of books at the shop.'

It's fifty centimetres square and painted pale blue with hand-drawn flowers all over it. It has my writing in black marker: *Mother*. I don't remember writing that; it's been years since I've seen it. I want Jack to leave the room, so I can look at the contents alone.

'Well?' he says.

'Well?' I repeat, in the hope he'll take the hint, but he sits on the edge of the sofa.

I sit on the rug and lift the lid off. Straight away I see my scrapbook. It's decorated with pictures of beaches in Tenerife from holiday brochures, models from *Mizz* and *Woman's Own* who I thought might look like her, and The Beatles. Inside the box are the 45rpm singles Gran gave me: 'Norwegian Wood' and 'Heart of Glass'. Dad always switched the car radio off if one of those songs came on.

After Gran died, I began asking him more questions about Debbie. He gave me a telephone number, saying it was for Debbie's old mobile. At first, I rang it every day, but there was never a reply, obviously. I used to tell the answer machine my problems, what was happening at school, how much I missed her. It only dawned on me a few years later that it can't have been Debbie's — she wouldn't have had a mobile phone in 1986. It was probably one of Monica or Dad's old numbers; there must be at least a thousand missed calls on it. I don't want to imagine them listening to the messages I left.

'That's an unusual collection of pictures,' says Jack, making me jump.

I had forgotten he was here.

'I was a child when I decorated it.'

I shouldn't feel embarrassed in front of him, but I do.

'But why beaches?' he says.

'It's Tenerife. It was where she was last seen.'

'That's a bit macabre, isn't it? What if she was . . . '

He stops himself from saying what he usually says after he's been drinking.

'I just thought she must have really liked Tenerife,' I say, 'to have never come back.'

It's like my eleven-year-old self is saying the words.

Jack gets up and heads towards the door. Before he leaves, he turns around.

'Why didn't you just put a picture of Debbie on it — instead of models who look like her?'

He doesn't wait for me to answer. He looks away from me and tilts his head as though pondering. He hasn't seen the memories inside my shell box. He might have feigned interest when we first started going out, but he isn't bothered about the details of her as a person. He would rather pontificate at length about what happened to her — as though he were discussing a murder victim on the television.

I lay everything out on the floor as I take it out of the box. The records, the scrapbook, the old cigar box Debbie decorated with seashells — half of which are chipped. I know what's in it without opening it, but I flip the lid anyway. It's quite pathetic really, the number of things in there: my hospital wristband, a stick of Blackpool rock — now a mass of crumbled sugar held together by a cylinder of cellophane. There's also a pen with a moving ship and a silver pendant depicting the Virgin Mary with the words *Bless This Child*, threaded on a piece of pink string. Dad can't remember buying any of the items in the box, so I like to think Debbie chose them just for me.

I open my scrapbook.

She wore flip-flops in the summer and Doc
 Martens boots in the winter.
She had a birthmark in the shape of
 Australia on the top of her leg.
She 'couldn't take her drink' after having
 children.

The front door shuts — I hadn't heard it open. Jack walks into the living room carrying a box the same size as my seashell one.

'I forgot this,' he says, placing it on the floor beside me.

It's decorated with what looks like real Liquorice Allsorts. I pick it up; it smells sugary, medicinal.

'They're real sweets,' I say. 'Where did this come from?'

He shrugs, and walks towards the door.

'It was packed next to your box. I'm going upstairs to make an important phone call. Don't just walk in, if that's okay? It'll seem unprofessional.'

I wave my hand in reply. His phone call might be far from professional, but I can't take my eyes off the box covered in sweets. It must be Robert's. It's an old King Edward cigar box like mine. I knew he must have had one, but I've never seen it before. I assumed he'd thrown it away. What was it doing in our storage?

I don't open it straight away. Like with presents, an unopened object is far more interesting than an unwrapped one. I turn it in my hands and hold it. She must have spent ages gluing them on like this.

I place it on the floor and slowly lift the lid.

There are more items in this one than in mine. Robert probably added some pieces himself. There's his conker that Grandad told him to bake in the oven for seven hours. After that, he painted it with five coats of Ronseal in mahogany. I would have been three or four years old. I bring it up to my nose — I remember the scent as he painted it, but it doesn't smell of anything now. The treatment was effective; it still looks as smooth and shiny as it did then.

I take out his other things: hospital wristband; a Pez dispenser, with a few rectangular sweets still inside; his first report from primary school; and birthday cards signed from *Mummy and Daddy*. I don't have any birthday cards with my mother's name inside. I run my fingers along the writing in one of them.

Underneath all of these is an old photo processing envelope. It lists different sizes and finishes of photographs — our old home address is scrawled on the form in childish handwriting. It's dated 20 February 1987 — nearly seven months after my mother disappeared. There is a cylinder inside it. I stick my hand in and pull out a black plastic container. I peel the cap off it, praying there's something inside.

There is.

A whole roll of film that might contain pictures of my mother that I've never seen before.

8

Friday, 4 July 1986
Debbie

The sun on my face is delicious. I feel like I haven't been outside for weeks, when it's only been days. Being inside feels so oppressive, like there are a hundred faces watching every move I make.

Outside, I feel free, away from prying eyes. Annie's sleeping in her pram, and even though I've only had two hours' sleep I feel calm for the first time in days.

Peter's finally back at work (I didn't tell him it was silly starting back on a Friday) and Bobby's at school until half three so I've over two hours of freedom. I park the pram outside the newsagents and pull the hood up.

The bell dings as I push the door.

'Is it okay if I leave it open? The baby's asleep outside.'

'Right you are, love,' says Mrs Abernathy.

There's that new song on the radio playing: 'The Lady in Red'. It's not like Mrs Abernathy to have the radio on. For a love song, it sounds pretty dreary — it's no 'Addicted to Love', that's for sure. I can't remember it on *Top of the Pops* last Thursday, but then I can't remember what I had for breakfast this morning. I *do* remember the 'Spirit in the Sky' video though, because it cheered me up. Mum wouldn't approve. She keeps harping on about Bobby being baptised so he can go to a better secondary school. I told her that's hardly the Christian way of thinking about things, but she just spouted her usual words of eternal damnation. I'll probably be waiting for my children in the burning fires of hell, if my mother's prediction comes true. It'll be more fun there anyway. Though the temperature might get a bit much; it's far too hot today.

Under the window is a giant freezer. I used to love picking an ice cream out of those as a kid — when Mum and Dad could afford one, that is.

I choose a lemonade ice lolly and, as I close the lid, I see him outside.

He's getting out of his car across the road. I quickly pay for the ice and dash out of the shop. He's walking in the opposite direction; he hasn't seen me. I've never been an attractive runner, so I try to walk a little faster. He's still a fair distance away from me. My flip-flops are smacking my heels — I'm surprised he can't hear me. I look around; there aren't many people.

'Nathan!'

He stops and turns around. I stop trotting just in time, and the breeze blows my long dress so it clings to my legs. He's still looking at it when I reach him.

'Hi, Debs.' He lifts his sunglasses and puts them on the top of his head. 'Pete let you out of the house, did he?'

I just nod. There are tiny freckles on his nose.

'Are you all right?' he says. 'Fancy a quick coffee?'

'Okay.' It seems the ability to think and speak has abandoned me.

He takes me by the hand and doesn't let go as we cross the road. I should be worried that someone we know might see us, but I'm not. He only lets go of my hand when he pushes the door of the café.

There are at least six tables free, but he chooses one at the back next to the door to the toilets. He pulls a chair out for me, and I sit. I feel like my head's out of my body — this whole situation feels so weird. We've not been alone since we were an item ten years ago.

That summer was so intense. We were sixteen, and secondary school had finished. We had no distractions from each other. Both of his parents went out to work, and we'd spend lazy days lying on his bed, listening to records and smoking cigarettes.

'Promise you'll never leave me for someone else,' he said to me one hot afternoon.

We'd closed the curtains for shade and they blew gently in the breeze.

'I'm not going anywhere,' I said, staring at the ceiling.

He rested his hand on my tummy and I placed my hand on his.

'Good,' he said. 'I don't know what I'd do if you did.'

He's still as good-looking now — better even. He's holding the menu, but staring into my eyes. I know, without glancing in the mirror, that my chest and neck will be red and blotchy.

'I'm sorry I was a bit quiet at yours the other day,' he says.

'I didn't notice.'

He laughs. 'You didn't notice? You were giving me evils.' He leans forward and puts his hand on mine. 'You won't tell Monica you've seen me today, will you? It's just — '

The waitress clears her throat — she's standing at the side of the table. How long has she been there? I swipe my hand from under Nathan's. I don't recognise her, but then, I'm not the best with faces these days. She's holding a notepad, a pen poised in her other hand.

'What can I get you?' she says.

I look down at my skirt. The top of my leg feels cold and wet. I grab a serviette, but it's no good. Something must've fallen from the table. I reach into my pocket and there's a wrapper. I take it out.

'Oh God.'

The ice lolly. From the paper shop.

I run out of the café without saying goodbye, and sprint down the street.

How could I have forgotten my little Annie? What if Mrs Abernathy tells the police and they're waiting for me. They might send me to prison.

I'm only seconds away. I can hear Nathan shouting my name, but I don't turn around.

What if Annie's not where I left her?

It'll be my punishment. What would I do without her?

As I cross the side street, I see the hood of her

69

pram outside the shop.

Please be in there, please be in there.

I reach it, and push the hood of the pram down.

'Oh, thank God.'

I bend over to catch my breath.

Annie's still fast asleep. My beautiful, sleeping baby is where I left her.

Mrs Abernathy comes to the doorway. 'Did you get what you went for?'

I try to work out if there's a hidden meaning in what she's asking, but when I look at her face, I realise there's no agenda behind her words. She's not as dishonest as I am.

I can never see Nathan again.

'Yes,' I say to her. 'Thanks for keeping an eye on her.'

'Anytime, dear.' She turns and walks back into the shop.

I'm nearly at my house when the tears start streaming down my face. How could I have been so stupid? I reach under the pram for a tissue.

I see his shoes, his legs, walking towards me.

'Are you okay, Debbie?' Nathan can barely speak, he's breathing so hard. 'Did I say something to upset you? I didn't realise you had Annie with you.'

I'm still crouching near the floor, dabbing my face. I must look a right mess.

I stand to face him.

'I forgot about her . . . left her outside the shop. Please don't tell Peter.'

He frowns. Is he angry with me as well?

'What do you take me for, Debs? Course I

won't tell him. What would I say? *Sorry, Pete, but while I took your wife for a sneaky coffee, she left the baby outside a shop?'*

I bury my face in the tissue. He strokes the top of my arm; I step away from him.

'I can't see you again,' I say, sniffing away the last of my tears.

'Why are you being so serious? We have to see each other. I'm married to your best friend.'

'What time is it?'

He looks at his watch. 'Ten to three.'

I turn around and walk away. I've forty minutes to get to Bobby's school. I can't forget another child. I dab my face to wipe away the remaining tears. I can't be seen crying at the school gates.

★   ★   ★

The phone's ringing as I open the front door. I back into the hallway, pulling the pram over the step and into the house.

If it's still ringing when I'm properly inside, then I'll answer it. I'm not in the mood to speak to anyone on the phone. Sometimes it can ring and ring and ring until the sound buries itself into the middle of my brain and I want to rip the cord from the socket.

I shut the front door and wheel Annie into the living room.

The phone's still ringing.

It might be Peter. I haven't spoken to him since this morning. The thought of him covers me in a warm hug. But I don't deserve that

71

— not after the way I've behaved.

'Hello?'

'Debbie?'

Oh. It's Monica.

'Yes,' I say. 'It's me.' Who else would it be?

'You sound funny,' she says.

'No, I don't.'

'Hmm.' She says it in that disapproving way of hers. 'I've just seen you running up and down the high street in your bare feet — are you wearing a nightie?'

'What?'

My blood feels as though it's been replaced with antifreeze.

'Up and down the street. Are you okay? Do you need me to pop round? Is Annie all right — only I didn't see her with you.'

I don't understand what she's talking about.

'When?'

'Just now. I was driving back from work.'

'Oh,' I say. 'Did you see Nathan too? I saw him near the shops.'

'Debbie, are you sure you're okay? I can be there in five, no problem. I can watch Annie while you have a sleep.'

'I don't need a sleep. I'm getting Bobby at half three.'

'I know, but even half an hour might help.'

'Help? Are you sure you didn't see Nathan? He'll tell you I wasn't running around in my nightdress without my shoes on.'

I almost want to laugh at the image.

'Debbie, Nathan's at work. He's just telephoned me from his office.'

'Oh,' I say.

'I can come after school. Would that be better?'

'No,' I say, but I can't think straight. How could Nathan have phoned her from the street? I can't remember where the nearest phone box is . . . where is it? 'It's okay — Peter's coming home early today.'

He isn't, but it gets her off the phone.

Why the hell would she think I was running around without shoes? And in a nightie?

I feel the soft fabric of the carpet, underneath my toes.

I look down.

My flip-flops aren't on my feet any more.

9

Anna

The rain is battering against the bookshop window; it's going to be quiet today. Even though it's not Sunday, I'm hoping Grandad will come in today. I left him a message to say that Sheila's not coming in, so he can have free rein of the till, but I haven't heard back from him. Dad doesn't seem worried — perhaps he's been to see him. Maybe Grandad's angry with me. If I don't see him today, I'm going to bang on his door and sit on the doorstep until he opens it . . . or until I need to collect Sophie from after-school club.

Ellen's in the back room, pricing books that she thinks might be valuable. She said she has never used the Internet before, but I find that hard to believe. Prisons must have computers these days.

'Annie?' she says. 'Can you just help me again with this — the page is blank. I'm not sure it's connecting.'

I have given up trying to tell her that I don't like being called Annie, but it doesn't seem to register. I sit next to her, checking the side of the laptop. I click to slide a switch to the left.

'You must have put it into *airplane* mode by mistake,' I say.

'But why would I do that if I'm not on an aeroplane?'

I look at her as she stares at the screen, frowning. Surely she must know how laptops work. I click on the refresh button and the Amazon page loads. As I'm getting up, I notice there is another tab in the background. It's a site I'm familiar with: *Missing People*.

★ ★ ★

Ellen has been on the computer for nearly an hour. I keep trying to catch her looking at the missing persons' website again, but she's too quick, and both times I've gone into the storeroom she's minimised what she was looking at. I should warn her about using the Internet for personal use, but I haven't introduced a policy for that yet; we've only had the laptop in the bookshop for a fortnight. And once she's gone, I'll probably use it myself.

I'm still looking towards the back room when I smell a waft of Obsession.

'Anna?'

It's Isobel. Luckily, I have the accounts on the counter so at least I look busy. She glances at them and wrinkles her nose.

'I do hope you don't have those in view when we have clientele,' she says. 'It's highly confidential.'

I can't win.

'I was just having a quick check while the shop was empty.'

I slam the book shut and shove it under the counter.

'I've popped in to see how your new volunteer

is getting on. Is she in?'

Isobel breezes past — the smell of her hairspray never fails to nauseate me.

I try to listen in, but they are talking too quietly. It's not like Isobel at all. Perhaps she knows Ellen more than she's letting on.

After nearly half an hour, all I have managed to overhear are the words 'vicar' and 'they might not want to know.' Now they're saying their good-byes, I rush to the window so they don't think I've been listening. I move the elephant bookend a fraction, concentrating on it as though it were the most interesting thing in the world.

'See you soon, Anna,' says Isobel. She hesitates at the door, glancing at the window display. 'I must think of some other paperwork for you to do. We can't have you twiddling your thumbs all day.'

She hums to herself, putting sunglasses over her eyes before leaving the shop. That woman notices more than I thought. I wish I could tell her what I'm going through — that I can't concentrate on anything because the mother I can't remember has come back into our lives and, at the same time, my marriage might be falling apart. But I can't. She'll tell the whole of Lancashire.

'Annie.'

I turn quickly.

'Sorry,' says Ellen. She's already in her jacket. 'Isobel said it was okay if I left a bit early. I hope you don't mind, but I've got an interview for a new flat.'

'Oh, okay. Yes, I suppose that's all right.'

'Sorry. I hope you don't think I've gone above

you . . . it was just she was asking about me finding a place to live and — '

'Don't worry about it. I know what she's like.'

'She told me about your mum.'

'Excuse me?'

'I'm sorry,' she says. She keeps saying sorry. 'I shouldn't have mentioned it.'

'I'm just surprised. I'm sure everyone knows about it anyway . . . it's not a big secret.'

'Do you still think about her?'

'What? I . . . Of course. Why?'

She shrugs. 'I'm getting too personal.' She looks at her watch. 'I've corrected my time now. I'd better go. See you next week.'

I watch her walk away until she disappears from view. I hurry into the back room and click on the Internet icon, then the 'History' button. Who was she looking for on that website?

I will never know: she's deleted today's history.

★   ★   ★

I've been standing outside Grandad's for five minutes. People walking past are looking at me. I have thirty minutes until I need to collect Sophie from school. The curtains are closed, but when I press my ear against the window, I can hear the television on low. Today's silver-top milk is still on the doorstep.

'I know you're in there, Grandad. Are you okay? Are you hurt?'

There's a shadow moving behind the curtains.

'Grandad! If you don't answer the door in a minute, I'll call the police — they'll break the door down, you know. Then everyone will come and have a nosy — even Yvonne from across the road. She's in, I can see her net curtains flapping. I've got my mobile right here, I *will* ring them.'

The left curtain flashes open.

Grandad's standing at the window. He hasn't shaved for days; he's still in his tartan dressing gown.

'Are you going to let me in?'

His shoulders rise and fall as he sighs. He rolls his eyes.

Moments later, he opens the door, but stands behind it so no one can see him.

'Well, come in then,' he says. 'Don't make a show of me.'

I do as he says and follow him down the hallway.

'I'll make you a cup of tea,' he says. 'Go through to the living room.'

'I didn't come here for a drink, Grandad. I came to see if you were all right.'

I sit on the sofa anyway. He always makes a drink for visitors, so at least I know he still has his senses. Dad said that when Gran, Debbie's mother, was alive, Grandad was never allowed to touch the kettle. Dad was probably exaggerating.

Diagnosis Murder is on the television, but it's barely audible. I look to the mantelpiece. There have always been three pictures of Debbie on there: one on her Christening day; a faded school photo, her hair flicked at the sides like a Charlie's Angel; and a third with Gran and Grandad — Debbie the only child.

Grandad comes into the living room carrying a tray of tea and biscuits. He's changed from his dressing gown into his usual beige cords and burgundy jumper over a checked shirt. He must have a wardrobe full of the same clothes. He places the tray on the coffee table. I wait until he's finished pouring the tea until I speak.

'I take it Dad's told you about the email.'

'He has.'

'At least we know she's alive, that's something isn't it?'

'Do we? How can we know if it's really her? Anyone could've written that. What we should be asking is *why?* If it is her, then why now?' He plucks a white cotton handkerchief from up his sleeve and presses it against his nose. 'I wish to God it were her. I'd give anything to see her face again. I just can't see her not picking up the phone, to tell us she was all right. She was our only child. A miracle, we called her at the time. She came to us later in life — we thought we'd never . . . I didn't believe in all that religious stuff before Marion died. But you have to believe they go somewhere, don't you?' He looks up to the ceiling. 'I hope to God we find out the truth about my girl.'

'I'm sorry, Grandad. This must be so hard for you. But I have to believe that she's out there. Perhaps she got into trouble? She might have been in prison. Or maybe she had an accident and has only just recovered her memory.'

He raises his eyebrows. 'You've been watching too many films, Anna.' He picks up his mug of tea and takes a sip. 'It can't be your mum. She'd have written to me, too.'

I stare at my cup on the tray.

'But no one could've known about the shells. It could only have come from her.'

'Hmm,' he says. 'Don't go getting your hopes up, love. At least one good thing may come from this: we might find out what happened to her.'

'I'm going to try and find her — or trace who wrote the email,' I say. 'If the police think it's a crank, then I'm going to get to the bottom of it.' I pull out the roll of film from my handbag. 'I found this in Robert's keepsake box. It might have some clues.'

Grandad shakes his head. 'This is only going to lead to heartache, Anna. The police will say it's some lunatic, obsessed with her or something — they won't even be interested, they weren't last time. It's been too long.'

'Last time? What happened last time?'

He flaps his hand.

'A letter, in strange writing. I took it to the police and they said it might be her, or it might not. They logged it and that was that. Said she was an adult — that she left of her own accord.'

My shoulders slump. Robert mentioned another letter the other day, and now Grandad. But I can't ask him more about it now — he looks exhausted. His eyes are bloodshot, even though he's tried to hide it with reading glasses. I shouldn't be talking to him like this. His only child. The bed she slept in upstairs still has the same duvet cover; her record player is still by the window.

'I'm sorry, Grandad.'

He doesn't look at me when he says, 'It's been hard for us all.'

The carriage clock chimes five.

'I have to go,' I say. 'The after-school club closes in half an hour.'

'They never had such things in my day.'

I smile a little as a tiny glimpse of the Grandad I know shows through. I lean over and kiss him on the cheek.

'I'll see myself out.'

* * *

I'm turning the roll of film in my hands, waiting in the queue. Who knew Max Spielmann would be so busy?

'What are we buying here?' says Sophie. 'I'm hungry.'

She says it like she's auditioning for *Oliver Twist*.

'Pictures.' I hold up the film. 'This shop can change this little thing into photographs.'

Her mouth drops open and her eyes widen. She steps closer to me.

'Is this a magic shop?'

'Yes.'

The man in front leaves, but the woman behind the counter is typing something into the computer. She has one long coarse hair growing from her chin and she's stroking it as though it were a beard.

'Is that woman a wizard?' says Sophie.

She hasn't got the hang of whispering yet. My cheeks are burning.

The woman looks up quickly; I've half a mind to run out of the shop.

'Not quite, young lady,' she says, looking up. 'I'm a witch. And you have to be good for your mum or you'll end up in my rabbit stew.' She smiles. 'How can I help you?'

I put the film on the counter.

'Can you develop this? I think it's nearly thirty years old.'

'That shouldn't be a problem. As long as it's been kept in its container.' She opens the lid and slides out the film. 'It looks intact. I'll have to send it off though — we don't do 34 mm any more in store. No demand, you see. I'll post it off tonight and it should be back in two or three days.'

I fill out my details and she winks at Sophie as we leave. Sophie doesn't smile back.

Out on the street, I feel like celebrating. I thought they'd say it couldn't be done — that they didn't do things like that these days.

But the pictures might not even come out.

I take Sophie's hand and pull her away from the kerb.

'Is there a word for that?' she says.

'Word for what?'

'You always walk on the pavement near the cars.'

'I don't know. I've never thought about it.'

'What would happen if a car crashed into us and got you first? Who'd look after me?'

'Don't think like that.'

'But who would? Daddy's always working.'

'He's not *always* working. I work too. I'll think of the word.'

'What word?'

'For protecting you on the pavement. I'll Google it. And I'm glad you're thinking so practically.'

She starts skipping. My hands go up and down with hers.

I wish I were in her head.

The back of my neck prickles; I feel as though someone's watching me. I turn around quickly.

There's no one there.

I shouldn't get my hopes up about the photographs. Grandad always says I should manage my expectations. But if I had a choice between forgetting everything over the past few days, or being hurt from finding the truth, then I'd choose the truth.

10

I've been watching her for weeks and she hasn't noticed. She's too busy living in that head of hers. I watch in the rearview mirror as she gazes out of the window. She's looking around.

I glance over at the pile of pink notepaper on the passenger seat. It's surprising how much meaning can be conveyed in so few words. Will it mean anything to her, to them?

I slide down in the seat of the car as someone passes. I don't recognise him; he mustn't be a neighbour. Streets have gone all Neighbourhood Watch nowadays.

The radio plays 'Norwegian Wood' by The Beatles. My fingers go to the radio — a reflex — and switch it off. Shutting the memories down. We used to listen to that together, didn't we? I can't remember if it was your favourite song, or mine.

11

Friday, 4 July 1986
Debbie

The oil from Bobby's fish fingers spits from the frying pan; a drop touches my lips. I put my finger on my mouth to rub the sting away.

I can't have imagined Nathan this afternoon. We had a conversation.

'We *have* to see each other,' he said. There must be meaning in that. But why would Monica say Nathan was at work? And if she was so worried about me looking hysterical in the street, why didn't she pull over?

The front door slams shut. It must be ten past five. Bobby's banging his legs against the chair under the dining table. Thump-thump, thump-thump.

'Stop it!'

He doesn't look up, but stops his legs.

It'll take Peter another five seconds to hang up his jacket. Five, four, three, two —

I hear him throw his newspaper onto the settee. He usually says hello.

'Everything okay?' I say, peering through the kitchen doorway into the living room.

'Hmm.' He pulls off his tie. 'I've brought in your flip-flops. They were on the doorstep.'

'What? Again?'

I can feel my heart banging in my chest. Has Monica told him about this afternoon? Has Nathan? I'm sure I had them on after I picked Bobby up from school.

'Oh,' I say. 'They probably slipped off again when I was getting the pram in.'

'It didn't look like it. They were placed together, just outside the front door — like someone had put them there like that.'

'How odd. Did Monica ring you?'

He looks at me, wrinkling his nose. 'Are you being serious?'

Bobby must've seen my flip-flops slip off, picked them up. Or I might've put them there before I closed the front door. That could've happened. Monica must've mistaken my flip-flops for bare feet earlier — they must keep coming off without me noticing. Easily done. I'll wear sandals next time I go out.

I don't tell Peter I haven't prepared our tea. Instead I say, 'I thought I'd go to the chippy for us tonight. A treat for you — after working so hard.'

I sound like my fifty-two-year-old mother.

I should've become a Career Woman. I heard that Michelle Watkinson from college flew to the Bahamas last year, first class. Though she probably has to put up with letches feeling up her arse as she pushes the trolley up and down the aisle. She hasn't spoken to me since I had children. And I haven't put make-up on since Annie was born, so I wouldn't be any good at her job.

I'm stuck, in limbo.

I don't know why I'm trying to appease Peter

anyway. It wouldn't hurt him to offer to cook tea once in a blue moon. But I'd never say that. What if he knows something? What if he can read my thoughts?

'Hmm,' he says, again.

I interpret that as: *You've done nothing all day. The least you could've done is stick a Fray Bentos in the oven and some chips in the fryer.*

'I'll make you a cup of tea while you think about it,' I say.

He goes straight to the baby; she's lying on the blanket on the living-room floor.

'Hello, my little angel,' he says.

I fill the kettle, roll my eyes at the wall, and immediately feel guilty for it. I put a bowl of beans in the microwave and turn the dial. It's handier than I thought it'd be. It pings, and I burn my fingers taking the bowl out. Peter's already sitting in his chair at the table.

'Had a nice day, have you?' His tone is neutral.

'Well, you know. Been stuck in the house for most of it.'

'You should get yourself out and about.' He leans back in the chair. 'If I had the day to myself, I'd be out there. Spot of fishing, trip to the park.'

Day to myself? I want to shout. If I had the day to myself, I wouldn't choose to be inside all day. But I don't want to appear ungrateful.

'But you don't even fish.'

'I'd take it up, probably.'

'You can't take a baby fishing.'

★   ★   ★

The kettle clicks off and the beeper sounds in his pocket.

'For God's sake,' he says, the chair nearly toppling behind him as he gets up to use the phone in the hall.

I pour hot water into the mug with *Mr Tea* on it.

When did we become people like this? We used to laugh about friends who turned into their parents. We said we'd never be like that when we had kids. We said we'd go out all the time, cook nouvelle cuisine, and listen to records. Trisha over the road is always zipping about here and there. They've got a car seat for their precious Tristan and they've been to Marbella twice since she had him. *And* she has highlights. They've got the money, I suppose. She's got a white Ford Escort cabriolet that she loves showing off. It's a C reg; Peter says that's only last year's. She's went back to work at the hairdressers' when her little one was seven months. I heard her shouting about it outside to her friend. It's exhausting just thinking about work.

I dump three sugars into Peter's mug.

His face is red when he comes back into the kitchen. He's breathing hard through his nose.

'What's happened?' I say.

'I've got to go back in. The alarm's going off in the shop and there's nobody else answering their bloody phone.'

'Have a sip of tea before you go.'

I grab his cup from the counter and hold it out to him.

He frowns. 'I haven't got time for that.' He flicks his wrist.

The cup flies out of my hand and smashes onto the floor. Tea splats like paint from a tin. For a moment, we lock eyes.

He shakes his head, turns around and walks out, slamming the front door behind him.

⋆ ⋆ ⋆

I've managed to get both the kids asleep at the same time. It might only last a few minutes. Peter still isn't home. I hope he doesn't come back while I'm watching *EastEnders*. Since I became pregnant with Annie, I've become obsessed with soap operas — especially this new one. They empty my brain just enough.

A few minutes after the opening titles, the key goes into the front door. I press pause. I don't want him to think I've just been lounging around. He comes straight into the living room — without hanging up his jacket — just as I'm getting up. He glances at the telly.

'I didn't know this was on on a Friday.'

'I taped it.'

He takes off his jacket and flings it onto the opposite couch.

'Everything okay?' I say.

I cleaned up your mess and swept your favourite mug into the bin.

He slumps onto the settee. I look at him, and I don't think I know him at all. He can't have been at Woolworths for nearly three hours — it doesn't take that long to turn an alarm off. His eyes aren't meeting mine. He's not usually this secretive — perhaps he's planning something. I glance around the room. He might've been watching me while he was out. I've seen those hidden cameras on *Game for a Laugh*.

'I'm tired,' he says. 'All these broken nights.'

'Oh,' I say, narrowing my eyes. 'I'm sorry. I didn't realise you woke up too. You always seem so fast asleep.'

He waves his hand. 'Never mind.' He sits up. 'I'm going to book a holiday — or rather, I was hoping you could do it. It'll get you out of the house for a bit. I can get some brochures this weekend. We can get one of those last-minute deal things. You could let your hair down.'

I want to tell him it's a ridiculous idea, but all I say is, 'We can't go with a newborn. It's a stupid idea.'

'No, it isn't,' he says. 'These first few weeks are the easiest — she won't take much looking after.'

'Easiest for who?' I whisper.

'They always sleep at this age,' he says. 'I was thinking. We could ask Nathan and Monica to come. Leo could keep Bobby entertained. It'll be fun.'

'I don't know if a holiday's such a good idea. Anyway, wouldn't it be better just the four of us? Me, you and the kids. Annie's so young, she might keep everyone awake.'

'We don't have to share accommodation . . . though that would make sense financially. She'll be sleeping soon, if Bobby's anything to go by.'

I feel the urge to scream and laugh hysterically in his face.

'And,' he continues, 'I was thinking of going abroad. We've not been anywhere hot together before, have we? And it'll be something to look forward to. I've seen loads of last-minute deals on Teletext.'

'Hmm. I'll speak to Monica about it tomorrow.'

The thought of going on an aeroplane makes my stomach churn. I've always hated heights.

'Ha!' he says, leaning forward. 'I know what you're like: if you're not keen on something, you go quiet, hope it gets forgotten.'

I open my mouth to speak. He gets up quickly.

'I'll give Nathan a ring now.'

'But it's twenty to nine — you might wake Leo.'

My mother would never telephone anyone after eight o'clock at night — nor would she answer it. 'If it's an emergency,' she says, 'then they know where we live.'

'It's fine,' he says, getting up and turning on the hall light.

'Don't talk too loud,' I say, 'or you'll disturb the kids.'

My heart thumps as I hear him speak. I want to listen in and hear what Nathan says in reply . . . or grab the receiver out of Peter's hands and talk to him myself.

Why is he being so stubborn about a holiday? It's not like him to be this impulsive, or sociable. I turn my ears off, and only switch them on when he's preparing to say goodbye.

'I'll get Debs to give you a bell when it's arranged.'

Me? Why is he suggesting I ring Nathan?

'Okay then,' he says down the line. 'Will do. Bye, Monica.'

I stand up quickly.

'You were talking to Monica?'

He shrugs as he walks into the living room.

'Yeah. Nathan was out.'

'Where?' It comes out of my mouth before I think.

Peter wrinkles his nose. 'I don't know. I didn't think to ask.'

He's the least curious person I know. 'Why didn't you pass the phone to me?'

'Because it was my idea . . . and Monica *is* my friend too.'

Don't I know it. He looks so pleased with himself.

'I'm making a brew,' he says, walking into the kitchen. 'Do you want one?'

'No. It'll only keep me awake. Think I'll head upstairs, early night.'

'Night then,' he shouts, above the sound of the kettle.

I switch off the telly, which was frozen on Lofty behind the bar at the Queen Vic. Poor Lofty, always taken advantage of . . . being messed around by Michelle. I used to think that about Peter, but now I'm not so sure. Maybe he's not so predictable after all.

My hand's reaching for the switch in the hall, when I notice a pink envelope on the doormat. It's no one's birthday, I think, as I bend down to pick it up. Didn't Peter notice it when he came in?

There's no name on the front. The flap isn't stuck down; it's tucked inside. I open it and take out the piece of paper. There are only six words. I hold on to the wall to steady myself.

I know your dirty little secret.

12

Anna

I wait until Sophie has gone to bed before I mention Debbie. I didn't want to confuse her by talking about another grandmother — who she thinks has passed away. How am I going to explain to her that Debbie *is* alive after all?

'Don't get your hopes up,' says Jack — words I have heard many times — while he pours himself a glass of white wine.

'I'm not,' I say. 'But the woman behind the counter said photos usually come out well, even after all that time.'

I grab my laptop and take it into the living room. I still don't know what to say in my reply to Debbie. It is too important to just fire off a few words when I have a whole lifetime to write about. She won't be expecting a message from me, but I doubt Monica or Dad have replied yet. They would have told me if they had, though I'm not sure of anything these days.

'Just ask to meet,' says Jack, reading my mind. 'You don't have to write an essay. If she is who she says she is, then you'll find out soon enough.'

Perhaps it is as simple as that. There is a tiny part of me — self-preservation, again — that tells me not to give too much away in an email. She must earn the right to hear my news. The least

94

she could do is meet me.

I click on the email forwarded by Dad. I already know her words off by heart, but I still read it. 'The memories of shells and sweet things . . .' No one else could know about that.

I type out the reply before I can think about it, and press send.

I look up and flinch. Jack is standing just centimetres away from me.

He laughs.

'You were off in dreamland then.' He hands me a piece of paper. 'These are a few of the private investigators we use at work. The other partners hire them to find people for court summonses. One of them might be able to help if you don't get a reply. Tell them to charge it to my account.'

'What makes you think she won't reply?' I say. He shrugs. I look at the list. 'So, are these PIs like Magnum?'

'Er, no. Unfortunately not. They're more likely to drive a Volvo estate than a Ferrari.' He laughs at his own joke.

I settle back into the sofa. Some names to research; it makes me feel useful. I've never spoken to a private investigator before; they must lead such exciting lives.

'They'll probably jump at the chance of this job,' says Jack. 'They're usually sitting in a car for eight hours at a time, pissing into a Coke bottle.'

'Oh.'

'I'm just nipping down to the shop for more wine. Tough case at the moment.'

'But it's Friday night.'

'If I can get this done, I can relax for the rest of the weekend.'

'You can't drive — you've already had a glass.'

He tuts. 'I'm walking to the offy on the corner.'

It's what I hoped he'd say.

As soon as I hear the front door shut, I race up the two flights of stairs to Jack's office in the loft. *Tough case*, my arse. He's a conveyancing solicitor, not a human rights lawyer.

There's no door to open — the whole of the loft is his work space. Three walls are hidden by bookcases filled with leather-bound books I'm certain he's never read, and sports trophies from his university days. There's a sofa bed to the left and a large mahogany desk under the roof window. The blue screen of his laptop is reflected in the skylight. If I'm quick enough, the screen-saver won't have kicked in yet. He's protective over his passwords.

I slide onto his chair. His Facebook account is open. I click on the messages tab, but there are none. Not even the link to our old house for sale that I sent him last week. I check the archive folder. Still nothing. I must have at least fifty messages archived in mine. He must have deleted every one. Who does that? Especially someone who professes to hardly ever use Facebook.

Francesca was the name of the woman who signed her name at the bottom of the letter. I go to his friends list, my hands shaking. Jack might only be minutes from walking through the door.

He only has fifty-nine friends. She's not hard to find. I could have looked on his friends list

96

from my account. Francesca King. Even her name sounds glamorous. She has long chestnut-coloured hair and her photo looks professionally taken. I click on her profile, and jot down everything I can see in her *About* section. *Partner at Gerald & Co, Winckley Square, Preston.* She works across town from Jack. I want to look through her posts and photos, but I don't have time.

I tear off my notes from Jack's pad, scrunching the paper into my jeans pocket. I click back to his news feed. As I put both my hands on the chair arms to get up, a red notification appears over the message icon. He has it on silent . . . of course he does.

I should leave it. If I read it, he will know — there's no way of marking them as unread.

But I can't stop myself.

A sharp intake of breath as I read the words.

Have you told her yet?

I look to the sender. It's not Francesca King, but a name that is vaguely familiar: Simon Howarth. Where do I know it from? I thought I had met all of Jack's colleagues, but they aren't the most interesting of people — I can't remember all of their names. It can't be a relative of Jack's; he's an only child, as are both of his parents.

The front door clicks shut. I race down the loft stairs and go straight into the bathroom. I stand behind the closed door. The kitchen is directly below me; I bet he's pouring another glass of wine. I hear him put the bottle noisily into the fridge.

If he sees my face, he'll know what I've been

doing. I flush the toilet and run the taps, waiting until I hear him tread the stairs.

I have a lot of research to do.

★ ★ ★

The information I found about Francesca King was the same limited details from her Facebook account. On her firm's website — no win, no fee ambulance chasers — was a notice for a drop-in consultancy clinic on Monday nights. I wouldn't have the bottle to face her — what if she'd seen the picture of Sophie and me on Jack's desk at work?

After firing a quick email to several of the private investigators, I slam my laptop shut.

Jack probably won't come down for the rest of the evening — too busy in the company of wine and Facebook. It's ridiculous really. Why aren't I saying anything to him?

Because of what I did six years ago.

He had to get me out of the mess I'd got myself into. It wasn't about him cheating, it was about me, chasing ghosts. It happened before, when I was at college, but Jack doesn't know about that. It's not like that now: this isn't stalking, per se. Everyone looks at what their husbands and partners are up to online, don't they?

Anyway, I have proof. I took a picture of the letter on my phone. Jack would be the first to say it: you can't argue with evidence.

I look in on Sophie before I go to bed, as I do every night. She looks so angelic when she's asleep; I imagine all children do. Debbie would have seen me sleeping as a baby. Did she think I was an angel, or an inconvenience? Before now, she was a ghost — I had idolised her, exalted her — thought she disappeared through no fault of her own. I believed it must have been something really awful for her to have left us. But if this email *is* from her, then I should accept that she *chose* to leave us.

If I found her after all this time, I'm not sure I'd even like her.

13

Monday, 7 July 1986
Debbie

When I worked, I hated Mondays. I'd spend the second half of Sunday under a cloud of dread, eating chocolate and watching videos from the corner shop. My colleagues weren't bad people, but being estate agents turned them into arseholes. I'd had dreams of being a fashion designer — leaving home, going to art school and pondering Andy Warhol soup cans, floating about in chiffon and sandals. But I should've known I wasn't good enough for that life. Dad said I was lucky to get a job at all. 'Get any job you can,' he said. 'That'll show Thatcher. She wants us to disappear into the woodwork like cockroaches.'

The trouble was, everyone thought estate agents were cockroaches too.

The office is a distant memory. Now, Mondays are the same as any other day. Peter's at work and Bobby's in school and gone is the pressure of playing happy families. Annie won't mind if I sit and cry all day or if I don't get out of bed and just stare at the ceiling for hours. As long as she's fed and changed, she's fine.

Today, though, I have a job to do: book a holiday I don't want to go on. It took too long to get out of the house, but we made it. It's a job in itself, but Annie is fast asleep in her pram.

The sun is shining and I'm not in the mood for it. Sunshine is for barbecuing with friends, spending the day at the beach; being happy. I want the weather to match my mood and never stop raining. I keep thinking about that note on the pink paper. I hid it in my knicker drawer. I thought about it at night when the noise of the day had faded. Who would send a letter like that to someone? I haven't got a dirty little secret. The more I thought about it, the more I reasoned that it wasn't for me. What if it's Peter who has the secret? Without a name on the envelope, I could pretend it didn't exist. That doubt means I can forget about it. For now.

Peter didn't stop going on about the bloody holiday all weekend. He got some brochures on Saturday, and dropped the same ones off with Monica. The prices are ridiculous. What's wrong with going to Wales like we always do? I tried telling him how much we'd save staying in Britain.

'In a year,' I said, 'we'll have enough for a deposit on a house. Property prices'll go up soon.'

He rolled his eyes and said, 'Working as a secretary in an estate agency doesn't make you a property expert. Anyway, what about what happened to Kevin? We have to make the most of things. You never know when your last holiday's going to be.'

Kevin Jackson was Peter's assistant manager at Woolies. He was only twenty-three when he was killed in a motorbike accident three months ago. Saturday was the first time Peter had mentioned him since the funeral.

The travel agents is a twenty-minute walk away, and the high street is quiet right now. I take my time; it's just after eleven and the deadline of the three thirty school pick-up isn't looming as much. There's an advert in Mrs Abernathy's shop for a weekend sales assistant, but I know what Peter will say: 'Family time is important.' His dad worked nearly every weekend when Peter was growing up. They're barely on speaking terms now, even though Peter's mother passed away three years ago, and his father only lives in Lytham. I can't face Mrs Abernathy after last week, anyway.

A dandelion clock passes through the air in front of my face. My uncle Charlie used to call them fairies. 'Catch them in your hand, make a wish, then let it go on its way.' Sometimes my wishes came true, which always surprised me. I doubt they would now.

I let go of the pram and try to clasp the clock between my hands.

Missed it.

I don't take my eyes off it; it floats on the breeze. If I could just catch it, I could wish for things to get better.

'Go on, grab it.'

I can't tell if that voice is inside, or outside, my head.

'I'm trying, Charlie,' I say.

I swipe again. It wafts down and down until landing perfectly still on the ground. It was meant for me.

'I've got it, Charlie,' I say, feeling the fluffiness of it in my hand. I close my eyes to make a —

A car horn sounds.

I turn around.

I'm in the road.

A car's coming straight for me. I look at the driver. I feel like I know everything about her as our eyes meet. My feet won't move. I'm going to die.

A hand grabs the top of my arm. I trip up the kerb and onto the pavement. The hand is still holding me. I look up the arm, up his body until I reach his face.

'Nathan.'

'What were you doing in the middle of the road?'

I look at the woman behind the wheel; she shakes her head at me and drives off.

'I don't know . . . I saw a fairy and . . . '

'A fairy?'

He frowns at me. He has that same look Peter gives me when I put sugar on my chips instead of salt. Please don't let Nathan look at me that way too.

'No, no. Not a real fairy . . . one of those dandelion clocks. You know?'

He lets go of my arm. 'I guess. You could've got yourself killed.'

'I didn't realise.' I look around me. There are people standing a few feet away — more on the other side of the road, just gawping at me. 'I . . . I thought it was quiet.'

The people on the street begin to wander off — it's not a big drama after all.

Why didn't I feel the step down from the kerb? I left Annie on her own again.

The car horn must've woken her. She's crying, but the sound is muffled, like she's in another room. How long has she been crying?

My cheeks burn.

I look down at my feet and my shoulders relax slightly.

At least I have my sandals on.

★　★　★

Nathan and I are sitting opposite the travel agent's assistant. Her hair is bleach blonde and curly. It's held in a scrunchie at the side of her neck. I used to do my hair in the morning, too. I want to tell her that I wasn't always this dowdy.

'So, Mr and Mrs Atherton — '

'No,' I say for the second time. 'I'm Mrs Atherton and this is Mr Bailey. We're booking for both of our families.'

She raises an eyebrow. She'll soon believe us when we list four adults and three children, but who cares?

I look at the wall behind her. There's a picture of a cruise liner floating on turquoise-blue water. What would it be like to jump from that ship? Would it hurt, or would I go unconscious before I hit the sea?

★　★　★

'I bet there'll be nothing to do there,' I say to Nathan outside. 'It'll be full of blokes in nylon

104

tracksuits and football shirts.'

'Didn't have you down as a snob, Debs.'

I sigh. 'I'm not. I just don't think I'm up to it. I only had a baby a couple of weeks ago. New mothers don't just swan off on holiday.'

'You're not that new.' He winks. 'Come on, cheer up. It'll give us something to look forward to. We could spend some time catching up — it'll be like old times. And with us sharing an apartment, it'll be so much cheaper. I didn't think we'd go on holiday at all this year. We're meant to be on a budget.'

'Good luck with that,' I say. 'Monica won't even buy a tin of baked beans less than thirty pence because it doesn't have the right label on it.'

He shrugs, frowning into the distance. I'm always saying the wrong things.

'Do you think we'll get under each other's feet?' I say. 'What if Annie doesn't sleep?'

'Then we'll all leave you to get up with her.'

'Yeah. Nothing new there.'

'Hey. I was joking.'

We start walking in silence. Annie's beginning to get wriggly — it's nearly time for her next bottle. It must be lunchtime because men in big suits and flashy ties are rushing around, tutting at Annie's pram as though I shouldn't be using the pavement between twelve and two. God forbid they miss a precious second of sitting in the pub with a pint.

'Shouldn't you be at work?' I say.

He goes to look at his watch, but it's not there. 'Good point.'

He bends down to say goodbye to Annie.

'Before I forget,' he says, standing up. 'You mentioned your uncle Charlie . . . when you were looking for fairies.' He puts a hand on my shoulder. 'Is everything okay with you, Debs?'

Nathan and I had just got together, nearly eleven years ago, when my uncle died. He and I were really close. It made me needier than I usually was. Perhaps Nathan liked that — perhaps he thinks I'm *still* like that.

'I don't know,' I tell him.

He lets his hand drop away from me.

'You know I'm here if you need to talk.'

'I can't talk to you,' I say. 'I should be talking to Peter.'

He looks at the pavement. 'Do you think we made the right choice?'

'What do you mean?' I say, but I know what he's talking about. But it was another lifetime. There's no point thinking about it now.

He opens his mouth, but he's already said enough. I pull my handbag-strap higher onto my shoulder and grip the pram.

'Bye, Nathan.'

★   ★   ★

Peter's been in a good mood since I told him the holiday's booked. He brought chips back from the chippy and it's not even Friday. He's offered to put Bobby to bed, which is probably for the first time ever, and said he'll take us to C & A in town to get holiday clothes. I should be excited. I've never been abroad. But I think about all the

106

things that could go wrong: the plane; Annie in the heat; that I won't be as jolly as everyone wants me to be. I might ruin it for everyone. I keep thinking about the note that came through the door. I couldn't mention it to Peter; it would only spoil his mood.

If the holiday had been arranged two years ago — a year ago, even — I'd be bouncing around, picturing sandy beaches, buying so many clothes — that we couldn't afford — along with miniatures of every toiletry I could think of, giant beach towels, and inflatables for the kids. I'd be ringing Monica every five minutes, asking her to order me things from her catalogue, and exchanging promises of babysitting while we were away.

But I was a different person then, and I don't know how to climb my way back.

I lie and rest my head on the settee, listening to Bobby running around upstairs whilst Peter chases after him with his pyjamas. He let Bobby stay in the bath for forty-five minutes. The boy must be freezing.

Finally, I hear Bobby's bed springs as he jumps onto his duvet. He'll be all clean and cuddly. I should be the one hugging him, but I suppose it'll do Peter some good to learn.

It's eight o'clock at night and Trisha's husband over the road is still playing loud music, showing off that they've got a four-foot-wide garage. It can't even fit their car in. I'm surprised Peter doesn't go out and ask him to turn it down. Actually, I'm not. I think he's a bit intimidated by Dean.

'Debs!' Peter's shouting down from the landing.

I know what's coming.

'Can you ask Dean to turn it down?'

I don't know why he thinks I'm braver than he is. Perhaps he doesn't care that he's about to send his very own wife out to talk to the local perv.

'Does that mean I get to miss the holiday?' I shout up to him, standing at the top of the stairs. 'Have a peaceful week here on my own?'

He frowns and shakes his head, and I feel like I'm the child again.

I stick my feet into my flip-flops, which I regret as soon as I shut the front door behind me: it's windy and blobs of freezing-cold rain drop on my toes. It's July, for God's sake.

Dean looks up from the Ford Cortina he's tinkering with on the roadside. Wham!'s 'I'm Your Man' is playing from tiny speakers in the open garage; a Samantha Fox calendar is nailed to one of the concrete walls inside. He's such a cliché. He wipes one of his screwdrivers with a cloth already covered in oil. He looks at his tool and winks at me. Good God. I almost retch. He's wearing one of those ghastly new shell suits in pale blue. Ugh.

'All right, Deborah?' His voice reminds me of Boycie from *Only Fools and Horses*. He puts it on though.

I never know how he's going to behave towards me. When we first moved in, he mistook my friendliness as a come-on, leaning towards me for a kiss at our first and only street

108

barbecue. I pushed him away of course, but these days he can either be civil or downright nasty.

'Do you mind turning your radio down, please, Dean? Peter's putting Bobby to bed.'

'Is he now?' He sits on his car bonnet like he's Kevin Webster. 'Don't let Trish hear you say that. Don't want her indoors getting any of those ideas about men doing women's work.'

'Trisha's out, isn't she? Anyway,' I say. 'It'd be much appreciated.'

He turns and walks slowly towards the garage, swinging his hips as he goes. He probably thinks I'm looking at his arse.

Oh shit — I am. I turn around quickly.

'Hey,' he shouts. 'Tell Pete not to blank me next time I see him in town.'

I look behind me. He's not angry; he's smiling. 'Yes, will do.'

'And that friend of yours — Margaret, is it? Him and her were thick as thieves. Not surprised they didn't see me. I'd keep my eye on those two if I were you.' His eyebrows go up and down.

I try and smile back, but it comes out as a grimace. 'It's Monica,' I say. 'Her name's Monica.'

I run back into the house, and shut the door. I kick off my flip-flops, my heart pounding. He must know something — or he's seen something.

Why would Peter be meeting up with Monica in town? He hasn't mentioned anything.

It must be Dean who sent the note.

But not to me, to Peter.

14

Anna

Jack must have slept on the sofa bed in his office upstairs last night, and then left before I woke, because he wasn't in the house this morning. There was no note. Usually he would scrawl something on a Post-it, or make a silly message with the fridge magnet letters. But nothing today. I'd fired off a quick text, asking if he was okay, but I probably won't get a response until lunchtime.

Jack said he'd be more relaxed this weekend, but he was the same. We took Sophie to an indoor play centre on Saturday, even though it was sunny — it's her favourite place — but Jack constantly checked his phone. As soon as we got home at three o'clock, when the rain started, he poured his first glass of wine. I spent the rest of the weekend with Sophie, drawing and making egg cups with her new air-dry clay.

As Sophie and I were leaving for the school run this morning, the landline rang. I almost didn't answer it.

'Anna. It's your grandad here . . . are you there?'

'Yes, Grandad.'

'Ah, good, good. Thought I was on your answerphone-majiggy-thing. I won't take up much of your time, love, I just wanted to ask if you'd mind popping over this morning. I've some of your mother's things I wanted to show you.'

'Oh, okay.'

'I'll tell you more when you're in front of me. Bye now.'

I rang Isobel, put on my croakiest voice, and told her I was taking the day off.

Thirty minutes later, with Sophie safely in school, I pull up outside his house. Robert's car is here too. I hadn't realised what Grandad was going to show me was that important — or that my brother would be here. I have left Robert countless messages on his mobile and he still hasn't got back to me.

Grandad's lived in this house most of his adult life. He married Gran when he was twenty-one and I'm sure everything inside is the same as it was in 1986. I think he stays here so Debbie would know where to come back to, with everything frozen in time so she would feel at home.

It's Robert who answers the door. He glances at me and walks back down the hallway.

'Are you all right, Robert?' I follow him into the living room. 'Robert?'

He's sitting in the chair next to the television, looking sideways at *The Jeremy Kyle Show*.

'Don't let Grandad see you've got that on,' I say. 'You know what he thinks about it.'

He grabs the remote control.

'We should go on it,' he says, switching it off. 'They'd have a field day with our family.'

He isn't smiling. He folds his arms across his chest. The sleeves of his tweed jacket are stretched at the shoulders — he must have had it for years. He dresses like a man twenty years older. His once-auburn hair has more flecks of grey than red, and there are deep frown lines across his forehead that I've not noticed before.

'Don't you want to know what happened to our mother?' I say.

'I wish you'd stop calling her that,' he says. 'What's she ever done for you, except give birth to you?'

'I . . . I just want . . . '

'Yes, because it's all about you. You're just like her. Have you thought about what this is doing to Monica?'

'Have you seen her? She didn't say much about the email when I went round last week.'

'You haven't seen her since last week? She probably thinks you've abandoned her . . . after everything she's done for you.'

'It's only Monday.'

I sit on the edge of the sofa, still in my coat, and glance at the painting of Jesus on the wall above the fireplace. He's always staring at me. His eyes are meant to be kind, but His chest is open, and a giant, graphic image of a heart takes centre stage.

'I do appreciate everything Monica's done for me,' I say. 'She's the only mother I've ever known — '

'Well then. We should forget about that email. It's probably some weirdo anyway.'

'But what about the shells?'

'A lucky guess. Everyone keeps shells.'

'Course they don't,' I say, turning my knees towards him. 'I found a roll of film from your memory box.'

'What? Oh that. I thought I'd got rid of it.'

'Are they your pictures?'

'I guess. Probably from the holiday. Grandad gave me an old camera to use while we were there.'

'*The* holiday?'

His eyes burn into mine, before they settle on the blank screen of the television. Why is he acting like he hates me? We've always got on, had a laugh.

It was only the week before last that he came to the bookshop to take me out for lunch.

'Well, I'm honoured that you've graced me with your presence,' I said that day, 'travelling all this way to the lovely town of St Annes.' I followed him out of the door and he linked his arm in mine as we walked.

'Yeah, very funny,' he said. 'I've an ulterior motive, actually.'

I sat opposite him in the café around the corner.

While we waited for our cheese toasties, he said, 'I've got wind that Monica's planning a surprise party for me in a few weeks.'

I zipped my lips with my finger and thumb. He rolled his eyes.

'She knows I'm not forty for a few years, doesn't she? It's not a special birthday.'

'You know how much Monica loves birthdays. She used to make our cakes from scratch. I

113

remember the time she made a house with chocolate fingers and apple slices for the roof.' I looked down at my cup. 'Although that was the year only two of my school friends came to my party. I suppose, at eleven years old, they'd grown out of kids' parties.'

'It was cruel of them, Anna. Gran had just died, and you were really upset — so was I. Kids don't get that sometimes. If I'd still been at the same school, I'd have given them hell.'

I smiled. 'Course you would.'

He shrugged, grinning at me. He never was a fighter.

'Anyway,' I said. 'Monica wants to do something nice for you. Especially after the D. I. V. O. R. — '

'Don't say it like that. It's too much like that song. You can't kick a man when he's down.'

'But *you* ended it with Kerry . . . said she had *stunted, intellectually* — '

He held up his hands. 'Okay, okay. That's what I said to you lot.' He looked around the café, and leant closer. 'It was only partially true. Oh God, it's such a cliché . . . '

'What is? What happened?'

I lean forward too.

'She ran off with — '

'The milkman? The postman?'

'It's not multiple choice. Be serious.' He sighed. 'She ran off with a bloke from the gym.'

'Ah,' I said. 'I see.'

He flapped his hand in the air. 'It's not so bad. Did I tell you that Marie Costigan friended me on Facebook last week?'

'Robert, I didn't even know you were on Facebook. Wasn't she your girlfriend at university? The one with the big — '

'Intellect. Yes.'

'I was going to say 'hair' . . . '

He shook his head at me, as our lunch was placed on the table. Robert took a bite and opened his mouth while waving his hand.

'Hot, is it?' I said.

I watched him chew quickly before gulping it down.

'Good God, yes.' Robert hardly ever swore; he didn't want it to come out accidentally in front of his students. 'And that's why the party is a no-no. I'd like to take Marie out, make a fresh start.'

'And you don't want to bring her to the party in case she sees what plebs your family are?' I smiled and patted his hand. 'I'll see what I can do, brother.'

But that was last week. The Robert sitting in front of me now, in Grandad's living room, is not the same person as he was just eleven days ago.

'Sorry,' I say to him, breaking the silence. 'I won't show the photographs to you, if you don't want to see.'

'I was six years old, and my mum didn't come back from holiday with us. The last thing on my mind would've been getting some shitty photos developed. They're probably full of lizards and grasshoppers. I can't stand the sound of grasshoppers.'

I take off my coat, and go into the hallway, hanging it on the bannister. Grandad appears at the kitchen doorway, the china rattling on the wooden tray.

'You didn't have to do anything fancy for us. Here, I'll take it for you.' I grab the tray, but he doesn't take his hands away. 'Grandad?'

'Your brother doesn't seem interested in finding your mum,' he says. 'Shall we do this another day? It might upset him.'

I give the tray a gentle tug and he releases his hands.

'Let him decide. I'm sure he'll leave if he wants to.'

He nods and goes back to the kitchen, grabbing a box from the counter. I place the tray on the coffee table in the living room, and Robert pours tea into one of the cups.

The cardboard box in Grandad's hands is the size of a shoebox. He sits on the end of his chair next to the gas fire.

'These are some of Deborah's belongings. I took in most of her things, when your dad — and you two, of course — moved in with Monica and Leo. Her clothes, shoes, you know ... I've had them such a long time. But I'm old and I can't hang on to things forever. You'd have to clear it out when I'm dead and buried. So, I had a sort out a few weeks ago, before all of this ... '

Robert's stirring his tea so loudly it's like a ringing bell. I glare at him, but he doesn't notice.

'You're not dying, are you, Grandad?' he says without looking up.

I want to put my hand over his mouth to shut him up.

Grandad's frowning.

'You're not, are you, Grandad?' I say.

He shakes his head.

'Not from anything specific, but I'm not getting any younger.'

Robert looks at his watch. He doesn't trust Grandad's carriage clock; apparently a gadget that old can't be reliable.

'I've got to get back to work soon,' he says. 'I'm lecturing at one. I need to prepare.'

This usually impresses Grandad; Robert was the first in the family to go to university, but it's like Grandad's not listening to him.

'What it is, you see,' says Grandad, 'is that I found her diary. Not a personal one — I mean the days of the week, you know, like a — '

'A pocket diary?' says Robert. He downs his tiny cup of tea.

'Yes, that's right. I didn't want to pry, but I had to look. She's my only child, you see.'

Robert's shifting in his chair. I wish he'd sit still and listen.

'I know, Grandad,' I say. 'It must be horrible not knowing.'

He edges forward in his chair.

'The diary was hidden amongst her — you know — her undergarments, which is why I only found *them* the other week. They were wrapped in a pair of tights.'

'What were, Grandad?' I say.

'The letters. Though God only knows who would send her words like that.' He looks to the painting of Jesus. Gran always did that if she heard or said anything that bordered on blasphemous. 'It was only when I found them, did I remember her talking about them — not long before she left . . . she said they weren't even addressed to her, though — she didn't seem that worried about them. They might not even mean anything . . . kids messing about.'

Grandad picks out a small shortbread tin from the cardboard box — a tartan one that I remember from a few Christmases ago. He lifts it open, and a few flecks of rust from the hinges fall onto his lap.

'There aren't many.'

He hands one to me, another to Robert. I take the letter out of the envelope carefully. It doesn't look as though it's been opened many times; the creases are still sharp.

I know your dirty little secret.

The skin on my arms turns to goosebumps; the hairs stand on end.

'Who would send her something like this?'

'I've no idea, love.'

'Would you mind if I took these home, to look at properly, I've . . . ' I was going to tell him about hiring an investigator, but Robert might get cross with me.

'Yes, I suppose. Unless Robert wants to take some too?'

Typical. Robert has barely spoken to Grandad today, he hardly ever comes round, but when he does, he gets treated like a prince.

'What does that one say, Robert?'

'You can read it for yourself. They're probably part of her silly little games,' says Robert, putting his note back into the envelope. 'Anna can take the stuff. Dad probably showed them to the police years ago. Nothing new.'

'I don't think he did, Robert,' says Grandad.

'Don't you want to find her?' I say to my brother.

Robert stands, tossing the envelope into the cardboard box.

'Find her? Do I want to *find her?* Why should I, when I never lost her?' He bends down and kisses Grandad's cheek. 'I can't be part of this any more.' He goes to the door, and turns before he leaves. 'I . . . sorry, Grandad. I'll call round next week.'

A few seconds later, the front door slams shut, making Grandad flinch slightly.

'I'm sorry about that,' I say.

He gets up and walks to the window, folding his arms.

'No,' he says. 'I know what he means. God forgive me for saying this, but she was ever so flighty, so impulsive.'

'But she wouldn't have left on some petty whim. There must be more to it than that.'

Grandad watches Robert from behind the net curtain; my brother rubs his face before getting into his car.

'That's what I thought, love. I hope we find some explanation. If only for the sake of that poor boy.'

* * *

What Robert said before, about the lizards and the grasshoppers, is the most he has ever mentioned about that holiday. I have the box of Debbie's letters next to me on the passenger seat. I want to dive in and look through it all, but there are pedestrians going past. I need to be at home, where I can concentrate.

I've been parked outside Francesca King's offices in Preston for forty minutes. Her name is etched on the glass alongside the names of the other partners. I thought that, because it's lunchtime, I'd catch her nipping to the shops for a sandwich. Perhaps it's just me who's so predictable — Francesca probably has food brought to her by one of her minions.

I go to her Facebook profile on my phone, so I can memorise, again, what she looks like. I slouch down in the seat; it would be just my luck to be spotted by my boss, Isobel, or one of the volunteers, when I'm meant to be off sick, even when I'm miles away from the bookshop.

A black cab pulls up alongside my car.

Oh God, I'm halfway down my seat. I push my feet into the footwell and slowly return to the upright position. I need to look to my right. Perhaps it is Francesca who's getting out of the taxi. I chance a quick glance: it's a woman with her back to me. Her hair is long and dark like Francesca's. She pays the driver and turns towards the pavement, passing the front of my car.

It's not her. This woman must be in her late fifties. She's waiting outside the solicitors. I put on my sunglasses, so she can't see me watching her.

Another woman is walking up the road. The

same long hair. I think it's *her*. I get out of my car, although I have no idea what I'm going to do. I can't see anything in these glasses — it's too cloudy. I push them onto the top of my head. She is only three metres away. Why did I get out? My face is hot.

'Francesca, love,' says the older woman, kissing the younger one on the cheek. 'Good timing. I've just got here myself.'

It *is* her. And I'm just standing here like a fool.

'Hi, Mum,' says Francesca. She looks at me and smiles. 'Hello.'

'Hello,' I say, like a parrot.

'Are you all right?' She's tilted her head to one side.

'I . . . er . . . I'm looking for a solicitor.'

She laughs a little laugh, like she's Snow White in the Disney film.

'Well, you've come to the right place,' she says. 'If you talk to Adam on reception, he'll arrange an appointment for you.'

'Thanks.'

It would look silly if I just walked away.

The letter, I want to say. *Why did you tell my husband you were forever his? It's not right.*

No words are coming out of my mouth. Francesca's mother looks slightly afraid of me — I've had those looks before, years ago. 'I'll come back later,' I say. 'I've got to get my son.' I pull the sunglasses back over my eyes and get into the car. I know they're looking at me, but as I pull away, I keep my eyes on the road ahead.

15

Friday, 11 July 1986
Debbie

Why is night-time so everlasting? It's been seventeen minutes since Annie finally dropped off, but my mind won't slow down. Thoughts are on repeat in my head: of the note through the letterbox; of Nathan; and of Peter and Monica together.

I've seen Nathan twice on our high street in the past week, yet he works the other side of Preston — at least five miles away. It can't be a coincidence. I should've asked him. Too caught up in my own head, that's my trouble. That's what Mum always says.

What were Peter and Monica talking about when Dean saw them? Why meet on their own and not mention it? Tomorrow I'll ask Peter; I just need to be brave. Even though he might lie; I'll be able to tell by the look on his face. The corners of his mouth turn up when he doesn't tell the truth. Perhaps they've fallen in love with each other. Or is that my guilty mind and wishful thinking? No, no, it's not that. I love Peter.

Infatuation: that's all it was with Nathan and me. But what is it now?

'*They can't be trusted, Debbie. You know what to do.*'

That voice again. It was clearly outside my head this time. Definitely.

'What?' I say.

I sit up quickly and look at Peter. His back is facing me. I lean over to look at his face; he's fast asleep.

Mum talks to God all the time, He must reply to her at least some of the time for her to keep doing it, surely.

'You spoke about your uncle Charlie,' Nathan said the other day. I can't remember talking about him in the street, but what if he's trying to contact me? I've heard people talk about voices from beyond the grave — I read it in a magazine a few months ago.

'Mummy!'

The voice makes me jump, but it's only Bobby calling out from his room.

As quietly as I can, I rush out of the bedroom in case he shouts again. I close the door behind me and flick on the landing light.

Bobby's sitting up in his bed, gripping Ted with both hands, his little cheeks wet with tears.

'What's wrong, sweetheart?'

'I got a bad dream,' he says. 'I dreamed a giant man trampled over the house. He crushed you and Daddy and took away me and Annie in his giant hands.'

I kneel on the floor next to him and pull him close to me. 'You know what that was?' I say.

He shakes his head.

'Did Daddy read you *The BFG* before you went to sleep?'

He nods, rubbing his left eye with his hand.

'It was just your dream remembering the story, that's all.'

'But the BFG was a goodie, not a child-catcher.'

'It must be two different stories put together . . . probably *Chitty Chitty Bang Bang*.' I stroke his hair. 'If you lie down and get to sleep now, I bet you have a good dream next.'

I don't want to talk to him too much, else he won't get back to sleep. I keep stroking his hair until his eyes begin to flicker. I kiss his damp cheek and tiptoe to the door.

I feel terrible for forgetting it was his birthday the day before yesterday. How could I have forgotten that? I always remember his birthday's not long after mine — I used to buy his presents with the birthday money *I* got.

I used to.

Who am I turning into? Bobby means the world to me, yet my mind feels only half present.

Thank God Monica made him a cake. She probably wanted to show me up. She'd brought round loads of presents, too, but I can't be angry with her for that.

'Night-night, my brave boy.'

'Mummy,' he says. 'Promise that a big giant won't come and get you and Daddy.'

'I promise, Bobs.' I leave his door ajar and peep through the gap. 'I'm not going anywhere.'

★　★　★

I don't know what day it is, but it's a school day, and it's lunch-time, and I'm at my parents' house: my childhood home. Mum's laid out some sandwiches, French Fancies and Wagon Wheels on posh plates on the coffee table. She's got out the Midwinter dinner service that Dad got from a jumble sale, complete with a sugar bowl and milk jug.

'You hardly ever visit these days,' she says. 'I wanted to make it more of an occasion.'

Dad's been in the loft and got out the baby bouncer; the same one I used as a baby. Annie's lying still on it — she's too small — but blinking her way around the room. Her eyes rest on the picture of Jesus with the bleeding heart. Poor child will have nightmares, like Bobby. I turn her round so she can watch *Rainbow*.

'I only gave birth a few weeks ago, Mum. I'm just getting back on my feet.'

If she tells me that she was out painting fences or making scones the day after I was born, I will scream.

'Where's Dad?'

'He's down at the library. He's got his routine now. Job centre every day first thing, then Monday he goes to the market, Tuesdays he . . . '

Oh, Jesus, I say in my head to the picture of His bleeding heart, *Please don't let me end up like this*.

I wait until she's reeled off Dad's weekly itinerary before I say, 'Are you happy, Mum?'

'What kind of question's that?' she says. 'What's happiness got to do with anything?'

'You always seem to be talking about everyone else. You never talk about yourself, or your hobbies. Do you have any hobbies?'

'What would I want to talk about myself for? I'm not the conceited sort. And anyway, I'm nothing special — no one'd want to hear about me.'

I pick up one of the fondant fancies and bite all the pink icing off. Mum rolls her eyes at me and smiles.

'Mum,' I say, mouth full of sponge. 'Do you ever wonder if this is all there is? You go to college, leave, get married, have kids. And then what?'

She frowns as she drops a cube of sugar in her tea.

'Sometimes you must accept the burden of what you've been given . . . and I was given your dad.' She takes a sip of tea. 'Anyway . . . Prince Andrew's marrying Sarah Ferguson next week. I suppose you could call that my hobby.'

'Good God, Mum.'

She nods to Jesus. 'He's listening, you know.'

I grab a tiny egg mayonnaise sandwich. I haven't eaten this much for weeks.

'Do you see much of Monica?' says Mum. 'You were always so close, always together.'

'Yeah. Though not much over the past few weeks. I think she's been busy.' Busy talking to my husband, I don't say.

'Well you need your friends,' says Mum. 'That's a mistake I made. I thought I didn't need them after I got married . . . didn't bother keeping in touch. I had this one friend — Sandra Birkette. She was what they called A Right One, but she was so much fun. She dragged me to one of those dances — got me a port and lemon

. . . it went right to my head. But that was the night I met your dad.'

'Ah, Mum. You should look her up in the Yellow Pages.'

'I wouldn't know where to start. She moved to Devon, I think.'

'I could look for her for you. It'd give me something useful to do.'

For just a second, I see a small light in her eye, but a second later it's gone.

'Don't be silly, Deborah,' she says. 'You've got enough to do with the children, the house, Peter.'

Hearing it out loud makes me feel pitiful. My essence, my identity, is defined by other people. I've become a shadow. And I don't know what to do about it.

16

Anna

I should not be nervous about seeing Monica, but I feel empty in the stomach. I rang the landline, but there was no answer. This is the first place I thought to go after seeing Francesca in the street. I knock on the front door, expecting no one to be in.

'Monica!'

'Hello, love. I saw you sitting outside in your car for ages. Are you okay? Your dad's doing the shopping at Morrisons.' She closes the door behind us and rubs the top of my arms. 'Why are you shivering? It's boiling outside. The weather doesn't know what it's meant to be doing — it was pouring down this morning.'

'I don't feel so well,' I say. 'I'm meant to be off sick.'

She turns into the living room and I follow. She bends down to their wood burner and throws in two more logs.

'How come you've got the fire on?' I say.

'You know how I feel the cold. This living room is always in the shade. What were you doing outside?'

She grabs the throw off the sofa, points for me to sit down, and wraps the soft material around me. I pull it up to my chin, for comfort rather than warmth.

'I don't know,' I say. 'I had to check something, and I haven't seen you for ages. You were a bit distant the last time I saw you. I hope I haven't upset you. Things are strange at the moment. I don't feel right.' I can't stop the tears. I wipe my face on the throw. 'I'm sorry.'

She sits next to me, putting her hand on my forehead.

'Oh, my darling girl.'

She grabs my shoulders and pulls me towards her, wrapping both arms around me. It makes me cry even more, the sobs shake my whole body.

'There, there. You let it out.'

She smells of apple shampoo and rose perfume. Like a delicious fruit salad, I used to say to her. She pulls away from me and takes hold of my hands.

'Is this about the email?'

'Yes. And about Jack. I think he might be having an affair.'

Monica frowns. She's always looked young for her age, but now I notice the deep lines between her eyebrows as though they have been excavated by worry.

'I can't believe that for a second,' she says. 'What makes you think that?'

Heat runs to my face.

'I was looking through his wallet and I found a letter from a woman called Francesca. I checked his Facebook and there she was: long hair, beautiful.'

Monica wipes the hair from my face.

'You're beautiful too, Anna. It's probably not what it seems. Have you talked to him about it?'

I shake my head.

'I can't say I've been through his things. He'll think I've had a relapse or something.'

'A relapse?' I see her eyes flicker; she frowns. 'But that was nothing to do with Jack,' she says. 'He can't expect you to have been through what you have and not be a tiny bit crazy.'

I laugh through my tears.

'I don't think that's a politically correct way of putting it, Mon.'

She shrugs.

'Well, maybe not. But you didn't hurt anyone, it wasn't the end of the world. And anyway — I've had my fair share of being off the wall.'

She says that, but I've never seen her be anything but calm, the voice of reason — the way she is now. She puts her hands on her knees. 'This calls for a cup of tea, I think. And extra sugar.'

I wipe my face with my sleeve.

'You're really spoiling me.'

'Very funny,' she says, standing up. 'All right. I might stretch to a chocolate digestive. That's if your dad hasn't eaten them all.'

She leaves the living room, and I bring my legs up onto the sofa. Sometimes I wish I could move back here and become a child again.

There aren't any photos of Debbie on the mantelpiece, there never have been, not like there are at Grandad's. There's one in the spare bedroom — the room that used to be mine

— but it's probably hidden in a drawer now.

I get up and go to the dresser, where all the photo albums are. All the pictures of Dad, Robert and Debbie are in a red-leather book with an imprint of a horse on the front cover. I open the glass door to reach for it, but it's not there.

Monica brings two cups of tea into the room.

'Where's the album?' I say.

'I . . . I was looking at it upstairs. Do you want me to get it?'

I know every picture by heart — there are only twenty-three. There's one of a Christmas day when Robert got an Action Man; another of his third birthday with the hedgehog cake Debbie made. There's only one of me. I'm lying on a quilt at maybe a few weeks old, and Robert is lying next to me, propping up his head with his hand. My tiny fingers grip his thumb and he's looking down at me. One of Debbie's, or Dad's, fingers covers the left side of the picture; it's an orange-and-white blur.

'No, it's okay,' I say. 'I've looked at them loads of times anyway.'

I sit back down on the sofa, and she sits next to me.

'This whole business,' she says, 'it's affecting your dad too. He'll never say it to you kids, but he's been quiet.' She takes a tiny sip of her tea. 'I couldn't tell you this before — not when you were a child, and since then, well, there's never been a right time to bring it up. But for a long time, Peter was in bits. Your gran moved in with you . . . sometimes your dad would just sit at the

131

kitchen table, staring out of the window.'

'For how long?'

She's looking into the wood burner.

'Monica, for how long was he like that?'

She shakes her head back to the present.

'I don't know. About two years.'

'Two years? How come I don't remember any of this?'

'You were only little, Anna. It's why you and your gran were so close. She doted on you. She said she treated you better than her own daughter. She was always honest like that. I still think of her today.'

'I wish I could remember.'

She looks at me.

'Oh, love. You've always been frustrated about not being able to remember the past, but there's nothing you can do about it . . . you shouldn't be so hard on yourself. Sometimes it's better to forget. And the mind protects you sometimes, I think. Like poor Robert. He asked when Debbie was coming home for about a year. Then he just stopped talking about her. The kids at school probably told him she was dead. That poor boy. It had an impact on him when he was growing up.'

I'd love to borrow Robert's memories for a day — or even for just a few moments. Perhaps once I had them, he would feel a burden lifted and he wouldn't want them back; he might be happy then.

'I do feel bad for Robert,' I say. 'But she left me too.'

She rubs my hand.

132

'I know, I know.'

I look out of the window. Outside, Mr Flowers is trying to grab something with his walking stick again.

'I wonder if he ever manages to pick up what he's looking for,' says Monica. 'It's always at the same time every day.'

'Have you ever offered to help him?'

She turns to me, her eyebrows raised. 'Do you know, I don't think I have.' She frowns again. Sometimes she is so hard to read. Is she thinking about the old man — or is she thinking about Debbie, Dad, or Robert?

'Have you told Leo about the email?'

'I mentioned it briefly when he Skyped on Sunday. But you know what he's like. He's living a whole new life out there, with Jocelyn and the kids . . . he looked bored when I mentioned it, uncomfortable. And his father . . . well, he hasn't been interested in my life since he left.'

'What you said the other day,' I say. 'About things going strange with Debbie. What did you mean?'

'I wasn't myself when you saw me last. I was talking rubbish.'

'No one has ever said anything like that before.'

'Hmm. It was before we went on holiday . . . your mum wasn't herself. But it wasn't just her . . . we all felt a change, I think, a shift in things — me, Nathan, your dad. We never should have booked that holiday. Things would have been so different. I should've been there for her more.'

133

'Do you know what happened that night?'

'Just bits,' she says, still staring out of the window. 'It's a lifetime ago.'

'What bits?'

She looks at me. 'About her and Nathan.'

17

Saturday, 12 July 1986
Debbie

The heat of the sun that shines through the window bathes me in warmth — even though it's freezing outside, in July. I'm wearing my terracotta duffle coat that won't even do up any more.

Monica comes back from the Ladies'. She's still as skinny as she was ten years ago — and she's showing it off in a skin-tight, sleeveless polo-neck dress; she doesn't have to worry about her arms.

'I had a big breakfast,' she says, sitting down opposite me. 'But you go ahead and order. You need to keep your strength up.'

'What do you think I am? An Olympic athlete?'

She flexes her arm. 'More like Supermum.'

'Hardly,' I say, ignoring the implication that I'm built like a brick shithouse. I grab the menu. 'Anyway, I can't do up my coat. I should go on that new cabbage-soup diet.'

'Jesus, Debs. You've just had a baby. Plus, you're only a size twelve.'

I'm closer to a fourteen, probably a sixteen, but I don't say it out loud. Monica's always been slimmer than me. She never ate dinner at school, but says being slender is in her genes.

'So, how does it feel to be free for a few hours?' she says. 'I wish my mum would offer to have Leo — we have to pay a babysitter. Mum must've seen him, what, ten times since he was born?'

'Don't exaggerate, Monica,' I say. 'That's only because she moved back down south.'

She rolls her eyes.

'You see? What kind of grandmother chooses a career over her only grandchild? It's unheard of.'

'At least she sends money to make up for it.'

'True,' she says, smiling. 'But I do envy the way your mum is with your two.'

'Me too.'

'Ha!' She shakes the sugar sachet before ripping it open. 'She's probably mellowed out since we were teenagers.'

'Not towards me, she hasn't.'

This idle chat isn't why I asked Monica to meet me, but I'm scared to say it. Why should I be? She's the closest thing I have to a sister.

'Do you remember,' she says, 'when you told your mum you were staying at mine, but really we were camping with Mark Saunders in his back garden?'

'I'd forgotten about that. I made you come home with me in the morning in case she could tell from my face I was hiding something.'

'You always were a shit liar.'

I smile at her. She was always the best at lying. Most of the time, she'd tell me stories that were so mundane, so ordinary, that I'd wonder why she'd bother to make them up in the first place.

But there was one that stuck with me.

'I remember you said Mark Saunders had a crush on me,' I say. 'I made a right fool of myself sending him that Valentine's card.'

The smile vanishes from her face. 'I didn't think I confessed to you about that.'

'You didn't. *He* told me.'

'Ah.' She sips her tea. 'Bugger, that's hot.'

I smile, not hiding my delight. 'You should add more milk.'

She looks up at me. 'Do you forgive me? I am sorry, you know. My mum said it was to get attention.'

'What was?'

'My making up stories. Though it was *her* attention I wanted, but didn't get, so it hardly worked.'

'It got *my* attention,' I say. 'It made me think you were crazy.'

She laughs. 'Only *you* would stick around with a weirdo like me. You're too nice for your own good.'

I look down at my frothy coffee sprinkled with chocolate powder. I dab the milky foam with my finger and put the mixture in my mouth.

'I doubt that,' I say.

'You've not been yourself these past few weeks, that's all.'

Sometimes, it's like she thinks she knows it all, but she doesn't. We sit in silence for a few minutes. It shouldn't feel this awkward.

'Why did you meet up with Peter the other day?' I say.

A redness appears on her neck and works its

way up to her cheeks. She puts her palms on the table and leans forward.

'I was going to tell you about that, but you beat me to it. What did Peter say about it?'

'Peter didn't tell me. It was Dean who lives opposite us. He saw you two in town.'

Saying *you two* makes me feel sick.

'Oh, Dirty Deano.' She laughs.

I narrow my eyes.

'Sorry.' She sits up straight and looks around the café, but no one's near us. 'Peter phoned me at work . . . said he was worried about you.'

'Worried? Why?'

'He said . . . ' She looks around again. 'He said that you didn't seem to enjoy life any more — that you weren't happy. You know what he's like: he's a sensitive soul.'

'It's only three weeks since I had Annie. And anyway, what's happy got to do with anything?'

I look out of the window at the busy road outside. I can't believe I've just quoted my mother.

'It's got everything to do with it, Debs.' She puts a hand on mine.

I want to swipe it from underneath hers. 'It must be the baby blues,' I say. 'That's a thing, right?'

She shrugs. 'I guess. But I thought the blues came a few days after.'

I lift my hand away from hers, using my coffee as the reason. I sip the drink, but it's cold and bitter.

'I think I've been hearing things . . . voices,' I say. 'It sounds like my uncle — Charlie, who died years ago. I know it's not really him. It must be the tiredness. Everyone hears voices from time to time, don't they?'

Monica's mouth drops open, her eyebrows rise. 'I've never heard voices,' she says.

Oh God. I've made a mistake telling her. She'll tell everyone. Peter might get me sectioned. For a moment, the idea sounds tempting: I'll get a break, away from everything.

No. Get a grip, Debbie.

Monica leans back in the chair, as though she's afraid I might take off all my clothes and run around naked.

'What are you smiling at?' she says.

'Nothing. I was just thinking about Annie.'

'How many times have you heard your uncle? What did he say?'

'Something about catching a fairy,' I say. Monica's frowning again. 'You know. Dandelion clocks.' I wave my hand. 'Never mind.'

She's never been into all that ghost stuff. I'm sure it was her who moved the glass when we did a Ouija board at secondary school.

'If it happens again,' she says, 'make an appointment with the doctor. They might give you something for it.'

'Something for it?' I pick up the coffee again to distract myself from her staring at me. 'It was probably Bobby talking in his sleep, or someone in the street.'

I feel silly telling her about it. I can see she doesn't believe me. But really, there's not much difference between the two of us: me hearing voices, her being a habitual liar.

139

'I'll come with you to the doctor's, if you're scared,' she says. 'There's nothing to be afraid of.'

There is, I think. They could take my children away from me.

'Thanks,' I say.

But I've no intention of mentioning it to anyone again. She looks at me as though there's something not quite right with me. I suppose that might be true.

18

Anna

The waiting room is beige, and the paintings on the wall are beige. I'd expected Francesca King's office to be more modern, minimalist. There's a television in the corner that's switched off. I could do with a distraction.

In the quiet, the conversation with Monica this afternoon at their house runs through my mind.

'What about Debbie and Nathan?' I had asked. 'What happened between them?'

'I can't talk to you before I've spoken to Peter,' she said. 'You might say something to him. I can't have your dad thinking I'm going behind his back. He didn't want you kids to know.'

'Don't you know me? I'd never do that.'

She placed the back of her hand on her forehead.

'I can't see properly,' she said. 'I think I'm getting a migraine. I can only see half of your face. I need to lie down in the dark.'

And that was the end of the conversation. That's what it has always been like — I only get part of the story.

There is another man in the waiting room. Divorce, I imagine. He keeps sniffing and wiping his face with a stringy tissue that's already soaked. I try not to stare; he doesn't notice me anyway.

141

The door opens. Before Francesca has a chance to come out, the snivelling man leaps from his seat and almost sprints towards her.

What am I even doing here? I don't think Jack believed there was an emergency at the shop.

'At a closed charity bookshop?' he'd said. 'At seven o'clock at night?'

'I think I left the heater on,' I said, putting on my coat. 'If those books catch fire . . . there are flats above it . . . I wouldn't be able to sleep for thinking about it.'

He was smiling at me as I walked into the hallway. I hadn't told him I'd rung in sick that day. Every time I looked at him, I pictured him with Francesca; stroking her hair, her legs, her face. I was almost sick.

But now I'm here, I don't know what I am going to say to her. Is this normal, what I'm doing? Most people would confront their other half, not sneak around visiting his mistress's place of work.

I get up to leave, but her door opens again. Have I been sitting here that long?

The man is still holding the tissue, but his eyes are no longer red.

'She's good, she is,' he says, pointing to Francesca. 'I can't let that bitch of an ex near my children. She's dangerous.'

'Oh, I see,' I say. 'Very good.' My hands tremble as they cling to my handbag in front of me.

Francesca waits until the man has gone, before she says, 'Sorry to keep you waiting. Come on through.' She says it so nicely, I have no choice but to follow her.

Her office has a large metal-and-glass desk. The bookcases either side of it are white and crammed with leather books, like Jack's. His office is mahogany, more traditional.

'We don't have to read them all,' she says, catching me looking at the shelves. She sits down in her bright-orange tub chair. It looks expensive; everything about her does. 'Only when we get an unusual case.'

I look around for photos of her family. If she has children, perhaps she would understand, be considerate of my situation. She might not have realised Jack's married.

But, on second thoughts, why would her being married with children make a difference? Either you're a person who cheats, or you're not.

'My husband's having an affair,' I say.

She doesn't flinch. 'I'm sorry to hear that.' Her tone is gentle; she's frowning. I almost believe her sincerity.

'I think it's with another . . . a colleague.'

She picks up a pen. Should I give Jack's name? Client confidentiality means she can't repeat anything I say.

'You might know him,' I say. 'Would that be a problem?'

'It shouldn't be. Everything stays professional.'

She hasn't asked who it is. She's like the counsellor I used to see: letting me do all the talking.

'I'm not sure I want a divorce, though,' I say.

She puts down her pen, and clasps her hands on the desk.

'If you decide to go ahead, it's best to be prepared by getting your marriage certificate,

143

records of incomings and outgoings, preferably from both of you. Also, details of any pensions, debts. And, of course, a list of your children and their dates of birth.'

'We've only the one.'

She reaches across her desk and takes one of the leaflets from a plastic holder. She hands it to me. *Putting Your Children First.*

The sick feeling that was in my stomach five minutes ago has reached my throat.

A timer on her desk gives a short, shrill ring.

Before she tells me that our time is up, I stand. I have to swallow before I speak.

'My husband's name is Jack Donnelly. Do you know him?'

This is what I came here for. I keep my eyes on her face. She frowns, opening her mouth, but it takes her a few moments to say, 'Jack. Yes, I know him.'

* ⋆ ⋆

She didn't elaborate on how she knew Jack, but I hadn't expected her to confess, either. She had given me her card, and said to call if I wanted to go ahead. How unprofessional would that be, to represent me while having an affair with the other party?

I take out the card I stuffed into my pocket. *Matthew Smith. Family Law Solicitor.*

It's not hers.

I reach my car and get in quickly. I grab an empty crisp packet, just in time, and I vomit into it.

19

Monday, 14 July 1986
Debbie

It took us nearly two hours to get out of the house. When I put on my jacket the first time, Annie decided that her feed shouldn't be in her little stomach, but all over me. After only three hours' sleep last night, and nightmares of shadows watching me through the window, I wanted to crawl up the stairs and never come down. But I needed to visit Uncle Charlie. I haven't been since Annie was born.

It's so peaceful here. The only sound is of the wind chimes over the graves of the little ones *gone too soon.* Mum said that Mrs Taunton, one of the more outspoken parishioners, tried to get the teddies and plastic windmills banned from the cemetery. But Father Matthew put a stop to her petition. 'There's enough to protest about these days,' he said, 'without upsetting those poor parents any further.'

I'd like to be buried here. Though that's a bit morbid, isn't it? I'm sitting on a bench facing the row of children's headstones. They're in front of Charlie's. I know all their names by heart, and every one of them is tended. There are no dead flowers or soggy cards, unlike some of the older ones behind them.

I used to see a woman visiting Albert Jenkins' grave every time I came here at two o'clock on a Monday. It was months between me last seeing her, and her name being added under Albert's — a fresh mound of earth on top. I didn't like to think of her, the woman with a twinkle in her eye, lying under the heavy soil. It didn't seem right. Lilian, she was called. I only found that out from her gravestone. I should've said hello to her, at least once.

Uncle Charlie's grave always has flowers on it. Mum comes every Sunday after Mass, 'To visit them all,' she says. I never met my grandmother or my grandfather. They'd been dead years before I was born. Poor Mum and Charlie, losing their parents so young. My grandfather had been a piano teacher: one of the few little details I know about him because it's so unlike anyone in our family to play the piano. 'It's something only wealthy folk do,' Dad used to say, ''cos they've got too much time on their hands.'

I reach under the pram for the three roses I snipped from the bush in our front garden (probably planted by the people who rented it before us). I leave Annie in her pram, next to the other children and make my way towards Charlie.

I place two on my grandparents' grave, before putting the other stem into Charlie's vase. I wipe the bits of mud from the year of his birth.

'All better now.'

I look around; there's no one else here.

'Now what's all this business of you talking to me?'

There's silence. What else did I expect?

'You're going to get me into trouble. The men in white coats are going to cart me off.'

A breeze blows across my face.

'I'll have to get going, Uncle Charlie.'

I stand and look over to Annie's pram.

There's a man crouching over it. Where the hell did he come from?

'Hey!' I shout.

My feet are unsteady as I run towards her pram. I'm running over graves, whispering, 'Sorry.'

The man stands.

'Nathan?' I blink several times. 'What are you doing here? Why are you dressed like that?'

He's usually in a shirt and tie during the day, but he's wearing a black tracksuit with white stripes down the side.

'I've just been jogging,' he says.

'Oh. You must have run a fair bit — it's miles from your work.'

His eyebrows rise, and he looks at his watch — it's different to the one he wore the other day. He used to love that expensive watch.

'Yes, I suppose it is. Must've got carried away.'

I pull the pram handles towards me. Annie's eyes are open; she's awake, staring at the sky.

'I didn't wake her,' he says. 'She was already like that. You should be more careful, leaving her like that.'

'I was only over there, it's — '

'Hey.' He raises his hands in front of him. 'I was only joking.'

'Hmm.' I get a wet wipe from the changing

bag and clean the mud from my hands. 'Did you know I'd be here?'

'What? No, of course not. How would I know that?'

I shrug. 'Did you know Monica met up with Peter in town?'

I don't know why I'm mentioning it — I'm trying to forget about it.

He frowns. 'No,' he says. 'Why would they meet on their own?'

'To talk about the holiday, probably.' I look at the ground. Monica's right: I'm rubbish at lying. 'Anyway. Shouldn't you be getting back?' I look at my wrist, but I've forgotten my watch. 'Oh no, what's the time?'

'Three o'clock.'

'I've got to get Bobby in half an hour.'

'I could give you a lift if you want?'

'It's okay. If I walk quickly, I should make it. Bye, Nathan.'

It's difficult to run while pushing a pram. I'm not that far from school, but I like to be early. It feels as though everyone's staring at me. Being unable to use my arms means that I'm panting by the time I get to the gates. Cue the dirty looks from the immaculate mothers. You'd think I was brandishing a chainsaw from the glances I'm getting.

I look down at my clothes. Okay, muddy knees on my jeans from the cemetery, but otherwise nothing inappropriate. Shoes on, top buttoned. My hair's probably a mess, but when isn't it these days?

I reach into my bag for my sunglasses, so I can

look at them without them seeing. There are no muddy patches or stains on *their* clothes. Their hairstyles are almost identical — all layered, either in the style of Princess Diana or Farah Fawcett, which says it all, really. They wouldn't know Blondie if she were standing in front of them.

Another member of their clan jogs up to them in her sports outfit, complete with leg warmers and a head band. Bloody hell — she thinks she's Jane Fonda.

I quickly look at my nails as she catches me grinning at her outfit. She actually tuts. I doubt she's run that far anyway; she's not even sweating.

Nathan.

He wasn't sweating either.

No, I'm reading too much into it.

I could give you a lift if you want?

He hadn't been jogging at all.

★ ★ ★

Everything's strange — it's like I'm watching an episode of *Tales of the Unexpected*. When I got home from school with Bobby, Peter was in the kitchen making spaghetti bolognese.

'Someone told me about it at work,' he said. 'Couldn't wait to get started.'

'Obviously,' I said. 'It's not even four o'clock.'

Now, we're sitting around the table at twenty to six, surrounded by every pan and utensil we own scattered on the kitchen work surfaces.

'Well,' says Peter. 'I think I did a good job. I

don't know what all the fuss is about with this cooking lark.'

I open my mouth, but I don't say what I'm thinking: that it took over two hours, my plate is swamped with watery liquid from the sauce, and I would've preferred chicken crispy pancakes.

'Well done,' I say, instead. Because that's what I ought to say, because I'm trying to be as nice as he is today.

Bobby's face is covered in red sauce; he looks like he's been in an accident. 'What's for pudding?' he says.

We both look to Peter.

'I ... er ... I thought we could have a banana.'

I try not to sigh out loud. 'I'll make some custard to go with it.'

I fill a pan with milk, and press the ignite switch so the gas hob lights with a whoosh.

I look outside through the kitchen window. The back yard looks so grey when it's raining. I wish we had a proper garden.

I jump as Peter puts his hands on my shoulders.

'I know what you're thinking,' he says, looking outside too. 'You're wishing I'd put that washing line up, aren't you?'

I don't think he knows me at all.

I just smile.

★   ★   ★

Peter didn't complain once through *Coronation Street*.

150

'Do you know,' he said halfway through, 'that there's a surge of electricity on the grid at exactly seven forty-five on Mondays and Wednesdays. Do you know why?'

I was already in my nightie, and held a hot-water bottle to my tummy. I'd forgotten how painful it is after birth.

'No,' I said.

'Because, at the EOPO, everyone puts the kettle on. Isn't that funny?'

'EOPO?'

'End of part one.'

He looked very pleased with this.

'I've taped that other one — *Albion Market*,' he says now, as the end credits of *Coronation Street* play. 'I thought we might watch it together.'

'Has someone new started at work?' I say.

'No. Why?'

'No reason.'

I wonder, briefly, what spurred him into watching programmes he's never seen, or to cook from scratch when he's never shown interest before.

I fake a stretch and get up from the settee, my hot-water bottle falling to the floor.

'Think I'll head up for an early night,' I say.

'Already? What about *Albion Market*? Tony Booth's in it, you know.'

If he says *Albion Market* one more time, I'll scream.

'It sounds very . . . fascinating, but I've had a long day.'

'Have you now.'

151

I don't take the bait. I go over to him and place a kiss on his cheek. 'See you up there.'

'Hmm.'

I haven't got the energy for it. Annie went to sleep two hours ago. I'll be lucky to get an hour's sleep before she wakes again.

I close the lounge door, and go to check the front door's locked.

There's another pink letter.

Has Dean nothing better to do?

I pick it up and put it in my dressing-gown pocket. I can't be bothered to deal with it right now.

20

I'd forgotten how cold it is in the North. It's July, but it's freezing in this bed and breakfast. There's a storage heater under the window — why are they always *under the window?* I don't think it's worked since the 1980s. I don't think this place has been decorated since then, either. There's a television on a stand in the corner near the ceiling, so you need to be lying on the bed to watch it. Next to the bed is the window. It's like being *in there* again.

It was the view outside that kept me going — the sounds that leaked through. The rain beating down and the birds singing when the sun came out.

I didn't have to think about when to eat, when to turn the lights off, because those decisions were made for me. I couldn't sleep most of the time. The noises at night were worse than in the day. I pretended to sleep, though. It was easier that way.

I get up from the bed. It's almost ten o'clock. There are things I must do.

21

Anna

I wish I could have called in sick again, but I think I would be pushing my luck asking Isobel to cover the bookshop again. It has been raining hard for an hour. It's going to be quiet — apart from the people who will use the shop as a shelter on their way to somewhere else. I will have conversations about the weather with every one of them, and answer each person as though they were the first to talk about it.

The rain tapping on the window makes me feel hemmed in, claustrophobic. It's like all the books on the shelves are gathering and closing in around me. It's too warm in here.

Ellen's due in ten minutes. I haven't seen her since she hid the fact she was looking at the missing persons' website. I should be giving her a chance. I always thought I was quite an open-minded person, but I find her presence intimidating.

The breeze from the shop door opening brings welcome relief.

'Grandad!' I get up from my stool. 'I wasn't expecting you to come in today.'

He turns, briefly, to shake the water from his umbrella onto the step outside. 'Typical weather,' he says. 'Can we not have a bit of sun without the rain spoiling it all the time?' He pats the top of my arm and walks towards the back room. 'I can't be stuck in the house today. The walls are starting to talk back at me.'

I lean against the door frame.

He's looking at the rota on the fridge.

'Oh, good,' he says. 'Sheila's not in today.'

'I thought you two got on.'

'Hmm. She never lets me have a go on the till. She sits there all morning, warming her behind on the heater. And she fancies herself as a church-goer, but she only goes for the tea and biscuits afterwards. She sleeps through most of the service on a Saturday evening. I reckon she thinks no one notices.' He hangs up his anorak and flicks on the kettle. He pulls a round tin from a carrier bag. 'I've made some scones for elevenses. Tea's too wet without a bit of cake.'

'You made scones?'

'I've had to keep myself busy, then I don't think too much,' he says. 'Your gran had a notebook with recipes in, but God rest her soul, she wasn't much of a cook. These are Mary Berry's.'

Ellen will be here in one minute, if she's on time.

'Grandad, I forgot to mention there's a new volunteer. She's called Ellen. She's a bit quiet.'

'I don't mind quiet. I can't bear people who go on and on about themselves.'

'Anyway — I don't think it's a secret, but she was released from prison a few months ago.'

'I see.' He folds the carrier bag and puts it in his coat pocket. 'Well, I suppose she's served her time. We all deserve a second chance.'

'Morning.'

Oh God. How long has Ellen been standing in the doorway? Grandad shrugs, and flicks on the kettle again — the water has to be freshly boiled.

'Cup of tea, Ellen?' says Grandad.

'Yes please, Frank. That's very kind.'

Ellen takes off her coat. 'It's okay, Annie. I'm used to people talking about me. You should've heard the things I got inside.'

'Were they awful to you?'

'Only a few. But you learn to stick up for yourself. Or just merge into the background, like I tried to.'

'I'm sorry.'

'Don't worry. It's okay — it's part of who I am. You don't have to be sensitive on my behalf.'

Grandad walks over, two cups of tea in his hands. He puts them on the sorting table before going into the bookshop. 'Now, stop gassing, you two,' he says. 'There'll be customers to serve.' He sits on the stool and drums his fingers on the counter. 'Any minute now.'

★   ★   ★

'These are the best scones I've had in a long time,' says Ellen.

'I dare say they are, love,' says Grandad.

It's eleven o'clock and the bookshop is quiet, so we're sitting around the sorting table.

'Do you read much, Ellen?' I say, trying to sweep Grandad's insinuation under the table.

'I do,' says Ellen. 'I quite like crime fiction.'

156

Grandad raises his eyebrows, and takes a bite of scone.

'What's your new flat like?' I say. 'Have you settled in?'

'I'm not in there yet. Next week. I'm in a B & B at the moment.'

'Well that sounds just the job,' says Grandad, no doubt picturing a grand establishment in the Lake District. 'Imagine, having your breakfast cooked for you every morning.'

'It's not like that,' says Ellen. 'I have to be out during the day. And I'm lucky if there's a mini box of cereal outside my door in the morning.'

'Oh, Ellen,' I say. 'That's awful. What do you do all day? What about your meals?'

'I have a wander around the shops. And there's the drop-in centre. They have soup every day.'

'Oh.' I feel ignorant and patronising.

'Really, Annie, you don't have to worry about me. I'm a big girl.'

'If you ever want more shifts here . . . I know it's not the most interesting of places, but — '

'Thank you.' She stands and takes each of our plates. 'And I love coming here.' She places the dishes in the sink and runs the hot tap. 'It's like coming home.'

★　★　★

My grandfather is very good at putting on a brave face. To see him today, mixing with the few customers who came in, you wouldn't know he has been trying to take his mind off his daughter.

He usually finishes at twelve, but I think he's hanging on until Ellen leaves, so he can talk about her. They have hardly spoken to each other, which is odd, as Grandad is usually a master of small talk. I've caught him looking at Ellen more than a few times.

He stays seated at the counter as she comes out of the back room with her coat on.

'Are you sure you want to go now?' I say to her. 'You're welcome to stay longer.'

'It's okay. I'm meeting a friend for lunch.' She walks towards the door. 'I'll see you next week — if I don't pop in before.'

The door is only closed for a second before Grandad says, 'How did she know my name?'

'What do you mean?'

'We'd not been introduced, but she addressed me by name.'

'She probably read the rota.'

'But I'm not down for . . . oh, never mind.'

'What is it? Grandad?'

'It's just this feeling I've got — like I've seen her before.'

'She's got the same birthday as Debbie. It's on her CV.'

Grandad narrows his eyes at me.

'You've got to stop saying things like that.' He gets off his stool, not looking at me. He goes into the back.

Why do I keep thinking stupid thoughts? Sometimes I think they won't go away. My counsellor said I should be honest with the people I'm closest to.

'I'm sorry,' I say into the other room. 'You're

158

not going, are you?'

He walks back into the bookshop with his anorak on.

'I'm just off down the road to get us some butties.'

★ ★ ★

He comes back in soaking wet after forgetting his umbrella.

'Well, that woke me up,' he says. 'I hope you're not still vegetarian because they only had beef or 'tuna surprise'.'

'I haven't been a vegetarian for over ten years.'

He sits on the stool behind the counter, so I grab a chair from the back and sit in the doorway, ready to jump up in case Isobel comes in. Grandad hands me the tuna sandwich.

'I can't be eating things like that,' he says. 'You never know what the *surprise* is going to be.'

I peel it open. 'I saw Monica yesterday,' I say.

'Hmm.' He swallows his mouthful with a gulp. 'Don't you see her every week anyway?'

'It wasn't Sophie's day there. Anyway, Monica mentioned something about Dad — how he was after Debbie went missing.'

Grandad straightens on the stool.

'She said Gran moved in with us — with Dad and me and Robert.'

He places his sandwich on the counter, using a sheet of paper as a plate. 'Why is she bringing that up now?'

'Because of the email. She wanted me to know why Robert's so upset.'

159

'But why tell *you*? You've been the only one who doesn't remember. Why is she doing this to you? We gave you the best start without all of this affecting you.'

'But . . . I know, Grandad. You're right. In some ways, I am fortunate I don't remember her . . . but I'd give anything to have a real memory of her in my mind — not just a photograph.'

He pats my knee. 'I understand, love,' he says. 'What exactly did she say?'

'Who?'

He rolls his eyes.

'Monica. About your dad.'

'That he couldn't cope — that he needed you and Gran's help for two years.'

'Two years is exaggerating it a bit . . . as if your gran would let me be on my own for two years. It was more like two months. And it was no bother to your gran. She loved being with you and Robert. Your father lasted two mornings at the school gates before the whispering and glances got to him. He couldn't do it . . . he called them vultures. They'd heard about it somehow . . . thought he'd done away with her.'

'Done away?'

'No smoke without fire. Don't look at me like that, Anna, it's not what *I* thought — it's what those busybodies without anything better to talk about said.'

I hadn't seriously considered that the police questioned Dad, and that strangers thought he might have killed his wife.

'It didn't help that he answered *no comment* to every question,' says Grandad.

160

'But that doesn't mean anything. Jack says suspects are told to say that.'

'Yes, they are . . . these days.'

Grandad presses his lips together.

'You don't believe he hurt her, do you, Grandad?'

He puts his barely-touched sandwich back in its wrapper.

'No,' he says, eventually. 'But something's not right. I mean . . . '

'What?'

'They got married, didn't they? Peter and Monica. Debbie would've been horrified.'

'You've never said that before. You really think that?'

He takes a deep breath. 'Oh, I don't know. Don't mention it to them, will you?'

'No, I won't,' I say. 'What do you think happened to her?'

'I've been through it hundreds of times in my head. I often thought it was down to us being so strict with her, that we expected too much from her . . . so she rebelled.' Tears gather in the corners of his eyes. He gets up from the stool. 'But I don't know. Something happened that night. She can't have vanished into thin air.'

★   ★   ★

I almost have to drag Sophie into the photo shop after last time.

'But what if the witch is there again?' she says.

'Shh,' I say. 'She was just joking.'

'It wasn't a funny joke.'

'Anna Donnelly,' I say to the man behind the counter. 'I've come for my photos.'

He raises his eyebrows: I'm stating the obvious.

'The witch isn't here, anyway,' I whisper, as the man goes into the back room.

'*He* could be her,' says Sophie. 'She has magic. And she prob'ly heard you say *witch*.'

The assistant brings out an A3 envelope and pulls out a packet of photographs. He goes through each one and I try not to look at them. I don't want the first time I see them to be in here. He looks at them so unsympathetically, I want to snatch them from his hands and tell him they're mine.

'A couple of them are over-exposed — they've got stickers on.' He shoves the pictures back into the wallet. 'Which means it's not our fault.'

'Right,' I say. 'I wouldn't have asked for my money back.'

He shrugs. 'You never know with people these days. They don't understand the equipment they're taking photos with.'

'A child took these photos, actually.'

'That explains it.'

I grab the envelope. 'Thank you.'

I stand outside the shop. Should I open them here?

Sophie is jumping up and down.

'I need a wee.'

'Can it wait two minutes?'

'No, Mummy. I'm bursting.'

'Come on then.'

We walk quickly to my car, parked around the corner.

Just one. If I could just look at one.

I reach into the envelope and pull out the wallet, my other hand opening the car door for Sophie.

'My seat belt, Mummy.'

'Yes, yes.'

I fasten her in, close the door, and get into the driver's seat.

I glance at the car parked opposite us. I've seen it a few times this week. There's someone in the driving seat, staring straight at me. I narrow my eyes as I lean towards the window. Is it a man or a woman? Whoever it is starts their engine, reverses and speeds off.

'I'm really bursting,' shouts Sophie.

'Okay, love.'

I close my eyes as I quickly pick out a photo at random.

I switch on the ignition and place the rest of the pictures on the passenger seat.

'We'll be home in five minutes,' I say.

I turn over the picture in my hands, my heart pounding.

I lift it up.

It's a picture of a bloody lizard.

★　★　★

'This is the best tea, me old china,' says Sophie.

'*Me old china?*'

She scoops up her beans with a spoon.

'It's cockney. Miss Graham taught us it.

Gramps said he'd get me a book from the library.'

'When did he say that?'

'Last time I was there . . . think it was last month.'

'You mean last week?'

'Yeah. It was June then.'

'Did you tell me about it?'

She nods. I feel awful.

I'm missing all of the little things because my head is taken up with the big things. From now on, all things 'Debbie' will have to be talked about when Sophie is asleep or at school.

The photos are still in their packet on the kitchen counter. I keep glancing at them.

No. I'll have to open them later.

'Did you know Monica was born in London?' says Sophie. 'But it wasn't near the bluebells, so she's not a real cockney.'

'I think you mean Bow bells, love.'

At exactly five thirty, the front door opens and closes. Jack hasn't been home on time this week.

He comes into the kitchen. There are bags under his eyes and he hasn't shaved for days.

'Daddy! Me old china.' Sophie puts together the knife and fork on her plate, slides off the chair and grabs her dad round the waist.

'*Me old china?*' whispers Jack. 'It sounds so strange in her little voice.'

'I think it's the one bit of cockney rhyming slang she's learnt.'

'Oh.' Jack smiles at Sophie — at least, he's trying to; his eyes have no shine.

'I've saved you some fish fingers,' I say. 'Only

164

five-star service here.' I pull the tray out of the oven — the golden crumb is now brown. 'I'll make something else. I haven't eaten yet either.'

'No, no. They're fine. I could do with some comfort food.'

'Elly's invited me to her swimming party,' says Sophie, sitting back at the table. 'Can I go?'

I open her book bag and take out the invitation, attaching it to the fridge with a magnet.

'Of course you can. Daddy'll take you.'

'Why can't *you* take me? You never go with me to swimming.'

'I just don't like the water, that's all. It . . . er . . . makes my hair go funny.'

'But you like water in the bath.'

'That's different.'

Monica had paid for private swimming lessons for me when I was eight years old, because at school I was the only one who would scream if the teacher tried to guide me into the water. 'Poor Orphan Annie,' my classmates would shout, flicking water at me from the pool. 'Boo hoo, boo hoo.'

The teacher would tell them off, of course, but that didn't stop the snide comments.

The nearest I got to the water, during these private lessons, was dangling my feet in, my little knees knocking together as they shook. 'Well, Annie,' Monica said after the third (and last) session, 'we can't say you didn't try.'

'Sorry, Sophie,' I say now. 'But Daddy loves swimming.'

'Hmm.' She pushes her empty plate into the

centre of the table. 'Can I go up the apples and pears? Harry in my class showed me how to make Minecraft figures from Lego.'

'Course you can.' Jack sits at the table as Sophie stands and runs out of the kitchen. 'Two phrases she's learned, then.'

Sophie thumps up the stairs as I sit down opposite Jack, handing him a plate with five frazzled fish fingers.

'You look really tired,' I say.

He rubs his eyes.

'I haven't been sleeping well.'

'What can be so bad at work that it's keeping you awake at night?'

'Did I say it was work?'

'The other day . . . you said you had a tough case.'

He cuts a fish finger and it almost snaps in half.

'Did I?' He shrugs. 'That must be it then.'

I take a deep breath.

'If there's something I should know — you can tell me.'

He crunches the food loudly; I try to not let it bother me this time. His eyes focus on the table. Has he even heard me?

'What? No,' he says. 'Where did that come from?'

'You've been distant . . . spending all of your time in your office . . . sleeping there.'

'You can talk,' he says.

'Pardon?'

'You've been obsessed with that email. It's just like that woman last time.'

166

'It's not like last time. This is something real.'

'Is it?'

He stands, and pours the rest of the fish fingers into the bin, slamming the plate onto the counter. He breathes slowly through his mouth.

'Look,' he says. 'I'm sorry. Really, I am, Anna. There's nothing wrong. It's *you* I'm worried about. It's just . . . I don't know why you're getting your hopes up, like the last time — however misguided you were then.'

I look down at my hands on the table; they're shaking. I'm with my husband — my hands shouldn't tremble with Jack.

'One of those private investigators called,' he says. 'Wanting to know if you were really my wife.'

'Why would he do that?'

'It was a woman. And I don't know . . . probably because we're charging it to my firm's account — she might have been ripped off in the past. At least we know she's thorough.'

'What did you say to her?'

'I said you *were* my wife, obviously.'

He grabs the plate and rinses it under the tap.

'What will she be investigating?' he says. 'It's just about Debbie, isn't it?'

'What else is there to investigate?'

'Just checking you didn't have any other long-lost relatives.' He tries to smile again. 'So I can estimate the cost.'

'No. It's just Debbie.'

He rubs my back between my shoulder blades.

'Good, good.' He kisses the top of my head, and walks to the door. 'I've got to do a bit of work upstairs, then I'll try to be back down before nine.'

I don't reply. He doesn't wait for one.

What just happened?

I asked him what was wrong, and he turned it back on me. Again.

But I lied as well. Francesca King must have said something to Jack.

It's not just Debbie I'm going to investigate. It's him as well.

★ ★ ★

It's eight o'clock and there is no sound from upstairs. Sophie is asleep, and I doubt Jack will come down again, so I've laid out Robert's photos on the kitchen table. There are twenty-seven altogether — seven of which are blurred; three of what I assume is Robert's hand, and four of lizards. The rest are pictures of Dad, Debbie, my pram, and Monica with her first husband, Nathan.

The photos displayed in our house when we were growing up were only ever of us five — Monica, Dad, Leo, Robert and me. Two partial families brought together. It's like Dad and Monica wanted to rewrite history: to erase the people who hurt them. I have always had an image of Nathan in my head that is like Dad, only a little bit different. But he is Dad's opposite. Dad is tall with red hair, which is mainly blonde and grey now, and his white skin is freckled. Nathan is also tall, but lean, tanned, and his hair is almost jet black. And he is very good-looking. In one photo, Monica and Nathan are sitting next to each other, leaning back against white plastic chairs. They are smiling, and Monica's head is leaning towards his, with Nathan's arm resting casually on her leg. Understated, yet intimate. Had they just said *cheese* at the command of the little boy taking their picture? They suit one another.

In another photo, Dad is standing at a huge barbecue, with a sausage on a fork in one hand, and a bottle of beer in another. His hair is a shiny chestnut colour and the freckles on the bridge of his nose have joined together to give him a tan. The skin around his eyes is creased as he smiles. It's like he had no worries at all, standing there in shorts and a T-shirt with his family and friends.

Poor Dad.

One of my tears drop onto the picture. I rush to get a piece of kitchen roll and dab it off before it makes a stain. I wipe my face with it and stuff the tissue up my sleeve.

There's a strange picture of green-neon stripes that I can't work out, but the next one is of Nathan kneeling at my buggy. My feet are resting on his chest; he must have put them there — I was too young to do that myself.

He's smiling at me, this stranger. Though I wasn't a stranger to *him*. He'd known me since the day I was born. It's a peculiar feeling, knowing someone was close to you and you don't recall them at all.

'What happened to you all?' I whisper.

The next photo is of a glass bottle of Coca

Cola, but in the distance, sitting at a table, are Debbie and Nathan. They look as though they're about to —

'Talking to yourself again?'

I stand up straight.

'Jack! How long have you been standing there? I didn't think you'd be back down tonight.'

'I couldn't leave you on your own again, could I?'

He has an empty wine glass in his hand, which he takes to the fridge to refill. It's probably the real reason he came downstairs.

'You got them then?' he says, looking down at the table. 'Wow — your brother had a thing for lizards.'

I smile. 'Seems like it. Though I don't think he appreciates them as much now.'

'Oh, I don't know — his ex-wife had a few reptilian characteristics.'

'Very funny. She wasn't that bad.'

I collect the photographs carefully into a pile and place them back into the wallet. 'Have you finished working for tonight?'

'There's nothing that can't wait until the morning. I thought we might watch a film together — try and switch off from everything for one night.'

'All right,' I say. 'I'll try.'

I grab a glass from the cupboard and pour myself a glass of wine. It's the only way I'll be able to forget about anything tonight.

22

Tuesday, 15 July 1986
Debbie

Two thirty in the morning. I'd forgotten about the tiredness with newborns. How could anyone forget that? I'm so exhausted I could sit and cry. I had to bring Annie downstairs; she won't settle. I've been pacing the living room for forty-five minutes. I tried singing 'Hush, Little Baby', but I couldn't hear my own voice over her screams. It used to work with Bobby.

It's been three hours since her last feed. Hungry. She must be hungry. Again. I thought she'd sleep at least four hours at night by now.

I grab a bottle from the fridge and place it into a jug of boiling water, carrying it back into the living room. I grab the flicker and turn on the telly: teletext is better than nothing. Don't the television people realise that not everyone is asleep after midnight? Not that I'd be able to watch anything, even on tape. Every time I stop pacing the living room, she shrieks.

I check the milk on my wrist. A tiny bit too warm, but it'll do. I put it to her mouth and she starts gulping it down; maybe she likes it hotter.

I fall back onto the settee, trying to concentrate on the words on the telly, but they're blurred. Blink, blink. I can't fall asleep while she's drinking.

It's so quiet at this time of the morning. All the little worries I have in the day double in size and it feels as though they're ganging up on me. Who is making Peter so happy? It certainly isn't me. And for him to cook tea; that hasn't happened for years, not since before the kids were born. He could be planning to leave me. He might leave in the middle of the night. No, that wouldn't happen — he never wakes once he's asleep.

Nathan.

Why was he pretending to be out jogging? Unless he wasn't pretending for my benefit, but so I'd tell Monica. Perhaps they're all in it together. They think I'm crazy and they're planning ways to tip me over the edge.

As I sit up, I hear the crackle of the envelope in my pocket. The note that came last night. I'd forgotten about it.

I hold Annie's bottle in the hand of the arm she's resting on, and take the letter from my pocket. The envelope's not hard to pull apart; it's not stuck down. I flick it open and shake the note from inside. I can see already it has more writing on the paper than the last one.

I place the letter on my lap and unfold it.

You ought to be more careful with that baby of yours — keep her close next time. You never know who's watching.

I throw the letter onto the carpet.

It can't be for Peter — he's not been alone with Annie since she was born. Someone knows

172

what I've been doing — that I left the baby outside the shop, and at the cemetery. I have to tell someone about these letters: Peter, the police.

My heart's thumping. Can Annie feel it?

She's looking up at me; the bottle's empty. Her lovely blue eyes are gazing at my face, trying to take me all in.

'I'll never let anyone hurt you, little girl.'

We both startle as a car door slams outside. I get up to turn the big light off, and tiptoe to the window. I don't know why I'm trying to be quiet — it's not as if anyone outside can hear me.

I place Annie on the armchair next to the window, putting a cushion along the edge of the seat.

I peer through the gap between the curtains.

There's someone standing next to Trisha's car, over the road — a man.

I open the curtains a few inches wider.

He takes something out of the boot and dumps it on the pavement. I stand on my toes, but I can't see anything, except the shine of a bin liner.

I look back to the man.

He's staring straight at me.

I duck down, almost catching my chin on the window sill. He must've seen me — the telly's giving off light; I should've switched it off.

My heart's thumping.

The car boot slams shut.

I wait a few seconds to give him time to leave, before slowly standing up again.

He's next to our gate, just looking at me.

It's Dean.

I can't move. My knees are shaking.

He brings his hand up. What's he doing?

He taps his nose three times. He's laughing at me, shaking his head.

I grab each curtain and pull them together sharply to close the small gap.

'There, there,' I say to Annie as I pick her up, even though she's perfectly fine. I hold her close to me as I climb the stairs.

She doesn't whimper or cry as I place her in the cot.

I wish Peter would wake at least once in the night, just to ask if I'm okay. Tonight, I'd tell him, no. No, I'm not okay.

★   ★   ★

I try to see things from other people's point of view. In the early hours of this morning, Dean probably thought I was a nosy housewife spying on him in the middle of the night. To him, I'm the crazy one. Did I think he'd killed Trisha and was getting rid of the body? Whatever was in that bin liner wasn't big enough for that.

Trisha's car's not outside this morning. Perhaps I fell asleep and dreamt the whole thing.

'She slept through the night then?' asks Peter, as he eats his toast. He walks into the living room, getting crumbs all over the carpet — not that it'll make any difference; I mustn't have hoovered this week.

'No,' I say. 'She woke three times.'

'Really? I didn't hear a thing.'

174

'You never do.'

'A bit tired, are we?'

Why can't he accept that sometimes it might be *him* I have the problem with, and it's not just my lack of sleep?

'Yes. I only had four hours' sleep at most.'

'It'll get better,' he says, kissing my forehead.

I wipe off the smear of butter he left on my skin.

'I would've helped get Bobby dressed,' he says, 'but I never know where anything is.'

'It's where it always is.' I don't have the strength to say more about it. 'Dean was outside last night,' I say. 'Getting something out of Trisha's boot. He saw me looking at him.'

Peter laughs. '*Coronation Street*'s got nothing on Dean, eh? Wonder what dodgy scheme he's involved with this time.'

I should've known that it was my imagination. Listening to myself describe it to Peter makes it sounds ridiculously dull — just a bloke going about his business. Not someone watching me, trying to scare me, which is far worse than him sending me notes.

'Peter . . . I've got something to show you. These letters came through the letterbox — I've kept them upstairs. I think — '

'Can we talk about this tonight, Debs? I've got an early meeting in Manchester this morning. Head office is thinking of having a twenty-five-million-pound sale at Woolies this Christmas. I know the company's doing well and everything, but that's just ridiculous. It'll never happen.'

'I suppose it can wait.'

175

He bends down to rub Bobby's hair; he's watching one of his videos before school.

'Catch you later, kid,' says Peter.

And then he's gone.

I get up and go to the window, watching Peter as he leaves. I should get rid of these old-fashioned net curtains, but they come in handy during the day when Annie's asleep and I want to watch the world go by. Peter's whistling as he strolls down the path and out of the gate. I wonder what it's like to be in his head — to know what being happy in the morning is like. He gets to go out and talk to people — people who answer him back, like he's a proper human being. I try to imagine going back to work and I can't. The feeling still fills me with panic. I'm safe here — with my children. I don't have to dread Sundays and feel the anxiety of mixing with strangers. That's what I tell myself.

'It's finished, Mummy,' says Bobby. 'Can I watch another?'

'What?'

I must remember my children are the important ones in my world. They depend on me.

'Sorry . . . yes. But we've got to leave for school in ten minutes, Bobs. Maybe just a short one.'

I sit on the settee and watch as he picks one of his three videos, ejecting the last, and putting in another. When did he get so independent? While I wasn't looking, I suppose. He's had to fend for himself a bit more now Annie's here. I've nothing to compare it to — it was only me as a child.

The theme to *Thomas the Tank Engine* blares into the living room. All the talk of useful engines reminds me that I can't just sit around being lazy. I go into the hall and grab Bobby's shoes. The letterbox rattles as something's pushed through it. I glance over, but it's just a folded leaflet — not another pink envelope, and I breathe again.

I pick it up from the mat and it drops open.

It's a flyer for Weight Watchers.

Bloody charming.

I look at the top and it has my name written on it in blue ink — the writing's loopy and slanted.

'The cheek of it!' I say aloud.

I open the front door and run to the gate. I look to my right and there's a boy at the end of the street, running away from me. I look to the left. No one else is posting leaflets — why would he just post it into our letterbox?

Dean and Trisha's door is pulled ajar.

God, I hope it's not Dean again.

My feet are stuck to the path. I need to get inside before it opens fully.

'All right, Debs?'

It's Trisha. Looking immaculate as ever. She must've got up at five o'clock in the morning for that make-up job.

'Yes, yes. Just getting the milk in.'

She looks at my hand, which is still holding the scrunched-up leaflet.

'Milkman ignored the note for one more today,' I say.

'Oh right.' She raises her eyebrows, not even

pretending to be interested in my boring life. She bends to pick her milk up. 'Have a nice day!'

She's in her own world, that one. Bet she doesn't even know who the Prime Minister is. Though if she does, I bet she loves Thatcher — people who own their own houses always do.

I look at our empty crate. We must be behind on the milk payments again — they build up too quickly. I slam the front door shut behind me and slump to the hall floor. Trisha must be in on it too. I'm sure she used to be nice to me. Didn't she? Or was it fake?

'*You've got to make yourself useful.*'

That voice, again.

'What?' I say. 'Who's that?'

I crawl into the living room. Bobby's already turned the telly off. How did *he* get so useful? He's standing in the middle of the living room, already wearing his shoes.

'Who put them on for you?'

'Me. Monica taught me.'

'Is she here? I think I heard her.'

'Are you all right, Mummy?' He walks over to me. I'm still on all fours. He puts his hand on my forehead. 'You look sad.'

'I'm fine, fine. I think I might've heard the telly.'

I slowly get up, looking behind Bobby, but there's no one there.

'Let's go a bit early,' I say, grabbing my jacket off the settee.

I help him into his coat, and place Annie in the pram.

As we walk down the street, I sense someone

watching me. Everyone's watching me. People stare at me as I walk past them.

What's happening to me?

★   ★   ★

I feel a little calmer on the walk home from school. Claire, one of the nice mums, talked to me at the gates. She's pregnant with her third child, God help her.

'What do you do all day?' I asked her.

'This one's a bit of a handful,' she said, tugging on the hand of her three-year-old daughter. 'I just aim to get through the day, keeping them alive until bedtime.' She smiled. 'If you're getting a bit . . . ' she leant closer, 'bored or lonely, feel free to pop round for a brew. Think I'm only around the corner from you. I'd suggest one of the mother-and-baby groups, but they're all run by Princess Diana over there.' She nodded to one of the clan, and straightened back up, rubbing her back. 'Nine months seems to take longer and longer each time.'

A new friend is just what I need. Monica's working full-time now, and I can't share my problems with my mother — it'd make her worry even more. The trouble is, though, how much do you confide to someone you hardly know?

I turn the corner onto our road. Trisha's car's back again. Dean's polishing the bonnet. Why isn't he using his own car? I grab the pram handles, intending to turn around, but I'm too slow. He's already seen me.

He stands and watches as I walk the last thirty yards to our gate.

Please don't talk to me, please don't —

'I'm surprised you're up and about so early,' he says, 'after your late-night shenanigans.'

I turn the pram ninety degrees so my back faces our front gate.

'You not speaking today?' he shouts. 'Peter in the doghouse?'

'Trisha not working today?' I say.

'Course. She's always working, isn't she?'

I shrug.

'I've got the day off,' he says.

He's walking towards me. He always has the day off.

I reach behind for the gate, but it's jammed. Come on, you stupid thing.

He's standing just a foot away from me. He leans his upper body towards me. I can smell stale beer on his breath. I close my eyes.

'Please don't hurt me.'

The gate swings into life and bangs against the fence.

I open my eyes as Dean pulls back his hand.

'Hurt you? I'm not gonna hurt you.' He's laughing at me again. 'Tell you something, Debs. When you women have babies, it turns you cuckoo.' He taps the side of his head as he walks backwards into the road.

The stupid, chauvinist bastard. Where's a speeding car when you need one?

He turns his head back and looks at me.

'Boo!'

I wish I hadn't jumped.

He laughs, and mutters something under his breath.

I wrestle the pram through the gate and walk backwards to the door. I'm going too slow.

I pick Annie out of the pram and open the front door, leaving the pram in the garden. I run into the kitchen and get a glass of water one-handed as I hold Annie tight.

I down it in one, but it doesn't help.

I walk into the lounge. There are toys everywhere . . . open video cases and at least three empty bowls of cereal, and four — five — cups, one of which has curdled tea inside, litter the living-room floor. Have they been there long? How have I missed them?

I pack a bag for Annie, grabbing her bottles from the fridge.

I need to get out of this house.

23

Anna

I'm on my own in the bookshop today, which is just as well as I have a headache from the two glasses of wine I drank last night. When had I become such a lightweight? Jack and I used to drink a bottle of wine each when we started going out. Before marriage, before Sophie.

Jack put on a rubbish action film last night and we sat in silence. There was a time we would have thought the film ridiculous, laughing at the ham-fisted fighting, before putting on something else.

I had glanced at him sideways. He didn't look much different from when we met — perhaps his hair was greyer at the sides, and he had dark circles under his eyes, but he wasn't sleeping properly. That's what he said, anyway.

I kept practising sentences in my head: *I know about you and Francesca, and the letter in your wallet.* But I couldn't get the words out — he would say I was losing my mind. Again. He'd turn something he had done wrong into something *I'd* done. I'd have to get evidence first, and then confront him with it. I should just ask him — tell him I found the letter when I was looking for something else.

Why did I keep thinking these thoughts? Jack

has never been unfaithful. What happened in the past was all me.

I met Gillian Crossley seven years ago — when I'd only been at the Preston branch of the charity-bookshop chain for a few weeks. I was pregnant with Sophie, and it was the first time I had been in the bakery she worked in; it was only a few doors down from my shop.

She treated me like an old friend. Her cheeks were flushed with the heat of the ovens and her long dark hair was captured in a net that rested on her shoulders.

'Hello,' I said to her. 'I'm the new manager of the charity bookshop.'

'Oh, you must be Annie!' she said the first time we met; her smile was beaming, infectious. 'I heard you replaced Evelyn as manager — and that you're a lot nicer than she is.' She winked at me. I didn't tell her that I preferred 'Anna', as it was nice hearing her call me Annie. People always got my name wrong.

I just smiled.

'I bet you like carrot cake, don't you?' she said.

'Yes,' I said, quietly, trying to find my voice. 'I can't eat too much though — I'm trying not to eat for two.'

She grabbed a piece from the display cabinet, wrapped it in a paper bag and carefully twisted the corners shut.

'Here's a slice on me,' she whispered, glancing to the back. 'Don't tell my boss, though. And don't worry about *your* boss, Isobel. She might give you a hard time, but she's like that with everyone . . . even us and we don't work for her.' She put the cake into a carrier bag with my sandwich. 'I love your bookshop — reading and contributing to charity at the same time. Nothing like a bit of escapism. If you ever get any books about Blondie in, I'll buy them. Obsessed, I am.'

I took the bag from her and muttered, 'Will do.'

Debbie liked Blondie, I thought. It was on my list.

I reached for my phone as I left the bakery, and took a picture of her through the window.

It had to be a sign.

Gillian looked about the same age as Debbie would be.

When I got home that day, Jack was sitting at the kitchen table on his laptop.

'There's a woman at the bakery who was really kind to me,' I said to him. 'She's called Gillian.'

'That's nice,' he said.

I doubted he was listening.

Back then, I kept a photograph of Debbie on the phone table in the hallway: close enough to see every day, but distant enough that she didn't look at me when I watched television.

Jack kept typing on his keyboard. I reached into my handbag and took out my mobile.

'Look,' I said. 'I've got a picture of her. Don't you think she looks like the picture of Debbie by the telephone?'

His fingers stopped mid-air.

'You took a photo of some stranger?'

I held my phone towards him. 'She's not *some stranger*.'

He frowned at me.

'What the hell are you on about, Anna? She looks nothing like Debbie. What are you getting at?'

I looked at the picture of Gillian again. Granted, it was hard to tell through the glass of a shop window, but she had the same hair and she was the same height, the same age. And she had called me Annie.

'Just wait till you see her in person,' I said.

He looked at me for a long time before he said, 'I'm not going to see her in person, am I?' He slammed his laptop shut. 'I'm working upstairs. You should get some sleep — you're not thinking straight.'

He looked at my pregnant belly when he said it — as though all those hormones running through my body were making me say strange things.

'Fine,' I said, taking four slices of bread out of the packet, a block of cheese from the fridge, and a jar of chilli jam up to bed.

That was just the start of it — though I didn't know that then. I hadn't thought anything I said had been out of the ordinary. I'd seen someone who reminded me of my mother. The mother I couldn't even remember.

I shiver, now, as I recall how much worse it got after that.

The shop door opens, and in walks a woman with curly hair and glasses. She looks to be in her late fifties or early sixties. She is wearing a beige raincoat with the belt straps dangling either side. She doesn't even glance at the bookshelves; she

185

strides straight towards me. I get up from the stool.

'Sally Munroe,' she says, holding her right hand out in front of me. 'Private investigator.'

I shake her hand. 'I — '

'You're Anna Donnelly. I would've come to your house but . . . ' She walks to the back room, grabbing each side of the doorway and leaning into it as she looks around.

'But what?' I say.

'There was something not quite right about what your husband said to me.'

She comes to stand in front of the counter again, only looking at me for the briefest of moments. Her eyes dart around as though she is looking for something. She glances at the clock and I make sure my mobile is still under the counter should I need to call for help.

'Your husband doesn't usually pop in at lunchtime, does he?' she says.

I look at the clock, too. I can't believe it's twelve thirty already. I've been daydreaming again.

'No, he doesn't,' I say, sitting back down on the stool, closer to my phone. Jack mentioned a woman telephoning him at work, but she hadn't contacted me in return. 'I wasn't expecting you. Why didn't you just email me back?'

She leans against the counter. She sighs heavily and relaxes her shoulders.

'Sorry about that,' she says. 'I like to get my bearings before talking about sensitive issues. We can't have any Tom or Dick listening in, can we?'

I shake my head. Did she mean to say that wrong?

186

'The reason I'm here,' she says, 'is for a preliminary meeting. I need to make sure I can work with you. Some people can be high maintenance — can't be doing with that. Can pick and choose my clients these days.'

She reaches into her massive handbag and pulls out a polythene pocket. She takes a sheet of paper from it, placing it in front of me.

'I take it you've read about my services online,' she says, 'and that you're happy with me going ahead with any necessary searches?'

'I haven't actually heard from any of the other firms I contacted — '

'Was it Tommy and Kev you contacted?'

'It might have been — are they the other local ones?'

'Yep. Tommy's in the Isle of Man — will be for another few days, I'd say. And Kev . . . well, no one's heard from him in weeks.' Her eyes drift to the side. 'I should look into that at some point. We might be each other's competition, but still . . . ' She blinks and looks back at me. 'So?'

'So?'

She rolls her eyes.

'So, if you're happy to sign this, I'll get working on it for you.'

'Sorry,' I say. 'You didn't mention a form to sign.'

She picks up a pen from the counter and hands it to me.

I look down at the paper.

Confidentiality Agreement.

Jack says I should scrutinise everything that needs signing.

'It just means,' says Sally, 'that I won't disclose to a third party the results of my investigation, unless specified by yourself — and, if it contains any evidence of a crime, that I'll be duty-bound to hand over to the local constabulary.'

Her signature is already on the document.

'You've spoken to my husband.' My pen hovers over the dotted line.

'Yes. I wanted to make sure you were who you said you were — and to make sure funds would be available to pay for my services. I've been let down in the past, you see. And I told him I'd deal with Janet, his secretary, about my future invoices.'

'I see.'

'Is something holding you back?' She speaks so quickly. 'Are you sure you want to dig into all of this?'

Hearing her say it makes me realise that I will be taking my search for Debbie to a different level. I won't just have conflicting things my family have told me — the unreliable memories, their feelings about her tainting the information they gave me.

That is, if Sally Munroe is any good at her job.

'Look,' she says. 'If I don't find anything that's of any use to you, then I'll only charge expenses. It's a personal guarantee of mine.'

I sign the piece of paper, already printed with my name.

She picks it up, blows the ink dry and puts it back into the polythene pocket.

'Very good,' she says. 'Now, as soon as is humanly possible, can you email me everything you have — including any little bits of information you think might be irrelevant? You never know. Then we can schedule a meeting convenient to us both. How does that sound?'

'Good,' I say. But I feel out of my depth. 'I have photos, do you want to see them?'

She fastens her bag and puts on a tweed flat cap.

'Well, of course, my dear! I want to see everything.'

She walks towards the door.

'Wait!' I say. 'You said something before — about what my husband said.'

She looks behind her before saying, 'Yes, that's right.' She frowns and pulls down the peak of her cap so it half-covers her eyes. 'He asked if I'd be investigating anything to do with him.'

'And what did you say?'

'I said, 'Of course I won't.''

'Oh.'

'But I didn't mean it,' she says, opening the shop door. 'You're the boss.'

She winks at me, and then she's gone.

★   ★   ★

I closed the bookshop fifteen minutes before I should have, but there is never a sudden late rush for second-hand books, so I headed over to Dad and Monica's. Sophie is in after-school club until five thirty, so I have at least an hour.

'I can't chat for too long,' Dad says. 'Monica reminded me that we've got a thing on at six.'

'What kind of thing?'

189

'Some wine-and-cheese evening,' he says, waving his hand. 'Seems we're back in the seventies.'

I'm holding the wallet of photos, and he glances at them as he pulls out a chair from under the table. I texted him after I got them, but he didn't reply. He leans forward, his hands clasped in front of him.

'I don't think we should look at them right now,' he says. 'Monica could be down any minute.'

'So?'

'It might upset her.'

'But aren't you curious? These are photos you've never seen of her.'

'We can meet up another day, we'll do lunch.'

He shifts in his chair, his eyes darting to the door, to the window.

'Since when have we ever done lunch? What's wrong, Dad? You look nervous.'

'Nothing. Well, not nothing. Jack phoned me this morning . . . said you've organised some sort of detective to find your mother.'

'Jack phoned you? But his office is going to be paying for the detective — it was his suggestion. I don't understand.'

'Don't think he's going behind your back again — he was just letting me know . . . thought it might've slipped your mind.'

'But that's what I wanted to talk to you about now. It wouldn't just slip my mind. Since when have you and Jack been having cosy chats about me?'

After all the times Jack said he doesn't believe

my dad's version of events, why would he phone my dad? It's just like six years ago, when everyone was speaking about me behind my back.

'It wasn't like that, Anna. He wanted to ask me a few questions about it.'

'What questions?'

'The ones he usually asks me when he's drunk . . . if I remembered anything I might have missed before.'

'Really? God. I'm sorry, Dad. I thought he was asking questions about me.'

'It was nothing like that, love.'

'I'll have a word with him later.'

'No, don't, really. It's nothing. I've had to answer questions about it for years.'

I place my hand over his.

'I'm sorry.'

He takes his hand from under mine and grasps it.

'Don't you ever say you're sorry. You've been through enough.'

'Do you think . . . '

'What?'

'Do you think, that if we find Debbie . . . that you'd want her back?'

He flattens his hands over mine; he shakes his head.

'I loved your mother . . . with all of my heart. I probably should've told her that more. I should've done a lot of things, but you can't go back in time. But no, in answer to your question. We'd be different people. I was fond of Monica all those years ago, but nothing ever happened between us when Debbie was alive. Now, I adore Monica. She has treated you and Robert as though you were her own. She's been there for me.' He closes his eyes for a few seconds before opening them again. 'I have to be honest with you, Anna. I really don't think this email is from Debbie. It can't be.'

'Why do you say that?'

'I thought it might've been, at first. But why would she just send an email? Why just say a few lines? It didn't even read like she would speak.'

'Did Grandad tell you that he found letters? Poison-pen letters, they looked like. They were with Debbie's things that he'd stored, from the house.'

Dad withdraws his hands from mine.

'No, he didn't. In those days after she left, when I was on my own looking after you and Robert, I remembered that Debbie tried to tell me something, but I was always too busy to listen. All I thought about then was keeping my job. I couldn't stay at home with you all, even when that was all I wanted to do. I had to pay for the roof over our heads. It wasn't like it is now — Debbie left her job six weeks before she had you, and that was that. There weren't day nurseries in abundance. We were meant to just get on with it. I wish I'd listened to her more. She wasn't herself. Perhaps it wasn't about the money — we should've found a way for her to go back to work. But after Robert had started school, we would've had to think about childcare for the holidays.' He rubs his forehead. 'We should've tried harder, I know that. But, like I said, you can't go back in time.'

'Was it because of me? That she left?'

'No, no, no. Don't ever think that, love. It was everything. I think she missed being with adults. I'd have felt the same.' He places his elbows on the table. 'But if there's a remote chance that this email is from Debbie, then no. We would never be together again. Debbie would say the same, I imagine. What I have with Monica is too precious. She was there for us all when I was at rock bottom. She has a heart of gold.'

'This is the most you've ever said to me about all of this.'

'I know. It's been really, really hard. I've not wanted to burden you with it. And Monica is my wife. I love her. She hasn't treated you and Robert any differently to Leo. I've had to put her first, above the memory of your mother. This is all difficult for Monica. She's always felt guilty about her and me.'

'I love Monica, too,' I say. I take a deep breath. 'I met the private investigator today. She's called Sally Munroe. She's going to start working on the investigation as soon as I've emailed her all the details — including the email Debbie sent us the other week.'

'I don't mean to be harsh, love, but whoever sent that message, sent it to Monica's email address. Why would someone do that? If it were Debbie, she'd contact me, or you or Robert. It might be from some crank again — you don't want to be wasting money on a wild-goose chase.'

'What do you mean, *again?* You all keep saying

that, but I don't remember anything specific. Robert wouldn't go into details when I asked him.'

Dad sighs.

'Because he doesn't know the details. It was about twenty years ago. A letter came through the post. Again, it was addressed to Monica, but using her old surname.'

He gets up and opens the cupboard above the fridge-freezer.

'Why didn't you tell me this? Why does everyone keep secrets from me all the time?'

'It was a long time ago, love. You were only ten years old and going through all that bother at school. I didn't intentionally keep it from you. In fact, I don't know why I kept it all these years anyway. I took it from Monica, and said I'd burned it.'

The envelope is white, creased. He doesn't open it, but pushes it across the table towards me.

'Best not look at it now,' he says, looking to the kitchen door. 'You'll have questions, and I don't have time to answer them.'

'Did you take it to the police?'

'Anna, the police wouldn't have been interested.'

'But they were interested when Grandad went to the police all those years ago.'

Dad's face drops. Why do I keep saying things that hurt people?

'That was an awful time,' he says. 'I was at the police station, being interrogated, for nearly eight hours. Their questions were relentless — Did Debbie have any financial problems? Was she having an affair? Had I found out and done something to harm her? — I thought that they knew something I didn't. What if I *had* hurt her, but couldn't remember?'

'But they let you go. I know you wouldn't hurt anyone.'

'They didn't look as kindly on me,' he says. 'It's because Debbie left a note.'

'She left a note? And no one thought to tell me this?'

He stands, the chair squeaking across the floor behind him.

'Anna!'

It's Monica.

I cover the envelope with my hand and slide it from the table and into my handbag.

'I didn't hear you come in. What have you got there?'

She's looking at the wallet of photographs on the table. She's wearing make-up, but there are still shadows under her eyes.

'Just some pictures Robert took when he was a kid.' I feel Dad's eyes boring into me. 'But I'll show you two another time. Dad says you have to get going soon.'

'We do?'

'Yes, Mon,' he says. 'We've got that thing tonight, remember?'

'Oh right, the thing.'

She's frowning at him.

I get up, kiss Monica on the cheek, and walk into the hall.

'I was just passing. I've got to get Sophie from after-school club.'

Debbie left a note. I want to ask where it is. My family has never been honest with me. It's too hard to ask what I want to know. If everything was out in the open, we could have had the answers years ago.

24

Tuesday, 15 July 1986
Debbie

It's still light outside. Downstairs, I can hear the telly on for Bobby, and Mum announced about five minutes ago that she was feeding Annie. All is well, and I don't have to get up. I can stay cocooned in my old single duvet for a while longer. It's bobbled with age, but I love it.

'Shall we ring him, Frank?' says Mum. 'Let him know they're here?'

'I'm not interfering in their marriage,' says Dad. 'Not unless Deborah asks me to.'

They must know I'm listening. I could always hear the pair of them from upstairs when I was growing up, but they never had anything interesting to say then. The rooms are too small, and the walls are too thin, in this house.

When I look up at the ceiling of my old bedroom, I could be fourteen again. I spot the tiny square I carved into the polystyrene tiles. If I remove it, there'll be the little note I put in there. I can't remember what it says. Probably a poem about being in love or my heart breaking or something equally as dramatic. One day, I'll look at it again.

Monica and I always spent time at her mother's house, mainly because she was always out working, and we could smoke cigarettes in their massive kitchen. Monica seemed so glamorous when she started at our school after she moved up from London. The closest I got to London was listening to the Sunday charts on Radio One. I was surprised she hung round with me, when I came from a council estate.

Our house was always freezing. I used to think it was because we'd run out of fifty pences for the meter, until Dad said it was because of Mum. 'She's having her sweats,' he said. 'It's like she's run a marathon.'

She had her hot flushes for years. It was only a few years ago, after Robert was born, that they stopped. She said, 'Why's it freezing in this house? We can't have a baby in a house that's as cold as a cave.'

Dad just rolled his eyes and got the extra fifty pees from a jar he kept in the cupboard under the stairs.

I turn onto my side. The little stereo Dad bought me is still on the wicker table. He's always loved gadgets — he'd buy anything electronic from the junk shop in town, even if it wasn't working. I used to be embarrassed by how little I had in my bedroom. Monica had a telly, a video — even a crimper and a set of heated rollers she never used. I envied her freedom — the fact her mother was always out — but now I'm glad my parents are always home, always here for me.

It's a shame Monica didn't come here more often when we were kids. Mum would've liked it, I think. If Monica lived here, she wouldn't have been as skinny. Mum shows love with food — even if her combinations are a little strange.

What does Mum do when no one's around? She only seems to do things for other people. I try to imagine her lying on a sun lounger, drinking Cinzano — a cigarette in a long holder dangling from her fingers. The thought of it makes me smile. Mum might be fifty-two, but she looks so much older, with her permed grey hair. She always wears that pale-blue tabard to save her clothes from her daily bleaching of the house. When I'm fifty-two, I'm going to look glamorous. If I fast-forward to then, the kids will've grown, and I won't have any responsibilities.

My old cot is at the end of my bed. Dad must've got it down from the loft. He's painted it pastel pink; last time I saw it, it was a deep blue.

There's a gentle tap on the door: it's Dad. Mum would've marched up the stairs and knocked as loudly as she could.

'I'm awake, Dad.'

The bedroom door opens slowly. He stands at the threshold — hands behind his back as though he were waiting for a bus.

'What time is it?' I say.

'Nearly ten past five. Did you manage to get some sleep?'

Peter'll be walking through our front door at any minute. He'll find an empty house.

'I thought it was later than that. I didn't hear you bring the cot in — you must've been quiet.'

'I got that down weeks ago,' he says, 'when Annie was born. We've been looking forward to you all coming round to stay. Will you be stopping long, love? If you are, then I've got a train set in the loft. I'd love to let Bobby have a go on it.'

I pull myself up to a sitting position.

'Since when have you had a train set?'

He shrugs. 'Since you were five. I bought it one Christmas — only second-hand, like — but you were more interested in the knitting set your mother got you.' He rolls his eyes. 'I thought I'd try and make you a tomboy, but you were having none of it.' He smiles.

'How do you remember about the knitting set?' I say. 'I'm sorry, Dad.'

'Give over. I'm only messing.'

He sits on the end of the bed.

'You know, love,' he says. 'You can stay here for as long as you like. It's been quiet since you left home, and what with me getting laid off at Leyland . . . well, I'm getting under your mum's feet. She wouldn't notice me as much with a house full.'

'Thanks, Dad. But we won't stop long.'

His eyes look to the floor. Poor Dad. He always talks like he lost his job at British Leyland a few weeks ago, but it's been four years. It must be so alien to him, not going out to work every day. I don't know how they manage, but you can't ask your parents how they afford to put food on the table.

'Peter won't know where we are,' I say. 'I didn't leave a note.'

Dad leans forward, resting his hand on my foot.

'He's not hurt you, has he?'

'What? No, of course he hasn't. Why do you ask that?'

'When we opened the front door earlier, you almost fell into the hall. You barely said a word . . . you just rushed upstairs and got into bed.'

'Did I? I can't remember . . . but that wasn't long ago. Are the kids okay?'

'Annie's asleep in her pram after her feed, and Bobby went straight to the telly — as usual. Anyway . . . it was like you'd just escaped from somewhere. You were frightened of something.'

He looks at the carpet, which has brown-and-orange swirls, immaculately hoovered every day, even though I'm never here. I used to hate it, but now it comforts me.

'I'm just worried about you,' he says. 'I've never seen you frightened at the thought of being in your own home.'

'You've known Peter for years. He's not like that.'

Dad purses his lips in a tight smile.

Then I remember the other day, when Peter whipped the cup out of my hands — it smashed into pieces. He slammed the front door.

'Frank!' Mum's shouting from the bottom of the stairs. 'Your tea's on the table. Hurry up or it'll get cold.'

Dad puts his hands on his knees and stands.

'Are you coming down, Debs? She'll have made a plate for you. It'll dry up if it's left in the oven.'

I flop back down against the pillow.

'In a minute.'

Dad walks to the door.

201

'You should get a microwave,' I say. 'They're like magic.'

'And they cost a small fortune,' he says. 'Anyway . . . your mother can't even program the video. Let's not let her loose on radiation.'

I hear Dad console Mum by saying my dinner won't be ruined. 'I'll have it for my supper if she's too poorly,' he says.

'She's not poorly, Frank. She's just got the melancholy.'

I don't know why they have to talk so loud. I look to the ceiling again. That would've been the perfect time to have told Dad about the letters I've been getting.

I was eleven and I'd just got back from secondary school, and a letter had arrived addressed to me. I looked at it for ages before taking it off the mantelpiece. I never received post and I'd sent a painting to *Blue Peter* a few weeks before. I felt the envelope, but couldn't feel a badge inside. I tore it open, and the note inside listed names and addresses to send the same letter to. If I didn't, I'd have twenty years of bad luck.

Dad grabbed it out of my hand as I read: *If you destroy this letter, someone you know will —*

'I'm not having that,' he said. 'It's one of those chain letters. I read about them in the paper.'

The tears welled in my eyes as he tore it to tiny pieces.

'But, Dad. It says if I destroy it, someone will die.'

He picked up the bits from the floor and scrunched them into a ball.

'*You* haven't destroyed it; *I* have. And no one's

going to die because of it.' He went into the kitchen and threw it in the bin. 'If I find out who sent you that, I'll bloody give them what-for.'

I ran to the window to see if there was anyone outside, which was silly as the post had come that morning. There was no villain lurking in the shadows of our estate. But someone had written my name. Did they write it out of fear — to share the burden?

Dad was right, though. No one died. Uncle Charlie had already passed away that year. Whoever is writing to me now, isn't writing out of fear, but hate. I couldn't tell Dad about the notes; it'd only upset him. I've already tried telling Peter, and he wasn't interested.

'There's peaches and Dream Topping for dessert, Bobby,' Mum shouts from the kitchen.

I pull the quilt up over my shoulders, and feel safer than I've done for weeks.

★　★　★

The phone's ringing downstairs. I turn and face the other way. Peter'll get it.

Whispers from the hallway.

I open my eyes, and the wall is in front of me, not our bedroom window or Annie's Moses basket. Because I'm not at home.

Thuds up the stairs.

Mum opens my bedroom door.

'Deborah,' she hisses. 'There's a telephone call for you.'

I fling back the covers and swing my feet onto the carpet.

'He woke the baby,' she says. 'I'll have to unplug it.'

I rub my face.

'How long have I been asleep?'

'It's ten to six.' Not long. She beckons me with her hand. 'Come on, love. He's waiting for you.'

'Hmm.' I get to my feet and follow Mum down the stairs. 'Did he sound angry?' I speak quietly so Peter won't hear me down the telephone line.

'Not at all. Why would he?'

'Mum, who's on the phone?'

We linger on the bottom stairs.

'It's your old friend, Nathan,' she whispers. 'Lovely man. Even asked how *I* was.' She's grinning at me, as though everything is just wonderful. 'I'll leave you to it.' She tiptoes across the hall and closes the living-room door.

It seems I'm living in the twilight zone.

I sit on the bottom step, like I'm sixteen again, and reach for the handset.

'Hello?'

'Debs! Your mum and dad still have the same number.'

'They do. Nothing seems to change in this house.'

He laughs.

'Is your wife there?' I say.

Why didn't I call Monica by her name?

'No. Don't know where she is, to be honest. I thought her and Leo would be here when I got home, but the house is empty.'

'How did you know I was here?'

'I didn't. I phoned yours and Peter's first to

see if Monica was there, but there was no answer.' He sighs loudly down the line. 'Is everything okay, Debs? You don't seem yourself.'

I twist the phone cord in my hands.

'I don't know. I just feel . . . different. It's the sleepless nights. Things should settle back down soon.'

'You know I'm here, if you want to talk.'

'Thanks, Nathan. But, like I said the other day, I should be talking to Peter about things.'

'Okay. I know Peter's busy at work at the moment, so the offer's there.'

'Thanks.'

I lean against the wall to my right and rest the handset on my shoulder. Nathan hasn't telephoned me in years. Hearing his voice, and him listening to mine, makes me feel as though I could close my eyes and float to the ceiling.

'We used to talk for hours, didn't we?' he says.

'We did.'

Mum used to walk past sighing loudly, pointing to her watch. 'It's okay,' I'd hiss, my hand covering the bottom of the phone. '*He* rang *me*.'

'We'd listen to your records all the time,' he says. 'Blondie and — what was that song you used to bring round to mine and made me put on again and again? By The Beatles — your dad bought it from a jumble sale or something.'

I smile. ' 'Norwegian Wood'. I haven't listened to it for years.'

'It came on the radio today. It made me think of you.'

I don't know what to say, so I say nothing.

'I think I can hear the car,' he says. 'I'd better go.'

'Okay.'

'Bye then, Debs.'

'Bye, Nathan.'

There's a brief silence before he hangs up. Still, I hold the phone against my ear. It's quiet for several seconds before the angry tone starts. I place the handset back in its cradle, and put my arms around my knees.

The living-room door opens. Mum probably listened in.

She stands at my feet.

'Deborah, love,' she says, towering above me. 'Why are you crying?'

25

Anna

My laptop and the photographs are scattered around me on the bedroom carpet. The letter Dad gave me this afternoon lies unopened in front of me. I won't be interrupted; it's ten o'clock and Sophie is asleep. Jack says he's at work, but I don't know. There is a part of me that is past caring. Everyone lies, don't they? I don't know why I expect so much from people. They always let me down.

Dad seemed angry that I had more questions about Debbie today. Have I exhausted the subject of my mother? When I was a child, I wanted to know everything about her, but this changed as I reached my teens. My curiosity turned into anger. No one else's mum had vanished — why had mine? I wasn't good enough to have a real mother. It wasn't enough that I had Monica. It singled me out, when all I wanted was to be like everyone else.

I cross my legs and pick up the envelope. It's addressed to Monica, written in capital letters. The date stamped is 1996 and the bright-green stamp is priced twenty pence; second class, probably. It came from Eastbourne, Sussex.

I flip it over; the seal is yellow with age, like the paper inside it.

The writing is slanted, scruffy.

Monica,
I know what you did. What will everyone think of you if they knew the truth?
x

I read it again and again.

Why would they think this is from Debbie? There's no signature, and no one has ever mentioned her being in Eastbourne. It must be from a stranger who saw Debbie's photo on the missing persons' website. Grandad put it up there when the site first started.

My laptop pings with an email notification from Sally Munroe.

Yes, send everything you have. I await.

She's straight to the point.

I use my phone to capture Robert's photographs, but most are ruined by the reflections of the main bedroom light. They will have to do.

I place the photo of Debbie and Nathan in front of me on the floor. Their faces are so close together, but I can't read their expressions. It looks like Debbie is frowning and Nathan is saying something to her. I wish I could have been there properly. It might be the last photo of her.

I upload them as attachments, and type out Debbie's date of birth, height, hair colour. I don't know what else would be useful. My childish list of facts is meaningless when searching the world for somebody. How would it help Sally to know that Debbie was terrible at cooking?

I am about to press send when I remember I also need to send her details about Jack. I type in Francesca's name, and the details of Simon Howarth, the man who sent my husband the Facebook message: *Have you told her yet?* I attach the photograph from my mobile of the letter Francesca wrote Jack, and send it before I change my mind.

I feel the adrenaline running from my heart to my feet.

I've sent it. I might finally get some answers.

It is almost ten thirty and Jack still isn't home. I get off the floor, turn the light off, and crawl onto the bed. I lie on top of the quilt — it's too hot to get under.

At times like these, I wish I had a close friend to call and talk about things with. I live in my head too much. But there's no one any more. I have my volunteers at the bookshop, but that isn't the same. I could never call them with my problems; it would be too unprofessional.

I feel so alone.

The voices from the bedroom in the house next door, on the other side of the wall, affirm it. The woman laughs at something her husband has said.

When I was younger, I had imagined my life to be just like hers.

I reach over and flick the lamp off. I turn my head to the side and smell Jack's pillow. It doesn't smell of him, just fabric softener. I can't remember the last time he slept next to me — I wish we'd never bought that sofa bed for his office.

The key goes into the front door downstairs. A few seconds later, the stairs creak as Jack creeps up. The floorboard next to the bedroom door groans as he pauses outside it. He must have seen our lamp light on from outside, minutes before.

'Are you awake, love?' he whispers.

He hasn't called me *love* for ages.

I don't answer. I'm not up to arguing or interrogating him about phoning my dad — as well as all the other things he is keeping from me.

The door handle turns; he pushes it open, and I close my eyes. I breathe in heavily, faking deep sleep.

He sighs, and walks out again.

26

Tuesday, 15 July 1986
Debbie

It's dark and Bobby should be getting ready for bed by now. I should get up from this single bed, but my body feels like it's made of stone: cold and heavy and no use to anyone. I glance at the record player on my left. A small collection of records lies on the wicker shelf underneath it. 'Norwegian Wood' will be amongst that pile. I'll try to remember to put it into Annie's changing bag before I leave.

A triangle of light on the carpet.

Mum's in the doorway. She comes into the bedroom; Annie's in her arms.

'I'll just put her down,' she whispers. 'Then I'll give Bobby his bath.'

I can't even sit up.

'I'll do it,' I say, anyway.

'You get your rest. And stop talking or you'll wake the little one.'

She wouldn't accept the irony, so I don't argue.

She lays Annie down in the cot.

'Thanks, Mum,' I whisper.

She nods, backing out of the room. When the door shuts the landing light away, I close my eyes.

Annie's stirring.

'Please don't wake up,' I whisper.

I must've been too loud: she whimpers.

I'm useless. Mum probably spent ages getting her to sleep.

She's about to cry, I know it.

I will myself to sit up, grabbing my pillow and placing it at the end of my bed. Moving from one end to another has robbed me of the small amount of energy I had.

I put my arm through one of the gaps in the cot and rest my hand on Annie's shoulder.

'I'm here, little one. I'm here.'

★ ★ ★

Annie's cries feel like they've pierced my ear drum. We've only been asleep for minutes, surely. There's no light under the door. She cries out again, and I leap out of bed to pick her up.

'There, there,' I whisper.

I half expect Mum to rush into the room, with the noise coming from here, but she must be asleep. There are no shouts coming from downstairs, no telly blaring, though it's hard to be sure with Annie screaming in my ears.

I creep onto the landing, avoiding the three places where the floorboards squeak. Annie's still shrieking; she's never slept here at night before. I tiptoe down the stairs, praying Mum's made up a bottle. I can't believe I only just remembered. What kind of mother am I?

They've left the lamp on in the living room. It's a gesture I appreciate, as Dad can't bear wasting electricity. I grab Annie's blanket from her pram near the window, and lay her on the living-room floor. Her little face is bright red from screaming.

'Shh, sweetheart. I won't be a sec.'

I almost cry with relief when I see three bottles lined up in the fridge. Dad must've bought two more from the chemist. I'll have to get Peter to pay him back.

The sound of the gas heating the kettle seems to soothe Annie. I take it off the heat at the first cheep of the whistle. The bottle doesn't take long to warm; Mum only made 4 oz bottles.

Annie gulps it down as I sit in Mum's chair, under Jesus with the bleeding heart. I feel His eyes burning into the side of my face, and I turn away from Him.

She stops drinking after only two ounces.

Screaming again.

I sit her forward and rub her back.

She burps twice, but she's still crying.

How did I end up here, alone in the near-dark at my parents' house, with a baby who hates me? I want to be Monica with her perfect house, perfect life. I want to be Michelle Watkinson, getting to fly on Concorde. They say in the news, it'll be able to carry passengers around the whole world soon. Dad says that plane is beautiful. 'A work of art, she is,' he said. 'If the British can help build something like that, just think of what else we can do in the future.' After working at the Leyland factory, he appreciates design.

'Be quiet, Annie!' I say. 'You'll wake everyone up.'

I try her with the bottle again, but she closes her mouth firmly whenever it touches her lips. I get up and pace the room. That doesn't work either.

'Please, baby. Please do this for me.'

As I walk, my tears fall onto her Babygro.

'I'm sorry, Annie.'

We walk up and down the room. The house is the same size as ours, yet this room feels smaller.

'I'm sorry, sweetie. I can't remember how to do this. Somewhere, there's someone who's totally right. Who wants to do this.'

I want to place her on the floor and run away.

I can't believe I said that to her out loud.

I hope she doesn't remember . . . use it in arguments against me.

My head is killing me — she's so loud.

'*You're ludicrous. You know it, don't you? You're not good enough for her. They're all going to find out about you. And what they think will be right. You're a piece of shit.*'

'What?' I look around the room; no one's there. 'You're wrong,' I say out loud, to the settee, to the wall, to Jesus. 'I *can* do this.'

I've done everything I'm supposed to do, and still she's not happy.

I sit on the edge of Mum's chair. The room spins.

I'm not really here. My body must be lying down somewhere, and it's just my mind living this nightmare. I give my little finger to Annie's palm and she clutches it. Instinct, I read once; not intention. Her skin is soft, warm. The dry creases on her hand are like hardened flakes of candle wax.

The time on the video flashes: 23.15. It's earlier than I thought.

I put Annie, still screaming, into her pram. We could both do with some fresh air; the whole house'll wake if she carries on like this. I grab Dad's jacket off the hook, and back the pram out of the front door.

I take a deep breath as the gentle breeze makes the tears on my face cold. The air outside smells sweeter than it has done for months. I close the gate behind me and am grateful there's no one around. Most of the houses in the street are in darkness — even Mrs Birchill's opposite. She's always been a nosy old cow. She used to tell me off for sitting on our own wall: 'You're staring at me, I know it. This estate's gone downhill.'

I don't even know if she's still alive. I don't pay attention when Mum announces that another acquaintance has popped their clogs. Mrs Birchill was wrong. This estate's all right. Growing up, there were a few of us from round here at the school in the next town, but some of the kids there turned their noses up at us. And then, those from our estate called us traitors for not going to the local secondary school. I felt like I didn't belong anywhere.

The houses are in rows of four. Some are rendered or pebble-dashed — the owners showing off that they exercised their *right to buy*. I miss the time when every house looked the same. Summers lasted forever, and we played outside all day, only coming back when we heard our mothers shout, 'Tea's ready!' We knew our own mother's voice from a distance.

Annie's eyes are wide open; can she see the stars, or is her eyesight not developed enough? I look up, too. There are a few wispy clouds and the stars look so near.

'Aren't they beautiful?' I say to her. She blinks, and I smile. 'I guess that's all I'm getting from you.'

I walk around the whole of the estate. It takes twenty minutes because I walk slowly. I've never known it so quiet. I turn the corner a few streets away from Mum and Dad's. The bench, lit with the harsh, orange light from the lamp post next to it, has only one plank left; the white concrete has been covered with graffiti. I don't remember it being like that. Perhaps Mrs Birchill was right after all.

At the top of the road, there's a car with its engine running. It wasn't there a moment ago; I didn't hear it start or pull up. I begin walking again, slowly, and reach the middle of the street. The car's engine idles. I can't see what make of car it is. I should turn around. It's waiting for me, I know it.

No, no. They're probably waiting for someone to come out of the house they're in front of. But the house has no lights on inside. My hands are sweating, shaking around the pram handle. My legs don't feel strong enough to run.

I stop, turn the pram around. The car engine growls as it starts to crawl along the pavement. I walk faster, glancing at it behind me. The lights are so bright, I can't tell who's driving — or even the colour of the car.

I run, the pram wheels gliding smoothly over

216

the cracks in the pavement. The car goes faster, matching my speed. A right, then another left, and I'll be at my parents' house. There's a short cut through a ginnel.

I look over my shoulder. A man's face is in the driver's window. Dark hair. Is it Nathan?

I look forward again, and turn down another street. The car follows. I'm nearly at the ginnel.

Oh God. It might be the person who sent me the letters. I should've told someone about them, made Peter listen to me. What if this is the end? No one knows where I am. I shouldn't have just sneaked out of the house; I should've left Mum and Dad a note.

I can hardly breathe; I'm running faster now. There's no one else on the streets. Where is everyone? I look down at Annie and she's fast asleep. How can she sleep now? I thought babies were meant to sense the emotions of their mother.

I come to the ginnel. The street light in the middle of it isn't working. I run down anyway — trees towering either side; rotten wooden faces lean towards me. The car lingers at the entrance behind before speeding away.

I didn't check on Bobby before I left. What if the man in the car has taken him? They *all* might have disappeared for all I know. They might be in the boot. I reach the end of the pathway and bend over. I want to vomit, but there's nothing in my stomach.

The car turns down my parents' road.

Oh God. He knows where they live.

It crawls along, stopping a hundred yards from the house, but I'm closer — only twenty feet from my parents' front door. I push the pram hard over the grass verge before it bounces off the kerb. The wind blows through my hair as I run down the road. The car doesn't move.

In seconds, I reach Mum and Dad's house. My heart's racing; my breaths are short.

Shit. I haven't got a key.

I put my hands into the pockets of Dad's jacket. There are only a few bus-ticket stubs, no keys.

I tap on the door. Oh Jesus. It's me who's going to be waking everyone up, not Annie. I crouch down and check under the terracotta pot. Thank God. Bless you, Mother. I grab the key from underneath and wipe off the dirt.

The car stops outside the house.

I hold my breath and duck behind the pram.

What am I doing? Making the baby a barrier between me and some crazy stalker?

I stand slowly. The car is silver, like ours. It's a battered Datsun, like ours.

My feet are frozen to the ground as the car door opens and closes. The driver walks round the front of the car and stands a few feet from the pram.

'Why the hell have you taken my children away from me?'

He doesn't look the same. His eyes are dark, wide; he looks unshaven, even though he was clean this morning.

'Peter. Calm down. I didn't take the children away. Stop being so loud and dramatic.'

'Loud and dramatic? You're a fine one to talk, aren't you?'

'Shh, you'll wake Annie.'

'Will I now? Why are you walking the streets at this time of night with my daughter? I was on my way round here, and I saw someone who looked just like you, wandering around at nearly midnight. I thought, *No, that can't be Debs — not in the dark, not when I've been so worried about her.* But then you came closer, and it *was* you. What were you thinking?'

'It's not that big a deal. People go for walks all the time. She wouldn't settle.'

'That's because she's not at home. I didn't know where you were. Why didn't you tell me you were here?'

'Didn't Mum ring you?'

His eyebrows are raised, his fists are clenched, and his feet are wide apart. I take a step back and lean against the front door.

'Anyway,' I say. 'What are *you* doing creeping about in the car? I thought it was someone trying to get me.'

'*Get* you? Why would anyone be trying to *get* you?' He's moving his head from side to side. He thinks I'm stupid.

'Keep your voice down. I've been getting these poison-pen letters . . . it's like someone's been watching me — and Annie.'

I almost fall into the house as the front door opens.

'What's going on out here?' It's Dad. 'The whole street'll wake up if you two keep shouting.'

'Sorry, Frank,' says Peter. His face has totally transformed into that of a person who looks calm. 'I had no idea where my family was. I needed to check they were safe.'

'At this time? Why didn't you just phone us?'

'I've been trying since seven — it just rung out.'

Dad rolls his eyes.

'Your mother,' he says, glancing at the sky. 'She must've unplugged the phone. She's been fretting about the baby waking in the night. I told her babies wake just fine all by themselves, but she was having none of it.' Dad pulls his dressing gown around his middle. 'As much as I would love to stand out here and have a chat, I think we should get this little one to bed.'

We all look at Annie, fast asleep in her pram.

Peter nods. 'I'm sorry, Frank, Debbie. You must understand how worried I was. I drove to Monica's, to the hospitals. I thought if you were here, someone would answer the phone . . . Are you staying here tonight, then?'

'Yes,' I say. 'Bobby's upstairs. I'll have to take him to school in the morning.'

He bends over the pram and blows a kiss to Annie, then backs away. His arms hang at his sides; his eyes are wet, dull. Poor man — what am I doing to him? He must've thought I'd left, taken his family away.

'Ring me tomorrow, okay?' he whispers.

I nod, and watch as he gets into the car and drives away.

'Come on, love,' says Dad, taking hold of the pram. 'Let's get you both back in the house.'

Inside, I peel back the pram cover.

'Wait,' says Dad. 'Just come into the living room for a minute, she'll be okay there.'

I follow him and sit on the settee as he gently closes the living-room door. He sits on the chair next to me.

'What are these letters you were talking about? Have you got them with you?'

'Were you listening at the door?'

'Just for a minute. I'm worried about you, love. It's like . . . I don't know . . . like the spark's gone out of you. There's no joy about you any more.'

'I'm just tired and out of sorts.'

'What did they say, these letters?'

I rub my forehead; my temples are throbbing.

'Something like *I know your dirty little secret* and *keep her close*. That sort of thing.'

'How odd.'

'I know. But, Dad, you're not to worry about it — they weren't even addressed to me. And before you ask, I don't have a dirty little secret.'

'I wasn't going to ask that.'

I smile at him. 'Yeah, right.'

'If you get any more, then I'll come with you to the police station.'

'What will they do? It's not illegal to send nasty letters, is it?'

'No, it's not. It should be, though . . . the effect it's having on you.'

I stand and take off Dad's jacket.

'It's not the letters that are affecting me. It's everything, I suppose. I'll get used to it . . . the shock of a new baby and all that. Don't tell Mum about them, I don't want her worrying more than usual.'

I open the living-room door, hang up the

jacket, and take Annie out of the pram. I turn to go up the stairs; Dad's standing right behind me.

'I know she wouldn't want me saying this,' he whispers. 'But your mum was a bit like this after you were born . . . with the melancholy.'

'What do you mean?' I whisper back. 'She said she was fine after she had me.'

He shakes his head. 'I don't know what she's told you, but no. She wasn't fine.' He glances up the stairs as though he's scared Mum'll hear. 'I shouldn't say any more. I'm only telling you because it was all right in the end, wasn't it? It'll be the same with you, won't it?'

I take a step up the stairs.

'Yes,' I say. 'Yes, it will.'

But I'm lying. Again.

'Night, Dad.'

27

Anna

I'm carrying a box of about a hundred books, and am at the bottom of two flights of stairs. You might have thought I'd be used to lugging them around, working in a bookshop, but my hands are shaking. Ellen's in front of me, carrying two boxes, and not at all out of breath. Why is there never a lift in these places?

'I really appreciate this, Annie,' she says. 'I know it was Isobel who offered your services. You could've said no, I would've understood.'

'It's okay, I don't mind.'

I try not to grit my teeth; this box is so heavy.

'I bet this was a lovely house before it was converted,' she says.

'I bet,' I say, trying not to let the strain of the weight show on my face. 'But you've answered my question about lifts.'

'Your question?'

'Never mind. Let's get these upstairs, shall we?' I walk past her. If I go quickly, my arms should still be able to hold the weight. Thank God it's the last batch. I almost drop the box at her door.

'Thank you so much,' she says, placing her two boxes down. 'That's the lot, I think.'

She looks at her boxes, and I feel terrible. This

was only the second trip; she hasn't many things, but I'm surprised how many books she has.

'My sister stored them for me in her garage . . . along with the rest of the stuff I managed to collect before . . . '

'That's nice,' I say.

That's nice? Jesus.

I look at my watch.

'I can take it from here,' says Ellen, 'if you have to be somewhere else.'

'I'm meeting someone in half an hour, but it's only in Lytham.'

I haven't seen the inside of Ellen's flat, having dumped the previous box on the landing.

'Can I get you a cup of tea?' she says. She unlocks the door, picks up a box, and backs in. 'I'll have to set the kettle up, though. Shouldn't take too long.'

'Don't worry about it. If I have a tea now, I'll have to go to the loo as soon as I get to the café.'

It seems I have verbal diarrhoea.

Ellen laughs. 'I know what you mean. I do have a bathroom here, but I'm not sure of the state of it.'

I should stay another five minutes — it won't take long to drive to the café.

'I didn't mean it to sound like that, Ellen. It's just — '

'Stop feeling so awkward around me, Annie.'

My mouth drops open.

'I'm not as violent as they said I was,' she says. 'Not any more, at least.'

She bends over and rips the Sellotape from a box at her feet. I'm waiting for her to say she's joking — smile or something, to cancel out what she just said.

She doesn't.

She picks out a kettle from her box and a Tupperware container. Without looking at me, she says, 'I'll put the tea on,' and walks into a tiny kitchenette off the lounge.

'Okay.'

My feet are glued to the floor. I want to run out of the door, down the stairs and onto the street. The noise of the kettle would mask the sound of my escape.

I jump when her head appears at the concertina door.

'Tea, white, without?' she says, smiling.

I nod; she goes back into the kitchen. I'm reading too much into what she says. As if she would *murder* me — I've just helped her move boxes. I don't think she realised that her comment earlier unnerved me. Perhaps she thought I'd take it as a joke. It's so out of character. Well, from the person she's shown me so far.

'Can I help you unpack?' I shout.

I'll make myself useful, then she won't get any ideas.

Stop being so ridiculous, Anna! It's just Ellen.

But I've only known her for a couple of weeks. I should have asked Isobel what she'd done.

Ellen comes out of the kitchen and places two mugs on the window sill on the other side of the living room. She kneels down next to an open box.

'You can help me unwrap these, if you like,'

she says. 'I haven't seen most of this stuff for years.'

My shoes thump the laminate flooring. I crouch opposite her and she passes me a parcel wrapped in the front cover of the *Daily Mirror*. It is yellow with age and dated Wednesday 28 January 1987. The headline reads: *Agony of Mrs Waite*.

'All of this would've been sent to the tip if it hadn't been for my sister saving it for me. I suppose she felt guilty. I didn't think I'd ever see it all again. Not that I've got much, anyway.'

She's holding a wooden picture frame that's been painted yellow, and has dried flowers glued around it.

'My son made me this,' she says, turning it round to show me.

'That's so sweet.'

'You have a little girl, don't you?'

'Yes, Sophie. She's six.'

'A lovely age. Treasure her, won't you.'

I feel the pang of guilt I always get when I think about her, that I don't give her enough attention.

'How old's your son now?' I ask her.

She looks up in surprise. It must be the first personal question I've asked her.

'He'll be forty next week. An important one.'

Her eyes haven't left mine. Why is she looking at me like that? It's as though she's waiting for me to ask more questions. Instead, I finish un-wrapping what's in my hand. Another photograph. It's in a silver-filigree frame, the glass is shiny as though frozen in time.

It's of a little boy. He's holding up a Lego construction to the camera, sitting next to a Moses basket.

'That's him,' says Ellen, leaning over the box towards me.

I pass the frame to her outstretched hands.

'What does he do now?' I ask her.

She's stroking the glass of the photo.

'I don't know, Annie. I've written to him three times, but he hasn't replied yet. He doesn't want to know me. He's ashamed.'

'But you might've written to the wrong address.'

She shakes her head.

My mobile phone beeps. I reach into my pocket. A message from Sally.

I'm here.

I get up from the floor.

'I'm sorry, Ellen. I have to go. Are you going to be okay?'

She doesn't get up.

'Of course.' She places the photo on top of the box. 'Are you all right to let yourself out?'

★ ★ ★

I drive to Lytham almost on autopilot. The little boy in Ellen's photo will be forty soon, but Robert is only thirty-seven on his next birthday.

No. I have to stop these idiotic thoughts. I want to forget I was in Ellen's flat. *I'm not as violent as they said I was.* Why would she say something like that?

I pull into a parking space on the main street,

to the annoyance of an elderly man waiting in the opposite lane. I get out and dash to the pavement before he starts waving his fist and shouting at me. I'm a few minutes from the café — one of about fifty in Lytham — so I walk as fast as I can without running.

I have to look twice, but Jack's car is parked alongside the pavement, not far from mine. He often comes to Lytham for work. He asked me this morning if I was free for lunch; I said I was working through. He must've been checking I wouldn't catch him. We were both lying.

I look into the window of the nearest café. He's always lucky with parking.

He's inside, to the left of the counter, sitting alone. I hold up my hand to tap on the window, but stop just in time. There's a half-empty glass across from his cup. He's waiting for someone to come back. If I tell him I'm here, I won't find out who's with him.

'Excuse me, love.'

An elderly couple want to get past; I'm in the doorway.

'Sorry.' I whisper, in case Jack hears me. I pretend to look at the menu in the window.

Oh God, I'm going to see them together. My heart starts pounding. Instinctively, I grab my mobile from my pocket. If he's with her, I need evidence. If I tell him I know about him and her, then he'll find a way to turn it around — say I was seeing things.

I keep the phone camera close to my chest; I don't want to draw attention to myself by waving it in the air.

Jack looks behind him at the door of the toilets. His companion is no doubt making herself look beautiful. The bitch.

A gust of sea wind blows, and the belt of my mac taps the window. Jack glances up, but I hide behind the menu again. I turn my back to the window. Two women, about my age, walk past, carrying takeaway coffees — heads together, chatting. My stomach tightens. What the hell am I doing, spying on my husband like this, outside a café, in front of everyone? Why can't I be normal like everyone else? If I look back inside and Jack's still alone, I'll just head to my meeting with Sally. I'm already late. She'll think I don't care.

One, two, three.

I turn around.

He's not alone. But he isn't with Francesca, either.

He's with a man.

★ ★ ★

I'm breathless when I get to Sally's table after running the few streets from the café Jack was in.

'Well, sit down then,' she says, looking up at me. 'We can't have you heavy breathing and scaring the other customers.'

'Sorry I'm late.'

'Only by five minutes. I'm always early.'

'I've just seen my husband.'

She raises her eyebrows. 'Either you've just had a really good time, or you've run away from him.'

229

I hang my coat on the back of the chair, and pull it out to sit down. 'Sorry, you don't want to hear about my problems,' I say. 'What did you find out?'

'I'm fine, thank you, Anna. It's so kind of you to ask.' She winks at me.

'Oh God, what's wrong with me?' I say. 'I'm so sorry.'

'I'm just kidding. If it were up to me, I wouldn't bother with hello or goodbye either.'

My hands shake as I get the photographs out of my bag.

'Are you okay?' she says. 'Did you have an argument with Jack?'

I imagine it's in her job description to be perceptive.

'I . . . '

She said the other day that anything said between her and me is confidential. She's virtually a stranger, but I don't want to burden Dad, Monica or Grandad with what is happening with my husband. I already emailed her a copy of the love letter from Francesca, so she already knows part of it.

I tell her about seeing Jack in the café and how he always turns things around, so it seems I'm crazy.

'But why would he want to make out that you're crazy?'

She makes quote marks with her fingers to frame the last word.

'Because I . . . I became obsessed with this woman who used to work near me, a few years ago. I thought she might have been my mother.'

It's too hot in here. I undo the collar button of my blouse. Why am I opening up to Sally? It'll only prove Jack right, won't it? If I tell her about all the things I have done in the past, she will look at me differently — like so many of my so-called friends I don't see any more. I used to time them to see how long it would take to distance themselves from me. Sometimes it would be immediate, others would just not reply to my texts or phone calls. Life is easier without friends anyway, no one can disappoint you.

But I have nothing to lose with Sally — she's being paid to be here.

'Go on,' she says, resting her chin in the cup of her hand.

'I suppose there's always been something there with me, since I was little. I've always known that Monica was Debbie's best friend, that she wasn't my real mother. Sometimes I wish they'd never told me about Debbie, pretended she didn't exist, so I could've led a normal life with a normal family — even just for the first ten, twelve, eighteen years of my life. But everyone was so honest about it all.'

'There's no such thing as a normal family, Anna.'

'There is.' I manage a smile as I dab a tear rolling down my cheek with a paper napkin. 'I met one once.'

I tell Sally about everything I went through before.

I had never been as bad before I met Gillian Crossley. She looked just like Debbie. I convinced myself that she *was* Debbie — that she'd chosen to work nearby to get close to me. I took it too far — started following her home to see if she had a replacement family.

Jack was there for me through all of this, but he didn't know about the ones before. I latched on to teachers, and my counsellor at college. What few friends I had, looked at me differently.

Daisy was my first counsellor. It was a sign, I thought, her having the same initial as my mother, yet she was only about five years older than I was. I thought we were friends. She listened to me for hours (an hour at a time, obviously). She knew everything about me. When I took her presents, she looked pleased.

But when I met her three times in a row at the library on a Saturday morning, she took a step back. 'This isn't a coincidence any more, is it, Anna? You knew I'd be here, didn't you? This has to stop. I'm sorry. I shouldn't have encouraged you. I should've said something the first time I saw you here.'

I only ever saw her in passing at college after that. I was too ashamed to even make eye contact with her. I gradually realised that she knew everything about me because she was paid to; I knew nothing about her, not really.

'I never told Jack about my time at college,' I say to Sally. 'It wasn't that I was embarrassed by it. By the time I met him, I didn't think about it. I lived at home when I was at university — I didn't see anyone from college who knew about it. I spent most of my spare time with Monica. She'd take me shopping, out for lunch.' I give a hollow laugh. 'It was like I was a project for her.

She'd taken early retirement from the council offices, so I kept her busy. But in a way, she built me back up again.'

'What changed?' says Sally. 'To make you so transfixed with this Gillian so many years after college?'

'I was pregnant. I suppose expecting a child myself made me question Debbie's decision to leave even more. I felt so close to Sophie when she was growing inside me — an unbreakable bond. How could someone just abandon that?'

The memory of it is still so vivid. The last time I visited the bakery, I was on maternity leave; Dad and Monica had looked after Sophie for the afternoon to give me some time to go into town and browse the shops, but I knew where I really wanted to go.

I stood outside the bakery, waiting for her to come into work. She hadn't been in for days; I'd walked past with the pram. Her colleagues said she was off sick. When I'd pressed them, they said she had a migraine.

But that day was different. Her boss came to the door as I waited on the doorstep.

'What are you doing standing outside again, Anna?' she said, her arms folded in the doorway. 'Gillian's off sick again. You realise all of this is making her ill, don't you?'

'I . . . I . . . '

I stepped back and a huge dollop of rain from the shop canopy landed on my head. I went to wipe it off and realised the rest of my hair was sopping wet. I was standing outside in the pouring rain, soaked to the skin.

I held up a silver picture frame.

'But I thought she might like this,' I said, getting closer to her, trying to get shelter. 'It's a photo of Robert and me when I was two. She won't have seen it before.'

The woman shook her head, went back into the bakery and slammed the door — a waft of warm air from inside hit my face.

'Get yourself some help, Anna!' she shouted through the glass.

Sally's face doesn't react as I finish my story.

'I don't understand why Jack would be horrible to you about that, when surely you needed love, empathy.'

I shrug. 'He's not horrible about it, really. He worries about me. He's very practical, strong. It's why I married him, I suppose. I'm in a good place now — well, I thought I was before all of this . . . '

Sally reaches over and pats my hand.

'While we're talking about Jack, we might as well start there.' She grabs a piece of paper off the empty chair next to her. 'The man who sent Jack the Facebook message: *Have you told her yet?* wasn't that hard to find. But what's interesting is that he had a sister called Francesca.'

'She's married then? Francesca King?'

It is so strange saying her name aloud. It's not just in my head any more: it's real.

'No. Not Francesca King — Simon Howarth's sister never married. Her name was Francesca Howarth.'

A different Francesca.

Oh God, what have I done?

I visited that woman at work — told her Jack was having an affair, hatred in my eyes.

'But, I'm afraid, it's past tense,' says Sally. 'Sadly, Simon's sister died as a result of a car accident. Recently, as it happens.'

She slides over a print-out of an online newspaper article.

It's dated three weeks ago.

One person has died and two are injured following a crash involving two cars in York.

A woman, driving a Ford Focus, sustained fatal injuries on the A64, between Copmanthorpe and Bishopthorpe, in the early hours of this morning (Wednesday), and was pronounced dead at the scene.

A man in the second vehicle suffered injuries that aren't believed to be life-threatening.

A cyclist, a man in his late fifties, sustained minor injuries.

Police are appealing for witnesses.

I look up at Sally.

'This wasn't that long ago.'

'That's right,' she says. 'She went to the same college as Jack. If Jack knows her brother, then chances are, he knew her. I believe this is the Francesca we're looking for.'

I glance at the time on my phone. It's one o'clock already.

'Thanks, Sally. That's great. I'm sorry, but I really must go. I'm not supposed to shut the bookshop at lunchtime. I'd like to hear more, but I can't get fired. My boss, Isobel, thinks I'm useless as it is.'

'I'm sure she doesn't.'

I stand, grabbing my coat from the back of the chair.

'Before you go, Anna, there's something I'd like you to ask your family about.'

'What?' I put on my coat, even though I'm boiling hot and the sun is shining outside.

'I spoke to my police contact. Deborah wasn't reported missing until two months after she disappeared. And it wasn't your father who reported it — it was Frank O'Reilley.'

Grandad.

'What? Why?'

'I don't know. It's what you should ask them.' She reaches into her bag and pulls out an estate agent's flyer. 'Also . . . sorry, I didn't expect this to be a rushed meeting, but the house you lived in as a baby . . . the one next door to it's for sale. The woman selling it owns your old house too. I'll arrange a viewing — perhaps we could ask her some information without just turning up on her doorstep?'

I stop my rushing.

'Do you think she'll let me see my old house?'

'I doubt that, but it's worth talking to her.'

Sally stands, holding out her right hand. I shake it.

'Yes. Thank you.'

28

Wednesday, 16 July 1986
Debbie

'*She's stolen your children. Get up!*'

Where's Annie? I only closed my eyes for five minutes, didn't I? A voice woke me up. I get out of bed and rush to the landing in Mum and Dad's house. Before I look in the room Bobby's sleeping in, I know the bed'll be empty. Mum and Dad aren't in their room either; their bed's perfectly made.

Nobody's stolen the children. It was just a dream.

I stand at the top of the landing, gripping the railings.

Oh no. It's happening again.

My right arm begins to tingle. I can't move it, but it won't stop shaking — my whole body's trembling.

The ringing in my ears is too loud.

My knees buckle, and I collapse onto the carpet. I can't breathe.

My heart is about to run out — it's beating too fast for the rest of me.

I'm dying.

My throat feels like it's closing; I shut my eyes.

My breaths are short.

Sick. I'm going to be sick.

There's nothing in my stomach.
Oh God, I can't breathe.
I want it to end; I want everything to end.
But I don't.

★ ★ ★

I'm on the landing, flat on my back.
Am I dead?
I look at my hand and pinch the skin on my arm.
No.
My poor parents, if they had to find me — what if Bobby had been the first?
Where is everyone? Where's all the noise?
I slowly get up.
There's something seriously wrong with me.
I had blood tests for months before Annie was born, though. They would've picked up something, wouldn't they?
I walk downstairs, holding the bannister tight; my knees are still weak. I feel as though I've been thrown against every wall in the house, yet there are no bruises on my skin.
Sounds of cars driving past outside. Everything's going on as normal. I can't remember what it's like to feel normal.
There's a note propped against the telephone.

Deborah,
Didn't want to wake you. Dad's taken Bobby to school, so I'm taking Annie out for a bit of fresh air.
Mum.

I wish she'd have put the note in Annie's cot.

I'm too ungrateful, I know that. When Annie starts to sleep through, I'll get more sleep myself and then I'll be a better person. I have to believe that, otherwise I'm going to sink into quicksand.

Perhaps it'd be easier for everyone if I wasn't around. I make people angry. I'm not how they want me to be. I'm not who *I* want to be.

Bang, bang, bang.

Someone's at the door.

I get down on my hands and knees and crawl into the living room, even though the front door is made from mottled glass and whoever it is can see me skulk away.

'Debs?' A man's voice through the letterbox.

Oh God, he must've seen me.

I look around the living room: nothing. If I were at home, there'd be an airer full of clothes to hide behind.

More voices at the door. What the hell is going on out there?

A key turns in the lock.

'Just wait there with the pram while I see what's going on.'

It's Mum.

'Deborah! What on earth are you doing on the floor like that?'

She's standing at the living-room doorway.

More footsteps in the hall. Nathan's cradling Annie in his arms. He peers over Mum's shoulder.

I stand quickly, grabbing a cushion to cover the 1950s nightie Mum laid out for me last night.

'I wondered where everyone was,' I say. 'But now that's been solved — seeing as half the people I know are standing right in front of me.'

'I dare say it has,' says Mum, looking at me as though I were parading naked. 'You've a visitor. You might want to run upstairs to make yourself presentable.' She's trying to direct me upstairs by flicking her eyes to the staircase without her head moving.

'Yes, yes, of course,' I say.

I smile and nod at Nathan — who's probably noticed my crimson face — and run two steps at a time up the stairs. I dress in the only outfit I brought with me. After only a few hours' sleep, I feel a bit more refreshed.

It can't be because Nathan's here.

My daughter's safe — that's it too. I hope he's not here on behalf of Peter, to try to convince me to come home.

In the bathroom, I splash water on my face. I look in the mirror as I pat it dry with a towel. I wish I'd brought make-up — I didn't bring anything. I can't even remember the journey here yesterday. I pinch my cheeks like Mum does before church when she thinks no one's looking.

I slowly go down the stairs and take a few breaths before grabbing the door handle to the living room. I want to listen in on what Nathan and Mum are talking about, but all I can hear is the telly.

The pair of them don't even glance up when I walk in. Nathan's long legs, crossed at the ankles, take up half the floor's width as he makes himself at home, and Mum's feeding Annie a bottle in her chair with Jesus above her as a witness. I'm glad Dad isn't here to see the way she's smiling at Nathan. She should be ashamed of herself, and in front of the son of God as well.

'Did you say something funny?' I say to Nathan.

He looks up, pretending to have only just noticed I've come into the room. More likely, he *has* just noticed me. I wish my teenage brain would leave me alone.

'I was just saying to Marion that I could take you all out to St Annes, if you fancied a breath of fresh air?'

Marion? Even Peter doesn't call my mother by her first name — in fact, I don't think he ever calls her anything. And why's everyone so bothered about fresh air? It's overrated.

'And I said to Nathan,' says Mum, 'that I'm going to wait in for your dad, make him lunch. Can you imagine what he'd think if I left him a note saying I've gone off gallivanting with a young man? You and Annie go. I'll be fine here.'

My cheeks are hot again. What's gotten into her? Sending me off on a day trip with another man. She's not this chatty when Peter comes round with me.

'Mum, I'm sure Dad wouldn't mind if he knew you were with Annie and me as well. He might appreciate the house to himself.'

'No, no. I'll stop in. Your dad'll have done two bus journeys after taking Bobby to school and going to the job centre. He'll need someone to come back to.'

'Oh no, poor Dad. I should've taken Bobby.'

241

'*Poor Dad* nothing. He likes to feel useful.'

'I don't think it'd be right for me to go. Peter might wonder where I am.'

'It's nearly ten o'clock. I plugged the phone back in at six this morning, and there's not been any phone calls. Just go out and let your hair down — it might get some colour in your cheeks.'

'I . . . well . . . if you're sure?' I'm still standing in the middle of the living room. 'But Annie'll be due another feed in a few hours.' I look to Nathan. 'I can't go out for long.'

Mum passes Annie to Nathan; doesn't she trust me with my own baby?

'Don't be silly,' she says. 'I've made a few bottles up for her. Take another two with you. I'll make a flask of hot water.'

My mouth drops open as she hands a bag over to Nathan.

'Are you sure, Mum?' I say, pulling her by the elbow into the kitchen. 'Wouldn't it be better if I stayed here? I don't think I'm well enough to go out.'

'What's wrong with you?' She puts her hand on my forehead. 'Your temperature's fine.' She leans her head towards mine. 'But your eyes look a bit different.' She tilts her head to the side. 'I know I'm usually one for plodding on with everything, but your old friend Nathan's a good sort.' She's blushing. 'I should've taken you out a bit more when you were little. I won't tell Peter if you don't want me to.'

'Mum! That's not a very Christian thing to say!'

'He can't see me in here,' she says, gesturing to Jesus on the wall in the other room.

I lean against the Formica worktop and look out of the window above the sink, then to the sill. There's a broken glass on a newspaper, waiting to be wrapped for the bin. Its glacier-like spikes sparkle in the sunshine. I could just slam my wrist over them — they're only inches away. It wouldn't hurt for long.

I turn to my mother.

'I wouldn't mind if you *did* tell Peter. He's been *off gallivanting*, as you call it, with Monica.'

'Just go and have a nice time. Dad'll pick Bobby up, so you don't have to worry about the time.'

'I suppose.'

At that moment, I realise I have no money on me at all. And the only money I have is the pittance left over from the family allowance and I don't even have my cheque book with me. How far did I think I'd get with no money when I fled the house yesterday? It doesn't matter anyway. Everything feels so pointless.

★   ★   ★

I feel like I'm in a taxi in Nathan's Sierra, with him in front and me in the back. Annie's lying in her carrycot, the seat belt strapped across it. Nathan's window's open and the breeze is refreshing.

'Am I okay to turn the radio on?' He shouts over the wind.

'Yes,' I holler back. 'Annie's awake.'

243

If she wasn't, she would be, after all this shouting.

Nathan keeps glancing at me in the rearview mirror. I look to the world outside the window, though we're on the dual carriageway and there are only fields.

'The Chicken Song' comes on the radio. Stupid fucking song; I don't know what all the fuss is about. Memories of my cousin's wedding two months ago flash into my mind. Me, eight months pregnant, sitting in the social club making half a pint of Guinness last two hours, while everyone danced the stupid chicken dance, pissed as farts. Even my mother, who'd had half a glass of sparkling wine, got up, self-consciously waving her hands about like the rest of them. Weddings are shit if you can't drink.

It finally ends and is replaced by 'West End Girls' by the Pet Shop Boys. At last some decent music. I imagine myself in the video, standing moodily next to Neil Tennant, smoking cigarettes. I could've had a different life had I aimed high enough, had I been bothered.

We've been driving for twenty minutes and Nathan and I haven't spoken much. He hasn't explained why he just turned up at my parents' house. Doesn't anyone use the phone any more? Why isn't he at work? It's a weekday, because Bobby's at school.

The sound and movement of the car has sent Annie to sleep. I'm so tired myself, but I can't sleep now. I close my eyes, anyway, and let the wind and the heat of the sun through the window warm me. If it weren't for Annie here next to me, I could be sixteen again — the pair of us driving round the coast in Nathan's fourth-hand Austin Metro.

We've just passed Lytham windmill. Nathan lowers the radio and rolls up the window. He glances at me over his left shoulder.

'I suppose Pete told you he came round to ours last night?'

'Hmm,' I say. 'Mum unplugged the phone. Annie's not been sleeping properly.'

I glance down at her, fast asleep: the irony.

'He said you took off in the middle of the night.'

I roll my eyes. 'Hardly. It was after I picked up Bobby from school.'

I don't tell him I was so scared of being in my own home that I almost couldn't breathe — that I felt that people were watching me through the window, through the walls.

We pass the White Church, where a bride in an ivory meringue is being helped out of a limousine by her dad. *Don't do it*, I want to shout.

'You know I'm here if you want to talk,' says Nathan.

He keeps saying that, doesn't he?

'I should talk to Monica, really. Peter might think it weird if I talk to you.'

Nathan shrugs. 'They have their own little chats, don't they?'

I lean forward, resting my hand on the front passenger seat.

'I thought it was only the one time they met. Have they spoken again?'

245

'Hang on a sec.'

He pulls up on the road next to the sand dunes and turns off the ignition. He takes off his seat belt, turning to face me.

'On the phone. I've heard them. First it was about the holiday — now he keeps ringing her, asking for advice.'

'Advice? About what?'

He takes a deep breath — his eyes dart around the car before they meet mine.

'You.'

★　★　★

I'm struggling to push the pram through the sand, so I turn it around and drag it.

'I can get that for you, Debs,' says Nathan. He goes to grab the handles, but I elbow him out of the way. I know I shouldn't take it out on him — it's not his fault Monica and Peter are conspiring against me. I shouldn't have to worry about those two at a time like this.

I stop at an area of sand that's far enough away from anyone else.

'Did you bring a blanket?' I say.

He's looking wide-eyed at me. He probably thinks I've gone crazy, like the rest of them do. He pulls out a tartan blanket from his Army & Navy bag, then unrolls it and places it on the sand.

'Do you want me to get Annie out?' he says.

'It's okay.' I pull up the hood to shade her from the sun peeking through the clouds. 'I'll let her sleep a while longer.'

246

'How many weeks is she now?' he says, sitting on the blanket. He grabs his bag and squashes it into the sand behind him, before laying his head on it, eyes closed.

'Four or five.'

I steal a glance at him while his eyes are shut. Such dark hair. If I hadn't known him since we were teenagers, I'd have thought his hair was dyed that colour. There's a St Christopher chain around his neck. It looks like the one I bought him all those years ago.

I sit down next to him, but not too close.

I look up to the sun and close my eyes.

It wasn't like this after I had Bobby. Everything was easy then. He'd sleep for hours at a time, letting me get myself ready for the day — and he slept through from two months old. But today is the first day in a long time that I've felt halfway human. I wish I could stay here, like this, forever. I might be getting better. I won't need to go to the doctor — I'll tell Monica that it was just lack of sleep, that I've healed myself. I'm a medical marvel.

'What are you smiling at?' says Nathan.

'I was just thinking about Monica,' I say, without thinking.

'Really? You don't mind her talking with Peter?'

I open my eyes to find him looking at me, shielding his eyes from the mid-morning sun. 'I'll speak to Peter about it tonight.' My stomach feels sick at the thought of confrontation. I doubt I'll even talk to him. I'm a coward. I don't want him bringing up the fact that I'm failing — as a mother and a wife. If we don't discuss it, I can try to get back to normal without any drama.

I glance at Nathan; he's lying down again with his face to the sky.

'Did Monica mention what they said about me?'

'You should talk to her about it,' he says. 'You know I'm not one for gossip.'

'What? How can it be gossip — I'm right here? You can talk to *me* about me.'

He props himself up, his elbow resting on the blanket, only inches from my arm.

'I know, Debs. It's just that . . . ' He takes a deep breath. 'Monica said Peter's been telling her that you two aren't getting along at the moment. He thinks you're *not yourself.*'

'What?'

It's one thing for *me* to think it, but for *him* to say it is another. The thought of it winds me in the stomach.

'I know, I know,' he says. 'It's a shit thing to say about anyone, baby or no baby. And he shouldn't be saying all of this to Monica. I told her I didn't want to hear what Peter's been saying — and you can imagine how she took that.' There's a light smirk on Nathan's face.

'Yes.'

I *can* imagine. There's nothing Monica likes more than to speak badly about others — she doesn't like it when people don't join in with her. She takes it as a slight. A few years ago, she came round on a Saturday afternoon after shopping with Rachel Kennedy, a woman we both went to school with.

'She's just got a promotion at GUS,' Monica

248

said. 'Office manager! Can you believe it? She's twenty-three and she only got one O Level. Thick as pig shit.'

'I'm sure she isn't. She's probably good at her job. She wasn't that bad at school.'

'I can't believe you're sticking up for her. Are you best friends with her or something?'

'Don't be silly, Mon. It's not that I like her,' I said. 'I don't know her.'

She folded her arms and didn't speak to me until she'd thought of someone else to talk about.

'Well,' I say to Nathan now. 'It serves her right. She shouldn't take so much joy in saying bad things about other people.'

'Amen to that.'

Annie whimpers in her pram. Just as I was about to relax.

I jump up and peer over her, but she's still asleep. I look over at the grey sea in the distance, and take off my socks.

'Nath, would you mind keeping an ear out for her? I fancy dipping my feet.'

'Yeah, course. Watch out for the dirty nappies, mind. And don't go walking too far in, Reggie Perrin.'

'Don't tempt me,' I say.

If he knew what was going on in my head, he wouldn't joke about something like that.

The first few steps, where the sand is bone dry, are the trickiest.

A football crosses my path, and a boy of about three or four rushes to grab it. He walks back to his mummy, who's lying on a towel, wearing a bikini. Her bronzed skin is frying in oil, like we're in bloody Marbella and not the lukewarm North of England.

'Mummy, will you play with me yet?' says the little boy. 'You said in five minutes and it's been a million.'

'I meant in ten minutes,' she says. 'And it's never been a million. Stop exaggerating.'

'What's pedgaterating?'

'Give it a rest, Barry.'

I wish I could be that woman. She doesn't care that she's being awful to her son in public because her thoughts are probably kinder, more honest, than mine. I can't let my feelings creep through my mask, though that's starting to slip. My children would be taken away and I'd be alone. As horrendous as it sounds, it's a thought that doesn't fill me with horror.

Shit, Debbie. Stop bloody overthinking things. I want to slap the side of my head, but instead, I grab the scrunchie from around my wrist and pull my hair into a ponytail.

The sand gets firmer as I near the sea. I bend to pick up a perfect ivory shell wedged in it. The sand gets under my finger nails, but I don't pick it out. There's another: a black shell — so thin it might break in my hands. I untuck my shirt from my trousers and use it as a pouch. I could decorate Annie's memory box with what I find.

I kneel when I see a tiny dried-out crab.

Eugh. Horrid, creepy little thing.

I run the pad of my finger on its miniature, smooth shell.

'Sorry, mate,' I say. 'I didn't mean to think that about you.'

I keep walking, closer to the tide. It has a scummy, white foam that I bet you wouldn't find in Tenerife.

I spot a perfect, white, spiral shell. It would look lovely in the centre of the box. I'll have to ask Dad for some proper, strong glue; it looks as though it'll never stay put on the cigar box.

I look down at my collection. I have about twenty shells. That should do it.

As I near the sea, my footsteps leave little pools of water inside them — like mini ponds. I stand at the point where the gentle tide ends, and the scummy water tickles the tips of my toes. I look to the horizon. Southport's just across the water. Dad used to take me there all the time. Mum never came, though. What did she do, all those times Dad and I went out together? I think of Peter and I can't picture him taking Bobby out on his own — he's always working. Little Bobby, he would've liked that dried-out crab.

I turn and see Nathan lying next to Annie's pram; they're little ants in the distance. I have to get that crab for Bobby. If I find it again, then everything will be all right.

I follow my footsteps, still fresh. I go slowly, scanning the ground. To my right is a couple: a man and a woman; their dog bounding along after a piece of driftwood they've thrown for it to fetch.

I stop when I see it: the perfect little crab, preserved in death like a mummy. How strange must it be to be hard on the outside and soft inside.

Before I reach for it, the piece of driftwood

lands in front of me. The dog grabs it in his teeth, taking the crab with it.

'No!' I shout. I stand, folding my shirt to protect my shells. 'You stupid dog! That was Bobby's.'

The woman looks at me, her hand reaching for the man next to her.

'Are you okay?' she says.

'Your dog took my crab.'

The man bends down and takes the wood from the dog's mouth.

'There's no crab here.'

'It's tiny. Really small.'

'Sorry, love. There's nothing here.'

They glance at each other. I know that look: *get away from the crazy lady*. I was on the receiving end of it when I was running down the street after leaving Annie outside the shop.

'You should keep that dog on a lead,' I shout to their backs as they walk away. 'It could kill someone.'

They walk faster in the opposite direction.

Good.

Annoying, happy people.

There are tears forming in my eyes, so I face the sea, briefly, to let them dry. I keep my eyelids open and the salt stings. But that's okay. At least I'm feeling something.

I turn and march towards Nathan and Annie, clutching the collection of shells to my fat, wobbly belly. I feel it as I walk, reminding me again that I'm nothing like that bronzed woman lying only a few yards from me. She still hasn't moved from the ground. With any luck, she'll fry.

Poor Barry is sitting cross-legged next to her, making piles of sand.

The ground is getting drier. Nathan is sitting up, waiting for me.

I kneel as soon as I reach the blanket and tip my finds out onto it.

'*She sells sea shells on the sea shore,*' says Nathan.

'Right.'

'*The shells she sells are surely sea shells, so if she sells sea shells on the sea shore, I'm sure she sells seashore shells.*'

'How the hell do you know all of that? It's just a silly tongue twister. It means nothing.'

'From my mum. And it does mean something. It's about a woman called Mary Anning.'

'What?'

He shrugs. 'The Mary bit was from a pub quiz. I only remember her name because we lost the tie-breaker with that stupid question. Who the fuck would know that?'

A passing woman tuts at him swearing.

'Do you ever think about running away from it all?' says Nathan, from nowhere. 'We could go now. There's nothing keeping us here.'

'Very funny,' I say, raking my fingers through the sand. 'Anyway, I haven't got Bobby with me.'

I blush as Nathan smiles. I always take a joke too far.

The clouds have gathered around the sun, and the wind from the sea sends a chill through the air.

'We should go,' I say. 'Dad's picking up

Bobby, but I want to be there when he gets back. I don't want them to think I don't care.'

★ ★ ★

We're travelling back to Preston, and the thought of talking to Peter tonight fills me with dread.

'*You're a worthless piece of shit.*'

The voice again. It doesn't sound like Uncle Charlie any more. It sounds like me. I should just get used to it — it's only telling me what I already know. I'm in a living nightmare where everything is foggy and dark.

At the beach, I had a little snippet of what normal feels like — just a few hours teasing me about what could've been. My mind feels like it's full of mud, of dark clouds and rain. If I were to just curl up and be left alone, I could dream of another life, far away. Everything would be okay. People around me could get on with their lives and be happier without me in it.

On the radio, Gary Davies is asking a contestant phone-in questions. Nathan has the volume so loud I want to throw Annie's bottle at him.

We pass the sign for Preston. The clouds are greyer, heavier. I don't want to go home — I don't even want to go to Mum and Dad's. I don't want to be anywhere. I open the window, hoping the wind masks the sounds of my sobbing.

254

29

Anna

I park up outside the bookshop after my meeting with Sally Munroe and luckily, there is no queue of people waiting at the door; there is only one person: Robert.

'You not in class today?' I say, slamming the car door shut.

'They're not classes — they're lectures.'

I shouldn't wind him up, but seeing him has cheered me a little. We haven't spoken much over the last few weeks and I have missed him. He still has a frown on his face, though. Even though it's a rare sunny day, he is still wearing a pale-green, cotton scarf — his 'English lecturer trademark', Dad calls it.

I unlock the door and he follows me inside.

'What brings you to St Annes?' I holler as I put my bag and coat in the back. 'Off to play the arcades on the pier?'

'Anna, stop it. I'm not in a joking mood today.'

He sits on the stool behind the counter. It reminds me of two summers ago, when he volunteered here. It was nice' to spend whole days with him again, and he charmed the volunteers, fetching them cups of tea.

'You haven't been in a happy mood for ages,' I

say, resting my elbows on the counter.

'Do you blame me? What makes you so chirpy today?'

I sigh. 'I'm not really. I've had a shit day, but I'm trying to be cheerful, for you.'

He looks at his hands, resting on his lap.

'I didn't expect you to be so honest.' He glances up at me with a brief smile. 'Sorry for being an idiot the other day at Grandad's. It's just . . . it's just that I remember the last time Monica received a letter that was supposed to be from Debbie. Dad told me he showed it to you the other day.'

'Yes, he did. Why did they think it was from Debbie?' I take a deep breath. 'Did no one ever question why the letter was sent to Monica and not Dad? I mean, if Debbie found out that those two had got married, she should have gone to the police. Dad's committed bigamy.'

'I don't know — probably because it's the same house Monica and Nathan lived in years ago. But Jesus, Anna, *those two?* Whose side are you on? To me, it sounds like you're angry with the wrong people. Dad brought us up — even when his heart was breaking, for God's sake. You've been dreaming about Debbie — this ghost of a mother who you've put on a pedestal. And you know what — I wish she *was* dead. If she *is* alive, she can stay the hell away from me.'

'I'm sorry, Robert. You're my brother — the one person I used to be myself around. Sometimes I forget what you've been through is far worse than what I have. It's just that I've no one to talk to about things. Jack's barely present,

I can't talk to Dad or Monica. The only person I've been able to talk to is the investigator — and she's being paid to listen. But I need to tell you something — '

He raises his palms. 'Stop! I don't want to hear any more. Really, Anna. I wish I were you — I wish I didn't remember her, that I could be distant in the way you can be. I want to get on with my life and forget she ever existed.'

'You see me as distant?'

He smiles wanly, shaking his head. 'That's what you got from all of that?' He stands from the stool, his eyes on mine. 'You're unbelievable sometimes.' He takes off his scarf and stuffs it in his pocket. 'Go on. What's this thing you want to tell me?'

'Sally Munroe, the investigator Jack organised for me,' — I stretch the truth a little — 'she said that Debbie wasn't reported missing until two months after she disappeared — and that it was Grandad who reported it, not Dad.'

His expression doesn't change. Why isn't he surprised?

He leans forward and rests his arms on the counter.

'Debbie left a note,' he says. 'In Tenerife.'

'I know. Dad only told me a few days ago.'

'I remember it. On holiday, Dad walked around with this piece of paper in his hands for days afterwards. It was the first time I'd ever seen him cry. A few years later, I was rummaging around — I can't remember what I was looking for, batteries probably — and I found it. Just lying in a drawer under all sorts of crap. Why would they still have it? I'd have burnt it . . . '

'What did it say?'

He rubs his forehead. 'God, I don't know. 'I'm sorry I have to leave', or something along those lines.' He looks up at me. 'I wasn't . . . I'm not . . . like you, Anna. I didn't want to cling on to everything she ever touched. That's if she *had* touched it. I just put it back where it was. And when I next went to look for it — though I don't know why I'd want to read it again — it'd gone.'

'What do you mean: *if* she had touched it?'

He shrugs and gives a heavy sigh. 'The writing . . . it was all over the place. I don't mean in a child's scrawl or anything like that . . . it was odd. I haven't seen many examples of Mum's handwriting, but it didn't feel like hers. It was on this horrid pink notepaper. It seemed contradictory that this note telling everyone she was going was on such bright paper.'

'Pink notepaper?' It doesn't take long for me to make the connection. 'The letters that Grandad had . . . that Debbie received a few weeks before you — we — went to Tenerife . . . they were on the same coloured notepaper.'

'But you haven't seen the note. You can't know it's the same paper.'

'No. No, I can't.'

I don't mention that he had just called Debbie, *Mum*.

I need to see that note. I know that when I see it, it *will* be the same notepaper.

'I know that look of yours, Anna. I know you want to keep digging, but I'm scared for you, for all of us. If I'm honest, I don't think I want to

258

know. Whatever it is, it won't be good.' He starts to walk away from the counter. 'I don't think Debbie wrote that email you're chasing. Really, I don't.'

I nod slowly. 'Okay.'

'Look, I *am* here for you if there's no one else to talk to. Other people don't know what we're going through — well, they don't know what *I'm* going through . . . *everyone* knows what you're going through.'

He gives a sad smile. He's always been the brave one, the one who tried to protect me from everything. Who's been there for him?

'Shit, I'm sorry, Rob. I've tried to think about what's best for everyone. I've tried to be kind. I've been selfish doing all of this, haven't I? I've hurt you.'

'No, you haven't hurt me, Anna. Stop feeling as though everything's your fault — it's not. And you should stop *trying* to be kind to everyone — you *are* a kind person. You make such an effort in trying to please people, but you should do what's best for you.'

He walks slowly towards the door, and I follow.

'That's the nicest thing you've ever said to me,' I say.

'Well, it's true.'

'I know I'm pushing my luck here, but you wouldn't mind if I carried on with the investigator?'

'I'd be contradicting myself if I said no,' he says, turning back into academic mode. He opens the door, lifting his hand in a wave. 'Bye, Anna.'

With the shop empty, I grab the laptop from the back room and open it on the counter. The sky is still cloudless, so it's likely be quiet this afternoon. Isobel hardly ever comes in when the weather is nice: too busy sunning herself in her back garden.

I type in Debbie's name. There are loads of results; Debbie Atherton is not an uncommon name. I sign in to LinkedIn, in the hope I see her face in one of the profile photos. I Google every one with the same estimated age, but I can't find her. It's something I've done countless times before. I don't know why I thought it would be different today.

There are no news articles about her disappearance — I already knew this. I assumed the reason was because it was in the eighties and there was no Internet. I had never queried the fact my dad never actively searched for her. It was always Grandad.

Why hadn't I questioned it? Jack often says I'm naive — he used to think it sweet — but now I feel stupid.

It's now two o'clock and there hasn't been a single customer since I came back. I log in to Facebook and scroll through Jack's friends list again. There is no Simon or Francesca Howarth. I type her name into the Facebook search bar; there are only a few in the UK, but I've no idea where she lived or what university she went to, if at all. Did she still live in Yorkshire? The article reported that her accident happened just outside York, so the chances are high, but the two I find in that area look to be in their teens. I wish I'd had more time to talk to Sally.

Before I left the café, she said that the house next door to the one I first lived in is for sale. I type the postcode into Rightmove, and recognise it straight away; I drive down that road at least once a month. The houses are small two-up two-down terraces, with tiny walled gardens at the front, yards at the back. The inside of next door looks as though it's been untouched for at least twenty years — large sofas and loud carpets. The kitchen is beige-and-brown melamine, but spotless.

My mobile phone sounds. A text from Sally.

Viewing for tomorrow morning okay?

Friday's my day off this week, so I reply yes.

It's not Dad's day to collect Sophie, but I need to see the letter Debbie wrote at the end. I make a call to Sophie's school to tell them not to send her to after-school club. I take the money from the till, quickly balancing it, and lock it, and the laptop, in the security cupboard. The chances of Isobel coming in are slim, but I leave a note on the counter saying I've gone home ill, just in case.

★   ★   ★

I rarely pick Sophie up from school at the normal time. If she's not at after-school club then my dad picks her up. It's a different world, standing at the school gates. There are a few strays, like me, but most of the parents are in groups of three or four, talking loudly about Marks & Spencer shoes or the new head teacher, Mr Hooper.

'Don't tell hubby I said this, but that Mr Hooper can teach me a lesson anytime.'

Ugh, *hubby*.

I'm probably jealous. I haven't even seen the new head teacher. Being around these parents makes me yearn to be the same.

Sophie's surprise as she sees me waiting for her makes my heart swell.

'Mummy!' she shouts, running towards me.

At six, she is not yet self-conscious or too embarrassed to show her eagerness in greeting me.

I open my arms and she runs into them, hitting me on the head with her lunch bag.

'Sorry, Mummy.'

'That's all right, love.' I stand, taking her by the hand. 'I thought we could pop and see Grandad and Grandma this afternoon. Would you like that?'

'Er. Okay. But it's not Wednesday, is it?'

'No.'

I feel guilty taking Sophie to Dad's after I promised myself I wouldn't talk about Debbie in front of her. I open the car door for her and she sits on her booster seat. As I pass her the seat belt, my phone vibrates. I take it out of my pocket.

It's a message from Dad.

I hold on to the sides of the car as I take in the words: *Monica's been injured. We're in Royal Preston Hospital.*

30

Wednesday, 16 July 1986
Debbie

I get home and my dad has already set off to fetch Bobby. Mum's still wearing her tabard as she waves Nathan off from the front step.

'Will you tell Peter you've been on a day out with his friend?' she says as his car disappears around the corner.

'Course I'll tell him. And Nathan was my friend before he was anyone else's.'

Mum tuts and rolls her eyes as she takes Annie out of my arms, and goes back into the house. I drag the pram into the hallway. No matter how old I am, Mum has this special talent for making me feel like a naughty fifteen-year-old.

'What was that for?' I say.

'You two always had your fights.'

'Who?'

'You and Monica. And now you're talking about who was friends with Nathan first!'

'But — '

Mum's already in the kitchen, putting on the kettle. I follow her, and lean back on a kitchen chair.

'Nathan said something to me earlier . . . ' says Mum, 'while you were changing upstairs. Are you sure everything's all right between you and

Peter? He'd never hurt you, would he?'

'No. What did Nathan say?'

'Oh, nothing. Just something about smashed cups. Ignore me . . . I've probably got the wrong end of the stick.' She takes a bottle out of the fridge. 'He really loved you, Nathan. Didn't he?'

I can't get away from it. I thought coming back to Mum and Dad's would give me a break.

'I'll get back home tonight if that's all right,' I say.

'Course it's all right,' she says. 'But your dad has loved having you all here. I dare say he'll be upset.'

She places Annie in the bouncer on the living-room floor and comes back into the kitchen.

'You will come round next Wednesday for the wedding, won't you? I'll put on a nice spread — it'll save you cooking.'

'Course. Wouldn't miss it for the world.'

'Eh, you sarky thing. This country would be on its knees if it weren't for the monarchy.'

'It's on its knees as it is. And don't let Dad hear you say that about the royals.'

'As if I would.'

She pours hot water into a plastic jug and puts Annie's bottle into it.

'Are you all right, Deborah?' she says, any hint of a smile gone from her face. 'Only I heard you mention to your dad last night about some letters you were getting.'

'Were you listening in?'

She feigns surprise; her hand rests on her heart.

'I don't eavesdrop! You know how sound carries in this house.'

'Well, you'll have heard that I didn't want to worry you then, won't you?'

'I'm your mother. I can't help it — I have to worry. Do you have the letters with you? It might be that creepy neighbour you've got opposite you?'

'Been thinking about it much, have you, Mum?' I smile at her. 'I didn't think you were listening when I talked about him in the past — or Dirty Dean as Monica calls him.'

'I always listen.'

The phone rings in the hallway.

'Get that, will you?' she says, shaking droplets of milk onto her wrist to test the temperature. 'I'll feed Annie . . . seeing as I'll not be getting the chance again for months.'

'Don't exaggerate, Mother,' I shout on my way to the phone.

I pick up the handset. 'Hello?'

'Debbie, it's me.' Peter's voice is quiet. 'I heard you went on a little jaunt with Nathan.'

'News travels fast. I've only been back fifteen minutes. You've been talking to Monica, haven't you?'

He sighs. 'She saw you in his car when she was on her lunch break. And you know what she's like . . . loves knowing information before anyone else.'

'Yes, I do know her. She's been my best friend for over ten years. How could she have seen us? We didn't go through town.'

'She's worried about you.'

'Then why doesn't she speak to *me* about it?'

'She said she tried to, but you started talking about hearing things — voices in your head.'

He whispers the last four words, as though afraid of being overheard.

'What?'

I shouldn't have believed Monica when she said she'd keep that quiet, but I can't believe she actually told him. Even for her, this is one step too far.

'I said I was tired . . . that I heard next door, that's all. Why does she have to make a big deal out of everything?'

'I know . . . ' he says. 'I told her she was being dramatic . . . overstating things. So you didn't say you heard voices? I told her you would've come to me about it first.'

I don't know what to say to him. I sit on the bottom step of the stairs.

'Debs, are you still there?'

'Yes.'

'You would tell me if you needed help, wouldn't you?'

Scenes flash through my mind: of me confessing I'm not all right, Peter and Monica getting together — of her taking over my life, my children.

I stand and walk over to the mirror. My hair is knotted and dull from the sea air. Shadows line the skin under my eyes. I look a mess, but I don't care.

'Yes, of course I'd tell you.' My voice is flat. I can't fake emotion any more. 'I'm not hearing things. She's making it up. She always was thrifty with the truth.'

There's movement behind me. Mum. She's probably been listening the whole time. I turn around, still holding the phone to my ear.

'Are you okay?' she whispers.

I nod and turn back to face the mirror.

'I suppose,' says Peter. 'Look. Can I pick you up? I've taken the afternoon off. I think we need to talk.'

I tell him yes, and replace the handset. But the last thing I want to do is talk to him.

I sit back on the bottom step.

'Have you ever thought of . . . ' I say aloud.

'Thought of what?' Mum stands at my feet, Annie in her arms.

'Nothing, nothing. I'm fine.'

'You're not thinking of doing anything stupid, are you?'

'No, no. Of course not.'

All I can think of is doing something stupid, but to me it makes perfect sense.

★　★　★

Peter and I barely said a word to each other on the drive back home, but Bobby's chatter masked any uneasiness. Now, he's sitting on the living-room carpet in front of the telly watching one of his videos, and Annie's still asleep in the new car seat Peter brought with him.

'This holiday is just what you need, Debs,' he says, putting a mug of milk in the microwave.

'Do you have to microwave everything?' I say.

'We've only got a few days to pack,' he says, ignoring me. 'Did you manage to get Annie's

267

name on your passport?'

He looks at me and holds up his hands.

'Don't worry,' he says. 'I'll see if I can sort it out.'

'I didn't say I wouldn't do it.'

'But you were thinking it.'

'Why do you always presume to know what's in my head? I wasn't thinking about anything.'

'Perhaps that's the problem.'

He says it so quietly I'm not sure I heard him right. I feel like the fight in me has gone, but then, it shouldn't be a fight, should it? I'm still the same person I always was, aren't I? I just do different things with my day.

Looking back at my life only seven years ago, I know I'm a different person. I'd been in my job a year, earning my own money, and I felt I was on the edge of something — freedom, travelling the world maybe. Now, everything feels such a chore; the hopelessness I've felt in the back of my mind has risen to the surface and it's taking over.

I stand straighter, levelling my head with Peter's.

'Nathan said you and Monica have been talking about me.'

He rolls his eyes.

'You make it sound like we're school kids. I've been worried about you.'

'Worried that I've not been making your tea, or doing your washing? Babies take up time and energy, you know.'

The dial on the microwave pings, relieving Peter of the awkward silence. He gives a stilted laugh and gets the mug out.

'Shi — sugar! Why don't they warn you that everything you put in that thing will come out the same temperature as the food?'

'They do,' I say flatly. 'That's why they do special cooking containers. I'm surprised you didn't know that, working at Woolies.'

It's typical of us these days, that whenever we try to have a serious conversation, it always ends up with something domestic. And then it hits me, as I look around our small kitchen: it's spotless. The mess that was there two nights ago has been cleared away.

I've never been domesticated. Mum usually did everything for me when I lived at home, and I went straight from home to living with Peter. We first lived together when we got back from our honeymoon in Wales. I started back at work at the estate agency, and Peter was at Woolworths — he was assistant manager then. I had visions of domestic bliss — of coming home before Peter, tidying around and having a cooked meal waiting for him. But after the first week, I realised it was just so boring.

The dishes began to pile up on the kitchen sides. I'd learn my kitchen skills from watching Mum, but Peter didn't like corned beef mashed with potato and peas. And he said I over-cooked chicken all the time, but Mum always worried about salmonella poisoning — I thought everyone did. So, he bought a freezer. From then on, whoever got home first would put tea in the oven. But then the house fairy didn't magically come and clean up after us.

I got the urge last year to make Bobby a birthday cake, but it looked like a pancake when I got it out of the oven. Luckily, Mrs Abernathy had boxes of cake mix. Everyone had said it was the best cake they'd ever eaten (I'd hidden the box in the outside dustbin).

'You'll have to make this every week,' said Peter.

'Once a year will do,' I said, smiling.

Smiling.

I used to smile.

Looking around our kitchen now, there's not a dirty dish in sight. Peter's been busy.

I turn my back on him and glance at the kitchen clock: only five thirty. Is it too early for bed?

'I know you said on the way back from your mum's not to mention Monica, but she's genuinely concerned about you. And I've arranged for, er . . .'

I turn back around; he's stirring powdered chocolate into the hot milk, clanging the spoon around the mug for longer than necessary.

'What have you arranged? If it's a doctor's appointment, then I can arrange that myself. I'm perfectly fine.'

'No, no. Not the doctor's. A night out with Monica on Friday night. I thought you could let your hair down for a few hours.'

I close my eyes. I suppose that's not such a bad idea. Before I escaped to Mum and Dad's, I felt the walls of this house closing in on me, people watching me. And Monica's tongue is always loose after a few drinks.

Nobody loves you. They'd rather you were

270

dead. They're thinking of ways to get rid of you.'

I open my eyes. 'What did you say?'

He swallows the hot chocolate.

'Nothing. I had my mouth full.'

I'm just tired, that's all it is. Perhaps if I have a few drinks, I'll get a decent night's sleep.

'Okay,' I say. 'I'll go on the night out.'

'Great. I'll let her know.'

I say nothing.

I picture what'll probably happen this evening. Me, putting on a happy face, watching bloody *Albion Market* or whatever it's called, and then going to bed knowing I'll be awake a few hours later. It doesn't even fill me with dread, because I feel nothing.

'If you don't mind,' I say, 'I'm going to have an early night. I didn't sleep well last night.'

I walk through the door to the lounge. Bobby's still engrossed in *Thomas the Tank Engine*.

'But I thought we were okay now?' says Peter. 'How will I do the kids' bedtime on my own?'

He thought we were all right? Did he think that a suggestion of a night out would make everything better? I don't know what planet he lives on.

'It'll be good practice for Friday,' I say. 'Mum made up some spare bottles for tonight — they're in Annie's bag.'

'Wait a sec, Deb.'

I stop and slowly turn around. I'm not in the mood for an argument. I just need to get under the bed covers and lie alone in the dark. I wait for another of his protests, but instead he gets something out of the drawer.

'This came for you yesterday.'

He's holding out a pink envelope. It has my name and address written on it. He's smiling — does he know who's written it?

I don't want it, I want to say. Whoever's writing to me is trying to break me. But I can't tell Peter that.

'Thanks,' I say.

I manage to stop the tremble in my hands as I take the letter. I walk through the lounge into the hall.

'Night, Debs,' he shouts after me. 'Hope you feel better in the morning.'

He talks as though I'm a colleague or someone at the corner shop. Why isn't he intrigued about the letter? I know I would be, if he were to receive one. We hardly ever get handwritten mail these days, people just phone each other. I shut the door to the living room and scrutinise the postmark. *Lancashire and South Lakes.* It's local. This is the first time one of these letters has been stamped. Perhaps it's just a fluke that it's the same colour.

I tear it open.

My hope that the colour is pure coincidence is shattered when I read it.

He wishes you were dead. They're thinking of ways to get rid of you.

I stand for a few moments as I take in the same carefully written capital letters. It's like the words in my head have been printed on paper, but I'm reading them as though I'm a thousand miles away — like it's happening to someone else.

It can't be Dean. I don't know why I even thought it would be. I can't understand why anyone would want to be so mean to me.

Unless they really know me.

Perhaps Peter wasn't curious about it because *he* wrote it.

I can't trust him. He's in on it too. With Monica. I don't think she's ever liked me, not really. But fuck her. I don't care what she thinks of me.

I want to tear the letter into pieces, but I don't. I leave it on the hall table. If it's still there in the morning, then I'm going to collect all of the notes and take them to someone who can help me.

But, for the moment, I haven't the energy to give a shit. Let whoever it is hurt me. They'll be doing me a favour.

31

Anna

I manage to find a parking space in the crammed hospital car park. I switch the engine off, and lean against the seat.

Thank God Jack finished work early and I could leave Sophie at home.

'Did your dad say what was wrong with her?' Jack whispered to me before I set off.

'No, nothing. Just that she was injured and in hospital.'

I was shaking so much my keys rattled as I held them. Jack took both of my hands in his.

'Try not to worry. Shall I drive you there?'

'No, no. I don't want to worry Sophie. I'll be fine.'

I turned to leave, but a thought stopped me.

'How come you're back so early? When I phoned, you were already home.'

'I . . . I just wanted to have a chat. But now's not the right time. Just go — go and see Monica.'

'Oh . . . okay.'

It's bad enough imagining what's wrong with Monica, without worrying even more about my marriage. Oh God. What if she isn't all right? Dad didn't say what happened, and when I tried to phone him, it went straight to answerphone. I get out of the car and walk slowly to the main reception.

I give Monica's name, and almost cry with relief when the man behind the desk says, 'Take the lift to level two, and then through the doors to your right. Bleasdale Ward.'

When Grandad was here three years ago with his knee, it took me at least half an hour to find him, but Monica's is easier to find. I push the hand sanitiser into my palms and spread it up to my wrist.

'Could you tell me where I can find Monica Atherton?' I say to the nurse at the station.

She points her pen to a room only two metres away.

I see Dad straight away, leaning against the window. The curtain around Monica's bed is pulled across, so I can't see her from the doorway.

'Dad!' I walk quickly towards him, trying to walk on tiptoes so as not to disturb the other patients. I don't know why I bother, though, because most of them are chatting away to the visitors milling around them.

It takes a few seconds for his eyes to focus, to recognise me.

'Anna! I didn't expect you to come here. Did I not put that in the text? Where's Sophie?'

'Jack left work early. I had to come — I was worried about Monica.'

She's sitting up in the bed, her eyes closed. Her right arm is in a cast and there are Steri-Strips on her forehead.

'Hey, Annie,' she says, her voice slurred.

'They gave her some pain relief,' says Dad.

I sit on the plastic chair next to the bed; Dad sits on the one opposite.

'What happened?'

'She fell down the stairs at the train station.'

'I was pushed,' Monica says quietly.

I look up at Dad.

'Pushed?' I say. 'Oh my God! Have you called the police?'

Dad purses his lips. 'I think it's the pain relief. I wasn't there, I was paying for the tickets. We were going to go for a day trip to Southport. There were a few other people who saw what happened, but they didn't see anyone push her. Remember when they gave your grandad morphine for his knee? He started talking to your grandmother . . . thought he was about to die too . . . that she was coming for him and after that, he was convinced there were spiders crawling all over him.'

Monica groans. She tries to open her eyes, but the one nearest me, the one with the strips above it, is too swollen.

'She was wearing those ridiculous shoes,' says Dad. 'The ones with the weird tassels on them.'

'I bought her those,' I say. 'And they're pom-poms, not tassels.'

I don't know why I'm taking offence about a pair of shoes at a time like this.

'Sorry, love,' says Dad. 'But they're not very practical.'

'I feel awful now.'

'It wasn't *your* fault, Anna,' says Dad. 'I said to Monica, 'They're shoes for sitting down in, not travelling in.''

'Did you?'

He shrugs. 'I suppose living with you two must've rubbed off on me.'

'Pushed,' says Monica.

'You weren't, love,' says Dad. 'But if it makes you feel better, I'll see if the station has CCTV.' He looks at me. 'I really don't think she was pushed.'

I look to Monica: an imperceptible shake of her head.

'Dad, Monica *can* hear you, you know.' I try to whisper, so my voice is lost among the chatter around us. 'Are you sure she's just imagining it? It's not as if she's seeing dead people or creepy crawlies everywhere.'

Dad frowns. 'We'll have a better idea when whatever medication they gave her wears off. She was in too much pain to talk before the ambulance came.'

After ten minutes, Monica seems to have fallen asleep.

Dad gets up carefully, so he doesn't scrape the chair on the floor.

'If you can stay for a few more minutes, love,' he says, 'would you mind if I go and grab a coffee from downstairs?'

'Of course.'

He's only been gone half a minute when Monica opens her eyes. She leans forwards, gently smacking her lips together. I reach over for the beaker of water on her cabinet. After taking a small sip, she leans back into her pillow, exhausted.

'So thirsty.' She pats around the bed with her

free hand; I put my hand in hers. She squeezes it. 'Darling, Annie. You should find the letters. The truth. Get me some clothes. Use your key.'

'What do you mean, *the truth*?'

Monica closes her eyes again.

'Everything okay here?'

'You were quick, Dad!'

'Was I?'

I take my hand from under Monica's and stand.

'I'm going to pop to yours and get Monica a change of clothes,' I say. 'So you don't have to worry about going back and forth in visiting hours.'

'Are you sure you don't mind?' says Dad.

'No, it's fine.' I walk over to him and kiss him on the cheek. 'I'll see you in an hour or so.'

'Thanks, love,' he says.

Poor Dad.

I don't think he knows as much as Monica.

★   ★   ★

It's six o'clock, still light, but the lamp at the far end of their hallway is still on, as always. 'It's the ambience more than the light,' Monica always says; it reminds me of Penelope Keith in *The Good Life*.

Robert said he found the letters years ago, in the junk drawer — the place where all the old phone chargers, screwdrivers, television and micro-wave receipts are kept. They probably won't have been put back there, but I check it anyway. There are still the same old Nokia chargers that were there years before. I search in the other drawers:

278

tea towels, cutlery, sharp knives. But no letters.

I head upstairs, going straight to Dad and Monica's room. They have fitted wardrobes and drawers along the wall to the left. Monica's clothes are in the cupboard near the window. I grab a weekend bag from the bottom and pull it open on their bed. I look at her clothes; most are unsuitable for a stay in hospital. There are at least twenty dry-clean only dresses, and five silk blouses. I don't think I have ever seen her in a pair of jeans. I go to the chest of drawers near the bedroom door. From what I remember, Monica's things are in the top three. It feels inappropriate to be looking in her underwear, so I just grab a few random items and shove them into the bag.

I open the second drawer and find neatly ironed and folded nightdresses and pyjamas. I take one of each, close the drawer, and grab her dressing gown from the back of the door. She might only be in one night, but you never know. I open the third drawer where she keeps her exercise gear. She's fifty-eight and still does aerobics three times a week. I pick out a pair of what look like yoga trousers and a matching top, still with their labels attached. She might not want to be in her nightwear in front of strangers.

I open the fourth and fifth drawers. Dad's underwear and pyjamas. I kneel on the floor and pull open the bottom drawer. There are three Clarks shoeboxes in a row at the back. I grab the nearest and take off the lid.

Inside are lots of little packages with Sellotape wrapped round them. *Anna 1992* is written on one of them in Monica's handwriting. There must be seven or eight with my name on. I pick at the tape on one and gently prise off the paper. Inside is a tiny white thing. I take it into the palm of my hand and see that it's a baby tooth. *My* baby tooth. She kept them.

I push the little packages of teeth to one side and pull out the wad of paper underneath. I sit cross-legged as I pick up the first. It's a handmade card with a picture of a woman and a dandelion on the front. *Happy Mother's Day, Monica. I love you. From Anna Bandana.*

Under my words, Monica has written *1993*.

Anna Bandana. I'd forgotten that's what she called me.

Did she mind that I never called her *Mummy?*

Under this are other cards I made her. The dates scribed underneath them end at 1997. Hadn't I written her a Mother's Day card since? My face grows cold with shame.

I remember Dad used to buy her flowers, telling her they were from all of us. 1997 was the year I started secondary school; I had only thought about myself, and the fact my mother didn't want me. But all along, I had Monica. Someone who talked to me about things Dad was too embarrassed to speak about. She stroked my hair when Jason Doherty in Year 10 said I was the ugliest person he had ever seen. 'You're not ugly, Anna. You're beautiful. He probably likes you. They're strange creatures, boys. And we should know, shouldn't we? We live with three of them.'

I lay down the Mother's Day cards, replacing

the little packages of teeth on top of them. I place the shoebox next to the other two and lift open the lid of the one next to mine. Inside are identical packages labelled 'Bobby'. I flick the lid of the third, expecting the same, labelled 'Leo', but it isn't.

Inside, there is a pink envelope addressed to Debbie. Underneath it, there are two folded notes in the same colour — the same pink as the awful letters Grandad gave me. My hands shake as I lift them out. I open the first one.

He wishes you were dead. They're thinking of ways to get rid of you.

It is written in identical handwriting to the ones Debbie received. Why does Monica have this one and not the rest?

The other note's folds are worn, as though it's been read hundreds of times. The paper is grubby.

I open it. Robert was right about the handwriting. It's not like the other envelope, but a strange, slurred scrawl.

To my family,
I'm sorry. I can't do this any more. I've tried.
I love you all.
Debbie.

I read it again and again. Is this all she wrote before abandoning her whole family? It's so vague. If she was intending to leave, then why

281

not say everything she wanted to?

I reach into Robert's shoebox. Underneath the Mother's Day cards are birthday cards from age one to six. *Love from Mummy and Daddy*, is written on each of them. Some have been written by my dad, but others have my mother's writing inside. I compare it to the writing on the pink note signed by Debbie.

It's not the same.

32

She suggested a café I've never been to before, but that wasn't difficult. Smooth FM plays quietly in the background, but I can still make out the song: 'Just the Way You Are' by Billy Joel.

She was already here when I arrived. I didn't tell her what I wanted, but she walks over to the counter and places a black coffee in front of me.

'I didn't mean to,' she says. 'I reached over to say hello and she just fell.'

'She wouldn't remember you,' I say. 'It was too long ago.'

'So, I'm that forgettable?'

'I didn't mean it like that.'

'Is she okay?'

'How would I know?'

'There's no need to be like that.'

'Sorry, sorry. It's just that . . . you could've ruined the whole thing.'

'Excuse me?'

'I'm so close. I'm nearly ready.'

'Why is everything about you?' She leans forward, her eyes boring into mine. 'You need to remember that I've kept your secret for all of these years. I didn't have to.'

'I know, I know. I said I'm sorry, didn't I?' I run my finger along the rim of the cup, but it's not like glass, it won't make a sound even though I wish it would. 'I'm thinking of confessing — it's been on my conscience for too long.'

'You know I think you're doing the right thing. Perhaps leave out the part where I'm involved, though.'

'I suppose. But they need to hear the whole truth. It's not fair on them. I started all of this — I have to see it to the end. They won't believe me if you don't back me up.'

She shakes her head. 'I really don't understand you.'

'I don't think I understand myself.'

She stands, her coffee barely touched, and puts on her jacket.

'If it all goes wrong,' she says, 'don't come running to me.'

I don't reply; I watch her leave, not looking back.

'Heart of Glass' plays on the radio.

You're following me, aren't you? I try putting my fingers in my ears, but it doesn't drown out the sound.

I push my coffee away and stand.

The bell dings as I open the door. I take a deep breath of fresh air, but there's a scent in the air.

I search for you.

Sometimes I think I see you.

I want to run to you and tell you that I'm sorry. But I can't.

Because you're dead.

33

Friday, 18 July 1986
Debbie

Monica's at the bar, probably asking for another couple of cocktails with umbrellas. They work, these ones. The umbrellas, I mean, not the cocktails (although they work too). You just push the little round bit up and down the cocktail stick, and there you have it: a working umbrella. If you're the size of a mouse. And I'm definitely not the size of a mouse.

Oh God, I should stop smiling to myself.

Shit, I'm pissed.

We've only had two, but I haven't had a drink for months. It feels like years since I've been out like this. From the time we started going to pubs, which was from about the age of fifteen (but don't tell my mother), Monica's always been the one to go to the bar. When I was twenty, I looked about twelve, so I've always handed her the money and she always got me what she wanted.

I suppose I could go to the bar myself, but it's a tradition now. Peter says it's lazy, but I've just had a baby — I'm practically an invalid.

And he's not here anyway, so I can do what I want.

Before I left the house, I went to prepare a few

bottles for Annie, but Peter had already made up four and put them in the fridge. Making me feel useless, again. Since when had he learned how to do all of that? Monica, probably. She must've been giving him lessons. She was probably the one who tidied our kitchen the other day. I won't tell her I'm onto them. Have to keep one step ahead.

If Peter saw me now, I'd tell him that I'm happy.

Right now, at this precise time, in this actual moment.

Time.

I look at my watch. It says eight thirty, though it could be nine thirty.

Ah fuck it, I'm out of the house. I'm me again.

I look down at my crap outfit. Leggings with a baggy grey top that has neon stripes across it. Neon. When did that become a thing? I'm so fat, I can't wear anything decent any more. Monica's wearing a denim skirt and a boob tube. Shit, even three weeks after she had Leo, she was in her old clothes.

I should be thin too by now. I can't remember the last time I enjoyed a meal. I must just stuff it in when no one's looking — including my own eyes. Anyway, it's not all love and roses and Milk Tray. Nathan's still a bit weird about Leo, even after five years.

'I'm Not in Love' by 10cc whines its way from the jukebox. God, it's such a depressing song. I roll my eyes at nobody. Someone should update that machine. We'll have to stick a few fifty-pence pieces in it later. We used to take it over, boring the whole pub with Blondie on repeat.

Monica's coming back. I've got to be sensible now — pretend I can hold my drink. I used to be able to drink Peter under the table, for God's sake.

Sit up, Debbie.

I shuffle my arse to the back of the seat and press my back to it.

'A Slow Comfortable Screw,' she says, setting the drinks on the table.

'First time for everything.' I put the straw to my mouth. 'Hmm, fruity.'

Monica crosses her legs as she sits on the little stool. She bends her body to the table and sucks from the straw without touching the glass with her hands. She must be as pissed as I am.

'Not bad,' she says. 'Though I think I'd prefer half a lager. I'm so thirsty today.'

'You're not pregnant, are you?'

'Since when has being thirsty been a symptom of pregnancy?'

I shrug.

'Anyway,' she says. 'It's so good to have a night out. We haven't done this for years.'

'What do you mean? We went out loads before I got pregnant with Annie.'

'I meant just us two. Like it used to be.'

'I suppose.'

'Do you remember those nights out on the Manx ferry nightclub? I thought we'd live like that forever. Working for the weekends — that's what we used to say. Then we'd meet up again on the Sunday and go to the pictures.'

'It feels like a lifetime ago.'

'Xanadu' sounds from the pub speakers.

'What the fuck is this song about?' I say.

'No idea.'

I want to ask her about her cosy chats with Peter, but I'm worried it'll turn the night into something darker. Every time I look at her, I picture her kissing him. God, I can't look at her any more.

'What's up?' she says.

'Nothing. Just looking at how much this place has changed.'

She looks around, her nose wrinkles.

'It hasn't changed at all.' She lifts her bum, and drags the stool closer to the table, picking up her drink, and throwing the umbrella on the table. 'How is everything?'

'You're as subtle as a brick. Is this why you suggested the night out? So you can report back to Peter with my little secrets?'

She almost drops her drink back down.

'Where the hell did that come from?' she says. 'What do you mean, your little secrets? I wouldn't tell Peter anything you told me.'

'But you told him that I was hearing things, didn't you? I told you in the café the other week. And then you went running to Peter with the latest bit of gossip.'

'Debbie, I swear I didn't tell him. Who else have you told?'

I don't know whether to believe her; she seems so sincere.

'I haven't told anyone else.'

She narrows her eyes. 'Are you sure?'

'Of course I'm sure.'

There's a hesitation in my voice. I don't even believe myself. Did I tell Nathan the other day?

'I know it's been hard for you since Annie was born, being stuck in the house all day. But is there anything else bothering you?'

Her eyes are wide. Is she acting? She was always so good at masking her feelings. Wasn't she? Or was that me? God, I shouldn't drink any more. I look at her again, squinting so I can focus on her properly. She could be lying. It could be *her* who wrote those letters to me.

I grab my handbag and take out the notes, laying them on the table side by side.

Monica bends down so she's inches away as she reads each one.

She scans them again before looking up at me.

'Holy shit, Debbie. When did you start getting these?'

'Only a few days after I got home from hospital.'

'Do you recognise the handwriting?' She picks one up and holds the letter up to her face.

'No. But it's hard to tell when it's written in capitals like that. It could be anyone.'

'Have you told anybody else about these?'

'My dad, Mum, Peter.'

'What did Peter say about it?'

'Nothing really. He didn't seem that interested at all.'

'Has he read them?'

'I . . . I can't remember. I'm sure I gave them to him to read. But he sort of batted me away. I left this one on the hall table the other night, and it was still there the following morning. If he has read it, then he's ignored it . . . he's not mentioned it.'

'How odd. Why didn't you bring it up again?' She holds up another. 'I mean — this one is really creepy. Who does he think wants you dead?'

'What makes you think a man wrote them?'

She puts the letter down as though it's given her an electric shock.

'It's just that . . . Oh, I don't know.' She picks up her drink and throws the straw on the table next to the discarded umbrella and downs the rest of her cocktail in one. She shivers as she places the glass on the table. 'I know a policeman through work. Can I take this one and show it to him?'

She picks up the last one I received. The one that mentions death. I suck up the rest of my drink.

'Sure.'

She folds it back up and puts it in her handbag.

'Are you not scared, Debs?'

I lean back against the back of the banquette.

'Should I be scared? I suppose it's made me afraid of being alone in the house, like I'm always being watched.'

'Shit, Debbie. You should've called me as soon as you got them — as soon as you got the first one.'

'But you're in cahoots with them. You'd say I was losing it.'

'What? I can't believe you're saying that to me. I care about you. You're like a sister to me.'

'Perhaps it was you.'

The colour drains from her face.

'What do you mean?'

'It was you who told Peter that I was hearing things.'

Her shoulders relax a little. Her chest rises as she takes a deep breath.

'Okay, okay. Yes, it was me. But it's only because I was worried.'

'I can't believe you lied to me.'

'It was only a little white lie. I didn't want it to spoil our night.'

'Right,' I say, picking up my jacket. 'Right. I understand.'

I put my arms in the sleeves and stand.

'Where are you going?' she says.

'Home. I don't want to look at your smug face any more.' I step aside from the table. 'With your perfect hair, your perfect clothes, your perfect life.'

I turn to leave, but she shouts after me.

'You don't know!' she says.

I stop and turn around. 'Don't know what?'

'My life is far from perfect. I think Nathan's having an affair.'

I shake my head at her. 'Whatever, Monica. You just can't stop lies spouting from that mouth of yours, can you?'

The door slams behind me and the fresh air hits me in the face.

★   ★   ★

It must be just after ten — it's only just going dark and there are still loads of people on the streets. I haven't been out in so long that the taxis aren't in the same place any more. Everything's a mass of lights and sounds. I don't want to be here, but I don't want to go home either. I'll walk it. It'll only take me ten minutes tops. Maybe thirty.

I stand at the traffic lights for ages, while other people cross regardless. They mustn't be as drunk as I am; they're giving me funny looks. Or are they? I wait another few minutes for the lights to change, even though there aren't any cars. Dad says you should never take safety for granted. Green cross code.

I cross and head up the hill. This is going to take me ages. I pull my jacket around me — it's freezing now. Why can't we have summers like they do abroad?

'All right, love?'

I ignore the man leaving the pub to my left. The cigarette smoke billows out of the place. I inhale, and it takes me back to when we had nothing better to do than spend all day in the pub.

There's a hand on my shoulder.

'I said, *All right, love?*'

I turn slowly. 'Oh, it's you.'

Dean. I can't get away from the man.

'That's not much of a hello, is it?' he says.

'Monica should be here any minute,' I say.

'Yeah right. She's a right bitch, she is. I don't know why you don't see it.'

'How come you know so much about Monica?'

He shrugs. 'I've got eyes everywhere.'

I bet you have, you slimy get, I think to myself. 'Anyway, I'd best get on.'

'Reckon you should be at home with your baby at this time of night, don't you?'

I turn and walk away.

'Whatever,' I mutter. 'Caveman.'

'I heard that, you know.'

I start to run — is he following me? I daren't turn around.

A bus pulls into the stop across the road; I run towards it.

Dean's laughing to himself. 'As if I'd chase after you, you fat cow.'

People stare at me as I get on the bus. I want to disappear. I shouldn't have agreed to go out — it's safer indoors.

I hand the driver two fifty-pence pieces and sit on the side furthest from Dean. I glance through the opposite window, but he's not in the street any more.

I don't know where this bus is going — it's not even going in the right direction to home.

Why has everyone in this world turned strange? Monica and Peter are conspiring against me, Nathan's following me everywhere (except tonight when I needed him), and Mum and Dad are being overprotective. What changed to make all of this happen? Are other people changing because of me?

I've never felt so alone.

I look at the reflection in the window as the bus starts off, and I see tears streaming down my face. I don't even feel them.

34

Anna

I am sitting outside the bathroom, leaning against the airing cupboard, listening to Sophie shout and squeal and splash as Jack baths her.

After dropping Monica's bag at the hospital, I just wanted to get home. I didn't tell Dad about the cards and letters I found. I'm meeting Sally tomorrow to see the house next door to our old place, but that will be the last time I'm actively getting involved with this investigation. I need to sort out issues closer to home.

Seeing the Mother's Day cards made me realise I should have appreciated what I had with Monica instead of yearning for someone who didn't even want me.

Sophie tears out of the bathroom in her *Paw Patrol* pyjamas, her hair wet.

'Mummy! You're back!'

'What are you doing creeping about?' says Jack, smiling as he comes out of the bathroom.

'I did shout hello, but you two were making a racket in there.' I ruffle the top of Sophie's hair. 'And I didn't want to disturb all that fun you were having.'

'We pretended,' says Sophie, 'that the water in the empty shampoo bottles was wee.'

'Oh, lovely.'

'It wasn't pretend,' says Jack, winking at me. 'It was real wee.'

Sophie wrinkles her nose.

'As if.'

'*As if?*' says Jack. 'Are you six or sixteen?'

'Don't be silly, Daddy. Come on.' Sophie walks into her bedroom. 'Read me a story.'

I get up from the floor.

'You go downstairs,' says Jack. 'Pour yourself a glass of wine. Then we can have a chat.'

He doesn't look me in the eye as he utters the last sentence. He's trying to sound more lighthearted than he feels, I'm sure of it. Jack has never requested a *chat*. In the past, he's always shuddered at the mention of a scheduled *chat*.

'Okay,' I say, as Sophie shouts for her daddy again. 'I'll see you down there.' I turn to go downstairs. 'Hey,' I say. Jack pops his head around Sophie's bedroom door. 'Did you see a car at the end of the street tonight? A red one — a new Honda, I think. I've seen it around a few times recently.'

'Nope,' he says. 'Can't say I've noticed.'

'I must be imagining things.'

★　★　★

By the time Jack gets downstairs, the wine in my glass is warm. Going by his expression, it seems he's looking forward to this talk as much as I am. Does he know that I found out about Francesca — that the girl he was once in love with has recently died? I have a terrible feeling of dread. Perhaps he's beginning to re-evaluate his life now that someone he was once close to has died. Maybe he doesn't see a future with me — thinks that life is too short to be miserable.

'Is that your second?' He points to my glass.

I look down at it. It's still three-quarters full.

'Yes.'

I don't know why I'm lying; perhaps it will make it easier for him to speak freely if he thinks I'm a little bit drunk.

'I'll just get myself a glass,' he says. 'Sophie's fast asleep.'

My heart is pounding. I sit a little straighter on the sofa; smooth my hair down with the palm of my hand. I haven't looked at my face since this morning — my make-up has probably worn off. I tiptoe to the mirror and place my wine glass on the mantelpiece. I pinch my cheeks to bring them colour — I used to see Gran do it, but this is the first time I've tried it and am surprised to find that it works. My lipstick has faded, but there is still a trace of eyeliner on my upper lids — at least my eyes don't look so tired. I really should make more of an effort.

I take a deep breath and a big gulp of wine. I almost retch, finding it hard to swallow. It's too warm and it tastes like vinegar. I have never really liked the taste of wine — I don't know why I pretend to. It's like the Emperor's new clothes, people always —

'So.' Jack's standing at the doorway. He walks over to the chair under the window and sits. 'I think you'd better sit down, too.'

He pats the edge of the sofa nearest him.

He sounds too cheerful for it to be terrible news. Doesn't he?

But as I sit and look at his hands, he can't keep them still.

'So,' he says, again. He takes a long sip of wine and stares at the floor. 'You remember when we first got together . . . you had this thing about asking me all about past relationships and stuff? And I told you that I was with someone when I was at college?'

'No. I didn't think we went into details about that.'

Have I remembered things wrong?

'Okay. I thought we did.' He shakes his head. 'Anyway, that's not the point . . . There was this girl called Francesca. She was only seventeen when we broke up — I was eighteen.' He takes a deep breath. 'It ended badly. She got pregnant and I said I couldn't deal with it . . . I felt like a kid myself at the time. Jesus what a cliché I was. She had a termination . . . she hated me for it. I never saw her after that. I moved to Lancashire for university and never left. We had no reason to contact each other.'

He pauses. He's speaking so pragmatically.

'So why are you bringing her up now?'

'She died in a car accident three weeks ago.'

I reach over to take hold of his hand. He squeezes mine before letting it go.

'The thing is, Anna, is that . . . God this is so hard.'

He puts a hand through his hair.

'Go on.'

My heart is thumping; my legs feel numb.

'Her brother told me that she got together with someone else pretty quickly after I left . . . but really, she was seeing him at the same time she was seeing me . . . You can see where this is going, can't you?'

I think I'm going to be sick.

'Just tell me, Jack,' I say quickly. 'I'm not going to try and guess.'

He takes another deep breath.

'Francesca had the baby.'

'What?'

I put my wine glass down before I drop it.

'She never told me. My parents moved to the south coast when I left — I had no contacts in the area.'

'You have another child?'

'I don't know.'

'What do you mean?'

'When Francesca was in hospital . . . after the accident . . . just before she died . . . she told her brother that the father of her son — it was a boy — was one of two people. The bloke she went out with after me . . . or during, whatever . . . didn't have anything to do with the baby.'

'Oh God, that poor child.'

'He didn't know any different, from what her brother Simon was telling me the other day. Francesca's family have been there for him, thank God.'

The taste of wine lingers in my mouth — I want to spit it out. My face feels hot.

I take a deep breath.

'He's sixteen,' I say aloud, more to myself than Jack.

'I know this is a lot to take in.'

'When did you find out?'

'That he existed — and the accident? Only a few weeks ago. Fran's brother contacted me on Facebook of all places. But you'd just received that email from someone claiming to be your mother.'

'Okay.' I stand. 'Right.'

And I walk out of the door.

35

Wednesday, 23 July 1986
Debbie

Mum's laid on a cold buffet of vol-au-vents with creamed mushrooms, crustless cucumber sandwiches, and fairy cakes decorated with red, white and blue icing. She's set it on the coffee table, which is quite casual for Mum, considering the occasion. And she's let Peter and me sit on the floor so we've easy access to the food, so it doesn't go to waste.

We're going on holiday tomorrow, and Peter's barely talking to me. It's because I can't remember getting home after the Friday night out with Monica. I must've drunk more than I thought.

'What time did you come home last night?' he'd said, standing over me as I lay in bed on Saturday morning. 'I went to bed at midnight and there was no sign of you. I've been up since six with Annie — I'm knackered.'

'I can't move,' I said, my voice monotone.

I couldn't even lift a hand. How could I tell him that I didn't remember what time I got in? I don't know what I was doing till after midnight. It was only about nine or ten when I left Monica.

'It's ten o'clock, Debs,' he said. 'I've got to go to work. I'm sorry.'

'I can't.'

'I know I said I'd cover the kids for you, but the duty manager's gone home sick.'

For me?

I threw the cover over my head, wanting a hole to swallow me into nothingness.

'I'm sick.'

'You're not sick, you're hungover.'

He whipped the quilt off my head; I brought my legs close to my chest, cowering against the pillow like a wounded animal. I hid my face with my arms. I didn't have the strength to sob, the tears just rolled down my face.

I heard him sigh as he stood next to me. I felt his breath as he crouched before me. His fingers reached through the gap in my arms and brushed the hair from my eyes.

'You didn't used to get this hungover.' He sighed. 'I'll call your mum and dad . . . see if they can come over.'

And they did, God bless them. They stayed until Peter came home from work, but I stayed in bed.

I wouldn't see Monica when she came round on Sunday. On Monday, I got up to pick Bobby up from school, waited until Peter got home, and then crawled up the stairs to bed. Annie was easy to look after. Bottle, nappy change, lie her next to me. She was fine. Tuesday was a repeat of Monday. If my children were still alive, then I was doing my job.

Monica visited again yesterday, Tuesday, evening. I heard her and Peter talking.

'You should call the doctor,' she said. 'It's not

normal. It's not like her to be like this.'

Yes, it is, I thought, staring at the bedroom ceiling. It's definitely like me. It's the real me who's been cocooned, pretending, just waiting for the chance to show my real colours.

'She was in a weird mood when she walked out of the pub on Friday night,' said Monica. 'It was only about ten o'clock.'

'So where the hell was she for all those hours?' said Peter.

They could ask all they want; I didn't know the answer. The last thing I remembered was walking out of the pub. I told Peter I got lost, took the wrong bus. For all I knew that could be true, but it didn't matter where I was. I didn't care what happened to me.

Now he's annoyed because I haven't packed yet and we're leaving tomorrow. It's his day off and we're round at my parents' house. I don't care if I go on holiday taking only the clothes I'm wearing.

'Has it started yet?' Dad's standing at the door-way between the living room and the kitchen.

'Not yet,' says Mum. She turns her bottom so quickly she nearly falls off her chair. 'Have you changed your mind?'

'No, I bloody haven't,' he says. 'Not if that b — ' He glances at Bobby running Matchbox cars along the skirting boards. 'Not if that woman's going. I'll be in my office if there's an emergency.'

He means his shed, where he has a sneaky packet of cigarettes and a portable black-and-white telly.

Poor Mum. She loves a royal wedding, but Dad won't watch anything that has Margaret Thatcher in it. The back door slams shut and Mum rolls her eyes, tutting.

'I wish he'd forgive and forget,' she says, as though Dad losing his job was just a falling out of friends.

Peter gives me that look — the one that says, *Your mum lives in a bubble of Jesus and Victoria sponge.*

'Oh, it's about to start,' she says, shifting further from the edge of her seat.

I bet she's dying to sit on the floor to get a closer look at Fergie's dress, but she never would.

'That Elton John,' she says, 'he gets invited to everything.'

★   ★   ★

It's been on the telly for hours already and they've only just got married. I will Annie to wake up, but she's barely stirring. Was Monica telling the truth when she thought Nathan was having an affair? He's not mentioned anything to me, but then, why would he?

I almost cheer when there's a knock at the door, and jump up from the floor — the most animated I've been in days. 'I'll go,' I say, taking advantage of Mum's abandonment of civility while she's engrossed in *ivory duchesse satin.*

I open the door, and it's Nathan.

'Hey, Debs. Come outside for a bit.'

I blink in the daylight — it feels like I haven't

303

been outside properly for weeks, even though we only arrived here a few hours ago.

'What? Why?'

He beckons me. I pull the door to after clicking the latch on.

He reaches into his pocket and pulls something out. I know what it is before he says anything.

'I got a letter, too,' he says.

He glances around as though looking for someone watching us.

I narrow my eyes.

'Did Monica tell you I was getting letters?'

'Not exactly. I didn't know you got more than one, though — I saw it on her bedside cabinet.'

'What does yours say?'

'Here.' He holds it out to me — his nails are bitten. 'See for yourself.'

I grab it.

Keep your hands to yourself, you dirty bastard.

My cheeks burn with the insinuation of what's been written.

'Do people think we're . . . ' I say. 'But we've only ever gone out once . . . everyone knew about that.'

I search for an emotion on his face, but find nothing.

'Monica said she had a contact at the police,' I continue, 'perhaps she should take that one too. What did she say when you showed it to her?'

'I haven't shown it to her. And the police won't care about things like — '

'You haven't shown her? But we haven't done

304

anything wrong.' I glance through the living-room window — Mum and Peter are where I left them. 'Look, I can't deal with all of this — I'm just about managing to get out of bed.'

I close my eyes. I can't believe I'm being so honest with him. I open my eyes again.

'Sorry, Debbie. I shouldn't have come round. I didn't know what to do. I couldn't tell Monica about it . . . she might ask about you.' He goes to put a hand on my shoulder, looks into the window, and puts it down by his side. 'To think someone's been watching us — it's creeping me out a bit.' He starts to walk backwards towards the gate. 'I'll see you tomorrow afternoon. I just didn't want to bring it up in front of everyone and spoil the holiday.'

I don't have the energy to ask why it would spoil the holiday, or tell him that I've been getting the letters for weeks. I watch him as he gets into his big white car and drives away. I want to run after him and shout, 'Don't leave me!'

I go back into the house and close the door behind me. There are cheers from the crowd on telly as Prince Andrew and Sarah Ferguson exit Westminster Abbey. They have everything they've ever wanted now. What would it be like to have a happy ever after?

36

Anna

I'm sitting in my car, across from the house I lived in as a baby. I arrived early to take in the atmosphere. I have driven down this road countless times and tried to peek in number fifty-seven, but I've never stopped, or walked down this street. I've seen the peach curtains open, closed; the airer in the front bedroom window, but never the occupants go in or out.

I'm not in the mood for this. I lay awake last night, thinking about a child on this earth who might be related to Jack, to Sophie. It all happened years before I met Jack, so I can't be angry about that — he didn't even know himself. I thought about that poor boy who has just lost his mother. The DNA test result will arrive any day now. I'm ashamed to think it, but I hope Jack isn't the father.

A tap on my car window interrupts my thoughts.

'Morning, love,' says Sally, not raising her voice to compensate for the closed window.

I get out, rubbing the tops of my arms. It might be July, but it's freezing. Sally's wearing the same beige mac, but today she's wearing jeans with at least a five-centimetre turn-up.

'Hi, Sally. Let's get this over and done with.'

She tilts her head to one side.

'Are you not feeling up to this? You haven't received any more emails, have you?'

'Actually, no, I haven't. She didn't reply to my suggestion of meeting up, and that was days ago. To be honest, I've had a lot on my mind since.'

'Anything you want to talk about?'

'Not right now.'

A front door slams shut opposite. A man opens a small garage at the side of his house and takes out a toolbox. He's in his sixties, with grey hair and a swagger like he's God's gift.

I look away when he catches me looking at him.

'Well, I never,' he says. 'It's like going back in time with you stood in front of number fifty-seven like that. You look just like my old neighbour. Same long dark hair, pale skin. Pretty too — not that I said that to her face.'

I want to wipe myself clean after feeling his eyes all over me.

'You remember Debbie Atherton?' says Sally.

'Course I do. There's been no one under sixty that's lived there since. Always thought she was too good for round here though, didn't she?' He opens the boot of his car, placing his toolkit inside, next to a bin bag full of women's clothes. 'What's it to you two? You Cagney and Lacey?' He laughs at his own joke, wheezing like he's only got one lung.

'We're just here to view the house next door,' says Sally.

'Ah, yeah. Old Mrs Sullivan, property tycoon.' He goes into his garage and presses play on a white stereo. Hanging on the wall above it is a 2017 David Beckham calendar. The song 'Gloria' from the film *Flashdance* booms out of the old speakers.

'If it's all right,' shouts Sally, over the music, 'I might come back another time to have a chat to you about Debbie.'

He salutes her. 'Right you are, Columbo.'

She smiles and rolls her eyes at me.

'Come on,' she says, holding me by the elbow and walking me towards number fifty-nine. 'The reason I dragged us both here, is that I've done a bit of research — obviously — and I discovered that the person not only owns the one for sale, but also your old house.'

'You mentioned it yesterday.'

Sally knocks on number fifty-nine and smiles in preparation. It opens slowly, to a woman of about eighty.

'Are you my ten o'clock?' she says.

'We are indeed, Mrs Sullivan,' says Sally.

'Well, come on in then. You don't have to take your shoes off. I keep mine on all the time now. You never know when you'll have to scarper, do you?'

'I suppose not,' I say.

'I was joking, love. They support my ankles. Weak as twigs.'

'Oh, I see.'

For someone who works in a shop, I've never been very good at small talk.

'Who do we have here then?' she says.

'I'm Sally and this is Anna.'

'Right you are. Do you mind if you see

yourselves round? Only, I've had three already this morning and I'm feeling a tad delicate.'

Sally purses her lips to stifle a laugh.

'That's fine, Mrs Sullivan. We'll not trouble you for too long.'

We go straight upstairs and stand in the bedroom overlooking the back yard.

'Why are we actually looking round the house?' I say to Sally. 'I thought we were asking about next door.'

'I know. But I didn't have the heart to not have a look round. Plus, I'm nosy.'

'Right, well, let's get back down there. I've got to get home.'

She puts a hand on my arm to stop me from going downstairs.

'Do you want me to keep looking for Debbie?'

I take a deep breath. 'Do you think you're close?'

'I've got a few leads. I've got to go down to Eastbourne.'

'Eastbourne? Where that other letter was from? Why didn't you tell me this before?'

'You said you had lots on your mind. Tell you what, I'll let you know as soon as I find anything while I'm down there. We can catch up when I get back. Okay?'

'Okay.'

I should be thinking that there's hope — a proper lead we've never had before. But another part of me is worried about how she will explain the cost of the trip to Jack's firm. I suppose it could be worse: she could've been travelling to Tenerife.

'She was a beautiful person, your mother,' says Sally. 'I feel as though I'm getting to know her. I'm like that with all the missing people I look for. I suppose some might think that's unprofessional, but I think it helps — to see them for who they were, not just a person in the news. Or *not* in the news, in this case.'

'Thanks, Sally. It's nice to hear someone else say it.'

She did what people always do: refer to Debbie in the past tense. She must know more than she's telling me.

We're still standing on the landing.

'If nothing comes of this,' she says, 'I was thinking of placing something on Facebook — it's actually quite effective these days. Though you have to be wary — violent partners use it to search for vulnerable ex-partners. Always check the source.'

'Will do,' I reply, wondering if she's actually talking to a Dictaphone hidden in her pocket.

I walk down the stairs and I feel as though my head will explode with the enormity of everything. All I can think about is Jack waiting for me at home. He needs my support, but I'm here. I should be the better person, swallow my pride and say that we will deal with anything together: him and me. I suppose Jack is having to do the same.

We shuffle into the hall; we're taking up too much space.

'Thanks for letting us view your house, Mrs Sullivan,' says Sally.

The lady isn't in her chair, but at the window.

She's parted her bright-white net curtains, not caring if she's seen by the outside world. We stand at the threshold.

'He insists on playing that God-awful music,' says Mrs Sullivan.

Sally clears her throat. 'I said thank you for — '

'Yes, yes, I heard you.' She drops the net curtain. 'I'm glad I'm moving . . . there's been so much sadness on this street. Even for that one over the road.' She's still looking at the man working on his car. 'Poor Dean.'

Sally and I look at each other with raised eyebrows.

'Had a lovely wife,' she continues. 'Trisha. Though I say lovely, she was rather fond of herself. She took off with a billionaire. No, I'm wrong. It was a millionaire, like the shortbread. Took their little son with her, she did.'

'That's awfully sad,' says Sally. 'What else do you remember about this street?'

'Well, around that time — actually, Trisha left before this — but next door . . . his wife ran away while they were on holiday in Tenerife.'

'Is that what people say?' I say.

'About Trisha?'

'No. About next door.'

She looks at me through narrowed eyes.

'You look familiar,' she says. 'Are you a relative?'

I look to Sally; she shrugs.

'I'm Debbie's daughter.'

Mrs Sullivan's eyes are still narrow, then they widen as she regards me afresh.

'Dear Lord, so you are. You're the spitting image. I bet you get that all the time.'

'Not really.'

'No? How odd.' She shakes her head. 'A terrible thing. I hope you don't think me awful for gossiping — only, it was a pretty big thing that happened on this street.'

Sally steps forward. 'The estate agent told me that you actually own the house next door, and that you're putting that on the market soon. Is that right?'

'It is, love,' she says to Sally, but she's still looking at me. 'Ah, of course. Is that why you're here? Did you want to have a look at next door?'

'I . . .'

'It's a bit of a mess right now. The last tenants left it in a right state. They were six months behind in the rent, but I was held to ransom — they have so many rights, you see.'

'I don't want to put you to any trouble,' I say.

Part of me wants to leave, to not see the house. I wouldn't be able to remember anything anyway. But I suppose we're not here for that; we're here to see if Mrs Sullivan or Dean remembers anything.

Mrs Sullivan grabs a set of keys from a silver cup on her bookcase, and we follow her out of the house. She steps over the small wall dividing the two properties and she opens the front door, pushing it hard against the pile of mail lying behind it.

'I've got cleaners coming in for me next week,' she says.

'Is it still decorated the same?' I ask.

312

'Good Lord, no,' says Mrs Sullivan.

We follow her into the house. There's a phone on the table in the hall; the carpet all the way through is brown. Like Mrs Sullivan's house, the only room off the hallway is the small living room, leading to the kitchen.

I was expecting a crack den the way she described it, but all that's been left behind are a few magazines and newspapers on the window sill, and several books on the shelf.

The kitchen is even smaller than the living room.

'We had the units replaced at the beginning of 2001,' says Mrs Sullivan. 'It was overdue then; I dare say it's well overdue now.'

I walk to the sink and look out of the window to the washing line hanging in the back yard. Debbie must have stood here and looked out at the same view. Concrete and a battered wooden gate, under grey clouds and drizzle.

I turn around, my back to the window. To my left is a small dining table under a clock on the wall. I can't picture Dad, with Debbie and Robert, sitting around a table like that. I close my eyes, yet I can't summon an image in my mind. On my right is a row of units — the right wall dominated by a fridge and a washing machine. The place is tiny, claustrophobic.

'I'll take you upstairs,' says Mrs Sullivan, who leads us back to the hall. 'Or rather, you go first — I'll see you up there. My knees are on their way out.'

I'm surprised, given how she manoeuvred over the wall a few minutes ago. I climb the stairs, feeling no connection to this place at all. After driving past it so many times, I thought if I were ever to go inside, I would instantly feel at home. But it feels so cold.

There's a small bathroom at the top of the stairs, a small double room, and a master bedroom at the front of the house. Sally and I go to the window, which is small, considering the room is the width of the whole house.

'My dad used to tinker on his car all the time,' says Sally, looking at Dean over the road. 'I always used to wonder what he actually did, but looking back, he probably used to just love the peace and quiet. Fancy Dean's wife leaving him and taking their kiddy.'

'It happens all the time, I expect,' I say.

It's a sentence that hangs in the air.

'You're not wrong.' Sally pats me on the shoulder. 'Let's hope there's a happy ending for you though, love.'

'Somehow, I doubt that,' I say.

Sally looks at me from the corner of her eye. I wonder if she instinctively knows how a case will end.

'You'll see that this is the biggest room in the house,' Mrs Sullivan says as she enters. She winks at us. 'I'm just practising my spiel. Obviously, it needs a lick of paint in here — you can tell where their pictures were hung.'

'Do you remember much about the time Peter Atherton came back from Tenerife with his children?'

'I remember it all too clearly,' she says. 'I lost my Dennis that spring. Days used to go on

314

forever and I used to spend a lot of time looking out of the window, pretending to watch television. When you hear of something unusual happening, the events around it seem to impress upon the mind.

'I didn't understand what was wrong at first. Just before they went on holiday, there was all this to-do with shouting and whatnot. He used to shout at her all the time. I remember being glad of the peace when they went. The baby would scream for hours before anyone would go to it, the poor little thing.'

My blood runs cold. I hadn't heard this version of the story. I don't know if I want to hear any more. Who would want to learn that no one came to you as a baby?

'Anyway, you don't want to hear about that, dear. I'm sure it's quite common. I used to let mine cry themselves to sleep.' She flaps a hand. 'Sorry — tell me if I go off on a tangent — I do it all the time. In the end, I was glad when they came back. I missed the sounds of the children — the sounds of life. I'm on the end terrace, you see. Then, after a few days, I realised I hadn't seen the mother out with the baby — it was that other woman . . . what was her name — with the dark hair, slim, dressed well.'

'Monica,' I say. 'Her name's Monica.'

'That's right,' she says conspiratorially — as though I'm not part of this story at all. 'Yes, it was her — she was round there all the time. I don't think she stayed the night though — I would've remembered that. But she hardly had her little boy at all. He must have been at his dad's. Complicated family that one.'

'Did you see her husband, Nathan, at all?'

'That tall, good-looking man? I definitely remember that one.' Mrs Sullivan laughs, but when she looks at me, her smile fades. 'I'm sorry, lovey. I keep forgetting all of this is so close to you. It's strange to think that that little baby was you.'

'So,' says Sally, she's beginning to sound a little impatient. 'Did you see Nathan at all after they came back from holiday?'

Mrs Sullivan frowns. 'No, dear,' she says. 'He wasn't the father of that Monica's little boy, was he? I never saw him again.'

Sally quickly thanks Mrs Sullivan, and takes me by the elbow, almost dragging me out of the house.

'Oh God. This is my fault,' she says. 'I had presumed when you had told me in your first email that *Leo lives in America with his father*, that you were referring to Nathan!' She looks around her as though searching for something. 'I've been lax. I should've asked for everyone's full names — I shouldn't have presumed anything, shouldn't have just gone from who went on the holiday.' She hits herself on the forehead. 'Damn!'

'But what difference would it have made? What's Nathan got to do with anything?'

'Anna,' she says, shaking her head. 'He might have *everything* to do with this.'

316

37

Friday, 25 July 1986
Tenerife, Canary Islands
Debbie

It's two o'clock in the morning and we're finally in the apartment. The journey was as bloody awful as I expected it to be. We were camped at Manchester airport for six hours because Peter didn't want to miss the plane. I'd never flown before and dreaded feeling the same panic I experienced in the house of horrors at the fair a few weeks ago — and that was only a few metres high. Monica and Nathan ordered a lager at the bar as soon as we'd checked our bags in, even though it was only four in the afternoon.

'The only way I'm getting on that plane,' I said, 'is if I'm anaesthetised.'

Monica smiled at me. 'Get this woman a double vodka.'

Peter frowned. 'Do you think you should, Debs?'

'It's either that or I'm not going.'

I prayed he wouldn't mention it taking me days to recover after my last bender of three cocktails.

'We could always inject you with something,' said Nathan. 'Works for B. A. Baracus.'

'If you've got it,' I said, 'I'll have it.' I said it without smiling. Monica's face dropped, her eyes darted around.

Let her feel uncomfortable, I thought. It'd serve her right.

On the flight, even though we'd chosen non-smoking seats, the whole cabin filled with grey, choking fog; my eyes constantly watered. It hid the tears, at least.

Luckily, Annie, Bobby and Leo slept for most of the flight, which was just as well as Peter sat on a different row with Nathan and Monica — who had her nose in *Jackie* magazine like she was fifteen again. I sat between the children, with Annie on my lap. Typical. It was like they'd planned it before we got on the plane.

But we're here at last. I'm wearing a white cotton T-shirt and matching trousers — the type of clothes magazines say you ought to wear 'on-board'. But mine are covered with Ribena splashes and cheesy Wotsits dust.

I glance over at Monica, who's trying to work out how to open the patio doors. I should've worn jeans like her — who'd have thought to wear denim to a hot country? And the way she has her sunglasses in her hair looks effortlessly cool. Well, as cool as someone can look, having sunglasses at night.

The kids woke up grumpy and groggy; I hope they get back to sleep now we're here. The boys are sitting on the dining chairs near the kitchenette, eyes wide and looking dazed. Annie's in a buggy, she can't support her own head in it, bless her.

This place looks nothing like the brochure, but I suppose nothing does. All the apartments look the same from the outside. The block next door reminds me of Preston Bus Station. At least it's clean inside. I refuse to do any housework while I'm here (though I can't remember the last time I did any at home).

'Shall we open this, then?' Peter's holding the bottle of red that was in the welcome pack, which also included a bottle of mineral water, a loaf of bread that looks like cake, and six eggs. Ten pounds down the drain — what a rip off.

I look at the wine and my heart starts to pound. I had two double vodkas at the airport, and they've worn off, but I daren't have any more. I feel like crawling under one of the beds as it is.

'It's a bit late for me,' I say. 'We have to get the kids to bed.'

By the time I utter the last three words, the rest of them are on the balcony, marvelling at the heat, 'even at this time in the morning'.

Peter and Nathan are still pissed from the flight. I knew I'd be looking after the children, the grown-ups letting their hair down after *working so bloody hard to pay for it*. I'll have a better time with the boys, anyway.

'Come on, kids,' I whisper. 'Let's see if we can get you to sleep.'

There are two bedrooms, and a bed-settee in the living area. Peter and I drew the short straw on that one.

I drag our massive suitcase into the room with two single beds, before taking Annie out of the buggy. In between the beds, against the back wall, is a white, wooden cot with a mattress that probably has hundreds of different babies' bodily fluids ingrained in it. I place her on one of the beds and unzip the suitcase to find a beach towel to cover it.

'Have you got your PJs, Leo?' I say.

Leo shrugs. It's a silly question, as I can hear Monica exclaiming that there's a barbecue area near the pool; she won't have unpacked yet. I take out two pairs of Bobby's shorts and hand them to the boys.

'It's too hot for proper pyjamas.'

'My daddy took me to Whitby last weekend,' says Leo.

'That's nice, love,' I say.

'Can I phone him tomorrow? He said I can. He said he'd wait by the phone to hear from me.'

'I'm sure they'll have a phone we can use at reception.'

'He'll go to sleep, won't he?'

'Who?'

'Daddy. I don't want him to wait by the phone all night.'

I peel the sheets back on the beds.

'Into bed, boys.' They both jump in and pull the covers up to their shoulders. I sit on the edge of Leo's bed. 'Don't worry, love. He'll have gone to sleep . . . it's the middle of the night. He'll think you're asleep.' He lies his head on the pillow and I bend to kiss his cheek. 'Night, sweetheart.'

I change Annie's nappy on the end of Bobby's bed. Her cheeks are so red — she's not used to this heat. I place her in the cot with her blanket and she looks at the net curtain blowing in the breeze from the open window. There's a sound of a moped in the distance.

A cork pops from the living room and they cheer as though they've never heard one before. God, they can't be starting again this late, can they? They're going to get us thrown out. Perhaps I should encourage them to shout louder.

'Shift up, Bobs,' I whisper. He slides across his bed, and I lie down next to him. There's only one, flat pillow. 'I'll just stay here until Annie goes to sleep.'

'I love you, Mummy,' he says, laying a hand on my shoulder.

'Love you too, Bobs.'

I think Leo's already asleep. He must be used to different beds — his dad has moved house about five times in the past two years. Poor boy. I glance over at Annie, and she's still mesmerised by the curtain — still unable to miss out on anything.

'Night, night, Annie,' I whisper.

But she doesn't even look my way.

★ ★ ★

I wake to Annie's screams and jump out of Bobby's bed. It's already light outside and I manage to pick the baby out of the cot and whisk her out of the room without waking the boys.

Shit. The three sterilised bottles I packed are in the suitcase back in the kids' bedroom.

Peter hasn't even changed the settee into a

321

bed, and he's sprawled on it with one leg on the floor. Did he assume I'd sleep in the children's room? The sight of him makes the rage reach my chest. I bet he didn't even check on how, or where, I was last night.

The empty bottle of wine is on the coffee table next to him, which isn't too bad between the three of them.

Annie is screaming in my ear.

I nudge Peter's leg with my foot.

'Peter!' I hiss as quietly as I can.

I nudge him again. Annie's cries aren't waking him. I'm tempted to pour a glass of cold water on him, but then I remember him ripping the quilt off me last Saturday morning, and how violated it made me feel.

I strap Annie into her buggy and tiptoe back into the boys' room, taking out the bag of bottles and formula from the already-open suitcase.

I pour mineral water into the kettle and flick it on.

Why hadn't I made up bottles last night? Why hadn't Peter? No, that would never do, would it?

After what feels like hours, I pour the boiling water into the bottle. Oh God, it'll take forever to cool. I fill the sink and place the bottle upright in it.

Still, Annie cries. She's going to wake everyone up. I knew it was going to be like this. It's roasting already in this apartment. I grab the buggy and walk backwards, opening the apartment door and shimmying out of it. As I swing the push-chair round, a cool breeze outside washes over me.

The door slams shut, but I don't care if it wakes Peter.

I don't know where I'm going, but I start walking down the light corridor. I pass three other doors before we get to the lift. We're only on the first floor, but I can't face dragging the buggy down the concrete steps. The lift doors open. Inside, it smells of cigarettes and BO. I press the button for the ground floor and hold my breath until we reach it.

The reception area is small. There's a woman on the telephone who doesn't look up as I go past and out of the glass doors. I walk down the side of the building — there are more apartments along it, their walled seating areas empty, except for the white plastic tables and chairs.

My face is colder than the rest of me, but at least Annie has quietened.

There's a woman walking towards me, a carton of milk in her hands. She's frowning at me. Only a few feet away from me now. Oh no, she's going to —

'Oh, love,' she says. She has a southern English accent; it sounds like she's out of *EastEnders*. 'Whatever is the matter?'

'What do you mean?'

'You seem to have . . . '

She points to my white T-shirt. My eyes follow hers. I'm covered in blood. I touch my face; there's blood pouring from my nose.

'Oh my God. I'm so sorry.'

I pull a blanket out from under Annie's pushchair, holding it against my nose.

'What are you sorry for?' She rubs the top of my arm. 'Don't worry, love. Come with me.'

She takes hold of the buggy, turns it around and pushes it down the path. We pass reception — the woman's still on the phone — and take a right along the other side of the block. She opens an apartment door and ushers me inside.

It's so much bigger than ours. There's a settee and two wicker chairs, plus a portable telly near the double patio doors. It takes me a moment to notice a child of about thirteen sitting on a chair outside — his knees brought up in front of him as he uses them to support the comic he's reading.

The woman pulls out one of the chairs around a large dining table and guides me down.

'How old is she?' the woman says, glancing at Annie in the pushchair.

'I . . . er, just over a month old.'

'I guess it's different these days,' she says. 'I used to count in weeks — until he was at least four months old.'

I don't tell her that people still do, but I can't remember how old Annie is off the top of my head. I'd have to count using my fingers. Is she five weeks in three days or four? I know today is Friday, because the next seven days are pictured in my head like white blocks that'll be shaded black for each one that passes.

'It's not that long ago, surely,' I say, looking to the lad on the patio.

'Oh, he's not mine. He's my nephew. But you're right. My son's nearly nine. Time goes by so quickly when they're young, doesn't it?'

She goes over to the glass doors and pulls across the light curtains. It gives the room an amber glow that mimics the sun.

'Will he not mind?' I say.

'He won't notice . . . he's in his own world most of the time.'

She smiles and walks into the kitchenette, picking out a bright white tea towel from one of the drawers.

'I couldn't use that,' I say. 'I'd ruin it.'

She sits down on the chair next to me.

'Don't worry. I'll just buy a new one.' She takes Annie's bloodied blanket. 'I can wash this for you, if you want — I've got loads of tokens for the washing machine. My Spanish isn't as good as it could be . . . I asked for too many by mistake.'

Now that she's sitting so close to me, I see she's probably about the same age as me. It's her short hair that makes her look older from a distance.

I put the tea towel against my nose. 'I've not had a nosebleed since I was a child.'

'Stress, perhaps? Or maybe it's the heat. It's probably nothing serious. Don't worry about it.'

'I think it's probably both,' I say, hoping she won't ask any questions about it.

I don't want to tell her that I think I'm either dying or losing my mind. What if it doesn't stop and I bleed to death? Oh God, I can't breathe again.

The woman places a hand on my arm. 'There, there. Don't panic. I've seen plenty of nose-bleeds. They usually stop after a few minutes.

325

Take a deep breath in.'

I do as she says. Her voice is soothing; it calms me.

'You're brave, bringing such a young one to Tenerife,' she says. 'Where have you come from?'

'Preston.'

'Oh. I've never been there. We're from the south coast, near Eastbourne.'

She's looking at me as I glance at the balcony.

'I know it's early,' she says, 'but I'm looking after him today. Even though he's probably old enough to look after himself. My husband and my sister have taken my little one to the water park. I can't swim — well, I can, but I'm not a strong swimmer. Doggy paddle mostly.' She smiles, but then the smile drops as she looks at the carton of milk still on the table. 'They're probably having an affair.'

My mouth drops open.

'Sorry,' she says. 'I'm always saying too much to total strangers.'

I take the tea towel from my nose. The blood has stopped.

'Don't worry,' I say. 'It makes a change from thinking about my own problems.'

Annie's been quiet since we got here, but she's starting to fret. I'm about to say we must go, when the woman says, 'I'm sure them going to the water park is just an excuse for them to spend the day together. She hated swimming when we were kids — more than I did.'

'I see.'

'I'm sorry,' she says. 'It's just that I haven't anyone to talk to. Everyone I know is friends with all of us. It's a bit tricky.'

For the first time since she was born, I'm glad when Annie starts bawling. I stand quickly.

'I'll have to go. Her milk will've cooled by now.'

'Yes, of course.'

She gets up to open the apartment door, and I wheel out the buggy.

'I never got your name,' she says.

'Debbie.'

'Debbie. Right. I'll make sure to get this blanket back to you nice and clean. I'll leave it at reception.' She leans against the door to stop it slamming shut. 'You take care of yourself. I'll probably see you around. I'm Ellen by the way.'

'Bye then. And thank you.'

'No problem.'

I turn and walk away.

She doesn't look like an Ellen.

38

Anna

I turn on the car stereo: it's Amy Winehouse singing 'Valerie'. When Jack and I started dating, it played on the radio all the time. He used to roll his eyes when it came on. 'The Zutons' version is far superior,' he said. He was a music snob then. He doesn't listen to music in the house these days.

There's still no news about the DNA test. It's been three days since he gave a sample and, apparently, it might be another two days before we get the result. Well, before *he* gets the result. I thought I knew everything about him. But you only ever know what a person chooses to reveal to you. He never told me his ex-girlfriend was pregnant when they split up. Is that something you would share with your wife?

It's one thing after another.

Yesterday, after we looked around my old house, Sally brought up Nathan as we stood by her car.

'Do you have any idea of what happened to him?' she asked.

'He and Monica divorced, I think. She said he'd moved somewhere down south. Leo barely remembered him . . . he didn't spend much time with him as a kid.'

'Does no one mention Nathan? Have you asked about him?'

'It's not the sort of thing I'd bring up. To be honest, Sally, there's a whole host of things I never ask about. I'm scared of hurting everyone's feelings all the time. I thought my dad and Monica fell in love and then she got divorced. I only knew about Nathan from Robert. There's been no need for Nathan to be in our lives.'

'Okay. I'll let you know if I find out anything else.'

She seemed annoyed at me, and I'm not surprised. I should've drawn her out a family tree — it's confusing even to me sometimes.

'I left my DS at home,' says a little voice from the back seat.

I forgot Sophie was sitting in the back. I'm driving on auto-pilot. I flick off the radio and bring myself back into the present.

'Do you want me to turn around and go back for it?' says my guilt.

'No, it's all right,' she says, with a touch of melancholy. 'I'll probably just watch the movie channel all day.'

'Sorry, love. I'm off next weekend. We can do something fun then.'

'Why is Daddy working on a Saturday too? He doesn't usually work on a weekend when you do.'

'It's just this once. And you love going to Nana and Grandad's, don't you?'

She sighs. 'Yeah.'

We pull up outside Dad's — at least my autopilot didn't take me straight to work. I open

329

the door for Sophie and she hops out.

'I need my backpack,' she says, grabbing it from the back seat.

She leads the way up the path. She's such a little individual. As much as I want her to grow into an independent young woman, I love her just as she is right now.

Sophie knocks twice on the door, but there's no answer.

There's a flap of a hand in the front window. I bend to peer through the letterbox and Dad's walking towards me. He opens the front door as I stand.

'Sorry, sorry,' he says.

I let Sophie go in first, ushering her into the living room before joining Dad back in the hall.

'Everything okay?'

There are sobbing noises coming from the kitchen.

'Is Monica all right? How's her arm?'

I scrutinise his face, trying to read his expression. There are remnants of tears coating his bottom eyelashes. I open the door of the kitchen and Monica's sitting at the kitchen table — an array of papers and letters in front of her.

She stands quickly, ripping a piece of kitchen roll from the holder on the wall.

'Is that the time?' she says, dabbing her cheeks, her make-up surprisingly intact. She puts the tissue into her trouser pocket and sweeps the pieces of paper with her left hand.

'How are you feeling?' I ask her. 'Has the pain lessened?'

'It's okay. The doctor said it'll heal in two or three weeks. It's only a sprain.'

'Shall I take Sophie to work with me? I don't mind — she can help in the back.'

'No, no. I love having her here. She stops me wallowing. I'm a terrible patient.'

'What's this?' I say, picking a pink letter up from the pile on the table. 'I've not seen this one before.'

She snatches it from my hand before I can read the writing.

'Nothing, nothing. Don't worry about it.'

'Are all of these about Debbie?'

She settles the pile into a neat square with her unbandaged arm. She sighs loudly.

'Yes.'

'Why are you crying?' I say.

I sense Dad behind me, not knowing where to put himself or what to say.

'I'm just being silly. Thinking about Debbie and everything else.'

I look down at the top of the pile and there's a photo of Nathan. It's not the time to bring it up, but I need to tell them anyway.

'I went to the old house yesterday,' I say. 'With Sally.'

'Sally?'

'The private investigator.'

There's a slight roll of Monica's eyes.

'I met Mrs Sullivan, who still lives next door. She said she never saw anything of Nathan after we came back from the holiday in Tenerife. When was the last time you heard from him?'

'I can't remember.'

Her eyes don't meet mine. Dad helps her to sit back in a chair.

'He phoned a few times, didn't he?' he's talking to Monica. 'He gave you an address he was staying at.'

Monica nods.

Dad looks at me.

'But you're right,' he says. 'I last saw him the night your mother left.' He sits down in the chair opposite. 'I always thought they ran away together. Did Monica ever tell you that Debbie and Nathan were a couple in their teens?'

'No,' I say, trying to catch Monica's eye again, but she's still looking at the picture of Nathan.

'He wrote a few times,' she says. 'And the odd phone call. But I didn't see him. After seven years of no contact, I divorced him.'

'Have you still got his letters?'

She shakes her head.

'Why didn't you keep them?'

'Because he hurt me.' Her shoulders shake as she sobs. 'And I didn't want to upset your dad. Peter and I — all of us — had already started living together. We'd moved on without the pair of them.'

Monica's mobile phone lights up; it's ringing on silent, the caller unknown.

'Aren't you going to answer that?' I say.

She shakes her head, just staring at it.

It stops flashing. I peer at the screen.

'There are eleven missed calls, Monica. What if it's her?'

'How could she know my number? It could be anyone.'

'Then why not answer it?'

She covers her eyes with both hands, elbows resting on the table.

I glance at the clock; it's already 9 a.m. — I should be opening the bookshop now. I really am going to get fired at this rate.

'But after all this time,' I say. 'I thought something might have happened to her — that she was dead. Why have you kept this from me?'

Dad makes a fist and pounds the table.

'Because it's not always about you, Anna!'

'Right, right.' I blink away the tears. 'Right. I'll phone you later to check on Sophie.'

I walk from the kitchen and dart my head around the living-room door.

'See you later, love.'

She nods, her eyes wide. She must have been listening.

'Do you want to come to work with me?' I say, trying to keep my voice even. 'You can help sort through the books — it'll be fun.'

She shakes her head. 'It's okay. I'll try and cheer Monica up. She's always crying.'

'I . . . ' I say, but I can't get into it with her now.

I reach into my pocket — and pull out Sophie's DS. 'Oh!' I look at it as though it were put in my pocket by magic — I thought the weight was my mobile phone. 'Look what I found!'

Her expression changes in an instant.

'Thanks, Mummy!' She gets up and takes it from my hands, then settles into the sofa next to her little rucksack.

'See you later,' I say. 'Don't forget to ring if you need me.'

She waves, her eyes on the console as it chimes into life.

I say a quiet goodbye to Dad and Monica in the kitchen, but Dad is towering over Monica, his arms wrapped around her. She's not crying about Nathan now. The letter she snatched from me wasn't like the rest — its ink hadn't faded, the creases were sharp. If I were to guess, she received that letter this morning.

★ ★ ★

I park around the corner from the bookshop and walk as fast as I can. I get my keys out. Ellen is standing outside the shop. She hasn't a coat; her hair has a fine mist of rain on it, like a halo.

'Sorry, Ellen,' I say. 'I got caught up with childcare.'

'That's okay,' she says, but she's biting her bottom lip, her eyes fixed on the ground.

She follows me inside, into the back room, and I hang up my damp coat.

'I'll make you a nice hot cup of tea,' I say.

'Thanks, Annie.'

I fill the kettle and flick it on, wishing, for the millionth time, that she wouldn't call me that. I get the float money from the safe and carry it through to the bookshop. I hold the blue cotton bag in my hands as I collapse onto the stool. I can't stop the tears falling, my breath is taken over by uncontrollable sobs, even though I'm trying to be quiet.

'Oh, love,' says Ellen, appearing at my side. 'Whatever's the matter?'

'Everything,' I manage to say through sharp breaths.

She goes into the back room and, a few minutes later, places a mug of tea on the counter.

'I've put two sugars in,' she says. 'Here, give me that.' She takes the money bag from me and opens the till drawer. 'Just in case Isobel comes in. She can't say we're slacking then, can she?' She winks at me.

'Thanks.'

I put my hands around the warm mug.

'You don't have to tell me what's going on,' she says. 'But it might help.'

She tilts her head to the side. Her tone is so kind that I do — I tell her everything — about Debbie, about Tenerife. I tell her that Jack might have a child with someone else, that my stepmother is hiding something, and my father always takes her side. I tell her that I've barely spoken to my brother these past few weeks, and I used to be so close to him.

When I finish, Ellen gets up from the chair she pulled in from the back. Her eyes are glossed with unshed tears.

'I met someone called Debbie once,' she says.

My own tears have dried.

'What?' I throw a damp tissue into the bin. 'It's quite a common name.'

'I met her in Tenerife.'

'Did you live there?'

'No, no. It was a holiday.'

335

There's a voice in my head screaming at me; I can't make out the words. It sounds like: *Don't trust her.*

'Ellen,' I say. 'Can I ask you something? I know I said I didn't want to know, but — '

'Why was I in prison?'

I nod slowly, and watch as she puts the coins in their allotted compartments.

She turns to me and says, 'Because I killed someone.'

39

When you kill someone, their soul becomes part of your own — you're together forever. Do you ever come to terms with what you've done? Are there different types of killers, or are we all the same?

They'll never forgive me.

I should never have sent that email. I still haven't replied to the one she sent back. What am I supposed to say? Some things are too big to say in so few words. I've learned that now.

40

Sunday, 27 July 1986
Debbie

We're all sitting around the pool, and I'm enjoying a quiet ten minutes while Annie sleeps in the pushchair next to me. She's not taken to the heat — she's like me. The others have started on the cocktails already while Leo and Bobby mess around in the pool. It's only eleven o'clock in the morning for God's sake.

'It's a scorcher today,' says Peter.

'Yes,' I say. 'We know.'

He's said it about fifty bloody times in two days and I bet he doesn't realise. No one else mentions it because they're nicer than I am. Or maybe life is just one long drama where we repeat ourselves against different backdrops over and over again.

I saw Ellen again yesterday, with her nephew. We were sitting around the pool like today when she approached me. She didn't have sunglasses; she squinted and used her hand to shield her eyes from the sun.

'I've put the blanket in the wash, love,' she said. 'I soaked it yesterday. It should be ready for the little one tonight.'

'Don't worry about it,' I said. 'I brought a spare.'

She glanced at Monica lying flat on the sun lounger in a black bikini — her skin glistening with baby oil, Walkman headphones on her ears.

'All right for some, eh?' said Ellen, wrinkling her nose.

'She's with me,' I said, with a little too much force. 'She's my friend.'

'Sorry, love,' she said. 'Didn't mean to offend.'

We exchanged an awkward goodbye, and she went off to get a slice of pizza for the teenager dressed in black.

Monica's in the same position this morning, only she's in a neon-green bikini. She hasn't one hair on her body. If only I had the time, the energy or inclination to be bothered with that. I've had the same pair of shorts over my swimsuit since we've been round the pool. I'd wear a wetsuit if I could.

'Are you going in the pool today, Debs?' says Monica, barely moving her lips.

Peter and Nathan don't look up from their card game; they're using pesetas with holes in the middle as poker chips.

'I'm not inflicting my blubber on everyone,' I say. 'I'm fine as I am.'

Monica sits up, removing her headphones. I don't think she has any music playing.

'Blubber? What are you like? You look gorgeous!'

'Hmm.'

'The water will cool you off nicely when it gets hotter later.'

I wish she'd shut up about the bloody swimming pool. But I look at it, glistening in the sun, and wish I could be like everyone else — jump in like Bobby and Leo, not care what anyone thinks.

'Why don't you get a cocktail?' says Monica. 'It might chill you out a bit.'

'I am chilled. I can't be drinking while I've got the baby. Peter's on his second drink already. He never drinks cocktails in England.'

She laughs and swings her legs to the side of the lounger.

'We're all here — everyone can help with the baby.'

'Yeah, right,' I mutter.

'I heard that.' Monica stands. 'And that's why I'm going to get you one.'

Before I can argue, she's sauntered off to the bar at the side of the pool. She returns five minutes later with half a pint of an orange creation.

'I'll never drink all of that.'

'Sure you will,' she says, handing me the deliciously cold glass.

She stands over me and I go to place it on the floor.

'No, no. Have a sip.'

I do as she says, my resolve weaker than my mind. I feel the cool drink run down my throat and into my stomach. It leaves a lovely warmth.

'How much alcohol's in that?' I say.

She settles back down and places the headphones over her ears.

'Enough.'

She closes her eyes. So much for her helping with the baby.

I take a longer sip from the straw. Perhaps this holiday would go a lot quicker if I were pissed.

★   ★   ★

I'm sitting on a stool, leaning against the bar. I'm kind of thinking that the mixture of sun and vodka has gone to my head. But at least I feel more like *me* again. This is what I used to be like: fun. Whatever was in those cocktails has done the trick.

Luckily, I had the foresight to make up a day's bottles for Annie and they're all neatly lined up in the fridge in the apartment — like I'm a proper earth mother, or something.

After the first cocktail — I think there were at least three different spirits in there — I stood up and announced: 'Peter!' (I was probably as wobbly as I am now.) Anyway, I said, 'Peter! Make that your last drink. You're looking after your daughter for the rest of the day.'

Monica sat bolt upright. Told you she wasn't listening to music.

'Good on you, girl,' she said. 'I'll get us more.'

Peter rolled his eyes at Nathan. Course he did. Though I don't know why they're suddenly so pally — they barely spoke at the airport. But here, in *Tenerife-ee*, they're getting on like a house on wheels — fire — whatever; it's too hot here. Peter gave the rest of his drink to Monica. I should've been pissed off about that, but I wasn't, because she downed it in one, laughed and dragged me here, to the tiniest bar in the world.

Only, it's an hour or so later, and it's not

341

Monica sitting next to me, but Nathan.

'And so, the trouble is, Debs . . . ' he says.

I think he's slurring his words more than I am. I'm only half concentrating on what he's saying as I've only got one eye open and it's taking in his face. He's got a really nice face, but he doesn't half go on and on and on.

' . . . don't you think?' he says.

'Yeah,' I say.

I can't be bothered to hear what I missed out on. It'll be nothing.

'Really? You agree? That we should start our own pool bar together in Blackpool?'

I feel my nose wrinkle. 'Eh?'

He turns and sips the rest of his drink, slurping the dregs with a straw.

'Knew you weren't listening,' he says.

He orders two more off the cocktail menu. I grab the drink and swivel on my stool so I can look over the pool. Monica and Peter are playing happy families, but I don't mind. I squint and see that Peter's trying to change Annie's nappy, and I smile to myself. Probably the first one he's changed of hers.

'Bet you've never changed a nappy, Nathan.'

He swivels around too, straw in his mouth.

'Hardly the most attractive of bets, Debs.' He pulls his sunglasses over his eyes. 'And no, I haven't. I've never seen myself with children. I mean, I know I have Leo and everything, but it's not the same. Not when her arsehole ex is ringing up all the time.'

'He's hardly an arsehole. He works at the Gas Board . . . or is it the Water Board? Nothing'll be a *Board* soon, the way things are going. Bloody Thatcher privatising everything . . . '

'Steady on, Debs. No need to get political — we're on holiday.'

'It's Ellen,' I say to Nathan, as subtly as I can.

'Why are you talking with your mouth closed?' he shouts, as loud as he can.

'Because she's right — '

'Hello, Debbie! You haven't met my Alan, have you?'

I shake my head, but the straw's still in my mouth. I clear my throat and sit up straighter. I've got to look more grown up.

Ellen's wearing a Hawaiian-print sarong, tied around the waist, and a bikini with cups that look like actual giant shells. Someone get that woman a Piña Colada. Nathan lifts his sunglasses, squints and puts them back on again.

Luckily, Ellen doesn't take offence; she's staring at him, tilting her head to the side.

Her face changes when she looks up and sees where her husband's eyes are; they're on the front of my swimming costume. Oh God.

Alan squeezes past Ellen and holds out his hand to me. His dyed-black hair is gelled back, and he's wearing the smallest swimming trunks I've ever seen. I try not to look at them, but he's got his other hand on his hip.

They must holiday often, as both have skin the colour of cinnamon. I must start wearing sunscreen; Ellen looks older with fewer clothes on.

I shake her husband's hand and it's slick with sweat.

'So this is the delightful new friend you've

been talking about, Ellen.'

She looks up to the sky. 'Can't you stop it, Alan, just this once.'

'You've just had a baby, eh?' he says. 'Nice and ripe, then?' He laughs.

I think I'm going to be sick.

'What did you just say?' Nathan places his drink on the bar behind him. 'You can't talk to a woman like that.'

Alan raises both palms. 'I didn't mean any harm. Ellen'll tell you what I'm like . . . a bit of a joker.'

'Bit of a wanker, more like.'

'What did you say?'

Ellen stands between Nathan and Alan. 'We must get going,' she says. 'I'd say let's meet up for a drink later, but I don't think you'd want to.'

Nathan stands, too.

'Course we should.' He lowers himself to Ellen's height. 'We can't have you isolated because of him.'

Ellen beams at him.

Typical. Everyone falls for his charm.

'That'd be great,' she says.

Nathan turns to the bar as they walk away.

'I think I've just sobered up,' I say.

I'm still facing the pool when Ellen turns and walks back towards me, her flip-flops slapping her heels.

She puts her head close to mine. I smile — thinking she's going to say how kind Nathan is.

'You won't do anything about it, will you?' she says.

'About what?'

I look to Nathan, willing him to see this exchange, but he's talking to the barman.

'I've seen it before with women like you,' she hisses. 'Pretending you're everyone's friend and then stealing their husbands from under their noses. I've seen the way you look at my husband.'

I smile at her. Has she been drinking too? I kick Nathan's ankle, but he doesn't look up.

'What do you mean?' I say. 'I've just had a baby. I've never stolen anyone's husband in my life.'

'I saw what you did just then — playing footsie with Nathan. They might not be happy together, but that's no reason to go stealing him in front of everyone.'

'What are you talking about, *not happy?* I'm not trying to steal him.' I slide down from my stool. 'And you're not invited later after all. You're talking crazy.'

She grabs me by the elbow.

'Oh, I'm the crazy one, am I? Not what your friend over there, holding your baby, said last night.'

She walks off as calmly as she walked over.

'Did you hear what that woman just said?' I say to Nathan.

I turn to him, but he's already standing next to me.

'Yes,' he says. 'Yes, I did. That is one weird bitch. We've been transported to the set of *EastEnders*.' He passes me. another drink. 'Get that down you. We'll not have those two with us for drinks tonight.'

I take too big a sip, and some of the cocktail slips out the sides of my mouth.

'Nathan,' I say, grabbing a napkin and wiping my face. 'You shouldn't call women bitches.'

He laughs and shakes his head at me.

'You're one of a kind, Debs. I'll tell you that for free.'

I'll tell you that for free. It's a phrase my dad uses all the time. I've a sudden pang to be with him and my mum right now. I've never had a confrontation like that before. My shoulders are tense and my stomach is churning.

I feel out of my depth here.

★ ★ ★

It's four o'clock and the pool is half empty. The cocktails are starting to wear off.

'Why don't you go in the pool now, Debs?' says Monica. 'There's a spare lilo over there.'

I pick up her Pimms and lemonade, and down it in one.

'Easy, tiger,' she says, laughing. 'You'll drown if you have any more.'

I stand and stretch, leaving my arms out beside me, enjoying the sun on my face. Annie's on a blanket under a parasol, staring at the logo. I take off my shorts.

'I'll take Annie with me,' I say, picking my baby up. 'I read in a magazine once that babies can swim.'

Monica sits up quickly; for a moment, I see two of her. She holds up her hand and shields her eyes.

'Don't worry,' she says. 'Have a break. I'll look after her.'

'Get off. She's mine. I can do what I want with her.'

'Okay, okay.'

I wait for her to say something else, but she doesn't. She's moving from side to side. Or is that me?

I kick off my flip-flops and walk over to the steps leading to the shallow end. The water feels deliciously cool against my scorched skin. I've been missing out on this feeling for days. Yeah, sod what everyone else thinks. Dad says that people are far too bothered about themselves to worry about what I'm doing.

I glance at a woman in her sixties sitting on a plastic chair beside the pool. She's resting her elbows on parted knees, smoking; her skin's like leather.

It's observations like those that make me realise what Dad says is rubbish. I judge people all the time.

No, no. Stop thinking.

Stop thinking, and start doing.

Another of my father's phrases.

I drag the lilo towards me and hold the bar at the side of the pool as I sit in the middle, causing it to sag.

I'm a whale.

But I don't care right now. I hold Annie close to my chest and it takes a few seconds to balance before I lay my head on the soft inflatable pillow. I kick the side of the pool, and Annie and I float away.

'Isn't the sky beautiful, little one?'

There are a few fluffy clouds. I turn Annie on

her side, so she can look at the water.

She's so beautiful and she came from inside me. How is that even possible? Everything is so new to her. What must that be like? To wipe everything clean and start again.

'You're perfect, Annie.'

I stroke her downy hair, skimming over the patches of cradle cap. A breeze wafts over us and a plane flies above, leaving its cottony trail in the sky.

'They're off on an adventure,' I say. 'Or going home.'

Just saying the word *home* feels strange — it seems so very far away.

Annie sighs noisily; it's the sweetest sound.

Right now, I am happy. I take in the image of the blue sky and my baby, and close my eyes.

This might be the best I'm ever going to feel.

★   ★   ★

Sprays of cold water are on my face.

Someone's shaking me.

I'm under water and I take a short breath by mistake.

My feet land on solid ground. I cough out the water from the back of my throat.

Peter's in the pool, standing. He's pulling Annie out from the water.

'What the fuck, Debbie?'

He holds the baby up. She blinks the water from her eyes before letting out a piercing scream.

'What happened?' I say.

'You fell asleep. Jesus fucking Christ. You feel

348

asleep with the baby on you. You — ' He cradles the baby into his torso. 'There, there. Thank God you're okay, Anna.' He turns his head. 'She could've fucking drowned, Debbie. You're a fucking liability.'

Peter strides towards the steps and hands my baby to Monica, who's standing at the side — tears streaming down her face.

My feet won't move. What have I done? Peter's words register in my mind. She must've slipped from my chest. I thought I was holding her tight, but I haven't slept properly in weeks. I should be running towards her, shouldn't I? Making sure she's okay.

I feel numb, yet I can feel warm tears on my hot skin. I don't know what's wrong with me. I look down, but I can't see the pounding that's coming from my chest. I feel the pulse on my wrist, yet it's the same as normal.

Why am I just standing here?

Annie's screams echo around the whole poolside. I wade across to the steps and climb them.

I'm not here any more. My body is doing everything for me. I just have to put one step in front of the other and I'll be with my family.

The ground is hard beneath my feet. People are staring at me. I can't let their gaze affect me or it'll consume me.

I reach them at the sun loungers. Annie's still crying. That's a good sign, isn't it?

I kneel at Peter's feet.

'I'm so sorry. I didn't mean to.'

He looks to the side before looking me in the eye.

'It's just as well Monica was watching you both.'

A hand grips my arm.

'I should've stopped you going in,' says Monica. 'It's my fault. You were in no fit state.'

No fit state.

'Calm down, everyone,' says Nathan. 'Debs fell asleep. It's hardly the crime of the century. Everything's okay. The baby's fine. Let's just forget it happened, eh?'

Everyone looks up at him. I want what he said to be true. I want everyone to forget. *I* want to forget.

'Where's Bobby?' I say.

Peter frowns. 'He went to the kids' club three hours ago.'

Monica places a hand on his. Her hands get everywhere. *She* gets everywhere. Where does she get the energy to be so bothered about other people?

She turns to me.

'Don't worry, Debs. It could happen to anyone. It probably happens all the time.'

I look up at Nathan, and he rolls his eyes.

'Nothing *happened*. The baby was in the water for two seconds, tops. Give Debs a break, for God's sake.'

I catch the briefest of glances between Peter and Monica. There's something there I've not seen before. They're ashamed of me. I'm a liability, like Peter said I was. I don't know what to do right now. I need someone to tell me the rules of everything.

Monica picks up a towel and wraps it around

my shoulders. It's damp and feels too hot on my skin.

Annie stops crying when Peter puts a dummy in her mouth.

'Where did you get that from?' I say. 'Bobby never needed a dummy. I don't want Annie to have one.'

'It was easier. She's been grizzly all day,' says Peter. 'And thank God I introduced it.'

Monica rubs my shoulders.

'It's all right now — Annie's fine. She'll not remember it anyway.'

Peter sits on a plastic chair next to me.

'I'm sorry, Peter. I've been so tired since she was born. I shouldn't have taken her with me in the pool. I'll not make that mistake again. I'm never going in a swimming pool again.'

His shoulders raise as he takes a deep breath in.

'Okay.' He won't meet my eyes. 'I'm sorry for swearing at you. I panicked.'

Monica stands and clasps her hands together like a *Blue Peter* presenter.

'It's half past four. Why don't we head back to the apartment to get ready for tonight's barbecue?'

'Good plan,' says Nathan.

Monica holds out her hand to him, but he holds his hand out to me.

'Come on, Debs. Let's get you inside.'

My eyes flit between them both.

Monica drops her hand and shrugs.

'I suppose she's the one who needs looking after.'

She mutters something at the end of the sentence, but I don't quite catch it. It sounded like *as usual*.

Peter gets up and walks away; Monica follows close behind. She briefly rubs the part of his back between the shoulder blades.

I look up to Nathan. He's still holding out his hand, so I take it.

41

Anna

As I stand outside Dad's house to collect Sophie, Ellen's words still ring in my ears. After she said those four words — *Because I killed someone* — I didn't know what to say to her. I've never knowingly met a murderer. I'd often wondered what questions I would ask if I discovered her crime, but in reality, I asked nothing. We were alone in the bookshop. What if she said that it was a random murder, someone who pissed her off?

A customer had come in, breaking the few minutes' silence.

'I'll tell you about it another time,' Ellen said, retreating to the back room.

That time didn't come. Instead, I texted Sally Munroe with Ellen's full name and date of birth, in the hope she will be able to find out more than my failed searches on Google. That's if the information on her CV is correct.

Monica opens the door.

'You look better than this morning,' I say, stepping inside, realising I should've called during the day to check on Sophie. 'Are you okay now?'

'I suppose. I guess I have good days and bad.' She holds the handle of the living-room door

353

and hesitates. 'I loved your mother, you know. She was like a sister to me. I would've done anything for her.'

'I know. You've said before.'

Her mouth drops open, her shoulders sag.

'I'm sorry,' I say. 'I didn't mean to snap.'

But she keeps doing that — blurting out that she loved my mother, talking about her in the past tense. These past few days, Monica has given up pretending to be cheerful. She has never admitted to having bad days before.

Dad and Sophie cheer in the living room.

'Your dad brought down his old computer games.' Monica moves her hand from the door and beckons me to follow her to the kitchen. 'Though *game* might be stretching it a little — it's basically a dot going from side to side on the television.'

She stops at the kitchen sink and turns, leaning against it, folding her arms. The letters and papers are still on the table, alongside the RSVPs for Robert's birthday party. Nathan's picture is no longer at the top of the pile; the most recent letter is.

'Can I read it?' I say.

She shrugs. 'Go ahead.'

I grab it before she changes her mind.

I study the envelope. The postmark is dated yesterday, and the writing is in the same small capital letters as the others.

I take out the letter and open it quickly.

Stop asking questions, or there will be consequences. I'm watching all of you. I know where each and every one of you live.

'What the hell?'

Monica's looking at the floor. When she looks up, her eyes are glistening.

'You have to stop looking, Anna.'

'But you got that email . . . that's what started all of this, not me. I'm just following up on it . . . trying to find answers. It's for everyone, not just for me.'

'Can't you see? Since your dad saw that email, we've been coming apart at the seams. Robert's barely been round — he's distracting himself with his work. I doubt he even remembers it's his party tomorrow afternoon.'

'His party . . . ? That's not all you're worried about, is it? Some stupid party?'

'It's not stupid to me! I've spent months organising it. I've got all his friends from school, from uni. I've made him a cake.'

She gestures to the kitchen counter. Under a glass cloche, is a massive chocolate cake, decorated with tiny books.

'But he hardly has any friends . . . ' I say. 'This isn't the point. Stop detracting from the important stuff — '

'Important stuff? You mean Debbie?' She lifts her arms and drops them as though deflated. 'She's always been the important one to you, hasn't she? You need to grow up, Anna. You have people all around you who love you . . . not some woman who abandoned everyone. It's been over thirty years, love. It was only a few years ago that Peter took her photo off the wall. I feel as though she's been looking over me for all of these years — taunting me for taking over her life.'

'But what if something bad happened to her that night, Monica?' I say, quietly. 'Don't you want to know what happened?'

'She left a note, Anna. It says everything in there.'

'How can you be sure it was her handwriting?'

'Because I recognise it, that's why.'

There are tears in her eyes. Why won't she just tell me the truth? She must know more than she's saying.

'Why did the police give up looking for her?' I say.

'Robert said he told you what happened when we got back from Tenerife.'

'But he was just a child. Grandad said Dad was questioned.'

She turns her back to me.

'We — or rather your grandfather — reported her missing a few weeks after we got back from the holiday. They came round, asking why Peter hadn't been to them, wasn't he worried something bad had happened to her? He showed them the note. Your gran and grandad confirmed it was her handwriting, but the police still searched the house . . . asked for her passport . . . it was like they were trying to trick us.'

Who would think like that? She's talking about her and Dad as *we* and *us*. Did she label them as a couple even then, or has it morphed into that?

'But she left the note and had taken her clothes and passport,' she says. 'What else were we to think?' She turns around, still not meeting my eye, tears streaming down her face. 'We all lost someone that night, Anna.'

* ★ ★ ★

It's only eight o'clock on a Saturday night, but Jack and I have already closed the bedroom curtains on today. For the first time in days, my husband is lying next to me. I can tell he's not asleep; he keeps sighing and changing positions.

He'd only worked in the morning, but had been drinking whiskey since three in the afternoon — he was drunk and silent when I got home with Sophie at tea time. He went to bed as I cooked Sophie's dinner, probably forgetting, in his drunken state, that he'd been sleeping in his office in the loft for the past few days. Perhaps because he confessed, he feels his conscience is clear — that he can share the burden of his problems.

It's Robert's party tomorrow night, yet my thoughts drift between Debbie and Jack. *What if Debbie were alive? What if she were dead? Does Jack have a son?*

I wish I had a sleeping pill or something to make my mind go blank, because I don't have the answers.

My mobile vibrates with a text on the bedside cabinet. I'm tempted to ignore it. Whatever it is, it's bound to keep me from sleep, and sleep is what I need. Sophie is fine, Jack is fine. It can't be anything important.

After ten minutes, I can't sleep for thinking about it. I grab the phone. It's a message from Sally Munroe.

En route to Tenerife after a development. Will contact you when I know more. S.

357

Tenerife.

It's going to cost a fortune, but it's the most obvious country to search — the place Debbie was last seen alive. I text my reply.

What have you found out? Would rather know ASAP x

She replies seconds later.

I'd rather tell you when I know more. Don't want to cause unnecessary alarm. S.

I sit up. My heart is banging in my chest. I stand and walk quietly out of the room, clutching the phone in my hand. I glance back at Jack and he's on his side, facing the window. I open Sophie's door and she's fast asleep, star-shaped across her bed. I pick up her quilt from the floor and gently drape it across her.

I pull the door slightly ajar and tiptoe downstairs.

The kitchen floor is cold under my feet. It might be July, but it's been cold today. Though that's not the reason I'm shivering.

The possibilities are running through my mind: *Sally's found Debbie, living abroad; she's found someone who knows her; she's found her grave.*

I hold up the phone and dial Sally's number.

She answers after three rings.

'Hey, Anna. Sorry. I shouldn't have texted you. I just didn't want you wondering where I was.'

'What have you found?'

She sighs. 'I didn't want to tell you over the phone. But I contacted the Spanish Consulate to ask if they have any . . .'

She stops talking.

'Unclaimed bodies,' I say, finishing her sentence.

'Yes,' she says quietly.

'And they do.'

'Yes. There were hundreds across mainland Spain, but there aren't as many in Tenerife. There are three that were found in 1987 and four in 1988. They've already been buried, but the person I spoke to said they've kept various personal items that were found with the bodies. Sorry . . . I know I'm talking in a blunt way about something so close to you. I might find nothing that's connected to your mother, but we must close this line of enquiry. It's where she was last seen alive.'

I pull my dressing gown around me — I'm still shaking. I sit on the nearest dining chair.

'Let me know as soon as you hear anything.'

'Of course. Try not to think about it too much until you hear back from me.'

'I think we both know that's impossible.'

'I know. I'm sorry. Take care, Anna. Speak soon.'

I end the call and throw the phone onto the table.

It's still light outside and the sun is low in the sky. It should be raining now; it should always rain with bad news.

I take a deep breath.

So, this is how it ends.

She died the night she disappeared.

I should've known that all these years, shouldn't I?

I stand and reach for my memory box and place it on the table, taking out my favourite picture of my mother. I hold it in my shaking hands just inches from my face. Her young face beaming into the camera, before I was born, before her troubles began.

Her twenty-seven-year-old face that's now decomposed, buried in an unmarked grave in a Spanish cemetery. My stomach churns as I picture it. I place the photo face down onto the table. I can't do this to myself.

I'm going to find out what happened to her. Has my father been covering up something for all of these years?

I jump. Jack's standing in the doorway.

'What's happened?' he says.

'Sally's on her way to Tenerife. She says there are unidentified bodies — they've been buried, but they kept the belongings they had on them.' My words flow out too fast. I look up at him. 'I should be crying, shouldn't I? I just can't believe it. Why hadn't anyone checked before?'

He walks towards me and grabs me in a hug. This is all it takes for me to break down.

'Oh, Anna.' He strokes my hair. 'Try not to think too much about it until you hear anything concrete.'

'That's what Sally said,' I say between sobs. 'But it'll be all I think about until she calls back.'

He kisses the top of my head, and goes to the cupboard above the kettle, taking out a bottle of whiskey. He pours large measures into two tumblers, adding ice from the freezer. He hands me a glass.

'It'll help you sleep.'

I take a sip. I've never liked whiskey. It burns my throat as I swallow, but the warmth is comforting. Jack pulls out the chair next to me and sits, taking a large gulp of whiskey. He winces as he swallows, leaning back against the chair.

'Oh God,' I say. 'It's going to cost your firm a fortune for Sally to travel abroad.'

'Jesus, Anna! Don't think about that. The amount of times Gerard has paid to have his mistress followed . . . don't worry about it.'

'Really?'

Jack raises his palms. 'Don't ask.'

'Okay,' I say. 'What if one of those bodies is Debbie's?'

'Then I'll help you get through it. I know it sounds crass, but then at least you'll have closure. You've been living under a cloud for most of your life — you need answers.' He reaches over and takes my hand in his. 'I can't imagine what it's like, wondering where your own mother is. I guess I've tried not to make a big deal about it over the years, but it's only because talking about it makes you so sad. I don't want you to feel sad. You're the most important person in my life. Apart from the little one upstairs, of course.'

He smiles.

'I feel as though I've neglected her over these past few weeks,' I say.

'Don't feel like that. She's her usual happy self. And you're a great mother.' He gently squeezes my hand.

'Shall I phone Dad, tell him what Sally said?'

He shakes his head. 'God, no. Think about how you feel, then times that by a hundred. They were married.' He looks up at me. 'Sorry. I didn't mean to be so frank.'

'It's okay. I know what you mean. You don't still think my dad did something to her, do you?'

He opens his mouth, but closes it. He leans back in his chair again.

'I've known your dad for nearly ten years . . . he's a decent man, I know that. When I say those things, I'm just speculating — it doesn't mean I think them.'

'You're just saying that.'

'I'm not. Shall I be truthful with you?'

'Of course.'

'Over these past years, I can see that your dad still mourns Debbie. It's Monica who's always been slightly strange about it all. Don't you think?'

I look up to the ceiling.

'I suppose,' I say. 'I can't go on thinking about what *might* have happened. But I do think Monica is — or she *and* Dad are — hiding something. I thought whatever it is, was kept from me so I wouldn't get hurt.' I look into Jack's eyes. 'As usual,' — I give a hollow laugh — 'I'm thinking everything's about me.'

'Don't be silly, Anna. You see things from your own point of view — most people are the same. Don't think you're any different. And, anyway, Sally Munroe might find nothing. It might be a wild-goose chase.'

He sips his drink.

There's a few minutes' silence before rain starts to patter on the kitchen window.

'What a strange few weeks,' he says. 'Why does everything have to come at once?'

'I've been thinking that. I'm glad I've got you back.'

He raises his eyebrows. 'I never left. I just didn't know how to deal with everything.' He runs a hand through his hair. 'I hadn't thought about Fran for years. It was always just you, you know. I haven't been pining after her for years. She was a girl I dated for a few months when I was seventeen.'

I nod and take another sip.

'I've a confession,' I say. 'That night, on my birthday, I was really pissed off with you — you came home late and had been out for a meal on your own. I went through your wallet.'

He takes his hand from mine and holds the tumbler with both hands.

'I know,' he says.

'What? How?'

'I found the letter years ago. It was in with my old GCSE certificates, but I never thought to get rid of it — it was a harmless teenage love letter. The day I heard about her accident — the day before your birthday — I dug it out — I don't know why. I guess I wanted to see her last words to me. Then I heard you coming up the stairs and I panicked, put it in my wallet. When I looked at the photo of you and Sophie a few days later, I could see something behind it — I knew I wouldn't have put it next to your picture. I felt such a shit, forgetting your birthday. I had so much on my mind, and then when I saw the letter had moved — I felt so guilty, I couldn't look you in the eye. I couldn't talk to you without feeling bad.'

'I thought you were having an affair.'

'I'm sorry. I should've just said what was going on. But you got that email, and everything changed. I didn't want to burden you with what was going on with me.'

I lift up my glass to take a sip, but I don't think I can stomach it. Jack takes the glass from me and places it on the kitchen counter. I watch as he pours milk into a mug and puts it in the microwave. When it beeps, he pours the whiskey into it and stirs in a teaspoon of sugar. He places the hot mug in front of me.

'That should do it. I saw my mum make it for my dad when I was a kid.'

I take a sip and it's delicious.

'Does it help?' he says.

'A little.'

'Are you still up for Robert's party tomorrow?'

'I have to be. I can't let him down — even though it's the last thing he wants. You're still coming, aren't you?'

'Of course.' He stands up and picks up both our drinks. 'Come on. Let's take these upstairs.'

We're walking up the stairs when Jack's phone pings with an email. We go into the bedroom and he places the drinks on my bedside table. I watch as he opens his mail.

He looks up after reading it.

'It's from Fran's brother,' he says. 'The other man has had his DNA result back.'

I sink onto the bed.

'And?'

'He's asked if I want to know from him or to wait for my own result.'

'What do you want to do?'

'I've prepared myself to hear by post.' He sits down next to me. 'But this will affect us both. I've kept you out of this, as you were going through enough shit, but this is about a child who's just lost his mother.'

I put my arm across his back.

'You know I'll support you whatever the outcome, don't you?'

'I'd hoped that. I didn't take it for granted.'

He leans back on the bed and takes out his phone, and scrolls to a picture.

'This is Matthew, when he was ten. Simon, Fran's brother, sent it to me. He said we looked alike. I can't see it though, can you?'

I take the mobile from his hands and look at the lovely little boy staring back at me.

'It's hard to tell, Jack. I look nothing like my dad.'

I bring the picture closer and see a nose that looks the same as Jack's, the tilt of the head and the closing of one eye in the sun. I've known what it's like for my biological mother to be absent, but Monica has been an amazing parent.

I look into the little boy's eyes: he knew his mother. The pain he must be going through must be unbearable. He must feel so lost. I just hope his family haven't told him about the uncertainty of his paternity. That shouldn't get in the way of the boy's grief.

I hand the picture back to Jack.

'Whatever he needs, we'll be there for him.'

Jack takes the phone, holds it against his stomach. He wipes away the single tear that rolls down his face.

42

Sunday, 27 July 1986
Debbie

Peter's letting me get ready in peace, as he's reserved a barbecue in the gardens at six and he doesn't want me to be late. *In peace*. He means I should sober up, and now I'm soaking in a bath of salty water with bubbles.

I'm an embarrassment to him. Why can't I just be normal? I almost killed our child, for God's sake. I don't want to think what would've happened if Monica hadn't been watching over us. She's our guardian angel, I suppose.

But Annie's fine. That's what I tell myself again and again.

I feel homesick. And I *am* drunk, I think. It's only the afternoon, but people get away with drinking earlier on holiday. Or rather, everyone else does. I shouldn't be allowed near water again. Perhaps that's what he wants now: me to fall asleep in this bath, into an oblivion of salt water and Mister Matey.

Before the swimming-pool incident, Nathan and I drank four cocktails at the bar. He must be able to take his drink, because he's fine. I can hear them all laughing at something he's said in the living area.

There's only a small mirror in this bathroom,

above the sink. It doesn't even have condensation it's so hot here. It's almost unbearable. I keep saying that: unbearable. It rolls too easily in my thoughts. I must say it all the time.

My thoughts are everywhere. That's the trouble with peace.

What the fuck was Ellen on about earlier? As if I'd go near her letch of a husband . . . and her thinking she knew my character. She couldn't be more wrong. I'm not interested in anything like that. It's bad enough having the trouble of one husband, without getting into the complications of having an affair. I can't even look after myself.

Peter and Monica are getting on well. Neither have mentioned my problems from home, though they might have talked about it amongst themselves. I'm past caring right now. It's all been trumped by my behaviour this afternoon. I thought Monica wasn't maternal before this holiday — she was only nineteen when she had Leo. She mothered him as though it were a job. But after today, and hearing her now with Annie, she's like a different person. The walls are so thin.

'I'm sure Annie just smiled, Nathan,' she's saying.

'It's probably wind,' says Peter, repeating what my mother said about Bobby at that age.

'Have we got any beers in the fridge?' says Nathan.

The water drips off me like I'm a washed-up whale as I sit up in the bath. The bubbles have slipped off me and my belly is hanging over like Father Christmas's. I prod my white, stretch-marked stomach and my finger goes in at least two inches. I should be bothered about it, but I'm not.

'Hurry up, Debs!' shouts Monica at the bathroom door. 'You've been in there an hour. I need to wash this chlorine off me before we go out.'

'Really? That long? Did you put your watch forward by mistake?'

'What?'

'Never mind. I'll be out in a minute.'

It doesn't matter what time her watch says compared to mine — time is passing the same, isn't it? I used to think like she did — I used to get excited about going out. It's probably because I've got two kids now, and she only has one. That's why she cares about what she looks like. It must be that.

I pull the plug and stand, grabbing the shower rail for balance as I climb out. It must be nice to have a shower — so much quicker. I think this for only a few seconds before realising showering would still be too much of an effort. What's the point of bathing or showering every day if you hardly go anywhere?

I grab the outfit from the hook on the back of the door. Monica must've selected it from my suitcase. It's my favourite baggy black dress and I love her for choosing it for me. She does know me after all.

I dress and look at the top half of myself in the mirror. My hair is frizzy, and my skin is blotchy, but it'll do.

I open the bathroom door and expect a waft of cold, but the air's stifled.

How much would it cost to telephone Mum and Dad from here?

★ ★ ★

I've been placed on a white plastic chair around a white plastic table next to Nathan and Monica. Peter's happy because he's *manning* the barbecue. He gave me a glass of sangria — almost half a pint. I tried to protest, but he said, 'You deserve a night off after the day you've had.' It's like he's a different person to this afternoon.

Monica's on baby duty. She put a roll of film in the old camera my dad gave Bobby, and gave Leo one of those new disposable ones. They're taking pictures of the floor — God knows what insects they'll find over here. At least it's keeping them quiet. Bobby's such a good boy. I used to call him Mummy's Special Soldier when he was smaller, but like most things, it passes.

He's been looking at me funny since this afternoon — like he doesn't believe it's really me, that an alien's possessed his own mother. Perhaps that's true.

Oh shit. Ellen's walking over. She's only fifty or so yards away. I slide down in the chair.

'Who the fuck invited her?' I hiss to Monica. 'I told her not to come.'

She follows my gaze.

'Oh. Sorry. I forgot to mention, Peter spoke with them earlier — they almost invited themselves, or rather, she did.'

'That bloody woman's a psycho. One minute she's really nice to me, the next she accused me

370

of eyeing up her perv of a husband.'

Monica turns sharply to face me.

'Are you kidding? Him?'

She turns to look at the vision that is Alan, complete with beer-belly overhang. We could almost be tummy twins.

'*Him?*' I say. 'You're meant to be shocked at the insinuation of *me* having an affair.'

'Yeah, that too,' she mutters under her breath; they're only a few feet away. 'That woman is deluded.'

In an instant, Monica plasters a smile on her face and stands, holding out a hand to the glorious couple. They're matching in neon green — her with a boob-tube dress, and him with long shorts (no T-shirt).

Bobby and Leo come towards us, sniggering. They both take a picture of them. That photo will really cheer me up when I get home.

Alan sits next to Nathan, and Ellen pulls out a chair next to me. She smiles when Peter hands her a glass of sangria.

'Well, isn't this nice,' she says, sitting back, admiring the view of the concrete apartment block next door. She leans towards me. 'Heard about your *Miami Vice* episode in the swimming pool today. It could've gone so wrong if your Don Johnson over there hadn't come to your rescue.'

She's looking at Monica. My mouth drops open. Ellen hated the sight of her yesterday. I feel uneasy just being next to her.

'I was overtired,' I say. 'It's having a newborn.'

'Hardly. You were necking those cocktails back. Still,' — she pats me on the hand — 'we

371

can't all be Wonder Woman, can we?'

'Quite,' I say, sucking my straw. 'I'm more Miss Piggy than Wonder Woman.'

Ellen bends over, and her shoulders shake. It's like she's laughing, but there's no sound.

'Oh, you're a card,' she says.

She raises her head; her face glowing after too much sun.

'Is your sister not joining us tonight?' I say.

She glances at me from the corner of her eye, her smile gone.

'I forgot I told you about her. Don't say anything, will you? You caught me at a bad time.' She sucks sangria through her straw. 'She's babysitting our boy. No more nosebleeds, then?'

'No.'

Monica pushes a sleeping Annie in her buggy away from the table when Alan lights up a cigarette. She leaves my baby a few feet away from us all. Nathan stands and walks over, kneeling in front of her. I watch as he places her foot on his chest and smiles at her. I should warn him that he might wake her, but I don't want to interrupt the moment. I've never seen him like this with a child before.

'You're all doe-eyed watching them two,' Ellen says in my ear. 'Be careful his wife doesn't see. I must say, though, he's a bit of a dish.'

I don't reply. If she continues whispering in my ear like this, I'm going to move.

Nathan stands. He leaves Annie and walks behind me to get to his chair, ruffling my hair as he passes.

'Sorry, Debs,' he says. 'I couldn't resist. She's

just the most beautiful baby. She looks just like you.'

The banter between Monica and Alan quietens as Nathan returns to his seat.

Ellen's voice is in my ear again. 'Awkward.'

Thank God Bobby and Leo are walking towards us.

'Can I have a picture, please?' Bobby says to Monica and Nathan.

Nathan leans towards her, placing a hand on her lap. If you saw that, you'd think them a happy couple. But they're not. They've barely spoken today; they've barely spoken all holiday.

They smile their *cheese*, which fades as the boys leave.

Seconds later, Alan's leering over Monica.

'Doesn't Nathan mind all of that in front of his face?' Ellen's lit a cigarette; she takes a long drag. 'I know *I* would. But I'm used to it.' She leans closer again. 'He gives me a slap sometimes . . . when I give too much mouth. Does yours do that?'

'Mine?' The sangria's gone to my head. I look at Peter, and can't imagine him even thinking of hitting me. I shake my head. 'No.'

'You've got a good one there, then.' She takes another drag. 'Shit. I don't know why I'm telling you this — I tell no one, not even my family. You've got one of those faces, I suppose. The way you're sitting there like that . . . it's like you're apologising for fucking being alive.'

I didn't want to engage with her; I didn't want to talk to her, but I can't help it.

'Your husband shouldn't hurt you, Ellen,' I say.

373

'All the fellas I've been with have. Must be me then, mustn't it?'

My hand reaches over to hers.

'No,' I say. 'It's not you.'

She bats my hand away.

'Don't you start being kind to me. It'll set me off.'

She dabs the back of her hand on the tears in her eyes. Her blue eyeliner and mascara doesn't streak. She must know the right make-up to wear.

'I'm sorry about being off with you at the cocktail bar,' she says. 'I'm allowed to be feisty to other people especially when he's only had a few drinks — and as long as it's not targeted at him. It's when he's had too many that I have to keep my mouth shut.'

Nathan moves his seat next to me; Ellen turns her head to Monica. Alan saunters over to poor Peter at the barbecue.

'Not drinking the sangria?' says Nathan. 'You've still got half left.'

'I've had more than enough booze today.' I smooth the black fabric over my legs.

'One can *never* have enough booze, Deborah.' He downs what red drink is left in his glass, and we sit in silence. I listen in on the women next to me, which isn't hard: Ellen's voice is so loud it echoes.

'How long have you and Nathan been married?' she shouts.

'Two years.' Monica's voice is quieter.

'He's not the boy's father then?'

'No. I didn't marry Leo's father. I was only

nineteen when he was born. It was a fling, but Leo still sees his dad.'

'Isn't that modern?'

'That's one way of putting it. It was hard being a single parent, but I stayed at university — my mother paid for childcare. After uni, I managed to get a good job to support us both. I got together with Nathan when Leo was three . . . I met Nathan through Debbie — they went out with each other when they were teenagers. They bumped into each other on the street a few years later, and Debbie gave him my number. I'd met him myself when we were younger, but they spent a lot of time alone . . . I only got to know him properly all these years later.'

'I can see that those two used to have a thing,' says Ellen.

I shift in my seat. They must know I can hear.

'What makes you say that?' says Monica.

My face burns. I shouldn't listen, but I can't help it.

'He does seem rather taken with her, doesn't he?' Ellen's voice isn't as loud; she's leaning into Monica's ear.

'I . . . I don't know.'

Thank God Peter is far enough away. I've only met Ellen a few times, but she's poisonous. I turn to Nathan, thinking he won't have heard a thing, but he's looking at me, frowning.

'What's that silly cow talking about now?' he whispers. He takes my hand. 'Come on. Let's go for a walk, away from that crazy couple.'

'She's had a rough time with that shitty husband of hers.'

'That's no excuse.'

He pulls me up from the chair; it doesn't take much effort as my body is willing, betraying me.

'It's terrible timing, us going for a walk,' I say, glancing at Monica.

She's narrowing her eyes at Ellen. I hope she sees that Ellen's shit-stirring — trying to deflect from her own awful home life.

'I'm just taking your wife for a wander,' Nathan hollers to Peter.

Peter gives a salute with the barbecue tongs. My husband's such a lovely man.

Nathan tugs at my hand until I follow.

'We can't be long,' I say. 'The food'll be ready soon.'

He releases my hand and puts both of his in his pockets. I look at his arms. He's always tanned quickly — his skin would turn golden in a conservatory, whereas mine would turn pink, like a pig's.

We walk down the side of the apartment block and out onto the sandy road. Topless men on mopeds whizz past. English tourists, wearing socks and sandals, walk along miserably, laden with carrier bags of food. Probably full of tea bags, baked beans and digestives.

'I found this gorgeous view the other day,' says Nathan. 'I know there are plenty of lovely sights around here, but even though there's a road right next to it, it feels so peaceful. The sound of the waves drowns out the cars. It has a bench, too — perfectly placed. It's not far away.'

We walk in silence, going uphill until we reach a bend in the road. There's an area of dried, yellow grass with a small seating area. Nathan takes my hand and leads me over rocks and stones. About five feet from the bench, there's a drop, with the blue sea below.

'Are we on the cliffs?' I say.

'Yeah. This one's called La Gran Caída.'

We sit on the bench. There are cars speeding past on the road behind us, but the sound of them quickly fades in my ears.

'This is beautiful,' I say.

'I thought you'd like it.'

'What do you mean?'

'You must know.' He's staring straight ahead at the waves, crashing on whatever's below — I can't see from this angle. 'There was only ever you, Debs.'

'But . . . but we're married. To other people! Nothing can ever happen between us.'

He turns his body to face me, raising a leg and resting it on the seat.

'You feel the same, then?' he says. 'I knew it.'

'No . . . I've just had a baby. My hormones are all over the place.'

He puts his arm around my shoulders.

'I can keep you safe. Peter can't.'

'Safe from what?'

'Those letters we've been getting. I know who sent them. I'll stop them.'

'Who sent them?'

He taps the side of his nose.

'Don't you worry about that.'

'Nathan! Stop being weird. What's wrong with you?'

He slumps against the back of the bench, as

though I've winded him.

'I'm not being weird. I'm looking out for you.' He turns his gaze back to the ocean. 'And Monica's too busy fawning over Peter to bloody notice anything I do.'

I nod slowly. 'Okay. So *that's* what this is really about. You're feeling neglected by your wife.'

'If anything, it's the other way around.'

I look at Nathan: I loved this man once. But he was a boy then — intense, troubled. He could still be like that now.

'Just talk to her, Nathan. Get everything out in the open. You love each other. Don't waste it all on some idea you have of me. It's not even real. If you lived with me for five minutes, you'd go off me.'

'No, I wouldn't. Before you had Annie, Peter used to rave about how relaxed you were. Monica's so caught up with what everyone thinks of her — the dad she never sees, the mother who doesn't give a shit.'

'Hang on. Before I had Annie?'

'I'm not saying you're a nightmare now,' says Nathan, smiling, 'I'm just saying that I haven't spoken to Peter properly since.'

I lean back against the warm concrete of the seat.

'What does it all matter, anyway?' I say.

'What do you mean?'

I stand. The dress sticks to the back of my legs. I peel it away.

'*See, the only person who loves you is as crazy as you are — you're making him that way. You might as well do your family a favour and leave*

*them in peace. They're better off without you
— can you see that now?'*

'Oh, shut up,' I say.

'What?'

Oh God.

I'm replying to the voice in my head.

'Doesn't matter,' I say. 'Let's head back.'

We walk back to the apartments in silence. Only Monica looks up as we get back to the barbecue area. Ellen's standing next to Peter near the barbecue, twirling her hair with her fingers. If she's trying to make her husband jealous, it's not working; Alan's face is just twelve inches away from Monica's, whose chair is backed up against a tree.

'I think you'd better rescue your wife,' I say to Nathan.

'She'll be fine.'

Annie's still in the buggy. Nathan sits at her feet on the grass.

I tut loudly at him and walk towards Monica.

'Would you mind taking a look at something for me?' I shout to her.

She stands straight up, and shimmies sideways against the table to escape.

'That sounds interesting,' says Alan. 'Room for a third?'

I narrow my eyes at him.

'You stuck-up bitch,' he says. 'Who do you think you are?'

Nathan gets up from the grass.

'What's your problem? Do you have an issue with women? You can't talk to Debbie like that.'

He walks towards Alan, his chest puffed.

'I just did.'

Alan leans over the table.

'Hey, hey.' Peter walks towards them, tongs in one hand and a bottle of beer in the other. 'The food shouldn't be long. How about a bit of music?'

He reaches under the table for his cordless tape recorder (probably got it on special with his discount at Woolies) and puts on 'Club Tropicana'.

Alan sits back down; Ellen sits in the chair next to him. She strokes the side of his face, but he bats her away.

Monica puts a hand on my wrist, and guides me away from them.

'What did you want to show me?'

'Nothing,' I say. 'I was trying to rescue you from that twat.'

'Thanks, Debs.' She frowns at Nathan, who's sitting back on the grass next to the pram, a bottle of beer in his hand. 'No thanks to you,' she says to him. 'He could've attacked me for all you care.'

'Don't be silly,' he says. 'You can handle yourself just fine.'

'What?' She walks towards him. 'He's twice the size of me.'

'Monica, *everyone* is twice the size of you.'

She glares at him, but he looks away.

'Where did you go with Debbie before?'

It's like I'm not standing here, next to them.

'Just a place.'

Why can't he just lie? He's still not looking at her; he's pulling out tufts of grass and flicking them away.

'It's embarrassing,' hisses Monica, 'you fawning over Debbie. Everyone can see it, you know.'

'I don't give a shit what you or anyone else thinks.'

Monica's face is red. She glances at me, her eyes glistening.

'Sorry, Debs,' she says. 'He must really annoy you.'

'Monica! Stop that.' Nathan's looking at her now. He gets up slowly. 'What makes you dictator over everyone? You can't control my feelings. It doesn't matter if I like Debbie. I won't do anything about it.'

'Only because she wouldn't let you.'

The talking has stopped behind us. I turn and see the three of them looking at us, the song has ended. Peter's standing next to the stereo. His head jerks back — he's wide-eyed. He blinks several times before 'Agadoo' booms out from the cassette player. He looks so hurt that I feel a pain in my chest. I walk towards him and reach a hand out to touch his, but he moves it away.

'Do you love Nathan?' he asks.

My eyes meet his.

'Of course I don't. I don't think I ever did, even when we were kids. I've just been a bit lost recently. I — '

'I don't believe you. You've been acting strange for weeks. Nathan's always around . . . that little outing you went on to St Annes . . . '

'I thought you didn't mind about that. Nathan said he. mentioned it to you before.'

Peter raises his eyebrows, looking at Nathan, shaking his head.

'You don't have to pretend any more, Debbie,' says Nathan, striding towards me. He takes hold of my hand. 'It's all out in the open now.'

I wrench my hand from his.

'No. That's not right. Why are you making this up? You're deluded.'

He looks up to the sky before looking at me — his eyes slightly bulging.

'Oh, I'm the deluded one, am I? I'm not the one hearing voices.'

It's like he's taken the air from my lungs. I bend over to catch my breath.

'Fucking hell, Nathan,' says Monica. 'What did you say that for?'

My knees buckle, and I fall to the ground.

'Why did you tell him?' I whisper to Monica.

'I thought it would help to try to . . . Oh God, I don't know. I don't know what's happening here. It's not my fault. I've always tried to help you.'

'See.' It's Alan, behind me. He's revelling in this. 'Told you she was a crazy bitch.'

There are footsteps towards the table behind me.

'Just fuck off, will you.' It's Peter.

'What?' says Alan.

'You heard. Get lost. You're not welcome any more.'

'How bloody rude!'

'Alan,' says Ellen. 'We have to go.'

I turn around and Ellen takes hold of her husband's arm, pulling him from behind the table. He shakes her off. I see Bobby and Leo fifty feet away — their cameras pointed at the ground. They haven't noticed the commotion, thank God.

'I was going to leave anyway,' Alan says, putting his sunglasses on, walking down the path. 'Worst barbecue I've ever been to.'

Ellen follows behind him.

Peter's standing there, holding the metal tongs. Annie lets off a piercing scream.

'Well, just great, everyone,' he says.

'I'll see to her,' I say, crawling on my knees towards her. I unclip the straps and lift her into my arms. 'There, there.' I reach under the pram and there's a bottle of milk that's cooled. I take off the lid and place it to her lips. She jams her mouth shut. 'Come on, little one.'

I try again, droplets of milk spill down her chin. It's like she's holding her breath — her face gets redder and redder. I take the bottle away and she opens her mouth with a big scream. I stand and rock her in my arms.

'There, there,' I whisper. I kiss the top of her head and hold my little finger against her tiny hand. She doesn't grab it like she usually does. I walk up and down; still she screams. 'Shh, Annie. It's okay. Everything's okay now.'

The other three are just standing there, watching. Monica shakes her head and walks over to us.

'Do you want me to have a try?' she says.

'No, no. I can do this. I'm her mother.'

'I know, Debs. But you're stressed. She'll be able to sense it.'

'What? I'm not stressed! It's you lot arguing that's upset her. Can't you see that?'

'We weren't exactly arguing. We were only talking.'

I look to Peter, to Nathan.

'You were arguing, weren't you?'

Nathan shrugs.

'We didn't raise our voices,' says Peter.

'Oh, great. You're ganging up on me as usual.' Annie's face is almost purple as she screams.

'We're not,' says Monica. 'It's just that you're out of sorts — '

'Have you forgotten what you and Nathan were just talking about? It wasn't me causing all of this — it was you.'

'But can't you see, you're acting strange right now? You're pacing back and forth so quickly — you're almost shaking Annie.'

Peter lets the tongs drop from his hands.

I stop moving. Is that why I'm breathless? Was I really doing what she says I was doing?

'Here.' Monica walks towards me slowly. Her smile is false, I can sense it, she's nervous — I know her too well. Her hands tremble as she reaches for Annie. 'Just let me see if I can stop her crying.'

I let her take my baby from my arms.

Monica cradles Annie close to her chest. 'There, there.'

She says the same words as I did, but her voice is so calm. I don't think mine was.

It only takes a few seconds for Annie to stop crying.

They're all looking at me again. I walk away, still facing them.

'I tried,' I say. 'You all saw that I tried.'

I turn, and I run.

I'm lying on Bobby's bed as it's the one nearest the window. The breeze makes the net curtain billow like my mother's skirt when she hangs the washing out. I'm so homesick, but not for mine and Peter's home: for my parents' house. Dad always knows what to say to make me feel better. He probably knows because of what happened to Mum after I was born.

I haven't been abroad before — never been on a plane. Had I told Peter that, or had he assumed I had? Mum and Dad couldn't afford foreign holidays when I was growing up, not with Dad being constantly threatened with redundancy. I've been ashamed about it in the past, not wanting to draw attention to our poverty, but everyone probably knew anyway — we weren't the only ones.

Gleeful screams come through the window from the pool. I kneel up and pull across the net curtains. Peter's watching over Bobby and Leo as they jump in and out of the water. Annie's buggy is next to him and he's pushing it backwards and forwards; she must be asleep — I can't hear her crying.

Bobby's made friends already; it's so easy at that age. The temporary nature of life is more visible when they're young.

His hair looks darker when it's wet — it doesn't look as red. Luckily his skin doesn't burn as easily as his dad's and mine.

Just look at him. He's not even wearing arm bands and he's jumping in and out of the pool.

And he's swimming! Who taught him that?

I lie back on the bed.

Annie was so distressed at being anywhere near me. Everyone's better off without me.

I sit up and swing my legs to the floor, slipping on my sandals. I stand and lift out one of Annie's blankets, and inhale the smell. But it's the one Ellen washed. It doesn't smell the same. I throw it back into the cot. Now isn't the time to be sentimental, anyway.

I know what to do now to make everything better for everyone.

I walk to the front door of the apartment and take a last look around. I shan't miss it.

I open the door, but there's someone already standing there: Nathan.

He's following me around like death's shadow.

He pushes me back inside and closes the door. He leans against it.

'I thought you'd come back here,' he says.

He presses his hands behind him, against the door, and pushes himself towards me.

'Why are you acting so strange, Nathan?'

'Me acting strange? Look in the mirror! You were all over the place twenty minutes ago, and now you're all calm.'

'I haven't got time for this.'

I try to push him aside to get to the door, but he puts his arm across it.

'Look, Debs, I'm sorry. I didn't mean that — saying you're acting strange. It's Monica. It's all her fault, isn't it?'

I stop struggling to get away from him.

Standing back, I look at his face. He's usually cool in the heat, but he's dripping with sweat; his sideburns are so wet they've gone curly.

'I've seen how jealous she is of you,' he says. 'How do you think it makes me feel? Realising my wife hates me — that she's in love with her best friend's husband?'

I fall against the wall.

'That's not true. She wouldn't do that to me. We're like sisters.'

'Are you, now?' he says. 'So why have you been fantasising about me?'

'I . . . ' I think back to the time when I was pregnant, and just after I had Annie. My head, my hormones, had been everywhere. But how did he know? Was I that obvious? 'It was just a silly crush,' I say. 'For God's sake . . . when I was expecting Bobby, I had a crush on the postman.'

He wrinkles his nose. He moves towards me and puts a hand on my shoulder; the other strokes my face.

'I know it's not a silly crush, Debs,' he says softly. 'We were meant to be together . . . childhood sweethearts.'

I take hold of the finger stroking my cheek and push it away.

'We were never sweethearts.'

'But we were in love.'

'We had a great few months, but you wouldn't give me space. You even hated me spending time with my parents.'

He breaks into laughter.

'Jesus Christ, Debbie. Who wants to spend time with their own parents — especially at that age?'

'I was seventeen. I pretended to be street-smart, but I was immature.' I look away from his gaze. 'I probably still am. I'm letting them down.'

'Who?'

Nathan tilts his head to the side. The squeals of delight from the swimming pool float through the window.

'Everyone.'

'It's Monica who made you think you're crazy. She's been telling everyone you've been hearing voices . . . that you've been wandering the streets in bare feet.'

'She hasn't told everyone.'

'You don't understand. She's a lot sneakier than you realise. She gets into people's heads — makes them think she's oh-so innocent, so helpful.'

'That's not true.'

'She's really got you fooled, hasn't she? She's played a long game, I'll give her that.'

'I've known her since I was fourteen — longer than I've known you or Peter. She'd never have an affair with my husband . . . or make me think I'm going crazy. What would she gain from that?'

He shrugs and walks to the fridge, pulling out a bottle of beer. He opens the lid with a can opener and drinks almost half of it.

'Ahh. Just what I needed.' He wipes his mouth. 'I know she doesn't love me. She's never home. I don't know why we're still together

— it's not as if I'm the kid's father. She's always wanted more children. But I can't be arsed with all of that.'

'*The kid?* You can't call him that. And Monica loves you. She's always saying so.'

'All lies, I'm afraid, Debs.'

He holds my gaze; he's no longer sweating. Nathan always was a good liar. *No, I didn't make silent phone calls to your house,* he said all those years ago. *It wasn't me who threw stones at your bedroom window.*

I thought he'd grown out of lying — that Monica got the better version of Nathan. But she didn't, did she?

'I can't do this any more,' I say.

I go to the door, expecting him to stop me, but he doesn't. I open it, and he doesn't move.

'Where are you going?'

'For a walk.'

'I'm telling the truth.'

'Whatever, Nathan.'

He reaches into his pocket and pulls out a pink note.

'She wrote these letters.'

He's holding the paper in the air. I swipe it from him and put it in my pocket.

'I don't believe you.'

'Why would I lie to you?' he says. 'You'll find out the truth soon enough.'

He grabs the top of my arm and pushes me against the wall. He brings his hand up, his thumb and index finger circle my neck.

'Just do it,' I say, closing my eyes.

'Really?'

He pushes his knee between my legs; he raises it.

'No, not that.'

His hand grips tighter around my throat; I open my eyes.

'No!'

He tilts his head to one side.

His other hand rests on the wall above me.

With my right hand, I grab the bottle out of his hand and smash it on the wall at my side; cold beer drips onto my feet.

I bring the jagged glass towards his neck. He takes his hand away from me. He holds both up in surrender.

We turn our heads to face the apartment door as it opens. Monica.

She looks from me to Nathan, her eyes wide.

'What the hell is going on? What are you doing, Debbie?'

I drop the shattered bottle and run out of the open door.

I sprint down the corridor, to the road, and past the row of shops. Tears are running down my face and my lungs burn.

'*Don't stop*,' says the voice. '*Keep running.*'

'I *can't* stop,' I whisper back. 'I never want to stop.'

★ ★ ★

I must've been going round in circles, because it's dark and I've reached the clifftop Nathan showed me earlier. I flick off my sandals and walk close to the edge.

The rock I'm standing on is only twelve inches long — just a foot stopping me falling into the water nearly five hundred feet below. The stone is cool under my bare feet.

It's quiet; there aren't many cars going past behind me. It must be late, or early. There's a lovely warm breeze, one you don't get in England when it's dark. If it gets stronger, it might push me over the edge. Hitting water from this height is meant to be like landing on tarmac.

I've always been afraid of heights. What a strange time to conquer my fear. Nathan said this part of the cliffs is called La Gran Caída. Perhaps the name will be imprinted on my soul, alongside Bobby's and Annie's. I thought that when I had children, I'd become a better person. I think I've always had a badness, a sadness, inside me.

Why are my thoughts everywhere? They need to be here. I'm ridiculous, silly; my mother's right. She's always right. I'm useless to everyone. Everyone will be happier without me. Especially the children.

Oh God, no.

I can't think about the children.

They have Peter. I'd only let them down again. What if I were left on my own with Annie again? I might kill her.

They'll forget me soon enough. They're young enough to erase me from their memory.

Breathe, breathe.

I'm surprised by how calm I am.

It's like my mind was coated in tar, but now it's been wiped clean.

I close my eyes.

So, this is how it ends.

I thought I'd be scared if ever I fell from such a height, but if I jump there'll be nothing I can do about it.

The warm breeze skims my face again. I should be with my children right now, lying next to them, watching them sleep.

But I can't. I'm not good enough for them. They'll end up hating me.

Bobby, Annie, you were the loves of my life.

'Debbie! For God's sake, what are you doing?'

Is that the voice inside my head again?

I close my eyes. I don't want anyone to stop me. I just want darkness.

Don't look back. I can't look back.

'Debbie, come away from there!'

Before I have time to think, I'm turning around.

'Oh,' I say. 'It's you.'

'What are you doing so close to the edge?'

I visualise the picture of Jesus my mother has hanging in the living room. It isn't a graphic depiction of His death: it's the Sacred Heart. I can't believe I've not made that connection before: life is eternal. Perhaps it's Him who's been talking to me all along.

'Leave me alone, Ellen. I know what I'm doing.'

She walks closer to me, and my body begins to shake.

43

Anna

I stop the alarm before it goes off. I've barely slept, and when I managed to drift off, my dreams were of my mother.

In the first one, she walked along the edge of a bridge as though she were balancing on a tightrope just inches from the ground.

'Come on, Annie,' she said. 'Come and have a go. It's fun — you'll like it.'

I was older than her. I had wrinkles around my eyes, yet her skin was so smooth, iridescent and glowing in the sunshine.

In the next dream, I was crawling in a ventilation shaft — like the ones in American films where the victim hides. The bottom of it, instead of being made from metal, was dirt. Worms wriggled beneath my hands and knees — their shiny skin catching the shards of light that leaked into the darkness. I came to a junction and took a left, but stopped as soon as my hand became tangled in strands of hair. I pulled my hand away, but it was covered in maggots and ants.

I knew it was Debbie. I didn't have to look further to know her rotting corpse lay before me.

Jack turns over in the bed so he's facing me.

'Did the alarm go off?' he says, his throat croaky.

'No. I was awake. It's Sunday, anyway.'

'Nice one,' he says. 'What time can I sleep till?'

I wish I were more like Jack. He never wakes and thinks of his worries; he just wants to sleep more.

'Whenever Sophie wakes you,' I say. 'The party's at three. I'm going to see Dad before it starts.'

Jack groans. He folds the pillow and lays his head on it.

'I thought we talked about this last night. We said it was best that we wait until we know more.'

'I know it's going to be bad news. I can feel it. I've never felt this before.'

My pillow is damp from tears I must have cried in my sleep. I've never cried for her before — I've always cried for myself.

'Anna,' says Jack. 'Why don't we just forget about everything for a day? A few hours aren't going to make a difference after thirty years.'

I get up and grab the outfit that's hanging on the back of the door.

'I don't think this can wait,' I say, before heading to the bathroom.

The shower is hot on my skin. Every time I close my eyes, I see her face. Soon, I'm going to find out what happened to my mother. It's like every cell of my body has known that this is the moment I'm meant to find out — that I'm ready to hear it.

I step out of the shower. The mirror is steamed

up, so my face is blurred. I could be Debbie — it could be her face staring back at me.

I swipe off the condensation, flick on the tap and splash my face with cold water. I grip the side of the wash basin. I want to go back to not knowing. At least there was hope.

There's a knock on the bathroom door.

'Mummy, I really need the toilet.'

'Coming, sweetheart. Won't be a sec.'

Thank God for Sophie.

★ ★ ★

I stand next to the lounge window with a small mirror to check my make-up. The living room is draped in darkness; outside is overcast. My eyes are swollen with shadows that can't be hidden with concealer. What's the point anyway? I slam shut the compact and throw it onto the chair. I rest my palms on the sill.

I don't see anyone watching the house, but there is a red car parked a few doors, down. I lean closer to the window, but I can't see if it's a man or a woman in the driver's seat. Whoever it is, is looking in my direction. Can they see me, too?

I rush out of the front door to the gate. The person in the car puts on a baseball cap, turns on the engine and reverses around the corner of the next street. It's a new car — I can't tell the make from here, but it looks like the one I've been seeing these past few days. It speeds off in the opposite direction.

It probably has nothing to do with me. I've

probably caught them spying on someone else. But my heart is pounding; I feel like I'm being watched.

I look down the other side of the street.

'Oh!'

Mr Robinson from next door is right next to me.

'Sorry, love,' he says. 'This was posted through our letterbox by mistake yesterday.'

He hands me a brown envelope.

'Thank you.'

'You jumped about ten metres off the ground then, Mummy,' Sophie says as I walk back into the living room.

She's standing on the sofa, looking out of the window.

'Mr Robinson gave me a fright, that's all.'

'I saw a car speed off. They must've been watching Fl like me and Daddy.'

'Yeah . . . they must have.'

I look down at the envelope, and race up the stairs, opening our bedroom door.

Jack has the pillow over his head.

'I think this is it,' I say.

He groans again and takes the pillow away.

He sits up, taking the letter from me.

'I'll open it later,' he says. 'All of this can wait until after the party. We have to be there for Robert.'

'But don't you need to know? What if you have a son?'

He gets out of bed and puts on his dressing gown.

'I need to do it in my own time, Anna.'

396

He walks out of the room and slams the bathroom door shut.

★ ★ ★

It took Jack two hours to come out of the bathroom, and another hour to get ready. I watched as he did his hair in the hall mirror.

'Why are you in such a good mood?' I said.

'Because we are forgetting everything for a few hours and I'm practising now.'

He must've read the results, I thought. He must've been digesting the news while getting ready.

I put sparkly gel in Sophie's hair — glad that she's not into plaits, because I would be useless — and all I could think of was the boy who might be Jack's son, although he's almost a teenager now. Would he want to live here? We would have to convert Jack's office into a bedroom for him. It would be a fresh start for all of us. I could move on from Debbie and concentrate on someone else.

But then it struck me how selfish my thoughts were.

This boy has just lost his mother — a mother who he'd grown up with — a mother that was his sole parent. Jack would be a stranger to him. And there I was, planning happy families in my head — trying to fill a hole in my own life.

Now, we're on the way to the party. *No, I think to myself*, in the passenger seat of Jack's car, *I will plan nothing*. I will let other people decide what they want to do. I can't control everything, everyone. I must let go, stop being so anxious. However much I've tried to keep everything together, I can't control everything. Perhaps realising that is what will make me happy.

'There's a good turnout,' says Jack as we pull into the car park of The Continental.

'There must be a lot of customers, too,' I say.

Jack rolls his eyes at me, and I smile.

'Sorry. Yes. It'll be a lovely party for Robert.'

Jack takes off his seat belt and leans over, kissing me on the cheek.

'I have to tell you now,' he whispers, 'my DNA test was negative.'

'What? Why didn't you tell me when you first read the results?'

He gazes out of the windscreen.

'Because I made a big deal out of waiting until after the party . . . I don't know . . . I had to process it all.' He turns, his eyes meet mine. 'You look disappointed. Are you?'

'I don't know . . . perhaps.'

He shakes his head a little, smiling.

'You're always yearning for something,' he says. 'Isn't what we have together enough?'

We both look behind us at Sophie in the back seat, engrossed in a game on her DS.

'This is enough,' I say, looking back at him. 'It's more than enough.'

Jack puts a hand on the door handle.

'So, how about we party like it's 1999?'

'Er, you've been to my family's parties before, right?'

He opens the door. '1999 was a pretty bad

year for me, to be honest.'

I playfully slap his thigh before opening the car door. Jack and I each hold one of Sophie's hands. We swing her all the way to the entrance.

'Can I have a wine?' she says.

'No,' Jack and I say at the same time.

Inside, I scan the place for Robert. I recognise some of his friends from university, sitting round a large table on the left, but he's not with them.

'Hello, Annie.'

It's Ellen, standing at the bar.

'Oh. It's you,' I say. 'What are you doing here?'

'My son gave me a lift. He got back in touch.'

It didn't answer my question. She lives nearly twenty miles away — why pick the same pub? Did I mention that Robert's party would be here? I can't remember telling her.

'Your family's over there.' She points to the other side of the room, a strange smile on her face.

'Thanks, Ellen.'

I turn my back on her and walk over to Dad and Robert. They're standing next to each other, completely still.

'What's going on?' I say. 'Happy Birthday, Robert! Shall we get you a drink? Maybe you could push the boat out and have a vodka.'

They both turn around.

'What's wrong?' I say. 'Are you drunk already, Robert?'

I look behind them. Monica's standing with her arms around someone.

'Monica?'

She turns around, tears and mascara run down her face.

'She came back.'

I look to the person standing next to her.

It's my mother.

44

2 a.m. Monday, 28 July 1986
Debbie

Ellen stops five feet away from me.

'I'm not going to touch you, Debbie,' she says. 'But you need to come away from the edge. This isn't the way to solve everything.'

'You don't know me . . . you don't know what's been going on in my life.'

'I've seen a snapshot. I've seen a husband who loves you, and a best friend that would do anything for you.'

'Well, you've got the wrong picture, haven't you?'

'I don't think so. I'm good at reading people and situations. I've listened to them when you're not there. Monica is really worried about you — she was in tears yesterday talking about you, about how you're like a sister to her. She feels you're slipping away from her.'

'Really? Nathan thinks her and Peter are having an affair.'

Ellen gives a laugh — almost like a cackling witch.

'Haven't you heard the way Peter talks to her? It's so formal, polite.'

'I've never noticed,' I say. 'Monica's right, though. She's been telling Peter and Nathan that I hear things — voices — telling me to do things.

401

God, I can't believe I'm telling you. A virtual stranger.' I give a dry laugh. 'I'm scared to be with my baby. I'll do her real harm next time, I know it.'

'You could see a doctor for that.'

'They'd lock me up. I'd never see my children again, anyway.'

A car screeches to the left — it swerves before stopping. The window rolls down and a man waves a fist.

'*Sal de la carretera, estupido ingles borracho!*'

There's a man, staggering in the road.

I should've guessed: Nathan.

'Oh, fuck off, Manuel,' he shouts to the driver.

He laughs as the man pulls away.

'I knew you'd come to our special spot, Debs. Didn't think it'd take you this long, though. You've been hours.'

He stands next to Ellen, not registering her presence.

'Why are you so close to the edge?' he says.

'Are the children okay?'

'Course. Monica's looking after them — they're fine.'

'Has Bobby asked about me?'

He shrugs. 'Not that I heard.'

I look back into the darkness of the sea. The light of the moon makes it easy to tell where the sea ends and the sky begins. Soon, I'll be part of that darkness. I close my eyes.

'Please,' says Ellen. 'Come away from there.'

'What are *you* doing here?' Nathan's slurring his words. He must've had more to drink after I left.

402

Everyone's better off without you. You heard what he said.

Why am I waiting? I should just jump.

'So, when are we leaving?' he says.

'What?'

Don't turn around again, I tell myself. Don't.

'I've brought a bag . . . packed our passports, too. I've got some savings . . . from my redundancy.'

'You lost your job?'

He shrugs. 'I lost it weeks ago. I was lucky to get a few quid. Not that Monica knows — she'd have spent it by now. I got up every morning in my suit as usual and didn't come back until tea time. She didn't suspect a thing. I knew it happened for a reason. I've been planning this for ages . . . since we booked the holiday.'

'Planned what?'

'All of this.' He swings his arms around and sways as though he might fall over. 'Okay, well not the bit about you standing on the edge of a cliff.' He frowns. 'What *are* you doing there? You're not going to jump, are you?'

'You're pissed, Nathan,' I say. 'Go away.'

'Go away? But I thought . . . we could go somewhere together. It's what you wanted.'

'I don't want any of this. I want nothing.'

Footsteps are coming towards me. A thud.

I turn.

He's dropped the bag; he's coming closer.

'Don't come near me, Nathan.'

A small rock next to my feet falls over the edge. It takes a few seconds before it lands loudly. No splash — just a crack as it hits another rock.

'That's what would happen to you,' says Ellen. 'No splash. Just you and a rock.'

Ellen notices more than I realised . . . this person I met only a few days ago. I thought she was drunk all the time, but she picks up on the smallest of things.

Nathan grabs my right arm, the one closest to the edge, as I turn to face him.

'Come on,' he says. 'Don't be silly. You heard what she said.'

I yank my arm away, but he doesn't let go.

'Please don't,' I shriek.

Adrenaline pulses through me.

I step back from the edge with my left foot, leaning heavily on it, but Nathan won't let go of me. He goes to put his other arm around my left shoulder, but I push it away.

His foot falters on the edge; his weight pulls me closer to him.

He slips.

'Ahhh!'

He cries out in pain as his left knee lands on a rock ten inches down. He's trying to balance, but he's faltering. His leg gives way and he lands on his elbows — he howls in pain. I grab both of his hands in mine as the rest of his body flails below. Ellen grabs hold of my waist — trying to pull me and Nathan away from the drop.

'Try and climb back up, Nathan!' she says. 'Keep still! Debbie, lie down on the floor. I'll grab your feet and pull.'

I do as she says, but my hands burn.

'I don't know if I can hold on much longer,' he says, his eyes wide, his face contorted in pain. 'I must've broken my arms — they're so weak.'

There are tears in his eyes. We're holding him, but he's too heavy — Ellen's too slight, she has barely the strength to keep me from the edge.

'I don't want to die,' he whispers.

'Pull us back, Ellen!' I shout.

Nathan's weight is dragging me towards him, I feel myself slide slowly along the ground.

'I don't know what to do!' I scream.

Ellen looks behind her. 'There's no one here to help us. I can't hold on much longer.'

'I love you, Debbie,' says Nathan.

He lets go of my hands.

Silence.

I cover my ears — I can't bear to hear what follows.

I lie there for what feels like hours before Ellen sits beside me. I push myself up, onto my knees.

It feels as though something's blocking my throat — I can't breathe.

I try to speak, but instead collapse next to Ellen.

'Here.' She takes off her sarong and wraps it around my face. 'I know it's not the same as a paper bag, but breathe — the carbon dioxide will help you.'

Inhale, exhale.

Slowly, slowly, my breathing calms.

'What happened?' My voice is barely a whisper. 'It was all too fast. I didn't know he was going to let go. Do you think he's all right?'

Ellen shakes her head. There are tears pouring down her face.

'No.'

I crawl forward on my hands and knees, trying to look down at the rocks below.

'I can't see him.'

'You wouldn't want to.'

I put my head in my hands, tugging at sections of my hair. I need to feel something.

'We have to get out of here,' says Ellen. 'He won't be washed away for a few hours. They're going to think we pushed him. People might've seen a struggle.'

I turn around, crawl back, and land next to her.

'Washed away? Oh God. He can't be gone just like that!'

'We have to go, Debbie!'

'I can't go back, Ellen. What will I tell everyone? How could I look Monica in the eyes, knowing I just killed her husband?'

'But you didn't — he fell.'

'But Monica saw me threaten him earlier with a broken bottle — she'll tell the police. Everyone will think I pushed him. He wouldn't have been here if it weren't for me. I can't. Oh God. What am I going to do? What would my children think of me . . . my parents? The shame of it. This can't be happening.'

Ellen reaches over for Nathan's bag. She unzips it.

'He wasn't lying,' she says. 'There's an envelope full of money here. And passports. He even brought some of your clothes.' She looks up at me. 'What a crazy bastard.' She looks back in the bag and pulls out a paper wallet. 'Looks like he was planning on writing to people back at home after he left.'

'Can I see that?'

She hands it to me. Inside are sheets of unused pink notepaper.

'I should've realised,' I say. 'It could never have been Monica.'

'What do you mean?'

'It doesn't matter. I've been so wrong. I'm not right, not for anybody. I need to leave.'

'What? You can't!'

'It's better than leaving the way I planned to. You can see that, can't you?'

'I don't know, Debbie. This is all madness.' She stares at the grass, then rubs her eyes with the heels of her hands. 'What shall I say to your family?'

'Say nothing. Pretend this night didn't happen.'

'You have to let them know where you're going. They'll worry about you.'

I take a piece of the pink paper out of the bag with shaking hands.

'Have you got a pen?'

45

Anna

Debbie has her arm around Monica's shoulder. Dad's face is completely white, his mouth open.

'I . . . I thought you were dead,' he says. He walks towards her; Monica stands aside. He touches Debbie's arm. 'Is it really you?'

She nods. 'I'm so sorry, Peter. I . . . I know I shouldn't have come — I didn't want to upset you, you've all moved on with your lives . . . I just wanted — '

'You don't have to say sorry, Debbie,' says Dad. 'I'm just glad you're alive.' He looks at Monica. 'I can't believe it, can you?'

Monica shakes her head, make-up like slug-trails down her face.

'Annie,' says Debbie. 'I'd know you anywhere. I'm so sorry, love. I didn't know whether I was right coming here . . . I . . . '

I run over to her and put my arms around her.

'You were right,' I whisper. 'I'm so happy to see you. I never thought I would. I've been looking for you for years.'

She holds the top of my arms and stands back to look at me.

'Look at you. You're beautiful. You look just like my mother.' She strokes my hair, my face. 'Just look at you.' She looks at Jack and Sophie behind me. 'And with a family, too. I'm so proud of you.'

They are the words I have wanted to hear from her for all of my life.

Tears flood my eyes; my body is overcome. I fall into my mother's arms.

'I missed you so much,' she says. 'I wanted to come and see you for such a long time. I thought you were better off without me — that the longer I left it, the more you'd hate me.'

'You should have come,' I say. 'I don't hate you — I love you. I'm not angry with you.'

Her tears fall onto my neck.

'Thank you, Annie. That's all I've ever wanted to hear. I love you so very much — I never stopped loving you. Have you been happy?'

'Yes, but I . . . yes. I have.'

She pulls away from me and looks at Robert.

'Bobby.' She holds an arm out to him.

He looks at us all — his eyes glistening.

He runs out of the door.

★   ★   ★

I glance around the beer garden. Robert's sitting on a wooden bench; he lights up a cigarette.

'I didn't know you still smoked,' I say.

He blows out the smoke, his bottom lip quivering.

'I thought I'd hate her if I saw her again. But . . . I don't. I can't believe it. I just need a moment.' He takes a deep breath and rests his elbows on his legs. 'Do you think she'll still be there when I go back in? I haven't upset her, have I?'

409

I rub his back.

'You haven't upset her, Rob.' I sit down next to him. 'Shit. I can't believe it either.'

'Did you know she'd be here?'

'No, not at all. I didn't even get a reply to that email I sent.'

'We should get back in.' He flicks his cigarette onto the ground and grinds it with his shoe. He stands. 'Right. I'm ready now.'

I follow him inside.

Debbie's sitting with Monica — they're holding both hands together on the table, both still crying.

Debbie stands when she sees Robert.

'Bobby, love. I'm so sorry.'

He walks slowly to her. He reaches out to touch her hair.

'It's really you, Mum. I've missed you.'

Debbie puts her hands on his shoulders and pulls him towards her.

He lets her — his head below her chin, like he was half the size. For a second, his arms dangle at his side. Then he puts them around her waist.

'My lovely boy.'

A few moments later, he pulls away.

'I'm sorry if I did something to upset you . . . to make you leave.'

'Darling.' Debbie strokes the tears away from his face. 'It was nothing you did . . . it was nothing anyone did. I wasn't very well. I was ill, though I wouldn't have known it then. I felt I didn't deserve to have you. I couldn't take care of myself, let alone you. You deserved better. I love you so much, Bobby.'

'You won't go away again, will you?'

'No, love. No, I won't.'

Jack pulls out a chair for me and pushes me gently onto it. He leans towards Debbie — his arm outstretched.

'Nice to finally meet you,' he says. 'I've heard a lot about you.'

Debbie holds up a shaking hand to meet his. She holds the wrist with her other hand to steady it.

'Sorry,' she says. 'I'm really nervous.'

There's a sound of smashing glass behind us.

Cold liquid sprays over my legs.

Grandad.

He stands amongst the broken shards; droplets of beer drip down the wood panelling.

'Is it really you?' He looks at each of us. 'Is it really my girl?'

'It is, Frank,' says Jack.

The glass crunches beneath his feet as he walks over to her.

He brings his hands to her face.

'It's really you,' he says. He strokes her cheeks and her hair. 'It's been so long, love. Are you all right?'

'I don't know, Dad. I'm trying to be.'

He holds her by the shoulders.

'I'm so pleased to see you. I never thought I'd see you again. You're staying for a bit, aren't you? You won't just leave me again, will you? At least give me a phone number I can reach you on.'

Debbie puts her arms on his.

'I'm staying for a while, Dad. If that's okay? If you forgive me?'

411

He takes her in his arms.

'My darling girl.' He pulls away, wiping the tears from his face with the back of his hands. 'There's nothing to forgive. I'm just so happy you're alive.' He pats her arms, her back, her hair, with his arms. 'You're real, aren't you? You're really here?'

'I'm really here, Dad.'

★   ★   ★

Dad and Monica are huddled together on the table next to Debbie and Grandad. He has a hand over hers like he never wants to let go of her again. Jack and Sophie are sitting with me, opposite them. Sophie looks at Debbie, then at me.

'You two have the same face,' she says. 'Only yours has a more wrinkles.' She's looking at Debbie, who laughs.

I take in Debbie's face, her hair. She must dye it, because there are no signs of grey. How long has she been dyeing it? What went through her mind when she did mundane things like that?

'Did you ever think of us?' I say.

'Every second of every day.' She reaches across the table to put a hand on mine. 'I know it's unforgivable, but I wasn't well. I didn't know where I was, half the time. And then there was that terrible accident.'

'What accident?'

'I . . . Did Ellen not tell you?'

'You know Ellen?'

Debbie nods.

'Yes. She got out of prison a few months ago. I thought I'd made the whole thing up in my head, but she tracked me down . . . said I had to make things right. I didn't know if I had the courage after all of these years, but then Ellen found you — she's good with the Internet and all of that stuff . . . she told me where you lived, but I couldn't just knock on your door. She'd done some volunteer work in the past, so she managed to get a position at your bookshop. I hope you don't think that's weird, Annie.'

I remember the feeling of being watched over the past few days — in town, outside my house. It must have been my mother.

'I . . . I suppose not,' I say. 'I've made some questionable decisions myself in the past, so I'm not really one to talk.'

She frowns slightly.

'But I won't go into all of that now,' I say. 'Go on . . . '

'Ellen had been thinking about everything when she was in prison, you see. About what happened with Nathan.'

I shift my chair back a little.

'What happened to Nathan?'

Debbie glances at Monica.

'I need to tell Monica first. If that's okay?'

'And that was why you came back? Not because you wanted to see us?'

'I just needed that push. The longer I was away, the harder it was to come back. I've a lot to tell you. If you want to hear it.'

Jack's looking at me. He reaches over, and I place my hand on his. Sophie, thinking it's a game, does the same — both her hands are on top of ours.

'I've waited a long time,' I say. 'I do want to hear it.'

46

I thought I'd imagined the whole story of that night in my head. I haven't told it out loud before.

Monica's looking at me, frowning. Her eyes never left mine as I told her what happened to Nathan. Dad and Peter were listening silently from the next table. I felt the shame I knew I would feel — my poor dad listening to me describe how I killed my best friend's husband.

'But why didn't you just come to me?' says Monica. 'Tell me what happened? I wouldn't have thought you'd done it on purpose. You didn't murder him, Debbie. It was an accident.' She breaks eye contact, and looks down at her lap; her left arm is in a support bandage. 'Poor Nathan. All these years, no one has been grieving for him.' Tears drip onto her hands. 'I thought you'd run away together — started again.'

'I wasn't in love with Nathan.' I glance at Peter, but he looks away. He's moved on. Some people find it easier than others. 'My mind was in a strange place. I didn't know what was real or not. And after what happened with Annie in the swimming pool, I thought everyone would be better off without me. If I'd been left alone with her again, something worse might've happened.'

Monica grabs a serviette from the table and dabs her cheeks.

'I know this is too late, but I would've helped

415

you, you know.' She leans closer and whispers, 'I never told anyone about the broken bottle. My loyalty was always with you.' She glances at the ceiling, blinking to stop more tears. 'What have you been doing for all of these years?'

I fold my arms around me.

I'd imagined her telling everyone about me threatening Nathan with the broken glass. I'd got so many things wrong.

'I went straight back to England, but on the train and then the ferry. I haven't flown since Tenerife. All the time, I felt people looking at me, was paranoid they could read my mind. If it hadn't been for my passport, I don't think I'd have remembered my name. For days, I wore the same dress as that night. Once I reached Dover, I didn't know where to go. I didn't have the capacity to book a room at a hotel. I found a café I was comfortable in and stayed there. But it came to closing time and I was lost again. I found a bench and couldn't stop crying and that's where the memory ends. Someone must've called an ambulance or something, because the next thing I knew I was in hospital. I didn't know how I got there. The two years were a blur of Valium and Clozapine. I had a bed near the window . . . it had a view of the car park . . . like I was looking into the world through the glass. I could curl up and sleep, but if I wanted to see life, I could just sit up and gaze out of the window.'

Annie and her husband are sitting a few tables down, their heads together, deep in conversation. They're close, I think. Anyone watching could tell he adores her. I'm so glad she found happiness.

'Why did you send that pink note a few days ago?' says Monica.

'I . . . I got scared. I wanted to run away again. But then I realised that I had to face everything. Otherwise you'd never have known what happened. I'm so sorry, Monica.'

She purses her lips, but her eyes still glisten.

'Anna and Robert need your apologies more than I do.'

My beautiful children, now grown up. I've missed so much. Would it have been best for them to see me at my worst, and grow up resenting me, or let them start afresh without me? Either way, they must hate me.

'Did you hear about Mum?' says Dad, breaking my thoughts.

I turn my chair around and shuffle it towards Dad's table.

'A few months after she died. I'm so sorry, Dad. I'm sorry I wasn't here to help you through it. I couldn't believe it. I thought . . . I thought there was always enough time to come back. I left it too long, didn't I?'

'She thought she was going to be with you . . . at the end,' says Dad. 'It wasn't like these dramatic heart attacks you see on television. She was standing in the kitchen. 'I don't feel so good,' she said. 'I think I must've eaten something off.' She was out of breath, but she hadn't done anything strenuous . . . her face was damp with sweat. I grabbed her a chair and sat her down, but she slumped in it . . . said she had.

417

a pain in her jaw. That's when I knew. I phoned for an ambulance, and when I went back to her, her face was pale, full of pain . . . I'd never seen her like that before.'

'Oh, Dad. Poor Mum.'

I want to close my ears, put my hands over them, shut my eyes. But I must listen to it. I have to know. It's not cowardice, though, is it? If my mind doesn't work the same way as other people's. One of my doctors told me that. She said it wasn't me being lazy or weak, it was my illness. I've battled through years to believe that.

'What did she say?' I ask him.

I clasp my hands together tightly. I'm right here, I'm listening, I'm in the present. This is real and I'm about to hear my mother's last words.

Breathe in, breathe out.

Everything'll be okay if I just breathe.

'She said, 'I'm going to be with our little girl now, Frank.'' Dad glances at the smashed glass on the floor to his right before looking back up at me. 'I begged her not to leave me, but she did.'

I put my face in my hands and can't stop the sobs.

'I'm so sorry, Dad.'

He stands and rests a hand on my shoulder.

'There, there, love,' he says. 'You let it all out.' He puts a hand on my head and smooths down my hair. 'I never thought I'd see you again, love.' He kisses the top of my head. 'I'm so happy that you're back. I always knew you'd come back to me.'

I've been away for so many years, yet I feel his

418

love as though it were yesterday that I left. I'm going to spend the rest of my life making it up to him, to everyone.

47

Anna

Debbie whispered quietly, after speaking to Monica, telling me what happened the night she disappeared. Her eyes were swollen and red from crying.

None of it has sunk in yet. I still can't believe she's alive, but what happened that night . . . it was like she was describing a film she had just seen.

'Didn't anyone look for Nathan?' I asked her.

'His parents are dead,' she said. 'They died years before he did.'

'But that didn't make it right,' I said. 'He deserved to be missed.'

'I know, I know. I made the note sound as though we were about to run off together,' she said. 'I had his passport, clothes.' She couldn't talk about him without crying. 'I was desperate, Annie. I didn't know what to do. He'd written me all of these horrible letters. It was one thing after the other. I had — have — depression. I know that now. It was an awful time.'

'What changed?' I said. I couldn't believe I was so calm, but I knew the enormity of it wouldn't hit me until later. 'What made you contact us?'

'Ellen. She looked for me. I'd read about her

in the paper. Did she tell you that she killed her husband? He was such an awful man. He used to hit her, control her — not that that meant he deserved to die. One day, she lost it. Had a kitchen knife ready. That poor woman. She's been through so much.

'But I wrote back to her because I had to know if what happened that night in Tenerife was real, or just a dream — if my whole life before that had been a dream. It was like myself, my history, had vanished after that night. I barely remembered who I was, my past.'

As she spoke, the only person I could think about was Nathan.

He might've been obsessed with her, but he deserved a life — he deserved to be grieved for by someone.

Now, we're on our way home.

I broke down in tears after closing the car door. I couldn't speak for half an hour.

Jack rubbed my back.

'We won't set off until you're okay,' he said.

I tried to speak, to tell him that it might be ages before I'm okay, but I couldn't.

'What's wrong with Mummy?' said Sophie.

'She's had a shock. She hasn't seen her mummy since . . . well, I don't think she can ever remember seeing her.'

'But Monica's her mummy.'

'Yes, that's right,' said Jack. 'But the other lady is Mummy's biological mother. She was very ill and wanted to get better.'

'What's a biological mummy? Is it like a robot?'

421

I almost laughed.

I sat up, wiping the tears with my cardigan.

'No, love,' I say. 'But I think that's a talk for another day.' I reached over for Jack's hand. 'Let's go home, shall we?'

We're passing through town and everything looks the same.

Debbie promised to visit me and talk properly. I hope she does — I have to trust that she won't leave again. I want to get to know her — show her the box of things I've kept. I think she'll like that — to know that she was missed, and loved.

Robert talked to her again after drinking four double vodkas. I don't know what he said to her, but I hope he was kind. I hope he saw that she's a person, with troubles all of us have. It wasn't our fault — it wasn't anyone's fault. She thought she prevented us from having an awful life with her, but I wish we'd been given the chance to see for ourselves. But we can't turn back time, can we? Debbie must've known she'd left us in good hands with Dad and Monica.

Just before I left, she gave me a canvas shopping bag, with seven or eight books inside.

'Don't look at them now,' she said. 'But these are my diaries . . . though they might be a little sparse . . . they don't cover the whole time I was away. I thought . . . well, there's nothing in there that I wouldn't tell you. You don't have to read them. It's probably mostly boring stuff any-way — '

'I'd love to read them,' I said. 'Thank you.'

I'm now holding the bag tight, almost hugging it. My mobile phone rings.

It's Sally Munroe.

'Hi Anna. I've got some news, but it's not what I thought it'd be.' She sighs loudly down the phone. 'I found there were two unidentified bodies found on the island. One of those was female, but was aged between fifty and sixty. The other was male. It'd been in the water for about twenty years before it was discovered. They found a silver St Christopher in the skin of his neck. I think it might be — '

'Nathan. Sally, I'm sorry. I should've texted you as soon as I saw her.'

'Saw who?'

'My mother. She was just — there — in the pub for Robert's birthday. Her friend must've told her where the party was.'

'What? Just *there*? I don't understand.'

'I don't understand either, not really. I think she had a nervous breakdown, or post-natal depression, or psychosis, I don't know. I've read so much about different conditions — but no one person is the same.' I look behind me, and luckily Sophie is playing on her beloved game console. 'When they — we — were on holiday, she said there was an accident — that Nathan fell.'

'Has she gone to the police about the accident?'

I don't think so. 'What would happen to her if she did?'

'I don't know,' she says. 'There might be a trial — depends what the coroner says.' There's a brief pause. 'I didn't think it would end like this.'

'No,' I say. 'Me neither.'

'Oh, before I go . . . Ellen wasn't hard to find — she uses her maiden name now. She was sent to prison in 1990 for the murder of her husband, Alan. She pleaded self-defence, but the prosecution went for her.'

'Was it self-defence? No . . . sorry, I shouldn't ask.'

'From what I read in the reports from the time, it seemed so.'

There's too much to take in. I need to sleep, to process all of this.

'Thank you, Sally. For all you've done.'

'You're welcome. My bill's in the post.' She laughs. 'I'm glad it worked out for the best for you, Anna.'

We say our goodbyes, and I throw my phone into my bag in the footwell.

'I still can't believe it,' I say to Jack. 'I started the day thinking my mother was dead, yet she was living in England all of this time.'

'I don't think she's had a happy life, though. Are you okay? It must've been a shock.'

'I'm *still* in shock to be honest.'

Mum said I was lying on her chest while we were on a lilo in the hotel swimming pool. She fell asleep, and I slipped from her, almost drowning. She asked if there were any lasting effects — was I afraid of water, but I lied. I said no.

She said Monica saved me that day.

I know, I wanted to say. She's been saving me for years.

'I thought Robert would be angry with Debbie,' says Jack.

'I suppose, when you think about it, all that matters is that she's back, she's alive.' The anxiety, that knot in the pit of my stomach that I've lived with for years, has vanished. I look out of the window. 'Thank God she's alive.'

★   ★   ★

I have been waiting for this moment all day. Jack is reading to Sophie upstairs, and I'm settled on the sofa with Debbie's journals. Some are like school exercise books, others are notebooks with different designs. It might feel as though I'm prying when I read them, like Dad and Monica would have felt listening to the messages I left for Debbie when I was a child. Perhaps if Dad still has the phone, he could give it to her, so she can hear all the calls she missed.

Before reading them all from cover to cover, I flick through the different books. Her handwriting is sometimes neat, at other times, erratic. There's a sentence crossed out too.

12 September 1987

I've been told — or rather, it has been suggested to me — that I should start writing in this journal. I haven't written in a diary since I was about fourteen years old. They assure me no one will read it, that my thoughts will be private, but I don't believe them. It's weird, though, I seem to be able to think a bit more clearly when I'm writing.

I'm in a secure ward — I've been here for

425

nearly a year, under S3 of the MHA (because, apparently, I'm a risk to myself. ~~Which is ridiculous because I'd be doing everyone a favour if I were to succeed~~. At any time, the police could come in and take me away for what I did last year.

Prison might be better than this place, though. It's so noisy here — especially at night. Everyone must have bad dreams. I know I do. I see his face, so close to mine, as he let go of my hand. When I close my eyes during the day, too. They used to say I shouted his name in my sleep — that I saw people in the corner of the room. 'I hear things,' I told them. 'I've never seen things.' But what if they're right? I could've seen lots of things and they felt real to me. I've no idea, really.

Sometimes, I can't remember what I look like. They're not big on mirrors in this place. Some days I push my food away; other days I eat everything they put in front of me — even taking food others don't want.

I must be fat right now because my clothes feel snug around my belly. I think I was skinny three months ago. When I look down at what I'm wearing, I don't recognise the top and the jeans. No wonder they don't fit properly.

Depression with postnatal psychosis is what they say I have now. At first, they thought I was schizophrenic after I told them God — or my dead uncle — was talking to me. But I don't hear anyone any more.

They won't tell me why that is. They must think they've cured me. They can't explain much, if you ask me, just prescribed different pills after the first time I tried to . . . Well, they just keep giving me different ones. I've no choice.

Give it a few months, they say. 'A few months?' I want to scream. I don't think I have a few months. I've got nothing to live for, and I'm absolutely no use to anyone else. Why don't they let me just do what I want to do? It'd save them a fortune in fucking medication.

6 January 1988

I've realised they don't actually read my diary. I've been keeping this one in my packet of sanitary towels (and no one likes to pry in there). To test this, I made up some disturbing thoughts about nurse Adrian and they haven't kept him away from me so far. And that was two months ago.

They say I've been 'doing well' for a few months now — that this new medication must be working after all. (Doing well — what a shit description of a life.) Now they say I'm nearly ready to leave. I'm not under constant obs any more, which is a relief because that was like being haunted.

I don't think I'm ready to leave, but I don't want to be in here any more. I feel so very, very low. Sometimes my thoughts are so dark, I constantly think of ways to end all of this. Which would be the least painful method? I've no blade — they give us plastic cutlery, and we don't get enough pills to save. I want to talk to Karen in the next bed — she's always talking about it — but when I want to speak, she just looks at the picture opposite us. It's the one with the fucking sheep in a fucking meadow. The bastards probably hung that picture there to remind us of what we are.

I'd be able to get what I want outside. That's what I need. To get out and have my freedom. Freedom of choice. Here, I'm like a child being babysat.

Would I do it somewhere no one would find me — or somewhere I'd be found? It's a constant chatter in my head. One that I tell no one about. I'd not want to involve anyone else directly by stepping or jumping in front of their car or train. No, it has to be clean. I wish I could look up ways, talk to people, but there is nothing. The books on our paltry shelf are all stupid novels by privileged people.

What else could I do if I get out of this place? People will know what I've done just by seeing the guilt and shame in my eyes. I won't be able to make friends — you have to be honest with friends, don't you? How could I tell them I'm a mother, but haven't seen my children for nearly a year and a half? Not to mention the fact I killed some-one and have misplaced my mind. They'd *think I'm a monster. They'd probably be right.*

5 November 1990

I've been out for one year, seven months and thirty-two days.

I'm still alive.

The thought of seeing my children is stopping me from doing anything 'stupid' again. Bobby and Annie are out in the world and they are getting older. Soon they will be old enough to want to come and find me. It's a hope I must cling to.

I'm starting a new job tomorrow. When I say job, I mean volunteering in a soup kitchen (not sure they call them that these days). When I went for the interview, it was humbling seeing people without a place to eat or somewhere to sleep. At least I have my benefits, a room (which is pretty grotty, but . . .).

So why do I still feel so fucking low?

Sleep. I need sleep.

Another pill. About the fiftieth bloody pill I've taken today.

When will this end?

19 January 1998

I can't believe it. I thought she would live forever. I thought we'd have a chance to meet again. That's been wiped away. I don't know if I can [words illegible] always thought I'd have the time. They'll never want me back now. [words illegible]

[words illegible] showed me how to work the internet, and I typed in my mother's name first and her death was what came up!

Six months ago.

Why am I writing in here? I should be going to see my dad.

I'm fucking useless.

Useless and I don't deserve to be on this fucking earth.

I'm going to go to the registry office tomorrow to get a copy of the death certificate. It might not even be real. This Internet thing might all be made up — hardly anywhere has it.

My name was listed as her daughter. My children as her grandchildren.

I can't fucking bear it. My mother is dead.

What use is writing when [ends]

24 June 2002

It's Annie's birthday today — she's sixteen years old. I wonder what she's doing to celebrate it. Having a party with all of her friends, I guess. I bet she has loads of friends.

She probably doesn't know I exist. It's easier for them if they never mention me, I imagine. I'm a dark stain they want to blot out. The only thing that keeps me going is the thought that I created two beautiful children and no one can take that from me: the only useful thing that I've done. One day, I might even see them again. Though they won't want to see me. Why would they?

I'm back here again. I didn't get very far, did I?

I still can't believe my lovely mother is dead.

She was so far away, yet I knew she loved me. I hurt her by leaving. I might have killed her. It was her heart, got too much for her.

It's been six years since she died, but I wake up thinking it's just happened.

Why do I keep going? Is it the thought of one day seeing my children again?

It must be.

The theme tune to 'Mistral's Daughter' is blaring out from the communal area. It's fucking annoying and that series is so bloody old! If I knew anyone outside, I'd ask them to bring in 'The Exorcist'. That would give them something to take their minds off their problems. Dad is out there somewhere. Bobby, Annie and Peter, too. How is Monica dealing with Nathan being gone? Does she think we're together living the high life? How much more wrong could she be?

I remember after I had Annie, there was another mum on the ward. We would watch 'Coronation Street' in the lounge. I can't remember her name, though — it began with an S. I bet she's having a good life.

God. I couldn't do it. However hard I tried out there, the memories and the nightmares always caught up with me. They still do. I don't know what I can do to stop them.

I'm seeing a new doctor tomorrow: Jemima O'Keefe. Her first name makes me think of that kids' programme 'Play School' — Bobby used to watch it. I'm going to have to be sensible and keep those thoughts to myself.

Stacy. The woman in the maternity ward was called Stacy.

28 August 2013

Patrick's finished with me.

It's stupid when I re-read that.

I'm forty-nine years old for God's sake.

Talking about a man who's dumped me.

Why do I always write in here when things turn to shit? I've no happy memories written down. It's always about things gone wrong.

It's because of Nathan.

Karma, probably.

Perhaps it's because I don't deserve happiness. I have tried so hard to get better. I even took up jogging. Endorphins, my doctor said.

And I felt great for ages — my longest time yet.

But then Patrick said he couldn't be with someone like me.

I didn't open up enough to him.

Every time I laughed I felt guilty: remembering my children I never see; picturing Nathan's face as he fell.

Who'd want to be with a murderer who abandoned her children, anyway?

Not that Patrick ever knew about that. The murderer part, I mean. I'd shown him pictures of my children, but Annie was a baby and Bobby was six. The picture was so . . .

Four years we were together, yet we lived separately. We met at the café I was working in. He had an engineering contract with some technology group — something to do with pumps or hoses or something. God, I didn't listen, did I?

Patrick was so kind. Physically, he wasn't someone I was normally attracted to (though I couldn't be bothered with all of that shit for years), but he was so kind, and he liked me back. He was divorced, had three grown-up children he saw every other weekend. He liked Chelsea FC, cooking for us on a Saturday while listening to Queen ('Still classics, Deb,' he said. 'No one will ever come close to Freddie Mercury.').

Why am I talking about him in the past tense? He's still alive — just not with me.

He taught me to drive, was so patient with me. He said I could achieve anything if I wanted it enough . . . even bought me a car when I passed my test. He was so pleased . . . said I was on my way to becoming the person I could be.

But I already was the person I could be.

He mustn't have been happy with that.

And I wasn't happy with him trying to change me, to fix me. I don't want a carer — I want someone who accepts me the way I am.

I'll never find that person, will I? Maybe I'm too broken.

It's for me to fix, not him.

I've asked for more shifts at the café. I'm someone else when I'm there. I pretend I'm a jolly soul to the customers, and after being on my feet all day, I collapse, exhausted, at night. When I sleep, I dream I'm someone else.

It's like having two lives.

Neither are mine.

At least the nightmares have stopped.

12 December 2016

Blast from the horrible past. I have heard from Ellen. It feels so wrong that she's been in prison for killing her husband, yet I've been free after killing Nathan.

She said it wasn't killing, though.

We didn't kill him.

He fell.

She's so kind. She tells me that it was on her mind for years when she was in there (though she says that, I'm sure she would've had internet in there and known how to contact me before this).

She couldn't believe it when I told her I hadn't seen my family. If it were her son, she would never have let him go.

Easy for you to say, I said.

This whole thing hasn't been easy for anyone, she said. Damn that Nathan, the crazy bastard. Gave me all sorts of confidence.

I have no idea what she meant by that.

30 June 2017

My darling Annie has replied. I was expecting Monica to send a message back, but my original one was probably too cryptic. I had to test the water — needed to know if they'd actually want to hear from me.

Annie's message was only one line (it was amazingly lifting to hear from her), but mine was only a couple. I wish Annie would have told me about her life. I guess that's selfish of me. She owes me nothing. She probably hates me. I know I would if I were her.

I only had half an hour on the computer at the library and there was a queue. I didn't know what to write back.

This B & B is pretty cheap, but it's basic. The television is an old-style portable. I switched it on one night when I couldn't sleep, but the reception was so crap I turned it off.

There are some people who actually live here. I know that feeling. Of homelessness, hopelessness. Never having roots. Simply existing from one day to the next. Not wanting to die, but not having a life either. Such a fine line.

From just flicking through Debbie's words, I don't know if I can read every entry. Those few pages were so raw, so honest. I so wish she hadn't have left that night in Tenerife. We could have made it better for her. Couldn't we?

48

Present Day
Debbie

It's strange standing outside Monica and Nathan's house, knowing my children were brought up in it. I used to spend so much time here. We — Peter and I — would come round on sunny afternoons to have barbecues in the back garden. Leo and Bobby were so close, but it's not like that now. When I visited Robert yesterday, he said that since they were teenagers, they didn't get on as well. They barely speak now. If they hadn't been made to live together, would it have been different?

But I can't change the past. It is what it is.

Monica opens the door. She's still as slim as she always was — food must be of no comfort to her.

We stand there, just looking at each other.

Her face is so familiar to me, yet different at the same time.

She takes me by the hand and pulls me inside the house.

'I'm so pleased you came,' she says. 'I was half afraid that . . . '

'I'd leave again?'

She's looking at me. To her, I've aged so quickly — in an instant, almost.

'Perhaps,' she says. 'Come on through to the kitchen. Peter won't be long.'

'It's so odd hearing you talk about him like that,' I say, following her. 'Wow, this has changed. It's spotless.'

She flicks on the kettle. 'I took early retirement. Can't bear a mess if I've got to look at it all bloody day.'

On the fridge are photographs of Bobby, Annie and her family. I feel a knot in my stomach.

'You can make new memories,' she says.

'Stop being so nice to me, Mon. I don't deserve it.'

'It's not up to me to decide what you deserve — it's up to you.'

I sigh. 'Since when did you get so wise?'

'Since I got so fucking old,' she says.

'You're not old. You look great — you always did.'

She turns her back to me and looks out of the kitchen window.

'I didn't have my eye on Peter the whole time you were married, you know. We were in such a difficult situation . . . we were there for each other. I was always fond of him.'

'I understand,' I say. She turns around. 'Really I do. Who am I to judge?'

'I thought you'd be so angry with me.'

'How could I be? You and Peter have brought up my children. They're a credit to you, they really are.'

'Oh, Debbie.'

She walks towards me, and rests a hand on my

shoulder, then embraces me in a hug.

We're still crying in each other's arms when the front door opens and closes.

'Shall I go out and come back in again?' says Peter.

'No, no,' says Monica, pulling away from me and dabbing her face with the back of her hand. 'I'll just pop upstairs . . . freshen up.'

I want to grab her hand and beg her not to leave me alone with Peter, but I don't. We have to talk. We haven't been alone since I got back.

'I'm sorry,' I say. The words don't seem enough.

He nods slowly. 'I know.' He pulls out a chair and sits, gesturing for me to do the same. 'I should've known there was something wrong, after you had Anna. I've blamed myself every day since you . . . left.'

'You shouldn't have. It was no one's fault. Though it's taken me so many years to realise that.'

'The children have been happy. I won't lie and say there weren't times when they withdrew into themselves as such, but overall, I think we've done pretty well.'

'I know you have. Thank you.'

'You don't have to thank me — they're my children too.' He shifts in his seat. 'What you said . . . about what happened that night . . . you must go to the police.'

'I know,' I say. 'It's what I should have done a long time ago. But I'll visit Annie first, if that's okay?'

'Of course,' he says. 'But just one thing. Anna hates being called Annie.'

439

49

Anna

I've been looking out of the window since midday, and Debbie's finally pulled up outside, driving the car that I've been seeing for days. It's a strange thought, but I never imagined she would drive a car. Dad never mentioned her ever driving; she always took the bus. At some point in her life after us, she would have taken lessons, a test. She must have done so many normal, everyday things without us. Like I have done without *her*.

Thirty years is a long time. What sort of life has she had? We didn't get a chance to talk much at Robert's party, but I'm hoping this afternoon I will get some answers.

I open the door to her.

'I never imagined you'd come to my house,' I say to her, as she greets me with a hug. She smells of Dewberry from the Body Shop.

She stands in the hallway, rubbing the tops of her arms — the rucksack she brought is at her feet.

'I'm not cold,' she says. 'I'm really nervous.'

'Me too,' I say. 'Jack's taken Sophie out for a while, but they'll be back soon. I'll make us some tea.'

She follows me through to the kitchen. I

prepared the teapot, cups and saucers, a plate of biscuits and cakes, and a jug of milk, hours ago. I've been up since five o'clock this morning. Everything had to be just right.

'Oh, you kept it!' says Debbie, bending so she's eye level with the shell box she made me that I placed on the dining table. 'I remember choosing the shells, but I can barely recall sticking them on the box.'

'Oh.'

'Annie — I mean Anna, sorry. No. I know I did it . . . sorry. All the talking therapy I've had over the years . . . encouraging me to tell the truth . . . it's not always the best way, is it? Oh, fondant fancies!' She picks one up, turning it round in her hand. 'I haven't had one of these for years.'

Her train of thought is all over the place. I always thought we'd be similar people, but we aren't at all.

'Gran told me you liked them,' I say, pouring hot water into the teapot.

'Really?'

Her face drops, and her lips press together when I mention her mother. I shouldn't push the subject.

'Please, have a seat,' I tell her.

I can't help staring at her all the time. I can barely believe she's here. She seems so small, so vulnerable. I feel as though I want to look after her.

I put a cup on the saucer; it rattles slightly. I can't believe I'm so nervous being alone with her.

'Do you take sugar?' I say.

Such a strange question to ask your own mother.

'No thanks.'

She smiles at me; her eyes are glistening.

'This is lovely,' she says, 'isn't it?'

I nod. 'What made you get in touch now?' I can't help blurting it out. 'I know you said before about Ellen convincing you after she left prison, but . . . '

'She tracked me down a few days after coming out of prison . . . She didn't want me to mention anything about Nathan, though. She was so scared of the thought of going back inside. It took me a few months to find the courage to even send that email at the library. It was only when I looked for Peter, that I found out he was married to Monica.'

'What? You haven't been on Facebook or anything to search for us?'

She shakes her head slowly.

'It was too painful. What would've been the point when I couldn't be in your lives? I know it sounds flaky, what I'm saying, but after so many years of being away, I got used to feeling alone — the feeling of missing everyone as though you were all dead.'

My mouth drops open.

She looks up at me. 'God, that sounds terrible,' she says. 'I didn't mean . . . I . . . I'm not very good at explaining things. I missed you very much, Anna.'

'I missed you too,' I say, looking at her and realising I don't know her very well at all — not the person she is now. I stir my tea, even though it's probably stone cold by now. 'Gran talked about you all the time. She encouraged me to keep a scrapbook about you. Would you like to see it?'

'Did she?' A tear rolls down her cheek. 'I thought everyone would've forgotten about me. Yes please, Anna. I'd love to see it.'

I jump up from the chair and almost run into the living room to get my book of facts about her. I leave the photographs Robert took in Tenerife in the box; she wouldn't want to see them after what happened there.

I hand her the scrapbook; she pushes her cup to one side and places the book in front, stroking the cover with her fingers. She opens it. My cheeks warm a little; no one has read it before. Those facts were all mine, but they are, actually, all hers.

She laughs. 'I wish I still had those Doc Martens.'

'Grandad might still have them. He kept all of your clothes, well until recently. He's had a sort through them.'

'I don't blame him for having a clear out — I had so many things I didn't even wear.'

'Did you . . . have you ever . . . '

'Met someone else?'

'Yes.'

'There was someone a few years ago — serious, I think, but I guess you have to love yourself before you love someone else, don't you? I suppose I've always believed I didn't deserve happiness.' She reaches over and strokes my hand. 'I'm not going anywhere. You do believe me, don't you?'

The front door opens, and there are whispers in the hallway.

Debbie and I look to the kitchen door, and Jack appears. Sophie's hiding behind him.

'Is that you, Sophie?' says Debbie softly.

My little girl peeks her head around her dad's waist and nods, before retreating.

Debbie points to one of the cakes, and I nod.

'Would you like a fondant fancy, Sophie?' says Debbie. 'They're my favourite.'

Sophie walks to the table and pulls out a chair before sitting down.

'Yes please,' she says shyly.

I push the plate towards her and she picks up a pink cake, biting the icing off from around the edges.

'I used to do that,' Debbie says, dabbing her cheeks with the back of her sleeve.

'I thought you were dead,' says Sophie.

Silence.

Debbie looks at each of us.

'I've been away. I wasn't well.'

'Are you going to stay now?' my little girl says.

'Yes,' says Debbie without hesitation. 'Yes, I am.'

Acknowledgements

A massive thank you to my brilliant editor, Phoebe Morgan, whose insight and support has been invaluable. Thanks too to Sabah Khan, Elon Woodman-Worrell, Elke Desanghere, and the fantastic team at Avon.

A big thank you to my agent, Caroline Hardman and everyone at Hardman & Swainson.

To Lydia Devadason and Sam Carrington, who have read nearly everything I've ever written.Your support and friendship has been unwavering, supportive, and much appreciated.

To WU for the chat and laughter (and . . . er . . . we do talk about writing some of the time . . .).

Thanks to Ami and Dan at Waterstones, Preston, to Steve and Denise at Nantwich Bookshop, and to Tom Earnshaw at the *Lancashire Post*.

Thanks to my mum, Carmel, for the patience in answering all of my questions about the 1980s — from maternity wards to bad food. To Rosemary McFarlane for the advice on Lytham Club days of the past.

Thank you to Janet Dyer and the lovely ladies at the art group for the tea, cake, laughs and support.

A big shout-out to the bloggers for the time and energy you spend reading, reviewing and blogging.

To Dea Parkin at the CWA, to Claire

Reynolds, Louise Fiorentino, Alison Stokes. A big thank you for your support.

A shout-out to Chris, Loretta, Oliver, Nick, James, Conor, Sam, Janny, Maralyn, Jackie, Anne, Carolyn, and Caroline.

To my family: Dom, Dan and Joe, who (mostly) allow me to write in peace (the caravan helps).

And last, but definitely not least, thank you to my lovely readers.

We do hope that you have enjoyed reading this large print book.

Did you know that all of our titles are available for purchase?

We publish a wide range of high quality large print books including:
**Romances, Mysteries, Classics
General Fiction
Non Fiction and Westerns**

Special interest titles available in large print are:
**The Little Oxford Dictionary
Music Book
Song Book
Hymn Book
Service Book**

Also available from us courtesy of Oxford University Press:
**Young Readers' Dictionary
(large print edition)
Young Readers' Thesaurus
(large print edition)**

For further information or a free brochure, please contact us at:
**Ulverscroft Large Print Books Ltd.,
The Green, Bradgate Road, Anstey,
Leicester, LE7 7FU, England.
Tel:** (00 44) 0116 236 4325
Fax: (00 44) 0116 234 0205

Other titles published by Ulverscroft:

99 RED BALLOONS

Elisabeth Carpenter

Eight-year-old Grace is last seen in a sweet shop. Her mother Emma is living a nightmare. But as her loved ones rally around her, cracks begin to emerge. What are the emails sent between her husband and her sister? Why does her mother take so long to join the search? And is there more to the disappearance of her daughter than meets the eye? Meanwhile, ageing widow Maggie Taylor sees a familiar face in the newspaper. A face that jolts her from the pain of her existence into a spiralling obsession with another girl — the first girl who disappeared . . .

PENGUIN BOOKS

Published by the Penguin Group
Penguin Books Ltd, 27 Wrights Lane, London W8 5TZ, England
Penguin Books USA Inc., 375 Hudson Street, New York, New York 10014, USA
Penguin Books Australia Ltd, Ringwood, Victoria, Australia
Penguin Books Canada Ltd, 10 Alcorn Avenue, Toronto, Ontario, Canada M4V 3B2
Penguin Books (NZ) Ltd, 182–190 Wairau Road, Auckland 10, New Zealand

Penguin Books Ltd, Registered Offices: Harmondsworth, Middlesex, England

First published 1990
Published in Penguin Classics 1991
9 10 8

Introduction and translation copyright © David West, 1990
All rights reserved

The moral right of the author has been asserted

Filmset in 10/12 Lasercomp Bembo
Printed in England by Clays Ltd, St Ives plc

CONTENTS

I

STORM AND BANQUET

I sing of arms and of the man, fated to be an exile, who long since left the land of Troy and came to Italy to the shores of Lavinium; and a great pounding he took by land and sea at the hands of the heavenly gods because of the fierce and unforgetting anger of Juno. Great too were his sufferings in war before he could found his city and carry his gods into Latium. This was the beginning of the Latin race, the Alban fathers and the high walls of Rome. Tell me, Muse, the causes of her anger. How did he violate the will of the Queen of the Gods? What was his offence? Why did she drive a man famous for his piety to such endless hardship and such suffering? Can there be so much anger in the hearts of the heavenly gods?

There was an ancient city held by colonists from Tyre, opposite Italy and the distant mouth of the river Tiber. It was a city of great wealth and ruthless in the pursuit of war. Its name was Carthage, and Juno is said to have loved it more than any other place, more even than Samos. Here the goddess kept her armour. Here was her chariot, and this was the city she had long favoured, intending to give it sovereignty over the peoples of the earth, if only the Fates would allow it. But she had heard that there was rising from the blood of Troy a race of men who in days to come would overthrow this Tyrian citadel; a people proud in war and rulers of a great empire would come to sack the land of Libya; this is the destiny the Fates were

wheels touching the crests of the waves. As when disorder arises among the people of a great city and the
common mob runs riot, wild passion finds weapons for
150 men's hands and torches and rocks start flying; at such a
time if people chance to see a man who has some weight
among them for his goodness and his services to the state,
they fall silent, standing and listening with all their attention
while his words command their passions and soothe their
hearts — so did all the crashing of the sea fall silent and
Father Neptune, looking out over the waves, drove the
horses of his chariot beneath a clear sky and gave them rein
to fly before the wind.

Aeneas and his men were exhausted, and making what
speed they could for the nearest land, they set course for
160 the coast of Libya. There is a place where a harbour is
formed by an island blocking the mouth of a long sound.
As the waves come in from the open sea and break on the
sides of this island, they are divided into the deep inlets of
the bay. Rock cliffs are everywhere. A great pinnacle
threatens the sky on either side, and beneath all this the
broad water lies still and safe. At the end of the bay there
rises a backcloth of shimmering trees, a dark wood with
quivering shadows, looming over the water, and there, at
the foot of this scene, is a cave of hanging rocks, a home
for the nymphs, with fresh spring water inside it and seats
in the virgin rock. Here there is no need of chains to moor
the weary ships, or of anchors with hooked teeth to hold
170 them fast. This is where Aeneas put in with seven ships
gathered from all the Trojan fleet, and great was their
longing for the land as they disembarked and stepped at
last on to the shore and threw their sea-wasted bodies
down on the sand. First of all Achates struck a spark from
the flint, caught it in some leaves, fed the flame by putting
dry twigs round it and set the fire going with brushwood.
Then weary as they were after all their labours, they laid
out their corn, the gift of the goddess Ceres, all tainted

2

THE FALL OF TROY

They all fell silent, gazing at Father Aeneas, and he began
to speak from his raised couch: 'O Queen, the sorrow you
bid me bring to life again is past all words, the destruction
by the Greeks of the wealth of Troy and of the kingdom
that will be mourned for ever, and all the horrors I have
seen, and in which I played a large part. No man could
speak of such things and not weep, none of the Myrmidons
of Achilles or the Dolopians of Neoptolemus, not even a
follower of Ulixes, a man not prone to pity. Besides, the
dewy night is already falling fast from the sky and the
setting stars are speaking to us of sleep. But if you have   10
such a great desire to know what we suffered, to hear in
brief about the last agony of Troy, although my mind
recoiled in anguish when you asked and I shudder to
remember, I shall begin:

Year after year the leaders of the Greeks had been broken
in war and denied by the Fates, until, with the aid of the
divine skill of Pallas Athene, they built a horse the size of a
mountain, cutting pine trees to weave into it for ribs. They
pretended it was a votive offering for their safe return to
Greece, and that was the story on men's lips. Then they
chose some men by lot from their best warriors and shut
them up in the darkness of its belly, filling the vast cavern   20
of its womb with armed soldiers.

Within sight of the mainland is the island of Tenedos,

shouted together that it should be taken to a proper place
and prayers offered up to the goddess. We breached the
walls and laid open the buildings of our city. They all
buckled to the task, setting wheels to roll beneath the
horse's feet and stretching ropes of flax to its neck. The
engine of Fate mounted our walls, teeming with armed
men. Unmarried girls and boys sang their hymns around it
and rejoiced to have a hand on the rope. On it came,   240
gliding smoothly, looking down on the heart of the city.
O my native land! O Ilium, home of the gods! O walls of
the people of Dardanus, famous in war! Four times it
stopped on the very threshold of the gate, and four times
the armour clanged in its womb. But we paid no heed and
pressed on blindly, madly, and stood the accursed monster
on our consecrated citadel. Even at this last moment Cassandra was still opening her lips to foretell the future, but God
had willed that these were lips the Trojans would never
believe. This was the last day of a doomed people and we
spent it adorning the shrines of the gods all through the
city with festal garlands.

Meanwhile the sky was turning and night was rushing   250
up from the Ocean to envelop in its great shadow the
earth, the sky and the treachery of the Greeks, while the
Trojans were lying quiet in their homes, their weary
bodies wrapped in sleep. The Greek fleet in full array was
already taking the army from Tenedos through the friendly
silence of the moon and making for the shore they knew
so well, when the royal flagship raised high the fire signal
and Sinon, preserved by the cruelty of the divine Fates,
stealthily undid the pine bolts of the horse and freed the
Greeks from its womb. The wooden horse was open, and   260
the Greeks were pouring gratefully out of its hollow
chambers into the fresh air, the commanders Thessandrus
and Sthenelus and fierce Ulixes sliding down the rope they
had lowered, and with them Acamas, Thoas, Neoptolemus
of the line of Peleus, Machaon, who came out first, Mene-

PENGUIN CLASSICS

THE AENEID

Publius Vergilius Maro was born in 70 B.C. near Mantua in the north of Italy, where his parents owned a farm. He had a good education and went to perfect it in Rome. There he came under the influence of Epicureanism and later joined an Epicurean colony on the Gulf of Naples where he was based for the rest of his life. In 42 B.C. he began to write the *Eclogues*, which he completed in 37 B.C., the year in which he accompanied Horace to Brindisi. The *Georgics* were finished in 29 B.C., and he devoted the rest of his life to the composition of the *Aeneid*. In his last year he started on a journey to Greece; meeting Augustus at Athens, he decided to travel back with him but he fell ill at Megara. He died in 19 B.C. on reaching Brindisi.

David West is an Aberdonian, educated at the local grammar school and university and then at Sidney Sussex College, Cambridge. He has taught in the Universities of Sheffield and Edinburgh and since 1969 has been Professor of Latin at Newcastle upon Tyne. His publications include *Reading Horace* (1967) and *The Imagery and Poetry of Lucretius* (1969). He notes with sorrow that no such career would now be possible, since the departments of Classics at Aberdeen and Sheffield are both defunct.

VIRGIL

THE
AENEID

A NEW PROSE TRANSLATION BY
DAVID WEST

PENGUIN BOOKS

PENGUIN BOOKS

Published by the Penguin Group
Penguin Books Ltd, 27 Wrights Lane, London W8 5TZ, England
Penguin Books USA Inc., 375 Hudson Street, New York, New York 10014, USA
Penguin Books Australia Ltd, Ringwood, Victoria, Australia
Penguin Books Canada Ltd, 10 Alcorn Avenue, Toronto, Ontario, Canada M4V 3B2
Penguin Books (NZ) Ltd, 182–190 Wairau Road, Auckland 10, New Zealand

Penguin Books Ltd, Registered Offices: Harmondsworth, Middlesex, England

First published 1990
Published in Penguin Classics 1991
9 10 8

Filmset in 10/12 Lasercomp Bembo
Printed in England by Clays Ltd, St Ives plc

CONTENTS

To the great dead who will not die

INTRODUCTION

I. A POEM FOR OUR TIME

The *Aeneid* is the story of a man who lived three thousand years ago in the city of Troy in the north-west tip of Asia Minor. What has that to do with us?

Troy was besieged and sacked by the Greeks. After a series of disasters Aeneas met and loved a woman, Dido, queen of Carthage, but obeyed the call of duty to his people and his gods and left her to her death. Then, after long years of wandering, he reached Italy, fought a bitter war against the peoples of Latium and in the end formed an alliance with them which enabled him to found his city of Lavinium. From these beginnings, in 333 years, in 753 B.C., the city of Rome was to be founded. The Romans had arrived in Italy.

The *Aeneid* is still read and still resonates because it is a great poem. Part of its relevance to us is that it is the story of a human being who knew defeat and dispossession, love and the loss of love, whose life was ruled by his sense of duty to his gods, his people and his family, particularly to his beloved son Ascanius. But it was a hard duty and he sometimes wearied in it. He knew about war and hated the waste and ugliness of it, but fought, when he had to fight, with hatred and passion. At the end of the twentieth century the world is full of such people. While we are of them and feel for them we shall find something in the

Aeneid. The gods have changed, but for men there is not much difference:

Pitiless Mars was now dealing grief and death to both sides with impartial hand. Victors and vanquished killed and were killed and neither side thought of flight. In the halls of Jupiter the gods pitied the futile anger of the two armies and grieved that men had so much suffering . . .

                                        10.755–9

But the *Aeneid* is not simply a contemplation of the general human predicament. It is also full of individual human beings behaving as human beings still do. Take the charm and humour of Dido putting the Trojans at their ease at 1.562–78; the grief of Andromache when she meets the Trojan youth who is the same age as her son Astyanax would have been if he had been allowed to live – we do not need to be told that Astyanax is the name on the second altar at 3.305; the cunning of Acestes and Aeneas as they shame the great old champion back into the ring at 5.389–408; the childish joke of Iulus at 7.116 and its momentous interpretation; the aged hero feasting his eyes on his old friend's son at 8.152 or realizing at 8.560 that he can do nothing now except talk; the native's abuse of the foreigners from 9.598; the lying harridans at the beginning of Book Ten or the death of Mezentius and his horse from 10.858; the growling of Aeneas and the fussing and fumbling of the doctor as he plies his mute, inglorious art from 12.387.

The *Aeneid* presents a heroic view of the life of man in all its splendour and anguish, but it is also full of just observation of the details of individual behaviour. It is not yet out of date.

2. THE *AENEID* IN ITS OWN TIME

Virgil was born seventy years before Christ. In 44 B.C., after a century of civil war and disorder, Julius Caesar was assassinated by Brutus and Cassius in the name of liberty. His heir was his nineteen-year-old grand-nephew and adopted son, Octavian, astute, ruthless and determined. In 42 B.C. Brutus and Cassius were defeated and the fortunes of Virgil were at their lowest ebb. His family estates at Mantua were confiscated by the victors to provide land for their soldiers to settle on. But he won the patronage of Maecenas, one of the two chief aides of Octavian, and published his pastoral *Eclogues* in 37 B.C. In 29 B.C., after Octavian had made himself master of the known world by defeating Antony and Cleopatra at Actium, Virgil finished what Dryden called 'the best poem of the best poet', the *Georgics*, on the agriculture of Italy. Throughout the twenties Virgil was at work on his *Aeneid*, a poem in imitation of Homer's *Iliad* and *Odyssey* and in praise of Augustus, the name Octavian had taken on 16 January 27 B.C. Virgil died before finishing it, on his way back from Athens with Augustus in 19 B.C. To qualify for membership of the Senate, a Roman had to be extremely wealthy. When Virgil died, he owned property ten times that requirement. He left instructions that the *Aeneid* was to be burned. These instructions were countermanded by Augustus.

It is therefore clear that Virgil wrote and wrote acceptably in praise of his patron, the ruler of Rome. The *Aeneid* is successful panegyric.

It would be easy to despise or dislike the poem for that. But wrong, for the following reasons:

(1) Rome had endured a century of violence, discord, corruption and insecurity of life and property. Augustus, after intense effort and suffering, notably in his disastrous campaign in Sicily in 37 B.C., by his victory at Actium promised peace, order, prosperity and moral regeneration. He even, according to Suetonius (*Life of Augustus* 89), fostered the talents of his generation in

every possible way. It was the promise of a Golden Age, and in this euphoria Virgil and his friend Horace, another client of Maecenas and Augustus, wrote their great patriotic poems. In that day it was not foolish to hope and to believe.

(2) Although Virgil wrote in praise of Augustus and the ideal of empire, he was no Chauvin. He loved country people and country ways, their traditions and their stubborn independence. He responded to human love, between man and woman, between father and son, between men and their homes (consider only 6.450ff., 12.435ff., 10.779ff.), and he knew that empire had to be bought with the coin of human suffering and deprivation. He also knew the other side – the hard work and danger, the dedication and sacrifice which empire demanded of those who had made it and who maintained it, notably Augustus. Virgil does not solve the problems inherent in all this. He does not even pose them. The *Aeneid* is a story. But behind that story we have all the issues which would have moved a contemporary Roman, and may still move us.

(3) Praise is one thing. Flattery is another, and the *Aeneid* is not flattery. The action of the epic is set a thousand years before Augustus and it praises him in two ways: first, by telling the story of his great ancestor, the first founder of Rome, in such a way as resembles the story of Augustus himself, its third founder. The resemblances are not pointed out. The reader is left to observe and ponder them for himself if he wishes. The second mode of praise is direct allusion to Augustus in prophecies and visions, notably near the beginning and end of the poem, in the descent of Aeneas to consult his father in the underworld at the end of Book Six and on the great shield of Aeneas at the end of Book Eight.

The *Aeneid* is, among other things, a search for a vision

of peace and order for Rome and for humanity. To see its outlines through the mists of time nothing is more helpful than the family tree of the Julians on page 339. Allusions to these names in the *Aeneid* are often to be heard as praise of Augustus, the contemporary Julian.

3. THIS TRANSLATION

Received wisdom, as represented by *The Proceedings of the Virgil Society* 19(1988)14, states that 'to translate poetry into prose is always a folly'. Leaving aside the fact that I am not a poet, I have had to reject this because I know of nobody at the end of our century who reads long narrative poems in English, and I want the *Aeneid* to be read. I believe also that this view does less than justice to the range, power and music of contemporary English prose. As written by our best novelists and journalists and even sometimes by ordinary letter-writers, it daily moves us towards pity, terror or laughter, and does so at least as effectively as the voices of contemporary poets. Further – this is ungentle but the argument requires that it be said – the English poets who have translated the *Aeneid* since Dryden have not done well. We may accept that poetic translation need not be true to the tone or detail of the original. A poet's first concern is with his own poem. But if we grant this freedom, we must then judge their works as poems, and as such the poetic translations of the *Aeneid* are low in interest and inspiration.

The ruling prose version is Jackson Knight's Penguin Classic of 1956. This is lovingly faithful to the author's vision of Virgil but the language is dated. It would be difficult to disagree with Sandbach's judgement in *The Proceedings of the Virgil Society* 10(1970–71)35 (reprinted in *Meminisse Iuvabit* (1989), ed. F. Robertson): '. . . too often the attempt to grasp and represent each of Virgil's words has pushed aside the need to give the sentence rhythm and cohesion and the emphasis that goes with form.'

The present version has two objectives. When Peter Schidlof died, one of the other members of the Amadeus Quartet was asked what their approach had been, and he replied: 'Loyalty to the spirit and the letter.' As a translator I think of the letter and the spirit. I have tried to be utterly faithful to everything I see and hear in the Latin, the rhetoric, nuances, colour, tone, pace, passion, even the peerless music of Virgil's verse, which Tennyson thought 'the stateliest measure ever moulded by the lips of man'. This, of course, is impossible, as Neruda well realizes:

> Now it is clear this couldn't be done –
> that in this net it's not just the strings that count
> but also the air that escapes through the meshes.
>
> Pablo Neruda, 'Isla Negra', trs. Alastair Reid

My second aim has been to write readable English which does honour to the richness and sublimity of Virgil's language – ebullient, for example in the utterances of Aeneas at the games in Book Five, charged with grief for the death of Marcellus at the end of Book Six and ringing with the courage and cruelty of war in the four great last books. Another impossible task. But if it is to be attempted, the translator must be ready to jettison the idiom of Latin and search for the English words that will carry as much as possible of the spirit of the Latin.

By this creed there are two great sins: to fall short of Virgil through sloth or ineptitude or self-love; and to write what is dull. If it is dull, it is not a translation of Virgil. This version admits defeat in every line, but where it seems to abandon some feature of the Latin, I hope it is always in an attempt to respond in living English to the poetic eloquence of its great original.

FURTHER READING

Anyone who is new to Virgil and would like to learn more about him would be well advised to start with W. A. Camps, *An Introduction to Virgil's 'Aeneid'* (1969), Oxford, and the Penguin translations of the *Georgics* and the *Eclogues*.

ACKNOWLEDGEMENTS

The text used, with very few exceptions, is the Oxford Classical Text by Sir Roger Mynors. This translation is of course based on such of the vast scholarly literature as I have been able to read. Previous translations have been plundered. Standard commentaries have been consulted, notably R. G. Austin on Books 1, 2, 4 and 6, R. D. Williams on 3 and 5, C. J. Fordyce on 7 and 8. Particularly valuable have been E. Norden on 6, P. T. Eden on 8 and Stephen Harrison who gave me access to his forthcoming commentary on 10 and corresponded vigorously with me for a whole summer. The *Aeneidea* of James Henry have been an inspiration.

For years now my friends have been set to work daily on Virgilian problems, and have saved me from many errors. Rosemary Burton and E. L. Harrison criticized the whole translation. Stephen Harrison, James Morwood and Nicholas Horsfall have commented on whole books or extended passages. Pamela West, Janet Watson and Jane Curran have been shrewd and generous consultants. To all of these I owe a debt that cannot be paid, as I do to my wonderful colleagues in the best of all imaginable university departments of Classics.

DAVID WEST
Newcastle upon Tyne

THE AENEID

Paris, son of Priam, king of Troy, has judged Venus to be more beautiful than Juno and Pallas Athene, and claimed his reward, Helen, wife of Menelaus, king of Sparta. The Greeks have gathered an army and sacked the city of Troy. Aeneas has escaped with his son Ascanius Iulus and his father Anchises. Driven by the jealous hatred of Juno, he has wandered across the Mediterranean for six years, trying to found a new city. At the beginning of the poem, his father has just died in Sicily and Aeneas is sailing at last for Italy . . .

I

STORM AND BANQUET

I sing of arms and of the man, fated to be an exile, who long since left the land of Troy and came to Italy to the shores of Lavinium; and a great pounding he took by land and sea at the hands of the heavenly gods because of the fierce and unforgetting anger of Juno. Great too were his sufferings in war before he could found his city and carry his gods into Latium. This was the beginning of the Latin race, the Alban fathers and the high walls of Rome. Tell me, Muse, the causes of her anger. How did he violate the will of the Queen of the Gods? What was his offence? Why did she drive a man famous for his piety to such $_{10}$ endless hardship and such suffering? Can there be so much anger in the hearts of the heavenly gods?

There was an ancient city held by colonists from Tyre, opposite Italy and the distant mouth of the river Tiber. It was a city of great wealth and ruthless in the pursuit of war. Its name was Carthage, and Juno is said to have loved it more than any other place, more even than Samos. Here the goddess kept her armour. Here was her chariot, and this was the city she had long favoured, intending to give it sovereignty over the peoples of the earth, if only the Fates would allow it. But she had heard that there was rising from the blood of Troy a race of men who in days to come would overthrow this Tyrian citadel; a people $_{20}$ proud in war and rulers of a great empire would come to sack the land of Libya; this is the destiny the Fates were

unrolling. These were the fears of the daughter of Saturn, and she had not forgotten the war she had fought long since at Troy for her beloved Argos, nor had her bitter resentment and the reasons for it ever left her mind. There still rankled deep in her heart the judgement of Paris and the injustice of the slight to her beauty, her loathing for the whole stock of Dardanus and her fury at the honours done to Ganymede, whom her husband Jupiter had carried off to be his cup-bearer. With all this fuelling her anger she
30 was keeping the remnants of the Trojans, those who had escaped the savagery of Achilles and the Greeks, far away from Latium, driven by the Fates to wander year after year round all the oceans of the world. So heavy was the cost of founding the Roman race.

The Trojans were in high spirits. They were almost out of sight of Sicily and heading for the open sea with the wind astern and their bronze prows churning the salt sea to foam, as Juno brooded, still nursing the eternal wound deep in her breast: 'Am I to admit defeat and give up my attempt to keep the king of the Trojans away from Italy? So the Fates do not approve! Yet Pallas Athene could fire
40 the fleet and drown my own Argives in the sea because of the guilt of one man, the mad passion of Ajax, son of Oileus. With her own hand she threw the consuming fire of Jupiter from the clouds, shattering his ships and sending winds to churn up the level sea. Then, as he breathed out flame from his breast where the thunderbolt had pierced it, she caught him up in a whirlwind and impaled him on a jagged rock. But here am I, the Queen of the Gods, the sister of Jupiter and his wife, and I have waged war all these years against a whole race of men! Is there no one left who worships the godhead of Juno? Will there be no one in the future to pray to me and lay an offering on my altars?'
50 These are the thoughts the goddess turned over in her burning heart as she came to Aeolia, the home of the clouds, a place teeming with the raging winds of the south.

Here Aeolus is king and here in a vast cavern he keeps in subjection the brawling winds and howling storms, chained and
bridled in their prison. They murmur in loud protest round
bolted gates in the mountainside while Aeolus sits in his
high citadel, holding his sceptre, soothing their spirits and
tempering their angry passions. But for him they would
catch up the sea, the earth and the deeps of the sky and
sweep them along through space. In fear of this, the
All-powerful Father banished them to these black caverns 60
with massive mountains heaped over them, and gave them
under a fixed charter a king who knew how to hold them
in check or, when ordered, to let them run with free rein.
It was to him that Juno made supplication in these words:
'I come to you, Aeolus, because the Father of the Gods and
King of Men has given you the power to calm the waves
of the sea or raise them by your winds. A race of men
hateful to me is sailing the Tyrrhenian sea carrying Ilium
to Italy, along with the Penates, their defeated gods. Whip
up your winds. Overwhelm their ships and sink them.
Drive their fleet in all directions and scatter their bodies 70
over the sea. I have fourteen nymphs of the rarest beauty
and the loveliest of them all is Deiopea. I shall make her
yours and join you in lawful wedlock. If you do me this
service, she shall spend all her years with you and make
you the father of beautiful children.'

To this Aeolus made answer: 'Your task, O queen, is to
decide your wishes; my duty is to carry out your orders. It
is thanks to you that I rule this little kingdom and enjoy
this sceptre and the blessing of Jupiter. Through you I have
a couch to lie on at the feasts of the gods, and my power 80
over cloud and storm comes from you.'

At these words he struck the side of the hollow mountain
with the butt of his spear and the winds seemed to form a
column and pour out through an open gate to blow a
hurricane over the whole earth. The east wind and the
south and the south-west with its squalls all fell upon the

sea at once, whipping it up from its bottom-most depths
and rolling huge waves towards its shores. Men shouted,
ropes screamed, clouds suddenly blotted out the light of
the sky from the eyes of the Trojans and black night
90 brooded over the sea as the heavens thundered and lightning flashed again and again across the sky. Wherever the
Trojans looked, death stared them in the face. A sudden
chill went through Aeneas and his limbs grew weak.
Groaning, he lifted his hands palms upward to the stars and
cried: 'Those whose fate it was to die beneath the high
walls of Troy with their fathers looking down on them
were many, many times more fortunate than I. O Diomede, bravest of the Greeks, why could I not have fallen
to your right hand and breathed out my life on the plains
of Troy, where fierce Hector was killed by the sword of
100 Achilles, where great Sarpedon lies and where the river
Simois caught up so many shields and helmets and bodies
of brave men and rolled them down its current?'

Even as he threw out these words, a squall came howling
from the north, catching his sail full on and raising the
waves to the stars. The oars broke, the prow was wrenched
round, and as they lay beam on to the seas, there came
towering over them a sheer mountain of water. Some of
the ships were hanging on the crests of the waves; for
others the waters opened and in the troughs could be seen
the sea-bed and the seething sand. Three of them were
caught by the south wind and driven off course on to a
reef hidden in mid-ocean – Italians know it as the Altars –
110 a huge spine of rock just under the surface; three of them
the southeaster took and carried helplessly from the high
sea on to the sandbanks of the Syrtes, ran them aground
and blocked them in with walls of sand; before the very
eyes of Aeneas, the ship that carried the faithful Orontes
and his Lycians was struck on the stern by a great sea and
the helmsman was swept away head first into the water.
Three times she spun round on the same spot till the swift

whirlpool sucked her down. Here and there men could be seen swimming in the vast ocean, and with them in the waves their armour, spars of wood and the treasures of Troy. One by one the stout ships of Ilioneus and brave Achates, then Abas and old Aletes, succumbed to the storm. The fastenings of the ships' sides were loosened, the deadly water poured in and the timbers sprang.

Neptune, meanwhile, observed the loud disturbance of the ocean, the release of storms, the draining of his deepest pools, and was moved to anger. Rising from the depths, he lifted his head high above the crests of the waves and looked serenely out over the sea at Aeneas' fleet scattered over the face of the waters and the Trojans overwhelmed by the waves and by the rending of the sky. He recognized at once the anger and the cunning of his sister Juno and instantly summoned the east wind and the west and spoke to them in these words: 'Is it your noble birth that has made you so sure of yourselves? Do you winds now dare to move heaven and earth and raise these great masses of water without my divine authority? I could take you now and . . . but first I must still the waves you have stirred up. For any crimes you commit in the future, you will pay a dearer price. Away with you and take this message to your king: "He is not the one who has jurisdiction over the sea or holds the trident that knows no pity. That is my responsibility, given to me by lot. His domain, O Eurus, wind of the east, is the huge crags where you have your home. That is where Aeolus can do his swaggering, confining his rule to the closed walls of the prison of the winds." '

These were his words, and before he had finished speaking, he was calming the swell, dispersing the banked clouds and bringing back the sun. Triton and the sea nymph Cymothoe heaved and strained as they pushed the ships off jagged rocks, while Neptune himself lifted them out of the sandbanks with his trident and opened up the vast Syrtes, restraining the sea as he skimmed along with his chariot wheels touching the crests of the waves. As when disorder arises among the people of a great city and the common mob runs riot, wild passion finds weapons for men's hands and torches and rocks start flying; at such a time if people chance to see a man who has some weight among them for his goodness and his services to the state, they fall silent, standing and listening with all their attention while his words command their passions and soothe their hearts – so did all the crashing of the sea fall silent and Father Neptune, looking out over the waves, drove the horses of his chariot beneath a clear sky and gave them rein to fly before the wind.

Aeneas and his men were exhausted, and making what speed they could for the nearest land, they set course for the coast of Libya. There is a place where a harbour is formed by an island blocking the mouth of a long sound. As the waves come in from the open sea and break on the sides of this island, they are divided into the deep inlets of the bay. Rock cliffs are everywhere. A great pinnacle threatens the sky on either side, and beneath all this the broad water lies still and safe. At the end of the bay there rises a backcloth of shimmering trees, a dark wood with quivering shadows, looming over the water, and there, at the foot of this scene, is a cave of hanging rocks, a home for the nymphs, with fresh spring water inside it and seats in the virgin rock. Here there is no need of chains to moor the weary ships, or of anchors with hooked teeth to hold them fast. This is where Aeneas put in with seven ships gathered from all the Trojan fleet, and great was their longing for the land as they disembarked and stepped at last on to the shore and threw their sea-wasted bodies down on the sand. First of all Achates struck a spark from the flint, caught it in some leaves, fed the flame by putting dry twigs round it and set the fire going with brushwood. Then weary as they were after all their labours, they laid out their corn, the gift of the goddess Ceres, all tainted with salt, and the goddess's own implements and set themselves to scorch with flame this grain they had saved from the sea and to grind it on stone.

Meanwhile Aeneas climbed a rock to get a view over 180 the whole breadth of the ocean and see if there was any trace of the storm-tossed Antheus or of the double-banked Trojan galleys, Capys perhaps, or Caicus' armour high on the poop. There was not a ship to be seen, but he did see three stags wandering about the shore with all their herd behind them grazing the low ground in a long line. He stopped in his tracks and snatched his bow and swift arrows from the trusty Achates. First he took down the 190 three leaders with their high heads of branching antlers. The whole of the rest of the herd scattered into the leafy cover of the wood, but not before he succeeded in stretching seven huge carcasses on the ground, one for each of the ships. He then made for the harbour and gave them out to all his men. Last of all he shared out the wine the good Acestes with a hero's generosity had poured into casks for them as they left the shores of Sicily. Then, as they mourned, he comforted them, saying: 'My friends, this is not the first trouble we have known. We have suffered worse before, and this too will pass. God will see to it. You 200 have been to Scylla's cave and heard the mad dogs howling in the depths of it. You have even survived rocks thrown by the Cyclops. So summon up your courage once again. This is no time for gloom or fear. The day will come, perhaps, when it will give you pleasure to remember even this. Whatever chance may bring, however many hardships we suffer, we are making for Latium, where the Fates show us our place of rest. There it is the will of God that the kingdom of Troy shall rise again. Your task is to endure and save yourselves for better days.' These were his words, but he was sick with all his cares. He showed them the face of hope and kept his misery deep in his heart.

His men went briskly to work preparing the coming 210

feast. They flayed the hide off the ribs and exposed the flesh. Some cut it into quivering slices and speared it on spits. Others laid out cauldrons of water on the shore and lit fires. Then at last they ate, and recovered their strength, lying on the grass and taking their fill of old wine and rich venison. When their hunger was satisfied and the remains of the feast removed, they talked at length about their missing comrades, not knowing whether to hope or fear, wondering whether they were still alive or whether at that very moment they were drawing their last breath and
220 beyond all calling. Most of all did Aeneas, who loved his men, mourn to himself the loss of eager Orontes and Amycus and the cruel death of Lycus, then brave Gyas, and brave Cloanthus.

Now the feast was ended and Jupiter was looking down from the height of heaven on the sea flying with sails and the land far beneath him, on the shores of the seas and the far-spread peoples, when suddenly he stopped in his survey at the highest point of the sky and fixed his eyes upon the kingdom of Libya. Even as he was turning over in his mind all the suffering that he saw, his daughter Venus came to him, her shining eyes brimming with tears, and
230 spoke with a sadness greater than his own: 'You who rule the affairs of gods and men with your eternal law and at whose lightning we are all afraid, what great harm has my son Aeneas been able to do to you? What crime have the Trojans committed that they should suffer all this loss of life and the whole world be closed to them for the sake of Italy? Did you not promise that with the rolling years there would come a time when from this stock the Romans would arise? From this blood of Teucer, recalled to Italian soil, there would come leaders of men who would hold power over every land and sea. O father, father, has some argument changed your mind? As for me, I used to console myself with this for the cruel fall and sack of Troy, by
240 weighing one destiny against another. But unrelieved mis-

fortune is now hounding these men from disaster to disaster. O great king, what end do you set to their labours? The Greeks were all around Antenor, but he escaped them, made his way safely into the Illyrian Gulf and the heartlands of the kingdom of the Liburnians, and then went beyond the mouth of the Timavus. From there with a great roar from inside the mountain, a sea of water bursts out of nine mouths and covers the fields with a sounding ocean. But in this place he founded the city of Patavium as a home for his Trojans and gave them a name. There he dedicated the arms with which he fought at Troy and there he now lives in settled peace and quiet. But as for us, your own children, 250 to whom you grant a place in the citadel of heaven, we lose our ships. It is unspeakable. We are betrayed and kept far away from the shores of Italy because there is one who hates us. Is this our reward for piety and obedience? Is this how you bring us to our kingdom?'

The Father of Gods and Men, looking at his daughter with the smile that clears the sky and dispels the storms, kissed her lightly on the lips, and said: 'Spare yourself these fears, my lady from Cythera. The destiny of your descendants remains unchanged. You will see the city of Lavinium and its promised walls. You will take great-hearted Aeneas 260 up to the stars of heaven. No argument changes my mind. But now, since you are tormented by this anxiety, I shall tell you more, unrolling for you the secrets of the scroll of the Fates. He will wage a great war in Italy and crush its fierce tribes. He will build walls for his people and establish their way of life, until a third summer has seen him reigning in Latium and a third winter has passed after the subjection of the Rutulians. But the reign of his son Ascanius, who now receives the second name Iulus (it was Ilus while the kingdom of Ilium still stood), shall last while thirty long years revolve, and he shall transfer his kingdom 270 from its seat at Lavinium and build a city with powerful fortifications at Alba Longa. Here the rule of the race of

Hector will last for three hundred long years until Ilia the royal priestess, heavy with the seed of Mars, shall give birth to twin sons. Then Romulus shall receive the people, wearing with joy the tawny hide of the wolf which nursed him. The walls he builds will be the walls of Mars and he shall give his own name to his people, the Romans. On them I impose no limits of time or place. I have given them an empire that will know no end. Even angry Juno,
280 who is now wearying sea and land and sky with her terrors, will come to better counsel and join with me in cherishing the people of Rome, the rulers of the world, the race that wears the toga. So it has been decreed. There will come a day, as the years glide by, when the house of Assaracus will reduce Achilles' Pthia and glorious Mycenae to slavery and will conquer and rule the city of Argos. From this noble stock there will be born a Trojan Caesar to bound his empire by Oceanus at the limits of the world, and his fame by the stars. He will be called Julius, a name
290 passed down to him from the great Iulus. In time to come, have no fear, you will receive him in the sky, laden with the spoils of the East. He too will be called upon in prayer. Then wars will be laid aside and the years of bitterness will be over. Silver-haired Truth and Vesta, and Romulus Quirinus with his brother Remus, will sit dispensing justice. The dread Gates of War with their tight fastenings of steel will then be closed, and godless Strife will sit inside them on his murderous armour roaring hideously from bloody mouth, hands shackled behind his back with a hundred bands of bronze.'

So spoke Jupiter, and he sent down Mercury, the son of Maia, to make the lands and the citadel of the new city of Carthage hospitable to the Trojans, in case Dido, in her
300 ignorance of destiny, should bar her country to them. Through the great expanse of air he flew, wielding his wings like oars, and soon alighted on the shores of Libya. There he lost no time in carrying out the commands of

Jupiter, and in accordance with the divine will the Carthaginians laid aside their fiery temper. Most of all the queen took into her heart a feeling of quiet and kindness towards the Trojans.

But all that night the dutiful Aeneas was turning many things over in his mind. As soon as life-giving morning came, he decided to go out and explore this new land and bring back to his men a true account of the shores to which the winds had driven him, and the beasts and men who lived there, if there were any men, for he saw no signs of cultivation. So, leaving his ships hidden in the 310 wooded cove under the overhanging rocks, and shut in on every side by trees and quivering shade, he set out alone with Achates, gripping two broad-bladed steel spears in his hand. As he walked through the middle of the wood, his mother came to meet him looking like a Spartan girl out hunting, wearing the dress of a Spartan girl and carrying her weapons, or like the Thracian Harpalyce, as she wearies horses with her running and outstrips the swift current of the river Hebrus. She had a light bow hanging from her shoulders in hunting style, her hair was unbound and streaming in the wind and her flowing dress was caught up 320 above the knee. 'Hey there, soldiers,' she called out to them, 'do you happen to have seen one of my sisters wandering about here or in full cry after the foaming boar? She was wearing a spotted lynx skin and had a quiver hanging from her belt.'

So spoke Venus, and Venus' son so began his reply: 'I have neither seen nor heard any of your sisters. But how am I to address a girl like you? Your face is not the face of a mortal, and you do not speak like a human being. Surely you must be a goddess? Are you Diana, sister of Apollo? Are you one of the sister nymphs? Be gracious to us, 330 whoever you may be, and lighten our distress. Tell us what sky this is we now find ourselves beneath. What shore of the world is this on which we now wander,

tossed here by the fury of wind and wave? We do not
know the place. We do not know the people. Tell us and
many a victim will fall by my right hand before your
altars.'

Venus replied: 'I am sure I deserve no such honour.
Tyrian girls all carry the quiver and wear purple boots
with this high ankle binding. This is a Phoenician kingdom
you are looking at. We are Tyrians. This is the city of the
people of Agenor, but the land belongs to the Libyans, a
race not easy to handle in war. Dido, who came from the
340 city of Tyre to escape her brother, holds sway here. There
was a crime long ago. It is a long and winding story, but I
shall trace its outlines for you. Her father had given her in
marriage to Sychaeus, the wealthiest of the Phoenicians.
They were joined with all the due rites of a first marriage
and great was the love the poor queen bore for him. But
the kingdom of Tyre was ruled by her brother Pygmalion,
the vilest of criminals. A mad passion came between the
350 two men. In blind lust for his gold the godless Pygmalion
attacked him without warning, ambushing him at the
altar. With no thought for his sister's love he killed Sychaeus and for a long time concealed what he had done.
Dido was sick with love and he deceived her with false
hopes and empty pretences. But one night there appeared
to her in a dream the very ghost of her unburied husband.
He lifted up his face, pale with the strange pallor of the
dead, and, baring the sword wounds on his breast, he
pointed to the altar where he had been killed and revealed
the whole horror of the crime that had been hidden in
their house. He then urged her to escape with all speed
from their native land, and to help her on her wanderings
he showed her where to find an ancient treasure buried in
the earth, an incalculable weight of silver and gold. This
360 moved Dido to plan her escape and gather followers, men
driven by savage hatred or lively fear of the tyrant. They
seized some ships which happened to be ready for sea.

They loaded them with the gold and sailed away with the wealth Pygmalion had coveted. The woman led the whole undertaking. When they arrived at the place where you will now see the great walls and rising citadel of the new city of Carthage, they bought a piece of land called the "Byrsa", the animal's hide, as large an area as they could include within the hide of a bull. But now tell me, who are you? What country have you sailed from? Where are you making for?' 370

In reply to her questions Aeneas drew a great sigh from the bottom of his heart and said: 'O goddess, if I were to start at the beginning and retrace our whole story, and if you had the time to listen to the annals of our suffering, before I finish the doors of Olympus would close and the Evening Star would lay the day to rest. We come from the ancient city of Troy, if the name of Troy has ever reached your ears. We have sailed many seas and by the chance of the winds we have been driven ashore here in Libya. I am Aeneas, known for my devotion. I carry with me on my ships the gods of my home, the Penates, wrested from my enemies, and my fame has reached beyond the skies. I am searching for my fatherland in Italy. My descent is from 380 highest Jupiter. With my goddess mother to show the way, I embarked upon the Phrygian sea with twenty ships, following the destiny which had been given to me, and now a bare seven of them remain, and these torn to pieces by wind and wave. I am a helpless stranger, driven out of Europe and out of Asia, tramping the desert wastes of Libya.'

Venus could listen to no more. She broke in on the tale of his sufferings, saying: 'Whoever you are, you breathe the breath of life and you have come to this Tyrian city. I do not believe you are hated by the gods. Go on now from here to the queen's door. I can tell you that your comrades 390 are restored and your fleet returned to you. The winds have veered to the north and blown them safe to shore. All

this is true unless my parents have failed in their efforts to teach me to interpret the flight of birds. Look at these twelve swans flying joyfully in formation. The eagle of Jupiter was swooping down on them from the heights of heaven and scattering them over the open sky, but now look at them in their long column. Some are reaching land. Some have already reached it and are looking down on it. Just as they have come to their home and their flock has circled the sky in play, singing as they fly with whirring
400 wings, so your ships and your warriors are either already in port or crossing the bar in full sail. Go on now, and follow where the road takes you.'

When she had finished speaking and was turning away, her neck shone with a rosy light and her hair breathed the divine odour of ambrosia. Her dress flowed free to her feet and as she walked he knew she was truly a goddess. As she hastened away, he recognized her as his mother and called after her: 'Why do you so often mock your own son by taking on these disguises? You too are cruel. Why am I never allowed to take your hand in mine, to hear your true voice and speak to you as you really are?'

410 With these reproaches he took the road that led to the city, but Venus hedged them about with a thick mist as they walked. The goddess spread a great veil of cloud over them so that no one could see them or touch them or cause any delay or ask the reason for their coming. She herself soared high into the sky and departed for Paphos, returning happily to her beloved home where she has her temple, and a hundred altars steam with the incense of Sheba and breathe the fragrance of fresh-cut flowers.

Meanwhile Aeneas and Achates hurried on their way, following the track, and they were soon climbing the great
420 hill which towered over the city and looked down upon the citadel opposite. Aeneas was amazed by the size of it where recently there had been nothing but shepherds' huts, amazed too by the gates, the paved streets and all the stir.

The Tyrians were working with a will: some of them were laying out the line of walls or rolling up great stones for building the citadel; others were choosing sites for building and marking them out with the plough; others were drawing up laws and electing magistrates and a senate whom they could revere; on one side they were excavating a harbour; on the other laying deep foundations for a theatre and quarrying huge columns from the rock to make a handsome backdrop for the stage that was to be. They were like bees at the beginning of summer, busy in the sunshine all through the flowery meadows, bringing out the young of the race, just come of age, or treading the oozing honey and swelling the cells with sweet nectar, or taking the loads as they come in or mounting guard to keep the herds of idle drones out of their farmstead. The hive seethes with activity and the fragrance of honey flavoured with thyme is everywhere. 'How fortunate they are!' cried Aeneas, now looking up at the high tops of the buildings. '*Their* walls are already rising!' and he moved on through the middle of the people, hedged about by the miraculous cloud, and no one saw him.

There was a wooded grove which gave abundant shade in the middle of the city. When first the Phoenicians had been driven there by wind and wave, Juno, the Queen of the Gods, had led them to this spot where they had dug up the head of a spirited stallion. This was a sign that from generation to generation they would be a race glorious in war and would have no difficulty in finding fields to graze. Here Sidonian Dido was building for Juno a huge temple rich with offerings and rich, too, with the presence of the goddess. It was a raised temple, and at the top of its steps the threshold was of bronze, the beams were jointed with bronze and the bronze doors grated as they turned in their sockets. Here in this grove Aeneas saw a strange sight which for the first time allayed his fears. Here for the first time he dared to hope, and despite all the calamities of the

430

440

450

past to have better confidence in the future. While waiting
for the queen and studying everything there was to see
under the roof of this huge temple, as he marvelled at the
good fortune of the city, the skill of the workmen and all
the works of their hands, he suddenly saw, laid out in
order, depictions of the battles fought at Troy. The Trojan
War was already famous throughout the world. The two
sons of Atreus were there, and Priam, and Achilles who
hated both sides. Aeneas stopped, and wept, and said to
460 Achates: 'Is there anywhere now on the face of this earth
that is not full of the knowledge of our misfortunes? Look
at Priam. Here too there is just reward for merit, there are
tears for suffering and men's hearts are touched by what
man has to bear. Forget your fears. We are known here.
This will give you some hope for the future.'

As he spoke these words, he was feeding his spirit with
the empty images and groaning, and rivers of tears washed
down his cheeks as he gazed at the fighting round the walls
of Troy. On one side Greeks were in flight with Trojan
warriors hard on their heels; on the other Trojans were
retreating and Achilles with his crested helmet was pursu-
470 ing them in his chariot. He wept, too, when he recognized
the white canvas of the tents of Rhesus nearby. It was the
first sleep of the night. The tents had been betrayed, and
were being torn down by Diomede, red with the blood
of all the men he had slaughtered. He stole the fiery
horses and took them back to the Greek camp before they
could crop the grass of Troy or drink the water of the
Xanthus. In another part of the picture poor Troilus, a
mere boy and no match for Achilles, had lost his armour
and was in full flight. His horses had run away with the
chariot and he was being dragged along helpless on his
back behind it, still holding on to the reins. His neck and
hair were trailing along the ground and the end of his
480 spear was scoring the dust behind him. The women of
Troy, meanwhile, were going in supplication to the temple

of Pallas Athene, but the goddess was hostile to them. Their hair was unbound, and they were carrying a robe to offer her, beating their breasts in grief, but her head was turned from them and her eyes were fixed upon the ground. There too was Achilles. He had dragged Hector three times round the walls of Troy, and now was selling his dead body for gold. Aeneas groaned from the depths of his heart to see the armour stripped off him, the chariot, the corpse of his dear friend and Priam stretching out his feeble hands. Aeneas even recognized himself in the confusion of battle, with the leaders of the Greeks all around him. There were the warriors of the East, the armour of Memnon and his dark skin. The Amazons were there in 490 their thousands with crescent shields and their leader Penthesilea in the middle of her army, ablaze with passion for war. There, showing her naked breast supported by a band of gold, was the warrior maiden, daring to clash with men in battle.

While Trojan Aeneas stood gazing, rooted to the spot and lost in amazement at what he saw, queen Dido in all her beauty arrived at the temple with a great crowd of warriors around her. She was like Diana leading the dance on the banks of the Eurotas or along the ridges of Mount Cynthus with a thousand mountain nymphs thronging 500 behind her on either side. She carries her quiver on her shoulder, and as she walks, she is the tallest of all the goddesses. Her mother Latona does not speak, but a great joy stirs her heart at the sight of her. Dido was like Diana, and like Diana she bore herself joyfully among her people, urging on their work for the kingdom that was to be. Then she sat on her high throne under the coffered roof, in the middle of the temple before the doors of the shrine of the goddess. There, as she was giving laws and rules of conduct to her people, and dividing the work that had to be done in equal parts or allocating it by lot, Aeneas suddenly saw a great throng approaching, Antheus, Ser- 510 gestus, brave Cloanthus and the other Trojans who had been scattered over the sea by the dark storm and swept away to distant shores. He was astounded, and Achates, too, was stunned with joy and fear. They burned with longing to clasp the hands of their comrades, but were at a loss because they did not understand what they saw. They did nothing, but stayed hidden in their cloak of cloud, waiting to learn how Fortune had dealt with their comrades. On what shore had they left their fleet? Why were they here? For these were picked men coming from each of the ships to plead their case, and they were now walking to the temple with shouting all about them.

520   They came in and were allowed to address the queen. Ilioneus, the oldest of them, made this appeal: 'You are a queen whom Jupiter has allowed to found a new city and curb proud peoples with your justice; we are the unhappy men of Troy, blown by the winds over all the oceans of the world, and we come to you as suppliants. Save our ships from the impious threat of fire. We are god-fearing men. Take pity on us. Look more closely at us – we have not come to Libya to pillage your homes and their gods, to take plunder and drive it down to the shore. Such violence and arrogance are not to be found in the hearts of the defeated.

530   'There is a place which Greeks know by the name Hesperia. It is an ancient land, strong in war and rich in the fertility of its soil. It was once tilled by Oenotrians, but now we believe their descendants have called themselves Italians after their king Italus. This is where we were steering when suddenly Orion rose in cloud and tempest and drove us on to hidden shallows, the sea overwhelmed us and fierce southerly squalls scattered us far and wide among breakers and uncharted rocks. A few of us drifted ashore here to your land. What manner of men are these?
540   Is this a country of barbarians that allows its people to act in this way? Sailors have a right to the shore and we are

refused it. They make war on us and will not let us set foot on land. You may be no respecters of men. You may fear no men's arms, but think of the gods, who see right and wrong and do not forget. Our king was Aeneas. He had no equal for his piety and his care for justice, and no equal in the field of battle. If the Fates still protect him, if he still breathes the air of heaven, if he is not even now laid low among the merciless shades, you would have nothing to fear or to regret by taking the lead in a contest of kindness. In the land of Sicily we have arms and cities and the great 550 Acestes, sprung from Trojan blood. Allow us to draw up our storm-battered ships, to hew timbers in your woods and shape new oars, so that we can make for Italy and Latium with joy in our hearts, if indeed we go to Italy with our comrades and our king; but if they are lost, if you, great Father of the Trojans, are drowned in the sea off Libya, and there are no hopes left in Iulus, then we can at least go back to where we came from across the Sicilian sea, to the place that is prepared for us, and return to king Acestes.' So spoke Ilioneus and all the Trojans to a man 560 murmured in agreement.

Then Dido looked down at them and made a brief answer: 'Have no fear, men of Troy. Put every anxious thought out of your hearts. This is a new kingdom, and it is harsh necessity that forces me to take these precautions and to post guards on all our frontiers. But who could fail to know about the people of Aeneas and his ancestry, or the city of Troy, the valour of its men and the flames of war that engulfed it? We here in Carthage are not so dull in mind as that. The sun does spare a glance for our Tyrian city when he yokes his horses in the morning. Whether you choose to go to great Hesperia and the fields of Saturn, or to the land of Eryx and king Acestes, you will 570 leave here safe under my protection, and I shall give you supplies to help you on your way. Or do you wish to settle here with me on an equal footing, even here in this

kingdom of Carthage? The city which I am founding is
yours. Draw up your ships on the beach. Trojan and
Tyrian shall be as one in my eyes. I wish only that your
king Aeneas had been driven by the same south wind, and
were here with you now. But what I can, I shall do. I shall
send men whom I can trust all along the coast, and order
them to cover every furthest corner of Libya, in case he has
been shipwrecked and is wandering in any of the woods or
cities.'

580   The brave Achates and Father Aeneas had long been
impatient to break out of the cloud, and at Dido's words
their eagerness increased. 'Aeneas,' said Achates, 'son of the
goddess, what thoughts are now rising in your heart? You
see there is no danger. Our ships are safe. Our comrades
are rescued. Only one of them is missing, and we saw him
with our own eyes founder in mid-ocean. Everything else
is as your mother Venus said it would be.'

He had scarcely finished speaking when the cloud that
was all about them suddenly parted and dissolved into the
clear sky. Aeneas stood there resplendent in the bright light
of day with the head and shoulders of a god. His own
mother had breathed upon her son and given beauty to his
590   hair and the sparkle of joy to his eyes, and the glow of
youth shone all about him. It was as though skilled hands
had added embellishments to ivory or applied gilding to
silver or Parian marble. Then suddenly, to the surprise of
all, he addressed the queen: 'The man you are looking for
is standing before you. I am Aeneas the Trojan, saved from
the Libyan sea. And you, Dido, alone have pitied the
unspeakable griefs of Troy. We are the remnants left by
the Greeks. We have suffered every calamity that land and
sea could inflict upon us. We have lost everything. And
600   now you offer to share your city and your home with us.
It is not within our power to repay you as you deserve,
nor could whatever survives of the Trojan race, scattered as
it is over the face of the wide earth. May the gods bring

you the reward you deserve, if there are any gods who
have regard for goodness, if there is any justice in the
world, if their minds have any sense of right. What happy
age has brought you to the light of life? What manner of
parents have produced such a daughter? While rivers run
into the sea, while shadows of mountains move in procession round the curves of valleys, while the sky feeds the
stars, your honour, your name, and your praise will remain
for ever in every land to which I am called.' As he spoke,   610
he put out his right hand to his friend Ilioneus and his left
to Serestus, then greeted the others, brave Gyas, and brave
Cloanthus.

Dido of Sidon was amazed at her first sight of him and
then at the thought of the ill fortune he had endured.
'What sort of chance is this,' she exclaimed, 'that hounds
the son of a goddess through all these dangers? What
power has driven you to these wild shores? Are you that
Aeneas whom the loving goddess Venus bore to Dardanian
Anchises in Phrygia by the river waters of the Simois? I
myself remember the Greek Teucer coming to Sidon after   620
being exiled from his native Salamis. He was looking to
found a new kingdom, and was helped by my father
Belus, who in those days was laying waste the wealth of
Cyprus. He had conquered the island and it was under his
control. From that day on I knew all the misfortunes of the
city of Troy. I knew your name and the names of the
Greek kings. Teucer himself, your enemy, held the Teucrians, the people of Troy, in highest respect and claimed
descent from an ancient Teucrian family. This is why I
now invite your warriors to come into my house. I, too,
have known ill fortune like yours and been tossed from
one wretchedness to another until at last I have been
allowed to settle in this land. Through my own suffering, I   630
am learning to help those who suffer.'

With these words she led Aeneas into her royal palace,
and as she went she appointed sacrifices to be offered in the

temples of the gods. Nor at that moment did she forget
Aeneas' comrades on the shore, but sent down to them
twenty bulls, a hundred great bristling hogs' backs and a
hundred fat lambs with their mothers, rich gifts to celebrate
the day. Meanwhile the inside of her palace was being
prepared with all royal luxury and splendour. They were
laying out a banquet in the central hall and the draperies
640 were of proud purple, richly worked. The silver was
massive on the tables, with the brave deeds of their ancestors embossed in gold, a long tradition of feats of arms
traced through many heroes from the ancient origins of the
race.

But a father's love allowed Aeneas' mind no rest, and he
asked Achates to go quickly ahead to the ships to take the
news to Ascanius and bring him back to the city. All his
thoughts were on his dear son Ascanius. He also told
Achates to bring back with him as gifts for Dido some of
the treasures that had been rescued from the ruins of Troy,
a cloak stiff with gold-embroidered figures and a dress
with a border woven of yellow acanthus flowers. These
650 miracles of workmanship had been given to Helen of
Argos by her mother Leda, and she had taken them from
Mycenae when she came to Troy for her illicit marriage
with Paris. There was also the sceptre which had once been
carried by Ilione, the eldest daughter of Priam, a necklace
of pearls and a double gold coronet set with jewels. Achates
set off for the ships in great haste to carry out his instructions.

Venus meanwhile was turning over new schemes in her
mind and devising new plans. She decided to change the
form and features of Cupid, and send him in place of the
660 lovely young Ascanius to inflame the heart of the queen,
driving her to madness by the gifts and winding the fire of
passion round her bones. For Venus was afraid of the
treacherous house of Carthage and the double-tongued
people of Tyre. The thought of the bitterness of Juno's

hatred burned in her heart, and as night began to fall and
her anxiety kept returning, she spoke to the winged god of
love in these words: 'My dear son, you are the source of
my power. You are my great strength. Only you, my son,
can laugh at the thunderbolts which my father, highest
Jupiter, hurled against the Giant Typhoeus. To you I come
for help. I am your suppliant, begging the aid of your
divine power. You well know how Juno's bitter hatred is
tossing your own brother from shore to shore round all
the seas of the world and you have often grieved to see me
grieving. Now he is in the hands of the Phoenician Dido, 670
who is delaying him with honeyed words, and I am afraid
of Juno's hospitality and what it may bring. She will not
stand idle when the gate of the future is turning. That is
why I am resolved to act first, taking possession of the
queen by a stratagem and surrounding her with fire. No
power in heaven will change her. I shall grapple her to
myself in love for Aeneas. As for how you are to achieve
this, listen now and I shall tell you my mind. Aeneas has
sent for his son, whom I so love, and the young prince is
preparing to go to the city of Carthage, bringing gifts
which have survived the burning of Troy and the hazards
of the sea. I shall put him into a deep sleep and hide him in 680
one of my sacred shrines on Mount Idalium or on the
heights of Cythera, so that he will not know of my scheme
or suddenly arrive to interrupt it. You will have to use
your cunning and take on his appearance for just one
night. He is a boy like yourself and you know him, so put
on his features, and when the royal table is flowing with
wine that brings release, and Dido takes you happily on to
her lap and gives you sweet kisses, you can then breathe
fire and poison into her and she will not know.'

Cupid obeyed his beloved mother. He took off his 690
wings and strutted about copying Iulus' walk and laughing.
But the goddess poured quiet and rest into all the limbs of
Ascanius, and holding him to the warmth of her breast, she

lifted him into the high Idalian woods, where the soft
amaracus breathed its fragrant shade and twined its flowers
around him.

Now Cupid was obeying his instructions and taking the
royal gifts, amused to be escorted by Achates. When he
came in, the queen was already sitting under a rich awning
on a golden couch in the middle of the palace. Presently
700 Father Aeneas and after him the men of Troy arrived and
reclined on purple coverlets. Attendants gave them water
for their hands, plied them with bread from baskets and
brought them fine woollen napkins with close-cut nap.
Inside were fifty serving-women, whose task it was to lay
out the food in order in long lines and honour the Penates
by tending their fires. There were a hundred other female
slaves and a hundred men, all of the same age, to load the
tables for the banquet and set out the drinking cups. The
Tyrians, too, came thronging through the doors, and the
palace was full of joy as they took their appointed places
on the embroidered couches. They admired the gifts Aeneas
710 had given. They admired Iulus, the glowing face of the
god and his false words, the cloak and the dress embroidered with yellow acanthus flowers. But most of all
the unfortunate Dido, doomed to be the victim of a plague
that was yet to come, could not have her fill of gazing, and
as she gazed, moved by the boy as much as by the gifts, the
fire within her grew. After he had embraced Aeneas and
hung on his neck to satisfy the great love of his father who
was not his father, he went to the queen. She fixed her eyes
and her whole heart on him and sometimes dandled him
on her knee, without knowing what a great god was
sitting there marking her out to suffer. But he was re-
720 membering his mother, the goddess of the Acidalian spring,
and he began gradually to erase the memory of Sychaeus,
trying to turn towards a living love, a heart that had long
been at peace and long unused to passion.

As soon as the first pause came in the feasting and the

tables were cleared away, they set up great mixing bowls full of wine and garlanded them with flowers. The palace was ringing with noise and their voices swelled through the spacious hall. Lamps were lit and hung from the gold-coffered ceilings and the flame of torches routed the darkness. The queen now asked for a golden bowl heavy with jewels, and filled it with wine unmixed with water. From this bowl Belus had drunk, and all the royal line descended 730 from Belus. They called for silence in the great chamber as Dido spoke: 'Jupiter, to you we pray, since men say that you ordain the laws of hospitality. Grant that this day may be a day of happiness for the Tyrians and the men from Troy, and may our descendants long remember it. Let Bacchus, giver of good cheer, be among us, and kindly Juno, and you, Tyrians, celebrate this gathering with welcome in your hearts.'

At these words she poured a libation of wine on the table to honour the gods, and having poured it, she took it first and just touched it to her lips. She then passed it to Bitias with a smile and a challenge. Nothing loth, he took a great draught from the golden bowl foaming to the brim, and bathed himself in wine. The other leaders of the 740 Carthaginians did the same after him. Long-haired Iopas, the pupil of mighty Atlas, then sang to his gilded lyre of the wanderings of the moon and the labours of the sun, the origin of the human race and of the animals, the causes of rain and of the fires of heaven, of Arcturus, of the Hyades, bringers of rain, of the two Triones, the oxen of the Plough; why the winter suns are so eager to immerse themselves in the ocean, and what it is that slows down the passage of the nights. The Tyrians applauded again and again and the Trojans followed their lead.

So the doomed Dido was drawing out the night with all manner of talk, drinking long draughts of love as she asked question after question about Priam and Hector, what 750 armour Memnon, son of the Dawn, was wearing when he came, what kind of horses did Diomede have, how tall was Achilles. 'But no,' she said, 'come tell your hosts from the beginning about the treachery of the Greeks, the sufferings of your people and your own wanderings, for this is now the seventh summer that has carried you as a wanderer over every land and sea.'

2

THE FALL OF TROY

They all fell silent, gazing at Father Aeneas, and he began to speak from his raised couch: 'O Queen, the sorrow you bid me bring to life again is past all words, the destruction by the Greeks of the wealth of Troy and of the kingdom that will be mourned for ever, and all the horrors I have seen, and in which I played a large part. No man could speak of such things and not weep, none of the Myrmidons of Achilles or the Dolopians of Neoptolemus, not even a follower of Ulixes, a man not prone to pity. Besides, the dewy night is already falling fast from the sky and the setting stars are speaking to us of sleep. But if you have such a great desire to know what we suffered, to hear in brief about the last agony of Troy, although my mind recoiled in anguish when you asked and I shudder to remember, I shall begin:

Year after year the leaders of the Greeks had been broken in war and denied by the Fates, until, with the aid of the divine skill of Pallas Athene, they built a horse the size of a mountain, cutting pine trees to weave into it for ribs. They pretended it was a votive offering for their safe return to Greece, and that was the story on men's lips. Then they chose some men by lot from their best warriors and shut them up in the darkness of its belly, filling the vast cavern of its womb with armed soldiers.

Within sight of the mainland is the island of Tenedos,

famous in story. While the kingdom of Priam stood, it was
rich and prosperous, but now there is only a bay giving a
none too safe anchorage for ships. The Greeks sailed here
and took cover on its lonely shore. We thought they had
left us and sailed for Mycenae with favouring winds. The
whole of Troy then shook itself free of its long sorrow.
The gates were thrown open and the people went out
rejoicing to see the Greek encampment, the deserted shore
and all the places abandoned by the enemy. Here was the
30 Dolopian camp and here fierce Achilles had his tent. This
was where the fleet was drawn up. This was where they
used to fight their battles. Some gazed at the fatal offering
to the virgin goddess Minerva and marvelled at the huge
size of the horse. Thymoetes was the first to urge them to
drag it inside their walls and set it on their citadel, whether
it was treachery that made him speak, or whether the Fates
of Troy were already moving towards that end. But
Capys, and those of sounder judgement, did not trust this
offering. They thought it was some trick of the Greeks and
should be thrown into the sea, or set fire to and burned, or
that they should bore holes in its hollow belly and probe
for hiding places. The people were uncertain and their
passions were divided.

40   Then suddenly at the head of a great throng Laocoon
came running down in a blaze of fury from the heights of
the citadel, shouting from a distance as he came: 'O you
poor fools! Are you out of your minds, you Trojans? Do
you seriously believe that your enemies have sailed away?
Do you imagine Greeks ever give gifts without some
devious purpose? Is this all you know about Ulixes? I tell
you there are Greeks hiding in here, shut up in all this
wood, or else it is a siege engine designed for use against
our walls, to spy on our homes and come down on the city
from above, or else there is some other trick we cannot see.
Do not trust the horse, Trojans. Whatever it is, I am afraid
of Greeks, particularly when they bring gifts.'

With these words he threw a great spear with all his 50
strength into the beast's side, into the curved timbers of its
belly. It stuck there vibrating, the creature's womb
quivered and the hollow caverns boomed and groaned. If
divine Fate, if the minds of the gods had not been set
against us, Laocoon would surely have forced us to tear
open the hiding places of the Greeks with our swords,
Troy would still be standing and the high citadel of Priam
would still be in its place.

While this was going on, there was a sudden outcry, and
some Trojan shepherds came before the king, dragging a
man with his hands tied behind his back. They knew
nothing about him. They had come upon him and he had
given himself up. This was all part of his scheme. His 60
purpose was to open Troy to the Greeks. He knew exactly
what he wanted to do, and he was ready for either outcome, to spin his web or to meet certain death if he failed.
In their eagerness to see the prisoner, Trojan soldiers came
running up from all sides, and gathered round to join in
jeering at him. Listen now to this story of Greek treachery,
and from this one indictment, learn the ways of a whole
people. Dishevelled and defenceless, he stood there with
every eye upon him, looking all round him at the warriors
of Troy, and said with a great sigh: 'There is nowhere for
me now on sea or land. There is nothing left for a man like 70
me, who has no place among the Greeks, and now here are
my enemies the Trojans, baying for my blood.'

He groaned. We had a change of heart, and all our
passions were checked. We fell to asking him what his
family was, and what he had come to tell us. We wanted
to hear why he had allowed himself to be taken prisoner.

'O king Priam,' he replied, 'I am the sort of man who
will confess the whole truth to you, whatever it may be.
First of all, I am a Greek from Argos, and I will not deny
it. Fortune may have made Sinon an object of pity, but for 80
all her malice, she will never make him a cheat or a liar.

You may perhaps have heard tell of the name of Palamedes, son of Belus, and the great glory that was his. Although he was innocent, false information was infamously laid against him. His offence was that he objected to the war, and the Greeks put him to death. They murdered him and now they mourn him. This Palamedes was my comrade and my kinsman. My father was a poor man, and sent me here to the war to be with him from my earliest years. While Palamedes was secure in his kingship and had authority in the council of the kings, we too had some standing and some credit. But after he left the shores of this upper world, the victim of the jealousy of Ulixes and his smooth tongue (you all know about Ulixes), I was prostrate and dragged out my life in darkness and grief, brooding to myself over the downfall of my innocent friend, till, like a madman, I broke my silence and promised that I would miss no chance of revenge if ever I came back in victory to our native Argos. My words roused his bitter hatred. This was my first step on a slippery path. From this moment on, Ulixes kept me in a constant state of fear by one new accusation after another. From this moment on he spread vague rumours about me among the common soldiers. He knew he was guilty and was looking for weapons to use against me. Nor did he rest until with Calchas the priest as his lackey . . . but why do I waste time? Why go over this sordid story to no purpose? If in your eyes all Greeks are the same, and all you have to know is that a man is a Greek, then give me my punishment. It is long overdue. This would please Ulixes, our friend from Ithaca, and Agamemnon and Menelaus would pay you well for it.'

By this time we were burning to ask questions and find out why all this had happened. We had never met villainy on this scale before. We were not familiar with the arts of Greece. He went on with his lies, cringing with fear as he spoke:

'The Greeks have often wanted to make their escape

from here and leave Troy far behind them, abandoning
this long and weary war. And oh how I wish they had   110
done so! But again and again rough seas here kept them in
port or the south wind alarmed them as they were setting
sail. And most of all, when this construction of interwoven
maple beams, this horse, was at last in position here, the
black clouds thundered all round the sky. We were at a
loss and sent Eurypylus to consult the oracle of Phoebus
Apollo, and this is the grim response he brought back from
the shrine: "When you Greeks first came to Troy you
killed a virgin and appeased the winds with her blood.
With blood you must find a way to return. You must
sacrifice a Greek life." When this answer came to people's
ears, they did not know where to turn, and the cold fear   120
ran through the marrow of their bones. For whom were
they to prepare death? Whom did Apollo want? At this
point there was a great uproar, and the Ithacan dragged
out the prophet Calchas into the middle of us and
demanded to know what was the will of the gods. Many
people could detect even then the ruthless hand of the
schemer directed against me. They saw what was to come
and held their peace. For ten days Calchas gave no answer,
concealing himself and refusing to say the word that would
betray a man and send him to his death. But at long last,
all according to plan, he allowed the clamour raised by the
Ithacan to force him to break his silence and mark me out
for the altar. They all agreed. They had all been afraid, but 130
now one man was doomed, and this they could endure.

'The day of the abomination was soon upon us. The
sacred rites were all prepared for me. The salted meal was
sprinkled and the sacrificial ribbons were round my head. I
escaped from death, I admit it, I broke my bonds, and lay
hidden all night in the reeds of a marsh, waiting for them
to set sail, and wondering if they had. I have no hope now
of seeing the land which was once my home, or my
beloved children, or my father whom I have so often

140 longed for. Perhaps they will be punished for my escape, and wash away this guilt of mine with their own helpless blood. But I beg of you by the gods who know the truth, by any honesty that may survive unsullied between men, pity me in my great suffering. I know in my heart I have not deserved it.'

He wept. We spared him and and even began to pity him. Priam spoke first and ordered him to be freed from the manacles and the ropes that tied him, and spoke these friendly words: 'Whoever you are, from this moment on forget the Greeks whom you have lost. You will be one of us. But now give full and truthful answers to the questions
150 I ask you: why have they set up this huge monster of a horse? Who proposed it? What is the purpose of it? Does it have some supernatural power? Is it an engine of war?'

Sinon was ready with all his Greek arts and stratagems. Raising to the skies the hands we had just freed from their shackles, he cried: 'I call upon you, eternal fires of heaven and your inviolable godhead. I call upon the altars and the impious swords from which I have escaped. I call upon the sacred ribbons which I wore as sacrificial victim. It is no sin for me to break my sacred oaths of allegiance to the Greeks. It is no sin for me to hate these men and bring all their secrets out into the open. I am no longer subject to
160 the laws of my people. Only you must stand by your promises. If I keep Troy safe, Troy must keep its word and save me, if what I say is true, and what I offer is a full and fair exchange.

'All the hopes and confidence of the Greeks in this war they started have always depended upon the help of Pallas Athene. But ever since the impious Diomede and Ulixes, the schemer behind all their crimes, took it upon themselves to tear the fateful Palladium, the image of the goddess, from her own sacred temple in Troy, ever since they slew the guards on the heights of the citadel and dared to touch

the sacred bands on the head of the virgin goddess with
blood on their hands, from that moment their hopes   170
turned to water and ebbed away from them, their strength
was broken and the mind of the goddess was set against
them. Tritonian Pallas gave clear signs of this by sending
portents that could not be doubted. No sooner had they
laid down the image in the Greek camp, than its eyes
glared and flashed fire, the salt sweat streamed over its
limbs and by some miracle the image of the goddess leapt
three times from the ground with her shield and spear
quivering. Calchas declared that they had to take to instant
flight across the sea, and prophesied that Troy could not be
sacked by Argive weapons unless they first took the omens
again in Argos, and then brought back to Troy the divine
image which they have now carried away across the sea on
their curved ships. So now they have set sail for their   180
native Mycenae to rearm and to muster their gods to come
with them and they will soon remeasure the ocean and be
back here when you least expect them. This is how Calchas
interprets the omens, and on his advice they have set up
this effigy of a horse to atone for the violation of the
Palladium and the divinity of Pallas, and for their deadly
sin of sacrilege. But he told them to make it an immense
structure of interlaced timbers soaring to the sky, so that it
could not be taken through the gates and brought into the
city or protect the people should they receive it with their
traditional piety. For if your hands violate this offering to
Minerva, then total destruction shall fall upon the empire   190
of Priam and the Trojans (and may the gods rather send
that on his own head). But if your hands raise it up into
your city, Asia shall come unbidden in a mighty war to the
walls of Pelops, and that is the fate in store for our descendants.'

The trap was laid. These were the arts of the liar Sinon,
and we believed it all. Cunning and false tears had overcome the men who had not been subdued by Diomede,

son of Tydeus, nor Achilles of Larisa, not by ten years of siege nor a thousand ships.

200   And now there came upon this unhappy people another and yet greater sign, which caused them even greater fear. Their hearts were troubled and they could not see what the future held. Laocoon, the chosen priest of Neptune, was sacrificing a huge bull at the holy altar, when suddenly there came over the calm water from Tenedos (I shudder at the memory of it), two serpents leaning into the sea in great coils and making side by side for the shore. Breasting the waves, they held high their blood-stained crests, and the rest of their bodies ploughed the waves behind them, their backs winding, coil upon measureless coil, through the sounding foam of the sea. Now they were on land. Their 210 eyes were blazing and flecked with blood. They hissed as they licked their lips with quivering tongues. We grew pale at the sight and ran in all directions, but they made straight for Laocoon. First the two serpents seized his two young sons, twining round them both and feeding on their helpless limbs. Then, when Laocoon came to the rescue with his sword in his hand, they seized him and bound him in huge spirals, and soon their scaly backs were entwined twice round his body and twice round his throat, their 220 heads and necks high above him as he struggled to prise open their coils, his priestly ribbons befouled by gore and black venom, and all the time he was raising horrible cries to heaven like the bellowing of a wounded bull shaking the ineffectual axe out of its neck as it flees from the altar. But the two snakes escaped, gliding away to the highest temples of the city and making for the citadel of the heartless Pallas, the Tritonian goddess, where they sheltered under her feet and under the circle of her shield.

    At that moment a new fear crept into all their trembling 230 hearts. They said that Laocoon had been justly punished for his crime. He had violated the sacred timbers by hurling his sinful spear into the horse's back, and they all shouted together that it should be taken to a proper place and prayers offered up to the goddess. We breached the walls and laid open the buildings of our city. They all buckled to the task, setting wheels to roll beneath the horse's feet and stretching ropes of flax to its neck. The engine of Fate mounted our walls, teeming with armed men. Unmarried girls and boys sang their hymns around it and rejoiced to have a hand on the rope. On it came, gliding smoothly, looking down on the heart of the city. O my native land! O Ilium, home of the gods! O walls of the people of Dardanus, famous in war! Four times it stopped on the very threshold of the gate, and four times the armour clanged in its womb. But we paid no heed and pressed on blindly, madly, and stood the accursed monster on our consecrated citadel. Even at this last moment Cassandra was still opening her lips to foretell the future, but God had willed that these were lips the Trojans would never believe. This was the last day of a doomed people and we spent it adorning the shrines of the gods all through the city with festal garlands.

Meanwhile the sky was turning and night was rushing up from the Ocean to envelop in its great shadow the earth, the sky and the treachery of the Greeks, while the Trojans were lying quiet in their homes, their weary bodies wrapped in sleep. The Greek fleet in full array was already taking the army from Tenedos through the friendly silence of the moon and making for the shore they knew so well, when the royal flagship raised high the fire signal and Sinon, preserved by the cruelty of the divine Fates, stealthily undid the pine bolts of the horse and freed the Greeks from its womb. The wooden horse was open, and the Greeks were pouring gratefully out of its hollow chambers into the fresh air, the commanders Thessandrus and Sthenelus and fierce Ulixes sliding down the rope they had lowered, and with them Acamas, Thoas, Neoptolemus of the line of Peleus, Machaon, who came out first, Menelaus and Epeos himself, the maker of the horse that tricked the Trojans. They moved into a city buried in wine and sleep, slaying the guards and opening the gates to let in all their waiting comrades and join forces as they had planned.

It was the time when rest, the most grateful gift of the gods, was first beginning to creep over suffering mortals, when Hector suddenly appeared before my eyes in my sleep, full of sorrow and streaming with tears. He looked as he did when he had been dragged behind the chariot, black with dust and caked with blood, his feet swollen where they had been pierced for the leather thongs. What a sight he was! How changed from the Hector who had thrown Trojan fire on to the ships of the Greeks or come back clad in the spoils of Achilles. His beard was filthy, his hair matted with blood, and he had on his body all the wounds he had received around the walls of his native city. In my dream I spoke to him first, forcing out my words, and I too was weeping and full of sorrow: 'O light of Troy, best hope and trust of all Trojans, what has kept you so long from us? Long have we waited for you, Hector. From what shores have you come? With what eyes do we look upon you in our weariness after the death of so many of your countrymen, after all the sufferings of your people and your city? What has so shamefully disfigured the face that was once so serene? What wounds are these I see?'

There was no reply. He paid no heed to my futile questions, but heaved a great groan from the depths of his heart and said: 'You must escape, son of the goddess. You must save yourself from these flames. The enemy is master of the walls and Troy is falling from her highest pinnacle. You have given enough to your native land and to Priam. If any right hand could have saved Troy, mine would have saved it. Into your care she now commends her sacraments and her household gods. Take them to share your fate. Look for a great city to establish for them after long wanderings across the sea.' These were his words, and he brought out in his own hands from her inmost shrine the mighty goddess Vesta with the sacred ribbons on her head and her undying flame.

Meanwhile the city was in utter confusion and despair. Although the house of my father Anchises stood apart and was screened by trees, the noise was beginning to be heard and the din of battle was coming closer and closer. I shook the sleep from me and climbed to the top of the highest gable of the roof, and stood there with my ears pricked up like a shepherd when a furious south wind is carrying fire into a field of grain, or a mountain river whirls along in spate, flattening all the fields, the growing crops and all the labour of oxen, carrying great trees headlong down in its floods while the shepherd stands stupefied on the top of the rock, listening to the sound without knowing what it is. Then in that moment I knew the truth. The treacherous scheming of the Greeks was there to see. Soon the great house of Deiphobus yielded to the flames and fell in ruins. Soon his neighbour Ucalegon was burning and the broad waters of the strait of Sigeum reflected the flames. The clamour of men and the clangour of trumpets rose to high heaven. Mindlessly I put on my armour, for reason had little use for armour, but my heart was burning to gather comrades for battle and rush to the citadel with them. Frenzy and anger drove me on and suddenly it seemed a noble thing to die in arms.

I now caught sight of Panthus, just escaped from the weapons of the Greeks, Panthus, son of Othrys, priest of Apollo and of the citadel. He was carrying in his hands the sacraments and the defeated gods from the temple, and dragging his young grandson along behind him in a mad rush to the door of my father's house. 'Where is our strong-point? Where are we rallying?' I had scarcely time to speak before he replied, groaning: 'The last day has come for the people of Dardanus. This is the hour they cannot escape. The Trojans are no more. Ilium has come to an end and with it the great glory of the race of Teucer. Pitiless Jupiter has given everything over to Argos. The Greeks are masters of the burning city. The horse stands high in the heart of it, pouring out its armed men, and Sinon is in triumph, spreading the flames and gloating over us. The great double gates are open and Greeks are there in their thousands, as many as ever came from great Mycenae. Others have blocked the narrow streets with their weapons levelled. Their lines are drawn up and the naked steel is flashing, ready for slaughter. Only the first few guards on the gates are trying to fight and offering blind resistance.'

I went where I was driven by the words of Panthus and the will of the gods, into the fighting and the flames, where the grim Fury of war called me, where I could hear the din of battle and the shouts rising to heaven. I came across Rhipeus in the moonlight and Epytus, huge in his armour, and they threw in their lot with me. Hypanis and Dymas too came to my side, and so did Coroebus, son of Mygdon. He had happened to come to Troy just in these last few days, burning with mad love for Cassandra, and was fighting as son-in-law on the side of Priam and the Trojans. It was his misfortune not to heed the advice his bride had given him in her prophetic frenzy.

When I saw them standing shoulder to shoulder and spoiling for battle, I addressed them in these words: 'You are the bravest of all our warriors, and your bravery is in vain. If your desire is fixed to follow a man who fights to the end, you see how things stand with us. All the gods on whom this empire once depended have left their shrines and their altars. You are rushing to defend a burning city. Let us die. Let us rush into the thick of the fighting. The one safety for the defeated is to have no hope of safety.'

These words added madness to their courage. From that moment, like wolves foraging blindly on a misty night, driven out of their lairs by a ravening hunger that gives them no rest and leaving their young behind to wait for them with their throats all dry, we ran the gauntlet of the enemy to certain death, holding our course through the middle of the city, with the hollow blackness of dark night hanging over us. Who could unfold the horrors of that night? Who could speak of such slaughter? Who could weep tears to match that suffering? It was the fall of an ancient city that had long ruled an empire. The bodies of the dead lay through all its streets and houses and the sacred shrines of its gods. Nor was it only Trojans who paid their debts in blood; sometimes valour came back even to the hearts of the defeated and Greeks were cut down in their hour of triumph. Bitter grief was everywhere. Everywhere there was fear, and death in many forms.

The first of the Greeks to come to meet us was Androgeos, and he had a large contingent of men with him. Not knowing who we were, but thinking we were allies, he called out first to us: 'Move along there, friends! Why are you so slow? What is keeping you back? The citadel is on fire, and everyone else is pillaging and plundering. Have you just arrived from your tall ships?' He spoke, and when no convincing answer came, he instantly realized that he had fallen amongst enemies. He was stupefied and started backwards without another word. He was like a man going through rough briers who steps on a snake with all his weight without seeing it, and starts back in sudden panic as it raises its wrath and puffs up its blue-green neck: that is how Androgeos recoiled in terror at the sight of us. We fell upon them and surrounded them with a wall of weapons. They did not know the ground, and were stricken with fear, so we cut them down wherever we caught them. Fortune gave us a fair wind for our first efforts, and Coroebus, his spirits raised by our success, cried out: 'Come comrades, let us take the first road Fortune shows us to safety, and go where she shows that she approves. Let us change shields with the Greeks and put on their insignia. Is this treachery or is it courage? Who would ask in dealing with an enemy? The Greeks themselves will provide our armour.'

He spoke, and then put on the plumed helmet of Androgeos and his richly blazoned shield, and buckled the Greek sword to his side. Rhipeus cheerfully followed suit, then Dymas himself and the whole band. Every man armed himself with the spoils he had just taken, and, moving through the city, we mingled with the Greeks and fought many battles under gods not our own, clashing blindly in the night, and many a Greek did we send down to Orcus. Some scattered towards their ships, running for the safety of the shore. Some climbed back in abject fear into the huge horse, and hid themselves in its familiar belly.

But no man can put trust in gods who are opposed to him. Suddenly there was Cassandra, the maiden daughter of Priam, being dragged from the temple of Minerva, from her very sanctuary, with hair streaming and her burning eyes raised in vain to heaven, but only her eyes – they had tied her gentle hands. Coroebus could not endure the sight of this, but a wild frenzy took him and he hurled himself into the middle of the enemy to his death. We all went after him and ran upon their spears where they were thickest. First we were attacked by our own men and overwhelmed by their missiles thrown from the high gable of the temple roof, and the sight of our armour and the confusion caused by our Greek crests brought pitiable slaughter on us. Then the Greeks raised furious alarm at the rescue of Cassandra and gathered from every quarter to attack us, Ajax fiercest of them all, the two sons of Atreus and the whole army of the Dolopians. It was as though a whirlwind had burst and opposing winds were clashing, the west, the south, and the east wind glorying in the horses of the morning, with woods wailing and wild Nereus churning up the sea from its depths. Then also appeared all those Greeks who had been routed by our stratagem in the darkness of the night and scattered through the city. They realized that our shields and weapons were not our own and did not accord with the words on our lips. In an instant they overwhelmed us by the sheer weight of their numbers. Coroebus was the first to die. He fell by the right hand of Peneleus and lay there face down on the altar of Minerva, goddess mighty in arms. Rhipeus also fell. Of all the Trojans he was the most righteous, the greatest lover of justice. But the gods made their own judgements. Hypanis and Dymas were cut down by their fellow-Trojans, and as for you, Panthus, you found as you fell that your great devotion and the ribbon you wore as 430 priest of Apollo were no protection. I call to witness the ashes of Troy. I call upon the flames in which my people died. In the hour of your fall I did not flinch from the weapons of the Greeks or from anything they could do. If it had been my fate to fall, my right hand fully earned it.

From here we were swept along in the fighting, Iphitus and Pelias with me. Iphitus was no longer young, and Pelias had been slowed by a wound he had received from Ulixes. The noise of shouting drew us straight to Priam's palace and there we found the fighting so heavy that it seemed there were no battles anywhere else, that this was the only place in the city where men were dying. We saw 440 Mars, the irresistible God of War, Greeks rushing to the palace, men with shields locked over their backs packing the threshold, ladders hooked to the walls and men struggling to climb them right against the very doorposts, thrusting up their shields on their left arms to protect themselves while their right hands gripped the top of the walls. The Trojans for their part were tearing down their towers and the roofs of all their buildings. They saw the end was near, and these were the weapons they were preparing to defend themselves with in the very moment of death, rolling down on the heads of their enemies the gilded beams and richly ornamented ceilings of their

ancestors. Down on the ground others were standing shoul-
450 der to shoulder with drawn swords blocking the doorway.
My spirit was renewed and I rushed to bring relief to the
palace of my king, to help its defenders, to put heart into
men who were defeated.

There was a forgotten entrance at the rear, a secret
doorway entering into a passage which joined the different
parts of Priam's palace. While the kingdom of Troy still
stood, poor Andromache often used to come this way
unattended to visit Hector's parents, taking her son Astyanax to see his grandfather. I slipped through this door and
climbed to the highest gable of the roof, from where the
460 doomed Trojans were vainly hurling missiles. There was a
tower rising sheer towards the stars from the top of the
palace roof, from which we used to look out over the
whole of Troy, the Greek fleet and the camp of the
Achaeans. We set about this tower and worked round it
with iron bars where there was a join we could open up
above the top floor of the palace. Having loosened it from
its deep bed in the walls, we rocked it and suddenly sent it
toppling, spreading instant destruction and crushing great
columns of Greeks. But others still came on and the hail of
rocks and other missiles never slackened.

In the portico in front of the palace, on the very threshold, Pyrrhus, son of Achilles, whom men also call Neo-
470 ptolemus, was rampaging and the light flashed on the bronze
of his weapons. He was like a snake which has fed on
poisonous herbs and hidden all winter in the cold earth,
but now it emerges into the light, casts its slough and is
renewed. Glistening with youth, it coils its slithering back
and lifts its breast high to the sun with its triple tongue
flickering from its mouth. Huge Periphas was with him,
and Automedon, the charioteer and armour-bearer of
Achilles. With him too were all the young warriors of
Scyros coming to attack the palace and throwing firebrands
on to the roof. Pyrrhus himself at their head seized a

double-headed axe and with it smashed the hard stone of the 480
threshold, wrenching the bronze-plated doorposts from
their sockets. He then hacked a panel out of the mighty
timbers of the door and broke a gaping hole which gave
them a view into the house. There before their eyes were
the long colonnades and the inner chambers. There before
their eyes was the heart of the palace of Priam and the
ancient kings. They saw armed men standing in the doorway, but inside all was confusion and lamentation, and
deep into the house the hollow chambers rang with the
wailing of women, and their cries rose to strike the golden
stars. Frightened mothers were wandering through the
great palace, clinging to the doorposts and kissing them. 490
But Pyrrhus pressed on with all the violence of his father
Achilles, and no bolts or guards could hold him. The door
gave way under repeated battering and the posts he had
dislodged from their sockets fell to the ground. Brute force
made the breach and the Greeks went storming through,
butchering the guards who stood in their way and filling
the whole house with soldiers. No river foaming in spate
was ever like this, bursting its banks and leaving its channel
to overwhelm everything in its path with its swirling
current, as it bears down furiously on ploughed fields in a
great wave, and cattle and their pens are swept all over the
plains. I myself saw Neoptolemus in an orgy of killing and 500
both the sons of Atreus on the threshold. I saw Hecuba
with a hundred women, her daughters and the wives of
her sons. I saw Priam's blood all over the altar, polluting
the flame which he himself had sanctified. Down fell the
fifty bedchambers with all the hopes for generations yet to
come, and down came the proud doorposts with their
spoils of barbaric gold. Everything not claimed by fire was
now held by Greeks.

Perhaps you may also ask how Priam died. When he
saw the capture and fall of his city, the doors of his palace
torn down and his enemy in the innermost sanctuary of his

510 home, although he could achieve nothing, the old man
buckled his armour long unused on shoulders trembling
with age, girt on his feeble sword and made for the thick
of the fight, looking for his death. In the middle of the
palace, under the naked vault of heaven, there stood a
great altar, and nearby an ancient laurel tree leaning over it
and enfolding the household gods in its shade. Here, vainly
embracing the images of the gods, Hecuba and her daughters were sitting flocked round the altar, like doves driven
down in a black storm. When Hecuba saw that Priam had
now put on his youthful armour, 'O my poor husband,'
520 she cried, 'this is madness. Why have you put on this
armour? Where can you go? This is not the sort of help we
need. You are not the defender we are looking for. Not
even my Hector, if he were here now . . . Just come here
and sit by me. This altar will protect us all, or you will die
with us.' As she spoke she took the old man to her and led
him to a place by the holy altar.

Suddenly Polites, one of Priam's sons, came in sight. He
had escaped death at the hands of Pyrrhus and now,
wounded and with enemy weapons on every side, he was
running through the long porticos of the palace and across
530 the empty halls with Pyrrhus behind him in full cry,
almost within reach, pressing him hard with his spear and
poised to strike. As soon as he reached his father and
mother, he fell and vomited his life's blood before their
eyes. There was no escape for Priam. Death was now upon
him, but he did not check himself or spare the anger in his
voice. 'As for you,' he cried, 'and for what you have done,
if there is any power in heaven that cares for such things,
may the gods pay you well. May they give you the reward
you have deserved for making me see my own son dying
before my eyes, for defiling a father's face with the murder
540 of his son. You pretend that Achilles was your father, but
this is not how Achilles treated his enemy Priam. He had
respect for my rights as a suppliant and for the trust I

placed in him. He gave me back the bloodless body of
Hector for burial and allowed me to return to the city
where I was king.' With these words the old man feebly
threw his harmless spear. It rattled on the bronze of
Pyrrhus' shield and hung there useless sticking on the
surface of the central boss. Pyrrhus then made his reply. 'In
that case you will be my messenger and go to my father,
son of Peleus. Let him know about my wicked deeds and
do not forget to tell him about the degeneracy of his son
Neoptolemus. Now, die.' As he spoke the word, he was
dragging Priam to the very altar, his body trembling as it   550
slithered through pools of his son's blood. Winding Priam's
hair in his left hand, in his right he raised his sword with a
flash of light and buried it to the hilt in Priam's side.

So ended the destiny of Priam. This was the death that
fell to his lot. He who had once been the proud ruler over
so many lands and peoples of Asia died with Troy ablaze
before his eyes and the citadel of Pergamum in ruins. His
mighty trunk lay upon the shore, the head hacked from
the shoulders, a corpse without a name.

Then for the first time I knew the horror that was all
about me. What was I to do? There came into my mind   560
the image of my own dear father, as I looked at the king
who was his equal in age breathing out his life with that
cruel wound. There came into my mind also my wife
Creusa whom I had left behind, the plundering of my
home and the fate of young Iulus. I turned to look at the
men fighting by my side. Exhausted, they had all deserted
me and thrown themselves from the roof or given their
suffering bodies to the flames.

Now that I was alone, I caught sight of Helen keeping
watch on the doors of the temple of Vesta where she was
staying quietly in hiding. The fires gave a bright light and
I was gazing all around me wherever I went. This Helen,   570
this Fury sent to be the scourge both of Troy and of her
native Greece, was afraid of the Trojans, who hated her for

the overthrow of their city. She was afraid the Greeks would punish her and afraid of the wrath of the husband she had deserted, so, hated by all, she had gone into hiding and was sitting there at the altar. The passion flared in my heart and I longed in my anger to avenge my country even as it fell and to exact the penalty for her crimes. 'So this woman will live to set eyes on Sparta and her native Mycenae again, and walk as queen in the triumph she has won? Will she see her husband, her father's home and her children and be attended by women of Troy and Phrygian slaves, while Priam lies dead by the sword, Troy has been put to the flames and the shores of the land of Dardanus have sweated so much blood? This will not be. Although there is no fame worth remembering to be won by punishing a woman and such a victory wins no praise, nevertheless I *shall* win praise for blotting out this evil and exacting a punishment which is richly deserved. I shall also take pleasure in feeding the flames of vengeance and appeasing the ashes of my people.'

As I ran towards her ranting and raving, my loving mother suddenly appeared before my eyes. I had never before seen her so clearly, shining in perfect radiance through the darkness of the night. She revealed herself as a goddess as the gods in heaven see her, in all her majesty of form and stature. As she caught my right hand and held me back, she opened her rosy lips and spoke to me – 'O my son, what bitterness can have been enough to stir this wild anger in you? Why this raging passion? Where is all the love you used to have for me? Will you not first go and see where you have left your father, crippled with age, and find whether your wife Creusa is still alive, and your son Ascanius? The whole Greek army is prowling all around them and they would have been carried off by the flames or slashed by the swords of the enemy if my loving care were not defending them. It is not the hated beauty of the Spartan woman, the daughter of Tyndareus, that is overthrowing all this wealth and laying low the topmost towers of Troy, nor is it Paris although you all blame him, it is the gods, the cruelty of the gods. Look, for I shall tear away from all around you the dank cloud that veils your eyes and dulls your mortal vision. You are my son, do not be afraid to do what I command you, and do not disobey me. Here where you see shattered masonry, stone torn from stone, and waves of dust-laden smoke, Neptune has 610 loosened the foundations with his great trident and is shaking the walls, tearing up your whole city from the place where it is set. Here too is Juno, cruellest of all, the first to seize the Scaean Gate, standing there sword in hand, and furiously calling up the supporting columns from the ships. Now look behind you, Tritonian Pallas is already sitting on top of your citadel shining out of the cloud with her terrible Gorgon, while the Father of the Gods himself puts heart into the Greeks and gives them strength. It is Jupiter himself who is rousing the gods against the armies of Troy. Escape, my son, escape with all haste. Put an end to your struggle, I shall not leave your side till I see you 620 safely standing on the threshold of your father's door.' She finished speaking and melted into the dense shadows of that night, and there before my eyes I saw the dreadful vision of the gods in all their might, the enemies of Troy.

At that moment I seemed to see the whole of Ilium settling into the flames and Neptune's Troy toppling over from its foundations like an ancient ash tree high in the mountains which farmers have hacked with blow upon blow of their double axes, labouring to fell it; again and again it threatens to fall, its foliage shudders and its head trembles and nods until at last it succumbs to its wounds and 630 breaks with a dying groan, spreading ruin along the ridge. I came down from the roof and with the god to lead me a way opened through fire and sword. The weapons parted and the flames drew back before me.

When at last I had reached the door of my father's house

and our ancient home, my first wish was to find my father
and take him into the high mountains, but he refused to go
on living now that Troy had been levelled to the earth. He
would not hear of exile, but cried: 'Those of you with
young blood still thick in your veins, those of you whose
strength is sound and unimpaired, you are the ones who
640 must busy yourselves with escaping. If the gods in heaven
had wished me to go on living, they would have preserved
this place for me. I have already seen one sack of the city
and survived its capture, and that is more than enough.
Here I lie and here I stay. Take your farewells and leave
me. My own right hand will earn me my death. The
enemy will take pity on me. They will be looking for
spoils. I shall have no tomb, but that is an easy loss to bear.
For long years, ever since the Father of the Gods and King
of Men blew the wind of his thunderbolt upon me and
touched me with its fire, I have been lingering here hated
by the gods and useless to men.'

650   As he said these words he stood there rooted and no
power could move him. Streaming with tears, my wife
Creusa, Ascanius, all of us begged him not to bring everything down on his own head: when Fate batters a house,
the father should not add his weight to the blows. But he
still refused. He stood by his decision and stayed where he
was. I rushed to take up arms again in complete despair.
Death was the only thing I could hope for. What course
could I follow? What fate was in store for us? 'Did you
think I could run away and leave my father here?' I
exclaimed. 'How did such a sacrilege escape my father's
lips? If the gods above decree that nothing of this great city
660 is to survive, if your mind is fixed and it is your pleasure to
add yourself and those you love to the destruction of the
city, the door is open and the deaths you want will come.
Pyrrhus will soon be here, soaked in the blood of Priam.
He is the one who murders the son before the face of the
father, and the father at the altar. O my loving mother, is

this why you took me through fire and sword, so that I could see my enemy in the innermost sanctuary of my home, and Ascanius and my father and my wife Creusa with them lying sacrificed in each other's blood? Bring me my armour, comrades. Bring it here. This is the last light we shall see and it is calling the defeated. Give me back to the Greeks. Let me go back and rejoin the battle. Today 670 we die. But not all of us shall die unavenged.'

I buckled on my sword again and was fixing my left arm into the shield. But as I was leaving Creusa suddenly threw herself at my feet in the doorway and held me, stretching out our little son Iulus towards me. 'If you are going to your death,' she cried, 'take us with you to share your fate, whatever it is. But if you have reason to put any hope in arms, your first duty is to guard this house. If you leave us here, what fate is waiting for little Iulus, for your father and for the woman who used to be called your wife?'

Her cries of anguish were filling the whole house, when 680 suddenly there was a great miracle. At the very moment when we were both holding Iulus and he was there between our sorrowing faces, a light began to stream from the top of the pointed cap he was wearing and the flame seemed to lick his soft hair and feed round his forehead without harming him. We took fright and rushed to beat out the flames in his hair and quench the holy fire with water, but Father Anchises, looking joyfully up to the stars of heaven and raising his hands palms upward, lifted his voice in prayer: 'O All-powerful Jupiter, if ever you yield to prayers, look down upon us, that is all we ask, and if we 690 deserve anything for our devotion, give us help at last, Father Jupiter, and confirm this omen.'

Scarcely had he spoken when a sudden peal of thunder rang out on the left and a star fell from the sky, trailing a great torch of light in its course through the darkness. We watched it glide over the topmost pinnacles of the house

and bury itself, still bright, in the woods of Mount Ida, leaving its path marked out behind it, a broad furrow of light, and the whole place smoked all around with sulphur. Now at last my father was truly convinced. He rose up
700 and addressed the gods, praying to the sacred star: 'There is now no more delay. Now I follow, O gods of my fathers. Wherever you lead, there am I. Preserve this house. Preserve my grandson. This is your sign. Troy is in your mighty hands. Anchises yields. I am willing to go with you, my son, and be your companion.'

He had spoken. The noise of the fires was growing louder and louder through the city and the tide of flame was rolling nearer. 'Come then, dear father, up on my back. I shall take you on my shoulders. Your weight will be nothing to me.
710 Whatever may come, danger or safety, it will be the same for both of us. Young Iulus can walk by my side and my wife can follow in my footsteps at a distance. And you, the slaves of our house, must pay attention to what I am saying. As you leave the city there is a mound with a lonely old temple of Ceres. Near it is an ancient cypress preserved and revered for many long years by our ancestors. We shall go to that one place by different routes. You father, take in your arms the sacraments and the ancestral gods of our home. I am fresh from all the fighting and killing and it is not right
720 for me to touch them till I have washed in a running stream.'

When I had finished speaking, I put on a tawny lion's skin as a covering for my neck and the breadth of my shoulders and then I bowed down and took up my burden. Little Iulus twined his fingers in my right hand and kept up with me with his short steps. Creusa walked behind us and we moved along, keeping to the shadows. This was the man who had been unmoved by all the missiles of the Greeks and had long faced their serried ranks without a tremor, but now every breath of wind frightened me and I started at every sound, so anxious was I, so afraid both for the man I carried and for the child at my side.

I was now coming near the gates and it seemed that our
journey was nearly over and we had escaped, when I 730
suddenly thought I heard the sound of many marching feet
and my father looking out through the darkness cried:
'Run, my son, run. They are coming this way. I can see
the flames reflected on their shields and the bronze glinting.'
At that moment some hostile power confused me and
robbed me of my wits. I ran where there was no road,
leaving the familiar area of the streets. Then it was that my
wife Creusa was torn from me by the cruelty of Fate —
whether she stopped or lost her way or sat down exhausted,
no one can tell. I never saw her again. Nor did I look 740
behind me or think of her or realize that she was lost till
we arrived at the mound and the ancient sanctuary of
Ceres. But when at last everyone had gathered there, she
was the only one who was not with us and neither her
companions nor her son nor her husband knew how she
had been lost. I stormed and raged and blamed every god
and man that ever was. This was the cruellest thing I saw
in all the sack of the city. Leaving Ascanius, my father and
the gods of Troy with my companions and hiding them all
away in a winding valley, I put on my flashing armour
and went back to the city, resolved to face all its dangers 750
again, to go back through the whole of Troy and once
more put my life at peril. First I went back to the walls and
the dark gateway by which I had left the city. I found my
route and retraced it, gazing all around me through the
darkness. Horror was everywhere and the very silence
chilled the blood. Then I went on to our house, thinking it
was possible, just possible, that she had gone there. The
Greeks had come flooding in and were everywhere. Consuming flames, fanned by the winds, were soon rolling to
the top of the roof and leaping above it as their hot breath
raged at the sky. From there I went on to Priam's palace 760
and the citadel where Phoenix and the terrible Ulixes, who
had been chosen to keep watch, were already guarding the

loot in the empty porticos of the shrine of Juno. Here Greeks were piling up the treasures of Troy, pillaged from all the burning temples – the tables of the gods, mixing bowls of solid gold and all the robes they had plundered. Children and frightened mothers stood around in long lines. I even dared to call her name into the darkness, filling the streets with my shouts. Grief-stricken I called her
770 name 'Creusa! Creusa!' again and again, but there was no answer. I would not give up the search but was still rushing around the houses of the city when her likeness appeared in sorrow before my eyes, her very ghost, but larger than she was in life. I was paralysed. My hair stood on end. My voice stuck in my throat. Then she spoke to me and comforted my sorrow with these words: 'O husband that I love, why do you choose to give yourself to such wild grief? These things do not happen without the approval of the gods. It is not their will that Creusa should go with you when you leave this place. The King of High
780 Olympus does not allow it. Before you lies a long exile and a vast expanse of sea to plough before you come to the land of Hesperia where the Lydian river Thybris flows with smooth advance through a rich land of brave warriors. There prosperity is waiting for you, and a kingdom and a royal bride. Wipe away the tears you are shedding for Creusa whom you loved. I shall not have to see the proud palaces of the Myrmidons and Dolopians. I am a daughter of Dardanus and my husband was the son of Venus, and I shall never go to be a slave to any matron of Greece. The Great Mother of the Gods keeps me here in this land of Troy. Now fare you well. Do not fail in your love for our son.'

790 She spoke and faded into the insubstantial air, leaving me there in tears and longing to reply. Three times I tried to put my arms around her neck. Three times her phantom melted in my arms, as weightless as the wind, as light as the flight of sleep.

By now the night was over. I returned to my comrades without her. Here I found that new companions had streamed in and I was amazed at the numbers of them, men and women, an army collected for exile, a pitiable crowd. They had come from all directions ready to follow me with all their resources and all their hearts to whatever 800 land I should wish to lead them. And now Lucifer was rising above the ridges of Mount Ida and bringing on the day. The Greeks were on guard at the gates and there was no hope of helping the city. I yielded. I lifted up my father and set out for the mountains.

3

THE WANDERINGS

When the gods had seen fit to lay low the power of Asia
and the innocent people of Priam, when proud Ilium had
fallen and all Neptune's Troy lay smoking on the ground,
we were driven by signs from heaven into distant exile to
look for a home in some deserted land. There, hard by
Antandros under the Phrygian mountain range of Ida, we
were mustering men and building a fleet without knowing
where the Fates were leading us or where we would be
allowed to settle. The summer had barely started and
Father Anchises was bidding us hoist sail and put ourselves
10 in the hands of the Fates. I wept as I left the shores of my
native land and her harbours and the plains where once
had stood the city of Troy. I was an exile taking to the
high seas with my comrades and my son, with the gods of
our house and the great gods of our people.

At some distance from Troy lay the land of Mars, a land
of vast plains farmed by Thracians, once ruled by the
savage Lycurgus. This people had ancient ties with Troy,
while the fortunes of Troy remained, and our household
gods were linked in alliance. Here I sailed, and using the
name Aeneadae, formed after my own, I laid out my first
walls on the curved shore. But the Fates frowned on
these beginnings. I was worshipping my mother Venus,
20 the daughter of Dione, and the gods who preside over new
undertakings, and sacrificing a gleaming white bull to the
Most High King of the Heavenly Gods. Close by there

happened to be a mound on top of which there grew a
thicket bristling with spears of cornel and myrtle wood. I
had gone there and was beginning to pull green shoots out
of the ground to cover the altar with leafy branches, when
I saw a strange and horrible sight. As soon as I broke the
roots of a tree and was pulling it out of the ground, dark
gouts of blood dripped from it and stained the earth with
gore. The horror of it chilled me to the bone, I trembled   30
and my blood congealed with fear.

I went on, pulling up more tough shoots from another
tree, searching for the cause, however deep it might lie,
and the dark blood flowed from the bark of this second
tree. With my mind in turmoil I began to pray to the
country nymphs and to Father Mars Gradivus who rules
over the fields of the Getae, begging them to turn what I
was seeing to good and to make the omen blessed, but
after I had set about the spear-like shoots of a third shrub
with greater vigour and was on my knees struggling to
free it from the sandy soil (shall I speak? Or shall I be
silent?) I heard a heart-rending groan emerge from deep in   40
the mound and a voice rose into the air: 'Why do you tear
my poor flesh, Aeneas?' it cried. 'Take pity now on the
man who is buried here and do not pollute your righteous
hands. I am no stranger to you. It was Troy that bore me
and this is no tree that is oozing blood. Escape, I beg you,
from these cruel shores, from this land of greed. It is
Polydorus that speaks. This is where I was struck down
and an iron crop of weapons covered my body. Their
sharp points have rooted and grown in my flesh.' At this,
fear and doubt oppressed me. My hair stood on end with
horror and the voice stuck in my throat.

This was the Polydorus the doomed Priam had once   50
sent in secret with a great mass of gold, to be brought up
by the king of Thrace, when at last he was losing faith in
the arms of Troy and saw his city surrounded by besiegers.
When Fortune deserted the Trojans and their wealth was

in ruins, the king went over to the side of the victors and
joined the armies of Agamemnon. Breaking all the laws of
God, he murdered Polydorus and seized the gold. Greed
for gold is a curse. There is nothing to which it does not
drive the minds of men. When the fear had left my bones,
I told the chosen leaders of the people and first of all my
father about this portent sent by the gods and asked what
60 should be done. They were of one mind. We must leave
this accursed land where the laws of hospitality had been
violated and let our ships run before the wind. So we gave
Polydorus a second burial, heaping the earth high in a
mound and raising to his shade an altar dark with funeral
wreaths and black cypress, while the women of Troy stood
all around with their hair unbound in mourning. With
offerings of foaming cups of warm milk and bowls of
sacrificial blood we committed his soul to the grave and
lifted up our voices to call his name for the last time.

   Then as soon as we could trust ourselves to the waves,
70 when the winds had calmed the swell and a gentle breeze
was rattling the rigging to call us out to sea, my comrades
drew the ships down to the water and crowded the shore.
We sailed out of the harbour, and the land and its cities
soon fell away behind us. In the middle of the ocean lies a
beautiful island dear to Aegean Neptune and the mother of
the Nereids. It used to float from shore to shore until in
gratitude the Archer God Apollo moored it to Gyaros and
high Myconos, allowing it to stand firm and be inhabited
and mock the winds. Here I sailed, and in this peaceful
haven of Delos we came safe to land, weary from the sea.
We went ashore and were admiring Apollo's city when its
80 king Anius, king of men and priest of the god, came to
meet us, his forehead garlanded with ribbons and the
sacred laurel. Recognizing Anchises as an old friend, he
gave us his hand in hospitality and we entered his house.

   There I gazed in reverence at the god's temple built high
of ancient stone and made this prayer to Apollo: 'O god of

Thymbra, grant us a home of our own. We are weary. Grant us walls and descendants and a city that will endure. Preserve these remnants that have escaped the Greeks and pitiless Achilles, to be a second citadel for Troy. Whom are we to follow? Where do you bid us go? Where are we to settle? Send us a sign, O Father, and steal into our hearts.'

I had scarcely spoken when everything seemed to begin 90 to tremble. The threshold of the doors of the god, his laurel tree, and all the mountain round about were shaken. The sanctuary opened and a bellowing came from the bowl on the sacred tripod. We threw ourselves to the ground and these were the words that came to our ears: 'O much-enduring sons of Dardanus, the land which first bore you from your parents' stock will be the land that will take you back to her rich breast. Seek out your ancient mother. For that is where the house of Aeneas and his sons' sons and their sons after them will rule over the whole earth.'

So spoke Phoebus Apollo, and a great joy and tumult 100 arose among us, all asking what city this was, where Apollo was directing us in our wanderings, what this land was to which we were to return. Then spoke my father Anchises who had been turning over in his mind what he had heard from the men of old: 'Listen,' he said, 'you leaders of Troy, and learn what you have to hope for. In the middle of the ocean lies Crete, the island of great Jupiter, where there is a Mount Ida, the cradle of our race, and where the Cretans live in a hundred great cities, the richest of kingdoms. If I remember rightly what I have heard, our first father Teucer sailed from there to Asia, landing at Cape Rhoeteum, and chose that place to found his kingdom. Troy was not yet standing, nor was the citadel of Pergamum, and they lived low down in the 110 valleys. This is the origin of the Great Mother of Mount Cybele, the bronze cymbals of the Corybants, our grove of Ida, the inviolate silence of our worship and the yoked lions that draw the chariot of the mighty goddess. Come

then, let us follow where we are led by the bidding of the gods. Let us appease the winds and set forth for the kingdoms of Cnossus. It is not far to sail. If only Jupiter is with us, the third day will see our ships on the shores of Crete.' So he spoke, and made due sacrifice on the altars, a
120 bull to Neptune and a bull to fair Apollo, a black lamb to the storms and a white lamb to favouring breezes.

Rumour as she flew told the tale of the great Idomeneus, how he had been forced to leave his father's kingdom and how the shores of Crete were now deserted. Here was a place empty of our enemies, their homes abandoned, waiting for us. We left the harbour of Ortygia and flew over the sea to Naxos where Bacchants dance on the mountain ridges and to green Donusa, to Olearos, to Paros marble-white and the Cyclades scattered on the face of the sea, skimming over an ocean churned up by the coasts of a hundred islands. The sailors raised all manner of shouts as they vied with one another in their rowing and my comrades kept urging me to make for Crete and go back
130 to the home of their ancestors. The wind rising astern sped us on our way and we came to shore at last on the ancient land of the Curetes. Impatiently I set to work on walls for the city we all longed for. I called it Pergamea and the people rejoiced in the name. I urged them to love their hearths and homes and raise a citadel to protect them.

Our ships were soon drawn up on dry land, our young men were busy with marrying and putting new land under plough and I was giving them homes and laws to live by, when suddenly from a polluted quarter of the sky there came a cruel, suppurating plague upon our bodies and
140 upon the trees and crops. It was a time of death. Men were losing the lives they loved or dragging around their sickly bodies. The Dogstar burned the fields and made them barren, the grass dried, the crops were infected and gave us no food. My father bade me retrace our course back across the sea to Phoebus Apollo and his oracle at Ortygia, to

pray for his gracious favour and ask when he would put an end to our toil, where we were to look for help in our adversity and what course we were to steer.

It was night and sleep held in its grasp all living things upon the earth. There as I lay, the holy images of the gods, the Phrygian Penates whom I had rescued from the thick of the flames of the burning city of Troy, seemed to be standing bathed in clear light before my eyes, where the full moon streamed in through the unshuttered windows. At last they spoke to me and comforted my sorrow with these words: 'Apollo here speaks the prophecy he will give you if you sail back to Ortygia. By his own will he has sent us here and we stand at your door. We followed you and your arms when Troy was burned to ashes. With you to lead us we have sailed across unmeasured tracts of swelling seas, and in time to come we shall raise your sons to the stars and give dominion to your city. Your task is to build great walls to guard this great inheritance. You must never flag in the long toil of exile, and you must leave this place. Delian Apollo did not send you to these shores. Crete is not where he commanded you to settle. There is a place – Greeks call it Hesperia – an ancient land, strong in arms and in the richness of her soil. The Oenotrians lived there, but the descendants of that race are now said to have taken the name of their king Italus and call themselves Italians. This is our true home. This is where Dardanus sprang from and his father Iasius from whom our race took its beginning. Rise then with cheerful heart and pass on these words to Anchises your father, and let him be in no doubt. He must look for Corythus and the lands of Ausonia. Jupiter forbids you the Dictaean fields of Crete.'

I was astounded by this vision and by the words of the gods. This was no sleep. I seemed to be face to face with them and to recognize their features and the garlands on their heads, and at the sight my whole body was bathed in cold sweat. Leaping from my bed, I raised my hands palms upward to the sky and lifted up my voice in prayer, making pure offerings at the hearth. Having performed these rites, I went with joyful heart to Anchises and told him everything in order. He remembered that our race had two founders, Dardanus and Teucer, a double ancestry. He realized that he had fallen into a new mistake about these ancient places. 'O my son,' he said, 'you who have been so tested by the Fates of Troy, only Cassandra made such a prophecy to me. Now I remember how she used to foretell that this is what Fate had in store for us and she kept talking about Hesperia and about the kingdoms of Italy. But who would have believed that Trojans would land on the shores of Hesperia? Who in those days would have believed the prophecies of Cassandra? Let us yield to Phoebus Apollo. We have been advised. Let us follow the better course.' We all accepted his command with cries of joy and abandoned this second settlement, leaving only a few of our number behind, and set sail upon our hollow ships to run before the wind over the vast ocean.

When we were out at sea and no longer in sight of land, and all around was sky and all around was sea, I saw a dark cloud come over our heads bringing storm and black night, and the waves shivered in the darkness. The wind soon whipped up a great swell and the storm rose and scattered us all over the ocean. A pall of cloud obscured the light, rain fell from a sky we could not see, and lightning tore the clouds, flash upon flash. We were thrown off course and drifted blindly in the waves. Under that sky even Palinurus said he had lost his bearings in mid-ocean and could not tell day from night. For three long days, if days they were, of darkness, and three starless nights we ran before the storm, until at last on the fourth day we saw the first land rising before us and there opened a clear view of distant mountains and curling smoke. Down came the sails and we sprang to the oars. The sailors were not slow to sweep the blue sea and churn it into foam. I was saved

from the ocean and the shores of the Strophades were the ₂₁₀
first to receive me.

This is the Greek name for islands in the great Ionian
sea. This is where the deadly Celaeno and the other
Harpies have lived ever since the house of Phineus was
barred to them and they were frightened away from the
tables where they used to feed. These are the vilest of all
monsters. No plague or visitation of the gods sent up from
the waves of the river Styx has ever been worse than
these. They are birds with the faces of girls, with filth
oozing from their bellies, with hooked claws for hands and
faces pale with a hunger that is never satisfied.

As soon as we reached the Strophades and entered the
harbour, there we saw on every side rich herds of cattle on ₂₂₀
the level ground and flocks of goats unguarded on the
grass. We drew our swords and rushed upon them, calling
on the gods and on Jupiter himself to share our plunder.
Then we raised couches along the shore of the bay and
were feasting on this rich fare when suddenly the Harpies
were among us swooping down from the mountains with
a fearful clangour of their wings, tearing the food to pieces
and polluting everything with their foul contagion. The
stench was rank, and through all this we heard their
hideous screeching. Once again, in a sheltered spot far back ₂₂₉
under an overhanging rock, we relaid our tables and relit
the altar fires. Once again the noisy flock came from some
hidden roost in a different quarter of the sky and fluttered
round their prey, clutching it in their hooked claws and
fouling it in their mouths. Then it was I ordered my men
to arm themselves to make war against this fearsome tribe.
They did as ordered, hiding swords and shields here and
there in the grass. And so when Misenus in his high
lookout heard the sound of them swooping down along
the whole curved shore of the bay, he raised the alarm by
blowing on the hollow bronze of his trumpet and my ₂₄₀
comrades attacked. This was a new kind of battle – swords

against filthy sea birds. But these were feathers that felt no violence and backs that could receive no wounds. They soared in swift flight up towards the stars, leaving behind them the half-eaten food and their filthy droppings, all but one who remained, perched high on a pinnacle of rock (Celaeno was her name), and from her breast there burst this dire prophecy: 'Is it war you offer us now, sons of Laomedon, for the slaughter of our bullocks and the felling of our oxen? Is it your plan to make war against the innocent Harpies and drive us from the kingdom of our

250 ancestors? Listen to what I have to say and fix it in your minds. These words were spoken by the Almighty Father of the Gods to Phoebus Apollo, and Phoebus Apollo spoke them to me, and now I, the greatest of the Furies, speak them to you. You are calling upon the winds and trying to sail to Italy. To Italy you will go and you will be allowed to enter its harbours, but you will not be given a city, and you will not be allowed to build walls around it before a deadly famine has come upon you, and the guilt of our blood drives you to gnaw round the edges of your tables, to put them between your teeth and eat them.'

With these words she rose on her wings and flew into the forest. In that instant the blood of my comrades was

260 congealed with fear. Their spirits fell and they lost all stomach for fight, telling me to plead and pray to the creatures for peace, whether they were goddesses or foul and deadly birds. Then Father Anchises stood on the shore and raised his hands palms upward to heaven, calling upon the great gods and pledging to pay them all the honours that were their due. 'O you gods,' he cried, 'let not this threat be fulfilled. O gods, turn away this fate from us and graciously preserve your devoted people.' He then gave orders to pull in the cables, undo the sail-ropes and let them run. The south wind filled the canvas, and wind and helmsman each set the same course for us as we flew over

270 the foaming waves. Soon there appeared in mid-ocean the

woods of Zacynthus, and Dulichium, Same and the stone cliffs of Neritos. We raced away from the rocks of Ithaca, the kingdom of Laertes, and cursed the land that had nurtured the villain Ulixes. In no time there rose before us the cloudy cap of Mount Leucas and Apollo's temple, the terror of sailors. Being weary we set course for it and came to land at the little city. The anchors ran out from the prows and our ships stood to the shore.

So at last our feet were on dry land again – more than we had dared to hope for. We performed rites of purification to Jupiter and lit altar fires in fulfilment of our vows, crowding the shores of Actium with our Trojan games. My comrades stripped and made their bodies slippery with oil and wrestled in the style of their fathers, as we celebrated our escape and safe voyage past so many Greek cities, right through the middle of our enemies.

In due course the sun rolled on round the great circle of the year. Icy winter came and the north winds were roughening the seas. I then took a concave shield of bronze, the armour once carried by great Abas, and nailed it on the doors of the temple where all could see, proclaiming the dedication of it with this inscription:

AENEAS DEDICATES THESE ARMS
TAKEN FROM THE CONQUERING GREEKS

Then I gave orders to leave port and told the rowers to sit to their benches. They vied with one another to strike the sea and sweep the surface of it with their oars. We had soon put the cloud-capped citadels of Phaeacia down below the horizon and we coasted along Epirus until we entered the harbour of Chaonia and then walked up to the lofty city of Buthrotum.

Here there came to our ears a story almost beyond belief, that Helenus, a son of Priam, was king over these Greek cities of Epirus, having succeeded to the throne and the bed of Pyrrhus, son of Achilles and descendant of

Aeacus. Andromache, once wife of Hector, had for a second time taken a husband from her own people. I was astounded and the heart within me burned with love for the man and longing to meet him and find out about these 300 great events. I was walking away from the harbour leaving ships and shore behind me when I caught sight of Andromache, offering a ritual meal and performing rites to the dead in a grove in front of a city on the banks of a river Simois, but not the true Simois of Troy. She was pouring a libation to the ashes of her husband Hector, calling on his shade to come to the empty tomb, a mound of green grass on which she had consecrated two altars. There she used to go and weep. When she saw me approaching with armed Trojans all about me, she was beside herself, numb with fear the moment she saw this great miracle, and the warmth of life went out of her bones. She fainted, and only after a long time was she at last able to 310 speak to me: 'Is this a true vision? Is it a true messenger that comes to me, son of the goddess? Are you alive? If the light of life has left you, why are you here? Where is Hector?' As she spoke she burst into tears and her cries filled all the grove. I could hardly find an answer to these wild words, but stammered a few broken phrases. 'I am indeed alive. After all that has happened I still go on living. Do not doubt it. What you see is true. But tell me, what fate has overtaken you since you were deprived of such a husband? What has fallen to the lot of Hector's Andromache? Are you still the wife of Pyrrhus?'

320   She answered, and her voice was low and her eyes downcast: 'The happiest of all Trojan women was the virgin daughter of Priam who was made to die by the tomb of her enemy Achilles under the high walls of Troy. Polyxena did not have to endure the casting of lots or live to be the slave of a conqueror and lie in a master's bed! But we saw our home burned and sailed over many seas. We submitted to the arrogance of the house of Achilles and the

insolence of his son and bore him a child in slavery. In due
course he turned his attention to marrying a Spartan, Hermione, granddaughter of Leda, giving his slave Andromache
over to his slave Helenus. But Orestes loved Hermione and
had hoped to marry her. Incensed at losing her and driven   330
on by the madness brought upon him by his own crimes,
he caught Pyrrhus where Pyrrhus least expected him and
slaughtered him on the altar he had raised to his father
Achilles. At his death some of the kingdom he had ruled
over came into the possession of Helenus, who then called
the plains the Chaonian plains and the whole district Chaonia after Chaon of Troy. He then built a Pergamum, this
Trojan citadel on the ridge. But what winds and what fates
have given you passage here? Is it some god that has driven
you to these shores that you did not know were ours?
What about your boy Ascanius? Is he alive and breathing
the air? If he were with you now in Troy . . . But does he   340
ever think of the mother he has lost? Does the old courage
and manliness ever rise in him at the thought of his father
Aeneas and his uncle Hector?'

   She was weeping her useless tears and sobbing bitterly as
these words poured from her when the hero Helenus, son
of Priam, arrived from the walls of the city with a great
escort. He recognized his own people and took us gladly to
his home. He too was weeping and could speak only a few
broken words to us between his tears. As I walked I recog-   350
nized a little Troy, a citadel modelled on great Pergamum
and a dried-up stream they called the Xanthus. There was
the Scaean Gate and I embraced it. Nor were my Trojans
slow to enjoy this Trojan city with me. The king received
them in a broad colonnade and in the middle of the courtyard they poured libations of the wine of Bacchus and fed
off golden dishes and every man had a goblet in his hand.

   Day after day wore on with breezes tempting our sails
and the canvas filling and swelling in the south wind, until
I went to the prophet Helenus with this request: 'You are

Trojan born. You can read the signs sent by the gods. You
360 understand the will of Phoebus Apollo of Claros, his
tripods and his laurels. You know the meaning of the stars,
the cries of birds and the omens of their flight. Come tell
me – for every sign I have received from heaven has
spoken in favour of this journey, and I am persuaded by all
the divine powers to set course for Italy and try to find
that distant land. Only the Harpy Celaeno has prophesied a
strange and monstrous portent, threatening us with her
deadly anger and all the horrors of famine – come tell me
now, what dangers am I to avoid as I start upon this
journey? And as it goes on, what must I do to overcome
such adversities?'

Before replying Helenus first performed a ritual slaughter
370 of bullocks and asked for the blessing of the gods. He then
loosened the ribbons from his consecrated head, and taking
my hand, he led me in anxious expectation into the mighty
presence of the god. In due course he spoke as priest and
this was the prophecy that came from his hallowed lips. 'O
son of the goddess, the proof is full and clear that the
highest auspices favour your voyage. This is the fate allotted
to you by the King of the Gods. This is how your fortune
rolls and this is the order of its turning. My words will tell
you a small part of all there is to know so that you may
trust yourself more safely to cross the seas that are waiting
to receive you, and come to harbour in Ausonia. The Fates
380 do not allow Helenus to know the rest and Saturnian Juno
forbids it to be spoken. First, you are wrong to imagine
that it is a short voyage to Italy and that there are harbours
close at hand for you to enter. Far and pathless are the
ways that lie between you and that far distant land. You
must first bend the oar in the waves of Sicilian seas, then
cross the ocean of Ausonia and the lakes of the underworld,
and pass Aeaea, the island of Circe, before you can come to
the land which will be safe for the founding of your city. I
shall give you a sign and you must keep it deep within

your heart: when in an hour of perplexity by the flowing
waters of a lonely river you find under some holm-oaks on   390
the shore a great sow with the litter of thirty piglets she has
farrowed, lying there on her side all white, with her young
all white around her udders, that will be the place for your
city. There you will find the rest ordained for all your
labours. Nor is there any need for you to shudder at the
thought of eating your tables. The Fates will find a way.
Call upon Apollo and he will come. But you must quickly
leave this land of ours and keep well clear of the shore of
Italy that lies nearest us bathed by the tide of our sea, for
hostile Greeks live in all these cities. Here Locrians from
Narycum have built their walls and the army of the
Cretan Idomeneus of Lyctos has seized the Sallentine plains   400
in Calabria. Here too is the little town of Petelia perching
on the wall built for it by Philoctetes, leader of the
Meliboeans. And when you have passed all these and your
ships are moored across the sea, when you have raised
altars on the shore to fulfil your vows, do not forget to veil
your head in purple cloth so that when the altar fires are
burning to honour the gods, no enemy presence can intrude
and spoil the omens. Your comrades and you yourself
must keep this mode of sacrifice and your descendants
must maintain this purity of worship for ever.

'But when you sail on and the wind carries you near the   410
shore of Sicily, and the close-set barriers of Pelorus open
before you, make for the land to the south and the sea to
the south, taking the long way round Sicily and keeping
well clear of the breakers on the coast to starboard. Men
say these lands were originally one but were long ago
convulsed by some great upheaval and torn apart. Such
changes can occur in the long ageing of time. The waves
of the sea burst in between them and cut Sicily loose from
the flank of the land of Hesperia, putting coastlines between
their fields and cities and flowing in between them in a
narrow tide. On your right waits Scylla in ambush and on   420

your left the insatiable Charybdis. Three times a day with the deep vortex of her whirlpool Charybdis sucks great waves into the abyss and then throws them upwards again to lash the stars. But Scylla lurks in the dark recesses of her cave and shoots out her mouths to seize ships and drag them on to the rocks. She has a human face and as far as the groin she is a girl with lovely breasts, but below she is a monstrous sea creature, her womb full of wolves, each
430 with a dolphin's tail. It is better to lose time by taking the long course round Cape Pachynus rather than set eyes on the hideous Scylla deep in her cave or see those rocks loud with the barking of dogs as blue as the sea.

'One thing more: if the prophet Helenus has any insight into the future, if there is any reason to believe what I say, if Apollo fills my mind with the truth, there is one prophecy I shall make to you above all others, one counsel I shall repeat to you again and again – worship the godhead of great Juno first and foremost in your prayers, of your own free will submit your vows to Juno and win over the mighty Queen of Heaven with your offerings as you pray.
440 If you do this you will at last leave Sicily behind you and succeed in reaching the shores of Italy. When you have landed and come to the city of Cumae and the sacred lakes of Avernus among their sounding forests, there deep in a cave in the rock you will see a virgin priestess foretelling the future in prophetic frenzy by writing signs and names on leaves. After she has written her prophecies on these leaves she seals them all up in her cave where they stay in their appointed order. But the leaves are so light that when the door turns in its sockets the slightest breath of wind dislodges them. The draught from the door throws them
450 into confusion and the priestess never makes it her concern to catch them as they flutter round her rocky cave and put them back in order or join up the prophecies. So men depart without receiving advice and are disappointed in the house of the Sibyl. No matter how impatient your

comrades, no matter how the winds may cry out to your
sails to take to sea, though you know that you could fill
the canvas with favouring breezes, you must not begrudge
the time but must stay to visit the priestess. Approach her
oracle with prayers and beg her by her own gracious will
to prophesy to you herself, opening her lips and speaking
to you in her own voice. She will tell you of the peoples of 460
Italy and the wars that are to come, and how you are to
escape or endure all the labours that lie before you. If you
do her reverence she will give you a prosperous voyage.
This is as much as my voice may utter to give you
guidance. Now go forward and by your actions raise the
greatness of Troy to the skies.'

After the prophet Helenus had told us these things in the
friendliness of his heart, he then ordered his people to carry
gifts of solid gold and carved ivory down to our ships and
stowed a great quantity of silver in their hulls with cauldrons from Jupiter's temple at Dodona, a breastplate of
chain mail interwoven with triple threads of gold and a
noble helmet with crest and streaming plumes once worn
by Neoptolemus. There were other gifts for my father,
and he also gave us horses and leaders of men, rowers to 470
make up the crews and arms for my comrades.

Meanwhile Anchises was ordering us to fit out the ships
with their sails and not lose the following winds when the
priest of Apollo addressed him in deep respect: 'Anchises,
the gods love you. You have been thought worthy of the
highest of all honours, the love of Venus. You have been
twice rescued from the ruins of Troy, and now before you,
look, the land of Ausonia. Sail there and take possession of
it. But you must sail past the opposite coast. The part of
Ausonia which Apollo reveals to you is far from here. Go 480
then, Anchises, fortunate in the devotion of your son.
There is no more to say. Why do I keep you talking when
the wind is rising?'

Andromache also grieved at this parting that was to be

our last and brought us robes embroidered with gold thread and a Phrygian cloak for Ascanius. She was as generous as Helenus had been, heaping the gifts of her weaving upon him and saying: 'Take these too, my boy, and I hope the work of my hands may remind you of Andromache, wife of Hector, and be a token of my long-enduring love for you. Accept them. They are the last gifts you will receive from your own people. You are the only image left to me of my own son Astyanax. He had just

490 those eyes, and just those hands. His face was just like yours. He would have been growing up now, the same age as yourself.'

The tears were starting to my eyes as I was leaving them, and I spoke these words. 'Live on and enjoy the blessing of heaven. Your destiny has been accomplished. But we are called from fate to fate. Your rest is won. You do not need to plough tracts of ocean searching for the ever-receding Ausonian fields. You have before your eyes an image of the river Xanthus and a Troy made by your own hands, more fortunate, I pray, than the Troy that

500 was, and less of a stumbling-block to the Greeks. If ever I reach the river Thybris and the fields through which the Thybris flows and see my people with their own city walls, we shall in some future age unite our cities and the peoples of Hesperia and Epirus, for we are kith and kin, the same Dardanus is our founder and the same destiny attends us. We shall make them both one Troy in spirit. Let that be a duty for our descendants.'

Down the coast we sailed near the Ceraunian rocks where the crossing to Italy is shortest, and as we sailed the sun set and shadow darkened the mountains. At last we lay

510 down by the waves of the sea in the lap of earth, and after allotting the next day's order of rowing, we took our ease all along the dry beach and sleep washed into our weary limbs.

Night in its chariot drawn by the Hours was not yet

coming up to the middle of the sky, but there was no more sleep for Palinurus. He rose from his bed and studied all the winds, pricking up his ears to test the air and marking the path of every star gliding in the silent sky, Arcturus and the rainy Hyades and the two Triones, the oxen of the Plough, and he looked round to the south at Orion armed in gold, and saw that the whole sky was serene and settled. Clear came his signal from the high stern. We broke camp, started our voyage and spread the wings of our sails. 520

The stars had been put to flight and dawn was reddening in the sky when we sighted in the far distance the dim hills and plains of Italy. 'Italy!' – the first shout was from Achates – and 'Italy!' – the men took up the cry in cheerful salute. Then Father Anchises, standing on the high stern, garlanded a great mixing bowl, filled it with unwatered wine and called upon the gods: 'O you who rule sea, land and storm, give us an easy wind for our voyage. Blow kindly upon us.'

His prayer was answered. The breeze freshened and a 530 harbour opened up before us growing nearer and nearer till we could see the temple of Minerva on the citadel. My comrades furled their sails and pointed their prows to the shore. The harbour was shaped like a bow, curving away from the swell which came in from the east. The rocks at the mouth were foaming with salt spray but the harbour lay tucked away behind. Towering rocks on either side stretched down their arms to form a double wall and the temple stood well back from the shore. The first omen I saw here was four horses white as snow cropping the grass on a broad plain and my father Anchises interpreted it: 'This land that receives us is promising us war! Men arm 540 horses for war and so this troop of horses means threat of war. Yet at other times they are harnessed to chariots and accept reins under the yoke in harmony. There is hope of peace also.'

At that moment we prayed to the sacred godhead of Pallas, clasher of arms, the first goddess to welcome us in this hour of our joy. Standing at the altar we veiled our heads with Phrygian cloth, and in accordance with the instructions which Helenus had told us to follow before all others, duly paid the prescribed honour to Juno of Argos with our burnt offerings.

We did not linger there but as soon as we had performed the rites in due order we raised our sails, swung the yards 550 round and left behind us this home of Greeks, this land we could not trust. Next we saw the bay of Tarentum, the city of Hercules if the story is true, and over against it rose the temple of the goddess Juno at Lacinium, the citadel of Caulon and the bay of Scylaceum, that great breaker of ships. Then from far out at sea we sighted Mount Etna in Sicily and heard a loud moaning of waters and grinding of rocks and the voice of breakers beating on the shore, as the sea began to rise and swirl the sand in its surge. Father Anchises cried out: 'This must be the deadly Charybdis. These are the cliffs Helenus warned us against. These are 560 the terrible rocks. Use all your strength to save yourselves, comrades. Keep well in time and rise to the oar.' They did as they were bidden. Palinurus was the first to wrench his ship to port and out to sea with a loud creaking of the bow, and the whole fleet with every sail and oar steered to port with him. A great arching wave came and lifted us to the sky and a moment later as the wave was sucked down we plunged into the abyss of hell. Three times the cliffs roared between their hollow rocks. Three times we saw the foam shoot up and spatter the stars. Meanwhile the sun had set, the wind had fallen and we were weary and lost, drifting towards the shore of the Cyclopes.

570 The harbour there is out of the wind. It is still and spacious but close by Mount Etna thunders and hurls down its deadly debris. Sometimes it shoots a pitch-black cloud of swirling smoke and glowing ashes into the sky and

tosses up balls of flame to lick the stars. Sometimes it belches boulders, tearing out the bowels of the mountain and throwing molten rock up into the air, seething and groaning in its very depths. The story goes that the body of Enceladus, half-consumed by the fire of the thunderbolt, is crushed under this great mass. Mighty Etna lies on top of him breathing fire from its shattered furnaces and 580 every time he turns over from one weary flank to another the whole of Sicily trembles and murmurs and wreathes the sky with smoke. We hid in the woods and lived through a night of horror, not seeing what was making these monstrous sounds. The fire of the stars was quenched and the dark bowl of heaven was denied their radiance. Clouds darkened the sky and unbroken night obscured the moon.

At last the Morning Star appeared and the next day was beginning to rise. The Goddess of the Dawn had dispersed the dank mists from the sky when suddenly we saw a 590 strange sight coming out of the woods. It was a man we did not know, in pitiable plight and half-dead with hunger, coming towards us on the shore with his hands stretched out in supplication. We stared at him. The filth on his body was indescribable. He had a straggling beard and the rags he wore were pinned together by thorns, but for all that he was a Greek, one of those who had been sent to Troy bearing the arms of his country. When still at a distance he saw our Trojan clothes and Trojan armour, he checked his stride and stood in terror at the sight of us. But he soon rushed down to the shore weeping and pleading: 'I beg you, Trojans, by all the stars, by the gods above, by 600 the bright air of heaven which we breathe, take me aboard your ships. Take me anywhere. That is all I ask. I know I was one of those who sailed with the Greek fleet. I admit I made war against the gods of your homes in Troy. If that offence is so great, tear me limb from limb, scatter the pieces on the waves and let them sink into the vastness of the sea. If I am to die, I shall be pleased to die at the hands of men.'

When he had spoken he clasped our knees, he grovelled on his knees, and would not rise. We urged him to explain who he was, what family he came from and what
610 misfortune was driving him to this. Father Anchises himself was not slow to offer his right hand and that assurance gave him courage. He laid aside his fear and told his story: 'My native land is Ithaca. I am a comrade of the unfortunate Ulixes. My name is Achaemenides. My father Adamastus being poor, I went to Troy – cursed be the day! My comrades, distraught with fear, forgot me and left me here in the vast cave of the Cyclops when they crossed that cruel threshold to safety. This huge cavern was his home, deep and dark and filthy with the gore of his feasts. He himself
620 was so tall that his head knocked against the stars – O you gods, relieve the earth of all such monsters. No one dared to look at him or speak to him. He fed on the flesh of his victims and drank the black blood. I have seen him with my own eyes lolling in the middle of his cave with two of our men in one huge hand, bashing their bodies on the rock till the threshold was swimming with blood. I have seen him chewing arms and legs with black gore oozing from them and the warm limbs twitching between his teeth. But he met his punishment. The man from Ithaca did not submit to this. Whatever happened Ulixes was
630 always Ulixes. As soon as the Cyclops had his fill and was sunk in a drunken stupor, lying there with his head back and his neck exposed, sprawling all over the cave and belching blood and wine and pieces of flesh as he slept, we prayed to the great gods and after casting lots spread ourselves out all round him. Then, taking a sharp weapon we drilled the one huge eye that lay, like an Argive shield or the lamp of Apollo's sun, deep set in that dreadful forehead. That was how in the end we took sweet revenge for the death of our comrades. But you are in danger. You

must escape and escape now. Cut your moorings and put 640
to sea. You know what Polyphemus is and how huge he is,
keeping his woolly sheep penned there in his hollow cave
and squeezing the milk from their udders, but there are a
hundred other horrible Cyclopes living together near this
shore and roving the high mountains. This is now the third
time I have seen the horns of the moon filling with light as
I have dragged out my existence in the woods alone
among the dens and lairs of wild beasts, climbing rocks to
keep watch on the giant Cyclopes and trembling at the
sound of their voices and the tread of their feet. My food is 650
miserable. The trees yield me some berries and the fruit of
the cornel, hard as stone, and I tear up herbs by the root
and eat them. I have kept constant watch but this is the
first time I have seen ships coming near this shore. I have
put myself in your hands, and would have done so whoever
you had been. It is enough for me to escape from this
unspeakable people. You can take this life of mine by
whatever means you please.'

Scarcely had he finished speaking when we saw the
shepherd Polyphemus himself high up on the mountain
among his sheep, heaving his vast bulk down towards the
shore he knew so well. He was a terrifying sight, huge,
hideous, blinded in his one eye and using the trunk of a
pine tree to guide his hand and give him a firm footing.
His woolly sheep were coming with him. They were the 660
only pleasure he had left, his sole consolation in distress. As
soon as he felt the waves deepening and reached the level
ocean, he washed away with sea water the blood that was
still trickling from his gouged-out eye, grinding his teeth
and moaning, and as he strode now in mid-ocean, the waves
still did not wet his towering flanks.

We were terrified and lost no time in taking the fugitive
aboard – he had suffered enough – and making our escape.
Keeping silence as we cut the cables we churned the surface
of the sea, leaning forward and straining at the oars. He

heard us, and whirled round in the direction of our voices,
670 but he had no chance of laying a hand on us or keeping up
with the current of the Ionian sea, so he raised a great
clamour which set the ocean and all its waves shivering.
The whole land of Italy trembled with fear and the bellowing boomed in the hollow caverns of Mount Etna. The
tribe of Cyclopes was roused and came rushing down from
their woods and high mountains to the harbour and filled
the shore. We saw the brotherhood of Etna standing there
helpless, each with his one eye glaring and head held high
680 in the sky, a fearsome gathering, standing like high-topped
mountain oaks or cone-bearing cypresses in Jupiter's soaring
forest or the grove of Diana. With terror driving us along
we let the sheets full out and filled our sails with whatever
wind was blowing. This is what Helenus had told us not to
do. He had advised us that it was a narrow passage between
Scylla and Charybdis with death on either side if I did not
hold a steady course. I resolved to turn about, and sure
enough the north wind came to our rescue and blew down
the narrow strait from Cape Pelorus. I sailed south past the
mouth of the river Pantagias with its harbour of natural
rock, past the bay of Megara and low-lying Thapsus.
690 Achaemenides pointed out such places to us as we took
him back along the shores he had once sailed as the
comrade of the unfortunate Ulixes.

At the entrance to the bay of Syracuse, opposite the
wave-beaten headland of Plemyrium, there stands an island
which men of old called Ortygia. The story goes that the
river-god Alpheus of Elis forced his way here by hidden
passages under the sea and now mingles with Sicilian
waters at the mouth of Arethusa's fountain. Obeying the
instructions we had received, we worshipped the great
gods of the place and I then sailed on leaving behind the
rich lands around the marshy river Helorus. From here
700 we rounded Cape Pachynus, keeping close in to its jutting
cliffs of rock, and Camerina came into view in the distance,

the place the Fates forbade to move, and then the Geloan plains and Gela itself, called after its turbulent river. Then in the far distance appeared the great walls of Acragas on its crag, once famous for the breeding of high-mettled horses. Next the winds carried me past Selinus, named after the parsley it gave to crown the victors in Greek games, and I steered past the dangerous shoals and hidden rocks of Lilybaeum.

I then put into port at Drepanum, but had little joy of that shore. This was the place where weary as I was with all these batterings of sea and storm, to my great grief I lost my father Anchises who had been my support in every difficulty and disaster. This is where you left me, O best of fathers, whom I rescued from so many dangers and all to no purpose. Neither Helenus for all his fearsome predictions nor the Harpy Celaeno gave me any warning of this sorrow. This was the last of my labours. With this my long course was run. From here I sailed, and God drove me upon your shores.

In these words did Father Aeneas recount his wanderings and the fates the gods had sent him, and they all listened. At last he was silent. Here he made an end and was at peace.

4

DIDO

But the queen had long since been suffering from love's deadly wound, feeding it with her blood and being consumed by its hidden fire. Again and again there rushed into her mind thoughts of the great valour of the man and the high glories of his line. His features and the words he had spoken had pierced her heart and love gave her body no peace or rest. The next day's dawn was beginning to traverse the earth with the lamp of Phoebus' sunlight and had moved the dank shadow of night from the sky when she spoke these words from the depths of her affliction to her loved and loving sister: 'O Anna, what fearful dreams I have as I lie there between sleeping and waking! What a man is this who has just come as a stranger into our house! What a look on his face! What courage in his heart! What a warrior! I do believe, and I am sure it is true, he is descended from the gods. If there is any baseness in a man, it shows as cowardice. Oh how cruelly he has been hounded by the Fates! And did you hear him tell what a bitter cup of war he has had to drain? If my mind had not been set and immovably fixed against joining any man in the bonds of marriage ever since death cheated me of my first love, if I were not so utterly opposed to the marriage torch and bed, this is the one temptation to which I could possibly have succumbed. I will admit it, Anna, ever since the death of my poor husband Sychaeus, since my own brother spilt his blood and polluted the gods of our home,

this is the only man who has stirred my feelings and
moved my mind to waver: I sense the return of the old
fires. But I would pray that the earth open to its depths
and swallow me or that the All-powerful Father of the
Gods blast me with his thunderbolt and hurl me down to
the pale shades of Erebus and its bottomless night before I
go against my conscience and rescind its laws. The man
who first joined himself to me has carried away all my
love. He shall keep it for himself, safe in his grave.'

   The tears came when she had finished speaking, and ₃₀
streamed down upon her breast. But Anna replied: 'O
sister, dearer to me than the light of life, are you going to
waste away, living alone and in mourning all the days of
your youth, without knowing the delight of children and
the rewards of love? Do you believe this is what the dead
care about when they are buried in the grave? Since your
great sadness you have paid no heed to any man in Libya,
or before that in Tyre. You have rejected Iarbas and other
chiefs bred in Africa, this rich home of triumphant warriors.
Will you now resist even a love your heart accepts? Have
you forgotten what sort of people these are in whose land
you have settled? On the one side you are beset by in- ₄₀
vincible Gaetulians, by Numidians, a race not partial to the
bridle, and the inhospitable Syrtes; on the other, waterless
desert and fierce raiders from Barca. I do not need to tell
you about the war being raised against you in Tyre and
your brother's threats. I for my part believe that it is with
the blessing of the gods and the favour of Juno that the
Trojan ships have held course here through the winds. Just
think, O my sister, what a city and what a kingdom you
will see rising here if you are married to such a man! To
what a pinnacle of glory will Carthage be raised if Trojans
are marching at our side! You need only ask the blessing of ₅₀
the gods and prevail upon them with sacrifices. Indulge your
guest. Stitch together some reasons to keep him here while
stormy seas and the downpours of Orion are exhausting

their fury, while his ships are in pieces and it is no sky to sail under.'

With these words Anna lit a fire of wild love in her sister's breast. Where there had been doubt she gave hope and Dido's conscience was overcome. First they approached the shrines and went round the altars asking the blessing of the gods. They picked out yearling sheep, as ritual prescribed, and sacrificed them to Ceres the Lawgiver, to Phoebus Apollo, to Bacchus the Releaser and above all to 60 Juno, the guardian of the marriage bond. Dido in all her beauty would hold a sacred dish in her right hand and would pour wine from it between the horns of a white cow or she would walk in state to richly smoking altars before the faces of the gods, renewing her offerings all day long, and when the bellies of the victims were opened she would stare into their breathing entrails to read the signs. But priests, as we know, are ignorant. What use are prayers and shrines to a passionate woman? The flame was eating the soft marrow of her bones and the wound lived quietly under her breast. Dido was on fire with love and wandered all over the city in her misery and madness like a 70 wounded deer which a shepherd hunting in the woods of Crete has caught off guard, striking her from long range with steel-tipped shaft; the arrow flies and is left in her body without his knowing it; she runs away over all the wooded slopes of Mount Dicte, and sticking in her side is the arrow that will bring her death.

Sometimes she would take Aeneas through the middle of Carthage, showing him the wealth of Sidon and the city waiting for him, and she would be on the point of speaking her mind to him but checked the words on her lips. Sometimes, as the day was ending, she would call for more feasting and ask in her infatuation to hear once more about the sufferings of Troy and once more she would hang on 80 his lips as he told the story. Then, after they had parted, when the fading moon was dimming her light and the

setting stars seemed to speak of sleep, alone and wretched
in her empty house she would cling to the couch Aeneas
had left. There she would lie long after he had gone and
she would see him and hear him when he was not there for
her to see or hear. Or she would keep back Ascanius and
take him on her knee, overcome by the likeness to his
father, trying to beguile the love she could not declare.
The towers she was building ceased to rise. Her men gave
up the exercise of war and were no longer busy at the
harbours and fortifications making them safe from attack.
All the work that had been started, the threatening ramparts
of the great walls and the cranes soaring to the sky, all
stood idle.

As soon as Saturnian Juno, the dear wife of Jupiter, 90
realized that Dido was infected by this sickness and that
passion was sweeping away all thought for her reputation,
she went and spoke to Venus: 'You are covering yourselves
with glory. These are the supreme spoils you are bringing
home, you and that boy of yours — and what a noble and
notable specimen of the divine he is — one woman has been
overthrown by the arts of two gods! I do not fail to
see that you have long been afraid of our walls and looked
askance at the homes of lofty Carthage. But how is this
going to end? Where is all this rivalry going to lead us
now? Why do we not instead agree to arrange a marriage
and live at peace for ever? You have achieved what you 100
have set your whole heart on: Dido is passionately in love
and the madness is working through her bones. So let us
make one people of them and share authority equally over
them. Let us allow her to become the slave of a Phrygian
husband and to hand over her Tyrians to you as a dowry!'

Venus realized this was all pretence in order to divert the
empire of Italy to the shores of Libya, and made this
response to the Queen of Heaven: 'Who would be so
insane as to reject such an offer and choose instead to
contend with you in war? If only a happy outcome could

110 attend the plan you describe! But I am at the mercy of the Fates and do not know whether Jupiter would wish there to be one city for the Tyrians and those who have come from Troy or whether he would approve the merging of their peoples and the making of alliances. You are his wife. It could not be wrong for you to approach him with prayers and test his purpose. You proceed and I shall follow.'

'That will be my task,' replied Juno. 'But now listen and I shall explain in a few words how the first part of the plan may be carried out. Aeneas and poor Dido are preparing to go hunting together in the forest as soon as tomorrow's sun first rises and the rays of the Titan unveil the world. When the beaters are scurrying about and putting nets 120 round copses, I shall pour down a dark storm of rain and hail on them and shake the whole sky with thunder. Their companions will run away and be lost to sight in a pall of darkness. Dido and the leader of the Trojans will both take refuge in the same cave. I shall be there, and if your settled will is with me in this, I shall join them in lasting marriage and make her his. This will be their wedding.' This was what Juno asked and Venus of Cythera did not refuse her but nodded in assent. She saw through the deception and laughed.

Meanwhile Aurora rose from the ocean and when her 130 light came up into the sky, a picked band of men left the gates of Carthage carrying nets, wide-meshed and fine-meshed, and broad-bladed hunting spears, and with them came Massylian horsemen at the gallop and packs of keen-scented hounds. The queen was lingering in her chamber and the Carthaginian leaders waited at her door. There, resplendent in its purple and gold, stood her loud-hoofed, high-mettled horse champing its foaming bit. She came at last with a great entourage thronging round her. She was wearing a Sidonian cloak with an embroidered hem. Her quiver was of gold. Gold was the clasp that gathered up

her hair and her purple tunic was fastened with a golden
brooch. Nor was the Trojan company slow to move   140
forward, Ascanius with them in high glee. Aeneas himself
marched at their head, the most splendid of them all, as he
brought his men to join the queen's. He was like Apollo
leaving his winter home in Lycia and the waters of the
river Xanthus to visit his mother at Delos, there to start
the dancing again, while all around the altars gather noisy
throngs of Cretans and Dryopes and painted Agathyrsians;
the god himself strides the ridges of Mount Cynthus, his
streaming hair caught up and shaped into a soft garland of
green and twined round a band of gold, and the arrows
sound on his shoulders – with no less vigour moved   150
Aeneas and his face shone with equal radiance and grace.
When they had climbed high into the mountains above the
tracks of men where the animals make their lairs, suddenly
some wild goats were disturbed on the top of a crag and
came running down from the ridge. Then on the other
side there were deer running across the open plain. They
had gathered into a herd and were raising the dust as they
left the high ground far behind them. Down in the middle
of the valley young Ascanius was riding a lively horse and
revelling in it, galloping past the deer and the goats and
praying that among these flocks of feeble creatures he
could come across a foaming boar or that a tawny lion
would come down from the mountains.

   While all this was happening a great rumble of thunder   160
began to stir in the sky. Down came the rain and the hail,
and Tyrian huntsmen, men of Troy and Ascanius of the
line of Dardanus and grandson of Venus, scattered in fright
all over the fields, making for shelter as rivers of water
came rushing down the mountains. Dido and the leader of
the Trojans took refuge together in the same cave. The
sign was first given by Earth and by Juno as matron of
honour. Fires flashed and the heavens were witness to the
marriage while nymphs wailed on the mountain tops. This

170 day was the beginning of her death, the first cause of all
her sufferings. From now on Dido gave no thought to
appearance or her good name and no longer kept her love
as a secret in her own heart, but called it marriage, using
the word to cover her guilt.

Rumour did not take long to go through the great cities
of Libya. Of all the ills there are, Rumour is the swiftest.
She thrives on movement and gathers strength as she goes.
From small and timorous beginnings she soon lifts herself
up into the air, her feet still on the ground and her head
hidden in the clouds. They say she is the last daughter of
180 Mother Earth who bore her in rage against the gods, a
sister for Coeus and Enceladus. Rumour is quick of foot
and swift on the wing, a huge and horrible monster, and
under every feather of her body, strange to tell, there lies an
eye that never sleeps, a mouth and a tongue that are never
silent and an ear always pricked. By night she flies between
earth and sky, squawking through the darkness, and never
lowers her eyelids in sweet sleep. By day she keeps watch
perched on the tops of gables or on high towers and causes
fear in great cities, holding fast to her lies and distortions as
often as she tells the truth. At that time she was taking
190 delight in plying the tribes with all manner of stories, fact
and fiction mixed in equal parts: how Aeneas the Trojan
had come to Carthage and the lovely Dido had thought fit
to take him as her husband; how they were even now
indulging themselves and keeping each other warm the
whole winter through, forgetting about their kingdoms
and becoming the slaves of lust. When the foul goddess had
spread this gossip all around on the lips of men, she then
steered her course to king Iarbas to set his mind alight and
fuel his anger.

Jupiter had ravished a Garamantian nymph and Iarbas
was his son. Over his broad realm he had erected a
200 hundred huge temples to the god and set up a hundred
altars on which he had consecrated ever-burning fires to

keep undying holy vigil, enriching the earth with the blood of slaughtered victims and draping the doors with garlands of all kinds of flowers. Iarbas, they say, was driven out of his mind with anger when he heard this bitter news. Coming into the presence of the gods before their altars in a passion of rage, he offered up prayer upon prayer to Jupiter, raising his hands palms upward in supplication: 'Jupiter All-powerful, who now receives libations of wine from the Moorish people feasting on their embroidered couches, do you see all this? Or are we fools to be afraid of you, Father, when you hurl your thunderbolts? Are they unaimed, these fires in the clouds that cow our spirits? Is there no meaning in the murmur of your thunder? This woman was wandering about our land and we allowed her at a price to found her little city. We gave her a piece of shore to plough and laid down the laws of the place for her and she has spurned our offer of marriage and taken Aeneas into her kingdom as lord and master, and now this second Paris, with eunuchs in attendance and hair dripping with perfume and Maeonian bonnet tied under his chin, is enjoying what he has stolen while we bring gifts to temples we think are yours and keep warm with our worship the reputation of a useless god.'

As Iarbas prayed these prayers with his hand on the altar, the All-powerful god heard him and turned his eyes towards the royal city and the lovers who had lost all recollection of their good name. Then he spoke to Mercury and gave him these instructions: 'Up with you, my son. Call for the Zephyrs, glide down on your wings and speak to the Trojan leader who now lingers in Tyrian Carthage without a thought for the cities granted him by the Fates. Take these words of mine down to him through the swift winds and tell him that this is not the man promised us by his mother, the loveliest of the goddesses. It was not for this that she twice rescued him from the swords of the Greeks. She told us he would be the man to rule an Italy

pregnant with empire and clamouring for war, passing the
high blood of Teucer down to his descendants and subduing
the whole world under his laws. If the glory of such a
destiny does not fire his heart, if he does not strive to win
fame for himself, ask him if he grudges the citadel of
Rome to his son Ascanius. What does he have in mind?
What does he hope to achieve dallying among a hostile
people and sparing not a thought for the Lavinian fields
and his descendants yet to be born in Ausonia? He must
sail. That is all there is to say. Let that be our message.'

Jupiter had finished speaking and Mercury prepared to
obey the command of his mighty father. First of all he
240 fastened on his feet the golden sandals whose wings carry
him high above land and sea as swiftly as the wind. Then,
taking the rod which summons pale spirits out of Orcus or
sends them down to gloomy Tartarus, which gives sleep
and takes it away and opens the eyes of men in death, he
drove the winds before him and floated through the turbulent clouds till in his flight he saw the crest and steep flanks
of Atlas whose rocky head props up the sky. This is the
Atlas whose head, covered in pine trees and beaten by
250 wind and rain, never loses its dark cap of cloud. The snow
falls upon his shoulders and lies there, then rivers of water
roll down the old man's chin and his bristling beard is stiff
with ice. This is where Mercury the god of Mount Cyllene
first landed, fanning out his wings to check his flight.
From here he let his weight take him plummeting to the
wave tops, like a bird skimming the sea as it flies along the
shore, among the rocks where it finds the fish. So flew the
Cyllenian god between earth and sky to the sandy beaches
of Libya, cleaving the winds as he swooped down from the
mountain that had fathered his own mother, Maia.

As soon as his winged feet touched the roof of a Car-
260 thaginian hut, he caught sight of Aeneas laying the foundations of the citadel and putting up buildings. His sword
was studded with yellow stars of jasper, and glowing with

Tyrian purple there hung from his shoulders a rich cloak given him by Dido into which she had woven a fine cross-thread of gold. Mercury wasted no time: 'So now you are laying foundations for the high towers of Carthage and building a splendid city to please your wife? Have you entirely forgotten your own kingdom and your own destiny? The ruler of the gods himself, by whose divine will the heavens and the earth revolve, sends me down from bright Olympus and bids me bring these commands to you through the swift winds. What do you have in mind? What do you hope to achieve by idling your time away in the land of Libya? If the glory of such a destiny does not fire your heart, spare a thought for Ascanius as he grows to manhood, for the hopes of this Iulus who is your heir. You owe him the land of Rome and the kingdom of Italy.' 270

No sooner had these words passed the lips of the Cyllenian god than he disappeared from mortal view and faded far into the insubstantial air. But the sight of him left Aeneas dumb and senseless. His hair stood on end with horror and the voice stuck in his throat. He longed to be away and leave behind him this land he had found so sweet. The warning, the command from the gods, had struck him like a thunderbolt. But what, oh what, was he to do? What words dare he use to approach the queen in all her passion? How could he begin to speak to her? His thoughts moved swiftly now here, now there, darting in every possible direction and turning to every possible event, and as he pondered, this seemed to him a better course of action: he called Mnestheus, Sergestus and brave Serestus and ordered them to fit out the fleet and tell no one, to muster the men on the shore with their equipment at the ready, and keep secret the reason for the change of plan. In the meantime, since the good queen knew nothing and the last thing she expected was the shattering of such a great love, he himself would try to make approaches to her and find the kindest time to speak and the best way to 280 290 handle the matter. They were delighted to receive their orders and carried them out immediately.

But the queen – who can deceive a lover? – knew in advance some scheme was afoot. Afraid where there was nothing to fear, she was the first to catch wind of their plans to leave, and while she was already in a frenzy, that same wicked Rumour brought word that the Trojans were fitting out their fleet and preparing to sail away. Driven to distraction and burning with passion, she raged and raved round the whole city like a Bacchant stirred by the shaking of the sacred emblems and roused to frenzy when she hears the name of Bacchus at the biennial orgy and the shouting on Mount Cithaeron calls to her in the night. At last she went to Aeneas, and before he could speak, she cried: 'You traitor, did you imagine you could do this and keep it secret? Did you think you could slip away from this land of mine and say nothing? Does our love have no claim on you? Or the pledge your right hand once gave me? Or the prospect of Dido dying a cruel death? Why must you move your fleet in these winter storms and rush across the high seas into the teeth of the .north wind? You are heartless. Even if it were not other people's fields and some home unknown you were going to, if old Troy were still standing, would any fleet set sail even for Troy in such stormy seas? Is it me you are running away from? I beg you, by these tears, by the pledge you gave me with your own right hand – I have nothing else left me now in my misery – I beg you by our union, by the marriage we have begun – if I have deserved any kindness from you, if you have ever loved anything about me, pity my house that is falling around me, and I implore you, if it is not too late for prayers, give up this plan of yours. I am hated because of you by the peoples of Libya and the Numidian kings. My own Tyrians are against me. Because of you I have lost all conscience and self-respect and have thrown away the good name I once had, my only hope of reaching the stars.

My guest is leaving me to my fate and I shall die. "Guest"
is the only name I can now give the man who used to be
my husband. What am I waiting for? For my brother
Pygmalion to come and raze my city to the ground? For
the Gaetulian Iarbas to drag me off in chains? Oh if only
you had given me a child before you abandoned me! If
only there were a little Aeneas to play in my palace! In
spite of everything his face would remind me of yours and
I would not feel utterly betrayed and desolate.'   330

   She had finished speaking. Remembering the warnings
of Jupiter, Aeneas did not move his eyes and struggled to
fight down the anguish in his heart. At last he spoke these
few words: 'I know, O queen, you can list a multitude of
kindnesses you have done me. I shall never deny them and
never be sorry to remember Dido while I remember
myself, while my spirit still governs this body. Much could
be said. I shall say only a little. It never was my intention
to be deceitful or run away without your knowing, and do
not pretend that it was. Nor have I ever offered you
marriage or entered into that contract with you. If the   340
Fates were leaving me free to live my own life and settle
all my cares according to my own wishes, my first concern
would be to tend the city of Troy and my dear ones who
are still alive. The lofty palace of Priam would still be
standing and with my own hands I would have built a new
citadel at Pergamum for those who have been defeated.
But now Apollo of Gryneum has commanded me to claim
the great land of Italy and "Italy" is the word on the lots
cast at his Lycian oracle. That is my love, and that is my
homeland. You are a Phoenician from Asia and you care
for the citadel of Carthage and love the very sight of this
city in Libya; what objection can there be to Trojans   350
settling in the land of Ausonia? How can it be a sin if we
too look for distant kingdoms. Every night when the earth
is covered in mist and darkness, every time the burning
stars rise in the sky, I see in my dreams the troubled spirit

of my father Anchises coming to me with warnings and I am afraid. I see my son Ascanius and think of the wrong I am doing him, cheating him of his kingdom in Hesperia and the lands the Fates have decreed for him. And now even the messenger of the gods has come down through the swift winds – I swear it by the lives of both of us – and brought commands from Jupiter himself. With my own eyes I have seen the god in the clear light of day coming within the walls of your city. With my own ears I have
360 listened to his voice. Do not go on causing distress to yourself and to me by these complaints. It is not by my own will that I still search for Italy.'

All the time he had been speaking she was turned away from him, but looking at him, speechless and rolling her eyes, taking in every part of him. At last she replied on a blaze of passion: 'You are a traitor. You are not the son of a goddess and Dardanus was not the first founder of your family. It was the Caucasus that fathered you on its hard rocks and Hyrcanian tigers offered you their udders. Why should I keep up a pretence? Why should I keep myself in check in order to endure greater suffering in the future? He did not sigh when he saw me weep. He did not even turn
370 to look at me. Was he overcome and brought to tears? Had he any pity for the woman who loves him? Where can I begin when there is so much to say? Now, after all this, can mighty Juno and the son of Saturn, the father of all, can they now look at this with the eyes of justice? Is there nothing we can trust in this life? He was thrown helpless on my shores and I took him in and like a fool settled him as partner in my kingdom. He had lost his fleet and I found it and brought his companions back from the dead. It drives me to madness to think of it. And now we hear about the augur Apollo and lots cast in Lycia and now to crown all the messenger of the gods is bringing terrify-ing commands down through the winds from Jupiter himself, as though that is work for the gods in heaven, as

though that is an anxiety that disturbs their tranquillity. I ₃₈₀
do not hold you or bandy words with you. Away you go.
Keep on searching for your Italy with the winds to help
you. Look for your kingdom over the waves. But my
hope is that if the just gods have any power, you will drain
a bitter cup among the ocean rocks, calling the name of
Dido again and again, and I shall follow you not in the
flesh but in the black fires of death and when its cold hand
takes the breath from my body, my shade shall be with
you wherever you may be. You will receive the punishment you deserve, and the news of it will reach me deep
among the dead.'

At these words she broke off and rushed indoors in utter ₃₉₀
despair, leaving Aeneas with much to say and much to
fear. Her attendants caught her as she fainted and carried
her to her bed in her marble chamber. But Aeneas was
faithful to his duty. Much as he longed to soothe her and
console her sorrow, to talk to her and take away her pain,
with many a groan and with a heart shaken by his great
love, he nevertheless carried out the commands of the gods
and went back to his ships.

By then the Trojans were hard at work. All along the
shore they were hauling the tall ships down to the sea.
They set the well-caulked hulls afloat and in their eagerness ₄₀₀
to be away they were carrying down from the woods
unworked timber and green branches for oars. You could
see them pouring out of every part of the city, like ants
plundering a huge heap of wheat and storing it away in
their home against the winter, and their black column
advances over the plain as they gather in their booty along
a narrow path through the grass, some putting their shoulders to huge grains and pushing them along, others keeping
the column together and whipping in the stragglers, and
the whole track seethes with activity. What were your
feelings, Dido, as you looked at this? Did you not moan
as you gazed out from the top of your citadel and saw ₄₁₀

the broad shore seething before your eyes and confusion
and shouting all over the sea? Love is a cruel master. There
are no lengths to which it does not force the human heart.
Once again she had recourse to tears, once again she was
driven to try to move his heart with prayers, becoming a
suppliant and making her pride submit to her love, in case
she should die in vain, leaving some avenue unexplored.
'You see, Anna, the bustle all over the shore. They are all
gathered there, the canvas is calling for the winds, the
sailors are delighted and have set garlands on the ships'
420 sterns. I was able to imagine that this grief might come; I
shall be able to endure it. But Anna, do this one service for
your poor sister. You are the only one the traitor respected.
To you he entrusted his very deepest feelings. You are the
only one who knew the right time to approach him and
the right words to use. Go to him, sister. Kneel before our
proud enemy and tell him I was not at Aulis and made no
compact with the Greeks to wipe out the people of Troy. I
sent no fleet to Pergamum. I did not tear up the ashes of
his dead father Anchises. Why are his cruel ears closed to
what I am saying? Where is he rushing away to? Ask him
to do this last favour to the unhappy woman who loves
430 him and wait till there is a following wind and his escape is
easy. I am no longer begging for the marriage which we
once had and which he has now betrayed. I am not
pleading with him to do without his precious Latium and
abandon his kingdom. What I am asking for is some time,
nothing more, an interval, a respite for my anguish, so that
fortune can teach me to grieve and to endure defeat. This
is the last favour I shall beg. O Anna, pity your sister. I
shall repay it in good measure at my death.'

    These were Dido's pleas. These were the griefs her
unhappy sister brought and brought again. But no griefs
moved Aeneas. He heard but did not heed her words. The
440 Fates forbade it and God blocked his ears to all appeals. Just
as the north winds off the Alps vie with one another to

uproot the mighty oak whose timber has hardened over long years of life, blowing upon it from this side and from that and howling through it; the trunk feels the shock and the foliage from its head covers the ground, but it holds on to the rocks with roots plunged as deep into the world below as its crown soars towards the winds of heaven – just so the hero Aeneas was buffeted by all this pleading on this side and on that, and felt the pain deep in his mighty heart but his mind remained unmoved and the tears rolled in vain.

Then it was that unhappy Dido prayed for death. She had 450 seen her destiny and was afraid. She could bear no longer to look up to the bowl of heaven, and her resolve to leave the light was strengthened when she was laying offerings on the incense-breathing altars and saw to her horror the consecrated milk go black and the wine, as she poured it, turn to filthy gore. No one else saw it and she did not tell even her sister. There was more. She had in her palace a marble shrine dedicated to Sychaeus, who had been her husband. This she used to honour above all things, hanging it with white fleeces and sacred branches. When the darkness of night covered the earth, she thought she heard, coming from this 460 shrine, the voice of her husband and the words he uttered as he called to her, and all the while the lonely owl kept up its long dirge upon the roof, drawing out its doleful song of death. And there was more. She kept remembering the predictions of ancient prophets that terrified her with their dreadful warnings, and as she slept Aeneas himself would drive her relentlessly in her madness, and she was always alone and desolate, always going on a long road without companions, looking for her Tyrians in an empty land. She would be like Pentheus in his frenzy when he was seeing columns of Furies and a double sun and two cities of 470 Thebes; or like Orestes, son of Agamemnon, driven in flight across the stage by his own mother armed with her torches and black snakes, while the avenging Furies sat at the door.

And so Dido was overwhelmed by grief and possessed by madness. She decided to die and planned in her mind the time and the means. She went and spoke to her sorrowing sister with her face composed to conceal her plan and her brow bright with hope. 'My dear Anna, rejoice with your sister. I have found a way to bring him
480 back to me in love or else to free me from him. Near Oceanus and the setting of the sun is the home of the Ethiopians, the most distant part of our earth, where mightiest Atlas turns on his shoulders the axis of the sky, studded with its burning stars. From here, they say, there comes a Massylian priestess who was the guardian of the temple of the Hesperides. She used to keep watch over the branches of the sacred tree and bring rich foods for the serpent, spreading the oozing honey and sprinkling the sleep-bringing seeds of the poppy. She undertakes to free by her spells the mind of anyone she wishes and to send cruel cares to others, to stop the flow of rivers and turn stars
490 back in their courses. At night she raises the spirits of the dead and you will see the ash trees coming down from the mountains and hear the earth bellow beneath your feet. I call the gods and your own sweet self to witness, O my dearest sister, that it is not by my own will that I have recourse to magic arts. Go now, telling no one, and build up a pyre under the open sky in the inner courtyard of the palace and lay on it the armour this traitor has left hanging on the walls of my room, everything there is of his remaining, and the marriage bed on which I was destroyed. I want to wipe out everything that can remind me of such a man and that is what the priestess advises.'

500 She spoke, and spoke no more. Her face grew pale, but Anna did not understand that these strange rites were a pretence and that her sister meant to die. She had no inkling that such madness had seized Dido, no reason to fear that she would suffer more than she had at the death of Sychaeus. She did what she was asked.

But the queen knew what the future held. As soon as the
pine torches and the holm-oak were hewn and the huge
pyre raised under the open sky in the very heart of the
palace, she hung the place with garlands and crowned the
pyre with funeral branches. Then she laid on a bed an
effigy of Aeneas with his sword and everything of his he
had left behind. There were altars all around and the
priestess with hair streaming called with a voice of thunder 510
upon three hundred gods, Erebus, Chaos, triple Hecate and
virgin Diana of the three faces. She had also sprinkled
water to represent the spring of Lake Avernus. She also
sought out potent herbs with a milk of black poison in
their rich stems and harvested them by moonlight with a
bronze sickle. She found, too, a love charm, torn from the
forehead of a new-born foal before the mare could bite it
off. Dido herself took meal in her hands and worshipped,
standing by the altars with one foot freed from all fastenings
and her dress unbound, calling before she died to gods and
stars to be witnesses to her fate and praying to whatever 520
just and mindful power there is that watches over lovers
who have been betrayed.

It was night and weary living things were peacefully
taking their rest upon the earth. The woods and wild
waves of ocean had been stilled. The stars were rolling on
in mid-course. Silence reigned over field and flock and all
the gaily coloured birds were laid to sleep in the quiet of
night, those that haunt broad lakes and those that crowd
the thickets dotted over the countryside. But not Dido.
Her heart was broken and she found no relief in sleep. Her 530
eyes and mind would not accept the night, but her torment
redoubled and her raging love came again and again in
great surging tides of anger. These are the thoughts she
dwelt upon, this is what she kept turning over in her heart:
'So then, what am I to do? Shall I go back to those who
once wooed me and see if they will have me? I would be a
laughing stock. Shall I beg a husband from the Numidians

after I have so often scorned their offers of marriage? Shall I then go with the Trojan fleet and do whatever the Trojans ask? I suppose they would be delighted to take me after all the help I have given them! They are sure to remember what I have done and be properly grateful! No: even if I were willing to go with them, they will never allow a woman they hate to come aboard their proud ships. There is nothing left for you, Dido. Do you not know, have you not yet noticed, the treacheries of the race of Laomedon? But if they did agree to take me, what then? Shall I go alone into exile with a fleet of jubilant sailors? Or shall I go in force with all my Tyrian bands crowding at my side? It was not easy for me to uproot them from their homes in the city of Sidon. How can I make them take to the sea again and order them to hoist sail into the winds? No, you must die. That is what you have deserved. Let the sword be the cure for your suffering. You could not bear, Anna, to see your sister weeping. When the madness was taking me, you were the first to lay this load upon my back and put me at the mercy of my enemy. I was not allowed to live my life without marriage, in innocence, like a wild creature, and be untouched by such anguish as this – I have not kept faith with the ashes of Sychaeus.'

While these words of grief were bursting from Dido's heart, Aeneas was now resolved to leave and was taking his rest on the high stern of his ship with everything ready for sailing. There, as he slept, appeared before him the shape of the god, coming to him with the same features as before and once again giving advice, in every way like Mercury, the voice, the radiance, the golden hair, the youthful beauty of his body: 'Son of the goddess, how can you lie there sleeping at a time like this? Do you not see danger all around you at this moment? Have you lost your wits? Do you not hear the west wind blowing off the shore? Having decided to die, she is turning her schemes over in her mind

and planning some desperate act, stirring up the storm tides
of her anger. Why do you not go now with all speed
while speed you may? If morning comes and finds you
loitering here, you will soon see her ships churning the sea
and deadly torches blazing and the shore seething with
flames. Come then! No more delay! Women are un-   570
stable creatures, always changing.'

When he had spoken he melted into the blackness of
night and Aeneas was immediately awake, terrified by the
sudden apparition. There was no more rest for his men, as
he roused them to instant action: 'Wake up and sit to your
benches,' he shouted. 'Let out the sails and quick about it.
A god has been sent down again from the heights of
heaven – I have just seen him – spurring us on to cut our
plaited ropes and run from here. We are following you, O
blessed god, whoever you are. Once again we obey your
commands and rejoice. Stand beside us and graciously help
us. Put favouring stars in the sky for us.'

As he spoke he drew his sword from its scabbard like a
flash of lightning and struck the mooring cables with the   580
naked steel. In that instant they were all seized by the same
ardour and set to, hauling and hustling. The shore was
emptied. The sea could not be seen for ships. Bending to
the oars they whipped up the foam and swept the blue
surface of the sea.

Aurora was soon leaving the saffron bed of Tithonus
and beginning to sprinkle new light upon the earth. The
queen saw from her high tower the first light whitening
and the fleet moving out to sea with its sails square to the
following winds. She saw the deserted shore and harbour
and not an oarsman in sight. Three times and more she
beat her lovely breasts and tore her golden hair, crying 'O   590
Jupiter! Will this intruder just go, and make a mockery of
our kingdom? Why are they not running to arms and
coming from all over the city to pursue him? And others
should be rushing ships out of the docks. Move! Bring fire

and quick about it! Give out the weapons! Heave on the oars! – What am I saying? Where am I? What madness is this that changes my resolve? Poor Dido, you have done wrong and it is only now coming home to you. You should have thought of this when you were offering him your sceptre. So much for his right hand! So much for his pledge, the man who is supposed to be carrying with him the gods of his native land and to have lifted his weary old

600 father up on to his shoulders! Could I not have taken him and torn him limb from limb and scattered the pieces in the sea? Could I not have put his men to the sword, and Ascanius, too, and served his flesh at his father's table? I know the outcome of a battle would have been in doubt. So it would have been in doubt! Was I, who am about to die, afraid of anyone? I would have taken torches to his camp and filled the decks of his ships with fire, destroying the son and the father and the whole Trojan people before throwing myself on the flames. O heavenly Sun whose fires pass in review all the works of this earth, and you, Juno, who have been witness and party to all the anguish of this love, and Hecate whose name is heard in nightly

610 howling at crossroads all over our cities, and the avenging Furies and you, the gods of dying Dido, listen to these words, give a hearing to my sufferings, for they are great, and heed my prayers. If that monster of wickedness must reach harbour, if he must come to shore and that is what the Fates of Jupiter demand, if the boundary stone is set and may not be moved, then let him be harried in war by a people bold in arms; may he be driven from his own land and torn from the embrace of Iulus; may he have to beg for help and see his innocent people dying. Then, after he has submitted to the terms of an unjust peace, let him not enjoy the kingdom he longs for or the life he longs to

620 lead, but let him fall before his time and lie unburied on the broad sand. This is my prayer. With these last words I pour out my life's blood. As for you, my Tyrians, you

must pursue with hatred the whole line of his descendants in time to come. Make that your offering to my shade. Let there be no love between our peoples and no treaties. Arise from my dead bones, O my unknown avenger, and harry the race of Dardanus with fire and sword wherever they may settle, now and in the future, whenever our strength allows it. I pray that we may stand opposed, shore against shore, sea against sea and sword against sword. Let there be war between the nations and between their sons for ever.'

Even as she spoke Dido was casting about in her mind 630 how she could most quickly put an end to the life she hated. She then addressed these few words to Sychaeus' nurse, Barce, for the black ashes of her own now lay far away in her ancient homeland: 'My dear nurse, send my sister Anna quickly to me, telling her to sprinkle her body with river water and take with her the animals and the other offerings as instructed. That is how she is to come, and your own forehead must be veiled with a sacred ribbon. I have prepared with due care offerings to Jupiter of the Styx and I am now of a mind to complete them and put an end to the pain of love by giving the pyre of this Trojan to the flames.' 640

The old woman bustled away leaving Dido full of wild fears at the thought of what she was about to do. Her cheeks trembling and flecked with red, her bloodshot eyes rolling, she was pale with the pallor of approaching death. Rushing through the door into the inner courtyard, she climbed the high pyre in a frenzy and unsheathed the Trojan sword for which she had asked – though not for this purpose. Then her eyes lit on the Trojan clothes and the bed she knew so well, and pausing for a moment to weep and to remember, she lay down on the bed and spoke these last words: 'These are the possessions of Aeneas 650 which I so loved while God and the Fates allowed it. Let them receive my spirit and free me from this anguish. I have lived my life and completed the course that Fortune has set before me, and now my great spirit will go beneath the earth. I have founded a glorious city and lived to see the building of my own walls. I have avenged my husband and punished his enemy who was my brother. I would have been happy, more than happy, if only Trojan keels had never grounded on our shores.' She then buried her face for a moment in the bed and cried: 'We shall die 660 unavenged. But let us die. This, this, is how it pleases me to go down among the shades. Let the Trojan who knows no pity gaze his fill upon this fire from the high seas and take with him the omen of my death.'

So she spoke and while speaking fell upon the sword. Her attendants saw her fall. They saw the blood foaming on the blade and staining her hands, and filled the high walls of the palace with their screaming. Rumour ran raving like a Bacchant through the stricken city. The palace rang with lamentation and groaning and the wailing of women and the heavens gave back the sound of mourning. It was as though the enemy were within the gates and 670 the whole of Carthage or old Tyre were falling with flames raging and rolling over the roofs of men and gods. Anna heard and was beside herself. She came rushing in terror through the middle of the crowd, tearing her face and beating her breast, calling out her sister's name as she lay dying: 'So this is what it meant? It was all to deceive your sister! This was the purpose of the pyre and the flames and the altars! You have abandoned me. I do not know how to begin to reproach you. Did you not want your sister's company when you were dying? You could have called me to share your fate and we would both have 680 died in the same moment of the same grief. To think it was my hands that built the pyre, and my voice that called upon the gods of our fathers, so that you could be so cruel as to lay yourself down here to die without me. It is not only yourself you have destroyed, but also your sister and your people, their leaders who came with you from Sidon and the city you have built. Give me water. I shall wash her wounds and catch any last lingering breath with my lips.'

Saying these words, she had climbed to the top of the pyre and was now holding her dying sister to her breast and cherishing her, sobbing as she dried the dark blood with her own dress. Once more Dido tried to raise her 690 heavy eyes, but failed. The wound hissed round the sword beneath her breast. Three times she raised herself on her elbow. Three times she fell back on the bed. With wavering eyes she looked for light in the heights of heaven and groaned when she found it.

All-powerful Juno then took pity on her long anguish and difficult death and sent Iris down from Olympus to free her struggling spirit and loosen the fastenings of her limbs. For since she was dying not by the decree of Fate or by her own deserts but pitiably and before her time, in a sudden blaze of madness, Proserpina had not yet taken a lock of her golden hair or consigned her to Stygian Orcus. So Iris, bathed in dew, flew down on her saffron wings, 700 trailing all her colours across the sky opposite the sun, and hovered over Dido's head to say: 'I am commanded to take this lock of hair as a solemn offering to Dis, and now I free you from your body.'

With these words she raised her hand and cut the hair, and as she cut, all warmth went out of Dido's body and her life passed into the winds.

5

FUNERAL GAMES

Meanwhile Aeneas, without slackening in his resolve, kept his fleet on course well out at sea, cutting through waves darkened by the north wind and looking back at the walls of Carthage, glowing now in the flames of poor Dido's pyre. No one understood what had lit such a blaze, but since they all knew what bitter suffering is caused when a great love is desecrated and what a woman is capable of when driven to madness, the minds of the Trojans were filled with dark foreboding. The ships were now in mid-ocean, with no land in sight. All around was sky and all around was sea, when there came a cloud like lead and stood over Aeneas bringing storm and black night and the waves shivered in the darkness. Even Palinurus himself called out from the high stern: 'What can be the meaning of these great clouds filling the sky? What have you in mind for us, Father Neptune?' Not till then did he give orders to shorten sail and bend to the stout oars. Then, setting the canvas aslant to the winds, he turned to Aeneas and said: 'Great-hearted Aeneas, even if Jupiter himself gave me his guarantee, I would not expect to reach Italy under a sky like this. The wind has changed and is freshening, howling across us from the west where the sky is dark. We cannot struggle against it or make any real headway. Since Fortune is too strong for us to resist, let us follow her. Let us change course and go where she calls. I do not think we are far from the safety of the shores of your brother Eryx and the harbours of Sicily, if only my memory serves me right, and I can plot our course back by the stars I observed on the way out.'

The good Aeneas then replied: 'That is what the wind wants. I have seen it myself for some time and watched you fighting it to no effect. Change course then and adjust the sails. There is no land that would please me more, nowhere I would rather put in with our weary ships, than the place that gives a home to the Trojan Acestes and holds the bones of my father Anchises in the lap of earth.' As soon as this was said they set course for harbour and the wind blew from astern and stretched their sails. The fleet raced over the sea and the sailors were delighted to have their prows pointing at last towards a beach they knew.

Far away, on the top of a high mountain, Acestes saw his friends' ships arriving and was amazed. He came down to meet them bristling with javelins and the shaggy fur of a Libyan she-bear. Acestes had been born of a Trojan mother to the river-god Crinisus and he had not forgotten his ancestry, but welcomed the returning Trojans and gladly received them with all the treasures of the countryside, comforting their weariness with his loving care.

As soon as the next day had risen bright in the east and put the stars to flight, Aeneas called his men from all along the shore to a council and addressed them from a raised mound: 'Great sons of Dardanus, who draw your high blood from the gods, the months have passed and the cycle of the year is now complete since we laid in the ground the bones that were all that remained of my divine father and consecrated an altar of mourning. This is now the day, if I am right, which I shall always find bitter and always hold in honour, for so the gods have willed. If I were spending this day as an exile in the Syrtes among the Gaetulians, or if I had been caught in Greek waters and were a prisoner in the city of Mycenae, I would still offer up these annual vows, perform these processions in ritual order and lay due

offerings on altars. Today we find ourselves near the very place where the bones and ashes of my father lie (I for one do not believe this is without the wish and will of the gods), and the sea has taken us into this friendly harbour. Come then, let us all celebrate these rites with joy. Let us
60 ask for favouring winds and may it be his will that we found a city and offer him this worship in it every year in temples dedicated to his name. Trojan-born Acestes is giving you two head of oxen for each ship. Call to your feast the Penates, the gods of your ancestral home, and those of your host Acestes. After all this, when in nine days the dawn, god willing, lifts up her life-giving light among men and the round earth is revealed in her rays, I shall hold games for the Trojans, first a race for the ships, then for those who are fleet of foot, and a contest for those who take the arena in the boldness of their strength to compete with the javelin or the flying arrow, for those too who
70 dare to do battle in rawhide gauntlets. Let them all come and see who wins the prizes of victory. Keep holy silence, all of you, and crown your heads with shoots of living green.'

When he had spoken he shaded his temples with a garland of his mother's myrtle. So did Helymus. So did old Acestes. So did the boy Ascanius and all the men, while Aeneas, and many thousands with him, left the council and walked to the tomb in the middle of this great escort. Here he offered a libation, duly pouring two goblets of unmixed wine upon the ground with two of fresh milk and two of sacrificial blood. Then, scattering red flowers,
80 he spoke these words: 'Once more I greet you, my divine father. I come to greet your sacred ashes, the spirit and the shade of a father rescued in vain. Without you I must search for the land of Italy, for the fields decreed by Fate and for the Thybris of Ausonia, whatever that may be.'

When he had finished speaking, a snake slithered from under the shrine. Moving gently forward in seven great curves and seven great coils, it glided between the altars and twined itself round the tomb, its back flecked with blue and its scales flashing mottled gold like the thousand different colours cast by a rainbow on the clouds opposite the sun. Aeneas was struck dumb at the sight. At last it 90 dragged its long length among the polished bowls and goblets and tasted the offerings, then, harming no one, it left the altars where it had fed and went back under the tomb. Encouraged by this, Aeneas renewed the rites he had begun for his father, not knowing whether to think of the snake as the genius of the place or as his father's attendant spirit. He slew a pair of yearling sheep as ritual prescribed. two swine, and as many black-backed bullocks, pouring wine from bowls and calling repeatedly upon the spirit of great Anchises and his shade released from Acheron. His 100 comrades, too, each brought what gifts he could and gladly offered them. They heaped the altars and slaughtered bullocks while others laid out bronze vessels in due order, and all over the grass there was lighting of fires under spits and roasting of flesh.

The long-awaited day had come and the horses of Phaethon were now drawing the ninth dawn through a cloudless sky. Rumour and the famous name of Acestes had brought out all the surrounding peoples and a joyful crowd had filled the shore, some coming only to see Aeneas and his men, some also to compete. First the prizes were displayed before their eyes in the middle of the arena, 110 sacred tripods, crowns of green, palm leaves for the victors, arms, purple-dyed garments and talents of silver and gold. The trumpet gave the signal from a mound of earth in the middle. The games had started.

The first event was for four heavy-oared ships of the same class picked out of the fleet. The *Pristis* was a fast ship with a keen crew commanded by Mnestheus. He was soon to become the Italian Mnestheus, from whom the family of the Memmii take their name. The huge *Chimaera* was a

great hulk of a ship the size of a city, commanded by Gyas,
120 and to drive her through the water the Trojans sat in three
tiers and plied three banks of oars one above the other.
Sergestus sailed the great *Centaur* (he it was who gave his
name to the Sergii), and Cloanthus, the founder of the
Roman Cluentii, was in the blue-green *Scylla*.

Well out to sea off a wave-beaten shore there stands a
rock which in winter, when the north-westerly winds are
darkening the stars, is often submerged and battered by the
swell. But in calm weather all is quiet and the level top of
it stands up from a glassy sea and gulls love to bask on it.
130 Here Father Aeneas set up a green branch of holm-oak as a
mark round which the sailors would know they had to
turn to begin the long row home. They then drew lots for
their starting positions, and the captains stood on the high
sterns gleaming in the splendour of purple and gold. The
crews wore garlands of poplar leaves and the oil they had
poured on their shoulders glistened on the naked skin.
There they sat at the thwarts, straining their arms at the
oars and their ears to hear the starting signal. They were
shuddering with fear and their hearts were leaping and
pumping the blood for the sheer love of glory. When the
140 shrill trumpet sounded, in that one instant the ships all
surged forward from the line and the shouting of the
sailors rose and struck the heavens. Their arms drew the
oars back and the water was churned to foam. Side by side
they ploughed their furrows and tore open the whole sea
to its depths with their oars and triple beaks, like two-
horse chariots streaming full-pelt from the starting gates
and racing over the ground, or like charioteers at full
gallop cracking the rippling reins on their horses' backs and
hanging forward over them with the whip. All the woods
resounded with the din and cheers and roars of encourage-
150 ment. The echo of the shouting rolled round the curve of
the shore and bounced back off the hills.

In all this noise and excitement Gyas shot out in front

and took the lead over the first stretch of water. Cloanthus
was next. His rowers were better but he was slowed down
by the weight of his ship. Behind them the *Pristis* and the
Centaur were contesting third place. Now the *Pristis* has
it. Now the huge *Centaur* moves into the lead, and now
they are level, bow by bow, ploughing the salt sea with
their long keels. They were soon getting near the rock,
almost at the turning point, when Gyas, still in the lead at   160
this half-way stage, called out to his helmsman: 'Where are
you going, Menoetes? Who told you to steer to starboard?
Your line is over here, to port! Hug the shore. The oars on
the port side should be scraping the rocks. Leave the deep
water to the others!' These were his orders, but Menoetes
was afraid of hidden rocks and pulled the bows round to
the open sea. 'You're off course!' shouted Gyas, correcting
his line. 'Where do you think you're going? Make for the
rocks, Menoetes!' and even as he was shouting, he saw
Cloanthus close behind him and cutting in, just scraping   170
past on the port side between Gyas' ship and the roaring
rocks. He was past in a moment, safe in clear water and
sailing away from the mark. Young Gyas was incensed.
The rage burned in his bones and tears ran down his
cheeks. Without a thought for his own dignity or the
safety of his crew he took the sluggard Menoetes and
threw him off the high stern head first into the sea. He
then took over the tiller himself and became his own
helmsman, urging on the rowers and pulling the rudder
round to make for the shore. Menoetes was no lightweight
and was no longer young. He went straight to the bottom
and it was some time before he surfaced. At last he climbed   180
to the top of the dry rock and sat there with the water
streaming out of his clothes. The Trojans had laughed as he
fell and as he swam and they laughed as he spewed up
waves of salt water from his stomach.

Sergestus and Mnestheus in the last two boats were both
delighted that Gyas was losing time and both saw a hope

of overtaking the flying Gyas. Sergestus took the lead as
they came up to the rock, but not by a whole ship's length.
His bow was out in front but the *Pristis* was pressing him
hard and her beak was ahead of his stern. Her captain
Mnestheus was pacing the gangway between the rowers,
urging them on on either side: 'Now is the time!' he cried.
190 'Now you must rise to your oars. You are the men who
stood with Hector. You are the men I chose as comrades in
the last hours of Troy. Now let us see the courage and the
heart you showed off Gaetulia in the shoals of the Syrtes
and in the Ionian sea when the waves were driving us on
to Cape Malea. I am no longer hoping to be first. It is not
victory that Mnestheus is fighting for, though who
knows?. . . But let victory go to whom Neptune has given
it. The disgrace would be to be last. Prevent that shame,
my fellow-Trojans, and that will be our victory.' At this
they bent to the oars and strove with all their might. The
bronzed ship shuddered at their great thrusts and the
surface of the water sped away beneath them. Their breath-
200 ing quickened, chests heaved, mouths dried and the sweat
poured off their bodies in rivers. It was pure chance that
brought them the honour they longed for. Sergestus was
desperately forcing the bow of his ship close to the rocks
and cutting inside into dangerous water when all ended in
disaster as he ran aground on a projecting reef. The rock
quivered at the impact, the flailing oars grated on its
jagged edges and the shattered prow was left hanging in
mid-air. The crew leapt up and stood there shouting. Some
busied themselves with iron-tipped poles and their pointed
boat-hooks. Some were salvaging broken oars from the surf.
210 Mnestheus was exultant and success only made him more
determined. The oars pulled fast and true. He called upon
the winds and as he set course for the homeward stretch
and ran shoreward over the open sea, he was like a dove
startled out of the cave where it has its home and its
beloved nestlings in the secret honeycombs of the rock; it

flies off in terror to the fields with a great explosion of
wings inside the cave, but it soon swoops down through
the quiet air and glides along in the bright light; its wings
are swift but they scarcely move – just so was Mnestheus.
Just so was the *Pristis* as she cut through the last stretch of
water. Just so did she fly along under her own impetus.

First Mnestheus left Sergestus struggling behind him, 220
stuck on his rock high out of the water. There he was in
the shallows, shouting in vain for help and learning how to
row with broken oars. Next Mnestheus went after Gyas
and the huge *Chimaera* which soon fell behind for lack of
its helmsman. Now, at the very end of the race, only
Cloanthus was in front of him. He took up the pursuit and
pressed him hard, straining every nerve.

The shouting grew twice as loud. They all cheered him
on as he gave chase and the heavens rang with the noise.
Cloanthus and his men on the *Scylla* saw the honour as
theirs by right. They had already won the victory and had
no intention of giving it up. They would rather have lost 230
their lives than lose the glory. Mnestheus and his men on
the *Pristis* were feeding on success. They could win because
they thought they could. They drew level and would
perhaps have taken the prize if Cloanthus had not stretched
out his arms to the sea, pouring out his prayers and calling
on the gods to witness his vows: 'O you gods who rule the
sea and over whose waters I now race, this is my vow and
gladly will I keep it: I shall come to your altars on this
shore with a gleaming white bull. On the salt waves of the
sea I shall scatter its entrails and pour streams of wine.' He
spoke and was heard by the sea nymph Panopaea and all 240
the dancing bands of the Nereids and of Phorcys. As he
sailed on, Father Portunus pushed the ship with his own
great hand and it flew landward swifter than the wind
from the south or the flight of an arrow, till it arrived safe
in the deep waters of the harbour.

Then the son of Anchises called them all together in due

order and bade the herald loudly proclaim Cloanthus the
victor, and veiled his head with the green leaves of the
laurel. For each ship there was a gift of wine, three
bullocks of their choice and a great talent of silver. In
addition the captains were singled out for special honours.
250 The victor received a cloak embroidered with gold round
which there ran a broad double meander of Meliboean
purple, and woven into it was the royal prince running
with his javelin and wearying the swift stags on the leafy
slopes of Mount Ida. There he was, eager and breathless, so
it seemed, and down from Ida plunged the bird that carries
the thunderbolt of Jupiter and carried him off in its hooked
talons high into the heavens while the old men who were
there as his guards stretched their hands in vain towards the
stars and the dogs barked furiously up into the air. To
Mnestheus, whose courage had in the end won him second
260 place, Aeneas gave a breastplate interwoven with burnished
mail and triple threads of gold, which he had stripped with
his own hands from the defeated Demoleos on the banks
of the swift Simois under the high walls of Troy. For
Mnestheus this was to be a proud possession and his
protection in battle. His attendants Phegeus and Sagaris
hoisted it up on to their shoulders, all the many layers of it,
but they could hardly carry it away, yet Demoleos used to
wear it while running all over the battlefield in pursuit of
Trojans. The third prize was a pair of bronze drinking
cauldrons and some embossed drinking cups of solid silver.

At last they had all received rich gifts and were glorying
in them as they walked, their foreheads bound with purple
ribbons, when Sergestus appeared, taking in the boat that
was the object of all their laughter and had missed all the
270 honours. He had prised her off the cruel rock with great
difficulty and no mean skill, but she had lost oars and was
limping in with only one bank of them. Like a snake
caught crossing a raised road, as they often are, and run
over by a bronze wheel or battered by a traveller with a

heavy stone and left mangled and half-dead, it tries in vain
to escape by twisting its body into long curves, part of it
still fierce, the blazing eyes, the hissing, high-uplifted head,
but the wounded part holds it back as it writhes and coils
and twines itself into knots – this is how the *Centaur* 280
moved, rowing slowly along. But she put up sails and
came into the harbour mouth under full canvas. Aeneas,
delighted that Sergestus had saved his ship and brought his
men to port, gave him a prize, as promised, the Cretan
slave woman Pholoe, good with her hands and with two
sons at the breast.

After the boat race, dutiful Aeneas strode to a piece of
grassy level ground. All around it stood wooded hills and
in the middle of the valley there was a circle for a theatre.
When he reached this place – and many thousands went
with him – Aeneas sat down on a raised platform in the 290
middle of the concourse. Here he offered prizes for any
men who might wish to take part in a foot race, whetting
their ambition with rewards, and Trojans and Sicanians
flocked in from all sides. Nisus and Euryalus were first,
Euryalus standing out for the bloom of his youthful beauty
and Nisus for the loving care he showed to him. Then
came Diores, a prince of the noble line of Priam, and after
him Salius and Patron together, one an Acarnanian, the
other an Arcadian of Tegean stock. Then came two young 300
Sicilians, Helymus and Panopes, men of the woods, attendants of old Acestes, and many more whose names are
buried in oblivion. When they had gathered, Aeneas spoke
in the middle of them: 'Give your minds to what I have to
say. Mark it well and be of good cheer. No man of you
will leave without winning a prize from my hand. Two
Cretan arrows I shall give, their steel tips burnished and
gleaming, and a two-headed axe embossed with silver.
These rewards will be the same for all of you, but there
will be other prizes for the first three in the race and
crowns woven of golden olive for their heads. The winner 310

will have a horse with splendid trappings, the second an
Amazonian quiver full of Thracian arrows, slung on a belt
with a broad gold band and the clasp that fastens it is a
polished jewel. The third can leave the field content with
an Argive helmet.'

When he had finished speaking, they took their places,
the signal sounded and they were off, streaming away
from the starting-point in one great cloud. But as soon as
they came in sight of the finish, Nisus shot out a long way
in front of all of them, swifter than the wind and the wings
of the lightning. Second, but a long way behind, was Salius.
Then, after a gap, came Euryalus in third place. Behind
him was Helymus, then, immediately behind him and hard
on his heels, was Diores leaning over his shoulder, and if
there had been more course to run, he would have overtaken and passed him or they would have run a dead heat.

They were soon almost at the end of the course and
tiring as they came up to the line, when the unlucky Nisus
slid and fell on a slippery patch of blood that had been spilt
where they had killed bullocks and wet the earth and the
green grass that grew upon it. Here, as he pounded the
track exulting in the very moment of victory, he lost his
footing and fell on his face in the filthy dung and blood
from the sacrifice. But he was not the man to forget
Euryalus and the love he bore him. He rose from the slime
and threw himself in the path of Salius and knocked him
head over heels, sprawling on the hard-packed sand. Euryalus flashed past. Thanks to his friend he was in the lead
and speeding along to loud applause and cheers, Helymus
behind him with Diores now winning the third prize. But
Salius stood up before the faces of the fathers in the front
rows and filled the whole bowl of the huge assembly with
loud clamour, demanding the honour of which he had
been cheated. On the side of Euryalus were the favour in
which he was held, his beauty as he stood there weeping
and the manly spirit growing in that lovely body. On his

side too was Diores, protesting at the top of his voice. He
had come in third but there would be no third prize for
him if the first were to be given to Salius. Father Aeneas
then spoke: 'You young men will all keep your prizes. The
awards have been made and no one changes that. Let it be   350
my task to offer consolation to our friend for the downfall
he did nothing to deserve.' With these words he gave
Salius the hide of a huge Gaetulian lion, weighed down
with gilded claws and mane. This was too much for Nisus,
who burst out: 'If losers win prizes like this and you take
pity on people who fall, what gift will be enough to give
to Nisus? I would have won the victor's crown of glory
and deserved it if the same bad luck as brought down
Salius had not disposed of me,' and as he spoke he pointed
to the filthy wet dung on his face and body. Good Father
Aeneas laughed and ordered them to bring out a shield
made by the hand of Didymaon which had been dedicated   360
to Neptune and taken down from the doorposts of his
temple by Greeks, and he gave this superb gift to the noble
young Nisus.

The race was over and the prizes finally awarded. Then
spoke Aeneas: 'If there is any courage here, any man with a
heart in his breast, now is the time for him to come
forward with gloves on his hands and his guard up,'
and he set out two prizes for the fight, for the victor a
bullock with its head shadowed by ribbons and its horns
plated with gold, and a sword and splendid helmet as a
consolation prize for the loser. Dares did not hesitate.
Immediately that great face of his appeared and all his
mighty strength, and the people murmured as he hoisted
himself to his feet. He had been the only man who used to   370
stand against Paris. He was the man who had felled the
huge Butes and stretched him out to die on the yellow
sand by the mound where great Hector lay, when Butes
came as champion from the Bebrycian race of Amycus.
This was the Dares who stood there with his head held

high to begin the battle, flexing his shoulders, throwing lefts and rights and thrashing the air. They looked around for an opponent, but no one in all that company dared go 380 near him or put on the gloves. Thinking that no one was challenging him for the prize, he went straight up to Aeneas and stood there in front of him. Without more ado he took one of the bull's horns in his left hand and said: 'Son of the goddess, if no one dares trust himself to battle, how long are we going to stand here? What is the point of keeping me waiting? Tell them I can take away my prize,' and all the Trojans to a man murmured and told Aeneas to award the prize as promised.

At this Acestes had hard words for Entellus, sitting next him on a bank of green turf. 'Entellus,' he said, 'I have seen the day when you were the bravest of the heroes. Is it all in 390 the past? Are you going to sit there meekly when a prize like this is lifted and no opposition offered? Tell me, where is Eryx now, the god they say was once your teacher? Has all that come to nothing? What about that reputation of yours that used to ring round the whole island of Sicily? And what about the great trophies hanging in your house?' 'I am not afraid,' replied Entellus. 'I have still my pride and my love of honour. But old age is slowing me down. The blood is cold and sluggish. My strength is gone and my body is worn out. But if I were what I once was, if I had the youth that makes that puppy so full of himself, prancing 400 about there, I would not have needed the reward of a pretty bullock to bring me to my feet. I am not interested in prizes.' At these last words he threw into the middle the pair of prodigiously heavy gauntlets in which Eryx used to raise his guard, carrying them into battle with the hard leather stretched over his forearms. They were amazed. The hides of seven huge oxen were there, stiffened by lead and iron sewn into them. Dares was more amazed than anyone and stood well back at the sight of them, but the great-hearted son of Anchises picked them up and felt their weight, turning over the great folds of the jointed hides from one hand to another. Then spoke old Entellus, his voice deep in his chest: 'What would you have thought, 410 any of you, if you had seen the gauntlets that were the armour of Hercules himself and the cruel battle these two fought on this very shore? This, Aeneas, is the armour your brother Eryx used to wear. You see it is still caked with blood and spattered brains. With these he stood that day against great Hercules. With these I used to fight while there was still good blood in me to give me strength, before old age came to tangle with me and sprinkled both my temples with grey. But if Trojan Dares recoils from this armour of ours, and if good Aeneas is satisfied and my patron Acestes approves, let us level the odds. There's nothing to be afraid of, Dares. For you I give up the boxing leathers of Eryx, and you take off your Trojan 420 gauntlets,' and as he spoke he threw the double cloak off his shoulders and stripped to show the great joints of his limbs, the great bones and muscles on his arms, and stood there a giant in the middle of the arena.

Then the son of Anchises took out two matching pairs of gauntlets, and tied armour of equal weight on the hands of both men. There was no more delay. Each man took up his stance, poised on his toes, stretching to his full height, guard held high in the air and no sign of fear. They kept their towering heads well back from the punches and fist struck fist as they warmed to their work. Dares had youth 430 on his side and speed of foot. Entellus had the reach and the weight, but his knees were going. He was slow and shaky and his whole huge body heaved with the agony of breathing. Blow upon blow they threw at each other and missed. Blow upon blow drummed on the hollow rib cage, boomed on the chest and showered round the head and ears, and the cheekbones rattled with the weight of the punches. Entellus, being the heavier man, held firm in his stance, keeping watchful eyes on his opponent and swaying

away from the bombardment. For Dares it was like attacking some massive high-built city or besieging a mountain
fortress. This way and that he tried, covering all the
ground in his manoeuvres, pressing hard with all manner
of assaults and all to no avail. Then Entellus drew himself
up and showed his right hand raised for the blow, but
Dares was quick to see it coming down and backed away
smartly. Entellus' full force was in the blow and it met the
empty air. Great was his weight and great was the fall of
that huge body. He fell as a hollow pine tree falls, torn up
by the roots on great Mount Ida or on Erymanthus.
Trojans and Sicilians leapt to their feet as one man in their
excitement and the shouting rose to high heaven. Acestes
was the first to run to comfort his old friend and help
him from the ground. But the hero Entellus did not slow
down or lose heart because of a fall. He returned to the
fray with his ferocity renewed and anger rousing him to
new heights of violence. His strength was kindled by
shame at his fall and pride in his prowess, and in a white
heat of fury he drove Dares before him all over the arena,
hammering him with rights and lefts and allowing him no
rest or respite. Like hailstones from a dark cloud rattling
down on roofs, Entellus battered Dares with a shower of
blows from both hands and sent him spinning.

At this point Father Aeneas did not allow the anger of
Entellus to go any further but checked his savage passion
and put an end to the fight. As he rescued the exhausted
Dares he comforted him with these words: 'Unlucky Dares,
what madness is this that has taken possession of you? Do
you not see that your strength is not as his and the divine
will has turned against you? Yield to God.' He spoke and
his voice parted the combatants, and Dares was led back to
the ships by his faithful comrades, dragging his weary legs,
shaking his head from side to side and spitting out a
mixture of gore and teeth. His men were then called and
given the helmet and the sword, leaving the palm of

victory and the bull to Entellus. Then spoke the victor in all his pride of spirit, glorying in the bull he had won: 'Son of the goddess, know this, and you too, men of Troy: this is the strength there used to be in my body when I was in my prime and this is the death from which you have rescued Dares.' With these words he took up his stance in front of the bullock's head as it stood there as the prize of battle, then, drawing back his right hand and rising to his full height, he swung the brutal gauntlet straight down between its horns, shattering the brains and grinding them into the bone. The ox fell and lay full out on the ground, dead and twitching, and these are the words Entellus spoke and spoke them from the heart: 'The life of this ox is worth more than the life of Dares, and with it, Eryx, I pay my debt to you in full, and here and now in the moment of victory, I lay down my gauntlets and my art.'

Aeneas immediately summoned all those who wished to take part in the archery contest and announced the prizes. With his great hand he set up the mast taken from Serestus' ship and put a cord round a fluttering dove to hang it from the top of the mast as a target for the steel-tipped arrows. The contestants gathered. Lots were thrown into a bronze helmet, and the first to leap out, to loud acclaim, gave the first place to Hippocoon, son of Hyrtacus. Next came Mnestheus, fresh from his triumph in the boat race, Mnestheus with the green olive binding his hair. Third was Eurytion, brother of the famous Pandarus who in days long past had been ordered to break the truce, and had been the first to shoot an arrow into the middle of the Greeks. Last of all, at the bottom of the helmet, was Acestes. He too dared to try his hand at the test of warriors. Soon they were bending their bows with all their strength and taking the arrows out of their quivers. A string twanged and the first arrow, from young Hippocoon, cut through the breezes of heaven to strike home full in the wood of the mast. The mast quivered, there was a flash of wings from the frightened bird and all around rang out the loud applause. Next the eager Mnestheus took his stand and drew, aiming high, straining both eye and bow, but to his dismay he failed to hit the bird, cutting the knot in the linen cords which bound her feet as she hung there at the top of the mast. She made off, flying south towards some dark clouds. Eurytion lost no time (his bow had long been bent and his arrow at the ready), but called upon his brother Pandarus as he prayed, and took aim at the dove now glorying in the freedom of the sky. As she beat her wings just beneath the black cloud, the arrow struck her and she fell dead, leaving her life among the stars of heaven and bringing back as she fell the arrow that had pierced her.

Father Acestes alone remained and the victor's palm was lost to him, but he aimed an arrow high into the breezes of the air to display his old skill and let the sound of his bow be heard. At this a sudden miracle appeared before their eyes, a mighty sign of what the future held in store. In times to come was the great fulfilment revealed and awesome prophets interpreted the omens to future ages. As it flew through the vaporous clouds, the arrow burst into flames and marked its path with fire till it was consumed and faded into thin air, like those stars that leave their appointed places and race across the sky trailing their blazing hair behind them as they fly. Sicilians and Trojans stood stock still in amazement, praying to the gods above, but the mighty Aeneas welcomed the omen and embraced the exultant Acestes, heaping great gifts on him and saying these words: 'Accept these, Father Acestes, for the Great King of Olympus has shown by this sign that he has willed you to receive honours beyond the lot of other men. Here is a gift from my old father Anchises himself, a mixing bowl engraved with figures which he once received as a great tribute from Thracian Cisseus to be a memorial and pledge of his love.' With these words he put a wreath of

BOOK FIVE

laurel round Acestes' temples and declared him first 540
was already honour although he alone had brought
and guardian of young Iulus, who had cut the cord, and
Nor did good Eurytion grudge
heights of heaven. Next in order
with his flying arrow. Father Aeneas

'Go now, and if Ascanius has with him his troop of boys
all ready and the horses drawn up and prepared to move,
tell him to lead on his squadrons in honour of his grand- 550
father and show himself in arms.' The people had all
flooded into the circus, so Aeneas ordered them to clear
the whole long track and leave the level ground free. Then
came the boys, riding in perfect order on their bridled
mounts, resplendent in full view of their parents, and all
the men of Sicily and of Troy murmured in admiration as
they rode. They wore their hair close bound in trimmed
garlands in ceremonial style and each carried a pair of
cornel-wood spears tipped with steel. Some of them had
polished quivers hanging from their shoulders with circlets
of twisted gold round neck and chest. They spread out into 560
three separate squadrons of horse, each with its own leader
at the head of a dozen boys in two separate files of six, each
squadron with its own trainer, all of them gleaming in
the sunlight. The first of these three squadrons of young
warriors was led in triumph by a little Priam, the noble son
of Polites who bore the name of his grandfather and was
destined to give increase to the Italian race. His horse was a
piebald Thracian with white above its hooves and a white
forehead carried high. The second squadron was led by
Atys, the founder of the Atii of Latium. Young Atys was a
dear friend of the boy Iulus, and Iulus was last and comeliest 570
of them all, riding on a Sidonian horse given to him by the
lovely Dido as a memorial and pledge of her love. The

other youngsters rode Sicilian ... round the
Acestes. They were daunted ... to their loved ones,
the Trojans feasted their...
features the features ... Epytides, standing at a distance,
After they h... with a loud call and a crack of his whip and
whole gath...
when ...rriors wheeled apart into two separate sections, each
of the three troops dividing its ranks equally. At a second
command the two new formations turned and advanced
on each other with spears at the level. All over the arena
they charged and turned and charged again, winding in
circles now in one direction now in the other, fighting out
in full armour the very image of a battle, now exposing
their backs in flight, now turning to point their spears at
590 the enemy and now when peace is made riding along
side by side. They say there was a labyrinth once in the hills
of Crete where the way weaved between blind walls and
lost itself in a thousand treacherous paths; there was no
following of tracks in this maze, no finding of a way and
no retracing of steps — such was the pattern woven by
the paths of the sons of the Trojans as they wound their
movements of mock battle and retreat, like dolphins
swimming in the waters of the sea, cleaving the waves off
Carpathos or Libya. The tradition of these manoeuvres
and battles was first renewed by Ascanius, who taught
the native Latins to celebrate it as he was building his
600 walls round Alba Longa. The Albans taught their sons to
do as Ascanius himself and the Trojans had done with
him when they were boys. In due course great Rome
itself received this tradition from Alba and preserved it. The
boys are now called 'Troy' and their troop is called 'the
Trojan Troop'. Here ended the games held in honour of
the divine father of Aeneas.

At this moment Fortune first changed and turned against

them. While they were paying to the tomb the solemn tribute of all these games, Saturnian Juno sent Iris down from the sky to the Trojan fleet and breathed favouring winds upon her as she went. Juno had many schemes in her mind and her ancient bitterness remained unsatisfied. Unseen by human eye the virgin goddess ran her swift course down her bow of a thousand colours till she came within sight of the great assembly. She then passed along the shore and saw the empty harbour and unattended ships. But there, far apart on the deserted beach, were the women of Troy, weeping for the loss of Anchises and weeping, all of them, as they looked out over the unfathomable sea. How weary they were, how numberless the breakers and how vast the sea that still remained for them to cross! These were the words on all their lips. What they were praying for was a city – they were heart sick of toiling with the sea. Iris knew how to cause mischief. She rushed into the middle of them, laying aside her divine form and dress and appearing as Beroe, the aged wife of Doryclus of Tmaros, a woman of good birth, who had borne sons and been held in high regard. In this guise she mingled with the mothers of Troy and spoke these words: 'Our sadness is that Greek hands did not drag us off to our deaths in war under the walls of our native city. O my unhappy people, for what manner of destruction is Fortune preserving you? This is the seventh summer since the fall of Troy that we have been driven by the winds and have measured every sea and land, every inhospitable rock and every angry star, rolling for ever on the waves as we search the mighty ocean for an Italy that ever recedes. Here we are in the land of our brother Eryx and Acestes is our host. Who is to prevent us from laying down the foundations of walls and giving a city to our people? I call upon our native land and household gods snatched from the hands of our enemies to no purpose, tell us, will there never again be walls that will be called the walls of Troy? Shall I never see a place with

the rivers that Hector knew, the Xanthus and the Simois? It is too much to endure. Come with me now and set fire to these accursed ships and destroy them. I have seen in a dream the image of the priestess Cassandra putting blazing torches in my hands and saying: "This is your home. This is where you must find your Troy." Now is the time to act. Portents like these brook no delay. Look at these four
640 altars of Neptune. The god himself is giving us the fire and the courage.' While still speaking she took the lead and snatched up the deadly fire, brandished it in her right hand and threw it with all her force. The minds of the women of Troy were roused and their hearts were bewildered, but one of the many, the oldest of them all, Pyrgo, who had been royal nurse to all the sons of Priam, called out: 'This is not Beroe speaking to you, women of Troy. This is not the wife of Doryclus from Rhoeteum. Look at the marks of divine beauty, the blazing eyes. Look at her proud
650 bearing, her features, the sound of her voice, her walk. I have just left Beroe sick and fretting because she was the only one who could not come to this ceremony and would not be paying due honour to Anchises.'

These were the words of Pyrgo and at first the women were at a loss looking at the ships with loathing in their eyes, torn between their pitiable desire to stay where they were on land, and the kingdom to which destiny was calling them, when the goddess soared through the heavens on poised wings, cutting in her flight a great rainbow beneath the clouds. This portent overwhelmed them.
660 Driven at last to madness they began to scream and snatch flames from the innermost hearths of the encampment or rob the altar fires, hurling blazing branches and brushwood and torches. The God of Fire raged with unbridled fury over oars and benches and the fir wood of the painted sterns.

It was Eumelus who brought the news to the Trojans while they were still in the wedge-shaped blocks of seats in

the theatre near the tomb of Anchises, and they could see
for themselves the dark ash flying in clouds of smoke.
Ascanius was happily leading the cavalry manoeuvres, so
he made off to the troubled camp at full gallop although
the breathless trainers tried in vain to hold him back.
'What strange madness is this?' he cried. 'Where, oh where   670
is this leading you, you unhappy women of Troy? This is
not the camp of your Greek enemies. What you are
burning is your own hopes for the future! Look at me! I
am your own Ascanius!' He had been wearing a helmet as
he stirred the images of war in the mock battle and now he
took it off and threw it on the ground at his feet. At this
moment Aeneas came rushing up and columns of Trojans
with him, but the women took to flight and scattered all
over the shore making for the woods and caves in the
rocks, wherever they could hide. They were ashamed of
what they had done and ashamed to look upon the light of
day. Their wits were restored now and they recognized
their own people. Juno was cast out of their hearts.

But that did not cause the fire and flame to abate their   680
unquenchable fury. The pitch was still smouldering beneath
the wet timbers, oozing slow smoke, and a consuming heat
was creeping along the hulls. The canker was sinking deep
into the bodies of the ships and all the exertions of men
and the pouring on of water were achieving nothing. This
was when the devout Aeneas tore the cloak off his shoulders
and called upon the gods for help, stretching out his hands
and praying: 'All-powerful Jupiter, if you do not yet abhor
the whole race of Trojans, if your loving-kindness still
looks as of old on the labours of men, grant now, O
Father, that our fleet escape the flames. Save from destruc-   690
tion what little remains to the Trojans, or else with your
own angry thunder cast the remnants of us down to death
and, if that is what I deserve, overwhelm us here with your
own right hand.' Scarcely had he spoken, when a black
deluge of torrential rain came lashing down, mountain

peak and plain trembled at the thunder and from the whole sky streamed the wild tempest of rain, dark with the cloud-bearing winds of the south. It poured down and filled the ships and soaked the charred timbers till all the fire was quenched and, except for four that were lost, all the ships were saved from destruction.

700 But this was a bitter blow for Aeneas, and his heart was heavy as he turned his thoughts this way and that, wondering whether he should forget about his destiny and settle in the fields of Sicily, or whether he ought to make for the shores of Italy. Then spoke old Nautes. He was the one man Tritonian Pallas had chosen to instruct and make pre-eminent in his art, providing him with responses to explain what the great anger of the gods portended and what the settled order of the Fates demanded. These were the words of comfort he now began to address to Aeneas: 'Son of the goddess, let us follow the Fates, whether they lead us on or

710 lead us back. Whatever fortune may be ours, we must at all times rise above it by enduring it. Acestes is by your side and he is a Trojan, offspring of the gods. Take him into your counsels. Be one with him. He is willing. Hand over into his care the people from the ships that are lost and those who are heart-weary of your great enterprise and destiny. Choose the old men, the women who are worn out by the sea, all of your company who are frail and have no stomach for danger, and weary as they are, here in this land let them have their city. Acestes will give them his name and they will call it Acesta.'

Aeneas was fired by these words from his old friend, but

720 his heart was divided between all his cares as never before. Dark night had risen in her chariot to command the vault of heaven, when suddenly there appeared the form of his father Anchises gliding down from the sky and these were the words that came pouring from him: 'O my son, dearer to me than life itself in the days when life remained to me, O my son, who has been tested by the Fates of Troy, I

come here in fulfilment of the command of Jupiter. He it was who drove the fire from your ships and has at last looked down from the sky and pitied you. Follow now this most wise advice which old Nautes is giving you and choose warriors from your people, the bravest hearts among them, to take to Italy. There in Latium is a wild 730 and hardy people whom you have to overcome in war. But first you must come to the home of Dis in the underworld and go through the depths of hell to seek a meeting with me. I am not confined in the grim shades of impious Tartarus but live in Elysium in the radiant councils of the just. A chaste Sibyl will lead you to this place, shedding the blood of many black cattle in sacrifice. Then you will learn about all the descendants who will come after you and the city walls you are to be given. But now farewell. The dewy night is turning her chariot in mid-course. The cruel sun is beginning to rise in the east and I have felt the breath of his panting horses.' As he finished 740 speaking he fled into thin air like smoke dissolving. 'Where are you going in such haste? Who are you escaping from? Who is there to keep you from my arms?' So cried Aeneas, and he stirred the smouldering ashes of the fire to worship the Lar of Pergamum and the shrine of white-haired Vesta with a ritual offering of coarse meal and incense from a full censer.

Immediately then he called his allies, Acestes first of all, and explained the command of Jupiter, the instructions of his own dear father and the resolve now firm in his own mind. There was no time lost in words and no dissent from Acestes. They transferred the mothers to the city and 750 put ashore those who wished it, those spirits that felt no need for glory, while they themselves repaired the rowing benches, replaced the charred timbers and fitted out the ships with oars and ropes. They were a small band but their hearts were high for war. Meanwhile, Aeneas was ploughing the city bounds and allotting homes to his

people. This was to be Ilium, and this was to be Troy.
Trojan Acestes was delighting in his kingdom, choosing a
site for his forum, summoning a senate and laying down
760 a code of laws. Then they founded a temple to Venus of
Ida, soaring to the stars on the peak of Mount Eryx, and
appointed a priest to tend the tomb of Anchises, consecrating to his name a great grove all around it.

And now the whole people had feasted for nine days
and performed their rites at the altars. A gentle breeze had
calmed the waves and the breath of a steady south wind
was calling them again to sea. Loud was the weeping along
the curved shore of the bay as they lingered for a night and
a day in their last embraces. Even the women, even the
men who had been shuddering at the sight of the sea and
unable to face its god, were now eager to sail and endure
770 to the end the whole agony of exile, but good Aeneas
comforted them with words of love and wept as he
entrusted them to their kinsman Acestes. At last came the
command to sacrifice three calves to Eryx and a lamb to
the Storms and to cast off their moorings in due order.
There stood Aeneas alone on the prow, his head bound
with a wreath of trimmed olive leaves and holding a
goblet in his hands as he scattered the sacrificial entrails and
poured the streaming wine into the salt sea. His men vied
with one another to strike the waves, sweeping them with
their oars as a freshening wind from astern helped them on
their way.

But Venus, never resting all this time from her cares,
780 went to Neptune and poured out to him these words of
complaint from her heart: 'It is the deadly anger of Juno,
her implacable fury, that forces me to use every prayer I
can. No man's piety can soften her, nor does the long
passage of time. Her will is not broken by the Fates nor by
the command of Jupiter and she knows no rest. In black
hatred she has eaten the city of the Phrygians out of the
heart of their race and dragged the Trojans who survive

through every form of suffering, but she is still not satisfied.
She is still persecuting the dead bones and ashes of the city
she has destroyed. She alone can understand her reasons for
this terrible rage. You yourself, I know, were a witness of
the turmoil she has just created in the waves of the Libyan   790
ocean, stirring up sea and sky to no avail with the help of
Aeolus' winds. To think she took all this upon herself in
your kingdom! And now this! Look how she has driven
the mothers of the Trojans to wrong-doing. It is her
cruelty that has burned out their ships, lost them their fleet
and forced them to abandon their own dear ones in a
strange land. As for what is to come, if what I am asking is
readily conceded, if the Fates are giving them a city in that
land, I beg of you to allow them a safe crossing and let
them reach the Laurentine Thybris.'

Then Neptune, son of Saturn and master of the ocean
depths, answered in these words: 'O Venus of Cythera, it is   800
wholly right that you should put your trust in the sea,
which is my kingdom, for you are born from it. I also
have deserved your trust, for I have often checked the wild
fury of the sea and sky and my care for your Aeneas has
been no less on land – I call the rivers Xanthus and Simois
to testify to this. During Achilles' pursuit of the broken
army of Troy, when he was driving them against their
own walls and killing them in their thousands, when the
rivers were choked and groaning with corpses and Xanthus
could find no way to roll down to the sea, there was
Aeneas standing against the might of Achilles, his strength
not equal to it and the gods opposed, and it was I who   810
caught him up in a hollow cloud, although my own desire
was to take these walls that I had built with my own hands
for the treacherous Trojans and turn them over from top
to bottom. As my mind was then, so is it even now. Put
away your fears. He will arrive safely where you wish, at
the harbour of Avernus. One only will be lost. One only
will you look for in vain upon the sea, and that one life

will be given for many.' When these words had soothed and gladdened the heart of the goddess, Father Neptune put a golden yoke on the necks of his horses and bits between their wild and foaming jaws and gave them full rein. As his blue-green chariot skimmed the surface of the sea, the waves were stilled, the swell subsided beneath his thundering axle and the rain clouds fled from the vast vault of heaven. Then all his retinue appeared, the huge sea beasts, Glaucus and his band of ageing dancers, Palaemon, son of Ino, the swift Tritons and all the ranks of Phorcys' army, while there on the left was Thetis with Melite and the maiden Panopaea, Nisaee and Spio, Thalia and Cymodoce.

Now all indecision was past and it was the turn of glad joy to capture the heart of Aeneas. Instantly he ordered all masts to be put up and canvas stretched from the yardarms. As one man they all set their sails, letting them out in time, first to port and then to starboard. As one man they swung round the high ends of the yard-arms and swung them round again as fair winds carried the fleet on its way. They were sailing close, in line ahead with Palinurus in the lead, and their orders were to make all speed and take their course from him.

The dank night was near the mid-point of the sky. The sailors were taking their rest in peace and quiet, stretched out under their oars along the hard benches, when the God of Sleep, parting the dark and misty air, came gliding lightly down from the stars of heaven. He was coming to you, Palinurus, bringing deadly dreams you did not deserve. The god took the shape of Phorbas and sat on the high poop pouring these soft words into the ears of Palinurus: 'Son of Iasius, the sea is carrying the ships along itself. The breeze is gentle and steady. This is an hour for sleep. Put down your head and steal a little time from your labours to rest your tired eyes. I'll take over a short watch for you myself.'

Scarcely lifting his eyes, Palinurus replied: 'Are you asking me to forget what I know about the calm face of the sea and quiet waters? There is a strange power in the sea and I would never rely on it. Winds are liars and believe me, I would never trust them with Aeneas, I who 850 have so often been betrayed by a clear sky.' This was his answer, and he stood by the tiller, gripping it with no intention of letting it go or taking his eyes off the stars. But look! The god takes a branch dripping with the water of Lethe for forgetfulness and the water of Styx for sleep. He shakes it over Palinurus, first one temple, then the other, and for all his struggles it closes his swimming eyes. As soon as this sudden sleep came upon him and his limbs began to relax, the god leaned over him, broke off a part of the poop, tiller and all, and threw him with it into the waves of the sea. Down fell Palinurus, calling again and 860 again on his comrades, but they did not hear. The god then rose on his wings and flew off into the airy breezes, while the ships sped on their way none the worse, sailing safely on in accordance with the promises of Father Neptune.

They were soon coming near the Sirens' rocks, once a difficult coast and white with the bones of drowned men, and at that moment sounding far with the endless grinding of breaker upon rock, when Father Aeneas sensed that he was adrift without a helmsman. In mid-ocean in the dead of night he took control of the ship himself, and grieving to the heart at the loss of his friend, he cried out: 'You trusted too much, Palinurus, to a clear sky and a calm sea, 870 and your body will lie naked on an unknown shore.'

6

THE UNDERWORLD

So spoke Aeneas, weeping, and gave the ships their head and at long last they glided to land at the Euboean colony of Cumae. The prows were turned out to sea, the teeth of the anchors held and they moored with their curved sterns fringing the shore. Gleaming in the sun, an eager band of warriors rushed out on to the shore of the land of Hesperia, some searching for the seeds of flame hidden in the veins of flint, some raiding the dense woods, the haunts of wild beasts, and pointing the way to rivers they had found. But the devout Aeneas made for the citadel where Apollo sits throned on high and for the vast cave standing there apart, the retreat of the awesome Sibyl, into whom Delian Apollo, the God of Prophecy, breathes mind and spirit as he reveals to her the future. They were soon coming up into the grove of Diana Trivia and Apollo's golden shrine.

They say that when Daedalus was fleeing from the kingdom of Minos, he dared to trust his life to the sky, floating off on swiftly driving wings towards the cold stars of the north, the Greater and Lesser Bears, by a route no man had ever gone before, until at last he was hovering lightly in the air above the citadel of Chalcidian Cumae. Here he first returned to earth, dedicating to Phoebus Apollo the wings that had oared him through the sky, and founding a huge temple. On its doors were depicted the death of Androgeos, son of Minos, and then the Athenians, the descendants of Cecrops, ordered to pay a cruel penalty and yield up each year the living bodies of seven of their sons. The lots are drawn and there stands the urn. Answering this on the other door are Cnossus and the land of Crete rising from the sea. Here can be seen the loving of the savage bull and Pasiphae laid out to receive it and deceive her husband Minos. Here too is the hybrid offspring, the Minotaur, half-man and half-animal, the memorial to a perverted love, and here is its home, built with such great labour, the inextricable Labyrinth. But Daedalus takes pity on the great love of the princess Ariadne and unravels the winding paths of his own baffling maze, guiding the blind steps of Theseus with a thread. You too, Icarus, would have taken no small place in this great work had the grief of Daedalus allowed it. Twice your father tried to shape your fall in gold and twice his hands fell helpless. The Trojans would have gone on gazing and read the whole story through, but Achates, who had been sent ahead, now returned bringing with him Deiphobe, the daughter of Glaucus, priestess of Phoebus and Trivia, who spoke these words to the king: 'This is no time for you to be looking at sights like these. Rather at this moment you should be sacrificing seven bullocks from a herd the yoke has never touched and seven yearling sheep as ritual prescribes.' So she addressed Aeneas. Nor were the Trojans slow to obey, and when the sacrifices were performed she called them into the lofty temple.

This rocky citadel had been colonized by Chalcidians from Euboea, and one side of it had been hollowed out to form a vast cavern into which led a hundred broad shafts, a hundred mouths, from which streamed as many voices giving the responses of the Sibyl. They had reached the threshold of the cavern when the virgin priestess cried: 'Now is the time to ask your destinies. It is the god. The god is here.' At that moment, as she spoke in front of the doors, her face was transfigured, her colour changed, her hair fell in disorder about her head and she stood there

with heaving breast and her wild heart bursting in
50 ecstasy. She seemed to grow in stature and speak as no
mortal had ever spoken when the god came to her in his
power and breathed upon her. 'Why are you hesitating,
Trojan Aeneas?' she cried. 'Why are you so slow to offer
your vows and prayers? Until you have prayed the great
mouths of my house are dumb and will not open.' She
spake and said no more. A cold shiver ran through the
very bones of the Trojans and their king poured out the
prayers from the depths of his heart: 'Phoebus Apollo, you
have always pitied the cruel sufferings of the Trojans. You
guided the hands of Trojan Paris and the arrow he sent
into the body of Achilles. You were my leader as I set out
60 upon all the oceans that lap the great lands of the earth and
reached the far-flung peoples of Massylia and the fields that
lie out to sea in front of the Syrtes. Now at long last we
lay hold upon the shores of Italy that have so often receded
before us. I pray that from this moment the fortunes of
Troy may follow us no further. You too, you gods and goddesses who could not endure Troy and the great glory of
the race of Dardanus, it is now right that you should have
mercy upon the people of Pergamum. And you, O most
holy priestess, you who know in advance what is to be, grant
my prayer, for the kingdom I ask for is no more than
what is owed me by the Fates, and allow the Trojans and
70 their homeless and harried gods to settle in Latium. Then I
shall found a temple of solid marble to Phoebus and Trivia,
and holy days in the name of Phoebus. And for you too
there will be a great shrine in our kingdom. Here I shall establish your oracle and the riddling prophecies you have given
my people and I shall dedicate chosen priests to your gracious service, only do not consign your prophecies to leaves
to be confused and mocked by every wind that blows. Sing
them in your own voice, I beg of you.' He said no more.

But the priestess was still in wild frenzy in her cave and
still resisting Apollo. The more she tried to shake her body

free of the great god the harder he strained upon her foaming mouth, taming that wild heart and moulding her by his pressure. And now the hundred huge doors of her house opened of their own accord and gave her answer to the winds: 'At long last you have done with the perils of the ocean, but worse things remain for you to bear on land. The sons of Dardanus shall come into their kingdom in Lavinium (put that fear out of your mind), but it is a coming they will wish they had never known. I see wars, deadly wars, I see the Thybris foaming with torrents of blood. There you will find a Simois and a Xanthus. There, too, will be a Greek camp. A second Achilles is already born in Latium, and he too is the son of a goddess. Juno too is part of Trojan destiny and will never be far away when you are a suppliant begging in dire need among all the peoples and all the cities of Italy. Once again the cause of all this Trojan suffering will be a foreign bride, another marriage with a stranger. You must not give way to these adversities but must face them all the more boldly wherever your fortune allows it. Your road to safety, strange as it may seem, will start from a Greek city.'

With these words from her shrine the Sibyl of Cumae sang her fearful riddling prophecies, her voice booming in the cave as she wrapped the truth in darkness, while Apollo shook the reins upon her in her frenzy and dug the spurs into her flanks. The madness passed. The wild words died upon her lips, and the hero Aeneas began to speak: 'O virgin priestess, suffering cannot come to me in any new or unforeseen form. I have already known it. Deep in my heart I have lived it all before. One prayer I have. Since they say the gate of the king of the underworld is here and here too is the black swamp which the tide of Acheron floods, I pray to be allowed to go and look upon the face of my dear father. Show me the way and open the sacred doors for me. On these shoulders I carried him away through the flames and a hail of weapons and rescued him from the middle of his enemies. He went on my journey with me over all the oceans and endured all the threats of sea and sky, feeble as he was but finding a strength beyond his years. Besides, it was my father himself who begged and commanded me to come to you as a suppliant and approach your doors. Pity the father, O gracious one, and pity the son, I beg of you. All things are within your power and Hecate had her purpose in giving you charge of the grove of Avernus. Was not Orpheus

120 allowed to summon the shade of his wife with the sound of the strings of his Thracian lyre? And when Pollux was allowed to redeem his brother by sharing his death, did he not often travel that road and often return? Do I need to speak of Theseus? Or of great Hercules? I too am descended from highest Jupiter.'

While he was still speaking these words of prayer with his hand upon the altar, the prophetess began her answer: 'Trojan, son of Anchises, sprung from the blood of the gods, it is easy to go down to the underworld. The door of black Dis stands open night and day. But to retrace your steps and escape to the upper air, that is the task, that is the labour. Some few have succeeded, sons of the gods, loved

130 and favoured by Jupiter or raised to the heavens by the flame of their own virtue. The middle of that world is filled with woods and the river Cocytus glides round them, holding them in its dark embrace. But if your desire is so great, if you have so much longing to sail twice upon the pools of Styx and twice to see black Tartarus, if it is your pleasure to indulge this labour of madness, listen to what must first be done. Hidden in a dark tree, there is a golden bough. Golden are its leaves and its pliant stem and it is sacred to Proserpina, the Juno of the underworld. A whole grove conceals it and the shades of a dark, encircling

140 valley close it in. But no man may enter the hidden places of the earth before plucking the golden foliage and fruit from this tree. The beautiful Proserpina has ordained that

this is the offering that must be brought to her. When one
golden branch has been torn from that tree, another comes
to take its place and the stem puts forth leaves of the same
metal. So then, lift up your eyes and look for it, and when
in due time you find it, take it in your hand and pluck it. If
you are a man called by the Fates, it will come easily of its
own accord. But if not, no strength will prevail against it
and hard steel will not be able to hack it off. Besides, you
have a friend lying dead. Of this you know nothing, but   150
his body is polluting the whole fleet while you linger here
at our door asking for oracles. First you must carry him to
his place of rest and lay him in a tomb. Then you must
bring black cattle to begin the purification. When all this is
done, you will be able to see the groves of Styx and the
kingdom where no living man may set his foot.' So she
spoke and no other word would cross her lips.

    With downcast eyes and sorrowing face Aeneas walked
from the cave, revolving in his mind the fulfilment of
these dark prophecies. With him stride for stride went the
faithful Achates, and his heart was no less heavy. Long did   160
they talk and many different thoughts they shared. Who
was this dead comrade of whom the priestess spoke? Whose
body was this that had to be buried? And when they came
to the shore, there above the tide line they found the body
of Misenus, who had died a death he had not deserved.
Misenus, son of Aeolus, who had no equal at summoning
the troops with his trumpet and kindling the God of War
with his music, had been the comrade of great Hector, and
by Hector's side had borne the brunt of battle, excelling
not only with the trumpet but also with the spear. But
after Achilles had defeated Hector and taken his life, the
brave Misenus had found no less a hero to follow by   170
joining Aeneas of the stock of Dardanus. Then one day in
his folly he happened to be blowing into a sea shell,
sending the sound ringing over the waves, and challenged
the gods to play as well as he. At this his rival Triton, if the

tale is to be believed, had caught him up and drowned him in the surf among the rocks. So then they raised around his body a loud noise of lamentation, not least the dutiful Aeneas. Without delay they hastened, still weeping, to obey the commands of the Sibyl, gathering trees to build an altar which would be his tomb and striving to raise it to the skies. Into the ancient forest they went among the deep 180 lairs of wild beasts. Down came the pines. The ilex rang under the axe. Beams of ash and oak were split along the grain with wedges, and they rolled great manna ashes down from the mountains.

Aeneas took the lead in all this work, urging on his comrades and carrying at his side the same tools as they, but he was always gloomily turning one thought over in his mind as he looked at the measureless forest and he chanced to utter it in this prayer: 'If only that golden bough would now show itself to us in this great grove, since everything the priestess said about Misenus has proved 190 only too true.' No sooner had he spoken than two doves chanced to come flying out of the sky and settle there on the grass in front of him. Then the great Aeneas knew they were his mother's birds and he was glad. 'Be my guides,' he prayed, 'if there is a way, and direct your swift flight through the air into the grove where the rich branch shades the fertile soil. And you, goddess, my mother, do not fail me in my time of uncertainty.' So he spoke and waited to see what signs they would give and in what direction they would move. They flew and fed and flew 200 again, always keeping in sight of those who followed. Then, when they came to the evil-smelling throat of Avernus, first they soared and then they swooped down through the clear air and settled where Aeneas had prayed they would settle, on the top of the tree that was two trees, from whose green there gleamed the breath of gold along the branch. Just as the mistletoe, not sown by the tree on which it grows, puts out fresh foliage in the woods in the

cold of winter and twines its yellow fruit round slender
tree trunks, so shone the golden foliage on the dark ilex, so
rustled the golden foil in the gentle breeze. Aeneas seized   210
the branch instantly. It resisted, but he broke it off impatiently and carried it into the house of the priestess, the
Sibyl.

All this time the Trojans on the shore did not cease to
weep for Misenus and pay their last tributes to his ungrateful ashes. First they built a huge pyre with rich pine torches
and oak logs, and wove dark-leaved branches into its sides,
setting up funeral cypresses in front of it and crowning it
with his shining armour. Some prepared hot water in
cauldrons and when it was seething over the flames, they
washed and anointed the cold body and raised their lament.
When they had wept their fill, they placed him on the bier   220
and draped him in his familiar purple robes. Others then
performed their sad duty of carrying the bier and held
their torches to the bottom of the pyre with averted faces,
after the practice of their ancestors. Then all the heaped-up
offerings burned – the incense, the sacrificial food, the
bowls filled with oil. After the embers had collapsed and
the flames died down, they washed with wine the thirsty
ashes that were all that remained of him and Corynaeus
collected his bones and sealed them in a bronze casket.
Three times he carried them in solemn ritual round the comrades of Misenus and sprinkled the heroes lightly with pure   230
water from the branch of a fruitful olive tree, uttering
words of farewell as he performed the lustration. But dutiful Aeneas raised a great mound as a tomb and set on it the
hero's arms, the oars he rowed with and the trumpet he
had blown, there near the airy top of Mount Misenus which
bears his name now and for ever through all years to come.

As soon as this was done he hastened to carry out the
commands of the Sibyl. There was a huge, deep cave with
jagged pebbles underfoot and a gaping mouth guarded by
dark woods and the black waters of a lake. No bird could

240 wing its flight over this cave and live, so deadly was the
breath that streamed out of that black throat and up into
the vault of heaven. Hence the Greek name, 'Aornos', 'the
place without birds'. Here first of all the priestess stood
four black-backed bullocks and poured wine upon their
foreheads. She then plucked the bristles from the peak of
their foreheads between their horns to lay upon the altar
fires as a first offering and lifted up her voice to call on
Hecate, mighty in the sky and mighty in Erebus. Attendants
put the knife to the throat and caught the warm blood in
250 bowls. Aeneas himself took his sword and sacrificed a
black-fleeced lamb to Night, the mother of the Furies and
her sister Earth, and to Proserpina a barren cow. Then he
set up a night altar for the worship of the Stygian king and
laid whole carcasses of bulls on its flames and poured rich
oil on the burning entrails. Then suddenly, just before the
sun had crossed his threshold in the sky and begun to rise,
the earth bellowed underfoot, the wooded ridges quaked
and dogs could be heard howling in the darkness. It was
the arrival of the goddess. 'Stand apart, all you who are
unsanctified,' cried the priestess. 'Stand well apart. The
260 whole grove must be free of your presence. You, Aeneas,
must enter upon your journey. Draw your sword from the
sheath. Now you need your courage. Now let your heart
be strong.' With these words she moved in a trance into
the open cave and step for step Aeneas strode fearlessly
along behind her.

You gods who rule the world of the spirits, you silent
shades, and Chaos, and Phlegethon, you dark and silent
wastes, let it be right for me to tell what I have been told,
let it be with your divine blessing that I reveal what is
hidden deep in the mists beneath the earth.

They walked in the darkness of that lonely night with
shadows all about them, through the empty halls of Dis
270 and his desolate kingdom, as men walk in a wood by the
sinister light of a fitful moon when Jupiter has buried the

sky in shade and black night has robbed all things of their colour. Before the entrance hall of Orcus, in the very throat of hell, Grief and Revenge have made their beds and Old Age lives there in despair, with white faced Diseases and Fear and Hunger, corrupter of men, and squalid Poverty, things dreadful to look upon, and Death and Drudgery besides. Then there are Sleep, Death's sister, perverted Pleasures, murderous War astride the threshold, the iron chambers of the Furies and raving Discord with 280 blood-soaked ribbons binding her viperous hair. In the middle a huge dark elm spreads out its ancient arms, the resting-place, so they say, of flocks of idle dreams, one clinging under every leaf. Here too are all manner of monstrous beasts, Centaurs stabling inside the gate, Scyllas – half dogs, half women – Briareus with his hundred heads, the Hydra of Lerna hissing fiercely, the Chimaera armed in fire, Gorgons and Harpies and the triple phantom of Geryon. Now Aeneas drew his sword in sudden alarm to 290 meet them with naked steel as they came at him, and if his wise companion had not warned him that this was the fluttering of disembodied spirits, a mere semblance of living substance, he would have rushed upon them and parted empty shadows with steel.

Here begins the road that leads to the rolling waters of Acheron, the river of Tartarus. Here is a vast quagmire of boiling whirlpools which belches sand and slime into Cocytus, and these are the rivers and waters guarded by the terrible Charon in his filthy rags. On his chin there 300 grows a thick grey beard, never trimmed. His glaring eyes are lit with fire and a foul cloak hangs from a knot at his shoulder. With his own hands he plies the pole and sees to the sails as he ferries the dead in a boat the colour of burnt iron. He is no longer young but, being a god, enjoys rude strength and a green old age. The whole throng of the dead was rushing to this part of the bank, mothers, men, great-hearted heroes whose lives were ended, boys, unmarried

girls and young men laid on the pyre before the faces of
their parents, as many as are the leaves that fall in the
forest at the first chill of autumn, as many as the birds that
flock to land from deep ocean when the cold season of the
year drives them over the sea to lands bathed in sun. There
they stood begging to be allowed to be the first to cross
and stretching out their arms in longing for the further
shore. But the grim boatman takes some here and some
there, and others he pushes away far back from the sandy
shore.

Aeneas, amazed and distressed by all this tumult, cried
out: 'Tell me, virgin priestess, what is the meaning of this
crowding to the river? What do the spirits want? Why are
some pushed away from the bank while others sweep the
livid water with their oars?' The aged Sibyl made this brief
reply: 'Son of Anchises, beyond all doubt the offspring of
the gods, what you are seeing is the deep pools of the
Cocytus and the swamp of the Styx, by whose divine
power the gods are afraid to swear and lie. The throng you
see on this side are the helpless souls of the unburied. The
ferryman there is Charon. Those sailing the waters of the
Styx have all been buried. No man may be ferried from
fearful bank to fearful bank of this roaring current until his
bones are laid to rest. Instead they wander for a hundred
years, fluttering round these shores until they are at last
allowed to return to the pools they have so longed for.'
The son of Anchises checked his stride and stood stock still
with many thoughts coursing through his mind as he
pitied their cruel fate, when there among the sufferers,
lacking all honour in death, he caught sight of Leucaspis,
and Orontes, the captain of the Lycian fleet, men who had
started with him from Troy, sailed the wind-torn seas and
been overwhelmed by gales from the south that rolled
them in the ocean, ships and crews.

Next he saw coming towards him his helmsman Palinurus who had fallen from the ship's stern and plunged into

the sea while watching the stars on the recent crossing
from Libya. Aeneas recognized this sorrowing figure with   340
difficulty in the dark shadow and was the first to speak:
'What god was it, Palinurus, that took you from us and
drowned you in mid-ocean? Come tell me, for this is the
one response of Apollo that has misled me. I have never
found him false before. He prophesied that you would be
safe upon the sea and would reach the boundaries of
Ausonia. Is this how he has kept his promise?' 'O great
leader, son of Anchises,' replied Palinurus, 'the bowl on the
tripod of Apollo has not deceived you and no god drowned
me in the sea. While I was holding course and gripping the
tiller which it was my charge to guard, it was broken off   350
by some mighty force and I dragged it down with me as I
fell. I swear by the wild sea that I felt no fear for myself to
equal my fear that your ship might come to grief, stripped
of its steering and with its pilot pitched into the sea and
that great swell rising. Three long winter nights the wind
blew hard from the south and carried me over seas I could
not measure, till, when light came on the fourth day, and a
wave lifted me to its crest, I could just make out the land
of Italy. I swam slowly to shore and was on the point of
reaching safety when a tribe of ruffians set upon me with
their knives, weighed down as I was by my wet clothes
and clinging by my finger tips to the jagged rocks at the   360
foot of a cliff. Knowing nothing of me they made me their
plunder, and now I am at the mercy of the winds, and the
waves are turning my body over at the water's edge. But I
beg of you, by the joyous light and winds of heaven, by
your father, by your hopes of Iulus as he grows to manhood, you who have never known defeat, rescue me from
this anguish. Either throw some earth on my body – you
can do that. Just steer back to the harbours of Velia. Or
else if there is a way and the goddess who gave you life
shows it to you – for I do not believe you are preparing to
sail these great rivers and the swamp of the Styx unless

370 the blessing of the gods is with you – take pity on me, give
me your right hand, take me aboard and carry me with
you over the waves, so that in death at least I can be at
peace in a place of quiet.' These were the words of Palinurus
and this was the reply of the Sibyl: 'How did you conceive
this monstrous desire, Palinurus? How can you, who are
unburied, hope to set eyes on the river Styx and the
pitiless waters of the Furies? How can you come near the
bank unbidden? You must cease to hope that the Fates of
the gods can be altered by prayers. But hear my words,
remember them and find comfort for your sad case. The
people who live far and wide in all their cities round the
place where you died, will be driven by signs from heaven
380 to consecrate your bones. They will raise a burial mound
for you and to that mound will pay their annual tribute
and the place will bear the name of Palinurus for all time
to come.' At these words his sorrows were removed and
the grief was driven from that sad heart for a short time.
He rejoiced in the land that was to bear his name.

And so they carried on to the end of the road on which
they had started, and at last came near the river. When the
boatman, now in mid-stream, looked ashore from the
waves of the Styx and saw them coming through the silent
wood towards the bank, he called out to them and challenged them: 'You there, whoever you are, making for our
river with a sword by your side, come tell us why you are
here. Speak to us from where you stand. Take not another
390 step. This place belongs to the shades, to Sleep and to
Night, the bringer of Sleep. Living bodies may not be
carried on the boat that plies the Styx. It gave me little
enough pleasure to take even Hercules aboard when he
came, or Theseus, or Pirithous, although they said they
were born of gods and their strength was irresistible. It was
Hercules whose hand put chains on the watchdog of Tartarus and dragged him shivering from the very throne of
our king. The others had taken it upon themselves to steal

the queen, my mistress, from the chamber of Dis.' The
answer of the Amphrysian Sibyl was brief: 'Here there are
no such designs. You have no need for alarm. These
weapons of his bring no violence. The monstrous keeper of   400
the gate can bark in his cave and frighten the bloodless
shades till the end of time and Proserpina can stay chaste
behind her uncle's doors. Trojan Aeneas, famous for his
devotion and his feats of arms, is going down to his father
in the darkest depths of Erebus. If the sight of such devotion
does not move you, then look at this branch,' she said,
showing the branch that had been hidden in her robes,
'and realize what it is.' At this the swelling anger subsided
in his heart. No more words were needed. Seeing it again
after a long age, and marvelling at the fateful branch, the
holy offering, he turned his dark boat and steered towards   410
the bank. He then drove off the souls who were on board
with him sitting all along the cross benches, and cleared the
gangways. In the same moment he took the huge Aeneas
into the hull of his little boat. Being only sewn together, it
groaned under his weight, shipping great volumes of stag-
nant water through the seams, but in the end it carried
priestess and hero safely over and landed them on the foul
slime among the grey-green reeds.

The kingdom on this side resounded with barking from
the three throats of the huge monster Cerberus lying in a
cave in front of them. When the priestess was close enough
to see the snakes writhing on his neck, she threw him a   420
honey cake steeped in soporific drugs. He opened his three
jaws, each of them rabid with hunger, and snapped it up
where it fell. The massive back relaxed and he sprawled
full length on the ground, filling his cave. The sentry now
sunk in sleep, Aeneas leapt to take command of the entrance
and was soon free of the bank of that river which no man
may recross.

In that instant they heard voices, a great weeping and
wailing of the souls of infants who had lost their share of

the sweetness of life on its very threshold, torn from the breast on some black day and drowned in the bitterness of
430 death. Next to them were those who had been condemned to death on false charges, but they did not receive their places without the casting of lots and the appointment of juries. Minos, the president of the court, shakes the lots in the urn, summoning the silent dead to act as jurymen, and holds inquiry into the lives of the accused and the charges against them. Next to them were those unhappy people who had raised their innocent hands against themselves, who had so loathed the light that they had thrown away their own lives. But now how they would wish to be under high heaven, enduring poverty and drudgery, however hard! That cannot be, for they are bound in the coils of the hateful swamp of the waters of death, trapped in the
440 ninefold windings of the river Styx. Not far from here could be seen what they call the Mourning Plains, stretching away in every direction. Here are the victims of unhappy love, consumed by that cruel wasting sickness, hidden in the lonely byways of an encircling wood of myrtle trees, and their suffering does not leave them even in death. Here Aeneas saw Phaedra, and Procris, and Eriphyle in tears as she displayed the wounds her cruel son had given her. Here he saw Evadne and Pasiphae with Laodamia walking by their side, and Caeneus, once a young man, but now a woman restored by destiny to her former shape.

450   Wandering among them in that great wood was Phoenician Dido with her wound still fresh. When the Trojan hero stopped beside her, recognizing her dim form in the darkness, like a man who sees or thinks he has seen the new moon rising through the clouds at the beginning of the month, in that instant he wept and spoke sweet words of love to her: 'So the news they brought me was true, unhappy Dido? They told me you were dead and had ended your life with the sword. Alas! Alas! Was I the cause

of your dying? I swear by the stars, by the gods above, by
whatever there is to swear by in the depths of the earth, it 460
was against my will, O queen, that I left your shore. It was
the stern authority of the commands of the gods that drove
me on, as it drives me now through the shades of this dark
night in this foul and mouldering place. I could not have
believed that my leaving would cause you such sorrow.
Do not move away. Do not leave my sight. Who are you
running from? Fate has decreed that I shall not speak to
you again.' With these words Aeneas, shedding tears, tried
to comfort that burning spirit, but grim-faced she kept
her eyes upon the ground and did not look at him. Her 470
features moved no more when he began to speak than if
she had been a block of flint or Parian marble quarried on
Mount Marpessus. Then at last she rushed away, hating
him, into the shadows of the wood where Sychaeus, who
had been her husband, answered her grief with grief and
her love with love. Aeneas was no less stricken by the
injustice of her fate and long did he gaze after her, pitying
her as she went.

From here they continued on their appointed road and
they were soon on the most distant of these fields, the place
set apart for brave warriors. Here Tydeus came to meet
him, and Parthenopaeus, famous for his feats of arms, and 480
the pale phantom of Adrastus. Here he saw and groaned to
see standing in their long ranks all the sons of Dardanus
who had fallen in battle and been bitterly lamented in the
upper world, Glaucus, Medon and Thersilochus, the
three sons of Antenor, and Polyboetes, the consecrated
priest of Ceres, and Idaeus still keeping hold of Priam's
chariot, still keeping hold of his armour. The shades
crowded round him on the right and on the left and it was
not enough just to see him, they wished to delay him, to
walk with him, to learn the reasons for his coming. But 490
when the Greek leaders and the soldiers of Agamemnon in
their phalanxes saw the hero and his armour gleaming

through the shadows, a wild panic seized them. Some turned and ran as they had run once before to get back to their ships, while others lifted up their voices and raised a tiny cry, which started as a shout from mouth wide open, but no shout came.

Here too he saw Deiphobus, son of Priam, his whole body mutilated and his face cruelly torn. The face and both hands were in shreds. The ears had been ripped from the head. He was noseless and hideous. Aeneas, barely recognizing him as he tried frantically to hide the fearsome punishment he had received, went up to him and spoke in 500 the voice he knew so well: 'Deiphobus, mighty warrior, descended from the noble blood of Teucer, who could have wished to inflict such a punishment upon you? And who was able to do this? I was told that on that last night you wore yourself out killing the enemy and fell on a huge pile of Greek and Trojan dead. At that time I did all I could do, raising an empty tomb for you on the shore of Cape Rhoeteum and lifting up my voice to call three times upon your shade. Your name and your arms mark the place but you I could not find, my friend, to bury your body in our native land as I was leaving it.'

To this the son of Priam answered: 'You, my friend, 510 have left nothing undone. You have paid all that is owed to Deiphobus and to his dead shade. It is my own destiny and the crimes of the murderess from Sparta that have brought me to this. These are reminders of Helen. You know how we spent that last night in false joy. It is our lot to remember it only too well. When the horse that was the instrument of Fate, heavy with the brood of armed men in its belly, leapt over the high walls of Pergamum, Helen was pretending to be worshipping Bacchus, leading the women of Phrygia around the city, dancing and shrieking their ritual cries. There she was in the middle of them with a huge torch, signalling to the Greeks from the top of the citadel, and all the time I was sleeping soundly in our

accursed bed, worn out by all I had suffered and sunk in a ₅₂₀
sleep that was sweet and deep and like the peace of death.
Meanwhile this excellent wife of mine, after moving all
my armour out of the house and taking the good sword
from under my head, called in Menelaus and threw open
the doors, hoping no doubt that her loving husband would
take this as a great favour to wipe out the memory of her
past sins. You can guess the rest. They burst into the room,
taking with them the man who had incited them to their
crimes, their comrade Ulixes – they say he is descended from
Aeolus. You gods, if the punishment I ask is just, grant that ₅₃₀
a fate like mine should strike again and strike Greeks. But
come, it is now time for you to tell me what chance has
brought you here alive. Is it your sea wanderings that have
taken you here? Are you under the instructions of the gods?
What fortune is dogging you, that you should come here
to our sad and sunless homes in this troubled place?'

While they were speaking to one another, Dawn's rosy
chariot had already run its heavenly course past the mid-
point of the vault of the sky, and they might have spent all
the allotted time in talking but for Aeneas' companion.
The Sibyl gave her warning in few words: 'Night is
running quickly by, Aeneas, and we waste the hours in
weeping. This is where the way divides. On the right it ₅₄₀
leads up to the walls of great Dis. This is the road we take
for Elysium. On the left is the road of punishment for evil-
doers, leading to Tartarus, the place of the damned.' 'There
is no need for anger, great priestess,' replied Deiphobus. 'I
shall go to take my place among the dead and return to
darkness. Go, Aeneas, go, great glory of our Troy, and
enjoy a better fate than mine.' These were his only words,
and as he spoke he turned on his heel and strode away.

Aeneas looked back suddenly and saw under a cliff on
his left a broad city encircled by a triple wall and washed
all round by Phlegethon, one of the rivers of Tartarus, ₅₅₀
a torrent of fire and flame, rolling and grinding great

boulders in its current. There before him stood a huge
gate with columns of solid adamant so strong that neither
the violence of men nor of the heavenly gods themselves
could ever uproot them in war, and an iron tower rose into
the air where Tisiphone sat with her blood-soaked dress
girt up, guarding the entrance and never sleeping, night or
day. They could hear the groans from the city, the cruel
crack of the lash, the dragging and clanking of iron chains.
560 Aeneas stood in terror, listening to the noise. 'What kinds
of criminal are here? Tell me, virgin priestess, what punishments are inflicted on them? What is this wild lamentation
in the air?' The Sibyl replied: 'Great leader of the Trojans,
the chaste may not set foot upon the threshold of that evil
place, but when Hecate put me in charge of the groves of
Avernus, she herself explained the punishments the gods
had imposed and showed me them all. Here Rhada-
manthus, king of Cnossus, holds sway with his unbending
laws, chastising men, hearing all the frauds they have prac-
tised and forcing them to confess the undiscovered crimes
they have gloated over in the upper world — foolishly,
for they have only delayed the day of atonement till
570 after death. Immediately the avenging Tisiphone leaps
upon the guilty and flogs them till they writhe, waving
fearful serpents over them in her left hand and calling up
the cohorts of her savage sisters, the Furies. Then at last the
gates sacred to the gods below shriek in their sockets and
open wide. You see what a watch she keeps, sitting in the
entrance? What a sight she is guarding the threshold?
Inside, more savage still, the huge, black-throated, fifty-
headed Hydra has its lair. And then there is Tartarus itself,
stretching sheer down into its dark chasm twice as far as
580 we look up to the ethereal Olympus in the sky. Here,
rolling in the bottom of the abyss, is the ancient brood of
Earth, the army of Titans, hurled down by the thunderbolt.
Here too I saw the huge bodies of the twin sons of Aloeus
who laid violent hands on the immeasurable sky to wrench

it from its place and tear down Jupiter from his heavenly
kingdom. I saw too Salmoneus suffering cruel punishment,
still miming the flames of Jupiter and the rumblings of
Olympus. He it was who, riding his four-horse chariot and
brandishing a torch, used to go in glory through the
peoples of Greece and the city of Olympia in the heart of
Elis, laying claim to divine honours for himself – fool that   590
he was to copy the storm and the inimitable thunderbolt
with the rattle of the horn of his horses' hooves on bronze.
Through the thick clouds the All-powerful Father hurled
his lightning – no smoky light from pitchy torches for him
– and sent him spinning deep into the abyss. Tityos too I
could see, the nurseling of Earth, mother of all, his body
sprawling over nine whole acres while a huge vulture with
hooked beak cropped his immortal liver and the flesh that
was such a rich supplier of punishment. Deep in his breast   600
it roosts and forages for its dinners, while the filaments of
his liver know no rest but are restored as soon as they are
consumed. I do not need to speak of the Lapiths, of Ixion
or Pirithous, over whose heads the boulder of black flint is
always slipping, always seeming to be falling. The gold
gleams on the high supports of festal couches and a feast is
laid in regal splendour before the eyes of the guilty, but the
greatest of the Furies is reclining at table and allows no
hand to touch the food, but leaps up brandishing a torch
and shouting with a voice of thunder. Immured in this
place and waiting for punishment are those who in life
hated their brothers, beat their fathers, defrauded their
dependants, found wealth and brooded over it alone   610
without setting aside a share for their kinsmen – these are
most numerous of all – men caught and killed in adultery,
men who took up arms against their own people and did
not shrink from abusing their masters' trust. Do not ask to
know what their punishments are, what form of pain or
what misfortune has engulfed them. Some are rolling huge
rocks, or hang spreadeagled on the spokes of wheels.

Theseus is sitting there dejected, and there he will sit until the end of time, while Phlegyas, most wretched of them all, shouts this lesson for all men at the top of his voice in 620 the darkness: "Learn to be just and not to slight the gods. You have been warned." Here is the man who has sold his native land for gold, and set a tyrant over it, putting up tablets with new laws for a price and for a price removing them. Here is the man who forced his way into his daughter's bed and a forbidden union. They have all dared to attempt some monstrous crime against the gods and have succeeded in their attempt. If I had a hundred tongues, a hundred mouths and a voice of iron, I could not encompass all their different crimes or speak the names of all their different punishments.'

When the aged priestess of Apollo had finished her answer, she added these words: 'But come now, you must 630 take the road and complete the task you have begun. Let us hasten. I can see the high walls forged in the furnaces of the Cyclopes and the gates there in front of us in the arch. This is where we have been told to lay the gift that is required of us.' After these words they walked the dark road together, soon covering the distance and coming close to the doors. There Aeneas leapt on the threshold, sprinkled his body with fresh water and fixed the bough full in the doorway.

When this rite was at last performed and his duty to the goddess was done, they entered the land of joy, the lovely glades of the fortunate woods and the home of the blest. 640 Here a broader sky clothes the plains in glowing light, and the spirits have their own sun and their own stars. Some take exercise on grassy wrestling-grounds and hold athletic contests and wrestling bouts on the golden sand. Others pound the earth with dancing feet and sing their songs while Orpheus, the priest of Thrace, accompanies their measures on his seven-stringed lyre, plucking the notes sometimes with his fingers, sometimes with his ivory plec-

trum. Here was the ancient line of Teucer, the fairest of all
families, great-hearted heroes born in a better time, Ilus, 650
Assaracus and Dardanus, the founder of Troy. Aeneas
admired from a distance their armour and empty chariots.
Their swords were planted in the ground and their horses
wandered free on the plain cropping the grass. Reposing
there below the earth, they took the same joy in their
chariots and their armour as when alive, and the same care
to feed their sleek horses. Then suddenly he saw others on
both sides of him feasting on the grass, singing in a joyful
choir their paean to Apollo all through a grove of fragrant
laurels where the mighty river Eridanus rolls through the
forest to the upper world. Here were armies of men 660
bearing wounds received while fighting for their native
land, priests who had been chaste unto death and true
prophets whose words were worthy of Apollo; then those
who have raised human life to new heights by the skills
they have discovered and those whom men remember for
what they have done for men. All these with sacred
ribbons of white round their foreheads gathered round
Aeneas and the Sibyl, and she addressed these words to
them, especially to Musaeus, for the whole great throng
looked up to him as he stood there in the middle, head and
shoulders above them all: 'Tell me, blessed spirits, and you,
best of poets, which part of this world holds Anchises? 670
Where is he to be found? It is because of Anchises that we
have come here and crossed the great rivers of Erebus.'
The hero returned a short answer: 'None of us has a fixed
home. We live in these densely wooded groves and rest on
the soft couches of the river bank and in the fresh water-
meadows. But if that is the desire of your hearts, come
climb this ridge and I shall soon set you on an easy path.'
So saying, he walked on in front of them to a place from
where they could see the plains below them bathed in
light, and from that point Aeneas and the Sibyl came
down from the mountain tops.

Father Anchises was deep in a green valley, walking
among the souls who were enclosed there and eagerly
surveying them as they waited to rise into the upper light.
It so happened that at that moment he was counting the
number of his people, reviewing his dear descendants, their
fates and their fortunes, their characters and their courage
in war. When he saw Aeneas coming towards him over
the grass, he stretched out both hands in eager welcome,
with the tears streaming down his cheeks, and these were
the words that broke from his mouth: 'You have come at
last,' he cried. 'I knew your devotion would prevail over
all the rigour of the journey and bring you to your father.
Am I to be allowed to look upon your face, my son, to
hear the voice I know so well and answer it with my own?
I never doubted it. I counted the hours, knowing you
would come, and my love has not deceived me. I understand how many lands you have travelled and how many
seas you have sailed to come to me here. I know the
dangers that have beset you. I so feared the kingdom of
Libya would do you harm.' 'It was my vision of you,'
replied Aeneas, 'always before my eyes and always stricken
with sorrow, that drove me to the threshold of this place.
The fleet is moored in the Tyrrhenian sea on the shores of
Italy. Give me your right hand, father. Give it me. Do not
avoid my embrace.' As he spoke these words his cheeks
were washed with tears and three times he tried to put his
arms around his father's neck. Three times the phantom
melted in his hands, as weightless as the wind, as light as
the flight of sleep.

And now Aeneas saw in a side valley a secluded grove
with copses of rustling trees where the river Lethe glided
along past peaceful dwelling houses. Around it fluttered
numberless races and tribes of men, like bees in a meadow
on a clear summer day, settling on all the many-coloured
flowers and crowding round the gleaming white lilies
while the whole plain is loud with their buzzing. Not

understanding what he saw, Aeneas shuddered at the ⁷¹⁰
sudden sight of them and asked why this was, what was
that river in the distance and who were all those companies
of men crowding its banks. 'These are the souls to whom
Fate owes a second body,' replied Anchises. 'They come to
the waves of the river Lethe and drink the waters of
serenity and draughts of long oblivion. I have long been
eager to tell you who they are, to show them to you face
to face and count the generations of my people to you so
that you could rejoice the more with me at the finding of
Italy.' 'But are we to believe,' replied Aeneas to his dear
father, 'that there are some souls who rise from here to go ⁷²⁰
back under the sky and return to sluggish bodies? Why do
the poor wretches have this terrible longing for the light?'
'I shall tell you, my son, and leave you no longer in
doubt,' replied Anchises, and he began to explain all things
in due order.

'In the beginning Spirit fed all things from within, the
sky and the earth, the level waters, the shining globe of the
moon and the Titan's star, the sun. It was Mind that set all
this matter in motion. Infused through all the limbs, it
mingled with that great body, and from the union there
sprang the families of men and of animals, the living things
of the air and the strange creatures born beneath the
marble surface of the sea. The living force within them is ⁷³⁰
of fire and its seeds have their source in heaven, but their
guilt-ridden bodies make them slow and they are dulled by
earthly limbs and dying flesh. It is this that gives them
their fears and desires, their griefs and joys. Closed in the
blind darkness of this prison they do not see out to the
winds of air. Even when life leaves them on their last day
of light, they are not wholly freed from all the many ills
and miseries of the body which must harden in them over
the long years and become ingrained in ways we cannot
understand. And so they are put to punishment, to pay the ⁷⁴⁰
penalty for all their ancient sins. Some are stretched and

hung out empty to dry in the winds. Some have the stain of evil washed out of them under a vast tide of water or scorched out by fire. Each of us suffers his own fate in the after-life. From here we are sent over the broad plains of Elysium and some few of us possess these fields of joy until the circle of time is completed and the length of days has removed ingrained corruption and left us pure ethereal sense, the fire of elemental air. All these others whom you see, when they have rolled the wheel for a thousand years, are called out by God to come in great columns to the 750 river of Lethe, so that they may duly go back and see the vault of heaven again remembering nothing, and begin to be willing to return to bodies.'

When he had finished speaking, Anchises led his son and the Sibyl with him into the middle of this noisy crowd of souls, and took up his stance on a mound from which he could pick them all out as they came towards him in a long line and recognize their faces as they came.

'Come now, and I shall tell you of the glory that lies in store for the sons of Dardanus, for the men of Italian stock who will be our descendants, bright spirits that will inherit 760 our name, and I shall reveal to you your own destiny. That young warrior you see there leaning on the sword of valour, to him is allotted the place nearest to the light in this grove, and he will be the first of us to rise into the ethereal air with an admixture of Italic blood. He will be called Silvius, an Alban name, and he will be your son, born after your death. You will live long, but he will be born too late for you to know, and your wife Lavinia will rear him in the woods to be a king and father of kings and found our dynasty to rule in Alba Longa. Next to him is Procas, glory of the Trojan race, and Capys, and Numitor, 770 and the king who will renew your name, Silvius Aeneas, your equal in piety and in arms if ever he succeeds to his rightful throne in Alba. What warriors they are! Look at the strength of them! Look at the oak wreaths, the Civic

Crowns, that shade their foreheads! These are the men who
will build Nomentum for you, and Gabii, and the city of
Fidenae. They will set Collatia's citadel on the mountains,
and Pometia too, and Castrum Inui, and Bola and Cora.
These, my son, will be the names of places which are at
this moment places without names. And Romulus, son of
Mars, will march at his grandfather's side. He will be of
the stock of Assaracus, and his mother, who will rear him,
will be Ilia. Do you see how the double crest stands on his
head and the Father of the Gods himself already honours 780
him with his own emblem? Look at him, my son. Under
his auspices will be founded Rome in all her glory, whose
empire shall cover the earth and whose spirit shall rise to
the heights of Olympus. Her single city will enclose seven
citadels within its walls and she will be blest in the abundance of her sons, like Cybele, the Mother Goddess of
Mount Berecyntus riding in her chariot turret-crowned
through the cities of Phrygia, rejoicing in her divine offspring and embracing a hundred descendants, all of them
gods, all dwellers in the heights of heaven.

'Now turn your two eyes in this direction and look at
this family of yours, your own Romans. Here is Caesar,
and all the sons of Iulus about to come under the great 790
vault of the sky. Here is the man whose coming you so
often hear prophesied, here he is, Augustus Caesar, son of a
god, the man who will bring back the golden years to the
fields of Latium once ruled over by Saturn, and extend
Rome's empire beyond the Indians and the Garamantes to
a land beyond the stars, beyond the yearly path of the sun,
where Atlas holds on his shoulder the sky all studded with
burning stars and turns it on its axis. The kingdoms round
the Caspian sea and Lake Maeotis are even now quaking at
the prophecies of his coming. The seven mouths of the 800
Nile are in turmoil and alarm. Hercules himself did not
make his way to so many lands though his arrow pierced
the hind with hooves of bronze, though he gave peace to

the woods of Erymanthus and made Lerna tremble at his bow. Nor did triumphing Bacchus ride so far when he drove his tiger-drawn chariot down from the high peak of Nysa, and the reins that guided the yoke were the tendrils of the vine. And do we still hesitate to extend our courage by our actions? Does any fear deter us from taking our stand on the shore of Ausonia?

'But who is this at a distance resplendent in his crown of olive and carrying holy emblems? I know that white hair and beard. This is the man who will first found our city on laws, the Roman king called from the little town of Cures in the poor land of the Sabines into a mighty empire. Hard on his heels will come Tullus to shatter the leisure of his native land and rouse to battle men that have settled into idleness and armies that have lost the habit of triumph. Next to him, and more boastful, comes Ancus, too fond even now of the breath of popular favour. Do you wish to see now the Tarquin kings, the proud spirit of avenging Brutus and the rods of office he will retrieve? He will be the first to be given authority as consul and the stern axes of that office. When his sons raise again the standards of war, it is their own father that will call them to account in the glorious name of liberty. He is not favoured by fortune, however future ages may judge these actions – love of his country will prevail with him and his limitless desire for glory. Look too at the Decii and the Drusi over there and cruel Torquatus with his axe and Camillus carrying back the standards. Those two spirits you see gleaming there in their well-matched armour are in harmony now while they are buried in night, but if once they reach the light of life, what a terrible war they will stir up between them! What battles! What carnage when the father-in-law swoops from the ramparts of the Alps and his citadel of Monaco and his son-in-law leads against him the embattled armies of the East! O my sons, do not harden your hearts to such wars. Do not turn your strong hands against the flesh of your motherland. You who are sprung from Olympus, you must be the first to show clemency. Throw down your weapons. O blood of my blood! Here is the man who will triumph over Corinth, slaughtering the men of Achaea, and will ride his chariot in triumph to the hill of the Capitol. Here is the man who will raze Argos and Agamemnon's Mycenae to the ground, and will kill Perseus the Aeacid, descendant of the mighty warrior Achilles, avenging his Trojan ancestors and the violation of the 840 shrine of Minerva. Who would leave you unmentioned, great Cato? Or you, Cossus? Who would be without the Gracchi? Or the two Scipios, both of them thunderbolts of war, the bane of Libya? Or Fabricius, who will find power in poverty? Or you, Serranus, sowing your seed in the furrow? Where are you rushing that weary spirit along to, you Fabii? You there are the great Fabius Maximus, the one man who restores the state by delaying. Others, I do not doubt it, will beat bronze into figures that breathe more softly. Others will draw living likenesses out of marble. Others will plead cases better or describe with their rod the 850 courses of the stars across the sky and predict their risings. Your task, Roman, and do not forget it, will be to govern the peoples of the world in your empire. These will be your arts – and to impose a settled pattern upon peace, to pardon the defeated and war down the proud.'

Aeneas and the Sibyl wondered at what they heard, and Father Anchises continued: 'Look there at Marcellus marching in glory in spoils torn from the enemy commander he will fight and defeat. There he is, victorious and towering above all others. This is the man who will ride into battle and quell a great uprising, steadying the ranks of Rome and laying low the Carthaginian and the rebellious Gaul. He will be the third to dedicate the supreme spoils to Father Quirinus.'

At this Aeneas addressed his father, for he saw marching 860 with Marcellus a young man, noble in appearance and in gleaming armour, but his brow was dark and his eyes downcast. 'Who is that, father, marching at the side of Marcellus? Is it one of his sons or one of the great line of his descendants? What a stir his escort makes! And himself, what a presence! But round his head there hovers a shadow dark as night.'

Then his father Anchises began to speak through his tears: 'O my son, do not ask. This is the greatest grief that you and yours will ever suffer. Fate will just show him to

870 the earth – no more. The gods in heaven have judged that the Roman race would become too powerful if this gift were theirs to keep. What a noise of the mourning of men will come from the Field of Mars to Mars' great city. What a cortège will Tiber see as he glides past the new Mausoleum on his shore! No son of Troy will ever so raise the hopes of his Latin ancestors, nor will the land of Romulus so pride itself on any of its young. Alas for his goodness! Alas for his old-fashioned truthfulness and that

880 right hand undefeated in war! No enemies could ever have come against him in war and lived, whether he was armed to fight on foot or spurring the flanks of his foaming war-horse. Oh the pity of it! If only you could break the harsh laws of Fate! You will be Marcellus. Give lilies from full hands. Leave me to scatter red roses. These at least I can heap up for the spirit of my descendant and perform the rite although it will achieve nothing.'

So did they wander all over the broad fields of air and saw all there was to see, and after Anchises had shown each and every sight to his son and kindled in his mind a love

890 for the glory that was to come, he told them then of the wars he would in due course have to fight and of the Laurentine peoples, of the city of Latinus and how he could avoid or endure all the trials that lay before him.

There are two gates of sleep: one is called the Gate of Horn and it is an easy exit for true shades; the other is made all in gleaming white ivory, but through it the powers of the underworld send false dreams up towards the heavens. There on that night did Anchises walk with his son and with the Sibyl and spoke such words to them as he sent them on their journey through the Gate of Ivory.

Aeneas made his way back to his ships and his comrades, then steered a straight course to the harbour of Caieta. The 900 anchors were thrown from the prows and the ships stood along the shore.

For lines 756–892, see Appendix One

7

WAR IN LATIUM

You too, Caieta, nurse of Aeneas, have given by your death eternal fame to our shores; the honour paid you there even now protects your resting-place, and your name marks the place where your bones lie in great Hesperia, if that glory is of any value.

Good Aeneas duly performed the funeral rites and heaped up a barrow for the tomb, and when there was calm on the high seas, he set sail and left the port behind him. A fair breeze kept blowing as night came on, the white moon lit their course and the sea shone in its shimmering rays. Keeping close inshore, they skirted the land where Circe, the daughter of the Sun, lives among her riches. There she sets the untrodden groves ringing with never-ending singing and burns the fragrant cedar wood in her proud palace to lighten the darkness of the night as her sounding shuttle runs across the delicate warp. From her palace could be heard growls of anger from lions fretting at their chains and roaring late into the night, the raging of bristling boars and penned bears and howling from huge creatures in the shape of wolves. These had all been men, but with her irresistible herbs the savage goddess had given them the faces and hides of wild beasts. To protect the devout Trojans from suffering these monstrous changes, Neptune kept them from sailing into the harbour or coming near that deadly shore. He filled their sails with favouring winds and took them past the boiling breakers to safety.

And now the waves were beginning to be tinged with
red from the rays of the sun and Aurora on her rosy
chariot glowed in gold from the heights of heaven, when
of a sudden the wind fell, every breath was still and the
oars toiled in a sluggish sea. Here it was that Aeneas, still
well off shore, sighted a great forest and the river Tiber in   30
all its beauty bursting through it into the sea with its racing
waves and their burden of yellow sand. Around it and
above it all manner of birds that haunted the banks and
bed of the river were flying through the trees and sweeten-
ing the air with their singing. Aeneas gave the order to
change course and turn the prows to the land, and he came
into the dark river rejoicing.

Come now, Erato, and I shall tell of the kings of ancient   40
Latium, of its history, of the state of this land when first
the army of strangers beached their ships on the shores of
Ausonia. I shall recall too, the cause of the first battle —
come, goddess, come and instruct your prophet. I shall
speak of fearsome fighting, I shall speak of wars and of
kings driven into the ways of death by their pride of spirit,
of a band of fighting men from Etruria and the whole land
of Hesperia under arms. For me this is the birth of a higher
order of things. This is a greater work I now set in motion.

King Latinus was by this time an old man and he had
reigned over the countryside and the cities for many peaceful years. We are told that he was the son of Faunus and
the Laurentine nymph Marica. The father of Faunus was
Picus, and the father claimed by Picus was Saturn. Saturn
then was the first founder of the line. By divine Fate   50
Latinus had no male offspring. His son had been snatched
from him as he was rising into the first bloom of his youth.
An only daughter tended his home and preserved the
succession for this great palace. She was now grown to
womanhood and at the age for marriage and many were
seeking her hand from great Latium and the whole of
Ausonia, Turnus the handsomest of them all, his claim

supported by the long line of his forbears. The queen Amata longed above all things to see him married to her daughter, but many frightening portents from the gods forbade it.

Deep in the innermost courtyard of the palace there
60 stood a laurel tree. Its foliage was sacred and it had been preserved and held in awe for many years, ever since Father Latinus himself had found it, so the story went, when he was building his first citadel, and dedicated it to Phoebus Apollo, naming the settlers after it, the Laurentines. To this tree there came by some miracle a cloud of bees, buzzing loudly as they floated through the liquid air till suddenly they formed a swarm and settled on its very top, hanging there from a leafy branch with their feet intertwined. A prophet thus interpreted: 'What we see is a
70 stranger arriving, and an army coming from the same direction, making for the same place and gaining mastery over the heights of the citadel.' Then again when Lavinia was standing by her father's side tending the altar with her chaste torches, another fearful sight was seen. Her long hair caught fire and all its adornment was crackling in the flames. The princess's hair was blazing, her crown with all its lovely jewels was blazing, and soon she was wrapped in smoke and a yellow glare, and scattering fire all over the palace. The horror and miracle of it were on everyone's lips, and it was
80 prophesied that her own fate and fame would be bright, but that a great war would come upon the people.

Troubled by such portents, the king consulted the oracle of his prophetic father Faunus, visiting the grove under Mount Albunea, a huge forest sounding with the waters of its sacred fountain and breathing thick clouds of sulphurous vapour. Here the Italian tribes and the whole land of Oenotria came to consult the oracle in their times of doubt. Here the priest brought his offerings, and when he lay down to sleep in the silence of the night on a bed of the fleeces of slaughtered sheep, he would see many strange

fleeting visions, hear all manner of voices, enjoy the con- 90
verse of the gods and speak to Acheron in the depths of
Avernus. Here too on that day Father Latinus himself came
to consult the oracle, and after sacrificing a hundred unshorn yearling sheep as ritual prescribes, he was lying
propped on a bed of their hides and fleeces, when suddenly
a voice was heard from the depths of the forest: 'Do not
seek to join your daughter in marriage to a Latin. O my
son, do not place your trust in any union that lies to hand.
Strangers will come to be your sons-in-law and by their
blood to raise our name to the stars. The descendants of
that stock will see the whole world turning under their feet 100
and guided by their will, from where the rising Sun looks
down on the streams of Ocean to where he sees them as he
sets.' This was the reply of his father Faunus, the warning
that came in the silence of the night. Latinus did not keep
it locked in his heart, and Rumour as she flew had already
spread it far and wide through the cities of Ausonia when
the young warriors from Laomedon's Troy tied up their
ships to the grassy ramparts of the river bank.

Aeneas, the leading captains of Troy and lovely Iulus
had lain down on the grass under the branches of a tall tree
and were starting to eat a meal, setting out their banquets 110
on wheaten cakes — for Jupiter himself had so advised them
— and heaping country fruits on these foundations, the gift
of Ceres, the Goddess of Grain. When the fruit had all been
eaten and the sparseness of the diet had driven them to sink
their teeth into Ceres' bounty, scant as it was, to violate
with bold hand and jaw the fateful circles of crust and
show no mercy to the flat quarter-circles of bread, suddenly
Iulus said, as a joke: 'Look! We are eating even our tables!'
That was all. This was the first announcement they had
received of the end of their sufferings. Astounded by the
presence of the divine, Aeneas seized upon his son's first
words while he was still speaking and made him be silent.
In that instant he lifted up his voice and cried out: 'Hail to 120

the land owed to me by the Fates, and hail to the household gods of Troy who have kept faith with me! This is our home. This is our own land. For now I remember it, my father Anchises left me this riddle of the Fates. "When you sail to an unknown shore and your food is so scanty that hunger forces you to eat your tables, that is the time, weary as you are, to hope for a home. This is where you must with your own hand lay down the foundations of your first buildings and raise a rampart round them." This is the hunger of which he spoke. This is the last hunger we had to endure and it will put an end to our calamities. Come then, with joy in your hearts, and at the first light of the sun let us all go in different directions from the harbour to explore this place and find out who are the men that live here and where their cities are. And now pour libations from your goblets to Jupiter, call upon my father Anchises with your prayers and set the wine in due order on the tables.'

At these words he wound a branch of living green round his forehead and offered up prayers to the Genius of the place and to Earth the first of gods, to nymphs and rivers not yet known, then to Night and the stars of Night then rising, to Jupiter of Mount Ida and the Phrygian Mother in due order, to his mother in the heavens and his father in Erebus. In reply the All-powerful Father thundered clear three times from the heights of the sky and with his own hand he displayed in heaven a burning cloud, quivering with rays of golden light. In that instant the word spread through the Trojan ranks that the day had come for them to found their promised city. Eagerly they renewed their feast, and delighting in this great omen, they set up their mixing bowls and crowned the wine with garlands.

When the next day first rose and began to traverse the earth with its lamp, they set out in different directions to explore the city and the boundaries and shores of this people. Here were the pools where the river Numicus springs, here was the river Tiber and here were the homes of the stalwart Latins. Then Aeneas, son of Anchises, ordered one hundred men chosen as spokesmen from every rank of his people to go to the sacred walls of king Latinus all bearing branches of Pallas Athene's olive wreathed in wool, carrying gifts and asking for peace for the Trojans. They made no delay, but hastened with all speed to do as they were bidden, while Aeneas himself was marking out the line of his walls with a shallow ditch and beginning to build on the site, surrounding this first settlement on the shore with a stockade and rampart as though it were a camp. The warriors, meanwhile, their long journey ended, were 160 within sight of the towers and high roofs of the city of the Latins and came up to the wall. There in front of the city boys and young men in the first flower of their age were exercising with their horses, training chariot teams in clouds of dust, bending the springy bow, spinning the stiff-shafted javelin, racing and sparring, when a messenger riding ahead of the Trojans brought to the ear of the old king the news that huge men in strange costume had arrived. Latinus ordered them to be summoned into his palace while he took his seat in the middle on his ancestral throne.

A sacred building, massive and soaring to the sky with a 170 hundred columns, stood on the highest point of the city. This was the palace of Laurentine Picus, a building held in great awe because of an ancestral sense of the presence of the divine in the grove that surrounded it. Here the omens declared that kings should receive their sceptres and take up the rods of office for the first time. This temple was their senate-house, this the hall in which they held their sacred banquets and here the elders would sacrifice a ram and sit down to feast at long tables. Here too, carved in old cedar wood, stood in order in the forecourt the statues of their ancestors from time long past: Italus and Father Sabinus planter of the vine, still holding in effigy his curved pruning knife, old Saturn, the image of Janus with 180

his two faces, all the other kings since the foundation of the
city and with them the men who had been wounded while
fighting to defend their native land. Many too were the
weapons hung on the posts of the temple doors, captured chariots, curved axes, crests of helmets, great bolts
from the gates of cities, spears, shields and beaks broken off
the prows of ships. Here too, with his short toga, and the
augural staff of Quirinus in his left hand, sat the Horse-
Tamer, Picus himself, whose wife Circe, possessed by lust,
190 struck him with her rod of gold and changed him with her
potions into a bird, sprinkling colours on his wings.

Such was the temple of the gods where Latinus sat in the
seat of his fathers and called the Trojans to him in his
palace. When they entered he was the first to speak,
addressing them in these kindly words: 'Tell me, sons of
Dardanus – you see we know your city and your family
and had heard about you before you set your course here
– what are you searching for? What has taken your ships
over all the blue waters of ocean to the shore of Ausonia?
What need has brought you here? Whether you have lost
200 your way or been driven off course by the storms that
sailors have to endure so often on the high seas, you have
now sailed between the banks of our river and are sitting
in harbour. Do not refuse the guest-friendship we offer
you and do not forget that we Latins are Saturn's people,
righteous not because of laws and restraints but holding of
our own free will to the way of life of our ancient god.
Besides, I myself remember that the Auruncan elders used
to say – the story is dimmed by the mists of time – that
Dardanus was born in these fields and went far away to the
cities of Ida in Phrygia and the Thracian island of Samos
now known as Samothrace. He set out from here, from his
210 Tyrrhenian home in Corythus, and now sits on a throne in
the palace of gold in the starry sky, and his altars add a
name to the roll of the gods.'

He spoke these words, and these were the words in

which Ilioneus made answer: 'Great king, son of Faunus, it
is not black storms and heavy seas that have driven us to
this land of yours, nor have we lost our way by mistaking
a star or a coastline. It is by design and with willing hearts
that we all sail to this city, driven from our own kingdom
which was once the greatest the journeying Sun could see
from the highest part of the heavens. Our race begins with
Jupiter. The warriors of Dardanus' Troy rejoice in Jupiter   220
as their ancestor. Their king, Aeneas himself, is descended
from Jupiter's exalted stock, and Trojan Aeneas has sent us
to your door. The storm that gathered in merciless Mycenae and swept across the plains beneath Mount Ida, and
the fate that drove the worlds of Europe and of Asia to col-
lide, these are known to all men, those who live far to the
north where the ends of the earth beat back the stream of
Oceanus, and those who are separated from us by the zone
of the cruel sun whose expanse covers the middle zone of
five. Since that cataclysm we have sailed all those desolate
seas, and now we ask for a little piece of land for our   230
fathers' gods, for harmless refuge on the beach, for the air
and sea which are there for all men. We shall not bring
discredit on your kingdom. Great fame will be yours, and
our gratitude for such a service will never fade. The men
of Ausonia will never regret taking Troy to their hearts. I
swear by the destiny of Aeneas and his right arm, strong in
the truth to all who have tested it, and strong in war and
the weapons of war, that many nations have asked to enter
into alliance with us. Do not despise us because we choose
to come to you with words of supplication and olive
branches wreathed in wool in our hands. Many races have
wished to be joined to ours, but the commands of divine
destiny have driven us to seek out your country. This was   240
the first home of Dardanus. This is the land to which
Apollo calls us back, and urges us with his mighty decrees
towards the Tyrrhenian Thybris and the sacred shallows of
the fountain of Numicus. These gifts, besides, Aeneas offers

you, some small relics of his former fortunes rescued from the flames of Troy. From this gold cup his father Anchises used to pour libations at the altar. This was the sceptre Priam would hold in his hand as he gave solemn judgement before the concourse of the nations, and here are his sacred head-dress and the vestments woven for him by the women of Troy.'

250   When Ilioneus had finished speaking, Latinus kept his gaze fixed upon the ground and did not move. He never raised his burning eyes but they were never still. As a king he was moved to see the sceptre of Priam and his embroidered purple but much more was he moved by the thought of a marriage and a husband for his daughter, and long did he ponder in his heart the prophecy of old Faunus. So this was the fulfilment of the portents sent by the Fates! So this was the son-in-law who would come from a distant land and be called to share his kingdom with equal auspices. This was the man whose descendants would excel in valour and whose power would win the whole world. He spoke at last, and joyfully: 'May the gods
260   give their blessing to what we begin today and to their own prophecies! You will receive what you ask, Trojan, and I do not refuse your gifts. While Latinus is king, you will have rich land to farm and you will never feel the lack of the wealth of Troy. Only Aeneas must come here himself if he is so eager and impatient to join us in friendship and be called our ally. He has no need to recoil from the face of his friends. It will be a condition of the peace I offer that I must clasp the hand of your king. But now I charge you to take back this answer to him. Tell him I have a daughter, and the oracles from my father's
270   shrine agree with all the signs from heaven in forbidding me to join her in marriage to any man of our people. Strangers will come from a foreign land to be my sons-in-law — this is what is in store for Latium according to the prophecies — and by their blood they shall raise our name

to the stars. This Aeneas is the man the Fates demand. This I believe, and this is my will, if my mind has any true insight into the future.' After these words, Father Latinus made a choice from his whole stable where three hundred well-groomed horses stood in their high-built stalls, ordering one to be brought out instantly for each of the Trojans in due order. Their hooves were swift as wings, their saddle-cloths were of embroidered purple. Gold medallions hung at their breasts, their caparisons were of gold and they champed bright golden bits between their teeth. For Aeneas 280 in his absence, he chose a chariot and pair of heavenly descent breathing fire from their nostrils. They were sprung from a stock which cunning Circe had crossbred by stealing one of the stallions of her father the Sun to mate with a mare. With these gifts Aeneas' men returned riding high in the saddle and bringing messages of peace.

But at that very moment fierce Juno, wife of Jupiter, was coming back from Argos, city of Inachus, holding her course through the winds of the air, when from far away in the heavens, as far as Cape Pachynus in Sicily, she caught sight of the jubilant Aeneas and his Trojan fleet. When she saw that they were already at work on their 290 buildings, having abandoned their ships and committed themselves to the land, she stopped in mid-flight, pierced by bitter resentment. Then, shaking her head, she poured out these words from the depths of her heart: 'A curse on that detested race of Phrygians and on their destiny, so opposed to our own! Could they not have died on the Sigean plains? They were defeated. Why could they not accept defeat? Troy was set alight. Could they not have burned with it? But no! They found a way through the press of the battle and the thick of the flames. They must think my divine powers are exhausted and discredited, or that I have glutted my appetite for hatred and am now at peace. After all, when they were cast out of their native land, I dared to hound them over the waves and wherever 300 they ran across the face of the ocean I was there and set my face against them. I have used every resource of sea and sky against these Trojans, and what use have the Syrtes been to me? Or Scylla? Or the bottomless Charybdis? The Trojans are where they wanted to be in the valley of the Thybris, safe from the sea and safe from me. Mars had the strength to destroy the monstrous race of Lapiths. The Father of the Gods himself handed over the ancient kingdom of Calydon to the wrath of Diana, and what great crime had the Lapiths or Calydon committed? But here am I, great Juno, wife of Jupiter, thwarted, though I have tried everything 310 that could be tried. Nothing has been too bold for me. And I am being defeated by Aeneas! But if my own resources as a goddess are not enough, I am not the one to hesitate. I shall appeal to whatever powers there are. If I cannot prevail upon the gods above, I shall move hell. I cannot keep him from his kingdom in Latium: so be it. The decree of the Fates will stand and he will have Lavinia to wife. But I shall be able to delay it all and drag it out, I shall be able to cut the subjects of both those kings to pieces. This will be the cost of the meeting between father-in-law and son-in-law, and their peoples will bear it. Your dowry, Lavinia, will be the blood of Rutulians and Trojans, and your matron-of-honour will be the Goddess of War herself, 320 Bellona. Hecuba, daughter of Cisseus, was pregnant with a torch and gave birth to the marriage torches of Paris and Helen. But she is not alone. Venus, too, has a son, a second Paris, and torches will again be fatal, for this second Troy.'

With these words the fearsome goddess flew down to the earth and roused Allecto, bringer of grief, from the infernal darkness of her home among the Furies. Dear to her heart were the horrors of war, anger, treachery and vicious accusations. Her own father Pluto hated his monstrous daughter. Her own sisters in Tartarus loathed her. She had so many faces and such fearsome shapes, and her head crawled with so many black serpents. This was the

creature Juno now roused to action with these words: 'Do ₃₃₀
this service for me, O virgin daughter of Night. It is a task
after your own heart. See to it that my fame and the
honour in which I am held are not impaired or slighted,
and see to it that Aeneas and his men do not win Latinus
over with their offers of marriage and are not allowed to
settle on Italian soil. You can take brothers who love each
other and set them at each other's throats. You can turn a
house against itself in hatred and fill it with whips and
funeral torches. You have a thousand names and a thousand
ways of causing hurt. Your heart is teeming with them.
Shake them all out. Shatter this peace they have agreed
between them and sow the seeds of recrimination and war.
Make their young men long for weapons, demand them, ₃₄₀
seize them!'

In that moment Allecto, gorged with the poisons of the
Gorgons, went straight to Latium and the lofty palace of
the king of the Laurentines and settled on the quiet threshold of the chamber of Amata. There the queen was seething
with womanly anger and disappointment at the arrival of
the Trojans and the loss of the wedding with Turnus.
Taking one of the snakes from her dark hair the goddess
Allecto threw it on Amata's breast to enter deep into her
heart, a horror driving her to frenzy and bringing down
her whole house in ruin. It glided between her dress and ₃₅₀
her smooth breasts and she felt no touch of its coils.
Without her knowing it, it breathed its viper's breath into
her and made her mad. The serpent became a great necklace
of twisted gold round her neck. It became the trailing end
of a long ribbon twined round her hair. It slithered all over
her body. While the first infection of the liquid venom was
still oozing through all her senses and winding the fire
about her bones, before her mind in her breast had wholly
consumed the fever of it, she spoke with some gentleness,
as a mother might, and wept bitterly over the marriage of
her daughter to a Phrygian: 'Is Lavinia being given in

360 marriage to these Trojan exiles? You are her father. Have
you no feelings for your daughter or her mother or
yourself? When the first wind blows from the north, that
lying brigand will take to the high seas and carry off my
daughter, leaving me desolate. Is this not how the Phrygian
shepherd wormed his way into Sparta and carried Leda's
daughter Helen off to the cities of Troy? Where is your
sacred word of honour? Where is the care you used to
have for your kinsmen? And what of all the pledges you
have given Turnus, your own flesh and blood? But if you
are searching for a son-in-law among strangers and that is
decided, if the commands of your father Faunus weigh so
370 heavily upon you, then I maintain that all peoples who are
not subject to our sceptre are strangers. That is what the
gods are saying. Besides, if you were to trace the house of
Turnus back to its first beginnings, his forefathers were
Inachus and Acrisius of Argos and his home is in the heart
of Mycenae.'

When with these words she had tried in vain to move
Latinus and seen that he held firm, when the maddening
poison of the serpent had soaked deep into her flesh and
oozed all through her body, the unhappy Amata, driven
out of her mind by her monstrous affliction, raged in a
wild frenzy through the length and breadth of the city like
a spinning top flying under the plaited whip when boys
380 are engrossed in their play and make it go in great circles
round an empty hall; the whip drives it on its curved
course and the boys look down, puzzled and fascinated as
they lash the spinning boxwood into life – as swift as any
top Amata ran through the middle of the cities of the
fierce Latian people. Not content with this, she flew into
the forests, pretending that she was possessed by Bacchus,
and rose to greater impieties and greater madness by hiding
her daughter in the leafy woods, hoping to cheat the
Trojans out of the marriage or delay the lighting of the
390 torches. 'Euhoe, Bacchus!' she screamed. 'Only you are

worthy of the virgin. For you she takes up the soft-leaved
thyrsus. Round you she moves in ritual dance. She grows
her hair to consecrate it to you.' Rumour flew fast. The
same passion kindled in the hearts of all the mothers of
Latium and drove them out to search for new homes.
They left their houses, their throats bare and their hair
streaming in the winds. Others, clad in animal skins and
carrying vine shoots sharpened into spears, made the
heavens ring with whimpering and wailing. Amata herself,
in the fever of her madness, held high a burning torch in
the midst of them and sang a wedding hymn for Turnus
and her daughter, rolling her bloodshot eyes. Suddenly she
gave a dreadful cry: 'Io, Io, all you mothers of Latins   400
wherever you may be, if in your faithful hearts there
remains any regard for unhappy Amata, if your minds are
troubled by the thought of what is due to a mother, untie
the ribbons of your hair and take to the secret rites with
me.' This, then, was the queen whom Allecto drove with
the lash of Bacchus through the forests and the desolate
haunts of wild beasts.

After she saw that this first madness was well under
way, and that she had subverted Latinus' plans and all his
house, the deadly goddess rose on her dark wings and flew
straight to the walls of the bold prince of the Rutulians.
Danae is said to have been driven on to this coast by
southern gales and to have founded this city for settlers
who were subjects of her father Acrisius, king of Argos.   410
Our ancestors long ago gave it the name of Ardea, and
Ardea still keeps its great name though its fortune lies in
the past. Here in his lofty palace in the darkness of midnight
Turnus was lying deep in sleep. Allecto changed her appearance. No longer wild and raving, she took on the face of
an old woman, with her brow furrowed by horrible
wrinkles and her white hair tied in a sacred ribbon and
bound in a chaplet of olive leaves. She became Calybe, the
aged priestess of Juno and her temple, and appeared before   420

the eyes of young Turnus saying: 'Are you going to stand
by and see all your labours go for nothing, Turnus, and
your crown made over to these incomers from Troy? The
king is refusing to give you the marriage and the dowry
you have earned in blood and is searching for a stranger to
inherit his kingdom. So now, Turnus, go and expose
yourself to danger! Your reward is to be laughed at. Go
and cut down these Etruscans in their battle-lines! Go and
cover the Latins with the shield of peace. These are the
very words which the daughter of Saturn, All-powerful
Juno, has commanded me to say and say clearly to you as
430 you lie in the peace of night. So up with you, and with a
light heart prepare to arm your young warriors and move
them from inside the city gates and out to the fields to
burn the Phrygian captains and their painted ships where
they have made themselves at home on our lovely river.
The mighty power of heaven demands it. If king Latinus
does not agree to obey this command and allow you this
marriage, he must learn, he must in the end face Turnus
with his armour on.'

    Turnus was laughing as he made his reply to the priestess:
'You are wrong. The report has not failed to reach my
ears. I know a fleet has sailed into the waters of the
Thybris. Do not invent these fears for me. Royal Juno has
440 not entirely forgotten us. It is old age and decay that cause
you all this futile agitation and distress and make you
barren of truth, taking a prophetess among warring kings
and making a fool of her with false fears. Your duty is to
guard the statues of the gods and their temples. Leave
peace and war to men. War is the business of men.'

    When she heard the warrior's words Allecto burst into
blazing anger, and while he was still replying, a sudden
trembling came over his limbs and the eyes stared in his
head as the Fury revealed herself in her full size and set all
450 her hydras hissing. As he faltered and tried to go on
speaking, she flung him back with her eyes flashing fire,

two snakes stood up on her head and she cracked her whips as she spoke again from her now maddened lips: 'So I am old and decayed and barren of truth and old age is taking me among warring kings and making a fool of me with false fears! Have a look at these! I come here from the home of the dread Furies, my sisters, and in my hands I carry war and death.'

With these words she threw a burning torch at the warrior and it lodged deep in his heart, smoking with black light. A great terror burst in upon his sleep, and the sweat broke out all over his body and soaked him to the bone. In a frenzy of rage he roared for his armour. 'My armour!' he shouted, ransacking his bed and the whole palace for it. The lust for battle raged within him, the criminal madness of war and, above all, anger. It was as though a heap of brushwood were crackling and burning under the sides of a bronze vessel, making the water seethe and leap up, a great river of it raging in the pot, with boiling foam spilling over and dense steam flying into the air. The peace was violated. Turnus gave orders to the leaders of his army to march to king Latinus, to prepare for war, to defend Italy and thrust the enemy out of its borders. When he arrived, that would be enough for the Trojans, and enough for the Latins. These were his words and he called upon the gods to witness them. The eager Rutulians urged each other to arms, some of them inspired by the rare grace of his youthful beauty, some by the long line of kings that were his ancestors, some by his brilliant feats of arms.

While Turnus was filling the hearts of the Rutulians with boldness, Allecto flew off with all speed to the Trojans on her wings of Stygian black. Here, spying out the ground where lovely Iulus was hunting along the shore, trapping and coursing, she hatched a new plot. Into his hounds the virgin goddess of Cocytus put a sudden fit of madness by touching their nostrils with the familiar scent of a stag and sending them after it in full cry. This was the first cause of all the suffering. It was this that kindled the zeal for war in the hearts of the country people. It was a huge and beautiful stag with a fine head of antlers, which had been torn from the udders of its mother and fed by Tyrrhus and his young sons – Tyrrhus looked after the royal herds and was entrusted with the wardenship of the whole broad plain. Silvia, the boys' sister, had given this wild creature every care and trained it to obey her. She would weave soft garlands for its horns, combing and washing it in clear running water. It became tame to the hand and used to come to its master's table. It would wander through the woods and come back home of its own accord to the door it knew so well, no matter how late the night. This is the creature that was roaming far from home, floating down a river, cooling itself in the green shade of the bank when it was startled by the maddened dogs of the young huntsman Iulus. He himself, Ascanius, burning with a passionate love of glory, bent his bow and aimed the arrow. The god was with him and kept his hand from erring. The arrow flew with a great hiss and passed straight through the flank into the belly. Fleeing to the home it knew so well, the wounded stag came into its pen moaning, and stood there bleeding and filling the house with its cries of anguish, as though begging and pleading. Silvia was the first to call for help. She beat her own arms in grief and summoned the country people, who came long before she expected them, for savage Allecto was lurking in the silent woods. Some came armed with stakes burned to a point in the fire; some with clubs made from knotted tree trunks; each man searched for what he could find and anger taught him how to make a weapon of it. Tyrrhus was calling up the troops. He had been driving in wedges to split an oak into four and he snatched up his axe, breathing furiously.

The cruel goddess saw from her vantage point that this

was a moment when harm might be done and, flying to the top of the farm roof, from the highest gable she sounded the herdsman's signal with a loud call on the curved horn, and its voice was the voice of Tartarus. The trees shivered at the noise and the whole forest rang to its very depths. Far away the lake of Trivia heard it. The white sulphur-laden streams of the river Nar heard it and its springs in Lake Velinus, and terrified mothers pressed their babies to their breasts. Swift to answer the call of that 520 dread horn, the hardy countrymen snatched up their weapons and gathered from every side. The Trojans, for their part, opened the gates of their camp and streamed out to help Ascanius. They drew up in line of battle, and this was no longer a village brawl with knotted clubs and stakes sharpened in the fire. They fought with two-edged steel, and a dark crop of drawn swords sprouted all over the field while bronze gleamed in answer to the challenge of the sun and threw its light up to the clouds, like the sea whitening at the first breath of wind and slowly stirring itself, raising its waves higher and higher till it reaches 530 from the depths of the sea-bed to the heights of heaven. Suddenly there was the hiss of an arrow and a young man standing out in front of the leading line of battle fell to the ground. It was Almo, the eldest son of Tyrrhus. The shaft had stuck deep in his throat, blocking the moist passage of the voice and closing off the narrow channel of his life in blood. The bodies of slain men soon lay around him, among them old Galaesus, who died when he stepped between the armies to make peace. He was the justest man in the broad fields of Ausonia in these far days, and the richest. Five flocks of sheep and five herds of cattle came back at evening to his stalls and he turned the soil with a hundred ploughs.

While the battle was evenly poised on the plain, the 540 mighty goddess, having fulfilled her promise when the first blood was spilt in war and the first clash of arms had led to

death, left Hesperia and returned through the breezes of
the sky to address Juno in these words of proud triumph:
'You asked and I have given. Discord is made perfect in
the horror of war. Now tell them to come together and form
alliances when I have sprinkled the Trojans with Italian
blood! And I shall do more than this, if such be still your
will for me. I shall spread rumours to draw the neighbour-
550 ing cities into the war. I shall set their hearts ablaze with a
mad lust for battle and they will come from all sides to
join in the fray. I shall sow a crop of weapons in all their
fields.' Juno gave her answer: 'There is enough terror and
lying. The causes of war are established. They are fighting
at close quarters and fresh blood is staining whatever
weapons chance first puts into their hands. Let this be the
wedding they will celebrate, the noble son of Venus and
great king Latinus. Let this be their wedding hymn. The
Father of the Gods, the ruler of high Olympus, would not
wish you to rove too freely over the breezes of heaven.
You must withdraw. Should there be any need for further
560 effort, I shall take the guidance into my own hands.' No
sooner had the daughter of Saturn spoken these words than
Allecto lifted up her wings, hissing with snakes, and flew
down to her home on the banks of the Cocytus, leaving
the steeps of the sky. At the foot of high mountains in the
middle of Italy, there is a well-known place, whose fame
has spread to many lands, the valley of Amsanctus. A dark
forest presses in upon it from both sides with its dense
foliage and in the middle a crashing torrent roars over the
rocks, whipping up crests of foam. Here they point to a
fearful cave which is a vent for the breath of Dis, the cruel
570 god of the underworld. Into this cave bursts Acheron and
here a vast whirlpool opens its pestilential jaws, and here
the loathsome Fury disappeared, lightening heaven and
earth by her absence.

But none the less the Queen of the Gods, the daughter
of Saturn, was at that moment putting the finishing touches

to the war. A whole crowd of herdsmen came rushing
from the battlefield into the city, carrying the bodies of
young Almo and Galaesus with his face mutilated. They
were all imploring the help of the gods and appealing to
Latinus. Turnus was there, and when the fire of their fury
and the accusations of murder were at their height, he
heaped fear upon fear by claiming that the Trojans were
being invited to take a share in the kingdom; their own
Latin blood would be adulterated by Phrygians while he
was being turned from the door. At this there gathered
from all sides, wearying Mars with their clamour for war,   580
those whose mothers had been crazed by Bacchus and were
now dancing in wild rout in the pathless forests – the name
of Amata had great weight with them. In an instant they
were all demanding this wicked war against all the omens,
against divine destiny and contrary to the will of the gods.
They rushed to besiege the palace of king Latinus, who
stood unmoved like a rock in the ocean, like a solid rock in
the ocean pounded by breakers, standing fast with the
waves howling round it, while reefs and foam-soaked scars
roar in helpless anger and the seaweed is forced against its   590
side, then streams back with the undertow. But there was
no resisting the counsels of blind folly. All things were
taking their course according to the nod of savage Juno.
Again and again the king, the father of his people, called
upon the gods and the empty winds to witness: 'We are
caught in the gale of Fate,' he cried. 'Our ship is breaking
under us. You, my poor people, will pay for this sacrilege
with your blood. You are the guilty one, Turnus, and a
grim punishment lies in store for you. You will supplicate
the gods but your prayers will be too late. I have already
reached calm water and here at the harbour mouth I lose
all the happiness I might have had in the hour of my
death.' He said no more, but shut himself away in his
palace and gave up the reins of power.   600
     In Hesperia, in the lands of Latium, there was a custom,

later inherited and revered in the cities of Alba, and now
observed by Rome, the greatest of the great, when men
first rouse Mars for battle, whether they are preparing to
bring the sorrows of war to the Getae, the Hyrcani or the
Arabs, or whether they are heading for India and the rising
of the sun and reclaiming the standards from the Parthians.
There are two gates known as the Gates of War, sanctified
by religion and the fear of savage Mars. These gates are
closed by a hundred bolts of bronze and the everlasting
610 strength of iron, nor does their sentry Janus ever leave the
threshold. When the Fathers are resolved on war, the
consul himself, conspicuous in the short toga of Quirinus
girt about him in the Gabine manner, unbars the doors.
They grind in their sockets and he summons war. The
whole army takes up the call and the bronze horns breathe
their shrill assent. So too in those days Latinus was bidden
to declare war upon the men of Aeneas by opening these
grim gates. The old king, father of his people, would not
lay his hand upon them, but recoiled from this wickedness
and refused to perform the task, shutting himself up in the
620 darkness away from the sight of men. At this, the Queen
of the Gods came down from the sky and struck the
stubborn doors, bursting the iron-bound Gates of War and
turning them in their sockets. Till that moment Ausonia
had been at peace and unalarmed, but now the foot-soldiers
mustered on the plain and high in the saddle came the
excited horsemen stirring up the dust. Every man was
looking for weapons, polishing shields with rich fat till
they were smooth, burnishing spears till they shone and
grinding axes on the whetstone. What joy to raise the
standards and hear the trumpets sound! Five great cities, no
630 less, set up anvils to forge new weapons, mighty Atina,
proud Tibur, Ardea, Crustumerium and Antemnae with
its towers. They hollowed out helmets to protect the heads
of warriors. They wove frames of willow shoots to form
shields. They made bronze breastplates and smooth shields

of ductile silver. This is what had become of all their regard for the sickle and the share. This is what had become of all their love for the plough – the swords of their fathers were now retempered in the furnace. Now the trumpets blew and out went the signal that called them to war. In high excitement they tore down their helmets from the roof, yoked their trembling horses to the chariot, buckled on their shields and their breastplates of triple- 640 woven gold and girt their trusty swords about them.

Now goddesses, it is time to open up Mount Helicon, to set your songs in motion and tell what kings were roused to war, what armies followed each of them to fill the plains, the heroes that flowered and the weapons that blazed in those far-off days in the bountiful land of Italy. You are the divine Muses. You remember, goddesses, and can utter what you remember. Our ears can barely catch the faintest whisper of the story.

The first to enter upon the war and arm his columns was cruel Mezentius from Etruria, scorner of the gods. At his side was his son Lausus, who for his beauty was second to 650 none but the Laurentine Turnus. Lausus was a tamer of horses and a hunter of wild beasts, and he was at the head of a thousand men who had followed him and followed him in vain from the city of Agylla. He deserved a father whom it would have been more of a joy to obey, a father other than Mezentius.

Behind them, driving over the grassland and displaying his victorious horses and his chariot which proudly bore the palm of victory, came Aventinus, son of Hercules, fair son of a fair father, and on his shield he carried his father's blazon, the Hydra and its snakes, the hundred snakes encircling it. His mother, the priestess Rhea, had given 660 birth to him in secret, bringing him into the land of light in the wood on the Aventine hill. She had lain with Hercules, a woman with a god, when he had come in triumph to the land of the Laurentines, the hero of Tiryns who had slain Geryon and washed the cattle of Spain in the river of the Etruscans. His men carried javelins and fearsome pikes into battle and used the Sabine throwing spear with its round tapering point. He himself was on foot, swinging a great lion skin about him as he walked. It was matted and bristling, and he had put it with its white teeth over his head and a fearsome sight he was as he came up to the palace with his father's garb tied round his shoulders.

670 Next came two bold Argive warriors, the twin brothers Catillus and fierce Coras, leaving the walls of Tibur, which took its name from their brother Tiburtus. They would charge out in front of the first line of battle through showers of missiles, like two cloud-born Centaurs plunging down in wild career from the snow-clad tops of Mount Homole or Mount Othrys, crashing through the trees as the great forest opens to let them pass.

The founder of the city of Praeneste was also there, a king who ruled among the herds and flocks of the countryside. Men have always believed that he was the son of Vulcan, 680 Caeculus, found as a baby on the burning hearth. His rustic legion came from far and wide to follow him: from Praeneste on its hill-top; from the fields round Juno's city of Gabii, from the icy waters of the Anio and the streaming river rocks of the Hernici; men nurtured by the rich city of Anagnia and by your river, Father Amasenus. Not all of these came into battle with shields and arms and chariots sounding: most of them showered acorns of blue lead from slings; some carried a pair of hunting spears in one hand and wore on their heads tawny caps made from 690 the hides of wolves, their left foot leaving a naked print while a rawhide boot protected the right.

Now Messapus, breaker of horses, son of Neptune, whom neither fire nor steel might lay low, suddenly took up his sword again and called to arms tribes that had long lived at ease and armies that had lost the habit of war. These were the men who came from the ridges of Fescennium, from Aequum Faliscum, from the citadel of Soracte and the Flavinian fields, from the lake of Ciminius and its mountain and the groves of Capena. They marched in regular formations singing the praises of their king like white swans flying back from their feeding grounds through wisps of cloud and pouring out the measured music from their long necks while far and wide the echo of their singing beats back from the river and the Asian marsh. This great mingled swarm of men seemed not like a bronze-clad army, but an aery cloud of clamorous birds on the wing, straining in from the high seas to the shore. 700

There comes Clausus of the blood of the ancient Sabines, leading a great army, and a great army in himself. From Clausus are descended the tribe and family of the Claudii, spread all over Latium ever since the Sabines were given a share in Rome. With him came a large contingent from Amiternum and the first Quirites, all the troops from Eretum and from olive-bearing Mutusca, all who lived in the city of Nomentum and the Rosean plains round Lake Velinus, on the bristling rocks of Tetrica and its gloomy mountain, in Casperia and Foruli and on the banks of the Himella, men who drank the Tiber and the Fabaris, men sent by chilly Nursia, levies from Orta, tribes from old Latium and the peoples whose lands are cut by the Allia, that river of ill-omened name. They were as many as the waves that roll in from the Libyan ocean when fierce Orion is sinking into the winter sea, or as thick as the ears of corn scorched by the early sun on the plain of Hermus or the golden fields of Lycia. Their shields clanged and the earth quaked under the beat of their feet. 710 720

Halaesus next, one of Agamemnon's men and an enemy of all things Trojan, yoked his horses to his chariot and rushed a thousand fierce tribes to join Turnus: men whose mattocks turn the rich Massic soil for Bacchus: Auruncans sent by their fathers from their high hills; men sent from the nearby plains of Sidicinum; men who come from Cales

and the banks of the Volturnus, river of many fords, and
730 with them the tough Saticulan and bands of Oscans. Their
weapon was the aclys, a light spear, and it was their
practice to attach a supple thong to it. A leather shield
protected their left side and for close fighting they used
swords shaped like sickles.

Nor will you, Oebalus, go unmentioned in our song.
Men say you were the son of Telon by the nymph of the
river Sebethus, born when Telon was already an old man
and ruling over Capreae, the island of the Teleboae. But
the son no more than the father had been content with the
lands he had inherited and by now he had long held sway
over the tribes of the Sarrastes, the plains washed by the
river Sarnus, men who lived in Rufrae, Batulum and
740 the fields of Celemna and those on whom the walls of
apple-bearing Abella look down. Their missile was the
cateia, a weapon thrown like the Teuton boomerang.
Their heads were protected by helmets of bark stripped
from the cork oak. They carried gleaming half-moon
shields of plated bronze and their swords too were of
gleaming bronze.

You too, Ufens, famous for your feats of arms, were sent
into battle from the mountains of Nersae. These Aequi live
in a hard land and are the most rugged of races, schooled
in hunting the forests. They work the soil with their
armour on. Their delight is always to bring home new
plunder and live off what they take.

750 Then came a priest from Marruvium, his helmet
decorated by a sprig of fruitful olive, the bravest of men,
Umbro by name, sent by king Archippus. By his spells and
the touch of his hand he knew well how to sow the seed of
sleep on nests of vipers and on water-snakes, for all their
deadly breath. His arts could charm their anger and soothe
their bites, but he had no antidote for the sting of a Trojan
sword and not all his lullabies and herbs gathered in the
Marsian hills could help him with his wounds. For you

wept the grove of the goddess Angitia. For you wept the
glassy waves and clear pools of Lake Fucinus.   760

There too, sent by his mother Aricia, glorious Virbius
came to the war, the lovely son of Hippolytus. He had
grown to manhood in the grove of Egeria around the dank
lake-shores by the altar where rich sacrifices win the favour
of Diana. For after Hippolytus had been brought to his
death by the wiles of his stepmother Phaedra, torn to
pieces by bolting horses and paying with his blood the
penalty imposed by his father, men say he came back
under the stars of the sky and the winds of heaven, restored
by healing herbs and the love of Diana. Then the All-   770
powerful Father was enraged that any mortal should rise
from the shades below into the light of life and with his
own hand he took the inventor of those healing arts,
Asclepius, son of Apollo, and hurled him with his thunderbolt down into the wave of the river Styx. But Diana
Trivia, in her loving care, found a secret refuge for Hippolytus and consigned him to the nymph Egeria and her
grove, where, alone and unknown, his name changed to
Virbius, he might live out his days. Thus it is that horn-
hooved horses are not admitted to the sacred grove of the
temple of Trivia because in their terror at the monsters of   780
the deep the horses of Hippolytus had overturned his
chariot and thrown him on the shore. But none the less his
son was driving fiery horses across the level plain as he
rushed to the wars in a chariot.

There, looking around him and moving among the
leaders, was Turnus himself, in full armour, the fairest of
them all, and taller by a head than all the others. On the
towering top of his triple-plumed helmet there stood a
Chimaera breathing from its throat a fire like Etna's, and
the fiercer and bloodier the battle, the more savagely she
roared and belched the deadly flames. The blazon on his
polished shield showed a mighty theme, a golden figure of
Io, raising her horned head, with rough hair on her hide,   790

already changed into a heifer. And there was Argus, guarding her, and her father Inachus pouring his river from an urn embossed on the shield. Behind Turnus came a cloud of foot-soldiers and the whole plain was crowded with columns of men bearing shields, the youth of Argos, bands of Auruncans, Rutulians, Sicani, that ancient race, Sacrani in battle order and Labici with their painted shields; men who ploughed the Tiber valley and the sacred banks of the Numicus; men whose ploughshare worked the Rutulian hills and the ridge of Circeii; men from the fields ruled by 800 Jupiter of Anxur and the goddess Feronia delighting in her greenwood grove, and men from the black swamps of Satura where the icy River Ufens threads his way along his valley bottom to lose himself in ocean.

Last of all came Camilla, the warrior maiden of the Volsci, leading a cavalry squadron flowering in bronze. Not for her girlish hands the distaff and wool-basket of Minerva. She was a maid inured to battle, of a fleetness of foot to race the winds. She could have skimmed the tops of a standing crop without touching them and her passage would not have bruised the delicate ears of grain. She 810 could have run over the ocean, hovered over the swell and never wet her foot in the waves. Young men streamed from house and field and mothers came thronging to gaze at her as she went, lost in wonderment at the royal splendour of the purple veiling the smoothness of her shoulders, her hair weaving round its gold clasp, her Lycian quiver and the shepherd's staff of myrtle wood with the head of a lance.

8

AENEAS IN ROME

When Turnus raised the flag of war above the Laurentine citadel and the shrill horns blared, when he whipped up his eager horses and clashed his sword on his shield, there was instant confusion. In that moment the whole of Latium rose in a frenzy to take the oath and young warriors were baying for blood. Their great leaders Messapus and Ufens and the scorner of the gods Mezentius were levying men everywhere, stripping the fields of those who tilled them. They also sent Venulus to the city of great Diomede to ask for help and to let him know that Trojans were settling in Italy, that Aeneas had arrived with a fleet bringing the defeated household gods of Troy, claiming that he was being called by the Fates to be king; the tribes were flocking to join this Trojan, this descendant of Dardanus, and his name was on the lips of men all over Latium; what all this was leading up to, what Aeneas hoped to gain from the fighting if Fortune smiled upon him, Diomede himself would know better than king Turnus or than king Latinus.

This is what was happening in Latium. The Trojan hero, descendant of Laomedon, saw it all and great tides of grief flowed in his heart. His thoughts moved swiftly, now here, now there, darting in every possible direction and turning to every possible event, like light flickering from water in bronze vessels as it is reflected from the sun or its image the moon, now flying far and wide in all directions, now rising to strike the high coffers of a ceiling.

It was night, and over the whole earth the weary animals, all manner of birds and all manner of flocks, were already deep in sleep before Father Aeneas, on the bank of the river, under the cold vault of the sky, heart sick at the
30 sadness of war, lay down at last and gave rest to his body. There on that lovely river he saw in his sleep the god of the place, old Tiber himself, rising among the leaves of the poplars. He was veiled in a blue-green cloak of fine-spun flax and dark reeds shaded his hair. He then spoke to Aeneas and lightened his sadness with these words: 'O you who are born of the race of the gods, who are bringing back to us the city of Troy saved from its enemies, who are preserving its citadel Pergamum for all time, long have we waited for you in the land of the Laurentines and the fields of Latium. This is the home that is decreed for you. This is the home decreed for the gods of your household.
40 Do not give it up. Do not be intimidated by the threat of war. All the angry passions of the gods are now spent. But come now, so that you may not think what you are seeing is an empty dream, I tell you that you will find a great sow with a litter of thirty piglets lying beneath ilex trees on a shore. There she will lie all white on the ground and the young around her udders will be white. This will be a sign that after three times ten years revolve, Ascanius will found the city of Alba, white in name and bright in glory. What I prophesy will surely come to pass. Attend now and I shall
50 teach you in few words how you may triumphantly resolve the difficulties that lie before you.

'The Arcadians are a race descended from Pallas. They came to these shores following the standards of their king Evander, chose a site here and established in these hills a city called Pallanteum after their founder Pallas. This people wages continual war with the Latin race. Welcome them into your camp as your allies. Make a treaty with them. I will take you to them straight up my river between these banks and you will be able to row upstream into the

current. Up with you then, son of the goddess, for the first
stars are beginning to set. Offer due prayers to Juno and 60
overcome her angry threats with vows and supplications.
To me you will give honour and make repayment when
you are victorious. I am that full river whom you see
scouring these banks and cutting through the rich farmland.
I am the river Thybris, blue as the sky and favoured of
heaven. Here is my great home. My head waters rise
among lofty cities.'

So spoke the river-god and plunged to the bottom of a
deep pool. The night was over and so was Aeneas' sleep.
As he rose he looked up to the light of the sun rising in the
sky, took up water from the river in cupped hands and
poured out these words of prayer to the heavens: 'O you 70
Laurentine nymphs, nymphs who are the mothers of rivers,
and you, Father Thybris with your holy stream, receive
Aeneas, and now after all his suffering keep him safe from
peril. In whichever of your pools you may be, at whichever
of your sources, you who pity our misfortunes, in whatever
land you emerge in all your splendour, I will always pay
you honour and always make offerings to you, O hornèd
river, king of all the waters of Hesperia, only be with me
and by your presence confirm your divine will.' So speaking he picked out two biremes from the fleet, manned
them with rowers and at the same time put some of his 80
comrades on board in full armour.

Now suddenly before his astonished eyes there appeared
a portent. There through the trees he caught sight of a
white sow with offspring of the same colour, lying on the
green shore. This sow devout Aeneas offered to you as a
sacrifice, even to you, O greatest Juno, leading her to your
altar with all her young. And all that long night the
Thybris calmed his flood, reversing his current, and was as
still and silent as a peaceful lake or quiet marsh. There were
no ripples on the surface of his waters, and no toiling for
the oar. Thus they began their journey and made good 90

speed, raising a cheerful noise as the caulked hulls glided over the water. The waves were amazed and the woods were full of wonder at the unaccustomed sight of far-glinting shields of warriors and painted prows floating on the river. So did they wear out the night and the day with rowing and mastered all the long windings of the river, moving under the shade of all manner of trees and cleaving green woods in smooth water. The fiery sun had climbed to the middle of the vault of heaven when they saw in the distance walls and a citadel and the roofs of scattered 100 houses. What Roman power has now raised to the heights of the sky, in those days was a poor land ruled by Evander. Quickly they turned their prows to the bank and steered for the city.

It so happened that on that day the Arcadian king Evander was performing yearly rites in honour of the mighty Hercules, son of Amphitryon, and was sacrificing to the gods in a grove outside the city. His son Pallas was with him, and with him also were all the leading warriors and the senators, poor men as they were. They were offering incense and warm blood was smoking on the altars. When they saw the tall ships and saw them gliding through the dense grove with men bending to the oars in 110 silence, they were seized with sudden fright and rose in a body, abandoning the sacred tables. Not so Pallas. Boldly he told them not to disturb their holy feast, and seizing a weapon he rushed off to face the strangers by himself. 'What is it, warriors, that has driven you to try these new paths?' he called out from the top of a mound while he was still at a distance. 'Where are you going? What race are you? Where is your home? Is it peace you are bringing us or war?' Then Father Aeneas replied from the high poop of his ship, holding out in his hand the olive branch of peace: 'We are of the Trojan race. These weapons you see are for use against our enemies the Latins. It is they who have driven us here, exiles as we are, with all the

insolence of war. We are looking for Evander. Tell him of
this. Say to him that the chosen leaders of the race of ₁₂₀
Dardanus have come to ask him to be their ally in battle.'
At this great name Pallas was dumbfounded. 'Whoever
you may be,' he cried, 'leave your ship and come and
speak with my father face to face. Come as a guest into our
house.' With these words he took Aeneas by the right
hand in a long clasp, and they moved forward into the
grove, leaving the river behind them.

Then Aeneas addressed the king with words of friendship: 'O noblest of the race of the Greeks, Fortune has
willed that I should come to you as a suppliant with an
olive branch draped with wool. I was not alarmed at the
thought that you are a leader of Greeks, an Arcadian and ₁₃₀
joined by blood to the two sons of Atreus, for I am joined
to you by my courage and by the holy oracles of the gods,
by our fathers who were kinsmen and by your fame which
is known throughout the world. All these have driven me
here by the command of the Fates, and I have willingly
obeyed. Dardanus, the first founder and father of the city
of Troy, sailed to our Teucrian land. According to the
Greeks he was the son of Electra, and that same Electra was
the daughter of Atlas, the mighty Atlas who carries the
circle of the heavens on his shoulder. On your side you are
the son of Mercury and he was the son of Maia, conceived ₁₄₀
and born on the snow-clad top of Mount Cyllene. But the
father of Maia, if we put any trust in what we hear, was
Atlas, that same Atlas who supports the stars of the sky.
And so we are of one blood, two branches of the same
family. Trusting in this, I have not sent emissaries or made
trial of you in advance by any form of subterfuge, but
have come in person as a suppliant to your door, and laid
my life before you. The same race harries us both in bitter
war, the Rutulians of king Daunus, and they are persuaded
that if they were to drive us away, nothing would prevent
them from putting all the heartlands of Italy under their

yoke and becoming masters of the Tyrrhenian sea to the
150 south and the Adriatic to the north. Take the right hand of
friendship I offer and give me yours. Our hearts are strong
in war. Our spirits are high. Our fighting men are tried
and proved.'

So spoke Aeneas. All the time he was speaking, Evander
had been gazing at his face and his eyes and his whole
body. He then replied in these few words: 'Bravest of the
Trojans, I welcome you with great joy, and with great joy
I recognize who you are. Oh how well do I recall the
words of your father, the very voice and features of the
great Anchises! For I remember that when Priam, son of
Laomedon, was on a visit to his sister Hesione in the
kingdom of Salamis, he came on to visit us in the cold
160 lands of Arcadia. In those days the first bloom of youth
was still covering my cheeks, and I was full of admiration
for the leaders of Troy. Priam himself, too, I admired, but
taller than them all walked Anchises. With all a young
man's ardour, I longed to speak with him and put my
right hand in his, so I approached him and led him with
full heart to the walls of Pheneus. When he was leaving he
gave me a wonderful quiver filled with Lycian arrows, a
soldier's cloak interwoven with gold thread and a pair of
golden bridles which now belong to my son Pallas. So
then, the right hand of friendship for which you ask has
170 already been given in solemn pledge, and as soon as
tomorrow's sun returns to the earth, I shall send you on
your way and you will not be disappointed with the
reinforcements and supplies I shall give you. Meanwhile,
since you are here as friends, come favour these annual rites
of ours which it would be sinful to postpone, by celebrating
them with us. It is time you began to feel at home at the
tables of your allies.'

The food and drink had been cleared away, but as soon
as he was finished speaking, he ordered them to be replaced,
and the king himself showed the Trojans to seats on the

grass, but took Aeneas apart to a couch of maple wood and
seated him on a rough lion skin for a cushion. Then the
priest of the altar and some chosen warriors served with
great good will the roast flesh of bulls, loaded into baskets   180
the grain which is the gift of Ceres worked by the hand of
man, and poured out the juice of Bacchus. Aeneas and the
warriors of Troy then feasted together on the whole chine
and entrails of the sacrificial ox.

After their hunger was relieved and their appetite satisfied, king Evander spoke as follows: 'This annual rite, this
set feast and this altar to a great divinity have not been
imposed upon us by any vain superstition working in
ignorance of our ancient gods. It is because we have been
saved from desperate dangers, my Trojan friend, that we
perform this worship and renew it yearly in honour of one
who has well deserved it.

'First of all, look at this vaulted cavern among the rocks.   190
You see how this great massive home inside the mountain
has been torn apart and is now abandoned, with boulders
lying everywhere in ruins. Here, deep in the vast recesses
of the rock, was once a cave which the rays of the sun
never reached. This was the home of a foul-featured, half-
human monster by the name of Cacus. The floor of the
cave was always warm with freshly shed blood, and the
heads of men were nailed to his proud doors and hung
there pale and rotting. The father of this monster was
Vulcan, and it was his father's black fire he vomited from
his mouth as he moved his massive bulk. Long did we pray
and in the end we too were granted the help and the   200
presence of a god. For the great avenger was at hand.
Exulting in the slaughter of the triple-bodied Geryon and
the spoils he had taken, the victorious Hercules was driving
the huge bulls through our land and the herd was grazing
the valley and drinking the water of the river. But Cacus
was a robber, and thinking in the savagery of his heart not
to leave any crime or treachery undared or unattempted,

he stole from pasture four magnificent bulls and as many
lovely heifers. So that there would be no hoof prints
210 pointing forwards in the direction of the cave, he dragged
them in by their tails to reverse the tracks, and was now
keeping his plunder hidden deep in the darkness of the
rock. There were no tracks leading to the cave for any
searcher to see.

'Meanwhile, when his herd had grazed its fill, and the
son of Amphitryon was moving them out of pasture and
preparing to go on his way, the cows began to low
plaintively at leaving the place, filling the whole grove
with their complaints, and bellowing to the hills they were
leaving behind them. Then, deep in the cave, a single cow
lowed in reply. Cacus had guarded her well, but she
thwarted his hopes. At this Hercules blazed up in anger.
220 The black bile of his fury rose in him, and snatching up his
arms and heavy knotted club, he made off at a run for the
windswept heights of the mountain. Never before had our
people seen Cacus afraid. Never before had there been
terror in these eyes. He turned and fled, running to his
cave with the speed of the wind, fear lending wings to his
feet. There he shut himself up, dropping a huge rock
behind him and breaking the iron chains on which it had
been suspended by his father's art, so that its great mass
was jammed against the doorposts and blocked the entrance. There was Hercules in a passion, trying every
230 approach, turning his head this way and that and grinding
his teeth. Three times he went round the whole of Mount
Aventine in his anger. Three times he tried to force the
great rock doorway without success. Three times he sat
down exhausted in the valley.

'Above the ridge on top of the cave, there stood a sharp
needle of flint with sheer rocks falling away on either side.
It rose to a dizzy height and was a favourite nesting-place
of carrion birds. Hercules put his weight on the right-hand
side of it where it leaned over the ridge towards the river

on its left. He rocked it, loosened it, wrenched it free from
its deep base and then gave a sudden heave, a heave at
which the great heavens thundered, the banks of the river   240
leapt apart and the river flowed backwards in alarm. The
cave and whole huge palace of Cacus were unroofed and
exposed to view and his shadowy caverns were opened to
all their depths. It was as though the very depths of the
earth were to gape in some cataclysm and unbar the
chambers of the underworld, the pale kingdom loathed by
the gods, so that the vast abyss could be seen from above
with the shades of the dead in panic as the light floods in.

'So Cacus was caught in the sudden rush of light and
trapped in his cavern in the rock, howling as never before,
while Hercules bombarded him from above with any   250
missile that came to hand, belabouring him with branches
of trees and rocks the size of millstones. There was no
escape for him now, but he vomited thick smoke from his
monstrous throat and rolled clouds of it all round his den
to blot it from sight. Deep in his cave he churned out
fumes as black as night and the darkness was shot through
with fire. Hercules was past all patience. He threw himself
straight down, leaping through the flames where the smoke
spouted thickest and the black cloud boiled in the vast
cavern. There, as Cacus vainly belched his fire in the
darkness, Hercules caught him in a grip and held him,   260
forcing his eyes out of their sockets and squeezing his
throat till the blood was dry in it. Then, tearing out the
doors and opening up the dark house of Cacus, he brought
into the light of heaven the stolen cattle whose theft Cacus
had denied, and dragged the foul corpse out by the feet.
No one could have enough of gazing at his terrible eyes
and face, at the coarse bristles on his beastly chest and the
throat charred by fires now dead.

'Ever since that time we have honoured his name and
succeeding generations have celebrated this day with rejoicing. This altar was set up in its grove by Potitius, the first

270 founder of these rites of Hercules, and by the Pinarii, the
guardians of the rites. We shall always call it The Greatest
Altar, and the greatest altar it will always be. Come then
warriors, put a crown of leaves around your hair in honour
of this great exploit, and hold out your cups in your right
hands. Call upon the god who is a god for all of us and offer
him wine with willing hearts.' No sooner had he spoken
than his head was shaded by a wreath and pendant of the
green-silver leaves of Hercules' poplar woven into his hair,
and the sacred goblet filled his hand. Soon they were all
pouring their libations on the table and praying to the
gods.

280   Meanwhile the Evening Star was drawing nearer as the
day sank in the heavens and there came a procession of
priests led by Potitius, wearing their ritual garb of animal
skins and carrying torches. They were starting the feast
again with a second course of goodly offerings, and they
heaped the altar with loaded dishes. Then the Salii, the
priests of Mars, their heads bound with poplar leaves, came
to sing around the altar fires. On one side was a chorus of
young warriors, on the other a chorus of old men, hymning
the praise of Hercules and his great deeds: how he seized
the two snakes, the first monsters sent against him by his
stepmother, and throttled them, one in each hand; how
290 also he tore stone from stone the cities of Troy and
Oechalia, famous in war; how he endured a thousand
labours under king Eurystheus to fulfil the fate laid upon
him by the cruel will of Juno. 'O unconquered Hercules,'
they sang, 'you are the slayer of the half-men born of the
cloud, the Centaurs Hylaeus and Pholus; of the monstrous
Cretan bull and the huge lion of Nemea in its rocky lair;
the pools of the Styx trembled at your coming, and the
watchdog of Orcus cringed where he lay in his cave
weltering in blood on heaps of half-eaten bones. But
nothing you have seen has ever made you afraid, not even
Typhoeus himself, rising up to heaven with his weapons in

his hands. Nor did reason fail you when the hundred heads ₃₀₀
of the Lernaean Hydra hissed around you. Hail, true son of
Jupiter, the latest lustre added to the company of the gods,
come to us now, to your own holy rite, and bless us with
your favouring presence.' To end their hymn they sang of
the cave of Cacus, and Cacus himself breathing fire, till the
whole grove rang and all the hills re-echoed.

As soon as the sacred rites were completed, they all
returned to the city. The king, weighed down with age,
kept Aeneas and his son Pallas by his side as he walked, and
made the way seem shorter by all the things he told them.
Aeneas was lost in admiration and his eyes were never still ₃₁₀
as he looked about him enthralled by the places he saw,
asking questions about them and joyfully listening to Evander's explanations of all the relics of the men of old. This is
what was said that day by Evander, the founder of the
citadel of Rome: 'These woods used to be the haunt of
native fauns and nymphs and a race of men born from the
hard wood of oak-tree trunks. They had no rules of
conduct and no civilization. They did not know how to
yoke oxen for ploughing, how to gather wealth or husband
what they had, but they lived off the fruit of the tree and
the harsh diet of huntsmen. In those early days, in flight ₃₂₀
from the weapons of Jupiter, came Saturn from heavenly
Olympus, an exile who had lost his kingdom. He brought
together this wild and scattered mountain people, gave
them laws and resolved that the name of the land should
be changed to Latium, since he had *lain* hidden within its
borders. His reign was what men call the Golden Age,
such was the peace and serenity of the people under his
rule. But gradually a worse age of baser metal took its
place and with it came the madness of war and the lust for
possessions. Then bands of Ausonians arrived and Sicanian
peoples, and the land of Saturn lost its name many times.
Next there were kings, among them the cruel and mon- ₃₃₀
strous Thybris, after whom we Italians have in later years

called the river Thybris, and the old river Albula has lost its true name. I had been driven from my native land and was setting course for the most distant oceans when Fortune, that no man can resist, and Fate, that no man can escape, set me here in this place, driven by fearsome words of warning from my mother, the nymph Carmentis, and by the authority of the god Apollo.'

He had just finished saying this and moved on a little, when he pointed out the Altar of Carmentis and the Carmental Gate, as the Romans have called it from earliest times in honour of the nymph Carmentis. She had the gift of prophecy and was the first to foretell the future greatness of the sons of Aeneas and the future fame of Pallanteum. From here he pointed out the great grove which warlike Romulus set up as a sanctuary – he was to call it the Asylum – and also the Lupercal there under its cool rock, then called by Arcadian tradition they had brought from Parrhasia, the cave of Pan Lycaeus, the wolf god. He also pointed out the grove of the Argiletum, and, calling upon that consecrated spot to be his witness, he told the story of the killing of his guest Argus.

From here he led the way to the house of Tarpeia and the Capitol, now all gold, but in those distant days bristling with rough scrub. Even then a powerful sense of a divine presence in the place caused great fear among the country people, even then they went in awe of the wood and the rock. 'This grove,' said Evander, 'this leafy-topped hill, is the home of some god, we know not which. My Arcadians believe they have often seen Jupiter himself shaking the darkening aegis in his right hand to drive along the storm clouds. And then here are the ruined walls of these two towns. What you are looking at are relics of the men of old. These are their monuments. One of these citadels was founded by Father Janus; the other by Saturn. This one used to be called the Janiculum; the other, Saturnia.'

Talking in this way they were coming up to Evander's

humble home, and there were cattle everywhere, lowing
in the Roman Forum and the now luxurious district of the
Carinae. When they arrived at his house, Evander said:
'The victorious Hercules of the line of Alceus stooped to
enter this door. This was a palace large enough for him.
You are my guest, and you too must have the courage to
despise wealth. You must mould yourself to be worthy of
the god. Come into my poor home and do not judge it
too harshly.' With these words he led the mighty Aeneas
under the roof-tree of his narrow house and set him down
on a bed of leaves covered with the hide of a Libyan bear.
Night fell and its dark wings enfolded the earth.

But his mother Venus was terrified, and with good
reason, by the threats of the Laurentines and the savagery
of the fighting, so she spoke to her husband Vulcan.
Coming to him in his golden bedroom and breathing
divine love into her voice, she said: 'When the citadel of
Troy was being ravaged in war by the kings of Greece, it
was owed to Fate and was doomed to fall in the fires lit by
its enemies, but I asked for nothing for those who suffered.
I did not call upon the help of your art to make arms for
them. Although I owed much to the sons of Priam and
had often wept at the sufferings endured by Aeneas, I did
not wish, O my dearest husband, that you should exert
yourself to no purpose. But now, in obedience to the
commands of Jupiter, Aeneas is standing on Rutulian soil
and so now I come to you as a suppliant. I approach that
godhead which I so revere, and as a mother, I ask you to
make arms for my son. You yielded to Thetis, the daughter
of Nereus, you yielded to the wife of Tithonus when they
came and wept to you. Look at all the nations gathering.
Look at the walled cities that have closed their gates and
are sharpening their swords against me to destroy those I
love.' She had finished speaking and he was hesitating. The
goddess took him gently in her white arms and caressed
him, and caressed him again. Suddenly he caught fire as he

390 always did. The old heat he knew so well pierced to the marrow of his bones and coursed through them till they melted, as in a thunderstorm, when a fiery-flashing rift bursts the clouds and runs through them in dazzling brightness. His wife knew and was pleased. She was well aware of her beauty and she knew how to use it. Father Vulcan, bound to her by eternal love, made this reply: 'You need not delve so deep for arguments. Where is that trust, O goddess, which you used to have in me? If your care for Aeneas was then as it is now, it would have been right for us even then to arm the Trojans. Neither the All-powerful Father nor the Fates were forbidding Troy to stand and

400 Priam to go on living for ten more years. And now if you are preparing for war and this is what you wish, whatever care I can offer you in the exercise of my skill, whatever can be done by melting iron or electrum, anything that fire and bellows can achieve, you do not have to pray to me. You need not doubt your power.' At these words he gave his wife the embraces so much desired, and then, relaxed upon her breast, he sought and found peace and repose for all his limbs.

When the night had passed the middle of his course, when Vulcan's first sleep was over and there was no more rest, just when the ashes are first stirred to rouse the

410 slumbering fire by a woman whose task it is to support life by the humble work of spinning thread on a distaff; taking time from the night for her labours, she sets her slave women going by lamplight upon their long day's work, so that she can keep her husband's bed chaste and bring her young sons to manhood – with no less zeal than such a woman and not a moment later did the God of Fire rise from his soft bed and go to work at his forge.

Between Lipari in the Aeolian Islands and the flank of Sicily, an island of smoking rocks rises sheer from the sea. Deep within it is a great vault, and in that vault caves have been scooped out like those under Etna to serve as forges

for the Cyclopes. The noise within them is the noise of
thunder. Mighty blows can be heard booming on the ₄₂₀
groaning anvils, the caves are filled with the sound of
hissing as the Chalybes plunge bars of white-hot pig-iron
into water and all the time the fires are breathing in the
furnaces. This is the home of Vulcan, and Vulcania is the
name of the island. Into these depths the God of Fire
descended from the heights of heaven.

The Cyclopes were forging steel, working naked in that
vast cavern, Brontes, Sterope and Pyracmon. In their hands
was a thunderbolt which they had roughed out, one of
those the Father of the Gods and Men hurls down upon
the earth in such numbers from every part of the sky.
Some of it was already burnished, some of it unfinished.
They had attached three shafts of lashing rain to it, three
shafts of heavy rainclouds, three of glowing fire and three ₄₃₀
of the south wind in full flight. They were now adding to
the work the terrifying lightning and the sound of thunder,
then Fear and Anger with their pursuing flames. In another
part of the cave they were working for Mars, busy with
the wing-wheeled chariot in which he stirs up men and
cities to war. Others were hard at work polishing the
armour worn by Pallas Athene when roused, the fearsome
aegis and its weaving snakes with their reptilian scales of
gold, even the Gorgon rolling her eyes in the bodiless head
on the breast of the goddess. 'Put all this away!' he cried.
'Whatever work you have started, you Cyclopes of Etna, ₄₄₀
lay it aside and give your attention here. Armour has to be
made for a brave hero. You need strength and quick hands
now. Now you need all your arts to guide you. Let
nothing stand in your way.' He said no more, but instantly
they all bent to the work, dividing it equally between
them. The bronze was soon flowing in rivers. The gold
ore and iron, the dealer of death, were molten in a great
furnace. They were shaping one great shield to be a match
for all the weapons of the Latins, fastening the seven

450 thicknesses of it circle to circle. Bellows were taking in air
and breathing it out again. Bronze was being plunged into
troughs of water and hissing. The cave boomed with the
anvils standing on its floor while the Cyclopes raised their
arms with all their strength in time with one another and
turned the ore in tongs that did not slip.

While Father Vulcan, the god of Lemnos, was pressing
on with this work in the Aeolian Islands, Evander was
roused from sleep in his humble hut by the life-sustaining
light of day and the dawn chorus of the birds under his
eaves. The old man rose, put on his tunic and bound
Etruscan sandals on the soles of his feet. He then girt on a
460 Tegean sword with its baldric over the shoulder and threw
on a panther skin to hang down on his left side. Nor did the
sentinels from his high threshold fail to precede him – his
two dogs went with their master – as the hero walked to
the separate quarters of his guest Aeneas, remembering
their talk and remembering the help he had promised to
give. Aeneas was up and about just as early, walking with
Achates. Evander had his son Pallas with him. They met,
clasped right hands, and sitting there in the middle of
Evander's house, they were at last able to discuss affairs of
state.

470 The king spoke first: 'Great leader of the Trojans, while
you are alive I shall never accept that Troy and its kingdom
are defeated. Beside your mighty name, the power we
have to help you in this war is as nothing. On one side we
are hemmed in by the Tuscan river, on the other the
Rutulians press us hard and we can hear the clang of their
weapons round our walls. But I have a plan to join vast
peoples and the armies of wealthy kingdoms to your cause.
A chance that no man could have foreseen is showing us
the path to safety. Fate was calling you when you came to
this place.

'Not far from here is the site of Agylla, founded long
480 ago on its ancient rock by the warlike Lydians who once

settled there on the ridges of the Etruscan mountains. After
this city had flourished for many years, Mezentius eventually took it under his despotic rule as king and held it by
the ruthless use of armed force. I shall not speak of the foul
murders and other barbaric crimes committed by this
tyrant. May the gods heap equal suffering upon his own
head and the heads of his descendants! He even devised a
form of torture whereby living men were roped to dead
bodies, tying them hand to hand and face to face to die a
lingering death oozing with putrefying flesh in this cruel
embrace. But at last his subjects reached the end of their
endurance and took up arms against him. Roaring and
raging he was besieged in his palace, his men were   490
butchered and fire was thrown on his roof. In all this
bloodshed he himself escaped and took refuge in the land
of the Rutulians under the protection of the armies of his
guest friend, Turnus. At this the whole of Etruria rose in
righteous fury and has now come in arms to demand
that Mezentius be given up for punishment. They have
thousands of troops and I shall put you at their head. Their
ships are massed all along the shore, clamouring for the
signal for battle, but they are held in check by this warning
from an aged prophet: "O you chosen warriors from
Lydian Maeonia, flower of the chivalry of an ancient race,   500
it is a just grievance that drives you to war, and Mezentius
deserves the anger that blazes against him, but it is not the
will of heaven that such a race as the Etruscans should ever
obey an Italian. You must choose your leaders from across
the seas."

'At this the Etruscan army has settled down again on the
plain, held back by fear of these divine warnings. Tarchon
himself has sent envoys to me with crown and sceptre, and
offers me the royal insignia of Etruria if I agree to come to
their camp and take over the kingdom. But my powers
have passed with the passing of the generations. Age has
taken the speed from my feet and the warmth from my

blood. I am too old for command and no longer have the
510 strength for battle. I would be urging my son to go, but he
is of mixed stock through his Sabine mother and is therefore part Italian. It is you who are favoured of the Fates for
your years and your descent. You are the man the gods are
asking for. Go then, O bravest leader of all the men of
Troy and Italy, and I shall send with you this my son
Pallas, our hope and our comfort. Let him be hardened to
the rigours of war under your leadership. Let him daily see
your conduct and admire you from his earliest years. Two
hundred horsemen I shall give him, the flower of our
fighting men, and Pallas will give you two hundred more
in his own name.'

520 He had scarcely finished speaking, and Aeneas, son of
Anchises, and his faithful Achates were still looking sadly
down at the ground, and long would they have pondered in
the anguish of their hearts, had Venus not given a sign from
the clear sky. There came from the heavens a sudden flash of
lightning and a rumble of thunder and the whole sky seemed
to be crashing down upon them with the blast of an Etruscan
trumpet shrilling across the heavens. They looked up and
again and again great peals broke over their heads and in
bright sky in a break between the clouds they saw armour
530 glowing red and heard it thunder as it clashed. The others
were all astonished but the hero of Troy understood the
sound and knew this was the fulfilment of the promise of his
divine mother. At last he spoke: 'There is no need, my friend,
no need to ask what these portents mean. This is heaven
asking for me. The goddess who is my mother told me she
would send this sign if war were threatening, and bring
armour made by Vulcan down through the air to help me.
Alas! What slaughter waits upon the unhappy Laurentines!
What a punishment Turnus will endure at my hands! How
many shields and helmets and bodies of brave men will
Father Thybris roll down beneath his waves. Now let the
540 Laurentines ask for war! Now let them break their treaties!'

When he had said this, he rose from his high throne. First of all he stirred the fires smouldering on the altar of Hercules and approached with joy the humble gods of home and hearth whom he had worshipped on the day before, and then Evander and the warriors of Troy made sacrifice together of duly chosen yearling sheep. When this was done Aeneas went back from Evander's house to his ships and his comrades, from whom he chose men of outstanding courage to follow him to war. The rest sailed downstream, floating effortlessly on the current, to bring 550 Ascanius news of his father and tell him what had happened. The Trojans going to Etruria were given horses. The mount picked out for Aeneas was caparisoned in one great tawny lion skin with gleaming gold claws.

Swiftly round the little city flew the rumour that they were riding to the gates of the king of Etruria. Frightened mothers heaped prayer upon prayer, their fear increasing with the approach of danger, and the vision of Mars loomed ever larger before them. As they left, Evander took the right hand of his son Pallas and clung to it inconsolably: 'If only Jupiter would give me back the years 560 that are past,' he cried, 'when I laid low the front rank of the enemy's battle line under the very walls of Praeneste, heaping up their shields and burning them to celebrate my victory, with this right hand sending down to Tartarus their king Erulus, whose mother Feronia had given him three lives at birth – I shudder to remember it – three sets of armour to carry into battle, and three times I had to lay him dead on the ground, but in those days this one right hand was able to take all his lives and strip him of all those sets of armour . . . no power on earth would be tearing me from your arms, O my beloved son, and Mezentius would never have been able to trample upon his neighbour, 570 putting so many of my countrymen to the sword and emptying the city of so many of its people. But O you gods above, and you, Greatest Jupiter, ruler of the gods, I

beseech you, take pity on an Arcadian king, and hear a
father's prayers. If your divine powers and the Fates are
keeping Pallas safe for me, if I am going to live to see him
again and be with him again, then I pray for life and
harden my heart to endure any suffering. But if Fortune
has some horror in store, let me die now, let me break off
580 this cruel life here and now, before I can put a name to my
sorrow, before I know what the future will bring and
while I still hold you in my arms, O my dear son, my only
source of joy, given to me so late in life. I want no grim
news to come and wound my ears.' These are the words
that poured from the lips of Evander at his last parting
with his son. When he had uttered them, he collapsed and
was carried into his house by his attendants.

    And now the gates had been opened and the horsemen
had ridden out, Aeneas among the first of them and his
faithful Achates with him, then the other Trojan commanders with Pallas conspicuous in the middle of the
column in his Greek military cloak and brightly coloured
armour. He was like the Morning Star, which Venus loves
above all other starry fires, as he leaves his ocean bath and
590 lifts up his holy face into the sky to scatter the darkness.
Mothers stood on the city walls, full of dread and following
with their eyes the cloud of dust and the glint of bronze
from the squadrons. They were riding in their armour by
the shortest route over rough scrub and their shouts rose to
the sky as the four-hoofed beat of the galloping column
drummed on the dusty plain. Near Caere's cold river there
was a wide glade, revered for generations as a holy place
by peoples near and far. It was enclosed on every side by a
ring of hills clad in black firs. The story is told that the
ancient Pelasgians, who in days long past were the first
inhabitants of Latium, consecrated this grove and a holy
600 day to be observed in it to Silvanus, the god of field and
flock. Not far from here Tarcho and the Etruscans were
occupying a strong position and their whole army could be

seen from the heights of the hills, encamped on the broad
fields. Aeneas and his chosen warriors had come down to
the camp and, weary from the ride, were seeing to their
horses and refreshing themselves.

But the goddess Venus, bringing her gifts, was at hand,
shining among the clouds of heaven. When she saw her   610
son at some distance from the others, alone in a secluded
valley across the icy river, she spoke to him, coming
unasked before his eyes: 'Here now are the gifts I promised
you, perfected by my husband's skill. When the time
comes you need not hesitate, my son, to face the proud
Laurentines or challenge fierce Turnus to battle.' With
these words the goddess of Cythera came to her son's
embrace and laid the armour in all its shining splendour
before him under an oak tree.

Aeneas rejoiced at these gifts from the goddess and at the
honour she was paying him and could not have his fill of
gazing at them. He turned them over in his hands, in his
arms, admiring the terrible, crested, fire-spurting helmet,   620
the death-dealing sword, the huge, unyielding breastplate
of blood-red bronze like a dark cloud fired by the rays of
the sun and glowing far across the sky, then the polished
greaves of richly refined electrum and gold, the spear and
the fabric of the shield beyond all words to describe. There
the God of Fire, with his knowledge of the prophets and of
time that was to be, had laid out the story of Italy and the
triumphs of the Romans, and there in order were all the
generations that would spring from Ascanius and all the
wars they would fight.

He had made, too, a mother wolf stretched out in the   630
green cave of Mars with twin boys playing round her
udders, hanging there unafraid and sucking at her as she
bent her supple neck back to lick each of them in turn and
mould their bodies into shape with her tongue.

Near this he had put Rome and the violent rape of the
Sabines at the great games in the bowl of the crowded

Circus, and a new war suddenly breaking out between the
people of Romulus and the stern Sabines from Cures led
by their aged king Tatius. Then, after these same kings had
put an end to their conflict, they stood in their armour
before the altar of Jupiter with sacred vessels in their hands,
sacrificing a sow to ratify the treaty.

Close by, four-horse chariots had been driven hard in
opposite directions and had torn Mettus in two – the man
of Alba should have stood by his promises – and Tullus
was dragging the deceiver's body through a wood while a
dew of blood dripped from the brambles.

There too was Porsenna ordering the Romans to take
Tarquin back after they had expelled him, and mounting a
great siege against the city while the descendants of Aeneas
were running upon the drawn swords of the enemy in the
name of liberty. There you could see him as though raging
and blustering because Horatius Cocles was daring to tear
the bridge down and Cloelia had broken her chains and
was swimming the river.

At the top of the shield Manlius, the keeper of the citadel
on the Tarpeian rock, stood in front of the temple and kept
guard on the heights of the Capitol. The new thatch stood
out rough on the roof of Romulus' palace, and here was a
silver goose fluttering through the golden portico, honking
to announce that the Gauls were at the gates. There were the
Gauls close by, among the thorn bushes, climbing into the
citadel under the cover of darkness on that pitch-black
night. Their hair was gold, their clothing was gold, their
striped cloaks gleamed and their milk-white necks were
encircled by golden torques. In each right hand there glinted
two heavy Alpine spears and long shields protected their
bodies. Here too Vulcan had hammered out the leaping
Salii, the priests of Mars, and the naked Luperci, the priests'
conical hats tufted with wool, the figure-of-eight shields
which had fallen from heaven and chaste matrons leading
sacred processions through the city in cushioned carriages.

At some distance from these scenes he added the habitations of the dead in Tartarus, the tall gateway of Dis and the punishments of the damned, with Catiline hanging from his beetling crag and shivering at the faces of the Furies. There too were the righteous, in a place apart, and Cato administering justice.

Between all these there ran a representation of a broad expanse of swelling sea, golden, but dark blue beneath the white foam on the crests of the waves, and all round it in a circle swam dolphins picked out in silver, cleaving the sea and feathering its surface with their tails.

In the middle were the bronze-armoured fleets at the battle of Actium. There before your eyes the battle was drawn up with the whole of the headland of Leucas seething and all the waves gleaming in gold. On one side was Augustus Caesar, leading the men of Italy into battle alongside the Senate and the People of Rome, its gods of home and its great gods. High he stood on the poop of his ship while from his radiant forehead there streamed a double flame and his father's star shone above his head. On the other wing, towering above the battle as he led his ships in line ahead, sailed Agrippa with favouring winds and favouring gods, and the beaks of captured vessels flashed from the proud honour on his forehead, the Naval Crown. On the other side, with the wealth of the barbarian world and warriors in all kinds of different armour, came Antony in triumph from the shores of the Red Sea and the peoples of the Dawn. With him sailed Egypt and the power of the East from as far as distant Bactria, and there bringing up the rear was the greatest outrage of all, his Egyptian wife! On they came at speed, all together, and the whole surface of the sea was churned to foam by the pull of their oars and the bow-waves from their triple beaks. They steered for the high sea and you would have thought that the Cycladic Islands had been torn loose again and were floating on the ocean, or that mountains were colliding with mountains, to see men in action on those ships with their massive, turreted sterns, showering blazing torches of tow and flying steel as the fresh blood began to redden the furrows of Neptune's fields. In the middle of all this the queen summoned her warships by rattling her Egyptian timbrels – she was not yet seeing the two snakes there at her back – while Anubis barked and all manner of 700 monstrous gods levelled their weapons at Neptune and Venus and Minerva. There in the eye of battle raged Mars, engraved in iron, the grim Furies swooped from the sky and jubilant Discord strode along in her torn cloak with Bellona at her heels cracking her bloody whip. But high on the headland of Actium, Apollo saw it all and was drawing his bow. In terror at the sight the whole of Egypt and of India, all the Arabians and all the Shebans were turning tail and the queen herself could be seen calling for winds and setting her sails by them. She had untied the sail-ropes and was even now paying them out. There in all 710 the slaughter the God of Fire had set her, pale with the pallor of approaching death, driven over the waves by the Iapygian winds blowing off Calabria. Opposite her he had fashioned the Nile with grief in every line of his great body, opening his robes and with every fold of drapery beckoning his defeated people into his blue-grey breast and the secret waters of his river.

But Caesar was riding into Rome in triple triumph, paying undying vows to the gods of Italy and consecrating three hundred great shrines throughout the city. The streets resounded with joy and festivities and applause. There was a chorus of matrons at every temple, at every temple there were altars and the ground before the altars was strewn 720 with the bodies of slaughtered bullocks. He himself was seated at the white marble threshold of gleaming white Apollo, inspecting the gifts brought before him by the peoples of the earth and hanging them high on the posts of the doors of the temple, while the defeated nations walked in long procession in all their different costumes and in all their different armour, speaking all the tongues of the earth. Here Mulciber, the God of Fire, had moulded the Nomads and the Africans with their streaming robes; here, too, the Lelegeians and Carians of Asia and the Gelonians from Scythia with their arrows. The Euphrates was now moving with a chastened current, and here were the Gaulish Morini from the ends of the earth, the two-horned Rhine, the undefeated Dahae from beyond the Caspian and the river Araxes chafing at his bridge.

Such were the scenes spread over the shield that Vulcan made and Venus gave to her son. Marvelling at it, and 730 rejoicing at the things pictured on it without knowing what they were, Aeneas lifted on to his shoulder the fame and the fate of his descendants.

For lines 626–728, see Appendix Two

9

NISUS AND EURYALUS

While this was happening far away in Etruria, Juno, daughter of Saturn, sent Iris down from the sky to bold Turnus, who chanced at that moment to be sitting in a grove sacred to his ancestor Pilumnus. These were the words that came to him from the rosy lips of Iris, daughter of Thaumas: 'There, Turnus, time in its ever-rolling course has brought you unasked what none of the gods would have dared to promise you if you had prayed for it – Aeneas has left his city, his allies and his fleet, and gone to visit the royal seat of Evander on the Palatine. And as though that were not enough, he has travelled as far as the remotest cities of Corythus and is arming a band of Lydians, some country people he has collected. What are you waiting for? This is the moment to call for your horses and chariots. Do not allow any delay. Make a surprise attack on their camp and seize it.' At these words she soared into the sky on poised wings, cutting in her flight a great rainbow under the clouds. The warrior knew her, and raising his hands palms upward to the stars, he called out to her as she flew: 'Iris, glory of the sky, who has sent you here to me, riding the clouds down to the earth? Why this sudden brightness in the air? I see the heights of heaven parting and stars wandering through the vault of the sky. I follow this great sign, whoever you are that call me to arms.' When he had spoken these words, he walked to the river's edge and scooped up in his hands the water from its

surface as he offered up prayer upon prayer to the gods
and burdened heaven with his vows.

The whole army was soon moving across the open
plain, rich in its horses, rich in embroidered apparel, rich in
gold. The vanguard was controlled by Messapus, the rear
by the sons of Tyrrhus, while Turnus, the chief commander, was in the middle of the column. It was like the
Ganges fed by the steady flow of its seven rivers and
silently rising, or like the fertile waters of the Nile when it
withdraws from the plains and settles back at last into its
own channel. The Trojans saw this distant cloud of black
dust suddenly gathering and the darkness rising on the
plain. Caicus was on the rampart on that side and he was
the first to raise the alarm: 'What is that ball of dark dust
rolling along the plain? Fetch your weapons, fellow-
citizens, and fetch them now! Give out missiles! Mount the
walls! The enemy is upon us. To your posts!' With a great
clamour the Trojans streamed in by all the gates to man
the walls, for these were the orders they had received from
Aeneas, the greatest of warriors, as he left them: if anything
should happen in his absence, they were not to dare take
up position for a pitched battle or trust themselves to the
plain, but only to stay on the ramparts and defend the
camp and the walls. So, though shame and anger urged
them to join battle, they nevertheless obeyed orders and
closed the gates against the enemy, waiting for them in full
armour inside their towers.

By this time Turnus had taken wing and gone on ahead
of the slow-moving column. With twenty picked horsemen
he arrived at the city before he was expected, riding a
piebald Thracian charger and wearing his gold helmet
shaded by red plumes. 'Is there any man among you, my
friends, will come with me and be first upon the enemy?
There!' he cried, and sent his javelin spinning into the air as
a signal for battle, then, rising in the saddle he charged
across the plain. His comrades took up the cry and followed

him with blood-curdling shouts. They were amazed at the
faint-heartedness of the Trojans. Why did they not commit
themselves to a fair fight on the level plain? They were
men. Why did they huddle in their camp and not meet
arms with arms? Turnus in a fury prowled round the walls
this way and that, searching for an approach where there
was none, like a wolf in the dead of night, lying in wait in
60 all the wind and rain by a pen full of sheep, and growling
at the gaps in the fence, while the lambs keep up their
bleating, safe beneath their mothers; beside himself with
anger he storms and rages but cannot reach them; he is
worn out by the ravening hunger he has been so long in
gathering and many a day has passed since blood wet his
throat – so did the Rutulian blaze with anger as he
surveyed the walls of the Trojan camp and the pain burned
him to the bone. How could he try to come at them?
70 What device could shake out the Trojans shut up there
behind their rampart and spill them on to the plain? Ah!
The fleet! There it was moored in a sheltered position
along the side of the camp, protected by the water of the
river, and to the landward by ramparts. There he made his
attack. Burning with fury himself he demanded fire from
his exultant comrades and took up a great blazing pine
torch in his hand. At this they all bent to the task, with
Turnus there to urge them on. They plundered what fires
they could find, and their reeking torches smouldered with
a pitchy light as Vulcan whirled to the stars dense clouds of
smoke shot through with sparks.

Tell me, Muses, what god turned these fierce flames
away from the Trojans and drove such fire from their
ships. The tale was told in times long past but the fame of
80 it will live for ever. When Aeneas was first building his
fleet on Mount Ida in Phrygia and preparing to take to the
high seas, Berecyntian Cybele herself, the Mother of the
Gods, is said to have addressed these words to great Jupiter:
'O my son, grant my prayer. Now that Olympus is

subdued, grant what your dear mother asks of you. On
top of my citadel I had a wood of pine trees which I had
loved for many years, a dark grove of black pine and
maple where men would bring their offerings. These trees
I gladly gave to the Trojan warrior when he needed a fleet,
but now my heart is seized by anxiety and dread. Put all
my fears at rest and answer your mother's prayer. Grant
that my ships should not be wrecked on any of their
voyages or overwhelmed by any squall of wind. Let it
stand to their favour that they were born on our mountains.' Her son, who turns the stars of heaven in their
courses, made this reply to his mother: 'What is this you
are calling on the Fates to do? What do these words of
yours mean? Are ships made by mortal hands to have
immortal rights? Is Aeneas to face all his doubts and
dangers and never know uncertainty? Is there any god to
whom such a privilege has been granted? No. But when
the ships have done their duty, when in due course they
reach the end of their voyaging and are safe in harbour
in Ausonia, each one to survive the sea and reach the
Laurentine fields with the Trojan leader will lose its mortal
shape. I shall order all of them to become goddesses of the
great ocean, like Galatea and Doto, daughters of Nereus,
whose breasts cleave the foam of the waves of the sea.'
Jupiter had spoken, ratifying his words by the waters of
the Styx, his brother's river, by the banks and dark whirlpools of that pitch-black torrent, and at his nod the whole
of Olympus shook.

And so the promised day had come and the Fates had
completed the allotted time, when the violent attack of
Turnus warned the Mother Goddess to defend her sacred
ships from these burning brands. A strange light now
shone before men's eyes and a great cloud seemed to cross
the sky from the east, bearing with it votaries of the
goddess from Mount Ida. A fearsome voice then fell from
the air and filled the ears of Trojans and Rutulians in their

armed ranks: 'Do not trouble, Trojans, to defend my ships.
Do not take your weapons in your hands. Turnus will
burn the sea dry before he can burn these sacred pine trees.
Go then! You are freed. Go, you goddesses of the sea! The
Mother of the Gods commands.' In an instant every ship
burst the ropes that moored it to the bank, and they
120 plunged like dolphins, beak first to the bottom. When they
returned to the surface, they were miraculously changed,
each one a nymph swimming in the sea.

The Rutulians were astonished. Messapus himself was
afraid and his horses reared. Even Tiber checked his flow
with a harsh roaring of his waters as he called back his
current from the sea. But the boldness and confidence of
Turnus never wavered. Without hesitation he set about
haranguing his men and whipping up their spirits: 'These
portents strike at the Trojans: they mean that Jupiter has
taken from them the help they have become accustomed
130 to. The ships did not wait to taste Rutulian fire and sword!
So now the seas are barred to the Trojans and they have no
hope of escape. By this they have lost one half of the
world, and the land is already in our hands, so many
thousands of men are marching under arms from all the
races of Italy. This Phrygian talk of destiny and the oracles
of the gods does not dismay me. Destiny and Venus were
satisfied the moment Trojans set foot on the fertile fields of
Italy. I too have a destiny, of a different sort – to cut down
with the sword this vicious people that has robbed me of
my bride. The sons of Atreus are not the only ones who
have suffered, and the people of Mycenae are not the only
140 men who can take up arms. Let them not imagine it is
enough to have been destroyed once! It should have been
enough for them to sin once. They had no need to show
loathing and contempt for every woman in the world.
Look at them now, all courage and confidence because of
this rampart that keeps us from them and these ditches
they have dug to hold us back. This is no sort of barrier to

stand between them and death. Did they not see the walls of
Troy settling into the flames? And those were fashioned by
the hands of Neptune. You are my chosen few. Which one
of you is ready to cut through their rampart with the sword
and rush into that camp of cowards? To fight Trojans I do
not need the armour Vulcan made for Achilles. I do not need
a thousand ships, not if every man in Etruria went and joined   150
them as allies this instant. Nor do they need to be frightened
of the dark. We shall not be creeping up on them like
cowards to kill the guards all over their citadel and steal their
Palladium. We shall not be hiding in the blind belly of a
horse. Our plan is to come in daylight in full view and gird
their walls with fire. I shall soon make sure they realize it is
not Greeks they have to deal with or the army of Pelasgians
Hector held off into a tenth year. But the best part of the day
is already spent. For what remains of it you can now rest
yourselves. You have done well. Be of good cheer, in high
hopes that we can bring them to battle.' Meanwhile Messapus   160
was given the task of blockading the gates with a night guard
and ringing the walls with watch-fires. Fourteen Rutulians
were chosen to keep watch on the walls, each commanding a
hundred men with purple crests on their helmets and gleaming with gold. They dispersed, some going to their various
duties, others lying out on the grass, enjoying their wine and
tipping up the bronze mixing bowls. The watch-fires burned
and the guards kept awake by gaming the night away.

The Trojans looked out on all this from the top of their
rampart and kept armed guards on all the high points
while anxiously checking the gates, building bridges to   170
their outlying fortlets, and bringing up missiles. Mnestheus
and the zealous Serestus never relaxed their vigilance. They
were the men Father Aeneas had appointed to take over
the command of the troops and the government of the
people should adversity require it. The whole legion was
on the alert along the walls. Lots had been cast for posts of
danger and each man was taking his turn to stand guard.

Nisus, son of Hyrtacus, was keeper of a gate. This
formidable warrior, swift to throw the spear or send the
arrow flying, had been sent by Ida, the hunters' mountain,
to be the comrade of Aeneas, and with him came his own
comrade, Euryalus, a boy with the first signs of manhood
180 on cheeks as yet unshaven. There was no lovelier youth
among the people of Aeneas, and no lovelier youth ever
put on Trojan armour. They were one in love, and side by
side they used to charge into battle. So now too, they were
sharing guard duty on the gate, when Nisus said to Euryalus: 'Is it the gods who put this ardour into our minds, or
does every man's irresistible desire become his god? My
mind is not content to rest in peace and quiet but has long
been driving me to rush into battle or into some great
enterprise. You see the Rutulians there with just a few
scattered lights piercing the darkness, how sure they are of
190 everything, lying sunk in sleep and wine, and silence
everywhere. Just listen to what I am thinking and to the
plan beginning to form in my mind. The people and the
fathers, they are all clamouring for Aeneas to be summoned
and messengers sent to tell him exactly what is happening.
If they promise to give you what I ask – all I want is credit
for the deed – I think I can find a way round the foot of
that hill to the city of Pallanteum.' Euryalus was overcome,
pierced to the heart with a great love of glory, and in an
instant he replied in these words to his ardent friend: 'So
200 you do not want me as your comrade on this great
expedition, and I am to let you go alone into dangers like
this? This is not how I was brought up by my father
Opheltes during the Greek terror and our sufferings at
Troy, and he knew all about war. Nor is this how I have
conducted myself with you, in following to the end the
Fates of great-hearted Aeneas. I have here a heart that
despises the light, that would gladly spend life to buy the
honour you are striving for.' To this Nisus replied: 'So
may great Jupiter, or whatever god looks with favour on

this undertaking, bring me back to you in triumph, I swear I never had any such fears about you. That would have been a sin. But if some chance or some god were to lead me into disaster – and you know how many things can happen in dangerous affairs like this – I would wish you to go on living. You are young and your claim on life is greater than mine. There would then be someone to consign my body to the earth if it is rescued from the battlefield or recovered by ransom, or if some fortune forbids that – and we know her ways – to make offerings for me here and honour me with an empty tomb. Besides, let me not be the cause of such heartbreak to your mother, who of all the mothers of Troy is the only one who has dared to follow her son here with never a thought for the walls of great Acestes.' 'One feeble argument after another,' replied Euryalus, 'and all to no purpose. My mind is made up and you have done nothing to change it. Let us go, and quickly.' So saying, he woke sentries to take over and keep guard for Nisus and himself. They left their post and marched off side by side to look for prince Ascanius.

Over the whole world the creatures of the earth were relaxed in sleep, all resting from their cares, and their hearts had forgotten their labours; but the chosen warriors who were the great leaders of the Trojans were holding a council on matters of the highest importance to the kingdom. What were they to do now? Who would go as a messenger to Aeneas? As they stood there on the level ground in the middle of the camp, leaning on their long spears and carrying their shields, Nisus and Euryalus suddenly arrived in great haste and asked to be admitted, saying that their business was urgent and well worth listening to. Seeing their excitement, Iulus was the first to welcome them and invited Nisus to speak. These were the words of the son of Hyrtacus: 'Give us a fair hearing, sons of Aeneas. Do not judge what is said by the age of the speakers. The Rutulians have fallen quiet, deep in their

drunken sleep, and we have seen a place for an ambush, some open ground where the two roads meet by the gate nearest the sea. There the ring of watch-fires is broken and the smoke is rising black to the stars. If you allow us to
240 take this opportunity to go and look for Aeneas and the city of Pallanteum, you will soon see us coming back laden with booty and much slaughter done. We have no doubts about the way to go. We always hunt there and have seen the first houses of the city in the dark valleys. We have explored the whole river.'

It was Aletes, heavy with years and mature in judgement, who now replied: 'O gods of our fathers, in whose divine hands Troy still remains, in spite of all, it is not your will utterly to destroy the Trojans, if you have put such firmness
250 of mind and heart into our young warriors,' and as he spoke he clasped the right hands of both of them and laid his hands on their shoulders while the tears ran down his cheeks and face: 'Can any recompense be found for you?' he cried. 'Can anything match the glorious deeds you propose? The first and richest reward will come from the gods and from your own virtue, but the others will soon follow from a grateful Aeneas, and young Ascanius for the rest of his life will never forget such a service.' 'More than that,' interposed Ascanius, 'my whole life hangs upon the
260 return of my father and I call upon you both to witness, by the great Penates and Lar of Assaracus, and the shrine of white-haired Vesta, I now place all my fortunes and all my hopes for the future in your hands, Nisus. Call back my father. Bring him back to my sight. If he is restored there can be no cause for grief. I shall give you two solid silver embossed cups which he took at the fall of Arisba, and with them a pair of tripods, two great talents of gold and an ancient mixing bowl given him by Dido of Sidon. But if he succeeds in taking Italy and winning the crown, while he is presiding over the distribution of booty in his hour of victory – you have seen the horse that Turnus rides, you

have seen him all golden in his armour – I shall exclude 270
from the lot that horse, the shield and the scarlet plumes,
and these will now be yours, Nisus, as your reward. In
addition my father will give you twelve chosen matrons
and twelve prisoners of war, each with his armour, and all
the lands on the plain now held by king Latinus. But as for
you, Euryalus, although you are a boy and not so far ahead
of myself in the race of life, I revere you and take you
wholly into my heart, embracing you as my comrade,
whatever may lie before us. Whatever I may do, I shall
look for no glory that is not shared with you. In war or in
peace, whatever I say or do, my whole trust will be placed 280
in you.'

To this Euryalus replied: 'The day shall never come
when I shall be found unequal to acts of courage like this,
if only the fall of fortune is in our favour tonight, and not
against us. But one thing I ask of you, more precious than
any gifts: I grieve for my mother of the ancient line of
Priam. The land of Troy could not hold her when she
came away with me, nor did the walls of king Acestes. As
I now leave her, she knows nothing of the danger I am
entering upon, whether it be great or small, and I have
taken no farewell of her because – and I swear it by the
Night and your own right hand – I could not bear to see
my mother weep. But comfort her in her helplessness, I 290
beg you, and support her in her desolation. Let me take
with me the hope that you will do this and I shall go all
the more boldly into whatever dangers lie before me.' The
Trojans were overcome and wept, the fair Iulus most of
all, as this image of his love for his own father touched his
heart, and he replied: 'You can be certain that everything I
do will be worthy of your great enterprise. Your mother
will be my mother in everything but the name Creusa.
The woman who gave birth to such a son will receive no
ordinary gratitude. I have promised you rewards when
you return in triumph. Whatever the outcome of your

300 bravery, I swear by this head of mine, by which my father
used to swear, that these same promises will hold good for
your mother and your kin.' So he spoke, weeping, and in
that moment he took from his shoulder a gilded sword
that Lycaon of Cnossus had fashioned with consummate
art and fitted in an ivory scabbard to hang perfectly at his
side, while Mnestheus gave Nisus a rough hide stripped
from a lion, and trusty Aletes changed helmets with him.
As soon as they were armed they marched off, and all the
310 leading Trojans, young and old, escorted them to the gates
with their prayers. Foremost among them was the fair
Iulus, bearing beyond his years a man's load of cares and a
man's spirit. He gave them many commissions to bear to
his father, but they were all futile. The wind scattered
them among the clouds.

They moved off and crossed the ditch, making their
way under cover of night to the camp that would be their
death, but not before they had brought death to many
others. They could see men sprawling in drunken sleep all
over the grass and chariots standing along the river bank
with their poles in the air and a tangle of men's bodies and
armour and wine vessels among the reins and wheels.
320 Nisus was the first to speak: 'Now, Euryalus,' he said, 'my
right hand must show its mettle. The hour calls out for it.
Our road goes this way. You keep guard to the rear in case
a party of men creeps up on us from behind, and look well
into the distance. I shall make havoc here and clear a broad
path for you.' So he spoke and then had done with words.
With sword drawn he made for proud Rhamnes who
happened to be propped up there on a deep pile of rugs,
his whole chest heaving as he slept. A king he was, and a
prophet cherished by a king, by Turnus. But not all his
prophesying could drive from him the plague of death.
Nisus then caught three of Rhamnes' attendants lying in a
330 heap among their weapons, then the armour-bearer of
Remus and his charioteer among the hooves of the horses.

Their heads were lolling. He cut them off. Next he removed the head of their master Remus and left the blood gurgling out of his trunk and warming the ground as the black gore soaked through the bedding. Lamyrus also he slew, and Lamus and young Serranus, a handsome youth who had gambled late into the night. There he lay overcome by all the wine of Bacchus he had drunk. He would have been happy if he could have made his gambling last the night and kept it up till daylight. Nisus was like a 340 lion driven mad with hunger and ravening through pens full of sheep, dumb with fear, while he growls from jaws dripping with blood as he mauls and champs their soft flesh.

Meanwhile there was no less slaughter from the hand of Euryalus. He too was in a blazing frenzy as he crept up on a great crowd of nameless warriors lying unconscious in his path, Fadus and Herbesus, Rhoetus and Abaris. Rhoetus was awake and saw it all, so hid in panic behind a great mixing bowl. But when Euryalus came near him, he rose and Euryalus plunged his sword to the hilt in his chest. When he withdrew it, the whole life of Rhoetus flooded out after it. As he lay there dying, still vomiting his crimson life's breath and bringing up wine and gore to- 350 gether, Euryalus was already prowling on, hot for blood. He was soon making for Messapus and his comrades, where he saw the dying embers of the watch-fires and the horses tethered in good order cropping the grass, when Nisus had a few words to say to him – for he noticed that Euryalus was being carried away by bloodlust and greed: 'Let us make an end,' he said. 'Daylight is no friend of ours and it will soon be here. Our enemies have taken enough punishment and we have cut our path through the middle of them.' They left behind them many pieces of men's armour wrought in solid silver, and mixing bowls besides, and lovely rugs, but Euryalus took Rhamnes' medallions and his gold-studded belt. Long ago the wealthy Caedicus 360

had sent them from his home as gifts to Remulus of
Tibur to form a guest-friendship with him. When Remulus
was dying, he gave them to his grandson, and after his
death they passed to the Rutulians as spoils of war. Euryalus
now snatched them up and put them round his brave
shoulders, but little good were they to do him. He also put
on the helmet of Messapus with its gorgeous plumes, and
they left the camp and made for safety.

At this moment, while the rest of the Latin army was
waiting in battle order on the plain, a detachment of
cavalry had been sent out from their city and was now on
370 its way with dispatches to Turnus, three hundred of them,
all carrying shields, under the command of Volcens. They
were approaching the camp and coming up to its ramparts
when they saw Nisus and Euryalus in the distance, veering
off along the road to the left. Euryalus had forgotten about
the helmet, and its glittering betrayed him, reflecting the
rays of the moon in the dim shadows of the night. The
enemy saw and did not fail to act. 'Halt there, you men!'
shouted Volcens from the head of his column. 'Why are
you on the road? Who are you? Why are you armed?
Where are you going?' They offered no reply, but ran off
into the trees, putting their trust in the darkness of the
380 night. The horsemen spread out along each side of the
wood they knew so well, blocking the tracks that led in,
and putting guards on every approach. It was a rough
wood full of dense undergrowth and dark ilex trees, all of
it choked with thick brambles, and the path glimmered
only here and there among the faint tracks left by animals.
Euryalus was held back by the darkness under the trees and
by the weight of his booty, and in his fright he lost his
way. But Nisus escaped. Without knowing it he had come
through the enemy and the area later to be known as
Alban, taking its name from the city of Alba, but in
those days king Latinus had high-fenced enclosures there
for his cattle. He now stopped and looked back for his

friend, but could not see him. 'Poor Euryalus,' he cried. ₃₉₀
'Where have I left you? Where can I look for you?' and
even as he spoke, he was beginning to go back over his
path through the wood with all its deceptive twists and
turns, retracing every remembered step as he wandered
through the silent undergrowth. He heard horses. He heard
the noise of the pursuers and their signals, and in no time
shouts reached his ears and he saw Euryalus. Lost in the
treacherous darkness of the wood and confused by the
sudden tumult, he had been caught by the whole enemy
troop and was now being carried off, still struggling desperately against all the odds. What was Nisus to do? How
could he rescue his young friend? How should he attack? ₄₀₀
What weapons could he use? Should he throw himself into
the thick of their swords and rush through wound upon
wound to a glorious death? In that instant he drew back his
arm, and brandishing his throwing spear, he looked up to
the moon in heaven and prayed in these words: 'O goddess,
daughter of Latona, O glory of the stars and guardian of
the groves, be with me now and help me in my hour of
trouble. If ever my father Hyrtacus has offered gifts for me
at your altars, if ever I myself have enriched them with the
spoils of my hunting, hanging my offerings in the dome of
your temple or nailing them on your holy gables, guide
my weapons through the air and grant that I may throw
this troop of my enemies into confusion.' When he had ₄₁₀
spoken, he hurled his spear with the whole force of his
body. Parting the shadows of the night it flew towards
Sulmo, whose back was turned, and there it struck and
broke, sending a splinter through his diaphragm. He rolled
over, vomiting a stream of warm blood from his chest in
the chill of death, and heaving his flanks in deep-drawn
agonies. While the enemy were looking round in all directions, there was Nisus, emboldened by his success, with
another shaft ready by his ear, poised to aim. They were
still in tumult when the spear came whistling and caught

Tagus in the middle of the forehead, went through the
420 brain, and stuck there, growing warm. Volcens was wild
with rage, but nowhere could he see the thrower and he
could not decide where to direct the fury of his assault.
'Never mind!' he shouted. 'For the moment, you and your
warm blood will pay me for both of them!' and he drew
his sword and rushed at Euryalus. This was too much for
Nisus. Out of his mind with terror and unable to endure
his anguish, he broke cover, shouting at the top of his
voice: 'Here I am! Here I am! I am the one who did it!
Aim your weapons at me, you Rutulians! The whole
scheme was mine. He is innocent. He could not have done
it. I swear by this sky above me and the stars who know
430 the truth, his only offence is to have loved the wrong
friend too much!' He was still speaking as the sword was
driven through the ribs of Euryalus, full force, shattering
his white breast. He rolled on the ground in death, the
blood flowed over his beautiful body, his neck grew limp
and the head drooped on his shoulders, like a scarlet flower
languishing and dying when its stem has been cut by the
plough, or like poppies bowing their heads when the rain
burdens them and their necks grow weary. But Nisus
rushed into the thick of the enemy, looking only for
440 Volcens. Volcens was the only thought in his mind. The
Rutulians gathered round their leader and in close fighting
threw Nisus back again and again as he came at them from
one side after another, but he bore on none the less,
whirling a sword like lightning till he met the Rutulian
face to face and buried it in his mouth as he opened it to
shout. So, in the moment of his own dying, he cut off the
breath of his enemy. Then, pierced through and through,
he hurled himself on the dead body of his friend and rested
there at last in the peace of death.

Fortune has favoured you both! If there is any power in
my poetry, the day will never come when time will erase
you from the memory of man, while the house of Aeneas

remains by the immovable rock of the Capitol and the
Father of the Romans still keeps his empire.

The victorious Rutulians had collected their booty and   450
their spoils and carried the body of Volcens to their camp,
weeping as they went. There was no less sorrow waiting
for them there, when they found Rhamnes dead, and with
him Serranus and Numa and all their other leaders who
had been killed in that one night of slaughter. A great
crowd gathered round the dead and dying heroes and the
ground was running with rivers of newly shed blood, still
warm and foaming. Between them they recognized the
spoils, the shining helmet of Messapus, and the medallions
which had cost so much sweat to recover.

By now Aurora was just leaving the saffron bed of
Tithonus and sprinkling her new light upon the world. The   460
sun was soon streaming over the earth and soon all things
stood revealed in its light. Turnus, in full armour himself,
was rousing his men to arm, and each of the leaders was
taking his own troop into battle in ranks of bronze, whipping up their anger with different accounts of the night's
work. They even stuck the heads of Euryalus and Nisus on
spears – what a sight that was! – and paraded along behind
them shouting. Aeneas' men, long-enduring, drew up in
battle order to face them on the walls on their left flank –
the right was guarded by the river – and they manned   470
their great ditches and stood on their high towers stricken
with grief and shocked by the sight of the heads of the
comrades they knew so well, impaled on spears and dripping black gore.

Meanwhile Rumour flew with the news on her swift
wings through the whole terrified city of the Trojans, and
came gliding into the ears of the mother of Euryalus. In
that instant the warmth left her very bones, the shuttle was
dashed from her fingers and its thread unwound. Crazed
with grief she rushed out, and wailing as women do and
tearing her hair, she made for the front ranks of the army

on the walls. With no thought for the presence of men,
480 with no thought of the danger of flying weapons, she
stood there on the ramparts and filled heaven with her
cries of mourning: 'Is this you I am looking at, Euryalus?
How could you leave me alone, so cruelly, you who were
the last comfort of my old age? Could not your poor
mother have been allowed a few last words with you,
before you went on that dangerous expedition? So now
you lie in a strange land, and your body is food for the
dogs and the birds of Latium! I am your mother and did
not walk before you at your funeral; nor close your eyes,
nor wash your wounds, nor cover you with the robe I
have been weaving for you day and night with what speed
I could, finding in my loom some solace for the cares of
490 age. Where am I to go to look for you, my son? What
piece of earth holds your mutilated body and dismembered
limbs? Is this head all you bring back to me? Is that what I
have followed over land and sea? Strike me, you Rutulians,
if you have any human feelings! Throw all your spears at
me! Let me be the first to die. Or will you take pity on
me, Great Father of the Gods, and blast my detested body
into Tartarus with your lightning, since I can find no other
way to end this bitter life?' Sorrow like this was too much
for the Trojans to bear. The sound of mourning was heard
all through the army. Their strength was broken. They
were losing their appetite for battle and her presence was
500 fanning the flames of their grief. At a word from Ilioneus
and the bitterly weeping Iulus, Idaeus and Actor came and
took her between them back into her house.

The ringing bronze of the trumpet gave out its shrill and
terrible note from close at hand. The shouting rose and the
heavens bellowed in reply. The Volsci all at once rushed
the walls with their shields locked in tortoise formation
and tried to fill in the ditches and tear down the rampart.
Some were looking for a point of access and putting up
scaling ladders where the line of defenders was strung out

along the walls, and light could be seen in the breaks
between them. From their side the Trojans showered down 510
missiles of every kind, and pushed the ladders off with
stout poles – in their long war they had learned how to
defend walls – and they rolled great heavy rocks down on
the enemy to try to break their armoured formations, but
in their close-packed tortoise they cheerfully endured whatever fell on them. But they still did not succeed. For where
a solid mass of Rutulians was threatening the walls, the
Trojans rolled along a huge block of stone and sent it
crashing down on them to loosen their interlocking shields
and cut a great swathe through them. After this the bold
Rutulians no longer cared to fight blind under cover of
their shields but strove to clear the defenders off the
ramparts with a barrage of missiles. At another section of 520
the wall Mezentius was brandishing a torch of Etruscan
pine and a fearful sight he was as he came at them with fire
and smoke. Messapus, son of Neptune and tamer of horses,
was cutting a way through the rampart and shouting for
scaling ladders.

I pray to you, Calliope, and to your sister Muses, to
breathe upon me as I sing of the death and destruction
wrought by the sword of Turnus and to tell who sent
down to Orcus each warrior that died. Unroll with me
now the mighty scroll of war.

There was a tower, well placed and of commanding 530
height, with high connecting bridges. The Latins were
trying to take it by main force, striving with all their
powers to bring it down, while the Trojans packed inside
tried to defend it by throwing rocks and sending a hail
of weapons through the loopholes. Turnus, who was leading the attack, hurled a blazing torch which set fire to
the side of the tower. Fanned by the wind, the flames took
hold of the planking and ate into the upright posts. Inside
all was confusion, terror and desperate attempts to escape
the heat. As everyone crowded together to take refuge on

540 the side away from the flames, all at once the whole sky
seemed to thunder and the tower toppled over with the
weight, and men plunged to the ground in their death
throes with the massive fabric following them down, impal-
ing them on their own weapons and driving the broken
timbers through their breasts. Only Helenor and Lycus
were able to escape. Helenor was a young man, son of the
king of Maeonia and the slave girl Licymnia, who had
reared him in secret and sent him to Troy under arms
although this had been forbidden. His equipment was
light, a sword with no scabbard and an inglorious shield of
plain white, and he found himself caught in the middle of
the thousands of men who fought with Turnus, looking at
550 the battle lines of the Latins drawn up on all sides of him,
like a wild beast trapped in a dense ring of hunters; it rages
against the steel, and with full understanding it hurls itself
to its death by springing on to the hunting spears – just so
did young Helenor leap into the middle of his enemies,
rushing to his death where he saw the steel was thickest.
But Lycus was far fleeter of foot. He ran the gauntlet of
the enemy and their weapons as far as the wall. There as he
was trying to take hold of the top of the outworks and
reach the outstretched hands of his comrades, Turnus, who
560 had been pursuing him with his javelin, came to gloat over
him: 'You fool! Did you think you could escape my
hands?' and even as he shouted, he seized hold of him
where he hung and tore him down, taking a great section
of the wall with him, like the eagle, the armour-bearer of
Jupiter, seizing in his hooked talons a hare or the white
body of a swan and soaring into the air with it; or like the
wolf of Mars tearing a lamb out of the sheep pen, and loud
and long will be the bleating of its mother, as she looks for
it.

The shouting rose on every side. The attackers levelled
the rampart, filled in the ditch and tossed blazing torches
570 high on to the roofs. Lucetius, who was coming to set fire

to a gate, was laid low by a rock thrown by Ilioneus, a huge block torn out of a mountain. Liger felled Emathion with a javelin; Asilas brought down Corynaeus with an arrow he never saw in all its long flight. Caeneus slew Ortygius; Turnus slew the victorious Caeneus; Turnus also slew Itys and Clonius, Dioxippus and Promolus, then Sagaris and Idas, who was standing out in front of the highest towers. Privernus was killed by Capys: Themillas had first grazed him with a light spear and the fool had thrown his shield away to put his hand to the wound. So the winged arrow flew and, plunging deep into his left side, it broke the passages of his life's breath with a mortal 580 wound. The son of Arcens stood there in gorgeous armour, resplendent in his embroidered cloak and Spanish purple, a noble sight to see. He had been sent to war by his father, who had reared him in the grove of Mars on the banks of the river Symaethus where the people of Sicily made their offerings at the rich altar of the mild god Palicius. Mezentius laid down his spears. Then, whirling his sling three times round his head, he shot the hissing bolt and struck the son of Arcens full in the middle of the forehead. Melting in its flight, the lead bullet split his skull and stretched him full length on the sand.

It was then, men say, that Ascanius first shot in war the 590 swift arrow which till this time had only driven wild animals to terror and flight, and his was the hand that laid the brave Numanus low. This was a warrior whose family name was Remulus, and not long before he had been joined in marriage to the younger sister of Turnus. His heart was swollen with pride at the royal rank he had newly acquired, and he stepped out in front of the battle line, swaggering and shouting abuse, some fit and some unfit to be repeated: 'You have been sacked twice already, you Phrygians! Are you not ashamed to be cooped up again in a siege behind ramparts with only a wall between yourselves and death! Are you the men who came here to 600

fight us for our brides? Is it some god that has driven you
to Italy? Or some madness? You will not find here the sons
of Atreus or the fictions and fine words of Ulixes! We are
men of a hardy stock. We take our babies down to the
river the moment they are born and harden them in the
icy water. Our boys stay awake all night and weary
the woods with their hunting. For games they ride horses
and stretch the bow to the arrow. Our men endure
610 hard labour and live spare, subduing the land with the
mattock and shaking the towns of their enemies with war.
We are worn hard by iron all our lives and turn our spears
to goad our oxen. There is no sluggish old age for us to
impair the strength and vigour of our minds. We crush
our grey hair into the helmet, and our delight is always to
bring home new plunder and live off what we take. But
you like your clothes dyed with yellow saffron and the
bright juice of the purple fish. Your delight is in dancing
and idleness. You have sleeves to your tunics and ribbons
to keep your bonnets on. You are Phrygian women, not
Phrygian men! Away with you over the heights of Mount
Dindymus, where you can hear your favourite tunes on
the double pipe. The tambourines are calling you and the
boxwood fifes of the Berecyntian Mother of Mount Ida.
620 Leave weapons to the men. Make way for the iron of our
swords.'

   So he hurled his abuse and threats till Ascanius could
endure it no longer. Turning to face him, he drew his bow
and stretched the horsegut string, and as he stood there
with his arms straining wide apart, he prayed first to
Jupiter with this vow: 'All-powerful Jupiter, bless now this
my first trial of arms, and with my own hands I shall bring
yearly offerings to your temple and set before your altar a
milk-white bullock, with gilded horns, holding its head as
high as its mother's, already butting with its horns and
630 kicking up the sand with its hooves.' The Father heard and
thundered on the left from a clear sky, and the sound of

the death-dealing bow of Ascanius mingled with the sound of the thunder. The arrow had been drawn back, and it flew with a fearful hiss straight through the head of Remulus, its iron point piercing his hollow temples. 'Go, Remulus!' he cried, 'and mock brave men with proud words! This is the reply to the Rutulians from the twice-sacked Phrygians!' Ascanius said no more than this, but the Trojans followed it with a shout of joy, their spirits raised to the skies.

At that moment Apollo, the youthful god, whose hair is never cut, chanced to be seated on a cloud, looking down from the expanse of heaven on the armies and cities of Italy, and he addressed these words to the victorious Iulus: 'You have become a man, young Iulus, and we salute you! This is the way that leads to the stars. You are born of the gods and will live to be the father of gods. Justice demands that all the wars that Fate will bring will come to an end under the offspring of Assaracus. Troy is not large enough for you.' At these words he plunged down from the heights of heaven, parting the breathing winds, and made for Ascanius, taking on the features of old Butes. Butes had once been armour-bearer to the Dardan Anchises and the trusted guard of his door, and Aeneas had then appointed him as companion to his son Ascanius. This was the guise in which Apollo came, the old man Butes to the life – voice, colouring, white hair, weapons grimly clanking – and these were the words he spoke to Iulus in the flush of his victory: 'Let that be enough, son of Aeneas. Numanus has fallen to your arms and you are unhurt. Great Apollo has granted you this first taste of glory and does not grudge you arrows as sure as his own. You must ask for no more, my boy, in this war.' So began Apollo, but while speaking, he left the sight of men, fading from their eyes into the insubstantial air. The Trojan leaders recognized the god. They knew his divine arrows and the quiver that sounded as he flew. So, although Ascanius was thirsting for

battle, they held him back, urging upon him the words of
Phoebus Apollo and the will of the god. But they themselves went back into battle and put their lives into naked
danger. The shouting rang round the ramparts all along
the walls. They bent their deadly bows and twisted their
spear thongs till the ground was strewn with missiles.
Shield and round helmet rang with the blows as fiercer and
fiercer raged the battle. It was like a great shower from the
west drumming on the earth in the rainy season when the
Kids are rising, or like hailstones dropping from the clouds
670 into the sea when the south wind is blowing and Jupiter
hurls down squalls of rain in his fury and bursts the hollow
thunderclouds in the sky.

Pandarus and Bitias, sons of Alcanor of Mount Ida, had
been brought up by the wood nymph Iaera in the grove of
Jupiter and they were built like the pines and mountains
of their fatherland. So sure were they of their weapons that
they now flung open the gate that had been entrusted to
them by their leader's commands, and took it upon themselves to invite the enemy to come within the walls. They
themselves stood inside at the ready, like twin towers, one
on the right and one on the left, armed in steel, with their
crests flashing high on their heads. They were like a pair
680 of tall oaks by a flowing river, on the banks of the Po or
by the lovely Adige, holding their unshorn heads up to the
sky with their high tops nodding in the breeze. As soon as
they saw the gate open, the Rutulians came bursting in.
Quercens and Aquiculus in splendid armour, impetuous
Tmarus and Haemon, son of Mars, but instantly with all
their men they either turned and ran or gave up their lives
on the very threshold of the gate. The fury mounted in all
their hearts as they fought. Trojans now came crowding
690 to the spot and not only joined in the fray but also dared to
sally out further and further in front of the gate.

Meanwhile Turnus, the Rutulian commander, was
raging and storming and creating havoc in another part of

the field, when a message arrived to say that the enemy
were hot with the Rutulian blood they were now spilling
and that open gates were on offer. Turnus instantly abandoned the work he had in hand and rushed to the Trojan
gate in a savage rage to meet these arrogant brothers. The
first man to fall to his javelin was Antiphates – for he was
the first to confront him. Antiphates was the bastard son of
great Sarpedon by a Theban mother. The spear of Italian
cornel wood flew through the unresisting air, went in by   700
his belly and twisted upwards deep into his chest. A wave
of frothing blood welled out of the black hole of the
wound, and the steel grew warm where it had lodged in
the lung. Then Erymas and Meropes fell to his hand; then
Aphidnus; then Bitias himself for all the fire that flashed
from his eyes and the roaring fury of his heart. No javelin
for him. He was not the man to yield his life to a javelin. It
was an artillery spear with an iron head a cubit long and a
ball of lead at its butt which came rifling through the air
with a loud hiss and the force of a thunderbolt. The two
bull-hides of his shield did not resist it, nor did his trusty
breastplate with its overlapping scales of gold. His huge
body collapsed and fell. The earth groaned and the mighty
shield thundered as it came down on top of him. It was
like the fall of a stone pile by the shore at Euboean Baiae;   710
men first build it to its massive height and then they let it
down into the sea, and it spreads ruin all along its length,
grinding the sea-bed as it settles in the shallows; the water
boils, the black sand rises, the high rock of Procida is
shaken, and Inarime with it, the hard bed laid for Typhoeus
at Jupiter's command.

Now Mars, mighty in war, put new spirit and strength
into the Latins and twisted a sharp goad into their flesh,
while sending Flight and black Fear upon the Trojans.
Now that their chance had come to fight, the Latins   720
gathered from all sides and the God of War stormed their
hearts. When Pandarus saw his brother stretched out in

death and knew how his fortunes stood and the turn events were taking, he put his broad shoulder to the gate with all his force and heaved it shut on its hinges, leaving many of his own people cut off outside the walls with a hard battle to fight, but taking in those who came running, and shutting them in with himself. Fool that he was! He did not see the Rutulian king bursting into the city in the middle of the press. By his own act he penned him in like a

730 great tiger among helpless cattle. In that instant a new light shone from the eyes of Turnus. He clashed his armour with a fearsome noise, the blood-red crest trembled on his head, his shield flashed lightning. Suddenly Aeneas' men recognized him – the hated face, the huge body – and were thrown into confusion. But the giant Pandarus leapt forward to confront him, burning with anger at the death of his brother: 'This is not your bridal chamber in the palace of Amata!' he shouted. 'Turnus is not safe in the middle of Ardea behind his father's walls. This is the camp of your

740 enemies and there is no way out.' Turnus replied, smiling calmly: 'If there is any courage in you, then come and fight. You will soon be able to tell Priam that here too you found an Achilles!' At these words Pandarus took a spear of rough, knotted wood with its bark unplaned and hurled it with all his force. As it flew to wound Turnus, the winds caught it, Juno deflected it and it lodged in the gate. 'You will not escape this weapon of mine,' called out Turnus, 'which I brandish here in my right hand. This sword is wielded by a different arm, and gives a deeper wound.' With these words he lifted it above his head, rising with it,

750 and struck Pandarus between the temples. The blade went straight through the middle of the forehead and parted the smooth, young cheeks. The wound was hideous. He fell with a crash and the ground shook with the weight of him. As he lay dying he strewed around his nerveless limbs and armour blooded with brains, and the two halves of his head hung on his two shoulders.

The Trojans turned and ran in terror. If at that moment
the victor had thought of breaking the bolts and letting his
comrades in through the gates, that would have been the 760
end of the war and the end of the Trojan race, but instead
his mad lust for blood drove him upon his enemies in an
ecstasy of passion. First he caught Phaleris and Gyges,
slitting his hamstrings. He then took their spears, and with
Juno lending him strength and spirit, he hurled them into
the backs of the retreating enemy. Next he sent Halys to
keep them company and Phegeus, the spear passing
through his shield; then Alcander, Halius, Noemon and
Prytanis, who were on the walls in the thick of battle and
did not know he was inside. Now Lynceus was coming at
him and calling on his comrades for help. Turnus from the
rampart on his right stopped him short with one flashing 770
stroke of his sword, a blow from close range that severed
the head and sent it flying far from the body, helmet and
all. Next he brought down Amycus, that mighty hunter
and slayer of wild beasts – no man better to charge the
spear-point with poison or smear the tip of the arrow; then
Clytius, son of Aeolus, and Cretheus, that dear companion
of the Muses, Cretheus, a great lover of song and of the
lyre, a great setter of poems to the strings, always singing
of horses and armour and the battles of heroes.

At last the Trojan leaders, Mnestheus and the bold
Serestus, hearing of the slaughter of their men, came on
the scene to find their allies scattering and the enemy 780
within the walls. 'Where are you running to now, citizens?'
cried Mnestheus. 'Where is there to go? What other walls
have you? What other defences when you leave these? Can
one man, and one man hemmed in on every side by your
ramparts, cause all this slaughter and send so many of your
best fighting men to their deaths all over your city, and
still live? Have you no spirit? Have you no shame? No
thought for your fatherland in its anguish, for your ancient
gods or for great Aeneas?' These words fired them. They

rallied and held fast in close formation while Turnus
790 gradually began to disengage, making for the river and the
part of the camp in the bend of the river. Seeing this the
Trojans laid on all the harder, shouting at the top of their
voices and crowding him like a pack of huntsmen with
levelled spears pressing hard on a savage lion; the lion is
afraid and gives ground, but he is still dangerous, still
glaring at his attackers; his anger and his courage forbid
him to turn tail, and though he would dearly love to, he
cannot charge through the wall of steel and the press of
men — just so did Turnus give ground, uncertain but
800 unhurried, and his mind was boiling with rage. Twice he
even hurled himself into the middle of his enemies, breaking their ranks and sending them flying along the walls,
but a whole army came together in a rush against him
from the camp, and Juno, daughter of Saturn, did not dare
to renew his strength to withstand them, for Jupiter sent
Iris down from the sky bearing stern commands through
the air for his sister Juno if Turnus did not withdraw from the
high walls of the Trojans. So sword-arm and shield were
of no avail. The warrior could no longer stand his ground
in the hail of weapons that overwhelmed him from every
side. The helmet rang and rang again on his hollow
temples and the solid bronze was cracked by rocks. The
810 plumes were torn from his head and the boss of his shield
gave way under the blows. The Trojans doubled their
barrage and the spear of Mnestheus was like the lightning.
Sweat poured off the whole body of Turnus like a river of
pitch and he was given no breathing space. His lungs were
heaving. He was shaking and sick with weariness. Then,
and only then, he dived head first into the river in full
armour. The Tiber took him when he came into his
yellow tide, bore him up in his soft waves, washing away
the blood of slaughter, and gave him back in high heart to
his comrades.

IO

PALLAS AND MEZENTIUS

Meanwhile the house of All-powerful Olympus was thrown open and the Father of Gods and King of Men summoned a council to his palace among the stars, from whose steep heights he looked down upon all the lands of the earth, upon the Trojan camp and the peoples of Latium. The gods sat in their chamber open east and west to the light, and Jupiter began to speak: 'O great dwellers in the sky, why have you gone back on your word? Why do you contend with such bitterness of heart? I had forbidden Italy to clash with the Trojans. Why is there discord against my express command? What has made them afraid and induced them to take up arms and make each other draw the sword? The time will come for war – there is no need to hasten it – when barbarous Carthage will let destruction loose upon the citadels of Rome, opening up the Alps and sending them against Italy. That will be the time for pillaging, and for hate to vie with hate. But now let it be. A treaty has been decided upon. Accept it, and be content.'

These were the few words spoken by Jupiter, but when golden Venus replied, her words were not few: 'O Father, imperishable power over men and over all the world – how could there be any other to whom we might address our prayers? – you see the Rutulians rampant and Turnus riding in glory in the midst of them, swollen with the success of his arms. A closed ring of fortifications no longer offers protection to the Trojans. They now have to fight

hand to hand inside their gates, even on the ramparts of
their walls, and their ditches are swimming with blood.
Aeneas is far away and knows nothing of this. Will you
never allow them to be free of besiegers? Even as Troy is
being reborn, a new enemy is threatening its walls with a
new army behind him, and from Arpi the Aetolian Diomede is once more rising against the Trojans. I suppose I
30 shall soon be wounded again – after all, mortals are at war
and your daughter stands in their way!

'If the Trojans have come to Italy without your approval,
in defiance of your heavenly will, they must be punished
for their sins and you must not raise a finger to help them.
But if they have obeyed all the commands they have
received from the gods above and the shades below, how
can anyone overturn what you have ordered or fashion a
new destiny? You have seen their ships burned on the
shores of my own son Eryx. You have seen the king of the
storms and the raging winds roused out of their Aeolian
island. You have seen Iris driven down from the clouds.
40 And now she even turns to the one remaining part of the
world and stirs up the powers below – Allecto has suddenly
been let loose upon the earth and has run wild through all
the cities in the middle of Italy! I no longer give a thought
to empire. That was our hope, as you well know, while
our fortunes remained. But those who must prevail are
those you wish to prevail. If there is no region on earth
that your cruel queen could concede to the Trojans, I beg
of you, Father, by the smoking ruins of the sacred city of
Troy, allow Ascanius to have a safe discharge from battle.
Allow your own daughter's grandson to live. As for
Aeneas, let him be tossed by storms in unknown waters
50 and go the road that Fortune gives him, but grant me the
power to protect Ascanius and take him out of this fearful
battle. I have Amathus. I have lofty Paphos, and Cythera,
and my palace at Idalium. Let him lay down his arms and
live out his life in obscurity, while you give the order for

Italy to be crushed beneath the mighty empire of Carthage.
The cities of Tyre will have nothing to fear from Ascanius.
What good has it done him to escape the plague of war
and come safe through the middle of all the fires lit by the
Greeks, to have drained the cup of danger on the sea and
over all the earth while the Trojans have been searching
for Latium and a new Pergamum? Would it not have been
better for them to settle on the dead ashes of their native
land, on the soil that was once Troy? Take pity on them, I   60
beg you, and if the wretched Trojans must live again the
fall of Troy, give them back their Xanthus and their
Simois.'

At this Juno, Queen of Heaven, burst out, wild with
rage: 'Why do you force me to break my deep silence?
The scars have formed over my wounds. Why do you
make me speak and reopen them? Neither man nor god
compelled Aeneas to choose the ways of war and confront
king Latinus as an enemy. We are told he has the authority
of the Fates for coming to Italy. The Fates, indeed! He was
goaded into it by the ravings of Cassandra! And did we
urge him to abandon his camp or put his life at the mercy
of the winds? Did we advise him to entrust his fortifications 70
and the whole management of the war to a boy? To
disturb the loyalty of the Etruscans and stir up a peaceful
people? Was it a god that drove him to dishonesty? Was it
some cruel power of mine? Where is Juno in all this?
Where is Iris sent down from the clouds? It is wrong, we
hear, for Italians to ring Troy with fire at the moment of
its birth, and for Turnus to take his stand in the land of his
fathers, Turnus, whose grandfather was Pilumnus and
whose mother was the goddess Venilia. Why then is it
right for Trojans to raise the black-smoking torches of war
against Latins, to put other men's lands under their yoke,
to carry off plunder, to pick and choose who are to be
their fathers-in-law, to tear brides from their mothers' laps
and to hold out the olive branch of peace with their   80

weapons fixed on the high sterns of their ships? You can steal Aeneas away from the hands of the Greeks, and where there was a man you can spread a cloud with empty winds. You can change ships into sea nymphs. Is it an impiety if we in our turn have given some help to the Rutulians? Aeneas, you tell us, is far away and knows nothing of all this. Keep him in ignorance and let him stay away! You have Paphos and Idalium. You have the heights of Cythera. Why do you concern yourself with those rough-hearted Italians and their city teeming with war? You claim we are trying to overturn from the foundations the tottering fortunes of these Phrygians from Troy. No!

90 Who was it who put your wretched Trojans at the mercy of the Greeks? What caused Europe and Asia to rise in arms and betray the sacred ties of friendship? Was I in the lead when the Trojan adulterer stormed the walls of Sparta? Did I hand him his weapons? Was it I who kindled the fires of war with lust? That was when you should have feared for your people. Now, when it is too late, you get to your feet with these complaints and lies, and hurl this empty abuse.'

As Juno was making her plea, all the gods began to murmur in support or in dissent. It was like the murmuring of a storm when the first breeze is caught in a wood and the rustling rolls through the trees unseen, warning sailors

100 that winds are on the way. Then the All-powerful Father, the highest power in all the universe, began to speak, and at his voice the lofty palace of the gods fell silent, the earth trembled to its foundations and the heights of heaven were hushed. The winds in that moment were stilled and the sea kept its waves at peace. 'So be it,' he said. 'Hear my words and lay them to your hearts. Since you have not allowed the people of Ausonia to be joined in a treaty with the Trojans, and since there is no end to this discord of yours, this day let each man face his own fortune and set his course by his own hopes. Trojan and Rutulian I shall treat

alike. Whether this camp is blockaded by the destiny of 110
Italy or because of the folly and wickedness of the Trojans
and false prophecies they have received, as each man has set
up his loom, so will he endure the labour and the fortune
of it – I do not exempt the Rutulians. Jupiter is the same
king to all men. The Fates will find their way.' Then,
swearing an oath by the waves of the Styx, his brother's
river, by the banks and dark whirlpools of that pitch-black
torrent, he nodded and his nod shook the whole of
Olympus. There were no more words. He rose from his
golden throne, and the heavenly gods thronged around
him and escorted him to the threshold.

The Rutulians meanwhile were fighting hard round
each of the gates to bring down their enemies in blood and
ring their walls with fire, while Aeneas' legion was trapped 120
inside its own ramparts with no hope of escape. Helpless
and desperate, they stood on their high towers and manned
the circle of their walls with a thin line of defenders. Asius,
son of Imbrasus, Thymoetes, son of Hicetaon, the two
Assaraci and old Thymbris alongside Castor were there
in the forefront of the battle, and the two brothers of
Sarpedon were with them, Clarus and Thaemon from the
mountains of Lycia. Acmon of Lyrnesus, as great a warrior
as his father Clytius or his brother Mnestheus, was putting
out all his strength to carry a boulder, no small part of a
mountain, while they strove to defend their camp by
throwing rocks and javelins, or hurling fire and fitting 130
arrows to the string. There in the middle of them, with his
noble head bared, stood the boy Ascanius for whom the
goddess Venus cares above all others, and rightly cares. He
was like a gem sparkling in its gold setting, an adornment
for a head or neck, or like glowing ivory skilfully inlaid in
boxwood or Orician terebinth, and his long hair lay on his
milk-white neck, held in place by a circlet of soft gold.
There too was Ismarus. The warriors of those great-hearted
peoples could see him tipping his arrows with poison and 140

aiming them at the enemy. He was the offshoot of a noble house in Maeonia where men worked the rich lands and the river Pactolus watered them with gold. Mnestheus also was there, raised to the heights of glory for his recent repulse of Turnus out of the ring of the walls; Capys, too, who gives his name to the city of Capua in Campania.

These were the men who clashed that day in bitter fighting. In the middle of the night that followed, Aeneas was ploughing the waves of the ocean. After leaving king Evander, he had entered the Etruscan camp and gone to their king to tell him his name and nation, what he 150 wanted, what he offered and what armed forces Mezentius was winning to his support. He told him too of the violent passions of Turnus and reminded him that in human affairs there is no room for certainty, and to all this he added his appeal for help. Tarchon instantly joined forces with him and made a treaty. Then these Etruscans, these men of Lydian stock, having paid their debts to destiny, put to sea and committed themselves to a foreign leader in accordance with the will of the gods. Aeneas' ship took the lead. Phrygian lions were yoked to it for a beak, and above them the figurehead was Mount Ida, a sight most dear to the Trojan exiles. Here sat great Aeneas, turning over in 160 his mind the varied chances of war, and all the while young Pallas stayed close by his left side, asking him now about the stars and the course they were steering through the darkness of the night, now about all he had suffered by land and sea.

Now goddesses, it is time to open up Mount Helicon, to set your songs in motion and tell of the army which came that night with Aeneas from the shores of Etruria, to say who fitted out the ships and who sailed in them across the ocean.

Massicus was the first, cutting through the water on the bronze-plated *Tiger*. Under him sailed a band of a thousand warriors who had left behind them the walls of Clusium

and the city of Cosae. Their weapons were arrows carried
in light quivers on their shoulders, and death-dealing bows.

With them sailed grim Abas, whose whole troop shone   170
in brilliant armour, and a gilded Apollo gleamed on the
stern of his ship. Populonia, his motherland, had given
him six hundred fighting men, skilful in the wars, while
three hundred came from Ilua, the island of the Chalybes,
teeming with its inexhaustible ores.

The third ship was sailed by Asilas, the great mediator
between gods and men, master of the stars of the sky and
the entrails of the beasts of the field, of bird cries and the
prescient fires of lightning. He sped along leading a thousand men in close formation with their spears bristling. Pisa
put them under his command, a city on Etruscan soil but   180
founded by men from the Alpheus, the river of Olympia.

Next in line sailed fair Astyr, whose trust was in his
horse and his iridescent armour. To him were joined three
hundred men, and all were as one in their zeal to follow
him, men whose home was Caere, men from the fields of
Minio, from ancient Pyrgi and the unwholesome swamps
of Graviscae.

Nor could I pass over Cunarus, so brave in war, the leader
of the Ligurians, nor Cupavo with his small band of fighting
men. High above his head tossed the swan feathers that were
a token of his father's change of form – all the fault of the
God of Love. They say that Cycnus sought comfort from
the Muse for the sadness of his love, by singing of the loss of
his dear Phaethon in the green shade of the poplars that had   190
been Phaethon's sisters. There, when he grew old, he put on
soft white plumage and rose from the earth, singing as he
flew towards the stars. It was his son who now commanded
the huge *Centaur*, driving it along under oar, and with him
in his fleet he took a throng of his peers. The Centaur
figurehead loomed over the water, threatening to hurl
down a massive rock into the waves from its dizzy height,
and the long keel ploughed its furrow deep in the sea.

There too was Ocnus, driving on an army from his fatherland. He was the son of Manto the prophetess and the Tuscan river Tiber. To you, Mantua, he gave your walls and the name of his mother – Mantua, rich in the roll of its forefathers, and not all of one race, but of three, and in each race four peoples. Of all these peoples Mantua is the head, and its strength comes from its Etruscan blood. From here too, Mezentius had roused five hundred men to fight against him, and these the river Mincius, veiled in blue-green reeds, led down to the sea in their ships of war from his father, Lake Benacus. There sailed Aulestes, heavy in the water, but rising as his hundred oars thrashed the waves and churned the marble of the sea to foam. He sailed the monstrous *Triton*, which terrified the blue sea with its horn. As it swam along, its figurehead showed a shaggy front like a man as far as its flanks, but its belly ended in a monster of the deep, while under the breast of this creature, half-man half-beast, the waves foamed and murmured.

These were the chosen leaders who went to the help of Troy in their thirty ships, and ploughed the plains of salt with bronze.

By now the day had left the sky and Phoebe, the kindly Goddess of the Moon, was pounding the middle of Olympus with the hooves of her night-wandering horses. Duty allowed no rest to the limbs of Aeneas. As he sat controlling the tiller and seeing to the sails, a band of his old comrades came suddenly towards him in mid-voyage. They were nymphs, the nymphs into whom his ships had been changed at the bidding of the kindly Mother Goddess Cybele, and they now held divine power over the sea. There they were, swimming in line, as many of them now cleaving the waves as had then stood to the shore with bronze-plated prows. They recognized their king from a distance and danced around him in the water, and Cymodocea, the best speaker among them, came behind his ship

and putting her right hand on its stern, raised her back out
of the water, while her left hand was below the surface,
oaring silently along. Aeneas was still bewildered when she
began to speak to him: 'Are you awake, Aeneas,' she
asked, 'son of the gods? Wake then and let out the sail-
ropes. We are the pines from the sacred top of Mount Ida,   230
now sea nymphs. We are your fleet. When the treacherous
Rutulian was pressing us hard with fire and sword, against
our wishes we had to break the moorings you gave us, and
now we have been looking for you all over the ocean.
Mother Cybele took pity on us and gave us this new form,
allowing us to become goddesses and spend our lives
beneath the waves. But your son Ascanius is trapped
behind a wall and ditches, surrounded by missiles and by
Latins bristling with war. The Arcadian cavalry from
Pallanteum are in their places as ordered, along with the
brave Etruscans, but Turnus has firmly resolved to prevent
them joining forces with the Trojan camp by taking up   240
position between them with his own troops. Up with you
then, and at the coming of dawn, first order your allies to
arms and then take up the invincible shield with its rim of
gold given you by the God of Fire himself. Tomorrow's
light, unless you think these are empty words of mine, will
see the field of battle heaped high with Rutulian dead.' So
she spoke, and as she left him she gave the high stern a
push with her right hand – and well she knew the art of it.
The ship flew through the waves faster than a javelin or
wind-swift arrow, and the others sped along behind it. The
leader of the Trojans, the son of Anchises, was struck   250
dumb with bewilderment, but his heart lifted at the omen,
and looking up to the vault of heaven, he uttered this short
prayer: 'Kindly Mother of the Gods, dweller on Ida, who
takes delight in Mount Dindymus, in cities crowned with
towers and in the lion pair responsive to your chariot
reins, be now my leader in this battle. Bring near to us the
due fulfilment of your omen. Stand by the side of your

Phrygians and give us your divine blessing.' These were his words, and even as he spoke them the revolving day was already rushing back in its full brightness and had put the darkness to flight. His first thought was to order his allies to follow the standards, to fit their minds for the use of their weapons and prepare themselves for battle.

260 And now, as soon as Aeneas, standing high on the stern of his ship, could see the Trojans and his own camp, at that moment he lifted the shield on his left arm and made it flash. The Trojans on the wall raised a shout to heaven, fresh hope renewing their anger, and they hurled their spears, like cranes from the river Strymon in Thrace giving out their signals under the black clouds, trumpeting as they cross the sky and flying before the storm winds with exultant cries. The Rutulian king and the leaders of Italy were amazed until they turned round and saw a fleet making for the shore and a whole sea of ships coming in 270 towards them. On the head of Aeneas there blazed a tongue of fire, baleful flames poured from the top of his crest and the golden boss of his shield belched streams of fire, like the gloomy, blood-red glow of a comet on a clear night, or the dismal blaze of Sirius the Dogstar shedding its sinister light across the sky and bringing disease and thirst to suffering mortals.

But the bold confidence of Turnus never wavered as he quickly took up position on the shore to repel the landing. 'This is the answer to your prayer,' he cried, 'now is the 280 time to break them. Brave men have the God of War in their own right arms. Each of you must now think of his own wife and his own home and remember the great deeds which brought glory to our fathers. Let us go down to the sea to meet them while they are still in confusion and finding their feet after landing. Fortune favours the bold.' So he spoke and pondered in his mind who could be led against the fleet and who could be trusted to keep up the siege of the walls.

Meanwhile Aeneas was landing his allies by gang-planks
from the high sterns. Many waited for the spent waves to
be sucked back and then took a leap into the shallow
water. Others were clambering down the oars. Tarchon, 290
who had been looking out for a stretch of shore where
there seemed to be no shoals and no grumbling of broken
water, where the swelling tide could come in without
obstruction, suddenly swung his ship round and appealed
to his comrades: 'Now, my chosen band, now bend to
your stout oars. Up with your ships out of the water. Take
the weight of them. Split with your rams this land that we
hate, and let each keel plough its own furrow. I do not
care if my ship is wrecked by such a mooring, if only we
take possession of this land.' When Tarchon had spoken,
his comrades rose to their oars and drove their ships 300
foaming at the prow, hard on to the soil at Latium, till
their beaks struck home on dry land and their keels were
safely settled. But not yours, Tarchon. You ran aground
on a shoal and hung there see-sawing on a dangerous ridge
of rock, till at last the waves were weary of you and your
ship broke up, throwing your men into the sea to be
tangled in smashed oars and floating thwarts, as the undertow of the waves kept taking the feet from them.

Turnus was no sluggard. Wasting no time he eagerly led
his whole force to face the Trojans and drew them up at
the ready on the shore. The trumpets sounded, and Aeneas 310
was the first to move against the army of the country
people of Latium and lay them low. This was an omen of
the battle that was to come. Theron was the first to fall. He
was the tallest of their warriors, and had taken it upon
himself to attack Aeneas. Through the mesh of his chain
mail of bronze, through his tunic stiffened with threads of
gold, Aeneas tore a huge gash with his sword in the flesh
of his side. He then struck Lichas. His mother was already
dead when Lichas was cut from her womb and dedicated
to Phoebus Apollo, the God of Healing. Little good did it

do the baby to escape the hazard of steel at birth. Next
Aeneas saw huge Gyas and tough Cisseus felling the embattled Trojans with their clubs, and sent them down to
320 death. Nothing could help them now: not the weapons of
Hercules, nor the strength of their hands, nor their father
Melampus, who had stood by the side of Hercules as long
as the earth supplied him with heavy labours to perform.
There was Pharus, hurling his empty threats, till Aeneas
spun the javelin and planted it in his throat even as he
shouted. You too, Cydon, desperately following your latest
beloved Clytius, with the first gold down on his cheeks,
would have forgotten the young men you were always in
love with. You would have fallen by the right hand of a
Trojan and lain there for men to pity, had not Aeneas been
confronted by seven brothers in serried ranks, the sons of
330 Phorcus, hurling their seven spears. Some rebounded harm-
lessly from his helmet or his shield. Others his loving
mother Venus deflected so that they only grazed his body,
and Aeneas addressed his faithful Achates: 'Pile up some
javelins for me. No weapon that has stood in the body of a
Greek on the plains of Troy will spin in vain from my
right hand against Rutulians!' He then caught up a great
spear and hurled it. Flying through the air it beat through
the bronze of Maeon's shield and shattered in one instant
the breastplate and the breast. Alcanor came to help him as
he fell, a brother's right hand to support a brother. Through
340 Alcanor's arm went the spear of Aeneas and flew on its
way dripping with his blood, while the dying arm hung
by its tendons from the shoulder. Another brother, Numitor, snatched the weapon from Maeon's body and aimed
at Aeneas in return, but was not allowed to strike him,
only to graze the thigh of great Achates. Then came
Clausus of Cures in all the pride of his youthful strength
and with a long-range cast of his unbending spear he
struck Dryops full force under the chin. It went straight
through his throat and took from him in one moment,

even as he spoke, his voice and his life's breath. His forehead struck the ground and his mouth vomited great gouts of blood. Then Aeneas laid three Thracians low, men 350 from the exalted stock of Boreas, then three more sent by their father Idas from their fatherland Ismara, all by different forms of death. Halaesus came running to the spot with his Auruncans; Messapus too, son of Neptune, whose horses drew every eye. Trojans and Latins were battling on the very threshold of Italy, each striving to dislodge the other, like opposing winds fighting their wars in the great reaches of the sky, equal in spirit and equal in strength; they do not give way to one another, neither the winds themselves nor the clouds nor the sea, but long rages the fight, undecided, and they all stand locked in battle – just so clashed the 360 armies of Troy and the armies of Latium, foot planted against foot, and man face to face with man.

In another part of the battle, where a torrent had rolled down boulders and trees uprooted from its banks and strewn them everywhere, Pallas saw his Arcadians, who had for once advanced on foot, now retreating with Latins in hot pursuit – the floods had so roughened the ground that they had decided to abandon their horses. One course alone remained – to fire the valour of his men by appeals and bitter reproaches: 'Where are you running to, comrades? I beg you by your pride in yourselves, by your bravery in time past, by the name of Evander your leader, 370 by the wars you have won, by the hopes rising in me to gain glory like my father's, this is no time to trust to your feet! It is swords you need, to cut your way through the enemy. There, where the moil is thickest, where the attack is fiercest, that is where your proud fatherland requires you and your leader Pallas to go. These are not gods who are pressing you so hard; they are mortals pursuing mortals. Like us they have two hands, and like us they have one life to lose. Look about you! The great barrier of ocean closes us in. There is no more land to run to. Shall we take to the

sea? Shall we set course for Troy?' With these words he
threw himself into the thick of his enemies.

380   The first man to meet him, drawn there by an unkindly
fate, was Lagus. While he was trying to tear loose a great
heavy rock, Pallas hurled his spear and struck him in the
middle of the back where the spine divides the ribs. Pallas
was pulling out the weapon, which had wedged between
the bones, when Hisbo swooped on him, hoping to take
him by surprise, but Pallas caught him first in the fury of
his charge, made reckless by the cruel death of his comrade.
Hisbo's lungs were swollen. Pallas buried his sword in
them. He then turned on Sthenius; then on Anchemolus of
the ancient stock of Rhoetus, who had shamefully de-
390 bauched his own stepmother. You too fell on the Rutulian
fields, Larides and Thymber, sons of Daucus, identical
twins, a source of confusion and delight to your parents.
But Pallas made a grim difference between you: with the
sword of his father Evander he removed the head of
Thymber, and cut off the hand of Larides. As it lay there,
it groped for its owner and the fingers twitched, still half
alive, and kept clutching at the sword. The Arcadians were
stung by Pallas' reproaches, and as they watched his glorious feats, remorse and shame armed them against their
enemies.

400   Then Pallas put a spear through Rhoeteus as he fled past
on his two-horse chariot, and gave that much respite and
reprieve to Ilus. For it was against Ilus that Pallas had
aimed a long throw with his mighty spear, but Rhoeteus
had come between them and taken the blow while fleeing
from great Teuthras and his brother Tyres. He rolled from
his chariot, and died with his heels drumming on the
Rutulian ploughland. Just as a shepherd fires a wood at
different points when the summer winds get up at last, and
suddenly all the flames merge in the middle to make one
bristling battle-front of fire stretching over the broad plain,
and there he sits in triumph looking down on the exulting

blaze – just so, Pallas, did the valour of your men all come   410
together in one, and put joy in your heart. But Halaesus
was a fierce warrior, and he made straight for the enemies
that stood in front of him, gathering all his strength behind
his weapons. Ladon and Pheres and Demodocus he slew,
and his flashing sword ripped off the right hand of Stry-
monius as it was poised to lunge at his throat. Thoas he
struck with a rock in the face, shattering the bones and
grinding them into the blood-soaked brains. Halaesus was
next. His father, foreseeing the future, had hidden him in
the woods, but when the father grew old and his whitening
eyes dissolved in death, the Fates laid a hand on the son and
consecrated him to Evander's spear. This was the prayer of   420
Pallas before he attacked: 'Grant now, O Father Thybris,
that the spear I am holding poised to throw may reach the
mark and go through the stout breast of Halaesus, and I
shall strip these arms of his from his body and hang them
on your sacred oak as spoils.' The god heard his prayer. As
the hapless Halaesus protected Imaon, he left his breast
exposed to the Arcadian spear.

But Lausus, who was bearing the brunt of the battle, did
not allow his men to be dismayed by all this slaughter
done by Pallas. First of all he slew Abas as he stood before
him, the very knot and stumbling block of war. The youth
of Arcadia were laid low and the Etruscans fell beside
them, and you too, Trojans, who had faced the Greeks   430
unscathed. The armies clashed, equal in their leaders and in
their strength, and the wings of the battle line were forced
into the centre so that men could not raise a hand or a
weapon in the crowd. On the one side Pallas thrust and
pressed, on the other Lausus. They were almost of an age,
and noble in appearance, but Fortune had denied each of
them a homecoming. Yet the ruler of high Olympus did
not yet allow their paths to cross, reserving for each his
own death at the hand of a stronger enemy.

Meanwhile, after Juturna had advised her dear brother

440 Turnus to take the place of Lausus, he cut through the middle of the ranks of warriors on his swift chariot, and as soon as he saw his allies he called out: 'Time now to stand down from the fighting. I am the only one who attacks Pallas. Pallas is mine, and mine alone. I wish his father were here to see it.' So he spoke and his allies left the ground clear as ordered. When the Rutulians withdrew, Pallas marvelled at these proud commands and stood amazed at the sight of Turnus, running his eyes all over that mighty body, his grim stare taking it in part by part from where he stood, and these were the words he hurled in reply to the words of the insolent prince: 'I shall win rich renown today, either for stripping the corpse of the 450 leader of my country's enemies, or else for a glorious death. My father will bear the one fate as easily as the other. Do not waste your threats on me.' With these words he strode on to the level ground in the middle of the battlefield, and the blood of the Arcadians froze in their breasts. Turnus leapt down from his chariot and prepared to come to close quarters on foot, flying at him like a lion which has seen from some high vantage point a bull practising for combat far away on the plain – this is how Turnus appeared as he came on. Pallas made the first attack, judging that Turnus would be within range of a spearcast and hoping that Fortune would favour the weaker for his daring. Lifting up his voice to the wide expanse of heaven, he cried: 'I call upon you, Hercules of 460 the stock of Alceus, by my father's table and by the friendship he offered you when you came as a stranger to his home, stand at my side now as I set my hand to this great task. May Turnus as he dies see me tear the blood-stained armour off his body, and may the last sight he endures be the face of the man who has defeated him!' Hearing the young warrior, Hercules checked the great groan rising from the depths of his heart and the helpless tears streamed from his eyes. Then Father Jupiter spoke

these loving words to his son: 'Each man has his allotted day. All life is brief and time once past can never be restored. But the task of the brave man is to enlarge his fame by his actions. So many sons of gods fell under the high walls of Troy, and with them fell also my son Sarpedon. Turnus too is called by his own destiny and has reached the limits of the time he has been given.' So he spoke and instantly turned his eyes away from the Rutulian fields.

But Pallas hurled his spear with all his strength and tore his bright sword from its enclosing scabbard. The spear flew and fell where the armour stood highest on the shoulder of Turnus, forcing its way through the edge of the shield and grazing at last the skin of that huge body. Then Turnus took long aim at Pallas with his steel-pointed hardwood spear and threw it saying: 'Now see whether mine is any better at piercing!' With a shuddering blow it beat through the middle of the shield, through all the plates of iron and of bronze and all the ox-hides that covered it, and unchecked by the breastplate, it bored through that mighty breast. In desperation Pallas tore the warm blade out of the wound, and blood and life came out together after it, both by the same channel. He fell forward on the wound, his armour ringing on top of his body, and as he died his bleeding mouth bit the soil of his enemies. Turnus stood over him and said: 'Take this message of mine to Evander, you Arcadians, and do not forget it: I am giving him back the Pallas he deserves. Whatever honour there is in a tomb, and any comfort he finds in burying him, these I gladly give him. His hospitality to Aeneas will cost him dear!' With these words he planted his left foot on the dead body, and tore off the huge, heavy baldric. On this great belt an abominable crime was embossed, how in one dark night, the night of their marriage, a band of young men were foully slain, and their marriage chambers bathed in blood, all worked by Clonus,

₅₀₀ son of Eurytus, in a wealth of gold. This was the spoil in which Turnus now exulted and he gloried in the taking of it. The mind of man has no knowledge of what Fate holds in store, and observes no limit when Fortune raises him up. The time will come when Turnus would gladly pay, and pay richly, to see Pallas alive and unharmed. He will bitterly regret this spoil and the day he took it. A throng of Pallas' allies laid him on his shield and carried him back with tears of lamentation. O Pallas, a great grief and a great glory is coming home to your father! This one day gave you to war, and now takes you from it, and yet you leave behind you huge piles of Rutulian dead.

₅₁₀ First a rumour of this calamity came flying to Aeneas and then a reliable messenger, to tell him his men were on the very edge of destruction; the Trojans were in retreat; now was the time to help them. Everything that stood before him he harvested with the sword, cutting a broad swathe through the enemy ranks, and burning with rage as he looked for this Turnus flushed with slaughter. Before his eyes he could see Pallas, Evander, everything, the table he had sat down to that day when he first came to their house, and the right hands of friendship they had given him. Four warrior sons of Sulmo he now captured alive and four reared by Ufens, to sacrifice them as offerings to ₅₂₀ the shade of Pallas and pour their captive blood on the flames of his pyre. Next he aimed his deadly spear from long range at Magus, who cleverly ran under it. The quivering spear flew over his head and he clasped the knees of Aeneas with this prayer: 'By the shade of your own father and the hopes you have of Iulus as he grows to manhood, I beg you to spare this life of mine for the sake of my son and my father. Our home is a high-built palace, and buried deep within it I have talents of engraved silver and great weights of gold, both worked and unworked. A Trojan victory does not depend on me. My one life will ₅₃₀ not make so great a difference.' This was Aeneas' reply:

'Keep for your children all those talents of silver and gold you talk about. Turnus put an end to such war-trading the moment he murdered Pallas. So judges the shade of my father Anchises. And so judges Iulus.' When he had spoken he took Magus' helmet in his left hand, and bending back his neck when he was still begging for mercy, he drove the sword home to the hilt. Not far away was Haemonides, priest of Phoebus Apollo and Diana Trivia, his temples bound by a headband of sacred wool, all shining white in his white robes and insignia. Aeneas closed with him, 540 drove him across the plain, stood over him when he fell, darkening the whiteness with his great shadow, and took him as his victim. Serestus collected the spoils and carried them back on his shoulders as a trophy to Mars Gradivus.

Caeculus of the stock of Vulcan renewed the battle, and Umbro from the Marsian mountains with him. Aeneas confronted them in all his fury. His sword had already struck off the left hand of Anxur − a stroke of the blade had sent the whole circle of his shield to the ground. He had uttered some great threat, imagining that the strength would be there to make it good. It seemed he was trying to raise his spirits to the skies, and had promised himself that he would live to enjoy grey hairs and a long life. Next Aeneas in his fury was faced by Tarquitus, glorying in his 550 shining armour, the son of Faunus, God of the Woods, and the nymph Dryope. Drawing back his spear, Aeneas threw and pinned the great heavy shield to the breastplate. While he was still begging for mercy, and still had much to say, Aeneas smashed his head to the ground, and as he set the warm trunk rolling, these were the words he spoke with hatred in his heart: 'Lie there now, you fearsome warrior. Your good mother will not bury you in the earth or burden your body with the family tomb. You will be left for the wild birds, or thrown into the sea to be carried away by the waves, and the hungry fish will come and lick 560 your wounds!' Next he pursued and caught Antaeus and

Lucas, the front rank of Turnus, then brave Numa and
yellow-haired Camers, son of great-hearted Volcens, who
was richest in land of all the men of Italy and ruled over
silent Amyclae. Aeneas was like Aegaeon, who they say
had a hundred arms and a hundred hands, with fire flaming
from fifty breasts and mouths, and fifty was the number of
swords he drew against the lightning of Jupiter, fifty the
number of identical shields he clashed – so seemed Aeneas,
raging victorious all over the plain, when once his sword
570 blade had warmed to the work. Imagine him next bearing
down on the chariot of Niphaeus, with the four horses
showing their chests as they stood to meet him, but when
they saw Aeneas' great stride and heard his fearsome roar,
they wheeled in panic and bolted, throwing their master
out of the chariot and stampeding to the shore.

Meanwhile Lucagus was coming into the middle of
battle on a chariot drawn by two white horses. With him
was his brother Liger, handling the reins and controlling
the horses while Lucagus whirled his naked sword about
him. Aeneas could not endure to see such fury and such
fervour, but rushed forward and loomed huge before them
580 with his levelled spear. It was Liger who spoke: 'These are
not the horses of Diomede you are looking at, or the
chariot of Achilles. These are not the plains of Troy. Here
in this land today there will be an end to your wars and to
your life.' Far flew these wild words of Liger. The Trojan
was preparing a reply to his enemy, but it was not in
words – it was his javelin he hurled. Lucagus had been
leaning forward over his horses to urge them on by
beating them with the flat of his spear. Now, when he had
planted his left foot to the front and was preparing for
battle, through the bottom rim of his shining shield came
590 the spear of Aeneas and pierced his left groin. He was
pitched from his chariot and as he lay dying on the
ground, good Aeneas addressed these bitter words to him:
'It is not the panic of your horses, Lucagus, that has

brought your chariot to grief. They did not shy away
from the shadow of their enemy. It is your own doing,
leaping off the car and abandoning your team!' With these
words Aeneas caught the horses' bridles. The wretched
brother of Lucagus fell from the chariot and stretched out
his helpless hands to Aeneas: 'Great Trojan, I implore you
by your own self and by the parents who brought such a
man as you into the world, spare this life of mine and take
pity on a suppliant.' Aeneas cut short his appeal. 'This is   600
not what I heard you say a moment ago. Die now. A
brother's place is with his brother.' And as he spoke the
point of his sword opened the breast of Liger, the hiding
place of his soul. So did the Trojan leader deal out death all
over the plain like a raging torrent of water or a storm of
black wind, until at last the young Ascanius and his warriors
sallied forth and left the camp. The siege was lifted.

In the meanwhile Jupiter came to Juno and said to her:
'O my true sister and most pleasing of wives, you are
right, it is Venus, as you thought, who is maintaining the
strength of the Trojans, not the warlike vigour of their
right arms nor their fierce and danger-hardened spirit.'   610
Humbly Juno replied: 'O finest of husbands, why do you
cause me anguish when I am in despair and in terror of
your harsh commands? If your love for me had that power
which once it had, and should have still, you who can do
all things would not be refusing me this. I should be able
to withdraw Turnus from the battle and keep him safe for
his father Daunus. But as things are, let him die. Let him
pay the penalty to the Trojans with his righteous blood.
Nevertheless he is descended from our stock, Pilumnus was
his ancestor in the fourth generation and his generous hand
has often weighed down your threshold with abundant   620
gifts.' The King of Heavenly Olympus made brief reply:
'If what you ask is a stay of the death that is upon him and
respite for a young man who must die, and if you accept
that this is what I ordain, then rescue Turnus. Let him flee.

Snatch him from the Fates that tread upon his heels. There
is room for me to grant you indulgence thus far. But if
there is some deeper thought of mercy underlying these
appeals of yours, and if you believe that the whole course
of the war can be affected or its outcome changed, the
hopes which you nourish are empty.' Juno replied, weeping
as she spoke: 'What if your heart wished to give what your
words refuse? What if you listened to me and let Turnus
630 live? As it is, although he is innocent, a cruel death is
waiting for him, unless I am wide of the mark and there is
no truth in me. But oh how I wish my fears were false and
I were deluded! How I wish you would recast your plans,
for you can do so, and choose a better course!'

As soon as the goddess had finished speaking, she flew
down from the heights of heaven swathed in cloud and
driving a great storm before her towards the battle line of
the Trojans and the Laurentine camp. Then she fashioned
out of empty vapour an effigy in the form of Aeneas, a
weird sight, a shade without strength or substance, armed
with Trojan weapons. She copied his shield and the crest
on his godlike head and gave the phantom power to speak
640 its empty words. Sound without thought she gave it, and
moulded its strides as it moved. It was like the flitting
shapes which men say are the ghosts of the dead, or like
the dreams which delude our sleeping senses. There in high
glee in front of the first line of warriors pranced this
apparition and goaded Turnus by brandishing weapons
and shouting challenges. Turnus attacked, throwing his
whirring spear from long range. The apparition turned tail
and fled. At that moment Turnus believed that Aeneas had
turned his back on him and was running away. Taking a
wild draught from the empty cup of hope, he cried:
'Where are you running to, Aeneas? You must not leave.
Your marriage is arranged. This is the land you crossed the
seas to find and my right hand will give it to you!'
650 Shouting such taunts, he went in pursuit with his sword

drawn and flashing and did not see that all his exultation
was scattering to the winds.

The ship which king Osinius had sailed from the land of
Clusium happened to be moored to a high shelf of rock,
with her ladders and gangway out. Here the panic-stricken
phantom of Aeneas fled and hid itself, with Turnus hard
behind it. Nothing could delay him. He leapt across the
gangways, high above the water, and scarcely had he set
foot on the prow when Saturnian Juno tore the ship from
her moorings, breaking the ropes, and took her quickly   660
out to sea on the ebbing tide. But by this time the
phantom was no longer looking for a place to hide. It had
flown high into the air and melted into a black cloud.
Meanwhile, Aeneas was calling on Turnus to fight, and
there was no Turnus, but every man who crossed his path
he sent down to death, and all the time the wind was
blowing Turnus round and round in mid-ocean. Looking
back to the shore in bewilderment and thanking no one for
his safety, he raised his arms in prayer and lifted up his
voice to the stars of heaven: 'All-powerful Father, have you
decided that I deserve this disgrace? Have you decreed that
I must endure this punishment? Where am I being taken?   670
What have I left behind me? How can I go back after
running away? What sort of Turnus would that be? Shall I
ever see my camp and the walls of the Laurentines again?
And what about that band of great warriors who have
followed me and followed my sword? The horror of it – I
have left them all to die! I see them wandering about
without a leader. I hear them groaning as they fall. What
am I to do? If only the earth could open deep enough to
swallow me! Or rather I pray to the winds, and pray to
them from my heart, to take pity on me and drive my ship
on to the rocks and cliffs, or run it aground on some shoal
of deadly sand, where there will be no Rutulian and no
word of my shame can follow me.' Even as he spoke, his   680
mind was tossed this way and that, in despair at his

disgrace. Should he fall on his sword and drive the raw steel through his ribs? Should he throw himself into the sea and try to swim from mid-ocean back into the curve of the bay to face the weapons of the Trojans once again? Three times he tried each way, and three times mighty Juno held him back, pitying the young man in her heart, and would not let him move. Cutting the deep water, he floated on a favouring tide and following waves, and came to land in the ancient city of his father Daunus.

But Mezentius meanwhile, by the promptings of Jupiter,
690 took the place of Turnus in the battle and fell furiously on the triumphant Trojans. Instantly all the Etruscan troops converged on him alone, united in their hatred, and pressed him hard under a hail of weapons. He stood like a rock jutting out into the ocean wastes, exposed to the threats and fury of wind and wave and bearing all the violence of sea and sky, unmoved. He felled Hebrus, son of Dolichaon, and Latagus with him, and Palmus as he ran. Latagus he stopped by hitting him full in the face and mouth with a
700 rock, a huge block broken off a mountain, but he cut the hamstrings of Palmus and left him rolling helpless on the ground. His armour he gave to Lausus to put on his shoulders, and his crest to fix on his helmet. Then it was the turn of Euanthes the Phrygian, and Mimas, the same age as Paris and his comrade in war. In one night Theano, wife of Amycus, brought him into the light of life, while Hecuba, daughter of Cisseus, pregnant with a torch, was giving birth to Paris. Paris fell in the city of his fathers, but Mimas lies a stranger on the Laurentine shore. Like the wild boar who has long kept his citadel among the pines of
710 Mount Vesulus, and long have the Laurentine marshes fed him in the reed beds of the forest; when the great beast is driven down from the mountains with the dogs snapping at him, and is caught between the nets, he stands at bay snorting, and the bristles rise on his shoulders and no one has the courage to clash with him or go near him, but they

attack from a safe distance with javelins and shouts, while
he stands his ground unafraid and wondering in which
direction to charge, grinding his teeth and shaking the
spears out of his back – even so, none of those men who
had just cause of anger against Mezentius was minded to
draw the sword and run upon him, but instead they stood
well back and bombarded him with missiles and deafening
shouts.

Acron was a Greek who had come from the ancient land   720
of Corythus, driven into exile while waiting to be married.
Mezentius saw him from a distance causing havoc in the
middle of the battle line in the purple feathers and purple
cloak given him by his promised bride. Just as a ravening
lion scouring the deep lairs of wild beasts, driven mad by
the pangs of hunger, if he sights a frightened she-goat, or
sees a stag's antlers rising, he opens his great jaws in
delight, his mane bristles and he battens on the flesh with
foul gore washing his pitiless mouth – just so did Mezentius
charge hot-haste into the thick of the enemy and felled the   730
unlucky Acron, who breathed out his life drumming the
black earth with his heels and blooding the weapons broken
in his body. Orodes fled, but Mezentius did not deign to
cut him down as he ran, or deal him a wound, unseen,
from the back, but came to bar his way and meet him face
to face, proving himself the better man by strength in arms
and not by stealth. He then put his foot on his prostrate
enemy and leaned on his spear, calling out: 'Here,
comrades, lies no small part of their battle strength, Orodes,
that stood so tall.' His men shouted their glad paean of
victory after him, but with his dying breath Orodes replied:
'Whoever you are that have conquered me, I shall be
revenged. You will not enjoy your victory for long. The   740
same fate is looking out for you, and we shall soon be
lying in the same fields.' Half smiling, half in anger,
Mezentius replied: 'Die now. As for me, that will be a
matter for the Father of the Gods and the King of Men,'

and at these words he drew his spear out of the body of Orodes. A cruel rest then came to him, and an iron sleep bore down upon his eyes and closed them in everlasting night.

Caedicus cut down Alcathous, Sacrator Hydaspes; Rapo killed Parthenius and Orses, a strong and hardy warrior. Messapus put an end to Clonius and Erichaetes, son of Lycaon, Erichaetes being on foot, but Clonius lying on the 750 ground, having lost his reins and fallen from his horse. On foot also was Agis the Lycian, who had come out in front of the battle line, but Valerus had some spark of his family's courage and overthrew him. Thronius was killed by Salius, and Salius by Nealces, shooting his arrows and javelins from ambush at long range.

Pitiless Mars was now dealing grief and death to both sides with impartial hand. Victors and vanquished killed and were killed and neither side thought of flight. In the halls of Jupiter the gods pitied the futile anger of the two armies and grieved that men had so much suffering, Venus 760 looking on from one side and Saturnian Juno from the other, while in the thick of all the thousands raged the Fury Tisiphone, pale as death.

Then came Mezentius storming over the plain, brandishing a huge spear, and as tall as Orion who walks in midocean cleaving his path through its deepest pools with his shoulders rising clear of the waves, or strides along carrying an ancient ash from the mountain tops with his feet on the ground and his head hidden in the clouds – so did Mezentius advance in his massive armour. Aeneas had picked 770 him out in the long ranks of men in front of him and was going to meet him. Mezentius held his ground, unafraid, and the huge bulk of him stood fast waiting to receive his great-hearted enemy. Measuring a spear-cast with his eye, he cried: 'Let the right hand which is my god not fail me now, nor the spear which I brandish to throw. My vow is to strip the armour from that brigand's body and clothe

you with it, Lausus. My trophy over Aeneas will be my
own son!' With these words he threw his spear from long
range. Hissing as it flew, it bounced off Aeneas' shield and
struck the noble Antores as he stood some distance away,
entering his body between flank and groin. Antores had
been a comrade of Hercules. He had come from Argos but
attached himself to Evander, settling with him in his city in   780
Italy. And so, falling cruelly by a wound intended for
another, he looked up at the sky and remembered his
beloved Argos as he died.

Then the devout Aeneas hurled his spear. Through the
circle of Mezentius' convex shield it flew, the triple bronze,
the layers of linen, the three stitched bull hides, and it stuck
low in Mezentius' groin, but it had lost its force. Exultant
at the sight of the Etruscan's blood, Aeneas tore the sword
from the scabbard at his thigh. Seeing Mezentius in distress   790
and Aeneas bearing down on him in hot fury, Lausus
moaned bitterly for the father whom he loved and the
tears rolled down his face. Now Lausus, I shall tell of your
cruel death and glorious deeds in the hope that the distance
of time may lead men to believe your great exploit. Never
will it be my wish to be silent about you, Lausus – you are
a warrior who does not deserve to be forgotten. Mezentius
was falling back, defenceless and encumbered, dragging his
enemy's spear behind him, stuck in his shield, when young
Lausus leapt forward and threw himself between them. Just
as Aeneas was standing to his full height and raising his
arm to strike, he came in beneath the sword blade, blocking
Aeneas and checking his advance. Lausus' comrades raised
a great shout and supported him by bombarding Aeneas
and harassing him with their missiles from long range, till
the father could withdraw protected by the shield of the   800
son. Aeneas, enraged, kept under cover. Just as when the
clouds descend in a sudden storm of hail, and all the
ploughmen and all the workers in the fields scatter across
the open ground and the traveller finds a sure fortress to

hide in under a river bank or the arch of some high-vaulted rock till the rain stops falling on the earth, so that they can continue to do the work of the day when the sunshine is restored — just so Aeneas, overwhelmed by missiles from all sides, weathered the storm of war till the
810 last roll of its thunder, and then it was Lausus he challenged, and Lausus he threatened: 'Why are you in such a haste to die? Why do you take on tasks beyond your strength? You are too rash. Your love for your father is deceiving you.' But Lausus was in full cry and his madness knew no check. At this the anger rose even higher in the heart of the leader of the Trojans and the Fates gathered up the last threads for Lausus. Aeneas drove his mighty sword through the middle of the young man's body, burying it to the hilt, the point going straight through his light shield, no proper armour to match the threats he had uttered. It pierced, too, the tunic his mother had woven for him with a soft thread of gold and filled the folds of it with blood. Then did his life
820 leave his body and go in sorrow through the air to join the shades.

But when Aeneas, son of Anchises, saw the dying face and features, the face strangely white, he groaned from his heart in pity and held out his hand, as there came into his mind the thought of his own devoted love for his father, and he said: 'What will the devout Aeneas now give to match such merit? What gift can he give that will be worthy of a heart like yours? Take your armour, that gave you so much pleasure. Now I return you to the shades and the ashes of your ancestors, if that is any comfort for you. In your misfortune you will have one consolation for your
830 cruel death, that you fell by the hand of the great Aeneas.' At this he turned on Lausus' comrades, railing at them as they hung back, while he lifted Lausus off the ground where he was soiling his carefully tended hair with blood.

Meanwhile by the bank of the river Tiber Lausus' father was staunching his wounds with water and leaning

against the trunk of a tree to rest. Nearby, his bronze
helmet hung from the branches and his weighty armour
lay quiet on the grass. About him stood his chosen warriors
as he bathed his neck, gasping with pain, and his great
beard streamed down his chest. Again and again he asked
about Lausus, and kept sending men to recall him and take   840
him orders from his anxious father. But Lausus was dead.
and his weeping comrades were carrying him back on his
shield, a mighty warrior laid low by a mighty wound.
Mezentius had a presentiment of evil. He heard the wailing
in the distance and knew the truth. Then, fouling his grey
hair with dust, he raised both hands to heaven and flung
himself on his son's body: 'Was I so besotted with the
pleasure of living that I allowed my own son to take my
place under my enemy's sword? Is the father to be saved
by the wounds of the son? Have you died so that I might
live? Now for the first time is death bitter to me! Now for   850
the first time does a wound go deep. And I have even
stained your name, my son, by my crimes. Men hated me
and drove me from the throne and sceptre of my fathers. I
owed a debt to my country and my people who detested
me, and I would to heaven I had paid it with this guilty
life of mine by every death a man can die! But I am still
alive. I have still not left the world of men and the light of
day. But leave it I shall!' Even as he was speaking, he was
raising himself on his wounded thigh, and slow as he was
with the violence of the pain deep in his wound, his spirit
was unsubdued. He ordered his horse to be brought. This
was his glory and his comfort, and on it he had ridden
home victorious from all his wars. Seeing it pining, he   860
spoke to it in these words: 'We have lived a long time,
Rhaebus, if any mortal life is long. Either you will be
victorious today and carry back the head of Aeneas with
the blood-stained spoils stripped from his body, and you
and I shall avenge the sufferings of Lausus; or else, if that
road is barred and no force can open it, we shall fall

together. I do not think, with courage like yours, that you will accept instructions from any other man or take kindly to Trojan masters.' With these words Mezentius mounted and Rhaebus took on his back the weight of the rider he knew so well. Both his hands were laden with sharp-pointed javelins and on his head he wore his helmet of
870 gleaming bronze with its shaggy horsehair crest. So armed, he galloped into the thick of battle, fierce shame, frenzy and grief all seething together in his heart. Three times he shouted the name of Aeneas. Aeneas knew his voice and offered up this joyful prayer: 'Let this be the will of the Father of the Gods. Let this be the will of high Apollo. Stand and fight with me.' He said no more, but made for Mezentius with spear at the ready. Mezentius replied: 'Now that you have taken my son, you savage, you need not try to frighten me. That was the only way you could
880 have found to destroy me. Death holds no terrors for us and we give not a thought for the gods. Enough words. I have come here to die. But first I have these gifts for you.' He spoke and hurled a spear at his enemy, then another and another, planting them in Aeneas' shield as he flew round him in a great circle, but the golden boss of the shield held fast. Aeneas stood there and Mezentius rode round him three times hurling his spears and keeping Aeneas on his left side. Three times the Trojan pivoted with him, turning his huge bronze shield, with its bristling forest of bronze spears. Then, weary of all the delay, weary of plucking javelins out of his shield and hard-pressed in
890 this unequal battle, Aeneas, after turning many plans over in his mind, at last burst forward and threw his spear, catching Mezentius' warhorse in the hollow between its temples. Up it reared thrashing the air with its hooves and throwing its rider. Then as it came down with all its weight, dislocating its shoulder, it fell head first on top of Mezentius and pinned him to the ground. The sky blazed with the shouts of Trojans and Latins as Aeneas rushed up

tearing his sword from the sheath and crying: 'Where is the bold Mezentius now? Where is that fierce spirit of his?' The Etruscan looked up, drinking in the bright air of heaven as he came back to his senses, and replied: 'You are my bitter enemy. Why jeer at me and threaten me with death? There is no sin in killing. I did not come into battle on those terms and my son Lausus struck no such bargain with you on my behalf. One thing I ask, if the defeated can ask favours from their enemies, to let my body be buried in the earth. I know the bitter hatred of my people is all about me. Protect me, I beg you, from their fury and let me lie in the grave with my son.' These were his last words. He then took the sword in the throat with full knowledge and poured out his life's breath in wave upon wave of blood all over his armour.

I I

DRANCES AND CAMILLA

Meanwhile the Goddess of the Dawn had risen from
Ocean, and anxious and eager as Aeneas was to give time
to burying his comrades, distraught as he was in mind at
their deaths, at first light the victor was paying his vows to
the gods. Cutting all the branches off a huge oak, he set it
up on a mound as a trophy to the great god mighty in
war, and clothed it in the shining armour he had stripped
from the body of the enemy leader Mezentius. There he
set the hero's crest dripping its dew of blood, the broken
10 spears and the breastplate struck and pierced through in
twelve places. On the left he bound the bronze shield and
from the neck he hung the ivoried sword. He then addressed his comrades (for all the Trojan leaders were pressing close around him), and these were the words he spoke
to urge them on in their hour of triumph: 'The greatest
part of our work is done, my friends. In what remains
there is nothing to fear. These are spoils I have taken from
a proud king, the first fruits of this war. This is Mezentius,
and my hands have set him in this place. Our way now lies
towards the king of the Latins and the walls of their city.
Make ready your weapons. Fill your minds and your hopes
with the thought of war, so that no man shall hesitate or
20 not know what to do when the gods permit us to pull up
our standards and lead the army out of camp. When that
time comes, there must be no faintheartedness or slug-
gishness in our thoughts to slow us down. In the mean-

while, let us consign the unburied bodies of our comrades
to the earth, for that is the only honour a man has in the
underworld. Go,' he said, 'and grace these noble spirits
with their last rites, for they have shed their blood to win
this land for us. But first let Pallas be sent back to the
stricken city of Evander. This was a warrior who did not
fail in courage when his black day took him from us and
drowned him in the bitterness of death.'

So he spoke, weeping, and made his way back to his
own threshold where the body of Pallas lay guarded by
old Acoetes. Acoetes had once been the armour-bearer of
Arcadian Evander, but the auspices were no longer so
favourable when he was appointed as companion to his
dear ward, Pallas. About them stood the whole throng of
their attendants and all the Trojans and the women of
Troy with their hair unbound in mourning after the
manner of their people. But when Aeneas entered his high
doorway, they beat their breasts and raised their wild
lament to the sky till the palace rang with the sound of
their grief. When he himself saw the head of Pallas cushioned there and his white face, and the open wound torn in
that smooth breast by the Italian spear, the tears welled up
and he spoke these words: 'Oh the pity of it! Fortune came
to me with smiles, but took you from me while you were
still a boy, and would not let you live to see us in our
kingdom, or to ride back in triumph to your father's
house. This is not what I promised Evander for his son,
when he took me in his arms as I left him, and sent me out
to take up this great command, warning me with fear in
his heart that these were fierce warriors, that this was a
hardy race I had to meet in battle. Even now, deluded by
vain hopes, he may be making vows and heaping altars
with offerings, while we bring him with tears and useless
honours a young warrior who owes no more debts to any
heavenly power. With what eyes will you look at the dead
body of your son? Is this how we return from war? Are

these the triumphs expected of us? Is this my great pledge? But you will not see a wound on him, Evander, of which you need to be ashamed. You will not be a father who has the terrible wish that his son who is alive were dead. The land of Italy has lost a great bulwark, and great too is your loss, Iulus.'

60 After he had his fill of weeping, he ordered them to take up the pitiable corpse, and from the whole army he sent a thousand chosen men as escort to pay a last tribute and join their tears with those of Evander, a small comfort for a great sorrow, but a debt that was owed to the stricken father. Others were not slow to weave a soft wickerwork bier of arbutus and oak shoots to make a raised couch, shaded by a canopy of green, where they laid the young warrior high on his bed of country straw. There he lay like a flower cut by the thumbnail of a young girl, a soft violet
70 or drooping lily, still with its sheen and its shape, though Mother Earth no longer feeds it and gives it strength. Then Aeneas brought out two robes stiffened with gold and purple threads which Sidonian Dido had long since made for him with her own hands, picking out the warp in fine gold, and the work had been a joy to her. With grief in his heart he put one of these on the young man's body as his last tribute and in a fold of it he veiled the hair that would soon be burned. Then he gathered a great heap of spoil from the battle on the Laurentine fields and ordered it to be brought to the pyre in a long procession, adding to it
80 the horses and weapons he had taken from the enemy. Then came the captives, whose hands he had bound behind their backs to send them as offerings to the shades of the dead and sprinkle the funeral pyre with the blood of their sacrifice. He also commanded the leaders of the army to carry in their own arms tree trunks draped with weapons captured from the enemy and inscribed with their hated names. Acoetes, worn out with age, was led along in the procession, beating his breast with clenched fists and tearing

his face with his nails, but he collapsed and lay all his length on the ground. Chariots were drawn along drenched with Rutulian blood, and then came Pallas' warhorse 90 Aethon, stripped of all its trappings with the tears rolling down in great drops and soaking its face. There were men to carry his spear and his helmet. The victorious Turnus had the rest. A great phalanx of mourners followed, all the Trojans and the Etruscans and the Arcadians with their arms reversed. After this procession of all the comrades of Pallas had marched well clear of the camp, Aeneas halted, and with a deep groan he spoke these words: 'The same grim destiny of war calls us away from here to weep other tears. For ever hail, great Pallas, and farewell for ever.' He said no more but set off towards his high-built fortifications and marched back into camp.

And now envoys appeared from the city of the Latins 100 bearing olive branches wreathed in wool and asking for a truce. The bodies of their dead were all over the plain where the steel had laid them, and they begged Aeneas to give them back and let them go to their graves in the earth, for he could have no quarrel with men who were defeated and had lost the light of life; he must show mercy to those who had once been called his hosts and the kinsmen of his bride. Good Aeneas could not refuse this petition. He honoured the envoys, granted what they asked and added these words: 'What cruel fortune is this, men of Latium, that has embroiled you in war and made you run away from us, who are your friends? You ask me 110 for peace for the dead, whose destiny has been to die in battle: I for my part would have been willing to grant them peace when they were still alive. Nor would I ever have come to this land if the Fates had not offered me a place here to be my home. I do not wage war with your people. It was your king who abandoned our sworn friendship and preferred to put his trust in the weapons of Turnus. It is not these men who should have risked their

lives but Turnus. If it is his plan to put an end to this war by the strength of his arm, and drive out the Trojans, he should have faced me and these weapons of mine in battle. One of us would have lived. God or our own right hands would have seen to that. Go now and light fires beneath
120 the bodies of your unfortunate citizens.' Aeneas had spoken. They were astonished and stood looking at each other in silence.

Then Drances, an older man who had always hated the young warrior Turnus, and spoken against him, began to make his reply: 'O Trojan great in fame, and greater still in arms, what words of mine could raise you to the skies? What shall I first praise? Your justice, or your labours in war? Gratefully shall we carry these words of yours back to our native city, and if Fortune shows us a way, we shall reconcile you to our king Latinus. Turnus can make his
130 own treaties. We shall do more. We shall delight to raise the massive walls Fate has decreed for you and lift up the building stones of Troy on our shoulders!'

All to a man they murmured in agreement when he had finished speaking. Twelve days they decided on, and during that time, with peace as mediator between them, Trojans and Latins were together in the hills and wandered the woods, and no man harmed another. The iron axe rang upon tall ash trees and brought down skyward-thrusting pines. They never rested from their labours, splitting the oak and fragrant cedar with wedges and carrying down the ash trees on carts from the mountains.

140 But Rumour was already on the wing, overwhelming Evander and the house and city of Evander with the first warnings of anguish. The talk was no longer of Pallas, conqueror of Latium. The Arcadians rushed to the gates, snatching up funeral torches according to their ancient practice. The road was lit by a long line of flames which showed up the fields far on either side. Nearer and nearer came the throng of Trojans till it joined the columns of

mourners. When the mothers of Pallanteum saw them
entering the walls, the stricken city was ablaze with their
cries. No power on earth could restrain Evander. Coming
into the middle of the throng where the bier had been laid
on the ground, he threw himself on the body of Pallas and   150
clung to it weeping and moaning until at last grief freed a
path for his voice: 'O Pallas, this is not what you promised
your father! You said you would not be too rash in trusting
yourself to the cruel God of War. I well knew the glory
of one's first success in arms, the joy above all other joys of
one's first battle. These are bitter first fruits for a young
man. A hard schooling it has been in war, and you did not
have far to go for it. None of the gods listened to my vows
and prayers. O my dear wife, most blessed of women, you
were fortunate in your death, in not living to see this day.
But I have outstayed my time. A father should not survive   160
his son. If only I had followed our Trojan allies into battle
and the Rutulians had buried me under their spears! If only
I had given up my own life and this procession was
bringing home my body and not the body of Pallas. I
would not wish to blame you, Trojans, nor our treaties,
nor regret the joining of our right hands in friendship. The
death of my son was a debt I was fated to pay in my old
age. But if an early death was his destiny, I shall rejoice to
think that first he killed thousands of Volscians and fell
while leading the Trojans into Latium. Nor would I wish
you any other funeral than this, Pallas, given you by good   170
Aeneas and the great men from Phrygia, the leaders of the
Etruscans and all the soldiers of Etruria, bearing the great
trophies of the warriors your right hand has sent to their
deaths. And you too, Turnus, would now be standing in
the fields, a huge headless trophy, had Pallas been your
equal in age, had the years given you both equal strength.
But why does my grief keep the Trojans from their arms?
Go now, take this charge to your king and do not forget
it. If I drag out my hated life now that Pallas is killed, the

reason, Aeneas, lies in your right arm. You know it owes
the life of Turnus to the son and to the father. This is the
one field where you must put your courage and your
180 fortune to the test. I seek no joy in life – that is not what
the gods have willed – only to take this satisfaction down
to my son among the dead.'

Aurora meanwhile had lifted up her life-giving light for
miserable mortals, bringing back their toil and sufferings.
Both Tarchon and Father Aeneas soon built funeral pyres
on the curving shore and carried there the bodies of their
dead, each after the fashion of their fathers. They then set
black-burning torches to the fires and the heights of heaven
were plunged into pitchy darkness. Three times they ran
190 round the blazing pyres in gleaming armour. Three times
they rode in solemn procession round the fires of the dead
with wails of lamentation. Tears fell upon their armour
and fell upon the earth beneath. The clamour of men and
the clangour of trumpets rose to heaven as some threw
into the flames spoils torn from the corpses of the Latins,
their splendid swords and helmets, the bridles of horses and
scorching chariot wheels, while others burned the familiar
possessions of their dead friends, the shields and spears
which Fortune had not blessed. All around, oxen were
being sacrificed and their bodies offered to the God of
Death, while bristling swine and flocks carried off from the
fields were slaughtered over the fires. All along the shore
200 they watched the bodies of their comrades burn and tended
the dying flames, nor would they be torn away till dank
Night turned over the heavens and showed a sky studded
with burning stars.

The mourning Latins too had built countless pyres some
distance apart from the Trojans. Many bodies of men they
buried in the earth; many they took up and carried back to
the city or to their homes nearby in the countryside. The
rest they burned uncounted and unhonoured, a huge pile
of jumbled corpses, and all the wide land on every side was

lit by fire upon fire, each brighter than the other. When 210
the third day had risen and dispersed the chill darkness of
the sky, the mourners levelled on the pyres the deep ash in
which the bones of the dead were mingled, and weighed it
down with mounds of warm earth. That day in their
homes in the city of king Latinus, famous for his wealth,
the noise of grief was at its loudest. That day their long
mourning reached its height. Here were the mothers and
heart-broken wives of the dead. Here were loving sisters
beating their breasts, and children who had lost their
fathers, all cursing this deadly war and Turnus' marriage;
he was the man who should be deciding this matter with
his own sword and shield since he was the man who was
claiming the kingdom of Italy and the highest honours for
himself. The bitter Drances heaped fuel on the fire and 220
swore that Turnus was the only man whose name was
being called; nobody else was being asked to fight. But at
the same time many voices were raised for Turnus and
much was said on his behalf. The great name of the queen
cast its protecting shadow and also in his favour was all the
fame and all the trophies he had won in his wars.

In the middle of this disturbance, while the dispute was
still raging, to crown all, the envoys suddenly arrived back
with a gloomy answer from the city of Diomede. They
had achieved nothing for all the efforts they had expended;
their gifts, their gold, their earnest prayers had failed; the
Latins would have to look elsewhere for reinforcements or 230
plead for peace with the Trojan king. At this bitter blow
even king Latinus lost heart. Aeneas was chosen by Fate
and brought there by the express will of heaven – this was
what the anger of the gods was telling them; this was the
message of these tombs newly raised before their eyes.
With such thoughts in mind he summoned a great council,
commanding the leaders of his people to come within his
lofty doors. They duly gathered, filling the streets as they
streamed to the royal palace. Greatest in age and first of

those who carried the sceptre, Latinus sat in the middle
with sadness on his brow and asked the envoys who had
240 returned from the city of the Aetolians to tell what reply
they brought, demanding to hear every detail in due order.
The assembly was called to silence. Venulus obeyed the
command and began to speak: 'Fellow-citizens, we have
seen Diomede and the Argive camp. We have paced out
the road and lived through all the chances of the journey.
We have touched the hand that brought down the land of
Ilium. There in the fields near Mount Garganus, in the
Apulian kingdom of Iapyx, the victorious Diomede was
founding his city called Argyripa after the home of his
fathers at Argos. After we were admitted to his presence
and given leave to speak, we offered our gifts, telling him
our names and the land from which we came, who had
250 brought war among us and what had taken us to Arpi.
He heard us out and made this reply in words of peace:

'"The peoples of your land are blest by Fortune. Yours
are the kingdoms of Saturn, the ancient Ausonians, but
what Fortune is it that disturbs your peace and persuades
you to stir up wars you do not understand? Those of us
whose swords violated the fields of Ilium – let me not
speak of all we endured as we fought beneath her walls or
of our men drowned in her river Simois – we are scattered
over the round earth, paying unspeakable penalties and
suffering all manner of punishment for our crimes. We are
260 a band of men that even Priam might pity. The deadly star
of Minerva knows us well. So do the rocks of Euboea and
Caphereus, the cape of vengeance. From that campaign we
have been washed up on many a different shore: Menelaus,
son of Atreus, is in exile in distant Egypt at the pillars of
Proteus; Ulixes has seen the Cyclopes on Etna; shall I speak
of the kingdom of Neoptolemus in Epirus? Of the new
home of Idomeneus in Calabria? Of Locrians living on the
shores of Libya? Even the leader of the great Achivi from
Mycenae was struck down by the hand of his evil queen

the moment he stepped over his own threshold! The adulterous lover had been waiting for Asia to fall. To think that the envious gods forbade me to return to the altars of my fathers or to see the wife I longed for and my beautiful homeland of Calydon. Even now I am pursued by the sight of hideous portents. My lost comrades have taken to the sky on wings. They have become birds and haunt the rivers – so cruelly have my people been punished – weeping till the rocks ring with the sound of their voices. From that moment of madness when I attacked the body of a goddess and my spear defiled the hand of Venus, I should have known that this was bound to come. Do not, I beg you, do not urge me to take part in any such battle. I have had no quarrel with the Trojans since the uprooting of their citadel of Pergamum, and I do not remember old wrongs or take any pleasure in them. As for the gifts you bring me from your country, give them rather to Aeneas. We have faced each other, spear against deadly spear, and closed in battle. Believe me, for I have known it, how huge he rises behind his shield, with what a whirr he spins his javelin. If the land of Ilium had borne two other such heroes, the Trojan would have come in war to the cities of the Greek, the Fates would have changed and Greece would now be in mourning. As for all the long delay before the stubborn walls of Troy, it was the hands of Hector and Aeneas – both men noble in their courage, noble in their skill in arms, but Aeneas the greater in piety – that held back the victory of the Greeks and did not let it come till the tenth year. Let your hands join in a treaty of peace while the chance is offered, but take care not to let your weapons clash on his!"

'You have heard, O best of kings, the answer of a king. You have heard his judgement on this great war.'

The envoys had scarcely finished before a confused roar was running through the troubled ranks of the Italians, as when rocks resist a river in spate and the trapped waters

eddy and growl while the banks on either side roar with
the din of the waves. As soon as calm returned to their
minds and the words of fear were stilled on their lips, the
king on his high throne addressed the gods and then began.
'For my part, O men of Latium, I would have wished, and
it would have been better so, to have decided this great issue
long since, and not be summoning a council at a time like
this with the enemy sitting by our walls. We are fighting a
misguided war, fellow-citizens, against unconquerable
heroes and the sons of gods. Battle does not weary them,
and even in defeat they cannot take their hands from the
sword. If you had any hope of recruiting the Aetolians as
your allies, lay it aside. To everyone his own hopes, but
you can see how feeble this one is. All other resource is
shattered and lies in ruins. You can see this with your own
eyes. The whole truth is there at your finger tips. I accuse
no one. Courage has done all that courage could do. The
whole body of the kingdom has fought this fight. But now
the time has come for me to express an opinion which has
formed in my doubting mind. Give me your attention,
and I shall tell it in a few words. Near the Tuscan river
Tiber I have long owned some land which stretches away
to the west beyond the land of the Sicani. Here Auruncans
and Rutulians sow their seeds, wearying the stony hills
with the plough and grazing the roughest of them. Let this
whole area with the pine forests clothing its high mountains
be given to the Trojans as a token of our friendship, and let
us propose a treaty in just terms, inviting them to become
partners in our kingdom. Let them settle here, if their
hearts are so set on it, and build their walls. But if it is their
wish to go elsewhere and seize the land of some other
nation, and if it is within their power to leave this country
of ours, let us weave the timbers of twenty ships in Italian
oak, or more if they can man them. The wood is all lying
on the shore. Let them say what ships they want and how
many, and we can provide the bronze, the dockyards and

the hands to do the work. I propose also that a hundred 330
envoys, men of the highest rank in the Latin race, be sent
to carry this message and conclude this treaty, holding out
the branches of peace in their hands and bearing gifts,
talents of gold and ivory, and the throne and robe which
are the emblems of our royal power. Consider this together,
and rescue our crippled fortunes.'

Then rose Drances, hostile as ever, who always looked
askance at Turnus' great reputation and was goaded by
bitter jealousy. He was generous with his wealth and
readier still with his tongue, but his hand did not warm to
battle. His voice had some weight in council and was 340
always a force for discord. His mother's breeding gave him
pride of rank; his father's origins were unknown. These
were the words he spoke to add force and substance to
their anger: 'What you propose, good king Latinus, is clear
to all and needs no words of mine to support it. Everyone
knows, and admits that he knows, what fortune has in
store for the people, but they are all afraid to utter it. It is
time for the man whose auspices the gods reject to blow a
little less hard and give us freedom to speak. It is because of
his fatal recklessness – I, for one, shall not be silent though
he draw his sword and threaten me with death – we have
seen so many of our leaders, who have been the lights of
our people, extinguished, and the whole of our city now
slumped in grief, while he storms the Trojan camp and 350
frightens the sky with his weapons, knowing he can save
his own life by taking to his heels. There is still one thing
you must add, O best of kings, to all those many proposals
and gifts you tell us to send to the sons of Dardanus, one
thing only, and no man's violence should be able to
overrule your right as a father to give your own daughter
to a noble husband in a marriage that will be worthy of
her, sealing this peace in a treaty for all time. But if our
hearts and minds are so beset with fear of the man, let us
beg and beseech him to give her up and restore to his king

and to his fatherland the rights which are their due. Why
360   do you keep throwing your unfortunate fellow-citizens
into the jaws of danger, Turnus, you who are the single
source and cause of all these sufferings of Latium? War will
never save us. We are all asking you for peace, and the one
inviolable pledge of that peace. I am the first to come to
you as a suppliant – you imagine I am your enemy and
that causes me no distress – look at me! I beg you to pity
your people and lay down your pride. You are defeated.
You must leave the field. We have been routed often
enough and have seen enough funerals. We have stripped
our wide fields bare. But if fame drives you on, if you
have the strength in your heart, if you have such a yearning
370   to receive a palace as a dowry, then be bold, have the
confidence to go and stand face to face with your enemy.
So that Turnus can get himself a royal bride, our lives are
to be as chaff. We, the rank and file, are to litter the fields,
unburied and unwept. But you too, if there is any strength
in you, if you have any of the fighting spirit of your
fathers, stand up to your challenger and look him in the
face.'

At this, Turnus groaned, and blazed up into a violent
rage. The words seemed to burst from the depths of his
heart: 'You have always a good supply of words, Drances,
380   when war calls for action. When the senate is summoned,
you are the first to appear. But this is no time for filling
the council chamber with talk, for pouring out high-flown
speeches in comfort while our walls and ramparts are all
that keep the enemy from us, and we are waiting for the
ditches to fill with blood. By all means, Drances, you can
thunder out your eloquence in your usual style and accuse
me of cowardice, when your right hand has heaped up as
many Trojan corpses as mine has and all the fields are
studded with your trophies. But now is our chance to test
our vigour and our valour. We do not have to look too far
for enemies – they are standing all round the walls. Shall

we advance to meet them? You hesitate? Where is your
martial spirit? Will it always be in your long tongue and   390
nimble feet? You say I have been defeated. You scum of
the earth, who can say I am defeated when he sees the
Thybris rising, swollen with Trojan blood, the house of
Evander destroyed root and branch and the Arcadians
stripped of their arms? This is not how Pandarus and Bitias
found me, nor the thousand men I sent down to Tartarus
on my day of victory when I was trapped inside the walls
and rampart of the enemy. You say that war will never
save us. That prophecy is for the Trojan and for yourself,   400
you fool. But go on, stirring up panic everywhere and
praising to the skies the strength of a race of men who
have been twice defeated. Go on insulting the armies of
Latinus. Now, it seems, the leaders of the Myrmidons are
afraid of Phrygian weapons! Now it seems that Diomede
and Achilles of Larisa are taking fright, and the river
Aufidus is flowing backwards in full retreat from the
waves of the Adriatic! Drances even pretends to be terrified
when I speak – a rogue's trick! The fear is a pretence to
add sting to his charges against me. But there is no need
for you to be alarmed. My hand will never take the breath
of life from a man like you. It is welcome to stay where it
is in that breast of yours.

'But now, father, I come to you and to your great plan.   410
If you no longer hold out any hope for our arms, if we are
left to fight on utterly alone, if after one setback we are
completely destroyed, and Fortune has abandoned us never
to return, let us stretch out our defenceless arms and sue for
peace. But if only there were a spark of our old courage
left in us! Any man who has fallen and bitten the dust of
death rather than live to see such a thing, I count him
fortunate in his life's labours, the noblest spirit amongst us!
Surely we still have untapped resources and warriors who
have not yet engaged and there are still cities and peoples
in Italy to help us? And surely the Trojans have paid a

heavy price in blood for the glory they have won! They too have had their funerals. The same storm has fallen on all of us. Why then do we disgrace ourselves by stumbling on the threshold? Why do our knees start shaking before we hear the trumpet? Many things change for the better with the passing of the days and the ever-varying workings of time. Fortune comes and goes. She has mocked many a man, and then set his feet back on solid ground. So the Aetolian Diomede and his city of Arpi will not help us. But Messapus will, and Tolumnius, blessed by the gods, 430 and all the leaders who have come to us from so many peoples, and great will be the glory for the chosen men of Latium and the Laurentine fields. We have Camilla too, from the noble Volscian race, leading her mounted column and her squadrons flowering with bronze. But if I am the only one the Trojans want to meet in battle, if that is your will and I am such a great obstacle to the good of all, then the Goddess of Victory has not entirely abandoned me, nor is she so ill-disposed to these hands of mine that I should refuse any undertaking for which I have such hopes. I shall 440 go and face him with my spirits high were he mightier than Achilles and with armour the equal of his, made like his by the hands of Vulcan. To all of you, and to Latinus, father of my bride, I, Turnus, second in courage to none of those who have gone before me, have offered up my life. Is Aeneas challenging me, and me alone? Let him challenge. It is the answer to my prayer. If this is the anger of the gods I would not have Drances appease it; if it is a moment for courage and glory, I would not give it to Drances.'

So they disputed among themselves in deep uncertainty. Aeneas, meanwhile, had struck camp and was moving his army. Suddenly there came a messenger rushing wildly through the royal palace and causing panic all over the 450 city: the Trojans, drawn up in line of battle, the Etruscan squadron with them, were coming down the valley of the Tiber and filling the whole plain. There was instant confusion and dismay among the people and hearts were roused by the sharp spur of anger. With wild gestures the young men asked for arms. 'Arms!' they shouted, while their fathers wept and murmured. On every side a great clamour of dissenting voices rose to the winds like the sound of flocks of birds settling in groves of tall trees, or swans whose harsh calls ring across the chattering pools of the river Padusa, so rich in fish. 'Do not disturb yourselves, citizens!' shouted Turnus, seizing the moment. 'Convene your council and sit there praising peace while your enemies 460 invade your kingdom with swords in their hands.' These were his only words to them as he leapt to his feet and rushed from the lofty palace shouting: 'You, Volusus, tell the Volscian contingents to arm! And take the Rutulians with you! Deploy the cavalry, Messapus, and you too Coras with your brother, in battle array over the whole plain! Some of you reinforce the approaches to the city and man the towers. The rest of you come and advance with me where I order.'

In an instant they poured on to the walls from all over the city. Father Latinus himself left the council and aban- 470 doned his high designs till a later time, in deep distress at the troubles of the hour. Again and again he blamed himself for not eagerly welcoming Trojan Aeneas and taking him into the city as his son-in-law. Meanwhile men were digging pits in front of the gates and bringing up rocks and stakes. The shrill trumpet blew the signal for bloody battle and mothers and sons went to make a motley ring all round the city walls. Their last struggle called them and they came. The queen too, with a great retinue of the mothers of the city, rode in her carriage to bring offerings to the temple of Pallas on the heights of the citadel. With her went the maiden Lavinia, the cause of all this suffering, 480 her lovely eyes downcast. The mothers followed them and filled the temple with the smoke of incense, pouring out their sad prayers from its high threshold: 'Mighty in arms,

ruler of the battle, Tritonian maiden, break with your hand the spear of the Phrygian pirate and throw him to the ground. Spread out his body beneath your high gates.' Turnus in a fury was eagerly arming himself for battle, and soon had on his breastplate glowing red with bristling scales of bronze, and his golden greaves. His head was still
490 bare, but the sword was girt to his side as he ran down from the heights of the citadel in a blaze of gold, ardent and exulting and already grappling with the enemy in hope and expectation. He was like a stallion that has broken his tether and burst from his stall; free at last he gains the open plain and runs to the fields where the herds of mares are pastured or gallops off to bathe in the river which he used to know so well, tossing high his head and whinnying with delight while the mane streams over his neck and flanks.

The princess Camilla came to meet him with her Volscians in battle order. Under the very gates of the city she leapt down from her horse, and all her squadron followed
500 her example, dismounting in one flowing movement. These were her words: 'Turnus, if the brave are right to have faith in themselves, I dare to meet the Trojan cavalry – this is my undertaking – and go alone against the horsemen of Etruria. Give me leave to try the first hazard of war, while you stay on foot by the walls and guard the city.'

At these words Turnus fixed his eyes on this formidable warrior maiden and replied: 'O Camilla, glory of Italy, I cannot hope to express my gratitude in words or deeds.
510 But now, since that spirit of yours knows no limits, come share with me the heat of battle. According to a firm report my scouts have brought me, that scoundrel Aeneas has sent his light-armed cavalry ahead to scour the plains, while he himself is coming to the city along a ridge in deserted mountain country. I am planning an ambush where there is a sunken path through a wood, and shall post armed men where the road enters and where it leaves

the gorge. You go to meet the Etruscan cavalry and
engage them. Bold Messapus will be with you with the
horsemen of Latium and the squadron of Tiburtus, and
you will have the task of leading them.' So he spoke and   520
with like words urged Messapus and the leaders of his allies
into battle, while he went to meet his enemy.

There is a winding valley well suited to stealth and
stratagem in war. Hemmed in on both sides, it is darkened
by the dense foliage of trees, and a narrow path leads into
it making a treacherous approach through a ravine. Above
this valley, among the viewpoints on the hilltop, there lies
a little-known plateau which gives safe cover whether you
wish to engage the enemy on your right flank or on your
left or stand on the ridges rolling down great boulders.
Marching by paths he knew, Turnus took up position here   530
and settled into ambush in this dangerous forest.

Meanwhile in the palace of the heavens Diana, daughter
of Latona, spoke to swift Opis, one of the sacred company
of girls who were her companions, and these were her sad
words: 'Camilla is going to a cruel war. Dear as she is to
me above all others, she has put on our armour, and it will
avail her nothing. This is no new love, believe me, that has
come to move the heart of Diana with sudden sweetness.
When Metabus, hated by his people for his arrogant use of   540
power, was driven from his throne, he left the ancient city
of Privernum and took his infant daughter with him
through all his wars and battles, to be his companion in
exile. He called her Camilla, changing part of her mother's
name, Casmilla. Carrying her in his arms, he made for the
long ridges and the lonely woods, cruel spears pressing him
hard on every side and Volscian soldiers on the move all
about him. Suddenly he found his way blocked by the
river Amasenus in full spate, foaming to the top of its
banks – such a deluge of rain had burst from the clouds.
He was about to leap into the water to swim across, but
checked himself out of love for his child and fear for the   550

burden he so loved. As he pondered all the dangers, a painful resolve soon formed in his mind. He took the warrior's spear he chanced to have in his hand, a mighty weapon of solid, knotted, well-seasoned wood, and wrapping the baby in cork-tree pith and bark, he lashed her tightly to the middle of the spear. Then brandishing it in his mighty hand, he cried out to heaven: "To you, kindly maiden, lover of woods and daughter of Latona, I dedicate my daughter as your handmaiden. She is your suppliant, and as she flies through the air to escape her enemies, the
560 first weapon she holds in her hands is yours. O goddess, I solemnly pray, receive her as your own as I now commit her to the hazard of the winds." At these words he drew back his arm and sent the weapon spinning. The waters rang with the sound as helpless Camilla flew over the wild river on the whistling javelin. But by now a great throng of his enemies was pressing Metabus even closer, and he threw himself into the water. Then, in triumph on the other side, he wrenched from the turf spear and maiden together, his dedication to Diana.

'No cities took him under their roofs or within their walls – he himself was too savage to have submitted to them – but he spent his whole life on the lonely mountains
570 among the herdsmen. There in the scrub among the rough dens of beasts he fed his daughter with milk from the udders of wild brood-mares, putting the teats to her soft lips, and as soon as she had taken the first steps on her infant feet, he put a keen-edged javelin in her hand and slung a bow and arrows from her little shoulder. Instead of gold in her hair and a long cloak to cover her, a tiger skin hung from her head all down her back. While her hand was still soft, she was spinning her baby javelins and whirling the sling round her head on its tapering thong to
580 shoot the white swan or crane from the river Strymon. Many a mother in the towns of Etruria longed in vain to see her married to her son, but all she cared for was Diana.

Undefiled, she preserved a constant love for her weapons and her chastity. If only she had never been caught up in such a war as this, daring to challenge the Trojans! I would have loved her and she would now have been one of my companions. But come now, since a bitter fate is closing in on her, glide down from the sky, Opis my nymph, and visit the land of Latium, where a dreadful battle is being fought and all the omens are adverse. Take these weapons, and draw an avenging arrow from my quiver. Then, with that same shaft, whoever violates that sacred body with a wound, be he Trojan or Italian, must pay to me an equal penalty in blood. Then I shall put a cloud round her poor body and her armour and take them undespoiled to lie in a tomb in her own country.' The goddess spoke, and Opis, veiled in a dark storm, glided lightly down through the breezes of the sky, whirring as she flew.

But all this time nearer and nearer to the walls came the Trojan column, the Etruscan leaders and the whole cavalry army drawn up in regular squadrons. Horses were prancing and snorting all over the plain, fretting at the reins that held them in and plunging to one side after another. Far and wide the field bristled with the steel of the spears, and all the land was a blaze of light from uplifted weapons. There too, coming to oppose them, appeared Messapus and the swift Latins, Coras with his brother, and the squadron of Camilla. Their right arms were drawn back, their lances thrust forward with tips quivering. Men were arriving. Horses were neighing. The whole plain was ablaze. They had now come within a spear-cast of each other and stopped. Then, with a sudden shout, they galloped forward, urging their horses to frenzy, and showering weapons thick as snow till the sky was curtained with shadow. Tyrrhenus and bold Aconteus were first to charge each other, riding full force with levelled spears, and great was the din and fearful the fall as they crashed their warhorses against each other, smashing breast on breast.

Aconteus was thrown forward a great distance and fell like a thunderbolt, or a rock hurled from a catapult, scattering his life's breath into the breezes.

In that instant the battle lines were thrown into disorder. Putting their shields on to their backs, the Latins turned and rode back towards the city walls driven by the Trojan squadrons under Asilas. But when they were almost at the gates, they raised another shout and pulled round the supple necks of their horses, while the Trojans fled in their turn, galloping with slack reins in a long retreat. As the sea advances wave by wave, now rushing to the land, throwing foam over the rocks and soaking the edge of the sand in the bay; now turning and hurrying back, sucking down the stones and rolling them along in its undertow while the shallows retreat and the shore is left dry – just so the Etruscans twice turned and drove the Rutulians to the city walls, and twice they were repulsed and had to cover their backs with their shields and look over their shoulders at their enemies. But when they clashed in battle for the third time, and all the ranks were embroiled together, each man singled out his own enemy, and then the groans of the dying could be heard, weapons and bodies lay deep in blood, half-dead horses rolled about entangled with the corpses of men, and ever fiercer and fiercer grew the battle. Orsilochus did not dare go near Remulus, but hurled his spear at his horse and its steel point stuck under its ear. Maddened by the blow, it reared, heaving its chest high and lashing its hooves, unable to endure the pain of the wound. Remulus was thrown and sent rolling on the ground, Catillus felled Iollas and then Herminius, great in stature, in spirit, and in arms. His head of golden hair was bare, his shoulder bare, and he had no fear of wounds, so vast he stood and open to the weapons of his enemies. Catillus' spear drove right through him and stood out between his broad shoulders quivering, and Herminius doubled up in agony. Black blood was flowing everywhere as they dealt out slaughter with the steel, searching for death and glory among the wounds.

There in the middle of all this bloodshed, exulting in it, was the Amazon Camilla with the quiver on her shoulder, and one side bared for battle. Sometimes the pliant spears 650 came thick from her hand; sometimes, unwearied, she caught up her mighty double axe, and the golden bow and arrows of Diana rang on her shoulder. Whenever she was forced to retreat, she turned her bow and aimed her arrows while still in flight. The girls she had chosen as her companions were all about her, Larina, Tulla, and Tarpeia brandishing her bronze axe, all of them daughters of Italy, chosen by the servant of the gods Camilla to do her honour by their beauty and to be her own trusted attendants in peace and war. They were like the Amazons of 660 Thrace whose horses' hooves drum on the frozen waters of the river Thermodon when they fight round Hippolyte in their brightly coloured armour, or when Penthesilea, daughter of Mars, rides home in her chariot and her army of women with their crescent shields exult in a great howling tumult.

Whom first did your spear bring down from his horse? Whom last, fierce warrior maiden? How many bodies of dying men did you strew on the ground? Eunaeus, son of Clytius, was the first. When he stood face to face with Camilla and she drove the long pine shaft of her spear through his unprotected chest, he vomited rivers of blood and champed the gory earth with his teeth, twisting himself round his wound as he died. Then she brought down Liris 670 and Pagasus on top of him: Liris when he was trying to collect the reins after his wounded horse had reared and thrown him, Pagasus when he came and stretched out an undefended right hand to support Liris as he fell; but they both went flying head over heels. Then she sent Amastrus, the son of Hippotas, to join them, and raced after Tereus and Harpalycus, Demophoon and Chromis, pressing them

hard even at long range with her spear, and for every dart
that flew from her hand, a Trojan hero fell. The huntsman
Ornytus was rushing past in strange armour, mounted on
his horse Iapyx. This was a warrior who wore on his broad
680 shoulders the hide of a bullock, while his head was encased
in the huge gaping jaws of a wolf, complete with cheekbones and white teeth. A country spear shaped like a sickle
armed his hand as he moved in the middle of the press,
taller by a head than them all. She caught him – it was not
difficult, for the whole column had turned and run – and
when she had pierced him through, she spoke these bitter
taunts over him: 'So you thought you were driving game
in the woods, my Etruscan friend? The day has come when
you have been proved wrong by a woman's weapons! But
it is no mean name you will be taking to your fathers
when you tell them you fell by the spear of Camilla.'

690   Instantly then she struck Orsilochus and Butes, the two
tallest of the Trojans. Butes was turned away from her and
the tip of her spear went in between helmet and breastplate
where his neck shone white as he sat in the saddle with the
shield hanging loose on his left arm. She fled from Orsilochus, but after he had driven her in a great circle, she cut
inside the arc and began to pursue her pursuer. Then,
rising above him, she struck again and again with her
mighty axe, hacking through his armour and his bones as
he begged and pleaded with her and the axe-blows spilt
700 the hot brains down his face. The warrior son of Aunus of
the Apennines then came upon her and stood stock still in
sudden terror at the sight. He was not the least of the
Ligurians while the Fates gave him leave to tell his lies. So,
when he saw that it was too late to save himself by
running away, and that the princess was upon him and
would not be deflected, he began to play his tricks, using
all his cunning and calculation. 'What is so wonderful,' he
said, 'if a woman depends on the courage of a horse? Give
up your chance of running away, and risk your life in close

combat with me on level ground. Gird yourself to fight on
foot and you will soon discover that the winds are blowing
you only the illusion of glory.' These words stung Camilla
to a burning fury of resentment. Handing her horse to a   710
companion, she stood there to face him without a trace of
fear, armed like her enemy with a naked sword and a plain
light shield. The moment he thought his ruse had succeeded, the warrior took to his heels himself. Jerking the
reins around, he made off, driving his horse to the gallop
with steel spurs. 'You Ligurian fool!' she cried. 'You are
the one who has been carried away by the empty winds of
pride! You have taken to the slippery arts of your ancestors,
but little good will they do you. Trickery will not bring
you safe back home to your treacherous father Aunus.'
These were her words, and on nimble feet she ran as swift
as fire in front of the horse and stood full in its path. Then,
seizing the reins, she exacted punishment from her enemy   720
in blood, as easily as the sacred falcon flies from his crag to
pursue a dove high in the clouds, catches it, holds it and
rips out its entrails with hooked claws while blood and
torn feathers float down from the sky.

But the Father of Gods and Men was not blind to this as
he sat high above on the top of Olympus, and he roused
Tarchon the Etruscan to bitter battle, laying on him the
sharp goad of anger. So Tarchon rode among the slaughter   730
in the ranks of his retreating squadrons, whipping them up
with all manner of cries, calling on each man by name and
rallying the routed to do battle: 'What are you afraid of,
you Etruscans? Will you never know shame? Will you
always be so spiritless? This is rank cowardice! One woman
has turned this whole army and is scattering you to all
points of the compass! What are weapons for? Why do we
carry swords in our hands and not use them? You are not
so sluggish when it comes to lovemaking and night cam-
paigns, or when the curved pipe calls you up to the
dancing chorus of Bacchus! Wait, then, for feasts and

goblets from groaning tables. That is what you love. That
740 is what you care about. Do nothing till the soothsayer
gives his blessing and announces the festival and the fat
victim calls you into the deep groves.' When this harangue
was over, he spurred his horse into the thick of the enemy
– he too was willing to die – and made a wild charge at
Venulus. Tearing him off his horse and clasping him in his
right arm, he rode off at full gallop with his enemy held in
front of him. A shout rose to the sky and all the Latins
turned to look as Tarchon flew like fire across the plain
carrying man and armour with him. Then he broke off the
steel head of Venulus' spear and with it probed for exposed
flesh where he could give the fatal wound. Venulus fought
750 back to keep Tarchon's hand from his throat, pitting
strength against violence, just as when a tawny eagle has
seized a snake and flown up into the sky, winding its talons
round it and digging in its claws; meanwhile the wounded
serpent writhes in sinuous coils, its scales stiff and rough,
and hisses as it reaches up with its head; but for all its
struggles, the eagle never stops tearing at it with its great
hook of a beak, beating the air all the time with its wings –
just like such an eagle did the victorious Tarchon carry off
his prey from the Tiburtine ranks. Following their leader's
example, and seeking like success, the Etruscans, the men
from Maeonia, rushed into battle. Then Arruns, whose life
was owed to the Fates, circled round Camilla to find
760 where Fortune would offer the easiest approach. She was
swift of foot, but he was more than her equal with the
javelin and far superior in cunning. Wherever she went on
her wild forays through the thick of battle, Arruns was
behind her, quietly following in her tracks. Wherever she
went as she returned in triumph and withdrew from her
enemies, Arruns pulled on his swift reins and kept out of
sight. Round a whole circle he went, trying now one
approach, now another, brandishing the fatal spear that
never missed its mark.

It then so chanced that Chloreus appeared, a man who had been consecrated to Cybele on her mountain, and in days long past had been a priest. She saw him a long way off, resplendent in his Phrygian armour and spurring his foaming warhorse. The horse-cloth was of hide with gold stitching and overlapping brass scales in the shape of feathers. He himself shone with exotic indigo and purple. The arrows he shot from his Lycian bow were from Gortyn in Crete and the bow hanging from his shoulder was of gold. Gold too was the helm on the head of the priest, and on that day he had gathered the rustling linen folds of his saffron-yellow cloak into a knot with a golden brooch. He wore an embroidered tunic and barbaric embroidered trousers covered his legs. Whether her intention was to nail his Trojan armour to the temple doors or to sport captive gold on her hunting expeditions, she picked him out in the press of battle, and blind to all else and unthinking, she tracked him through the whole army, burning with all a woman's passion for spoil and plunder. At last the lurking Arruns saw his moment and hurled his spear, offering up this prayer to heaven: 'O highest of the gods, guardian of the holy mountain of Soracte, Apollo, we are the first to worship you. We heap up the wood of the pine to feed your flames, and in your holy rites, sure in our faith, we walk on fire, sinking our feet deep in the hot ash. Grant now, All-powerful Father, that our arms be wiped clean of this disgrace. My mind is not set on spoils won from a girl or a trophy set up for routing her or for any form of booty. My fame will come from my other feats of arms. But let this deadly scourge be defeated and fall to my spear, and I shall go back to the cities of my fathers and claim no credit.'

Phoebus Apollo heard, and part of his prayer he decided to answer, part he scattered to the swift breezes of air. He granted his prayer to surprise Camilla and lay her low in death, but did not allow the mountains of his native land

298

THE AENEID

to see him ever again. A sudden squall took these words
and blew them far away to the winds of the south. So,
when the spear that left his hand went whirring through
the air and the Volscians, all of them, turned their minds
and eyes intently to their queen, she was not thinking of
whirring or of air or of weapons coming out of the sky,
and the shaft struck home beneath her naked breast and
lodged there drinking deep of her virgin blood. Her companions rushed in panic to support their falling queen, and
Arruns fled, more terrified than anyone, joy mixed with
his fear. He had lost his faith in his spear and was afraid to
face the weapons of the warrior maiden. As when a wolf
has killed a shepherd or a great ox, and goes at once to
hide high in the trackless hills before the avenging spears
can come to look for him; he knows what he has done,
and takes fright, comforting his quivering tail by tucking it
under his belly as he makes for the woods – just so did
Arruns disappear from sight in wild confusion, happy to
escape and mingle in the press of battle. Camilla was
dying. She tried to pull out the spear, but its steel point
stood deep in the wound between the bones of her ribs.
She was swooning from loss of blood, her eyes dimming
in the chill of death, and the flush had faded from her
cheeks. With her dying breath she spoke to Acca, alone of
all her young friends. She was her most faithful companion
and to her alone she used to open her heart. 'I can do no
more, Acca my sister. This cruel wound is taking all my
strength, and everything is going dark around me. Run
from this place and take my last commands to Turnus. He
must come into battle and keep the Trojans away from the
city. And now, farewell.' Even as she was speaking she was
losing her hold on her reins and in spite of all her efforts
she slid to the ground. Then, growing cold, she little by
little freed herself from her body. Her neck drooped and
she laid down her head, yielding to death and letting go
her weapons, as her life left her with a groan and fled in

anger down to the shades. At this a measureless clamour
rose and struck the golden stars. Now that Camilla had
fallen, the battle raged as never before. Charging in one
solid mass came the whole army of the Trojans, the
Etruscan nobles and the Arcadian squadrons of Evander.

Opis, Diana's sentinel, had long been at her post high in
the mountains, watching the fighting and knowing no
fear. But when, far beneath her in the press of warriors
shouting in the frenzy of battle, she saw Camilla receive
the bitter stroke of death, she groaned and spoke these 840
words from the depths of her heart: 'Alas, Camilla! You
have paid too cruel a price for daring to challenge the
Trojans in war, nor has it profited you that alone in the
wild woods you have worshipped Diana and worn our
quiver on your shoulder. But your queen has not left you
unhonoured now at your last hour. This death of yours
will not be forgotten among the peoples of this earth, and
no one shall say that you have died unavenged. Whoever
has desecrated your body with a wound will pay just
penalty with his life.'

At the foot of a high mountain there was a huge mound
of earth shaded by dense ilex trees. It was the tomb of
Dercennus, an ancient king of the Laurentines. Here the 850
lovely goddess first alighted on her swift flight, keeping
watch for Arruns from the high mound. When she saw
him gleaming in his armour and swollen with empty
pride, she called out: 'Why are you leaving? Turn round
and come in this direction. Come here and die! You must
receive your reward for Camilla. Come, even a man can
die by the weapons of Diana!' When she had spoken, the
Thracian nymph took a winged arrow from her gilded
quiver and drew her deadly bow. Far back she stretched 860
the string until the curved horns of the bow were close
together, her hands level, the left on the steel point of the
arrow, the right holding the string against her breast.
Arruns heard the hiss of the arrow and the whirr in the air,

and in that same moment the steel was planted in his flesh. His comrades paid no heed. They left him breathing his last and groaning in some place unknown in the dust of the plain, while Opis soared on her wings to heavenly Olympus.

The light-armed squadron of Camilla were the first to flee when they lost their queen; then the Rutulians in a rout; then bold Asilas and all the scattered leaders and leaderless columns made for safety, wheeling their horses and galloping for the walls. No weapon could check the deadly onset of the Trojans and no one could stand against them. Back rode the Latins with slack bowstrings on slumped shoulders, and the four-hooved beat of their galloping horses drummed on the crumbling plain. As the black cloud of swirling dust rolled up to the walls, the mothers stood on the watch-towers beating their breasts and the wailing of women rose to the stars in the sky. The first Latins to burst into the open gates were pressed hard by a pursuing column of enemies mingled with friends and did not escape a pitiable death. There, on the very threshold, within the walls of their native city and in the safe refuge of their own homes, their bodies were pierced and they breathed out their life's breath. Some shut the gates and dared not open them to take their own people within the walls for all their pleading, and there was piteous slaughter of the armed men guarding the approaches and of men rushing to death on their weapons. Of those who were shut out before the weeping eyes of their own parents, some rolled headlong down into the ditches with the weight of the rout behind them, while others came on blindly at full gallop and crashed into the massive gates with their firm-set posts. Even the mothers strove their utmost – the true love of their native land showed them the way and Camilla was their example. Wildly they hurled missiles from the walls and rushed to do the work of steel with stumps and stakes of oak wood hardened in the fire, longing to be the first to die in defence of the walls of their city.

Meanwhile the warrior Turnus was still in the wood when the bitter news came and filled his heart to overflowing. The words of Acca brought him great turmoil of spirit: the battle forces of the Volscians were destroyed; Camilla had fallen; the enemy were attacking fiercely and had carried everything irresistibly before them; panic was 900 already reaching the city walls. In a frenzy – and this is what the implacable will of Jupiter decreed – he came down from the hills where he had kept his ambush and left the wild woods behind him. Scarcely was he out of sight and moving on to the plains when Father Aeneas entered the open pass, came over the ridge and then emerged from the woods. So then they were both making for the walls at speed, with their whole armies marching not many paces from each other. Aeneas saw the Laurentine columns and the long line of dust smoking on the plains at one and the same moment as Turnus recognized Aeneas advancing 910 relentlessly under arms and heard the drumming of approaching hooves and the breathing of horses. They would have joined battle instantly and tried the fortunes of war if the rose-red sun had not been dipping its weary horses in the Iberian sea, drawing down the light of day and bringing on the night. They both encamped before the city and built stockades on their ramparts.

12

TRUCE AND DUEL

When Turnus saw the line of the Latins broken, the battle going against them and their spirits flagging, when he realized that the time had come to honour his promises and that all eyes were upon him, no more was needed. He burned with implacable rage and his courage rose within him. Just as a lion in the fields round Carthage, who does not move into battle till he has received a great wound in his chest from the hunters, and then revels in it, shaking out the thick mane on his neck; fearlessly he snaps off the shaft left in his body by the ruffian that threw it, and opens his gory jaws to roar – just so did the violent passion rise in 10 Turnus. At last he spoke these wild words to the king: 'Turnus keeps no man waiting. There is no excuse for Aeneas and his cowards to go back on their word or fail to keep their agreement. I am coming to meet them. Bring out the sacraments, father, and draw up the terms of the treaty. Either this right hand of mine will send this Trojan who has deserted Asia down into Tartarus – the Latins can sit and watch – and one man's sword shall refute a charge brought against a whole people, or else he can rule over those he has defeated and have Lavinia as his wife.'

Latinus answered him, and his voice was calm: 'You are 20 a great-hearted young warrior. The more you excel in fierce courage, the more urgent is my duty to take thought, to weigh all possible chances and to be afraid. You have the kingdom of your father Daunus. You have all the cities

your right hand has taken. I too, Latinus, have some
wealth and some generosity of spirit. In Latium and the
Laurentine fields there are other women for you to marry,
and of the noblest families. This is not easy to say. Allow
me to speak openly and honestly, and as you listen, lay
these words to your heart. For me it would have been
wrong to unite my daughter with any of those who came
to ask for her in the past. It was forbidden by all the
prophecies of gods and men. But I gave way to my love
for you. I gave way to the kinship of blood and to the 30
grief and tears of my wife. Breaking all the ties that bound
me, I seized Lavinia from the man to whom she had been
promised and took up arms in an unjust cause. From that
moment you see the calamities of war that fall upon me,
and the suffering that you bear more than any other.
Twice we have been crushed in great battles, and we can
scarcely protect within our city the future hopes of Italy.
The current of the Thybris is even now warm with our
blood and the broad plains white with our bones. Why do
I always give way? Why do I change my resolve? What
folly this is! I am ready to accept them as allies if Turnus is
killed; why not put an end to the war while he is still alive?
What will your kinsmen the Rutulians, what will the 40
whole of the rest of Italy say if I betray you and send you
to your death – which Fortune forbid – when you are
asking to marry my daughter? Remember the many acci-
dents of war and take pity on your old father waiting with
heavy heart far away in your native Ardea.' These words
had no effect on Turnus. The violence of his fury mounted.
The healing only heightened the fever. As soon as he could
bring himself to speak, out came his reply: 'This concern
you are so kind as to show for my sake, I beg of you for
my sake, forget it, and allow me to barter my life for
glory. We too have weapons, father. We too have some 50
strength in our right arm to throw the steel around, and
when we strike a man, the blood flows from the wound.

His mother the goddess will not be at hand with her woman's tricks, lurking in the treacherous shadows and trying to hide him in a cloud when he turns tail!'

Terrified by this new turn in the fortunes of battle, queen Amata began to weep. Seeing her own death before her, she tried to check the frenzy of Turnus, the man she had chosen to be the husband of her daughter: 'By these tears, Turnus, by any respect for me that touches your
60 heart, Amata begs of you this one thing. You are the one hope and the one relief of my old age. In your hands rest the honour and the power of Latinus. Our whole house is falling and you are its one support. Do not persist in meeting the Trojans in battle. Whatever fate awaits you in that encounter, waits also for me. If you die, I too will leave the light I loathe. I shall never live to be a captive and see Aeneas married to Lavinia.' When Lavinia heard these words of her mother, her burning cheeks were bathed in tears and the deep flush glowed and spread over her face. As when Indian ivory has been stained with blood-red dye, or when white lilies are crowded by roses and take on their red, such were the colours on the maiden's face. Turnus
70 was distraught with love and fixed his eyes on Lavinia. Burning all the more for war, he then spoke these few words to Amata: 'Do not, I beg of you, mother, send me to the harsh encounters of war with tears and with such an evil omen. Turnus is not free to hold back the day of his death. Go as my messenger, Idmon, and take these words of mine to the leader of the Phrygians, and little pleasure will they give him: when tomorrow's dawn reddens in the sky, borne on the crimson wheels of Aurora's chariot, let him not lead Trojans against Rutulians. Let the Trojan and Rutulian armies be at peace. His blood, or mine, shall de-
80 cide this war. This is the field where the hand of Lavinia shall be won.'

When he had finished speaking and rushed back into the palace, he called for his horses and it gladdened his heart to

see them standing there before him neighing. Orithyia,
wife of Boreas, had given them to Turnus' grandfather
Pilumnus to honour him, and they were whiter than the
snow and swifter than the winds. The impatient charioteers
stood round them, drumming on the horses' chests with
cupped hands and combing their streaming manes. Then
Turnus himself drew over his shoulders the breastplate
with scales of gold and pale copper and fitted on his sword
and shield and his helmet with its red crests in horned
sockets. The God of Fire himself had made the sword for   90
Turnus' father Daunus, dipping it white-hot in the waters
of the Styx. Then instantly he snatched up his mighty
spear which was leaning there against a great column in
the middle of the palace, spoil taken from Actor the
Auruncan, and brandished it till it quivered, shouting:
'You, my spear, have never failed me when I have called
upon you. Now the time is here. Mighty Actor once
wielded you. Now it is the right of Turnus. Grant me the
power to bring down that effeminate Phrygian, to tear the
breastplate off his body and rend it with my bare hands, to
foul in the dust the hair he has curled with hot steel and   100
steeped in myrrh!' Such was the blazing fury that drove
him on. Sparks flew from his whole face and his piercing
eyes flashed fire. He was like a bull coming into his first
battle, bellowing fearfully and gathering his anger into his
horns by goring a tree-trunk and slashing the air, pawing
the sand and making it fly as he rehearses for battle.

Aeneas meanwhile, arrayed in the arms his mother had
given him, was no less ferocious. He too was sharpening his
spirit and rousing himself to anger, rejoicing that the war
was being settled by the treaty he had proposed. He then   110
reassured his allies and comforted the fears and anxieties of
Iulus, telling of the future that had been decreed, ordering
envoys to return a firm answer to Latinus and lay down the
conditions for peace.

The next day had scarcely risen, sprinkling the mountain

tops with brightness. When the horses of the Sun first reared up from the deep sea and raised their nostrils to breathe out the light, the Rutulians and Trojans were measuring a field for the duel under the walls of the great city, setting out braziers between the two armies and building altars of turf to the gods they shared. Others, wearing sacrificial aprons, their foreheads bound with holy leaves, brought fire and spring water. The Ausonian legion advanced, armed with javelins, filling the gateways as they streamed out of their city in serried ranks. On the other side the whole Trojan and Etruscan army came at the run in all their varied armour, drawn up with weapons at the ready as though it were the bitter business of battle that was calling them out. There too, in the middle of all these thousands, the leaders hovered in the pride of purple and gold, Mnestheus of the line of Assaracus, brave Asilas and Messapus, tamer of horses, son of Neptune. The signal was given. They all withdrew to their places, planting their spears in the ground and propping their shields against them. Then in a sudden rush the mothers, those who could not bear arms and the weak old men took up their seats on the towers and roofs of the city or stood high on the gates.

But Juno looked out from the top of what is now the Alban Mount – in those days it had neither name nor honour nor glory – and saw the plain, the two armies of Laurentines and Trojans, and the city of Latinus. Immediately the goddess Juno addressed the goddess who was the sister of Turnus, the ruler of lakes and roaring rivers, an honour granted by Jupiter the High King of Heaven as the price of her ravished virginity: 'Nymph, pride of all rivers, dearest to our heart, you know how I have favoured you above all the other women of Italy who have mounted the ungrateful bed of magnanimous Jupiter, and have gladly set you in your place in the skies, learn now the grief which is yours, Juturna, and do not lay the blame on me. As long as Fortune seemed to permit it, as long as

the Fates allowed all to go well with Latium, I have
protected the warrior Turnus and your walls. But now I
see he is confronting a destiny to which he is not equal.
The day of the Fates and the violence of his enemy are 150
upon him. My eyes cannot look at this battle or at this
treaty. If you dare to stand closer and help your brother,
go. It is right and proper. You suffer now. Perhaps a better
time will come.' She had scarcely spoken when the tears
flooded from Juturna's eyes, and three times and more she
beat her lovely breasts. 'This is no time for tears,' said
Juno, daughter of Saturn. 'Go quickly and if you can find a
way, snatch your brother from death or else stir up war
and dash from their hands this treaty they have drawn up.
You dare. I sanction.' With these words she urged her on,
then left her in doubt and confusion and wounded to the 160
heart.

Meanwhile the kings arrived, Latinus mighty in his
four-horse chariot, with twelve gold rays encircling his
shining temples, proof of his descent from his grandfather
the God of the Sun. Turnus was in his chariot drawn by
two white horses, gripping two broad-bladed spears in his
hand. From the other side, advancing from the camp, came
Father Aeneas, the founder of the Roman race, with his
divine armour blazing and his shield like a star. Beside him
were Ascanius, the second hope for the future greatness of
Rome, and a priest arrayed in pure white vestments, driving
to the burning altars a yearling ewe as yet unshorn and the 170
young of a breeding sow. Turning their eyes towards the
rising sun, the leaders stretched out their hands with offerings of salted meal, marked the peak of their victims'
foreheads with their blades and poured libations on the
altars from their goblets.

Then devout Aeneas drew his sword and prayed: 'I now
call the Sun to witness, and this land for which I have been
able to endure such toil; I call upon the All-powerful Father
of the Gods, and you his wife, Saturnian Juno – and I pray

you, goddess, from this moment look more kindly on us —
and you, glorious Mars, under whose sway all wars are
disposed; I call upon springs and rivers; I call upon all the
divinities of high heaven and all the gods of the blue sea: if
victory should chance to fall to Ausonian Turnus, it is
agreed that the defeated withdraw to the city of Evander.
Iulus will leave these lands, and after this the people of
Aeneas will not rise again in war, or bring their armies
here, or disturb this kingdom with the sword. But if
Victory grants the day to us and to our arms — as I believe
she will, and may the gods so rule — I shall not order
Italians to obey Trojans, nor do I seek royal power for
myself. Both nations shall move forward into an everlasting
treaty, undefeated, and equal before the law. I shall give
the sacraments and the gods. Latinus, the father of my
bride, will have the armies and solemn authority in the
state. For me the Trojans will build the walls of a city and
Lavinia will give it her name.'

So prayed Aeneas, and Latinus followed him, looking
up and stretching his right hand towards the sky: 'I too
swear, Aeneas, by the same: by earth and sea and stars; by
the two children of Latona and by two-browed Janus; by
the divine powers beneath the earth and the holy house of
unyielding Dis; and let the Father himself, who sanctions
treaties by the flash of his lightning, hear these my words. I
touch his altar. I call to witness the gods and the fires that
stand between us. The day shall not come when men of
Italy shall violate this treaty or break this peace, whatever
chance will bring. This is my will and no power will set it
aside, not if it dissolve the earth in flood and pour it into
the sea, not if it melt the sky into Tartarus, just as this
sceptre' — at that moment he was holding his sceptre in his
hand — 'will never sprout green or cast a shadow from
delicate leaves, now that it has been cut from the base of its
trunk in the forest, leaving its mother tree and losing its
limbs and leafy tresses to the steel. What was once a tree.

skilled hands have now clad in the beauty of bronze and given to the fathers of Latium to bear.' With such words they sealed the treaty between them in full view of the leaders of the peoples. Then, taking the duly consecrated victims, they cut their throats on to the altar fires, and, tearing the entrails from them while they still lived, they heaped the altars from laden platters.

But it had long seemed to the Rutulians that this was not an even contest and their hearts were still more confused and dismayed when the two men appeared before their eyes and they saw at close range the difference in their strength. Their fears were increased by the sight of Turnus stepping forward quietly with downcast eyes to 220 worship at the altar like a suppliant. His cheeks were like a boy's and there was a pallor over all his youthful body. As soon as his sister Juturna saw that such talk was spreading and that men's minds were weakening and wavering, she came into the battle lines in the guise of Camers, whose family had been great from his earliest ancestors, whose father had won fame for his courage, and who himself was the boldest of the bold in the use of arms. Into the middle of the battle lines she advanced, well knowing what she had to do, and there with these words she sowed the seeds of many different rumours: 'Is it not a disgrace, Rutulians, to sacrifice the life of one man for all of us? Are we not 230 their equals in numbers and in strength? Look, these few here are all they have, the Trojans, Arcadians and the army sent by Fate – the Etruscans who hate Turnus! We are short of enemies, even if only half our number were to engage them in battle. As things are, the fame of Turnus will rise to the gods on whose altars he now dedicates himself, and he will live on the lips of men, but if we lose our native land, we shall be forced to obey proud masters, who now sit here idling in our fields!'

By such words she more and more inflamed the minds of the warriors, and murmurs crept through their ranks.

240 Even the Laurentines had a change of heart, even the Latins, and men who a moment ago were longing for a rest from fighting and safety for their people, now wanted their weapons and prayed that the treaty would come to nothing, pitying Turnus and the injustice of his fate. At this moment Juturna did even more and showed a sign high in the sky, the most powerful portent that ever confused and misled men of Italy. The tawny eagle of Jupiter was flying in the red sky of morning, putting to clamorous flight the winged armies of birds along the shore, when he suddenly swooped down to the waves and 250 seized a noble swan in his pitiless talons. The men of Italy thrilled at the sight, the birds all shrieked and – a wonder to behold – they wheeled in their flight, darkening the heavens with their wings, and formed a cloud to mob their enemy high in the air until, exhausted by their attacks and the weight of his prey, he gave way, dropping it out of his talons into the river below and taking flight far away into the clouds.

The Rutulians greeted the portent with a shout and their hands were quick to their swords. Tolumnius, the augur, was the first to speak: 'At last!' he cried. 'At last! 260 This is what I have so often prayed to see. I accept the omen and acknowledge the gods. It is I who will lead you. Now take up your arms, O my poor countrymen, into whose hearts the pitiless stranger strikes the terror of war. You are like the feeble birds and he is attacking and plundering your shores. He will take to flight and sail far away over the sea, but you must all be of one mind, mass your forces into one flock and fight to defend your king whom he has seized.' When he had spoken he ran forward and hurled his cornel-wood spear at the enemy standing opposite. It whirred through the air and flew unerringly. In that moment a great shout arose. In that moment all the ranks drawn up in wedge formation were thrown into disorder, and in the confusion men's hearts blazed with

sudden passion. The spear flew on. By chance nine splendid   270
brothers had taken their stand opposite Tolumnius, all of
them sons borne by the faithful Tyrrhena to her Arcadian
husband Gylippus. It struck one of these in the waist where
the sewn belt chafed the belly and the buckle bit the side-
straps. He was noble in his looks and in the brilliance of his
armour, and the spear drove through his ribs and stretched
him on the yellow sand. Burning with grief, his brothers, a
whole phalanx of spirited warriors, drew their swords or
snatched up their throwing spears and rushed blindly forward. The ranks of the Laurentines ran to meet them while   280
from the other side the massed Trojans came flooding up
with Etruscans from Agylla and Arcadians in their brightly
coloured armour. One single passion drove them on – to
settle the matter by the sword. They tore down the altars
and a wild storm of missiles filled the whole sky and fell in
a rain of steel. The mixing bowls and braziers were
removed, and now that the treaty had come to nothing
even Latinus took to flight with his rejected gods. Some
bridled the teams of their chariots; some leapt on their
horses and stood at the ready with drawn swords.

Messapus, eager to wreck the treaty, rode straight at the   290
Etruscan Aulestes, a king wearing the insignia of a king,
and the charging horse drove him back in terror. He fell as
he retreated, and crashed violently head and shoulders into
the altar behind him. Riding furiously, Messapus flew to
him and, towering over him with a lance as long as a
housebeam, he struck him his death blow even as he
poured out prayers for mercy. 'So much for Aulestes!'
cried Messapus. 'This is a better victim to offer to the great
gods!' and the men of Italy ran to strip the body while it
was still warm. Corynaeus came to meet them, snatching a
half-burnt torch from an altar. Ebysus made for him, but
before he could strike a blow, Corynaeus filled his face   300
with fire. His great beard flared up and gave off a stench as
it burned. Corynaeus pressed his attack and, clutching the

hair of his helpless enemy in his left hand, he forced him to the ground, kneeling on him with all his weight, and sunk the hard steel in his flank. Meanwhile Podalirius had been following the shepherd Alsus as he rushed through the hail of missiles in the front line of battle and was now poised over him with the naked sword. But, drawing back his axe, Alsus struck him full in the middle of the forehead and split it to the chin, bathing all his armour in a shower of blood. It was a cruel rest then for Podalirius. An iron
310 sleep bore down upon him and closed his eyes in everlasting night.

But true to his vow Aeneas, unhelmeted, stretched out his weaponless right hand and called to his allies: 'Where are you rushing? What is this sudden discord rising among you? Control your anger! The treaty is already struck and its terms agreed. I alone have the right of conflict. Leave me to fight and forget your fears. We have a treaty, and my right hand will make it good. The rituals we have performed have made Turnus mine.' While he was still speaking, while words like these were still passing his lips, an arrow came whirring in its flight and struck him,
320 unknown the hand that shot it and the force that spun it to its target, unknown what chance or what god brought such honour to the Rutulians. The shining glory of the deed is lost in darkness, and no man boasted that he had wounded Aeneas.

When Turnus saw him leaving the field and the leaders of the allies in dismay, a sudden fire of hope kindled in his heart. Horses and arms he demanded both at once, and in a flash he leapt on his chariot with spirits soaring and gathered up the reins. Then many a brave hero he sent down to death as he flew along, and many half-dead
330 bodies he sent rolling on the ground, crushing whole columns of men under his chariot wheels as he caught up their spears and showered them on those who had taken to flight. Just as Mars, spattered with blood, charges along

the banks of the icy river Hebrus, clashing sword on shield and giving full rein to his furious horses as he stirs up war; they fly across the open plain before the winds of the south and the west, till Thrace roars to its furthest reaches with the drumming of their hooves as his escort gallops all round him, Rage, Treachery and the dark faces of Fear – just so did bold Turnus lash his horses through the thick of battle till they smoked with sweat, and as he trampled the pitiable bodies of his dead enemies, the flying hooves scattered a dew of blood and churned the gore into the 340 sand. Sthenelus he sent to his death with a throw from long range; then Thamyrus and Pholus, both in close combat. From long range, too, he struck down the Imbrasidae, Glaucus and Lades, whom their father Imbrasus himself had brought up in Lycia, and gave them armour that equipped them either to do battle or to outstrip the winds on horseback.

In another part of the field, Eumedes was charging into the fray. He was a famous warrior, son of old Dolon, bearing his grandfather's name, but his spirit and his hand for war were his father's. It was Dolon who dared to ask 350 for the chariot of Achilles as a reward for going to spy on the camp of the Greeks. But Diomede provided a different reward for his daring, and he soon ceased to aspire to the horses of Achilles. When Turnus caught sight of Eumedes far off on the open plain, he struck him first with a light javelin thrown over the vast space that lay between. Then, halting the two horses that drew his chariot, he leapt down and stood over his dying enemy with his foot on his neck. He wrenched the sword out of Eumedes' hand, and it flashed as he dipped it deep in his throat, saying: 'There they are, Trojan. These are the fields of Hesperia you tried 360 to take by war. Lie there and measure them! This is my reward for those who test me by the sword. This is how they build their cities.' Next, with a throw of his javelin, he sent Asbytes to join him, then Chloreus, Sybaris, Dares,

Thersilochus and Thymoetes, whose horse had fallen and thrown him over its head. Just as when the breath of Thracian Boreas sounds upon the deep Aegean as he pursues the waves to the shore, and wherever the winds put out their strength the clouds take to flight across the sky, just so, wherever Turnus cut his path, the enemy gave way before him, their ranks breaking and running, and his own impetus carried him forward with the plumes on his helmet tossing as he drove his chariot into the wind. Phegeus could not endure this onslaught of Turnus and his wild shouting, but leapt in front of the chariot and pulled round the horses' heads as they galloped at him, foaming at their bits. Then, as he was dragged along hanging from the yoke, the broad blade of Turnus' lance struck his unprotected side, piercing and breaking the double mesh of his breastplate and grazing the skin of his body. He put up his shield and was twisting round to face his enemy when he fell and was caught by the flying wheel and axle and stretched out on the ground. Turnus, following up, struck him between the bottom of the helmet and the top edge of the breastplate, cutting off his head and leaving the trunk on the sand.

While the victorious Turnus was dealing death on the plain, Aeneas was taken into the camp by Mnestheus and faithful Achates. Ascanius was with them. Aeneas was bleeding and leaning on his long spear at every other step. He was in a fury, tugging at the arrow-head broken in the wound and demanding that they should take the quickest way of helping him, make a broad cut with the blade of a sword, slice open the flesh where the arrow was embedded and get him back into battle. But now there came Iapyx, son of Iasus, whom Phoebus Apollo loved above all other men. Overcome by this fierce love, Apollo had long since offered freely and joyfully to give him all his arts and all his powers, prophecy, the lyre, the swift arrow, but, in order to prolong the life of his dying father, Iapyx chose

rather to ply a mute, inglorious art and know the virtues
of herbs and the practice of healing. There, with the
grieving Iulus, in the middle of a great crowd of warriors,   400
stood Aeneas, growling savagely, leaning on his great spear
and unmoved by their tears. The old man, with his robe
caught up and tied behind him after the fashion of Apollo
Paeon, tried anxiously and tried in vain all he could do
with his healing hands and the potent herbs of Apollo. In
vain his right hand worked at the dart. In vain the forceps
gripped the steel. Fortune did not show the way and his
patron Apollo gave no help. And all the time the horror of
battle grew fiercer and fiercer on the plain, and nearer and
nearer drew the danger. They soon could see a wall of dust
in the sky. The cavalry rode up, and showers of missiles
were falling into the middle of the camp. A hideous noise
of shouting rose to the heavens as young men fought and   410
fell under the iron hand of Mars.

At this Venus, dismayed by her son's undeserved suffering, picked some dittany on Mount Ida in Crete. The stalk
of this plant has a vigorous growth of leaves and its head is
crowned by a purple flower. It is a herb which wild goats
know well and feed on when arrows have flown and
stuck in their backs. This Venus brought down, veiled in a
blinding cloud, and with it tinctured the river water they
had poured into shining bowls, impregnating it secretly
and sprinkling in it fragrant panacea and the health-giving
juices of ambrosia. Such was the water with which old   420
Iapyx, without knowing it, bathed the wound, and
suddenly, in that moment, all the pain left Aeneas' body
and the blood was staunched in the depths of the wound.
Of its own accord the arrow came away in the hand of
Iapyx and fresh strength flowed into Aeneas, restoring him
to his former state. It was Iapyx who was the first to fire
their spirits to face the enemy. 'Bring the warrior his arms,
and quickly!' he cried. 'Why stand there? This cure was
not effected by human power, nor by the guidance of art.

It is not my right hand that saved you, Aeneas. Some
greater power, some god, is driving you and sending you
430 back to greater deeds.' Aeneas was hungry for battle. He
had already sheathed his calves in his golden greaves and
was brandishing his flashing spear, impatient of delay.
When the shield was fitted to his side and the breastplate to
his back, he took Ascanius in an armed embrace and kissed
him lightly through the helmet, saying: 'From me, my
son, you can learn courage and hard toil. Others will teach
you about fortune. My hand will now defend you in war
and lead you where the prizes are great. I charge you,
when in due course your years ripen and you become a
man, do not forget, but as you go over in your mind the
440 examples of your kinsmen, let your spirit rise at the
thought of your father Aeneas and your uncle Hector.'

When he had finished speaking, he moved through the
gates in all his massive might, brandishing his huge spear,
and there rushed with him in serried ranks Antheus and
Mnestheus and all his escort, streaming from the camp. A
blinding dust then darkened the plain. The very earth was
stirred and trembled under the drumming of their feet. As
they advanced, Turnus saw them from the rampart opposite. The men of Ausonia also saw them and cold tremors
of fear ran through the marrow of their bones. But before
all the Latins, Juturna heard the sound and knew its mean-
450 ing. She fled, trembling, but Aeneas came swiftly on
leading his dark army over the open plain. Just as when a
cloud blots out the sun and begins to move from mid-
ocean towards the land; long-suffering farmers see it in
the far distance and shudder to the heart, knowing what it
will bring, the ruin of trees, the slaughter of their crops
and destruction everywhere; the flying winds come first,
and their sound is first to reach the shore – just so the
Trojan leader from Rhoeteum drove his army forward
against the enemy in wedge formation, each man shoulder
to shoulder with his neighbour. Fierce Osiris was struck by

the sword of Thymbraeus. Mnestheus cut down Arcetius, Achates Epulo, and Gyas Ufens. Tolumnius himself fell, 460 the augur who had been the first to hurl a spear against his enemies. The shouting rose to the sky and now it was the Rutulians who turned and fled over the fields, raising the dust on their backs. Aeneas did not think fit to cut down men who had turned away from him, nor did he go after those who stood to meet him in equal combat or carried spears. He was looking for Turnus, and only Turnus, tracking him through the thick murk. Turnus was the only man he asked to fight.

Seeing this and being stricken with fear, the warrior maiden Juturna threw out Metiscus, the driver of Turnus' 470 chariot, from between the reins and left him lying where he fell, far from the chariot pole. She herself took over the reins and whipped them up to make them ripple, the very image of Metiscus in voice and form and armour, like a black swallow flying through the great house of some wealthy man, and collecting tiny scraps of food and dainties for her young chattering on the nest; sometimes her twittering is heard in empty colonnades, sometimes round marshy pools – just so did Juturna ride through the middle of the enemy and the swift chariot flew all over the field. Now here, now there she gave glimpses of her brother in triumph, but then she would fly off and not allow him to 480 join in the battle. But Aeneas was no less determined to meet him and followed his every twist and turn, tracking him and calling his name at the top of his voice all through the scattered lines of battle. Every time he caught sight of his enemy, he tried to match the speed of his wing-footed horses, and every time Juturna swung the chariot round and took to flight. What was Aeneas to do? Conflicting tides seethed in his mind, but no answer came, and different passions drove him to opposing thoughts. Then the nimble Messapus, who was running with two pliant steel-tipped javelins in his left hand, aimed one of them at Aeneas and 490 hurled it true. Aeneas checked himself and crouched on one knee behind his shield, but the flying spear sheared off the peak of his helmet and carried away the plumes from the top of it. At this his anger rose. Treachery had given him no choice. When he saw Turnus' horses pull the chariot round and withdraw, again and again he called upon Jupiter and the altars of the broken treaty, and then, and not till then, he plunged into the middle of his enemies. He was terrible in his might and Mars was aiding him. Sparing no man, he roused himself to savage slaughter and gave full rein to his anger.

500　　　What god could unfold all this bitter suffering for me? What god could express in song all the different ways of death for men and for their leaders, driven back and forth across the plain, now by Turnus, now by Trojan Aeneas? Was it your will, O Jupiter, that peoples who were to live at peace for all time should clash so violently in war?

　　Aeneas met Sucro the Rutulian – this was the first clash to check the Trojan charge – but Sucro did not detain them long. Aeneas caught him in the side and drove the raw steel through the cage of the ribs to the breast where

510　death comes quickest. Turnus, now on foot, met Diores and his brother Amycus who had been unhorsed. As Diores rode at him he struck him with his long spear; Amycus he despatched with his sword. Then, cutting off both their heads, he hung them from his chariot and carried them along with him, dripping their dew of blood. Aeneas sent Talos, Tanais and brave Cethegus to their deaths, all three in one encounter, then the gloomy Onites, who bore a name linked with Echion of Thebes and whose mother was Peridia. Turnus killed the brothers who came from the fields of Apollo in Lycia, then young Menoetes, who hated war – but that did not save him. He was an Arcadian who had plied his art all round the rivers of Lerna, rich in fish.

520　His home was poor and he never knew the munificence of the great. His father sowed his crops on hired land. Like

fires started in different places in a dry wood or in thickets
of crackling laurel; or like foaming rivers roaring as they
run down in spate from the high mountains to the sea,
sweeping away everything that lies in their path – no more
sluggish were Aeneas and Turnus as they rushed over the
field of battle. Now if ever did the anger seethe within
them; now burst their unconquerable hearts and every
wound they gave, they gave with all their might.

Murranus was sounding the names of his father's fathers
and their fathers before them, his whole lineage through all 530
the kings of Latium, when Aeneas knocked him flying from
his chariot with a rock, a huge boulder he sent whirling at
him, and stretched him out on the ground. The wheels
rolled him forward in a tangle of yoke and reins and his
galloping horses had no thought for their master as they
trampled him under their clattering hooves. Hyllus made a
wild charge, roaring hideously, but Turnus ran to meet him
and spun a javelin at his gilded forehead. Through the
helmet it went and stuck in his brain. As for you, Cretheus,
bravest of the Greeks, your right hand did not rescue you
from Turnus; nor was Cupencus protected by his gods
when Aeneas came near, but his breast met the steel and the 540
bronze shield did not hold back the moment of his death.
You too, Aeolus. The Laurentine plains saw you fall, and
your back cover a broad measure of their ground. The
Greek battalions could not bring you down, nor could
Achilles who overturned the kingdom of Priam, but here
you lie. This was the finishing line of your life. Your home
was in the hills below Mount Ida, a home in the hills of
Lyrnesus, but your grave is in Laurentine soil. The two
armies were now wholly turned to face one another. All the
Latins and all the Trojans – Mnestheus and bold Serestus,
Messapus, tamer of horses, and brave Asilas – the battalion 550
of Etruscans and the Arcadian squadrons of Evander were
striving each man with all his resources of strength and will,
waging this immense conflict with no rest and no respite.

At that moment Aeneas' mother, loveliest of the goddesses, put it into his mind to go to the city, to lead his
army instantly against the walls and throw the Latins into
confusion at this sudden calamity. Turning his eyes this
way and that as he tracked down Turnus through all the
different battle lines, he noticed the city, untouched by this
great war, quiet and unharmed, and his spirit was fired by
the sudden thought of a greater battle he could fight.
560 Calling the leaders of the Trojans together, Mnestheus,
Sergestus and the brave Serestus, he took up position on
some rising ground and the whole of the Trojan legion
joined them there in close formation without laying down
their shields or spears. Aeneas addressed them standing in
the middle of a high mound of earth: 'There must be no
delay in carrying out my commands. Jupiter is on our side.
No man must go to work half-heartedly, because my plan
is new to him. The city is the cause of this war. It is the
very kingdom of Latinus, and if they do not this day agree
to submit to the yoke, to accept defeat and to obey, I shall
570 root it out and level its smoking roofs to the ground. Am I
to wait until Turnus thinks fit to stand up to me in battle
and consents to meet the man who has already defeated
him? O my fellow-citizens, this city is the head and heart
of this wicked war. Bring your torches now and we shall
claim our treaty with fire!'

When he had finished speaking, they formed a wedge,
all of them striving with equal resolve in their hearts, and
moved towards the walls in a solid mass. Ladders suddenly
appeared. Fire came to hand. They rushed the gates and
cut to pieces the first guards that met them. They spun
their javelins and darkened the heavens with steel. Aeneas
himself, standing among the leaders under the city wall
580 with his right hand outstretched, lifted up his voice to
accuse Latinus, calling the gods to witness that this was the
second time he had been forced into battle; twice already
the Italians had shown themselves to be his enemies; this

was not the first treaty they had violated. Alarm and discord rose among the citizens. Some wanted the city to be opened up and the gates thrown wide to receive the Trojans and they even dragged the king himself on to the ramparts; others caught up their weapons and rushed to defend the walls: just as when a shepherd tracks some bees to their home, shut well away inside a porous rock, and fills it with acrid smoke; the bees, alarmed for their safety, rush in all directions through their wax-built camp, sharpening their wrath 590 and buzzing fiercely; then as the black stench rolls through their chambers, the inside of the rock booms with their blind complaints and the smoke flies to the empty winds.

Weary as they were, a new misfortune now befell the Latins and shook their whole city to its foundations with grief. As soon as the queen, standing on the palace roof, saw the enemy approaching the city, the walls under attack, fire flying up to the roofs, no Rutulian army anywhere to confront the enemy and no sign of Turnus' columns, she thought in her misery that he had been killed in the cut and thrust of battle. In that instant her mind was deranged with grief and she screamed that she was the 600 cause, the guilty one, the fountainhead of all these evils. Pouring her heart out in sorrow and madness, she resolved to die. Her hand rent her purple robes, and she died a hideous death in the noose of a rope tied to a high beam. When the unhappy women of Latium heard of this, her daughter Lavinia was the first to tear her golden hair and rosy cheeks. The whole household was wild with grief around her, and their lamentations rang all through the palace. From there the report spread through the whole city and gloom was everywhere. Latinus went with his garments torn, dazed by the death of his wife and the downfall of his city, fouling his grey hair with handfuls of 610 dirt and dust.

Meanwhile, on a distant part of the plain, the warrior Turnus was chasing a few stragglers. He was less vigorous

now, and less and less delighted with the triumphant
progress of his horses, when the wind carried to him this
sound of shouting and of unexplained terror. He pricked
up his ears. It was a confused noise from the city, a
620 murmuring with no hint of joy in it. 'What is this?' he
cried in wild dismay, pulling on the reins to stop the
chariot. 'Why such grief and distress on the walls and all
this clamour streaming from every part of the city?' His
sister, who was driving the chariot in the shape of Metiscus
and had control of the horses and the reins, protested: 'This
way, Turnus. Let us go after these Trojans. This is where
our first victories showed us the way. There are others
whose hands can defend the city. Aeneas is bearing hard on
Italians in all the confusion of battle; we too can deal out
630 death without pity to Trojans. You will kill as many as he
does and not fall short in the honours of war.'

Turnus made his reply: 'O my sister, I recognized you
some time ago when first you shattered the treaty with your
scheming and engaged in this war, and you do not deceive
me now, pretending not to be a goddess. But whose will is it
that you have been sent down from Olympus to endure this
agony? Was it all to see the cruel death of your pitiable
brother? For what am I to do? What stroke of Fortune could
grant me safety now? No one is left whom I love as much as
I loved Murranus, and I have seen him before my own eyes
640 calling for me as he fell, a mighty warrior laid low by a
mighty wound. The luckless Ufens has died rather than look
on my disgrace, and the Trojans have his body and his arms.
Shall I stand by and see our homes destroyed? This is the one
indignity that remained. And shall I not lift my hand to
refute the words of Drances? Shall I turn tail? Will this land
of Italy see Turnus on the run? Is it so bad a thing to die? Be
gracious to me, you gods of the underworld, since the gods
above have turned their faces from me. My spirit will come
down to you unstained, knowing nothing of such dishonour
and worthy of my great ancestors to the end.'

Scarcely had he finished speaking when Saces suddenly 650
came galloping up on his foaming horse having ridden
through the middle of the enemy with an arrow wound
full in his face. On he rushed calling the name of Turnus
and imploring him: 'You are our last hope of safety,
Turnus. You must take pity on your people. The sword
and spear of Aeneas are like the lightning and he is threatening to throw down the highest citadels of Italy and give
them over to destruction. Firebrands are already flying to
the roofs. Every Latin face, every Latin eye, is turned to
you. The king himself is at a loss. Whom should he choose
to marry our daughters? What treaties should he turn to?
And then the queen, who placed all her trust in you, has 660
taken her own life. Fear overcame her and she fled the
light of day. Alone in front of the gates Messapus and bold
Atinas are holding the line and all round them on every
side stand the battalions of the enemy in serried ranks.
Their drawn swords are a crop of steel bristling in the
fields. And you are out here wheeling your chariot in the
deserted grasslands.'

Turnus was thunderstruck, bewildered by the changing
shape of his fortune, and stood there dumb and staring. In
that one heart of his there seethed a bitter shame, a grief
shot through with madness, love driven on by fury, and a
consciousness of his own courage. As soon as the shadows
lifted from his mind and light returned, he forced his 670
burning eyes round towards the walls, looking back in
deep dismay from his chariot at the great city. There,
between the storeys of a tower came a tongue of flame,
rolling and billowing to the sky. It was taking hold of the
tower, which he had built himself, putting the wheels
under it and fitting the long gangways. 'Sister,' he said,
'the time has come at last. The Fates are too strong. You
must not delay them any longer. Let us go where God and
cruel fortune call me. I am resolved to meet Aeneas in
battle. I am resolved to suffer what bitterness there is in

death. You will not see me put to shame again. This is
680 madness, but before I die, I beg of you, let me be mad.'
No sooner had he spoken than he leapt to the ground from
his chariot and dashed through all his enemies and their
weapons, leaving his sister behind him to grieve as his
charge broke through the middle of their ranks. Just as a
boulder comes crashing down from the top of a mountain,
torn out by gales, washed out by flood water or loosened
by the stealthy passing of the years; it comes down the
sheer face with terrific force, an evil mountain of rock, and
bounds over the plain, rolling with it woods and flocks
690 and men – so did Turnus crash through the shattered ranks
of his enemies towards the walls of the city where all the
ground was wet with shed blood and the air sang with
flying spears. There he made a sign with his hand, and in
the same moment he called out in a loud voice: 'Enough,
Rutulians! Put up your weapons, and you too, Latins!
Whatever Fortune brings is mine. It is better that I should
be the one man who atones for this treaty for all of you,
and settles the matter with the sword.' At these words the
armies parted and left a clear space in the middle between
them.

But when Father Aeneas heard the name of Turnus, he
abandoned the walls and the lofty citadel, sweeping aside all
700 delay and breaking off all his works of war. He leapt for
joy and clashed his armour with a noise as terrible as
thunder. Huge he was as Mount Athos or Mount Eryx or
Father Appenninus himself roaring when the holm-oaks
shimmer on his flanks and delighting to raise his snowy
head into the winds. Now at last the Rutulians and the
Trojans and all the men of Italy, the defenders guarding
the high ramparts and the besiegers pounding the base of
the walls with their rams, they all turned their eyes eagerly
to see and took the armour off their shoulders. King
Latinus himself was amazed at the sight of these two huge
heroes born at opposite sides of the earth coming together

to decide the issue by the sword. There, on a piece of open   710
ground on the plain, they threw their spears at long range
as they charged, and when they clashed the bronze of their
shields rang out and the earth groaned. Blow upon blow
they dealt with their swords as chance and courage met
and mingled in confusion. Just as two enemy bulls on the
great mountain of Sila or on top of Taburnus bring their
horns to bear and charge into battle; the herdsmen stand
back in terror, the herd stands silent and afraid, and the
heifers low quietly together waiting to see who is to rule
the grove, who is to be the leader of the whole herd;
meanwhile the bulls are locked together exchanging blow   720
upon blow, gouging horn into hide till their necks and
shoulders are awash with blood and all the grove rings
with their lowing and groaning – just so did Aeneas of
Troy and Turnus son of Daunus rush together with shields
clashing and the din filled the heavens. Then Jupiter himself
lifted up a pair of scales with the tongue centred and put
the lives of the two men in them to decide who would be
condemned in the ordeal of battle, and with whose weight
death would descend.

Turnus leapt forward thinking he was safe, and lifting
his sword and rising to his full height, he struck with all his   730
strength behind it. The Trojans shouted and the Latins
cried out in their anxiety, while both armies watched
intently. But in the height of his passion the treacherous
sword broke in mid-blow and left him defenceless, had he
not sought help in flight. Faster than the east wind he flew,
when he saw his own right hand holding nothing but a
sword handle he did not recognize. The story goes that
when his horses were yoked and he was mounting his
chariot in headlong haste to begin the battle, he left his
father's sword behind and caught up the sword of his
charioteer Metiscus. For some time, while the Trojans
were scattered and in flight, that was enough. But when it
met the divine armour made by Vulcan, the mortal blade   740

was brittle as an icicle and shattered on impact, leaving its fragments glittering on the golden sand. At this Turnus fled in despair and tried to escape to another part of the plain, weaving his uncertain course now to this side now to that, for the Trojans formed a dense barrier round him, hemming him in between a huge marsh and the high walls.

Nor did Aeneas let up in his pursuit. Slowed down as he was by the arrow wound, his legs failing him sometimes and unable to run, he still was ablaze with fury and kept hard on the heels of the terrified Turnus, like a hunting 750 dog that happens to trap a stag in the bend of a river or in a ring of red feathers used as a scare, pressing him hard with his running and barking; the stag is terrified by the ambush he is caught in or by the high river bank; he runs and runs back a thousand ways, but the untiring Umbrian hound stays with him with jaws gaping; now he has him; now he seems to have him and the jaws snap shut, but he is thwarted and bites the empty air; then as the shouting rises louder than ever, all the river banks and pools return the sound and the whole sky thunders with the din. As he ran Turnus kept shouting at the Rutulians, calling each of them by name and demanding the sword he knew so well. 760 Aeneas on the other hand was threatening instant death and destruction to anyone who came near. Much as that alarmed them, he terrified them even more by threatening to raze their city to the ground, and though he was wounded he did not slacken in his pursuit. Five times round they ran in one direction, five times they rewound the circle. For this was no small prize they were trying to win at games. What they were competing for was the lifeblood of Turnus.

It so chanced that a bitter-leaved wild olive tree had stood on this spot, sacred to Faunus and long revered by sailors. On it men saved from storms at sea used to nail their offerings to the Laurentine god, and dedicate the

clothes they had vowed for their safety. But the Trojans, 770
making no exception for the sacred tree-trunk, had
removed it to clear space for the combat. In this stump the
spear of Aeneas was now embedded. The force of his
throw had carried it here and lodged it fast in the tough
wood of the root. He strained at it and tried to pull it out
so that he could hunt with a missile the quarry he could
not catch on foot. Wild now with fear, Turnus cried: 'Pity
me, I beg of you, Faunus, and you, good Mother Earth,
hold on to that spear, if I have always paid you those
honours which Aeneas and his men have profaned in war.'
So he prayed and he did not call for the help of the god in 780
vain. Aeneas was long delayed struggling with the stubborn
stump and no strength of his could prise open the bite of
the wood. While he was heaving and straining with all his
might, the goddess Juturna, daughter of Daunus, changed
once more into the shape of the charioteer Metiscus and
ran forward to give Turnus his sword. Venus was indignant
that the nymph was allowed to be so bold, so she came and
wrenched out Aeneas' spear from deep in the root. Then
these glorious warriors, their weapons and their spirits
restored to them, one relying on his sword, the other
towering and formidable behind his spear, stood there
breathing hard, ready to engage in the contest of war.   790

Meanwhile the King of All-powerful Olympus saw
Juno watching the battle from a golden cloud and spoke
these words to her: 'O my dear wife, what will be the end
of this? What is there left for you to do? You yourself
know, and admit that you know, that Aeneas is a god of
this land, that he has a right to heaven and is fated to be
raised to the stars. What are you scheming? What do you
hope to achieve by perching there in those chilly clouds?
Was it right that a god should suffer violence and be
wounded by the hand of a mortal? Was it right that
Turnus should be given back the sword that was taken
from him? For what could Juturna have done without

your help? Why have you put strength into the arm of the
800 defeated? The time has come at last for you to cease and
give way to our entreaties. Do not let this great sorrow
gnaw at your heart in silence, and do not make me listen
to grief and resentment for ever streaming from your
sweet lips. The end has come. You have been able to harry
the Trojans by sea and by land, to light the fires of an
unholy war, to soil a house with sorrow and mix the
sound of mourning with the marriage song. I forbid you
to go further.'

These were the words of Jupiter. With bowed head the
goddess Juno, daughter of Saturn, made this reply: 'Because
I have known your will, great Jupiter, against my own
wishes I have abandoned Turnus and abandoned the earth.
810 But for your will, you would not be seeing me sitting alone
in mid-air on a cloud, suffering whatever is sent me to
suffer. I would be clothed in fire, standing close in to the
line of battle and dragging Trojans into bloody combat. It
was I, I admit it, who persuaded Juturna to come to the
help of her unfortunate brother, and with my blessing to
show greater daring for the sake of his life, but not to shoot
arrows, not to stretch the bow. I swear it by the implacable
fountainhead of the River Styx, the one oath which binds
the gods of heaven. And now I, Juno, yield and quit these
820 battles which I so detest. But I entreat you for the sake of
Latium and the honour of your own kin, to allow what the
law of Fate does not forbid. When at last their marriages are
blessed – I offer no obstruction – when at last they come
together in peace and make their laws and treaties together,
do not command the Latins to change their ancient name in
their own land, to become Trojans and be called Teucrians.
They are men. Do not make them change their voice or
native dress. Let there be Latium. Let the Alban kings live
on from generation to generation and the stock of Rome
be made mighty by the manly courage of Italy. Troy has
fallen. Let it lie, Troy and the name of Troy.'

He who devised mankind and all the world smiled and replied: 'You are the true sister of Jupiter and the second 830 child of Saturn, such waves of anger do you set rolling from deep in your heart. But come now, lay aside this fury that arose in vain. I grant what you wish. I yield. I relent of my own free will. The people of Ausonia will keep the tongue of their fathers and their ancient ways. As their name is, so shall it remain. The Trojans will join them in body only and will then be submerged. Ritual I will give and the modes of worship, and I will make them all Latins, speaking one tongue. You will see that the people who arise from this admixture of Ausonian blood will be above all men, above the gods, in devotion and no other race will 840 be their equals in paying you honour.' Juno nodded in assent. She rejoiced and forced her mind to change, leaving the cloud behind her and withdrawing from the sky.

This done, the Father of the Gods pondered another task in his mind and prepared to dismiss Juturna from her brother's side. There are two monsters named Dirae borne to the goddess of the dead of night in one and the same litter with Megaera of Tartarus. The heads of all three she bound with coiling snakes and gave them wings to ride the wind. These attend the throne of savage Jupiter in his royal 850 palace, and sharpen the fears of suffering mortals whenever the King of the Gods sets plagues or hideous deaths in motion or terrifies guilty cities by the visitation of war. One of these Jupiter sent swiftly down from the heights of heaven with orders to confront Juturna as an omen. She flew to earth, carried in a swift whirlwind. Like an arrow going through a cloud, spun from the bowstring of a Parthian who has armed the barb with a virulent poison for which there is no cure, a Parthian, or a Cretan from Cydonia; and it whirrs as it flies unseen through the swift darkness – so flew the daughter of Night, making for the 860 earth. When she saw the Trojan battle lines and the army of Turnus, she took in an instant the shape of the little bird which perches on tombs and the gables of empty houses and sings late its ill-omened song among the shades of night. In this guise the monster flew again and again at Turnus' face, screeching and beating his shield with her wings. A strange numbness came over him and his bones melted with fear. His hair stood on end and the voice stuck in his throat.

His sister Juturna recognized the Dira from a long way
870 off by the whirring of her wings, and grieved. She loosened and tore her hair. She scratched her face and beat her breast, crying: 'What can your sister do to help you now, Turnus? Much have I endured but nothing now remains for me, and I have no art that could prolong your life. How can I set myself against such a portent? At last, at last, I leave the battle. Do not frighten me, you birds of evil omen. I am already afraid. I know the beating of your wings and the sound of death. I do not fail to understand the proud commands of great-hearted Jupiter. Is this his reward for my lost virginity? For what purpose has he granted me eternal life? Why has he deprived me of the
880 state of death? But for that I could at least have put an end to my suffering and borne my poor brother company through the shades. So this is immortality! Will anything that is mine be sweet to me without you, my brother? Is there no abyss that can open deep enough to take a goddess down to the deepest of the shades?' At these words, covering her head in a blue-green veil and moaning bitterly, the goddess plunged into the depths of her own river.

Aeneas kept pressing his pursuit with his huge spear flashing, as long as a tree, and these were the words he spoke in his anger: 'What is the delay now? Why are you
890 still shirking, Turnus? This is not a race! It is a fight with dangerous weapons at close quarters. Turn yourself into any shape you like. Scrape together all your resources of spirit and skill. Pray to sprout wings and fly to the stars of heaven, or shut yourself up and hide in a hole in the

ground!' Turnus replied, shaking his head: 'You are fierce,
Aeneas, but wild words do not frighten me. It is the gods
that cause me to fear, the gods and the enmity of Jupiter.'
He said no more but looked round and saw a huge rock, a
huge and ancient rock which happened to be lying on the
plain, a boundary stone put there to settle a dispute about
land. Twelve picked men like those the earth now produces   900
could scarcely lift it up on to their shoulders, but he caught
it up in his trembling hands and, rising to his full height
and running at speed, he hurled it at his enemy. But he had
no sense of running or going, of lifting or moving the
huge rock. His knees gave way. His blood chilled and
froze and the stone rolled away under its own impetus
over the open ground between them, but it did not go the
whole way and it did not strike its target. Just as when we
are asleep, when in the weariness of night, rest lies heavy
on our eyes, we dream we are trying desperately to run   910
further and not succeeding, till we fall exhausted in the
middle of our efforts; the tongue is useless; the strength we
know we have, fails our body; we have no voice, no
words to obey our will – so it was with Turnus. Wherever
his courage sought a way, the dread goddess barred his
progress. During these moments, the thoughts whirled in
his brain. He gazed at the Rutulians and the city. He
faltered with fear. He began to tremble at the death that
was upon him. He could see nowhere to run, no way to
come at his enemy, no chariot anywhere, no sister to drive
it.

   As he faltered the deadly spear of Aeneas flashed. His
eyes had picked the spot and he threw from long range   920
with all his weight behind the throw. Stones hurled by
siege artillery never roar like this. The crash of the bursting
thunderbolt is not so loud. Like a dark whirlwind it flew
carrying death and destruction with it. Piercing the outer
rings of the sevenfold shield and laying open the lower rim
of the breastplate, it went whistling through the middle of

the thigh. When the blow struck, down went great Turnus, bending his knee to the ground. The Rutulians rose with a groan which echoed round the whole mountain, and far and wide the high forests sent back the sound of their
930 voices. He lowered his eyes and stretched out his right hand to beg as a suppliant. 'I have brought this upon myself,' he said, 'and for myself I ask nothing. Make use of what Fortune has given you, but if any thought of my unhappy father can touch you, I beg of you – and you too had such a father in Anchises – take pity on the old age of Daunus, and give me back to my people, or if you prefer it, give them back my dead body. You have defeated me, and the men of Ausonia have seen me defeated and stretching out my hands to you. Lavinia is yours. Do not carry your hatred any further.'

There stood Aeneas, deadly in his armour, rolling his
940 eyes, but he checked his hand, hesitating more and more as the words of Turnus began to move him, when suddenly his eyes caught the fatal baldric of the boy Pallas high on Turnus' shoulder with the glittering studs he knew so well. Turnus had defeated and wounded him and then killed him, and now he was wearing his belt on his shoulder as a battle honour taken from an enemy. Aeneas feasted his eyes on the sight of this spoil, this reminder of his own wild grief, then, burning with mad passion and terrible in his wrath, he cried: 'Are you to escape me now, wearing the spoils stripped from the body of those I loved? By this wound which I now give, it is Pallas who makes sacrifice
950 of you. It is Pallas who exacts the penalty in your guilty blood.' Blazing with rage, he plunged the steel full into his enemy's breast. The limbs of Turnus were dissolved in cold and his life left him with a groan, fleeing in anger down to the shades.

THE PARADE OF FUTURE ROMANS IN THE UNDERWORLD
(Book Six, lines 756–892)

Silvius:	According to Jupiter's prophecy at 1.257–77, Rome is to be founded in four stages. Aeneas will build his city at Lavinium and live for three years. His son Ascanius Iulus will reign for thirty years and transfer the city to Alba Longa. After their descendants, the Alban kings, rule for three hundred years, Romulus (Quirinus), son of Mars and Ilia, will found his city at Rome. But here at 6.763, where Aeneas begins his survey of the Alban kings waiting in the underworld, Ascanius, being still alive, is not in the parade, and the first to be mentioned is Silvius, a son of Aeneas not yet born.
Alban kings:	Virgil offers five names to cover the years from about 1053 to 753 B.C.
Romulus:	Romulus restored his grandfather Numitor to the throne which Numitor's younger brother had usurped. Romulus then founded Rome in 753 B.C.
Caesar:	Julius Caesar, 102–44 B.C., adopted his grand-nephew Octavian as his son and heir.

Augustus:	Name adopted by Octavian in 27 B.C.
(Numa):	From the village of Cures, he gave Rome religion and laws. His traditional dates are 715–673 B.C.
Tullus:	Tullius Hostilius, the warrior king, 673–642 B.C.
Ancus:	Ancus Marcius, 642–617 B.C., here only appears as a king who courted popular favour.
Tarquins:	L. Tarquinius Priscus, 616–579 B.C., and L. Tarquinius Superbus, 534–510 B.C.
Brutus:	L. Junius Brutus led a rising against Tarquinius Superbus to avenge the rape of Lucretia. Later, as one of the first two consuls of Rome, in 510, he executed his own two sons who tried to restore the Tarquins. The rods and axes carried by the consuls signified their right to flog and execute. This passage alludes also to the other avenging Brutus who assassinated Julius Caesar in 44 B.C.
Decii:	P. Decius Mus, father and son of the same name, were famous for self-immolation, each taking his own life to secure victory for Roman armies, the father in 340 B.C. in the Latin War and the son in 295 B.C. in battle against the Samnites.
Drusi:	Livia, wife of Augustus from 38 B.C. till his death in A.D. 14, was a member of this notable Roman family.
Torquatus:	T. Manlius Torquatus led the Romans against the Gauls in 361 B.C., and in 340 B.C. in the Latin War he executed his own son for disobeying orders in engaging and defeating an enemy champion.

Camillus: M. Furius Camillus recovered the gold said to have been the price of the Gaulish withdrawal from Rome in 390 B.C. This passage may also be read as an oblique tribute to Augustus, who, after long negotiations, recovered in 20 B.C. the standards lost to the Parthians at Carrhae in 53 B.C.

(Pompey):   Gnaeus Pompeius and Julius Caesar are the two spirits in gleaming armour. Caesar defeated Pompey at the battle of Pharsalus in 48 B.C.

(Mummius):   L. Mummius sacked Corinth in 146 B.C.

(Paullus):   L. Aemilius Paullus is here credited with the conquest of Greece for his defeat of Pyrrhus, king of Epirus, at the battle of Pydna in 168 B.C.

Cato: M. Porcius Cato, Cato the Elder, 234–149 B.C., was famed as the custodian of traditional Roman virtues.

Cossus: A. Cornelius Cossus defeated Tolumnius, king of the Veientes, in single combat, perhaps in 246 B.C.

Gracchi: Tiberius Sempronius Gracchus (died 133 B.C.), and his brother Gaius Sempronius Gracchus (died 121 B.C.), the two reforming tribunes, were members of this famous Roman family.

Scipios: Scipio Africanus Maior defeated Hannibal at Zama in 202 B.C. Scipio Africanus Minor destroyed Carthage in 146 B.C.

Fabricius: Gaius Fabricius Luscinus fought against Pyrrhus, king of Epirus, in 80–79 B.C. The power he found in poverty is an allusion to his rejection of Pyrrhus' gifts.

Serranus: Gaius Atilius Regulus was sowing seed (*serere:* to sow) on his farm when he was

called to the consulship in 257 B.C. He
therefore acquired the name Serranus.

Fabii: Anchises at 6.845 calls out to his friends
the members of the great Fabian family
to ask why they are all in such a hurry to
reach the light of life that they are hustling one weary spirit along with them,
and then he realizes that the problem is
not weariness. This is the great Q. Fabius
Maximus Cunctator (*cunctator:* delayer)
who used Fabian tactics against Hannibal in 217–216 B.C. in the Second Punic
War. He is not tired. It is his nature to
delay!

Marcellus: M. Claudius Marcellus, consul five times,
killed the Gaulish chieftain Viridomarus
in single combat in 222 B.C., thus becoming the third Roman, after Romulus and
Cossus, to win the Supreme Spoils (*Spolia
Opima*). Augustus was eager to make sure
that there would not be a fourth (see
Livy 4.20.5). The younger M. Claudius
Marcellus (42–23 B.C.) was the son of
Augustus' sister Octavia, and was adopted
by Augustus in 25 B.C. An ancient life of
Virgil (*Vita Donati* 32) describes how,
when Virgil was reading this passage to
Octavia and Augustus, Octavia swooned
when he reached line 882.

APPENDIX 2

THE SHIELD OF AENEAS
(Book Eight, lines 626–728)

Most of the scenes on the shield are incidents from Italian wars (see lines 626 and 678), all depicted with vivid evocation of the colours, textures and materials used in this imaginary work of art and the sounds evoked by it.

Around the outside of the circle are six scenes described in forty-one lines:

(i) The wolf suckling Romulus and Remus, who are to found the city in 753 B.C.

(ii) The rape of the Sabine women as planned by Romulus and the subsequent war and reconciliation.

(iii) The punishment of Mettus Fufetius, dictator of Alba Longa who will make a treaty with Tullus Hostilius, king of Rome 673–642 B.C., and then desert him in battle.

(iv) Two famous scenes from the Etruscan attack on Rome in 508 B.C.

(v) At the top of the shield the attack of the Gauls in 390 B.C. and the origin of some traditional features of Roman religion. The matrons of Rome were permitted to drive in carriages to the games and temples in return for giving their gold and jewels to enable Camillus to build a temple to Apollo after the defeat of Veii in 396 B.C.

(vi) Presumably at the bottom of the shield, scenes in the underworld showing Catiline whose conspiracy was put down by Cicero in 63 B.C. and M. Porcius Cato who fought for the Republican cause against Caesar and committed suicide after his defeat at Thapsus in 46 B.C. Like his great ancestor Cato the Elder (6.841) he was regarded as a model of the uncompromising Republican virtues.

In the centre of the shield, in a ring of silver dolphins feathering with white foam the silver sea and its golden waves, is depicted Augustus' victory over Antony and Cleopatra at Actium in 31 B.C. and his triple triumph of 29 B.C. (Dalmatian, Actian and Alexandrian). To this Augustan theme Virgil devotes 54 lines.

APPENDIX 3

THE JULIAN FAMILY

```
                    Jupiter = Dione
                              |
                    Venus = Anchises ¹
                              |
                          Aeneas
          ┌───────────────────┴───────────────────┐
Ascanius Iulus (once Ilus)            Silvius (6.760–75)
(founder of Alba Longa)
      (1.267–8)                       The Alban kings
                                              |
                                       Mars = Ilia
                              ┌───────────────┴───────────────┐
                          Romulus                          Remus
                              ┊2
                  ┌───────────┴───────────┐
               Iulia              C. Iulius Caesar
                  |
   (5.568) Atia = C. Octavius      Iulia = Cn. Pompeius
                  |                         (6.826–35, 7.317)
      ┌───────────┴───────────┐
   Octavia        Scribonia = AUGUSTUS ³ = Livia Drusilla
      |                       |                 (6.824)
M. Claudius Marcellus = Iulia
      (6.863)
```

1. Anchises' grandfather Assaracus seems to be mentioned in a Julian connection at 1.284, 6.778, 9.259, 643.
2. This gap is variously filled (see S. Weinstock, *Divus Julius*, p. 183 n. 1.).
3 Augustus was born C. Octavius in 63 B.C. He was adopted as Julius Caesar's son by Caesar's will in 44 B.C. under the name of C. Iulius Caesar Octavianus (called Octavian in English), and took the name of Augustus in January 27 B.C.

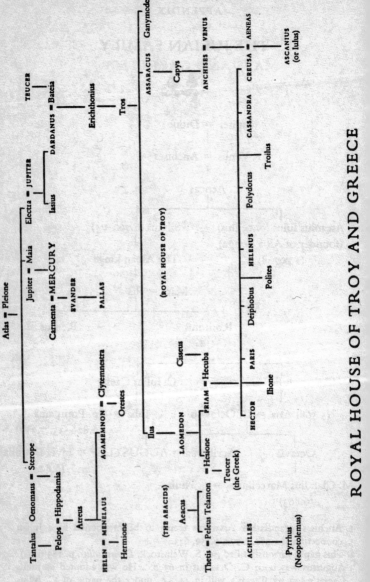

(ANCESTORS OF THE TROJANS)

Atlas = Pleione

Jupiter = Maia

Carmena = MERCURY

EVANDER

PALLAS

Electra = JUPITER

DARDANUS = Batea

Iasius

TEUCER

Erichthonius

Tros

ASSARACUS   Ganymede

Capys

ANCHISES = VENUS

ASCANIUS (or Iulus)

CREUSA   AENEAS

(ROYAL HOUSE OF TROY)

CASSANDRA

Troilus

Polydorus

HELENUS

Deiphobus   Polites

PARIS

Cisseus

PRIAM = Hecuba

Ilione

HECTOR

LAOMEDON

Hesione = Telamon   Teucer (the Greek)

Ilus

(HOUSE OF ATREUS)

Tantalus

Pelops = Hippodamia

Oenomaus   Sterope

Atreus

AGAMEMNON = Clytemnestra

Orestes

MENELAUS

HELEN =

Hermione

(THE AEACIDS)

Aeacus

Thetis = Peleus Telamon

ACHILLES

Pyrrhus (Neoptolemus)

ROYAL HOUSE OF TROY AND GREECE

MAPS AND GAZETTEER

THE VOYAGES OF AENEAS

AGATHYRSIANS

DACIA

R. Danube

GETAE

Caspian Sea

THRACE

MACEDONIA

Aeneadae

Arisba

Samothrace

Rhoeteum

PHRYGIA

Troy Thymbra

THESSALY

Lemnos

Antandros

Lyrnessus

Meliboea

Larisa

EPIRUS

Aegean

Gryneum

MAEONIA

Buthrotum

Dodona

HAONIA

Epirus

DOLOPIANS

MYRMIDONS

Scyros

DRYOPES

PTHIA

EUBOEA

Chalcis

Sea

LYDIA

Actium

Oechalia Narycum

Aulis

Claros

Leucas

ACARNANIA

BOEOTIA Thebes

C. Caphereus

Ithaca

Megara

Athenae

Samos

Same

Corinth

Nemea

Gyaros

Elis

Pheneus

Mycenae

Myconos

Zakynthos

ARCADIA

Argos

Salamis

Delos

Donusa

Lerna Tiryns

MESSENIA

Paros

Naxos

Strophades

Sparta

Olearos

Amyclae

C. Malea

Carpathos

Cythera

CRETE Gortyn

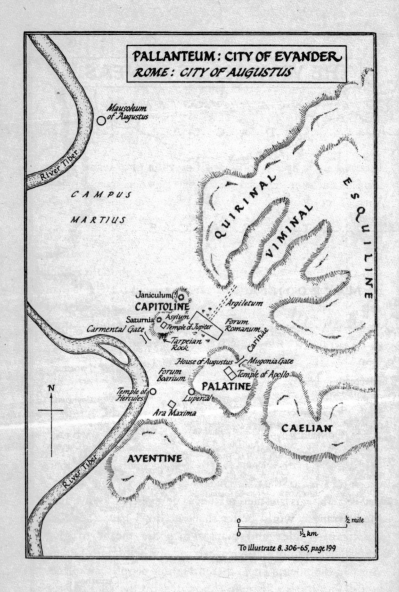

PALLANTEUM : CITY OF EVANDER
ROME : CITY OF AUGUSTUS

Mausoleum of Augustus

River Tiber

CAMPUS

MARTIUS

QUIRINAL

VIMINAL

ESQUILINE

Janiculum(?)

CAPITOLINE

Argiletum

Saturnia   Asylum

Carmental Gate   Temple of Jupiter

Forum Romanum

Tarpeian Rock

Carinae

House of Augustus   Mugonia Gate

Forum Boarium   Temple of Apollo

Temple of Hercules   PALATINE

Lupercal

Ara Maxima

N

CAELIAN

AVENTINE

River Tiber

½ mile

½ km

To illustrate 8. 306-65, page 199

GAZETTEER

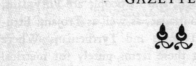

I started to compile a glossary of mythological terms in the *Aeneid*, but soon decided that it was not necessary. Such is Virgil's command of narration that the poem usually explains itself as it goes along. Where this is not so, explanations have been added to the text, for example at the beginning of Book Six where there is an unusual concentration of such difficulties. Here, the modern reader needs to be told that the Chalcidian citadel is the Chalcidian colony of Cumae; that Phoebus in line 18 is the same god as Apollo in line 9; that Androgeos was the son of Minos and that the Athenians were held to be the descendants of Cecrops. The *Aeneid* is first and foremost a narrative, and narratives do not thrive on interruptions. A glossary would drive readers to the end of the book. Even footnotes would take the eye to the foot of the page and the mind to scholarly furniture. It is a regrettable interference with the text of Virgil, but I have preferred to add such information to the body of the work where it is necessary rather than check the flow of the narrative.

Geography is another matter. The ancients knew their Mediterranean world better than we do. I have therefore supplied an index and maps which are meant to give topographical information which may be helpful for understanding the poem. These therefore omit peoples and places whose locality is sufficiently indicated by the context, for example the lists of the Latin enemies of Aeneas at the end of Book Seven and his Etruscan allies at 10. 163–214.

Virgil has many equivalent or nearly equivalent geographical terms at his disposal. Greeks are called Achaeans, Argives, Graians, and Pelasgians; Troy is Dardania, Ilium, Pergama (strictly its citadel), and its people are Phrygians, Teucrians, even Laomedontiadae, as well as Trojans; Etruscans are also Lydians, Tuscans and Tyrrhenians. Where Virgil seems to be using these terms purely for metrical convenience, the translation speaks of Greeks, Trojans and Etruscans. But the variants are preserved where they are used to some effect, rhetorical at 2. 324–6 for example, or emotive (the term 'Phrygian' usually carries a contemptuous allusion to the alleged effeminacy of the Trojans). In particular Italy is variously referred to as Ausonia, Oenotria, Hesperia (the Western Land), and sometimes these terms are used in prophecies not understood by those who hear them. This oracular obscurity is preserved in the translation since the progressive revelation of the divine will is an important aspect of the plot of the poem. The Tiber, for instance, is called the Lydian Thybris at 2. 781–2 and Aeneas can have no idea what is meant. The Italian river is always referred to by this Greek form of its name until 6. 873.

In the index below these equivalents will be noted but they will not occur on the maps. So too rivers and mountains appear in the list below, but normally not on the maps.

Names in brackets do not appear on the maps; names with map references appear on the map of The Voyages of Aeneas; other names appear on the map of Pallanteum/ Rome.